THE YEAR'S BEST DARK FANTASY AND HORROR

2011 EDITION

OTHER BOOKS EDITED BY
PAULA GURAN

Embraces
Best New Paranormal Romance
Best New Romantic Fantasy
Zombies: The Recent Dead
Vampires: The Recent Undead
Halloween (forthcoming)
New Cthulhu: The Recent Weird (forthcoming)

THE YEAR'S BEST DARK FANTASY AND HORROR

2011 EDITION

EDITED BY

PAULA GURAN

PRIME BOOKS

YEA

THE YEAR'S BEST DARK FANTASY AND HORROR 2011 EDITION

Cover art by Ivan Bliznetsov/Fotolia.
Cover design by Telegraphy Harness.

An extension of this copyright page can be found on pages 572-574.

Prime Books
www.prime-books.com

ISBN: 978-1-60701-281-8

To Gardner Dozois for (so far) twenty-eight editions of
The Year's Best Science Fiction
and ninety-four other anthologies.

(Thanks for the privilege of compiling the list!)

TABLE OF CONTENTS

BACK TO THE DARK

PAULA GURAN

For those of you who missed the introduction ("What the Hell Do you Mean by Dark Fantasy?") to the first volume of this series, and wish to read it, you can find it online at http://www.prime-books.com/intro-ybdfh2010. But, just so you've got the basics, here's the condensed version:

• "Dark fantasy" isn't universally defined—the definition depends on the context in which the phrase is used or who is elucidating it. You know it when you "feel" it.

• Darkness itself can be many things: nebulous, shadowy, tenebrous, mysterious, paradoxical (and thus illuminating) . . .

• A dark fantasy story might be only a bit unsettling or perhaps somewhat eerie. It might be revelatory or baffling. It can be simply a small glimpse of life seen "through a glass, darkly."

• Since horror is something we feel—it's an emotion, an affect—what each of us experiences, responds, or reacts to differs. What terrifies one may not frighten another.

• I'm not offering any definitions. I'm merely offering you, the reader, a diverse selection of stories that struck me as fitting the title of this tome. Each of them—no matter the style of the writing, theme, or shade of darkness—grabbed me from the start and kept me reading.

This selection of stories—all originally published in 2010—presents what I feel is an even wider range than included in last year's inaugural edition. There are tales of demons, ghosts, shapeshifters, vampires, zombies, and monsters of several varieties: supernatural, alien, merely human. You'll encounter stories based on myth, folklore, and fairy tale. Find stories with swords (with and without sorcery) and sorcery (with or without swords). There's also the science fictional, the amusing and quirky, retellings of the known and new tellings of the unknown, journeys into personal darkness and considerations of cosmic terrors. You will find yourself in future dystopias, the past, the present, and in between or outside any precise place in space or time. There are twists, turns, and, of course, terrific writing.

As far as writers: you'll be introduced to some new up-and-comers and renew acquaintances with established masters; there are well-known authors and those just beginning to be noted. Some writers are back who were in last year's edition. There may even be a few re-introductions: authors you've read previously but haven't recently come across.

Of course, this is far from *all* the "best" that was published last year, it just skims the surface of an amazing depth of talent currently writing dark fiction and being published in anthologies, collections, and periodicals on paper with ink or in pixels on screens. This year, I had many sources pointed out to me I'd not been aware of last year. I look foreword to discovering even more great fiction published in 2011 to consider for the next volume. But I'll continue to need your help finding it. Please keep sending suggestions, pointing out online publications, and submitting published anthologies and periodicals to darkecho@darkecho.com. (I prefer a PDF or Word .doc or RTF. But if you need to snail mail the actual book/magazine, email me for the address.)

One surprise this year was the number of stories from anthologies that made it into the final line-up. I read so many good stories in periodicals, I probably would have said—if asked along the way—that a great many selections this year were going to come from such publications. Then you get down to those final decisions and . . . you never know until you know. In the end, I chose more anthologized stories than first anticipated.

And—not really a surprise, but perhaps just one of those "things" about a particular year—the length of the stories averaged longer this year. More than a third fall into the longer-than-a-short-story (over 7500 words) but not-quite-a-novella length (starting at around 17,500 words or so) category some term "novelette."

As I write this, we're already a quarter of the way through 2011. By the time it goes to press, we'll be more than half way through the year—and I'll be considering short fiction for *The Year's Best Dark Fantasy and Horror: 2012*. What will it contain? No way to predict yet—and not just because the reading goes on (and on). There's an aspect of defining dark fantasy I didn't mention last year: the "Big Picture" of the times it is written and read in, the *Zeitgeist*, society's overall emotional attitude as well as one's personal feelings, reactions, hopes, fears, perceptions. What shade of darkness are we seeing right now?

As I mentioned in the acknowledgements last year for the inaugural volume, the scope, intent, and—allow me to add—theme of The Year's Best Dark Fantasy and Horror series is *unique*. I'll note it here this time as a more obvious reminder to those looking to compare it to other "year's best" compilations, past or present, or who are predisposed to assuming it is something it is not. There may be stories here that can be called "horror," but this is not a horror anthology per se. Not all of the dark is horrific.

One final note: Anthologies with titles including phrases like *Year's Best, Best of, Best (fill in the blank)* are what they are. When compiling such a volume, no editor can completely and absolutely fulfill the inference of the title. Fiction is not a race to be won, there are no absolutes with which to measure it. Yet I'm sure every person who edits a "best" anthology exerts tremendous effort in a genuine attempt to offer a book worthy of its grandiose moniker. Ultimately, decisions are arrived at with sincere intention, but personal taste is, of course, involved, and—like it or not—compromises must be made.

The job is somewhat onerous but, more often, enjoyable, and in the end, I'm sure we all hope you, the readers, find satisfaction in our selections. I know I hope you will.

Paula Guran
April 2011

Deputy Roy Barnes liked to talk about things, especially things he didn't understand, like those monsters that crawled out of corpses. The deputy called them lesser demons. He'd read about them in a book . . .

LESSER DEMONS

NORMAN PARTRIDGE

Down in the cemetery, the children were laughing.

They had another box open.

They had their axes out. Their knives, too.

I sat in the sheriff's department pickup, parked beneath a willow tree. Ropes of leaves hung before me like green curtains, but those curtains didn't stop the laughter. It climbed the ridge from the hollow below, carrying other noises—shovels biting hard-packed earth, axe blades splitting coffinwood, knives scraping flesh from bone. But the laughter was the worst of it. It spilled over teeth sharpened with files, chewed its way up the ridge, and did its best to strip the hard bark off my spine.

I didn't sit still. I grabbed a gas can from the back of the pickup. I jacked a full clip into my dead deputy's .45, slipped a couple spares into one of the leather pockets on my gun belt and buttoned it down. Then I fed shells into my shotgun and pumped one into the chamber.

I went for a little walk.

Five months before, I stood with my deputy, Roy Barnes, out on County Road 14. We weren't alone. There were others present. Most of them were dead, or something close to it.

I held that same shotgun in my hand. The barrel was hot. The deputy clutched his .45, a ribbon of bitter smoke coiling from the business end. It wasn't a stink you'd breathe if you had a choice, but we didn't have one.

Barnes reloaded, and so did I. The June sun was dropping behind the trees, but the shafts of late-afternoon light slanting through the gaps were as bright as high noon. The light played through black smoke rising from a Chrysler sedan's smoldering engine and white smoke simmering from the hot asphalt piled in the road gang's dump truck.

My gaze settled on the wrecked Chrysler. The deal must have started there. Fifteen or twenty minutes before, the big black car had piled into an old oak at a fork in the county road. Maybe the driver had nodded off, waking just in time to miss a flagman from the work gang. Over-corrected and hit the brakes too late. Said: *Hello tree, goodbye heartbeat.*

Maybe that was the way it happened. Maybe not. Barnes tried to piece it together later on, but in the end it really didn't matter much. What mattered was that the sedan was driven by a man who looked like something dredged up from the bottom of a stagnant pond. What mattered was that something exploded from the Chrysler's trunk after the accident. That thing was the size of a grizzly, but it wasn't a bear. It didn't look like a bear at all. Not unless you'd ever seen one turned inside out, it didn't.

Whatever it was, that skinned monster could move. It unhinged its sizable jaws and swallowed a man who weighed two-hundred-and-change in onelong ratcheting gulp, choking arms and legs and torso down a gullet lined with razor teeth. Sucked the guy into a blue-veined belly that hung from its ribs like a grave-robber's sack and then dragged that belly along fresh asphalt as it chased down the other men, slapping them onto the scorching roadbed and spitting bloody hunks of dead flesh in their faces. Some it let go, slaughtering others like so many chickens tossed live and squawking onto a hot skillet.

It killed four men before we showed up, fresh from handling a fender-bender on the detour route a couple miles up the road. Thanks to my shotgun and Roy Barnes' .45, allthat remained of the thing was a red mess with a corpse spilling out of its gutshot belly. As for the men from the work crew, there wasn't much you could say. They were either as dead as that poor bastard who'd ended his life in a monster's stomach, or they were whimpering with blood on their faces, or they were running like hell and halfway back to town. But whatever they were doing didn't make too much difference to me just then.

"What was it, Sheriff?" Barnes asked.

"I don't know."

"You sure it's dead?"

"I don't know that, either. All I know is we'd better stay away from it."

We backed off. The only things that lingered were the afternoon light slanting through the trees, and the smoke from that hot asphalt, and the smoke from the wrecked Chrysler. The light cut swirls through that smoke as it pooled around the dead thing, settling low and misty, as if the something beneath it were trying to swallow a chunk of the world, roadbed and all.

"I feel kind of dizzy," Barnes said.

"Hold on, Roy. You have to."

I grabbed my deputy by the shoulder and spun him around. He was just a kid, really—before this deal, he'd never even had his gun out of its holster while on duty. I'd been doing the job for fifteen years, but I could have clocked a hundred and never seen anything like this. Still, we both knew it wasn't over. We'd seen what we'd seen, we'd done what we'd done, and the only thing left to do was deal with whatever was coming next.

That meant checking out the Chrysler. I brought the shotgun barrel even with it, aiming at the driver's side door as we advanced. The driver's skull had slammed the steering wheel at the point of impact. Black blood smeared across his face, and filed teeth had slashed through his pale lips so that they hung from his gums like leavings you'd bury after gutting a fish. On top of that, words were carved on his face. Some were purpled over with scar tissue and others were still fresh scabs. None of them were words I'd seen before. I didn't know what to make of them.

"Jesus," Barnes said. "Will you look at that."

"Check the back seat, Roy."

Barnes did. There was other stuff there. Torn clothes. Several pairs of handcuffs. Ropes woven with fishhooks. A wrought-iron trident. And in the middle of all that was a cardboard box filled with books.

The deputy pulled one out. It was old. Leathery. As he opened it, the book started to come apart in his hands. Brittle pages fluttered across the road—

Something rustled in the open trunk. I pushed past Roy and fired point blank before I even looked. The spare tire exploded. On the other side of the trunk, a clawed hand scrabbled up through a pile of shotgunned clothes. I fired again. Those claws clacked together, and the thing beneath them didn't move again.

Using the shotgun barrel, I shifted the clothes to one side, uncovering a couple of dead kids in a nest of rags and blood. Both of them were handcuffed. The thing I'd killed had chewed its way out of one of their bellies. It had a grinning, wolfish muzzle and a tail like a dozen braided snakes. I slammed the trunk and chambered another shell. I stared down at the trunk, waiting for something else to happen, but nothing did.

Behind me . . . well, that was another story.

The men from the road gang were on the move.

Their boots scuffed over hot asphalt.

They gripped crow bars, and sledge hammers, and one of them even had a machete.

They came towards us with blood on their faces, laughing like children.

The children in the cemetery weren't laughing anymore. They were gathered around an open grave, eating.

Like always, a couple seconds passed before they noticed me. Then their brains sparked their bodies into motion, and the first one started for me with an axe. I pulled the trigger, and the shotgun turned his spine to jelly, and he went down in sections. The next one I took at longer range, so the blast chewed her over some. Dark blood from a hundred small wounds peppered her dress. Shrieking, she turned tail and ran.

Which gave the third bloodface a chance to charge me. He was faster than I expected, dodging the first blast, quickly closing the distance. There was barely enough room between the two of us for me to get off another shot, but I managed the job. The blast took off his head. That was that.

Or at least I thought it was. Behind me, something whispered through long grass that hadn't been cut in five months. I whirled, but the barefoot girl's knife was already coming at me. The blade ripped through my coat in a silver blur, slashing my right forearm. A twist of her wrist and she tried to come back for another piece, but I was faster and bashed her forehead with the shotgun butt. Her skull split like a popped blister and she went down hard, cracking the back of her head on a tombstone.

That double-punched her ticket. I sucked a deep breath and held it. Blood reddened the sleeve of my coat as the knife wound began to pump. A couple seconds later I began to think straight, and I got the idea going in my head that I should put down the shotgun and get my belt around my arm. I did that and tightened it good. Wounded, I'd have a walk to get back to the pickup. Then I'd have to find somewhere safe where I could take care of my arm. The pickup wasn't far distance-wise, but it was a steep climb up to the ridgeline. My heart would be pounding double-time the whole way. If I didn't watch it, I'd lose a lot of blood.

But first I had a job to finish. I grabbed the shotgun and moved toward the rifled grave. Even in the bright afternoon sun, the long grass was still damp with morning dew. I noticed that my boots were wet as I stepped over the dead girl. That bothered me, but the girl's corpse didn't. She couldn't bother me now that she was dead.

I left her behind me in the long grass, her body a home for the scarred words she'd carved on her face with the same knife she'd used to butcher the dead and butcher me. All that remained of her was a barbed rictus grin and a pair of dead eyes staring up into the afternoon sun, as if staring at nothing at all. And that's what she was to me—that's what they all were now that they were dead. They were nothing, no matter what they'd done to themselves with knives and files, no matter what they'd done to the living they'd murdered or the dead they'd pried out of burying boxes. They were nothing at all, and I didn't spare them another thought.

Because there were other things to worry about—things like the one that had infected the children with a mouthful of spit-up blood. Sometimes those things came out of graves. Other times they came out of car trunks or meat lockers or off slabs in a morgue. But wherever they came from they were always born of a corpse, and there were corpses here aplenty.

I didn't see anything worrisome down in the open grave. Just stripped bones and tatters of red meat, but it was meat that wasn't moving. That was good. So I took care of things. I rolled the dead bloodfaces into the grave. I walked back to the cottonwood thicket at the ridge side of the cemetery and grabbed the gas can I'd brought from the pickup. I emptied it into the hole, then tossed the can in, too. I wasn't carrying it back to the truck with a sliced-up arm.

I lit a match and let it fall.

The gas *thupped* alive and the hole growled fire.

Fat sizzled as I turned my back on the grave. Already, other sounds were rising in the hollow. Thick, rasping roars. Branches breaking somewhere in the treeline behind the old funeral home. The sound of something big moving through the timber—something that heard my shotgun bark three times and wasn't afraid of the sound.

Whatever that thing was, I didn't want to see it just now.

I disappeared into the cottonwood thicket before it saw me.

Barnes had lived in a converted hunting lodge on the far side of the lake. There weren't any other houses around it, and I hadn't been near the place in months. I'd left some stuff there, including medical supplies we'd scavenged from the local emergency room. If I was lucky, they would still be there.

Thick weeds bristled over the dirt road that led down to Roy's place. That meant no one had been around for a while. Of course, driving down the road would leave a trail, but I didn't have much choice. I'd been cut and needed to do something about it fast. You take chances. Some are large and some are small. Usually, the worries attached to the small ones amount to nothing.

I turned off the pavement. The dirt road was rutted, and I took it easy. My arm ached every time the truck hit a pothole. Finally, I parked under the carport on the east side of the old lodge. Porch steps groaned as I made my way to the door, and I entered behind the squared-off barrel of Barnes' .45.

Inside, nothing was much different than it had been a couple of months before. Barnes' blood-spattered coat hung on a hook by the door. His reading glasses rested on the coffee table. Next to it, a layer of mold floated on top of a cup of coffee he'd never finished. But I didn't care about any of that. I cared about the cabinet we'd stowed in the bathroom down the hall.

Good news. Nothing in the cabinet had been touched. I stripped to the waist, cleaned the knife wound with saline solution from an IV bag, then stopped the bleeding as best I could. The gash wasn't as deep as it might have been. I sewed it up with a hooked surgical needle, bandaged it, and gobbled down twice as many antibiotics as any doctor would have prescribed. That done, I remembered my wet boots. Sitting there on the toilet, I laughed at myself a little bit, because given the circumstances it seemed like a silly thing to worry about. Still, I went to the first-floor bedroom I'd used during the summer and changed into a dry pair of Wolverines I'd left behind.

Next I went to the kitchen. I popped the top on a can of chili, found a spoon, and started towards the old dock down by the lake. There was a rusty swing set behind the lodge that had been put up by a previous owner; it shadowed a kid's sandbox. Barnes hadn't had use for either—he wasn't even married—but he'd never bothered to change things around. Why would he? It would have been a lot of work for no good reason.

I stopped and stared at the shadows beneath the swing set, but I didn't stare long. The dock was narrow and more than a little rickety, with a small boathouse bordering one side. I walked past the boathouse and sat on the end of the dock for a while. I ate cold chili. Cattails whispered beneath a rising breeze. A flock of geese passed overhead, heading south. The sun set, and twilight settled in.

It was quiet. I liked it that way. With Barnes, it was seldom quiet. I guess you'd say he had a curious mind. The deputy liked to talk about things, especially things he didn't understand, like those monsters that crawled out of corpses. Barnes called them lesser demons. He'd read about them in one of those books we found in the wreck. He had ideas about them, too. Barnes talked about those ideas a lot over the summer, but I didn't want to talk about any of it. Talking just made me edgy. So did Barnes' ideas and explanations . . . all those *maybe's* and *what if's*. Barnes was big on those; he'd go on and on about them.

Me, I cared about simpler things. Things anyone could understand. Things you didn't need to discuss, or debate. Like waking up before a razor-throated monster had a chance to swallow me whole. Or not running out of shotgun shells. Or making sure one of those things never spit a dead man's blood in my face, so I wouldn't take a file to my teeth or go digging in a graveyard for food. That's what I'd cared about that summer, and I cared about the same things in the hours after a bloodfaced lunatic carved me up with a dirty knife.

I finished the chili. It was getting dark. Getting cold, too, because winter was coming on. I tossed the empty can in the lake and turned back toward the house. The last purple smear of twilight silhouetted the place, and a pair of birds darted into the chimney as I walked up the dock. I wouldn't have seen them if I hadn't looked at that exact moment, and I shook my head. Birds building nests in October? It was just another sign of a world gone nuts.

Inside, I settled on the couch and thought about lighting a fire. I didn't care about the birds—nesting in that chimney was their own bad luck. I'd got myself a chill out at the dock, and there was a cord of oak stacked under the carport. Twenty minutes and I could have a good blaze going. But I was tired, and my arm throbbed like it had grown its own heartbeat. I didn't want to tear the stitches toting a bunch of wood. I just wanted to sleep.

I took some painkillers—more than I should have—and washed them down with Jack Daniel's. After a while, the darkness pulled in close. The bedroom I'd used the summer before was on the ground floor. But I didn't want to be downstairs in case anything came around during the night, especially with a cool liquid fog pumping through my veins. I knew I'd be safer upstairs.

There was only one room upstairs—a big room, kind of like a loft.

It was Barnes' bedroom, and his blood was still on the wall.

I didn't care. I grabbed my shotgun. I climbed the stairs.

Like I said: I was tired.

Besides, I couldn't see Barnes' blood in the dark.

At first, Roy and I stuck to the sheriff's office, which was new enough to have pretty good security. When communication stopped and the whole world took a header, we decided that wasn't a good idea anymore. We started moving around.

My place wasn't an option. It was smack dab in the middle of town. You didn't want to be in town. There were too many blind corners, and too many fences you couldn't see over. Dig in there, and you'd never feel safe no how many bullets you had in your clip. So I burned down the house. It never meant much to me, anyway. It was just a house, and I burned it down mostly because it was mine and I didn't want anyone else rooting around in the stuff I kept there. I never went back after that.

Barnes' place was off the beaten path. Like I said, that made it a good choice. I knew I could get some sleep there. Not too much, if you know what I mean. Every board in the old lodge seemed to creak, and the brush was heavy around the property. If you were a light sleeper—like me—you'd most likely hear anything that was coming your way long before it had a chance to get you.

And I heard every noise that night in Barnes' bedroom. I didn't sleep well at all. Maybe it was my sliced-up arm or those painkillers mixing with the whiskey and antibiotics—but I tossed and turned for hours. The window was open a crack, and cold air cut through the gap like that barefooted girl's knife. And it seemed I heard another knife scraping somewhere deep in the house, but it must have been those birds in the chimney, scrabbling around in their nest.

Outside, the chained seats on the swing set squealed and squeaked in the wind. Empty, they swung back and forth, back and forth, over cool white sand.

After a couple months, Barnes wasn't doing so well. We'd scavenged a few of the larger summer houses on the other side of the lake, places that belonged to rich couples from down south. We'd even made a few trips into town when things seemed especially quiet. We'd gotten things to the point where we had everything we needed at the lodge. If something came around that needed killing, we killed it. Otherwise, we steered clear of the world.

But Barnes couldn't stop talking about those books he'd snatched from the wrecked Chrysler. He read the damned things every day. Somehow, he thought they had all the answers. I didn't know about that. If there were answers in those books, you'd have one hell of a time pronouncing them. I knew that much.

That wasn't a problem for Barnes. He read those books cover to cover, making notes about those lesser demons, consulting dictionaries and reference books he'd swiped from the library. When he finished, he read them again. After a while, I couldn't stand to look at him sitting there with those reading glasses on his face. I even got sick of the smell of his coffee. So I tried to keep busy. I'd do little things around the lodge, but none of them amounted to much. I chainsawed several oak trees and split the wood. Stacking it near the edge of the property to season would also give us some cover if we ever needed to defend the perimeter, so I did that, too. I even set some traps on the other side of the lodge, but after a while I got sloppy and began to forget where they were. Usually, that happened when I was thinking about something else while I was trying to work. Like Barnes' *maybe's* and *what if's*.

Sometimes I'd get jumpy. I'd hear noises while I was working. Or I'd think I did. I'd start looking for things that weren't there. Sometimes I'd even imagine something so clearly I could almost see it. I knew that was dangerous . . . and maybe a little crazy. So I found something else to do—something that would keep my mind from wandering.

I started going out alone during the day. Sometimes I'd run across a pack of bloodfaces. Sometimes one of those demons . . . or maybe two. You never saw more than two at a time. They never traveled in packs, and that was lucky for me. I doubted I could have handled more than a couple, and even handling two . . . well, that could be dicey.

But I did it on my own. And I didn't learn about the damn things by reading a book. I learned by reading them. Watching them operate when they didn't know I was there, hunting them down with the shotgun, blowing them apart. That's how I learned—reading tales written in muscle and blood, or told by a wind that carried bitter scent and shadows that fell where they shouldn't.

And you know what? I found out that those demons weren't so different. Not really. I didn't have to think it through much, because when you scratched off the paint and primer and got down to it those things had a spot in the food chain just like you and me. They took what they needed when they needed it, and they did their best to make sure anything below them didn't buck the line.

If there was anything above them—well, I hadn't seen it.

I hoped I never would.

I wouldn't waste time worrying about it until I did.

Come August, there were fewer of those things around. Maybe that meant the world was sorting itself out. Or maybe it just meant that in my little corner I was bucking that food chain hard enough to hacksaw a couple of links.

By that time I'd probably killed fifteen of them. Maybe twenty. During alate summer thunderstorm, I tracked a hoofed minotaur with centipede dread-locks to an abandoned barn deep in the hollow. The damn thing surprised me, nearly ripping open my belly with its black horns before I managed to jam a pitchfork through its throat. There was a gigantic worm with a dozen sucking maws; I burned it down to cinders in the water-treatment plant. Beneath the high school football stadium, a couple rat-faced spiders with a web strung across a cement tunnel nearly caught me in their trap, but I left them dying there, gore oozing from their fat bellies drop by thick drop. The bugs had a half-dozen cocooned bloodfaces for company, all of them nearly sucked dry but still squirming in that web. They screamed like tortured prisoners when I turned my back and left them alive in the darkness.

Yeah. I did my part, all right.

I did my part, and then some.

Certain situations were harder to handle. Like when you ran into other survivors. They'd see you with a gun, and a pickup truck, and a full belly, and they'd want to know how you were pulling it off. They'd push you. Sometimes with questions, sometimes with pleas that were on the far side of desperate. I didn't like that. To tell you the truth, it made me feel kind of sick. As soon as they spit their words my way, I'd want to snatch them out of the air and jam them back in their mouths.

Sometimes they'd get the idea, and shut up, and move on. Sometimes they wouldn't. When that happened I had to do something about it. Choice didn't enter in to it. When someone pushed you, you had to push back. That was just the way the world worked—before demons and after.

One day in late September, Barnes climbed out of his easy chair and made a field trip to the wrecked Chrysler. He took those books with him. I was so shocked when he walked out the door that I didn't say a word.

I was kind of surprised when he made it back to the lodge at nightfall. He brought those damn books back with him, too. Then he worked on me for a whole week, trying to get me to go out there. He said he wanted to try something and he needed some backup. I felt like telling him I could have used some backup myself on the days I'd been out dealing with those things while he'd been sitting on his ass reading, but I didn't say it. Finally I gave in. I don't know why—maybe I figured going back to the beginning would help Barnes get straight with the way things really were.

There was no sun the day we made the trip, if you judged by what you could see. No sky either. Fog hung low over the lake, following the roads running through the hollow like they were dry rivers that needed filling. The pickup burrowed through the fog, tires whispering over wet asphalt, halogen beams cutting through all that dull white and filling pockets of darkness that waited in the trees.

I didn't see anything worrisome in those pockets, but the quiet that hung in the cab was another story. Barnes and I didn't talk. Usually that would have suited me just fine, but not that day. The silence threw me off, and my hands were sweaty on the steering wheel. I can't say why. I only know they stayed that way when we climbed out of the truck on County Road 14.

Nothing much had changed on that patch of road. Corpses still lay on the asphalt—the road gang, and the bear-thing that had swallowed one of them whole before we blew it apart. They'd been chewed over by buzzards and rats and other miserable creatures, and they'd baked guts-and-all onto the road during the summer heat. You would have had a hell of a time scraping them off the asphalt, because nothing that mattered had bothered with them once they were dead.

Barnes didn't care about them, either. He went straight to the old Chrysler and hauled the dead driver from behind the steering wheel. The corpse hit the road like a sack of kindling ready for the flame. It was a sight. Crows must have been at the driver's face, because his fishgut lips were gone. Those scarred words carved on his skin still rode his jerky flesh like wormy bits of gristle, but now they were chiseled with little holes, as if those crows had pecked punctuation.

Barnes grabbed Mr. Fishguts by his necktie and dragged him to the spot in the road where the white line should have been but wasn't.

"You ready?" he asked.

"For what?"

"If I've got it figured right, in a few minutes the universe is going to squat down and have itself a bite. It'll be one big chunk of the apple—starting with this thing, finishing with all those others."

"Those books say so?"

"Oh, yeah," Barnes said, "and a whole lot more."

That wasn't any kind of answer, but it put a cork in me. So I did what I was told. I stood guard. Mr. Fishguts lay curled up in that busted-up fetal position. Barnes drew a skinning knife from a leather scabbard on his belt and started cutting off the corpse's clothes. I couldn't imagine what the hell he was doing. A minute later, the driver's corpse was naked, razored teeth grinning up at us through his lipless mouth.

Barnes knelt down on that unmarked road. He started to read.

First from the book. Then from Mr. Fishguts' skin.

The words sounded like a garbage disposal running backward. I couldn't understand any of them. Barnes' voice started off quiet, just a whisper buried in the fog. Then it grew louder, and louder still. Finally he was barking words, and screaming them, and spitting like a hellfire preacher. You could have heard him a quarter mile away.

That got my heart pounding. I squinted into the fog, which was getting heavier. I couldn't see a damn thing. I couldn't even see those corpses glued to the road anymore. Just me and Barnes and Mr. Fishguts, there in a tight circle in the middle of County Road 14.

My heart went trip-hammer, those words thumping in time, the syllables pumping. I tried to calm down, tried to tell myself that the only thing throwing me off was the damn fog. I didn't know what was out there. One of those inside-out grizzlies could have been twenty feet away and I wouldn't have known it. A rat-faced spider could have been stilting along on eight legs, and I wouldn't have seen it until the damn thing was chewing off my face. That minotaur thing with the centipede dreadlocks could have charged me at a dead gallop and I wouldn't have heard its hooves on pavement . . . not with Barnes roaring. That was all I heard. His voice filled up the hollow with words written in books and words carved on a dead man's flesh, and standing there blind in that fog I felt like those words were the only things in a very small world, and for a split second I think I understood just how those cocooned bloodfaces felt while trapped in that rat-spider's web.

And then it was quiet. Barnes had finished reading.

"Wait a minute," he said. "Wait right here."

I did. The deputy walked over to the Chrysler, and I lost sight of him as he rummaged around in the car. His boots whispered over pavement and he was back again. Quickly, he knelt down, rearing back with both hands wrapped around the hilt of that wrought-iron trident we'd found in the car that very first day, burying it in the center of Mr. Fishguts' chest.

Scarred words shredded, and brittle bones caved in, and an awful stink escaped the corpse. I waited for something to happen. The corpse didn't move. I didn't know about anything else. There could have been anything out there, wrapped up in that fog. Anything, coming straight at us. Anything, right on top of us. We wouldn't have seen it all. I was standing there with a shotgun in my hands with no idea where to point it. I could have pointed it anywhere and it wouldn't have made me feel any better. I could have pulled the trigger a hundred times and it wouldn't have mattered. I might as well have tried to shotgun the fog, or the sky, or the whole damn universe.

It had to be the strangest moment of my life.

It lasted a good long time.

Twenty minutes later, the fog began to clear a little. A half hour later, it wasn't any worse than when weleft thelodge. But nothing had happened in the meantime. That was the worst part. I couldn't stop waiting for it. I stood there, staring down at Mr. Fishguts' barbed grin, at the trident, at those words carved on the corpse's jerky flesh. I was still standing there when Barnes slammed the driver's door of the pickup. I hadn't even seen him move. I walked over and slipped in beside him, and he started back towards the lodge.

"Relax," he said finally. "It's all over."

That night it was quieter than it had been in a long time, but I couldn't sleep and neither could Barnes. We sat by the fire, waiting for something . . . or nothing. We barely talked at all. About four or five, we finally drifted off.

Around seven, a racket outside jarred me awake. Then there was a scream. I was up in a second. Shotgun in hand, I charged out of the house.

The fog had cleared overnight. I shielded my eyes and stared into the rising sun. A monster hovered over the beach—leathery wings laid over a jutting bone framework, skin clinging to its muscular body in a thin blistery layer, black veins slithering beneath that skin like stitches meant to mate a devil's muscle and flesh. The thing had a girl, her wrist trapped in one clawed talon. She screamed for help when she saw me coming, but the beast understood me better than she did. It grinned through a mouthful of teeth that jutted from its narrow jaws like nails driven by a drunken carpenter, and its gaze tracked the barrel of my gun, which was already swinging up in my grasp, the stock nestling tight against my shoulder as I took aim.

A sound like snapping sheets. A blast of downdraft from those red wings as the monster climbed a hunk of sky, wings spreading wider and driving down once more.

The motion sent the creature five feet higher in the air. The shotgun barrel followed, but not fast enough. Blistered lips stretched wide, and the creature screeched laughter at me like I was some kind of idiot. Quickly, I corrected my aim and fired.

The first shot was low and peppered the girl's naked legs. She screamed as I fired again, aiming higher this time. The thing's left wing wrenched in the socket as the shot found its mark, opening a pocket of holes large enough to strain sunlight. One more reflexive flap and that wing sent a message to the monster's brain. It screeched pain through its hammered mouth and let the girl go, bloody legs and all.

She fell fast. Her anguished scream told me she understood she was already dead, the same way she understood exactly who'd killed her.

She hit the beach hard. I barely heard the sound because the shotgun was louder. I fired twice more, and that monster fell out of the sky like a kite battered by a hurricane, and it twitched some when it hit, but not too much because I moved in fast and finished it from point-blank range.

Barnes came down to the water. He didn't say anything about the dead monster. He wanted to bury the girl, but I knew that wasn't a good idea. She might have one of those things inside her, or a pack of bloodfaces might catch her scent and come digging for her with a shovel. So we soaked her with gasoline instead, and we soaked the winged demon, too, and we tossed a match and burned down the both of them together.

After that, Barnes went back to the house.

He did the same thing to those books.

A few days later, I decided to check out the town. Things had been pretty quiet . . . so quiet that I was getting jumpy again.

They could have rolled up the streets, and it wouldn't have mattered. To tell the truth, there hadn't been too many folks in town to begin with, and now most of them were either dead or gone. I caught sight of a couple bloodfaces when I cruised the main street, but they vanished into a manhole before I got close.

I hit a market and grabbed some canned goods and other supplies, but my mind was wandering. I kept thinking about that day in the fog, and that winged harpy on the beach, and my deputy. Since burning those books, he'd barely left his room. I was beginning to think that the whole deal had done him some good. Maybe it was just taking some time for him to get used to the way things were. Mostly, I hoped he'd finally figured out what I'd known all along—that we'd learned everything we really needed to know about the way this world worked the day we blew apart the inside-out grizzly on County Road 14.

I figured that was the way it was, until I drove back to the house.

Until I heard screams down by the lake.

Barnes had one of the bloodfaces locked up in the boathouse. A woman no more than twenty. He'd stripped her and cuffed her wrists behind a support post. She jerked against the rough wood as Barnes slid the skinning knife across her ribs.

He peeled away a scarred patch of flesh that gleamed in the dusky light, but I didn't say a word. There were enough words in this room already. They were the same words I'd seen in those books, and they rode the crazy woman's skin. A couple dozen of them had been stripped from her body with Roy Barnes' skinning knife. With her own blood, he'd pasted each one to the boathouse wall.

I bit my tongue. I jacked a shell into the shotgun.

Barnes waved me off. "Not now, boss."

Planting the knife high in the post, he got closer to the girl. Close enough to whisper in her ear. With a red finger, he pointed at the bloody inscription he'd pasted to the wall. "*Read it,*" he said, but the woman only growled at him, snapping sharpened teeth so wildly that she shredded her own lips. But she didn't care about spilling her own blood. She probably didn't know she was doing it. She just licked her tattered lips and snapped some more, convinced she could take a hunk out of Barnes.

He didn't like that. He did some things to her, and her growls became screams.

"She'll come around," Barnes said.

"I don't think so, Roy."

"Yeah. She will—this time I figured things out."

"You said that when you read those books."

"But she's a book with a pulse. That's the difference. She's alive. That means she's got a connection—to those lesser demons, and to the things that lord it over them, too. Every one of them's some kind of key. But you can't unlock a gate with a bent-up key, even if it's the one that's supposed to fit. That's why things didn't work with the driver. After he piled up that Chrysler, he was a bent-up key. He lost his pulse. She's still got hers. If she reads the words instead of me—the words she wrote with a knife of her own—it'll all be different."

He'd approached me while he was talking, but I didn't look at him. I couldn't stand to. I looked at the bloodface instead. She screamed and spit. She wasn't even a woman anymore. She was just a naked, writhing thing that was going to end her days cuffed to a pole out here in the middle of nowhere. To think that she could spit a few words through tattered lips and change a world was crazy, as crazy as thinking that dead thing out on County Road 14 could do the job, as crazy as—

"Don't you understand, boss?"

"She digs up graves, Roy. She eats what she finds buried in them. That's all I need to understand."

"You're wrong. She knows—"

I raised the shotgun and blew off the bloodface's head, and then I put another load in her, and another. I blew everything off her skeleton that might have been a nest where a demon could grow. And when I was done with that little job I put a load in that wall, too, and all those scarred words went to hell in a spray of flesh and wood, and when they were gone they left a jagged window on the world outside.

Barnes stood there, the girl's blood all over his coat, the skinning knife gripped in his shaking hand.

I jacked another shell into the shotgun.

"I don't want to have this conversation again," I said.

After Barnes had gone, I unlocked the cuffs and got the bloodface down. I grabbed her by her hair and rolled her into the boat. Once the boathouse doors were opened, I yanked the outboard motor cord and was on my way.

I piloted the boat to the boggy section of the lake. Black trees rooted in the water, and Spanish moss hung in tatters from the branches. It was as good a place as any for a grave. I rolled the girl into the water, and she went under with a splash. I thought about Barnes, and the things he said, and those words on the wall. And I wished he could have seen the girl there, sinking in the murk. Yeah, I wished he could have seen that straight-on. Because this was the way the world worked, and the only change coming from this deal was that some catfish were going to eat good tonight.

The afternoon waned, and the evening light came on and faded. I sat there in the boat. I might have stayed until dark, but rain began to fall—at first gently, then hard enough to patter little divots in the calm surface of the lake. That was enough for me. I revved the outboard and headed back to the lodge.

Nothing bothered me along the way, and Roy didn't bother me once I came through the front door. He was upstairs in his room, and he was quiet . . . or trying to be.

But I heard him.

I heard him just fine.

Up there in his room, whispering those garbage-disposal words while he worked them into his own flesh with the skinning knife. That's what he was doing. I was sure of it. I heard his blood pattering on the floorboards the same way that rat-spiders' blood had pattered the cement floor in the football stadium. Sure it was raining outside, but I'd heard rain and I'd heard blood and I knew the difference.

Floorboards squealed as he shifted his weight, and it didn't take much figuring to decide that he was standing in front of his dresser mirror. It went on for an hour and then two, and I listened as the rain poured down. And when Deputy Barnes set his knife on the dresser and tried to sleep, I heard his little mewling complaints. They were much softer than the screams of those cocooned bloodfaces, but I heard them just the same.

Stairs creaked as I climbed to the second floor in the middle of the night. Barnes came awake when I slapped open the door. A black circle opened on his bloody face where his mouth must have been, but I didn't give him a chance to say a single word.

"I warned you," I said, and then I pulled the trigger.

When it was done, I rolled the deputy in a sheet and dragged him down the stairs. I buried him under the swing set. By then the rain was falling harder. It wasn't until I got Barnes in the hole that I discovered I didn't have much gas in the can I'd gotten from the boathouse. I drenched his body with what there was, but the rain was too much. I couldn't even light a match. So I tossed a road flare in the hole, and it caught for a few minutes and sent up sputters of blue flame, but it didn't do the job the way it needed to be done.

I tried a couple more flares with the same result. By then, Roy was disappearing in the downpour like a hunk of singed meat in a muddy soup. Large river rocks bordered the flowerbeds that surrounded the lodge, and I figured they might do the trick. One by one I tossed them on top of Roy. I did that for an hour, until the rocks were gone. Then I shoveled sand over the whole mess, wet and heavy as fresh cement.

It was hard work.

I wasn't afraid of it.

I did what needed to be done, and later on I slept like the dead.

And now, a month later, I tossed and turned in Barnes' bed, listening to that old swing set squeak and squeal in the wind and in my dreams.

The brittle sound of gunfire wiped all that away. I came off the bed quickly, grabbing Barnes' .45 from the nightstand as I hurried to the window. Morning sunlight streamed through the trees and painted reflections on the glass, but I squinted through them and spotted shadows stretching across the beach below.

Bloodfaces. One with a machete and two with knives, all three of them moving like rabbits flushed by one mean predator.

Two headed for the woods near the edge of the property. A rattling burst of automatic gunfire greeted them, and the bloodfaces went to meat and gristle in a cloud of red vapor.

More gunfire, and this time I spotted muzzle flash in the treeline, just past the place where I'd stacked a cord of wood the summer before. The bloodface with the machete saw it, too. He put on the brakes, but there was no place for him to run but the water or the house.

He wasn't stupid. He picked the house, sprinting with everything he had. I grabbed the bottom rail of the window and tossed it up as he passed the swing set, but by the time I got the .45 through the gap he was already on the porch.

I headed for the door, trading the .45 for my shotgun on the way. A quick glance through the side window in the hallway, and I spotted a couple soldiers armed with M4 carbines breaking from the treeline. I didn't have time to worry about them. Turning quickly, I started down the stairs.

What I should have done was take another look through that front window. If I'd done that, I might have noticed the burrowed-up tunnel in the sand over Roy Barnes' grave.

It was hard to move slowly, but I knew I had to keep my head. The staircase was long, and the walls were so tight the shotgun could easily cover the narrow gap below. If you wanted a definition of dangerous ground, that would be the bottom of the staircase. If the bloodface was close—his back against the near wall, or standing directly beside the stairwell—he'd have a chance to grab the shotgun barrel before I entered the room.

A sharp clatter on the hardwood floor below. Metallic . . . like a machete. I judged the distance and moved quickly, following the shotgun into the room. And there was the bloodface . . . over by the front door. He'd made it that far, but no further. And it wasn't gunfire that had brought him down. No. Nothing so simple as a bullet had killed him.

I saw the thing that had done the job, instantly remembering the sounds

I'd heard during the night—the scrapes and scrabbles I'd mistaken for nesting birds scratching in the chimney. The far wall of the room was plastered with bits of carved skin, each one of them scarred over with words, and each of those words had been skinned from the thing that had burrowed out of Roy Barnes' corpse.

That thing crouched in a patch of sunlight by the open door, naked and raw, exposed muscles alive with fresh slashes that wept red as it leaned over the dead bloodface. A clawed hand with long nails like skinning knives danced across a throat slashed to the bone. The demon didn't look up from its work as it carved the corpse's flesh with quick, precise strokes. It didn't seem to notice me at all. It wrote one word on the dead kid's throat . . . and then another on his face . . . and then it slashed open the bloodface's shirt and started a third.

I fired the shotgun and the monster bucked backwards. Its skinning knife nails rasped across the doorframe and dug into the wood. The thing's head snapped up, and it stared at me with a headful of eyes. Thirty eyes, and every one of them was the color of muddy water. They blinked, and their gaze fell everywhere at once—on the dead bloodface and on me, and on the words pasted to the wall.

Red lids blinked again as the thing heaved itself away from the door and started toward me.

Another lid snapped opened on its chin, revealing a black hole.

One suck of air and I knew it was a mouth.

I fired at the first syllable. The thing was blasted back, barking and screaming as it caught the doorframe again, all thirty eyes trained on me now, its splattered chest expanding as it drew another breath through that lidded mouth just as the soldiers outside opened fire with their M4s.

Bullets chopped through flesh. The thing's lungs collapsed and a single word died on its tongue. Its heart exploded. An instant later, it wasn't anything more than a corpse spread across a puddle on the living room floor.

"Hey, Old School," the private said. "Have a drink."

He tossed me a bottle, and I tipped it back. He was looking over my shotgun. "It's mean," he said, "but I don't know. I like some rock 'n' roll when I pull a trigger. All you got with this thing is *rock*."

"You use it right, it does the job."

The kid laughed. "Yeah. That's all that matters, right? Man, you should hear how people talk about this shit back in the Safe Zone. They actually made us watch some lame-ass stuff on the TV before they choppered us out here to the sticks. Scientists talking, ministers talking . . . like we was going to talk these things to death while they was trying to chew on our asses."

"I met a scientist once," the sergeant said. "He had some guy's guts stuck to his face, and he was down on his knees in a lab chewing on a dead janitor's leg. I put a bullet in his head."

Laughter went around the circle. I took one last drink and passed the bottle along with it.

"But, you know what?" the private said. "Who gives a shit, anyway? I mean, really?"

"Well," another kid said. "Some people say you can't fight something you can't understand. And maybe it's that way with these things. I mean, we don't know where they came from. Not really. We don't even know what they *are*."

"Shit, Mendez. Whatever they are, I've cleaned their guts off my boots. That's all I need to know."

"That works today, Q, but I'm talking long term. As in: What about tomorrow, when we go nose-to-nose with their daddy?"

None of the soldiers said anything for a minute. They were too busy trading uncertain glances.

Then the sergeant smiled and shook his head. "You want to be a philosopher, Private Mendez, you can take the point. You'll have lots of time to figure out the answers to any questions you might have while you're up there, and you can share them with the rest of the class if you don't get eaten before nightfall."

The men laughed, rummaging in their gear for MREs. The private handed over my shotgun, then shook my hand. "Jamal Quinlan," he said. "I'm from Detroit."

"John Dalton. I'm the sheriff around here."

It was the first time I'd said my own name in five months.

It gave me a funny feeling. I wasn't sure what it felt like.

Maybe it felt like turning a page.

The sergeant and his men did some mop-up. Mendez took pictures of the lodge, and the bloody words pasted to the living room wall, and that dead thing on the floor. Another private set up some communication equipment and they bounced everything off a satellite so some lieutenant in DC could look at it. I slipped on a headset and talked to him. He wanted to know if I remembered any strangers coming through town back in May, or anything out of the ordinary they might have had with them. Saying *yes* would mean more questions, so I said, "No, sir. I don't."

The soldiers moved north that afternoon. When they were gone, I boxed up food from the pantry and some medical supplies. Then I got a gas can out of the boathouse and dumped it in the living room. I sparked a road flare and tossed it through the doorway on my way out.

The place went up quicker than my house in town. It was older. I carried the box over to the truck, then grabbed that bottle the soldiers had passed around. There were a few swallows left. I carried it down to the dock and looked back just in time to see those birds dart from their nest in the chimney, but I didn't pay them any mind.

I took the boat out on the lake, and I finished the whiskey, and after a while I came back.

Things are getting better now. It's quieter than ever around here since the soldiers came through, and I've got some time to myself. Sometimes I sit and think about the things that might have happened instead of the things that did. Like that very first day, when I spotted that monster in the Chrysler's trunk out on County Road 14 and blasted it with the shotgun—the gas tank might have exploded and splattered me all over the road. Or that day down in the dark under the high school football stadium—those rat-spiders could have trapped me in their web and spent a couple months sucking me dry. Or with Roy Barnes—if he'd never seen those books in the backseat of that old sedan, and if he'd never read a word about lesser demons, where would he be right now?

But there's no sense wondering about things like that, any more than looking for explanations about what happened to Barnes, or me, or anyone else. I might as well ask myself why the thing that crawled out of Barnes looked the way it did or knew what it knew. I could do that and drive myself crazy chasing my own tail, the same way Barnes did with all those *maybe's* and *what if's*.

So I try to look forward. The rules are changing. Soon they'll be back to the way they used to be. Take that soldier. Private Quinlan. A year from now he'll be somewhere else, in a place where he won't do the things he's doing now. He might even have a hard time believing he ever did them. It won't be much different with me.

Maybe I'll have a new house by then. Maybe I'll take off work early on Friday and push around a shopping cart, toss steaks and a couple of six packs into it. Maybe I'll even do the things I used to do. Wear a badge. Find a new deputy. Sort things out and take care of trouble. People always need someone who can do that.

To tell the truth, that would be okay with me.

That would be just fine.

Countless people with no chance, no future; everyone failing at everything. Mass despair. "Collective emotional downwaves" is the latest psychology buzz; sociobiological impulses to self-destruction in an overpopulated world. And then Whim feels that bad beat coming in the numbers . . .

RAISE YOUR HAND IF YOU'RE DEAD

JOHN SHIRLEY

Sometimes I think I'm dead. Sometimes I think I'm not dead. So far, I can't figure it out, not definitely.

I should tell you who's sending this message to you. It's me, Mercedes' older brother, Whim. At least I think it's me. And I'm sending this to you, Syke, so maybe you can figure out if I'm dead, and you can do something about it. If you can fix that—you're my hodey. If you can't, you can't, and you're still my hodey.

Maybe I can figure it all out. This message, if that's what it is, will take a while to get to you, if it gets to you at all. I'm still working out what the rules are in here. If I think it all through, maybe I'll work out if I'm dead or not.

Mercedes was the one I was with you know, harvesting suicides, the night we looked the Empties in the eyes . . .

I was nervous, on my knees in the padded prow of the twelve-foot aluminum boat, as Mercedes piloted us up under the big supports for the Golden Gate Bridge. Dangerous out there anytime, sure, even when the seas aren't running rough, because you can get a black wind, that toxin laden fog, just sweeps down on you quick, no time to get to shore—or you can ship too much water and you might dump over, find yourself thrashing in that cold, dirty water, with the bay leeches fastening on your ankles and the waves smacking you on jagged rocks around the support towers.

But it was sheer superstition, really, making me nervous. I get superstitious about numbers. It has to do with my dad having been a gambler, between his subbing gigs; Dad rattling on about odds and numbers and how number patterns crop up in the cards. "You can feel that bad beat coming in the numbers," he'd say. "If you pay attention. If you don't feel the odds, the beat'll smack you upside the head."

He was an old school guy, born in Atlanta in 1970; he said things like "smack you upside the head." And "old school."

The thing is, Syke, as we ran the boat out there, the engine chugging in the moonlight, it just hit me that today was 3-5-35. March fifth, 2035. Now, three and five is eight plus three is eleven, plus five is sixteen. You write sixteen, 1 and 6; add them, it makes seven. My unlucky number. Nine's my lucky number, seven's unlucky. Maybe because my old man died when I was fourteen, twice seven, on the fourteenth of June.

On the night of 3-5-35 I looked up at the bridge, and thought: *Each cable is made of 27,572 strands of wire. 80,000 miles of wire in the main cables. The bridge has more than 1,200,000 rivets . . . Now if you add two and seven to five and seven and two . . .*

"We shouldn't be out here," I said to Mercedes. My sis was back by the little engine, working the tiller. I was out front with the grabbers and the sniffer. She wore her long brown leather jacket, gloves, boots; I had my oversized army jacket, without the insignia, army boots, waterproof pants. You've never seen me in physical person, Syke. In the social space I wear some nicer shit—seeing as how CG clothing is gratis with the access fee. I muttered once more, "Really shouldn't be out here."

"What?" she called. "Why? You cold? Told you to put on a slicker."

"It's not that," I said, though I was shivering, scanning the gray water with the sniffer. "It's the numbers . . . " I had the sniffer—that's for picking up human DNA fragments in the air—in my left hand. The mechanical grabber in my right.

I figure I gotta explain this stuff to you, Syke, since it's way, way far from your thing. You were always so indoors—you were the indoors of the indoors. Wandering around like an out of body experience in the social space and the subworlds with the likes of Pizzly and creeps like Mr. Dead Eyes hounding about in the background. Remember Mr. Dead Eyes, hodey, he'll come up again. You recall that perv, Mr. DE, dogging Mercedes in the subworlds?

There's my future girl, he'd say to my sister. *All good things come to them who wait.*

That night under the bridge I was thinking about Mr. Dead Eyes, and not knowing why and that spooked me too. I was just about to explain to little sis about the numbers, the date, and how we should go back, but then the sniffer tripped and I saw the first floater. He was floating face up in a patch of light from the lamp on the bridge support. His eyes were colorless—looked just like cocktail onions. So that told me he'd been dead a while, but not long as all that. Longer, and the gulls, or some adventurous crab would have gotten his eyes out.

He wasn't very waterlogged or bloated either. Which was good. It sucks when you got to handle them, even with a grabber and rubber gloves, when they're, you know, coming apart from being out there awhile.

"Got one," I called out to her. "At two o'clock. Not too soggy. But come up slow . . ."

She cut the engine and we coasted toward the floater. He might've been about fifty when he took the plunge, with long brown hair like seaweed washing around his pudgy, onion-eyed face. We hadn't found him soon enough to harvest his organs. A messy, nauseating job, anyhow, harvesting organs. I was always sort of relieved when I knew I wouldn't have to do it.

The guy in the suit might have some good pocket fruit. He had a decent suit on, and the one remaining shoe was pretty good quality leather. So maybe he had money, jewelry, stuff like that. The uneven light picked out a gold glint from a wristwatch; I hoped it was waterproof. (I remember when we found an elderly black guy one time had one of those old fashioned grills on his teeth, installed in the first decade of the century—diamonds and gold all over it. Nasty, prying that grill off him. Paid good though.)

I used the grabber on onion-eyes, then got the watch off with a quick movement of my rubber-gloved hand. Always afraid the body's going to grab my wrist as I do it. I saw too many zombie movies as a kid. But they never do move. It's almost disappointing.

I tucked the gold watch in the scavenge duffel, then grabbed his tie and pulled his body up against the boat. He had a nice oxblood tie, seemed like silk.

I'm always really careful when I pull the bodies close to the boat. It sucks ugly to fall in with them, hodey. You tend to grab the body to keep from sinking. They can fall apart when you grab them. It's better not to fall in.

I glanced back at Mercedes. Her curly black hair seemed like it was shining with an orange halo, in the light from the tower support behind her. Her big black eyes, her pale skin, her round face, those sound-wave face tattoos on her cheeks—you know how her face can come together and she seems so iconic. You'd know that better than anyone, Syke. She came to your little world in her real semblance. At twenty-one she's a year younger, but she seems like she's from a whole different race than me, not just a different family. Me being so dark-skinned and lean.

"You want to take him to shore?" I asked. "Looks too spongy for organ harvesting."

"Then just do the pockets, Whim," she said, like, *It's so obvious.*

I went through his pockets, came up with a wild-dog wallet which turned out to have a usable unicredit tab in it—and his ID, which we pitched, not being into identity theft.

I checked this floater for a gold necklace; nope, so I clipped off his wedding ring finger. He was too sponged up to just pull the ring off. Had to use the clipper to cut right through his finger. Just a crunch, a little ooze of blackened blood, releasing the rankness of dead man. He was good and cold.

He had a suicide note in a plastic sack in his pocket, as they often do. I took that too, in case it gave out any information I could sell to the family.

I glanced at it in with my pen light. Didn't see anything useful. Looked like the usual maudlin stuff. I caught the lines, *My wife got the treatment, now it's like she's dead to me, she's all empty, and I went to see my dad, he was empty too, and they're going to do it to me.*

I gave up on all this ranting and tossed the note away. Guy'd been losing his mind at the end, I figured.

I let him slide back into the water, and we went on toward the Marin side of the bridge, in case there was another floater. You might be surprised to hear we've found as many as four in one night, Syke. But now that the suicide nets are down again—and no, I wasn't the one who vandalized them this time, or any of the other times—we get three or four jumpers a week, sometimes several a day. It's been good and steady like that, since the Desperation came into its own. The climate change thing peaking, all that shoreland sucked up, all those people misplaced, all that desertification, tropical pests and diseases swarming north, crops either drowned or charred or eaten away. Population of the world doubling. More and more jobs outsourced, automated. Two hundred million people who used to have food in North America, used to *just assume* food would be there—barely eating now, many of them starving. Countless people with no chance, no future; everyone failing at everything. Mass despair. "Collective emotional downwaves" is the latest psychology buzz; sociobiological impulses to self-destruction in an overpopulated world. The Desperation . . .

You're so insular, in your little world, Syke. You never talked about this stuff. Maybe you took it for granted. Or maybe you were hardly aware of it—hell you were ten years living mostly in the virtual model, tripping your mind to the subworlds, sending your body on remote to exercise, all that stuff. The curse of being born with all those silver spoon annuities. And a touch of agoraphobia, I'd guess.

So, after harvesting onion-eyes, me and Mercedes weren't surprised to see another body come flying down off the bridge, within minutes. People travel from around the country, around the world to jump off the Big Orange

Arc now, and the bridge crew makes a lot of extra money taking bribes from suicide jumpers. Truth is, though, about a fourth of the "suicides" are murders. That's what I hear. Lot of women from the sex slave brothels get pitched off for trying to escape. A lesson to the others.

It was Mercedes who first spotted the woman coming down. We both heard the yell, getting higher pitched as the woman came down turning end over end, close to the northern tower.

I thought I caught of a flash of diamonds and I thought, *That's a good harvest, right there.*

And then she hit the water. *Whack.* We waited for her dead body to bob up, Mercedes piloting the boat a bit closer to the impact point, shipping some water in the rising waves from a barge passing five hundred yards away.

I shivered with the cold as we waited. Daydreamed about hot toddies in front of the holo, in a snug corner of Siggy's Allnighter.

Then the woman came thrashing up and I heard Mercedes cussing. I was only thinking it: *Shit—she's alive.*

Now and then it happens. Sure it's a long ways down from the deck of the Golden Gate Bridge, and people almost invariably die right off, because when they hit that water at that speed, with that much momentum, it's almost like hitting solid ground.

But a few live. They're always busted up; most tend to die in a few minutes. Once in a while a jumper gets pulled out of the water alive, tells his weepy story about how he knew he wanted to live the moment he let go, and how people should hang in there—though of course, with the Coast Guard no longer doing rescue, anywhere, survivors don't get pulled out much.

I remember the only other survivor we found. That guy, he was a short chunky Asian guy—maybe his fat saved him from being busted up too much. He begged us to help him. But he had a lot of jewelry on him and I could tell he wasn't going to make it to the shore alive no matter what we did. Mercedes said, "You want to help him on his way, or me?" I didn't want her to have to do it. I held his head under the water for awhile—he hardly thrashed at all.

I imagine you being all judgmental about that, Syke. Easy for you to raise your eyebrows. You inherited your mom's software income, never had to live off the streets. Anyway, I'd have pulled him out if I thought he'd live. I guess.

This woman, now, bobbing up, all sputtering, she was muscular, wearing some kind of tights. I could see she had a broken right arm, blood bubbling from her mouth. But something about her—maybe those high cheekbones, those cutting blue eyes, the really short-cut brown hair—made me think she was tough. She just might live.

I couldn't bring myself to drown her. I thought we ought to shove on out of there and let the broken woman do her dying, and then come back for the harvest. Just leave before she started asking for help.

She didn't ask for help, though—she ordered some up. She had us sized up pretty good.

"I'll pay you," she rasped. "You get me to shore."

I was figuring she was maybe not a suicide. Didn't seem the type. More likely someone thought they'd done her in.

"How much?" Mercedes asked her. "And how do we get it?"

"Ten thousand WD," the woman said, sputtering. "Transfer soon as we get to a hospital." She coughed up more blood, paddling a little with her good arm. "But you better hurry . . ."

Mercedes was against it. "We don't have any way to make her pay, Whim, once we get her there."

But I was kind of fascinated by this woman. And maybe drowning that fat Asian guy bothered me more than I like to admit.

So I said, "Let's take a chance."

We got her into the boat—that had to hurt like hell, with her broken arm and legs. I was impressed at how she didn't scream. She sucked air through her clenched teeth when the pain got bad, and squeezed her eyes tight shut, but she didn't scream.

We hauled her to shore—had to go all the way back to the south shore, where our truck was, and from there we could drive to the nearest ER. When we pulled her out of the boat she went all shivery with the pain, and she gasped—and then she went limp. I had to check to see she wasn't dead. Just out cold.

"I really, *really* don't know if we should risk this, Whim," Mercedes said as I tugged the woman, my arms under hers, into the back of the battered old Toyota hybrid pickup. "This woman—she didn't jump. Someone *tossed* her off that bridge. So maybe they're gonna wanna make sure . . . And we'll be in the way."

"She's giving us ten thousand WD," I pointed out.

"And I really, *really* think she could be fulla shit about that," Mercedes said. "I told you before, I'm telling you now." She sighed. "But I guess we're this far . . . " She banged the tailgate up on the truck.

"We could leave her right here. But we'll always wonder—it might be enough to start over in Canada . . . "

That was our dad's dream. He was a writer, sometimes, when he wasn't teaching or throwing money away on cards. Made most of a half-assed living substitute teaching. He raised us after our mom died in the first wave of the pigeon flu. He wanted to get us to Canada, where the weather is more predictable and there's fewer tropical diseases and there's some kind of health care, but then one of the kid gangs caught him outside, and busted him up pretty bad. He died a few months later.

Mercedes just nodded, when I brought up the Canadian thing. I remember getting a rush of hope, thinking maybe I'd added up the numbers wrong and this time they were coming out to nines, somehow, and we were going to win.

But first we had to get the jumper to the hospital. Mercedes drove, I rode shotgun. "You got that gun with you?" she asked suddenly, working the stick shift with quick, angry motions of her hand.

"Just the little plastic one."

Something came on TVnet in the truck cab about Senator Boxell's plan to harvest the kid gangs. Maybe it was the word *harvest* that caught my attention, that being some of my own jargon. "There's just no point in not facing the reality of today's world," he said, on the little screen. "If it weren't for the planetary climate change emergency, why, we could manage all this population. As it is, with millions of orphans—we estimate more than half a million of them on the street in every major American city—it's just cruel and nonsensical to leave these kids to starve to death. The right thing to do is euthanasia and organ harvesting. It's a matter of triage . . . "

Mercedes gave a bitter little laugh, hearing that. When dad died, she ran off on her own for awhile. I spent two weeks looking for her; finally found her living on the streets—in one of those orphan kid gangs.

After Senator Boxell was a news spot then about the war in Pakistan, another thousand men caught in a nerve-gas cloud, along with about four thousand civilians—that old prick General Marsh saying he had it all under control . . .

Then a commercial. A sexy woman's mouth appeared on the little dashboard screen, saying, "The SINGULARITY is here. Sign up for Singular! Search it. Do it. Free it."

"Someone's always claiming the Singularity is here or about to be, or something," Mercedes snorted, looking at a side street, as we passed. The street, down the hill a little, was flooded by the rising tide. "I wish they'd just let us hook into it and go somewhere else . . . Any fucking place else . . . "

I didn't say, *Could be worse, Mercedes. Least we have a place to live. We pull in some WD.*

I used to say that to her. But lately it gets her mad and there are still bruises on my shoulder from where she punched me last time.

I glanced in back again. The woman's eyes were tight shut but the hand on her good arm was making funny little clutching motions. Still alive.

We got to the hospital in about five minutes. We nosed the truck slowly through the indigent crowds outside, the homeless, people trying to get into the hospital. Lots of people sick with the mutated malaria.

We had no air conditioning, and away from the bay, when I rolled down the window, the air was thick, and muggy, smelled like unwashed people. Mosquitoes whined at us. Hostile faces turned toward us. Someone threw a bottle that clacked into the side of the truck. I rolled up the window again.

We drove slowly up to the wall next to the emergency line to the public ER entrance. But we ignored the line—Mercedes had the woman's Gold Medicard. If it was up to date, it'd get our jumper into any medical facility. Only the rich, the connected, and certain government types had them.

We pulled up by the high steel gate to the inner hospital lot, and the ExAd kiosk. I could see four paramil guards in full armor standing inside the gate, under the overhang, faces shut away in opaque, reflective helmets, idly toying with their recoil-reversal batons.

It started to rain, one of those glutinous, warm downpours we get now. I started the wipers and they left streaks of dark grease from the rain on the windshield. Rain clouds even more polluted than usual, probably just got here from overseas. Thanks for sharing, China.

Mercedes got out, hurried over to the reader in the Express Admissions kiosk, slipped the little card through and a screen flickered in response. From the truck, I could see she was talking to someone on the screen, pointing at the truck for the kiosk camera. I glanced back at the broken woman lying on the old, folded rug on the truckbed, next to my harvest bag, saw her grimacing, hands fisting, eyes shut. And then, out behind the truck, a sudden surge of motion—a kid gang, pushing through the crowd, coming our way.

This gang of little kids had those bullet-shaped slam-helmets they steal from the Japan Center. Some kind of trendy gear from Tokyo. They came ramming through the waiting crowd, heads down, using the helmets to penetrate the throng like bullets nosing through flesh.

"Those kids," Mercedes said, coming back to the truck, blinking in the rain. "I know 'em. We need to get the fuck out of their way . . . "

Then the gate slid back, for us, as Mercedes climbed in next to me, the guards stepping forward, one of them waving us through while the others brandished their RR sticks to keep the crowds back. Several of the kids charged the paramils, pretty kamikaze thing to do—the kids were half the guards' size. The RR sticks went crack, sparked with energy, the kids were flung back, spinning through the air.

I tried not to floor it, but I went too fast through the open gate, almost nailing one of the guards. He had to jump out of the way, shouting angrily, his amplified voice barking something that might've been, "Tweakin' sperm-puddle!"

I stopped the truck and we got out. Two burly orderlies were rolling a gurney through the sliding doors toward our truck. I was worried about leaving the harvest bag out there, where the guards might go through it, but no choice, we had to get that transfer out of the woman, and she had to be awake to do it . . .

So fuck it, we followed the gurney into the hospital. I was afraid that they'd pat me down, being as the metal detectors aren't much good anywhere, with the hardened plastic guns around, but they didn't . . .

Anytime things are urgent—you end up waiting. It's like life wants to make sure you get a chance to savor every last possible split-second of frustration; like it wants to make sure you torture yourself with hopeless impatience.

But finally they let us come in from that pisshole of a waiting room, to see the broken woman cleaned up and tubed, in her little clean white booth, one of the few private rooms in the hospital. A bank of monitors hooked up to her.

It was just us and a white-painted metal-and-plastic healthbot trundling around her, scanning, humming inside itself, whirring irritably when we got in the way.

Mercedes was on one side of the hospital bed, I was on the other. The woman was stripped to a green hospital gown. Both long legs and one arm in instacasts. Small breasts, wide apart, tenting the gown, her head going side to side in a druggy semi-delirium.

"Hey bridge lady," Mercedes said.

The broken woman opened her eyes to slit. "You got here," she croaked at us. "Same ones, from the bridge?"

"We're here," I said.

"Told 'em you had to . . . had to come in." She gave a bloodstained, sad little smile. "Said you were my only relatives."

"Heartwarming," Mercedes said. "How we do the transfer?"

"You got to do . . . " She cleared her throat. Took a breath. Managed, " . . . something else for me. First."

"That wasn't the deal!" Mercedes hissed, her dark eyes snapping.

"You got . . . " The woman swallowed hard. "You got a transpod?"

Mercedes snorted. "What you think?" She reached into her coat pocket, pulled it out, held it up: one of the flat models, slim as a playing card. We harvested it a month ago off what was left of a depressed accountant.

"Okay," the broken woman said, her voice barely audible. She paused and sighed as the healthbot extruded a needle from its utility column and squirted some meds into her IV. It trundled away, and the woman went on, "I'll give you half the money now. But . . . " She took a breath. "But to get the rest, you got to bodyguard me for an hour till my people get here. The soulless are pressin' em hard. You got to stick with me maybe hour and a half . . . "

I remember thinking: *Did she say "soulless"*?

"Bodyguard?" I said. "Lady there's guards all around this place. Plus the hospital has two city cops in it."

"They might be empties . . . soulless . . . or . . . the soulless'll push buttons on 'em . . . most of the empties, they're rich bigshots . . . I wasn't trying to jump off that bridge—it was that, or . . . "

Mercedes sniffed and shook her head so that her curls bounced. "You're in some kinda cult? Talking about soulless people and shit?"

The broken woman licked her lips. "I'm . . . was with the Justice Department. Field officer. Internal Affairs. Some of us found out about the empties . . . the Singularity thing. The soulless . . . " She was pretty stoned on the meds. Not making much sense. "Independent investigation . . . " She took a ragged breath. "They say we rogued out but . . . they're offering new bodies to everyone . . . "

"Which version of the Singularity you talking about?" I asked. Not knowing what else to say. Thinking we ought to just get the five grand and get out with that. But not wanting to leave her here either.

She lifted her good arm up, shakily wiped her mouth with the back of her hand. "Upload minds to new bodies . . . bodies fixed up to last longer . . . nanobot refreshers . . . Some of the bodies are vat grown. Some are, like, stolen."

Mercedes was shaking her head again. But I was feeling kind of funny, looking at this woman. This woman was *bad-ass*. This woman had lived through something that kills most people and she was all crunched up but she was still negotiating, working her situation. This woman had some kind of gravitas. Made me take her seriously. Gave me another feeling too . . . I looked at her name on the hospital's patient info sheet. Said she was Dresden Dennings. What a badass name, too. Dresden. Maybe I could find out her birthday, add up the numbers, see if they felt friendly to me. I looked at her, past all the bruises, thinking I could fall in love with this woman. Even if she was five or six years older than me.

Living with your sister gets old. Don't get me wrong Syke. I love Mercedes even more than you do. Different, is all.

"It's not a fucking cult," Dresden said. "It's just . . . what happens. They found a way to upload minds. The mind gets transferred but . . . turns out . . . souls are real. Mind goes, the soul . . . " She licked her lips. "Soul doesn't go with it. People end up soulless. Empties. What goes in the upload—it's not . . . holographic."

"What the fuck," Mercedes muttered.

"Holographic consciousness," Dresden said, a sort of awe in her voice. "What gets uploaded, it's missing a dimension. And empathy, love, all that—it's in that dimension, see . . . and they . . . the empties don't have it." She laughed raspily. "They don't even have a sense of humor anymore. The Singularity is mass producing sociopaths. Thousands, tens of thousands of sociopaths. They don't trust feeling people. We can't be predicted, see. Senator Boxell . . . " Her eyelids drooped. Her voice drooped too. "The Joint Chiefs. The President. The mayor. The police chief. They've all had it. Supposed to be a body that doesn't age . . . holes with eyes . . . empties . . . "

The meds were really kicking in now and her words slurred together, her eyes rolled back, mostly whites.

"She can't transfer the money all dozey like this, Mercedes," I said. "We got to wait for her."

Mercedes bitched and cussed but it was no good, Dresden was too stoned. There were two chairs, and we pulled them up, and waited . . . thinking over what she'd said.

We were supposed to be bodyguards protecting her from the soulless. From . . . *the empties.*

Lunacy. But someone had chased her off that bridge.

We did have that working gun—the hardened-plastic disposable pistol, use and lose, good for five shots, compacted-polymer slugs. Metal detectors don't pick it up. Use it and throw it away. Kill a man with it, if it doesn't break—some of them are made crappy. I had the gun in my baggy army coat pocket.

But bodyguarding? Not our specialty. Let's face it, we were water buzzards, not raptors.

"This is suck-ugly bullshit," Mercedes said. "Maybe I've got a stimpill I can put in her mouth, stim her up and get her to transfer the money."

"That might kill her," I said.

She looked at me defiantly. "So?"

"Um—I just . . . " I shrugged.

Mercedes shook her head in disgust. "You're getting all humpy for this woman."

"No, ... "

She shook her head again and got out her viddy, and that's when she called you up. You remember that, anyhow.

I remember when we met, me and you, Syke, if you want to call that meeting. Mercedes talked me into visiting the VR social space with her, though she knows I don't like them. She insisted I had to meet "Psych." I didn't know how you spelled it then. "He likes to psych people out but he's a good guy," she said. She seemed so *up* about it, and I hardly ever saw her up, so I gave in and there we were, in that neutral space, feeling like we're physically walking through a shiny digital hallway, passing people who were jabbering about this and that, people with their little 3D persicons floating over their heads.

Somehow Mercedes found you in that cloud room that's like your second home. I don't know how you can find your way around in there. Going from one weird little cluster of furniture to another in all that colored fog. But there you were, you popped up out of nowhere, arms spread to hug Mercedes, beaming with that big wide mouth and eyes. I wonder if you really look like that? Looked like a real face to me. I remember you had that persicon of some skinny twentieth century actor dancing in a top hat, around and around.

Mercedes said, "Hey Syke, this is my older brother Whim. Anyway he's a year older . . . "

And you said, "I heard you were gonna be a writer, like your dad, and then you decided to rob dead people instead."

You were smiling in that weirdly sympathetic way, and I just laughed. I don't know how you get away with saying shit like that without getting people mad. But I guess that's your talent.

"Mercedes talks too much," I said. Thinking that was strange because she normally doesn't talk too much. But she really trusted you, Syke.

"The thing is," you said, "being a writer is almost always about robbing dead people. 'Specially nowadays. Take other people's old ideas and use 'em like kiddy blocks and make castles. You want to go in a 'world?"

Then we went to that underwater subworld you like. All those caverns where we could fight monsters and laugh when their heads exploded with pretty silver confetti.

I'm thinking about all this, Syke, because it was that day that we met Mr. Dead Eyes. At first we thought he was one of the VR bots, a program simulating a ghost or something, but he was an avatar of somebody real somewhere, and he kept trying to find out where Mercedes lived in the physical world. He found her again and again down there—in that world.

When you looked at the guy—I swear there was this feeling like you could fall into him; like you lean over a deep well to look in and lose your balance and fall in. Big tall guy, his eyes always unfocussed, that red mouth, too red for a man's lips, and that big hunk of chin, and that archaic little faux hawk haircut . . . And when he talked he seemed so empty . . .

"You make me want to get all the way to the center of you, and out the other side," Mr. Dead Eyes said—that's what he said to Mercedes, and more than once. "It's so sad to have to run from the one you belong to," he said to her, another time. "Let me open you to big fat sensations, Mercedes."

Remember that one made you mad, Syke? You told him to fuck off and he just laughed and the laughter didn't show in his eyes.

And I think he was one of the first ones. Because I heard him talking up the Singularity, and his new body, and how he was going to live ten thousand years.

You remember, Syke?

Okay: The hospital. Mercedes squinting into that little screen she was holding, trying to see your VR semblance in that colored fog, asking you how to do a really secure transfer of funds, saying there was some worrying stuff about the transfer we were about to do, and you were your usual smarmily assured techno-nerd self, rattling off access protocols at her, which she recorded in a sidebar.

And then I saw that a man was standing in the door to Dresden's hospital cubby. And it was Mr. Dead Eyes, Syke. In physical person. Looking just like his semblance. Wearing a black and gray Federal Police uniform, headset, a mike clipped to his shoulder. Those same unfocused eyes, that red, red mouth, that big chin. Big hands. And one of those hands was on a gun butt, at his right hip.

"Why there you are," he said. "When I saw the scan from outside the hospital, I said, 'Is that Mercedes, Syke's little friend from the subworlds?' And by jiminy it's her in physical person. I always said we'd meet in the meat . . . "

Mercedes was gaping at him, blinking hard, like she thought something had gone wrong with her eyes. Just looking at the guy she'd had to ditch a dozen times when she was in the social space. The guy who'd stalked her through it. And here he was in person. His cop's name tag said Sgt. Imber.

Mercedes broke the connection with you, and then she stood up, glaring ice cold at Imber. "You found me." I never heard three words spoken with more loathing.

He grinned. "Not exactly coincidence. Your name popped up connected to our rogue here, I asked for this one . . . "

"Don't let him near me." Took me a second to work out who said that. It wasn't Mercedes—it was Dresden, her eyes cracked open. "Wants to kill me," she said. "Soulless. He's . . . empty."

"Empty of what?" Imber said, stepping into the little room, his hand tightening on the butt of his pistol. "No big ass deal. It's more like an appendectomy."

I felt a long, deep chill, that seemed to go on and on, when he said that. I was thinking, *It's true.*

Imber shook his head sadly at the broken woman. "You didn't have to go through this, Dresden. You didn't have to run onto the bridge. You didn't have to fight our people. Didn't have to jump just to get away from those boys—that was some crazy shit. You're lucky to be alive."

Dresden licked her dry lips. "Wasn't going to let them . . . take my body . . . push me out . . . "

I looked at Imber and he looked back at me. It was so clear to me, now, looking at him. The absence was nothing you could see—but it was nothing you could miss.

The empties. Maybe I'd known for awhile. I'd seen them on the streets. In the patrol cars. On TV. More and more of them with nothing behind their eyes; with those reasonable, flat tones, talking of triage and necessity and putting the good of society over the good of the parasites. Thinning the herd.

I guess I'd known they were soulless . . . I just didn't know why there were so many empties now. The Singularity . . .

I stepped between Dresden and Imber. And it was almost like that plastic gun jumped into my hand. It was a kind of spasmodic act of revulsion, drawing that gun, Syke—and I pointed it at Mr. Dead Eyes and squeezed the trigger. Fired almost point blank.

Imber was drawing his own gun when I shot him. He went over backwards, firing as he fell back. His bullet went between my left arm and my ribs, I could feel it cutting the air there, sizzling that close to me. I heard a despairing grunt and I turned to see that Imber's bullet had missed me but hit Dresden—it was a charged bullet, I could tell because the wound in her side was shooting sparks and her back was arching . . . and Mercedes was shouting something at me and I was turning to snap another furious shot at Imber. I missed.

He was flat on his back now, just outside the door, writhing around the first bullet I'd fired, the slug tearing up his brisket, and he was firing sloppily up at me. Bullets chewed the doorframe of the cubby to my left, made it smoke with the charges.

I aimed carefully this time and fired and that big chin of his shattered; must've been busted bits of it going up into his brain, because he shrieked once and then went silent and slack. Not the first guy I shot—but that's the first time I felt good doing it.

Down the hall, people were yelling for security. I turned to check on Dresden, but she was dead, her eyes glassy. "Shit," I said. "Dammit."

Then Mercedes was pushing me out the door. I had only a couple more shots in the disposable gun, and I used them as we ran out, heading for the back exits, firing over the heads of hospital security to keep them back.

Then we were banging through the door onto the wet asphalt of a back lot, past a row of dumpsters, gasping in the muggy air. We sprinted through the rain toward the hurricane fence topped with razor wire. Have to get over that fence somehow . . .

Mercedes ran ahead of me up to the fence, taking off her coat as she went. She tossed it up high, slung it over the razor wire on the fence, and I got to the fence, locked my hands together; she stepped into them and I boosted her up. She grabbed the coat, climbed up, was dropping over the other side, yelling at me to get over the fence—but I was hearing sirens, turned to see the patrol vans screaming around the corner of the hospital, the burly men and women jumping out, rushing toward me. I got maybe halfway up the fence when they grabbed me, dragged me down off it. I yelled at Mercedes to run but I didn't have to, I saw her back disappearing as she darted through a rubbishy lot, into the alley between two high rises . . .

They knocked me down but there was talk about being careful not to hurt me, he's a perfect specimen, he's young and in good shape, he's what they want . . .

I saw a man flip his mirror helmet back so he could look me over better. I saw his eyes. Empty.

They sprayed some sleep-you-creep into my mouth and I was gone.

I woke up in restraints, Syke. And naked. Lying on my back. There's nothing more horrible than waking up in restraints—naked. Trapped and vulnerable. It happened to me once before, when I was a teenager, flipped out on Icy Dust. Woke up in a jail infirmary strapped down. Scary feeling. But not so bad, that time, I knew they were going to let me go, eventually . . .

It was worse this time. Because I knew they'd never let me go.

I could hardly move. There was a clamp holding my head in place. My upper arms and elbows and wrists were clamped down too. My knees and ankles were locked down.

I couldn't see much. Too many lights shining at my face. I made out several pairs of eyes, the rest of the faces hidden by surgical masks. Those empty eyes. I caught the gleam of instruments. Heard healthbots muttering reports.

"Anybody want to tell me what the fuck?" I said.

"Don't see why we should," said a woman in a surgical mask. Her voice pleasant. A nurse—or some kind of biotechnician.

A man in uniform came into the ring of light. I got a look at his face. An old, lizardlike face I knew from the news. *General Marsh.*

"This him?" What a rumbly, gristly old voice General Marsh had.

"If you want one right away, this's the best one we have," the technician said. "There aren't any better in the vats. He's in excellent shape. He's the age and size you wanted. Not a bad looking kid."

"Kinda skinny. I guess he'll do. I'm sick. I need uploading quick . . . "

"We just put the nanos in him . . . If you'll go with the nurse to upload, we'll get you in there."

"Won't be any of his mind left in his brain to bother me?"

"No, no," the technician said soothingly. "All that—anything extraneous, his memories, consciousness, the holographic pattern—it's all going to be pushed out when we upload you into him. It just kind of gets lost in the circuits of the transfer interface. Sort of like when you do a vasectomy—where does the sperm go? The body absorbs it. Our gear will absorb him, and he won't be there to bother you . . . "

"That old fuck . . . taking my body . . . " I said. "Hey general, they're just uploading a copy of your mind—they're not sending all you, man."

"Everything important," he said distantly amused. "You believe in the soul, kid—that's such primitive thinking."

"Look at these people," I told him. "There's something missing from them. That Boxell's got no soul. He's one of 'em! You want to end up that empty, man? Like Boxell? Let me up out of this shit and we'll talk . . . "

The general chuckled. "Superstitious! I do hope none of him stays."

"None of him will . . . " The technician leaned close and told me, ever so sweetly: "Now, Whim . . . we're going to give you a mild tranquilizer—but we can't put you completely under. It won't feel like dying, really. More like going down a long, long slide . . . just slide on down and out and . . . it won't hurt at all." It's funny, what she said then. Not to me, to the computer about initiating the process. She said, "Three, five, thirty-five . . . " Reciting the date. The time: "Three Oh-five a.m . . . and thirty five seconds."

The numbers know. That was the last thing I heard, alive.

Then, all that was really me, mind and soul, went sliding down, down, and out . . .

Souls. They can't *send* them when they upload. Souls go where the universe wants—not where we want them to go. So when they try to put a shaky old General's consciousness in my body, only his personality and memory will go in. Probably had a shriveled little soul anyway. What's left of it will dissipate, during the uploading. It doesn't go where mine has gone—that's the difference between us, and the uploaded. Their souls just... disintegrate. Ours are shoved out of the way...

When they pushed me out, I found I was in a *somewhere*—I was drifting through the circuits of the interface computer. I got stuck in the transfer equipment. Lots of us are wandering around in here. Souls in databanks. I can see 'em sometimes, in my mind's eye. We can talk a little. I like to say to 'em, *Hey, raise your hand if you're dead.* Just to show I still have a sense of humor. The real joke is, there are people walking around in perfectly healthy physical bodies, who are more dead than we are...

And I found that I can follow the numbers, feel those 0s and 1s, reach out through these circuits and cables, and send a message to you, Syke, since one computer talks to another—and you're always interfacing with a computer.

I want to tell you: Come out of your virtual womb before it's your virtual tomb, Syke. They're going to come after you subworld people soon. You in particular.

Come out—and go find Mercedes, and take care of her. Ask around Siggy's Allnighter. You'll find her. Because I know she matters to you. You and her, you're soul mates.

Me—well, I think I've got it figured out now. I'm not in my body—and something else is. Not someone—some *thing.* So I'm not ever going to be able to go back to my body. I'm just a soul, organized into a mind; a soul floating in circles, in a machine. And if my mind was uploaded to another body, my soul wouldn't go with my mind.

I wouldn't want that.

So no—you can't help me. I answered my own question. I'm dead. One times zero equals zero. It all adds up. I'm only dead, though, in the physical way. Not in the way that matters.

Don't worry about me. I followed the numbers, and I'm about to lead the others out of here. I can feel them going into another computer, and then another—and then, one at a time, out through some kind of satellite transmission link. The soul, see, ends up flying through the sky, just like it was supposed to. And there's something up there waiting. I want to see what it is. Maybe I'll meet Dresden. I hardly knew her. But I feel cheated, losing her... But maybe I'll meet her somewhere, between here and there—wherever we are.

There's nothing to be afraid of, *she thinks.* No more here than in any bad dream. *But she finds the thought carries no conviction whatsoever. It's even less substantial than the dissolving wallpaper and bookcase . . .*

AS RED AS RED

CAITLÍN R. KIERNAN

1.

"So, you believe in vampires?" she asks, then takes another sip of her coffee and looks out at the rain pelting Thames Street beyond the café window. It's been pissing rain for almost an hour, a cold, stinging shower on an overcast afternoon near the end of March, a bitter Newport afternoon that would have been equally at home in January or February. But at least it's not pissing snow.

I put my own cup down—tea, not coffee—and stare across the booth at her for a moment or two before answering. "No," I tell Abby Gladding. "But, quite clearly, those people in Exeter who saw to it that Mercy Brown's body was exhumed, the ones who cut out her heart and burned it, clearly *they* believed in vampires. And that's what I'm studying, the psychology behind that hysteria, behind the superstitions."

"It was so long ago," she replies and smiles. There's no foreshadowing in that smile, not even in hindsight. It surely isn't a predatory smile. There's nothing malevolent, or hungry, or feral in the expression. She just watches the rain and smiles, as though something I've said amuses her.

"Not really," I say, glancing down at my steaming cup. "Not so long ago as people might *like* to think. The Mercy Brown incident, that was in 1892, and the most recent case of purported vampirism in the northeast I've been able to pin down dates from sometime in 1898, a mere hundred and eleven years ago."

Her smile lingers, and she traces a circle in the condensation on the plate-glass window, then traces another circle inside it.

"We're not so far removed from the villagers with their torches and pitchforks, from old Cotton Mather and his bunch. That's what you're saying."

"Well, not exactly, but . . ." and when I trail off, she turns her head towards me, and her blue-grey eyes seem as cold as the low-slung sky above Newport. You could almost freeze to death in eyes like those, I think, and I take another sip of my lukewarm Earl Grey with lemon. Her eyes seem somehow brighter than they should in the dim light of the coffeehouse, so there's your foreshadowing, I suppose, if you're the sort who needs it.

"You're pretty far from Exeter, Ms. Howard," she says, and takes another sip of her coffee. And me, I'm sitting here wishing we were talking about almost anything but Rhode Island vampires and the hysteria of crowds, tuberculosis and the Master's thesis I'd be defending at the end of May. It had been months since I'd had anything even resembling a date, and I didn't want to squander the next half hour or so talking shop.

"I think I've turned up something interesting," I tell her, because I can't think of any subtle way to steer the conversation in another direction; there are things I'd rather be talking with this mildly waiflike, comely girl than shop. "A case no one's documented before, right here in Newport."

She smiles that smile again.

"I got a tip from a folklorist up at Brown," I say. "Seems like maybe there was an incident here in 1785 or thereabouts. If it checks out, I might be onto the oldest case of suspected vampirism resulting in an exhumation anywhere in New England. So, now I'm trying to verify the rumors. But there's precious little to go on. Chasing vampires, it's not like studying the Salem witch trials, where you have all those court records, the indictments and depositions and what have you. Instead, it's necessary to spend a lot of time sifting and sorting fact from fiction, and, usually, there's not much of either to work with."

She nods, then glances back towards the big window and the rain. "Be a feather in your cap, though. If it's not just a rumor, I mean."

"Yes," I reply. "Yes, it certainly would."

And here, there's an unsettling wave of not-quite *déjà vu*, something closer to dissociation, perhaps, and for a few dizzying seconds I feel as if I'm watching this conversation, a voyeur listening in, or I'm only remembering it, but in no way actually, presently, taking part in it. And, too, the coffeehouse and our talk and the rain outside seem a lot less concrete—*less here and now*—than does the morning before. One day that might as well be the next, and it's raining, either way.

I'm standing alone on Bowen's Warf, staring out past the masts crowded into the marina at sleek white sailboats skimming over the glittering water, and there's the silhouette of Goat Island, half hidden in the fog. I'm about to turn and walk back up the hill to Washington Square and the library, about to leave the gaudy, Disney-World concessions catering to the tastes of tourists and return to the comforting maze of ancient gabled houses lining winding, narrow streets. And that's when I see her for the first time. She's standing alone near the "seal safari" kiosk, staring at a faded sign, at black-and-white photographs of harbor seals with eyes like the puppies and little girls from those hideous Margaret Keane paintings. She's wearing an old pea coat and shiny green galoshes that look new, but there's nothing on her head, and she doesn't have an umbrella. Her long black hair hangs wet and limp, and when she looks at me, it frames her pale face.

Then it passes, the blip or glitch in my psyche, and I've snapped back, into myself, into *this* present. I'm sitting across the booth from her once more, and the air smells almost oppressively of freshly roasted and freshly ground coffee beans.

"I'm sure it has a lot of secrets, this town," she says, fixing me again with those blue-grey eyes and smiling that irreproachable smile of hers.

"Can't swing a dead cat," I say, and she laughs.

"Well, did it ever work?" Abby asks. "I mean, digging up the dead, desecrating their mortal remains to appease the living. Did it tend to do the trick?"

"No," I reply. "Of course not. But that's beside the point. People do strange things when they're scared."

And there's more, mostly more questions from her about Colonial-Era vampirism, Newport's urban legends, and my research as a folklorist. I'm grateful that she's kind or polite enough not to ask the usual "you mean people get paid for this sort of thing" questions. She tells me a werewolf story dating back to the 1800s, a local priest supposedly locked away in the Portsmouth Poor Asylum after he committed a particularly gruesome murder, how he was spared the gallows because people believed he was a werewolf and so not in control of his actions. She even tells me about seeing his nameless grave in a cemetery up in Middletown, his tombstone bearing the head of a wolf. And I'm polite enough not to tell her that I've heard this one before.

Finally, I notice that it's stopped raining. "I really ought to get back to work," I say, and she nods and suggests that we should have dinner sometime soon. I agree, but we don't set a date. She has my cell number, after all, so we can figure that out later. She also mentions a movie playing at Jane Pickens that she hasn't seen and thinks I might enjoy. I leave her sitting there in the booth, in her pea coat and green galoshes, and she orders another cup of coffee as I'm exiting the café. On the way back to the library, I see a tree filled with noisy, cawing crows, and for some reason it reminds me of Abby Gladding.

2.

That was Monday, and there's nothing the least bit remarkable about Tuesday. I make the commute from Providence to Newport, crossing the West Passage of Narragansett Bay to Conanicut Island, and then the East Passage to Aquidneck Island and Newport. Most of the day is spent at the Redwood Library and Athenaeum on Bellevue, shut away with my newspaper clippings and microfiche, with frail yellowed books that were printed before the Revolutionary War. I wear the white cotton gloves they give me for handling archival materials, and make several pages of handwritten notes, pertaining primarily to the treatment of cases of consumption in Newport during the first two decades of the Eighteenth Century.

The library is open late on Tuesdays, and I don't leave until sometime after seven p.m. But nothing I find gets me any nearer to confirming that a corpse believed to have belonged to a vampire was exhumed from the Common Burying Ground in 1785. On the long drive home, I try not to think about the fact that she hasn't called, or my growing suspicion that she likely never will. I have a can of ravioli and a beer for dinner. I half watch something forgettable on television. I take a hot shower and brush my teeth. If there are any dreams—good, bad, or otherwise—they're nothing I recall upon waking. The day is sunny, and not quite as cold, and I do my best to summon a few shoddy scraps of optimism, enough to get me out the door and into the car.

But by the time I reach the library in Newport, I've got a headache, what feels like the beginnings of a migraine, railroad spikes in both my eyes, and I'm wishing I'd stayed in bed. I find a comfortable seat in the Roderick Terry Reading Room, one of the armchairs upholstered with dark green leather, and leave my sunglasses on while I flip through books pulled randomly from the shelf on my right. Novels by William Kennedy and Elia Kazan, familiar, friendly books, but trying to focus on the words only makes my head hurt worse. I return *The Arrangement* to its slot on the shelf, and pick up something called *Thousand Cranes* by a Japanese author, Yasunari Kawbata. I've never heard of him, but the blurb on the back of the dust jacket assures me he was awarded the Nobel Prize for Literature in 1968, and that he was the first Japanese author to receive it.

I don't open the book, but I don't reshelve it, either. It rests there in my lap, and I sit beneath the octagonal skylight with my eyes closed for a while. Five minutes maybe, maybe more, and the only sounds are muffled footsteps, the turning of pages, an old man clearing his throat, a passing police siren, one of the librarians at the front desk whispering a little louder than usual. Or maybe the migraine magnifies her voice and only makes it seem that way.

In fact, all these small, unremarkable sounds seem magnified, if only by the quiet of the library.

When I open my eyes, I have to blink a few times to bring the room back into focus. So I don't immediately notice the woman standing outside the window, looking in at me. Or only looking *in*, and I just happen to be in her line of sight. Maybe she's looking at nothing in particular, or at the bronze statue of Pheidippides perched on its wooden pedestal. Perhaps she's looking for someone else, someone who isn't me. The window is on the opposite side of the library from where I'm sitting, forty feet or so away. But even at that distance, I'm almost certain that the pale face and lank black hair belong to Abby Gladding. I raise a hand, half waving to her, but if she sees me, she doesn't acknowledge having seen me. She just stands there, perfectly still, staring in.

I get to my feet, and the copy of *Thousand Cranes* slides off my lap; the noise the book makes when it hits the floor is enough that a couple of people look up from their magazines and glare at me. I offer them an apologetic gesture—part shrug and part sheepish frown—and they shake their heads, almost in unison, and go back to reading. When I glance at the window again, the black-haired woman is no longer there. Suddenly, my headache is much worse (probably from standing so quickly, I think), and I feel a sudden, dizzying rush of adrenalin. No, it's more than that. I feel afraid. My heart races, and my mouth has gone very dry. Any plans I might have harbored of going outside to see if the woman looking in actually was Abby vanish immediately, and I sit down again. If it was her, I reason, then she'll come inside.

So I wait, and, very slowly, my pulse returns to its normal rhythm, but the adrenaline leaves me feeling jittery, and the pain behind my eyes doesn't get any better. I pick the novel by Yasunari Kawbata up off the floor and place it back upon the shelf. Leaning over makes my head pound even worse, and I'm starting to feel nauseous. I consider going to the restrooms, near the circulation desk, but part of me is still afraid, for whatever reason, and it seems to be the part of me that controls my legs. I stay in the seat and wait for the woman from the window to walk into the Roderick Terry Reading Room. I wait for her to be Abby, and I expect to hear her green galoshes squeaking against the lacquered hardwood. She'll say that she thought about calling, but then figured that I'd be in the library, so of course my phone would be switched off. She'll say something about the weather, and she'll want to know if I'm still up for dinner and the movie. I'll tell her about the migraine, and maybe she'll offer me Excedrin or Tylenol. Our hushed conversation will annoy someone, and he or she will shush us. We'll laugh about it later on.

But Abby doesn't appear, and so I sit for a while, gazing across the wide room at the window, a tree *outside* the window, at the houses lined up neat and tidy along Redwood Street. On Wednesday, the library is open until eight, but I leave as soon as I feel well enough to drive back to Providence.

3.

It's Thursday, and I'm sitting in that same green armchair in the Terry Roderick Reading Room. It's only 11:26 a.m., and already I understand that I've lost the day. I have no days to spare, but already, I know that the research that I should get done today isn't going to happen. Last night was too filled with uneasy dreaming, and this morning I can't concentrate. It's hard to think about anything but the nightmares, and the face of Abby Gladding at the window; her blue eyes, her black hair. And yes, I have grown quite certain that it *was* her face I saw peering in, and that she was peering in *at* me.

She hasn't called (and I didn't get her number, assuming she has one). An hour ago, I walked along the Newport waterfront looking for her, but to no avail. I stood a while beside the "seal safari" kiosk, hoping, irrationally I suppose, that she might turn up. I smoked a cigarette, and stood there in the cold, watching the sunlight on the bay, listening to traffic and the wind and a giggling flock of grey sea gulls. Just before I gave up and made my way back to the library, I noticed dog tracks in a muddy patch of ground near the kiosk. I thought that they seemed unusually large, and I couldn't help but recall the café on Monday and Abby relating the story of the werewolf priest buried in Middletown. But lots of people in Newport have big dogs, and they walk them along the wharf.

I'm sitting in the green leather chair, and there's a manila folder of photocopies and computer printouts in my lap. I've been picking through them, pretending this is work. It isn't. There's nothing in the folder I haven't read five or ten times over, nothing that hasn't been cited by other academics chasing stories of New England vampires. On top of the stack is "The 'Vampires' of Rhode Island," from *Yankee* magazine, October 1970. Beneath that, "They Burned Her Heart . . . Was Mercy Brown a Vampire?" from the *Narragansett Times*, October 25, 1979, and from the *Providence Sunday Journal*, also October 1979, "Did They Hear the Vampire Whisper?" So many of these popular pieces have October dates, a testament to journalism's attitude towards the subject, which it clearly views as nothing more than a convenient skeleton to pull from the closet every Halloween, something to dust off and trot out for laughs.

Salem has its witches. Sleepy Hollow its headless Hessian mercenary. And Rhode Island has its consumptive, consuming phantoms—Mercy Brown, Sarah Tillinghast, Nellie Vaughn, Ruth Ellen Rose, and all the rest. Beneath the *Providence Sunday Journal* piece is a black-and-white photograph I took a couple of years ago, Nellie Vaughn's vandalized headstone, with its infamous inscription: "I am waiting and watching for you." I stare at the photograph for a moment or two, and set it aside. Beneath it there's a copy of another October article, "When the Wind Howls and the Trees Moan," also from the Providence Sunday Journal. I close the manila folder and try not to stare at the window across the room.

It is only a window, and it only looks out on trees and houses and sunlight.

I open the folder again, and read from a much older article, "The Animistic Vampire in New England" from *American Anthropologist*, published in 1896, only four years after the Mercy Brown incident. I read it silently, to myself, but catch my lips moving:

In New England the vampire superstition is unknown by its proper name. It is believed that consumption is not a physical but spiritual disease, obsession, or visitation; that as long as the body of a dead consumptive relative hasblood in its heart it is proof that an occult influence steals from it for death and is at work draining the blood of the living into the heart of the dead and causing his rapid decline.

I close the folder again and return it to its place in my book bag. And then I stand and cross the wide reading room to the window and the alcove where I saw, or only thought I saw, Abby looking in at me. There's a marble bust of Cicero on the window ledge, and I've been staring out at the leafless trees and the brown grass, the sidewalk and the street, for several minutes before I notice the smudges on the pane of glass, only inches from my face. Sometime recently, when the window was wet, a finger traced a circle there, and then traced a circle within that first circle. When the glass dried, these smudges were left behind. And I remember Monday afternoon at the coffeehouse, Abby tracing an identical symbol (if "symbol" is the appropriate word here) in the condensation on the window while we talked and watched the rain.

I press my palm to the glass, which is much colder than I'd expected.

In my dream, I stood at another window, at the end of a long hallway, and looked down at the North Burial Ground. With some difficulty, I opened the window, hoping the air outside would be fresher than the stale air in the hallway. It was, and I thought it smelled faintly of clover and strawberries. And there was music. I saw, then, Abby standing beneath a tree, playing a violin. The music was very beautiful, though very sad, and completely unfamiliar. She drew the bow slowly across the strings, and I realized that somehow the music was shaping the night. There were clouds sailing past above the cemetery, and the chords she drew from the violin changed the shapes of those clouds, and also seemed to dictate the speed at which they moved. The moon was bloated, and shone an unhealthy shade of ivory, and the whole sky writhed like a Van Gogh painting. I wondered why she didn't tell me that she plays the violin.

Behind me, something clattered to the floor, and I looked over my shoulder. But there was only the long hallway, leading off into perfect darkness, leading back the way I'd apparently come. When I turned again to the open window and the cemetery, the music had ceased, and Abby was gone. There was only the tree and a row after row of tilted headstones, charcoal-colored slate, white marble, a few cut from slabs of reddish sandstone mined from Massachusetts or Connecticut. I was reminded of a platoon of drunken soldiers, lined up for a battle they knew they were going to lose.

I have never liked writing my dreams down.

It is late Thursday morning, almost noon, and I pull my hand back from the cold, smudged windowpane. I have to be in Providence for an evening lecture, and I gather my things and leave the Redwood Library and Athenaeum. On the drive back to the city, I do my best to stop thinking about the nightmare, my best not to dwell on what I saw sitting beneath the tree, after the music stopped and Abby Gladding disappeared. My best isn't good enough.

4.

The lecture goes well, quite a bit better than I'd expected it would, better, probably, than it had a right to, all things considered. "Mercy Brown as Inspiration for Bram Stoker's *Dracula*," presented to the Rhode Island Historical Society, and, somehow, I even manage not to make a fool of myself answering questions afterwards. It helps that I've answered these same questions so many times in the past. For example:

"I'm assuming you've also drawn connections between the Mercy Brown incident and Sheridan Le Fanu's *Carmilla*?"

"There are similarities, certainly, but so far as I know, no one has been able to demonstrate conclusively that Le Fanu knew of the New England phenomena. And, of course, the publication of *Carmilla* predates the exhumation of Mercy Brown's body by twenty years."

"Still, he might of known of the earlier cases."

"Certainly. He may well have. However, I have no *evidence* that he did."

But, the entire time, my mind is elsewhere, back across the water in Newport, in that coffeehouse on Thames, and the Redwood Library, and standing in a dream hallway, looking down on my subconscious rendering of the Common Burying Ground. A woman playing a violin beneath a tree. A woman with whom I have only actually spoken once, but about whom I cannot stop thinking.

It is believed that consumption is not a physical but spiritual disease, obsession, or visitation . . .

After the lecture, and the questions, after introductions are made and notable, influential hands are shaken, when I can finally slip away without seeming either rude or unprofessional, I spend an hour or so walking alone on College Hill. It's a cold, clear night, and I follow Benevolent Street west to Benefit and turn north. There's comfort in the uneven, buckled bricks of the sidewalk, in the bare limbs of the trees, in all the softly glowing windows. I pause at the granite steps leading up to the front door of what historians call the Stephen Harris House, built in 1764. One hundred and sixty years later, H. P. Lovecraft called this the "Babbitt House" and used it as the setting for an odd tale of lycanthropy and vampirism. I know this huge yellow house well. And I know, too, the four hand-painted signs nailed up on the gatepost, all of them in French. From the sidewalk, by the electric glow of a nearby street lamp, I can only make out the top half of the third sign in the series; the rest are lost in the gloom—*Oubliez le Chien*. Forget the Dog.

I start walking again, heading home to my tiny, cluttered apartment, only a couple of blocks east on Prospect. The side streets are notoriously steep, and I've been in better shape. I haven't gone twenty-five yards before I'm winded and have a nasty stitch in my side. I lean against a stone wall, cursing the cigarettes and the exercise I can't be bothered with, trying to catch my breath. The freezing air makes my sinuses and teeth ache. It burns my throat like whiskey.

And this is when I glimpse a sudden blur from out the corner of my right eye, hardly *more* than a blur. An impression or the shadow of something large and black, moving quickly across the street. It's no more than ten feet away from me, but downhill, back towards Benefit. By the time I turn to get a better look, it's gone, and I'm already beginning to doubt I saw anything, except, possibly, a stray dog.

I linger here a moment, squinting into the darkness and the yellow-orange sodium-vapor pool of streetlight that the blur seemed to cross before it disappeared. I want to laugh at myself, because I can actually feel the prick of goose bumps along my forearms, and the short, fine hairs at the nape of my neck standing on end. I've blundered into a horror-movie cliché, and I can't help but be reminded of Val Lewton's *Cat People*, the scene where Jane Rudolph walks quickly past Central Park, stalked by a vengeful Simone Simon, only to be rescued at the last possible moment by the fortuitous arrival of a city bus. But I know there's no helpful bus coming to intervene on my behalf, and, more importantly, I understand full fucking well that this night holds nothing more menacing than what my over-stimulated imagination has put there. I turn away from the street light and continue up the hill towards home. And I do not have to *pretend* that I don't hear footsteps following me, or the clack of claws on concrete, because I *don't*. The quick shadow, the peripheral blur, it was only a moment's misapprehension, no more than a trick of my exhausted, preoccupied mind, filled with the evening's morbid banter.

Oubliez le Chien.

Fifteen minutes later, I'm locking the front door of my apartment behind me. I make a hot cup of chamomile tea, which I drink standing at the kitchen counter. I'm in bed shortly after ten o'clock. By then, I've managed to completely dismiss whatever I only thought I saw crossing Jenckes Street.

5.

"Open your eyes, Ms. Howard," Abby Gladding says, and I do. Her voice does not in any way command me to open my eyes, and it is perfectly clear that I have a choice in the matter. But there's a certain *je-ne-sais-quoi* in the delivery, the inflection and intonation, in the measured conveyance of these four syllables, that makes it impossible for me to keep my eyes closed. It's not yet dawn, but sunrise cannot be very far away, and I am lying in my bed. I cannot say whether I am awake or dreaming, or if possibly I am stranded in some liminal state that is neither one nor the other. I am immediately conscious of an unseen weight bearing down painfully upon my chest, and I am having difficulty breathing.

"I promised that I'd call on you," she says, and, with great effort, I turn my head towards the sound of her voice, my cheek pressing deeply into my pillow. I am aware now that I am all but paralyzed, perhaps by the same force pushing down on my chest, and I strain for any glimpse of her. But there's only the bedside table, the clock radio and reading lamp and ashtray, an overcrowded bookcase with sagging shelves, and the floral calico wallpaper that came with the apartment. If I could move my arms, I would switch on the lamp. If I could move, I'd sit up, and maybe I would be able to breathe again.

And then I think that she must surely be singing, though her song has no words. There is no need for mere lyrics, not when texture and timbre, harmony and melody, are sufficient to unmake the mundane artifacts that comprise my bedroom, wiping aside the here and now that belie what I am meant to see, in this fleeting moment. And even as the wall and the bookshelf and the table beside my bed dissolve and fall away, I understand that her music is drawing me deeper into sleep again, though I must have been very nearly awake when she told me to open my eyes. I have no time to worry over apparent contradictions, and I can't move my head to look away from what she means for me to see.

There's nothing to be afraid of, I think, and *No more here than in any bad dream.* But I find the thought carries no conviction whatsoever. It's even less substantial than the dissolving wallpaper and bookcase.

And now I'm looking at the weed-choked shore of a misty pond or swamp, a bog or tidal marsh. The light is so dim it might be dusk, or it might be dawn, or merely an overcast day. There are huge trees bending low near the water, which seems almost perfectly smooth and the green of polished malachite. I hear frogs, hidden among the moss and reeds, the ferns and skunk cabbages, and now the calls of birds form a counterpoint to Abby's voice. Except, seeing her standing ankle deep in that stagnant green pool, I also see that she isn't singing. The music is coming from the violin braced against her shoulder, from the bow and strings and the movement of her left hand along the fingerboard of the instrument. She has her back to me, but I don't need to see her face to know it's her. Her black hair hangs down almost to her hips. And only now do I realize that she's naked.

Abruptly, she stops playing, and her arms fall to her sides, the violin in her left hand, the bow in her right. The tip of the bow breaks the surface of the pool, and ripples in concentric rings race away from it.

"I wear this rough garment to deceive," she says, and, at that, all the birds and frogs fall silent. "Aren't you the clever girl? Aren't you canny? I would not think appearances would so easily lead you astray. Not for long as this."

No words escape my rigid, sleeping jaws, but she hears me, all the same, my answer that needs no voice, and she turns to face me. Her eyes are golden, not blue. And in the low light, they briefly flash a bright, iridescent yellow. She smiles, showing me teeth as sharp as razors, and then she quotes from the Gospel of Matthew.

"Inwardly, they were ravening wolves," she says to me, though her tone is not unkind. "You've seen all that you need to see, and probably more, I'd wager." And with this, she turns away again, turning to face the fog shrouding the wide green pool. As I watch, helpless to divert my gaze or even shut my eyes, she lets the violin and bow slip from her hands; they fall into the water with quiet splashes. The bow sinks, though the violin floats. And then she goes down on all fours. She laps at the pool, and her hair has begun to writhe like a nest of serpents.

And now I'm awake, disoriented and my chest aching, gasping for air as if a moment before I was drowning and have only just been pulled to the safety of dry land. The wallpaper is only dingy calico again, and the bookcase is only a bookcase. The clock radio and the lamp and the ashtray sit in their appointed places upon the bedside table.

The sheets are soaked through with sweat, and I'm shivering. I sit up, my back braced against the headboard, and my eyes go to the second-story window on the other side of the small room. The sun is still down, but it's a little lighter out there than it is in the bedroom. And for a fraction of a moment, clearly silhouetted against that false dawn, I see the head and shoulders of a young woman. I also see the muzzle and alert ears of a wolf, and that golden eyeshine watching me. Then it's gone, she or it, whichever pronoun might best apply. It doesn't seem to matter. Because now I do know exactly what I'm looking for, and I know that I've seen it before, years before I first caught sight of Abby Gladding standing in the rain without an umbrella.

6.

Friday morning I drive back to Newport, and it doesn't take me long at all to find the grave. It's just a little ways south of the chain-link fence dividing the North Burial Ground from the older Common Burying Ground and Island Cemetery. I turn off Warner Street onto the rutted, unpaved road winding between the indistinct rows of monuments. I find a place that's wide enough to pull over and park. The trees have only just begun to bud, and their bare limbs are stark against a sky so blue-white it hurts my eyes to look directly into it. The grass is mostly still brown from long months of snow and frost, though there are small clumps of new green showing here and there.

The cemetery has been in use since 1640 or so. There are three Colonial-era governors buried here (one a delegate to the Continental Congress), along with the founder of Freemasonry in Rhode Island, a signatory to the Declaration of Independence, various Civil-War generals, lighthouse keepers, and hundreds of African slaves stolen from Gambia and Sierra Leone, the Gold and Ivory coasts and brought to Newport in the hey-day of whaling and the Rhode Island rum trade. The grave of Abby Gladding is marked by a weathered slate headstone, badly scabbed over with lichen. But, despite the centuries, the shallow inscription is still easy enough to read:

HERE LYETH INTERED Y^e^ BODY
OF ABBY MARY GLADDING
DAUGHTER OF SOLOMON CLADDING ^esq^
& MARY HIS WYFE WHO
DEPARTED THIS LIFE Y^e^ 2^d^ DAY OF
SEPT 1785 AGED 22 YEARS
SHE WAS DROWN'D & DEPARTED & SLEEPS
^ZECH 4:1^ NEITHER SHALL THEY WEAR
A HAIRY GARMENT TO DECEIVE

Above the inscription, in place of the usual death's head, is a crude carving of a violin. I sit down in the dry, dead grass in front of the marker, and I don't know how long I've been sitting there when I hear crows cawing. I look over my shoulder, and there's tree back towards Farewell Street filled with the big black birds. The watch me, and I take that as my cue to leave. I know now that I have to go back to the library, that whatever remains of this mystery is waiting for me there. I might find it tucked away in an old journal a newspaper clipping, or in crumbling church records. I only know I'll find it, because now I have the missing pieces. But there is an odd reluctance to leave the grave of Abby Gladding. There's no fear in me, no shock or stubborn disbelief at what I've discovered or at its impossible ramifications. And some part of me notes the oddness of this, that I am not afraid. I leave her alone in that narrow house, watched over by the wary crows, and go back to my car. Less than fifteen minutes later I'm in the Redwood Library, asking for anything they can find on a Solomon Gladding, and his daughter, Abby.

"Are you sick?" the librarian asks, and I wonder what she sees in my face, in my eyes, to elicit such a question. "Are you feeling well?"

"I'm fine," I assure her. "I was up a little too late last night, that's all. A little too much to drink, most likely."

She nods, and I smile.

"Well, then. I'll see what we might have," she says, and, cutting to the chase, it ends with a short article that appeared in the *Newport Mercury* early in November 1785, hardly more than two months after Abby Gladding's death. It begins, "We hear a ftrange account from laft Thursday evening, the Night of the 3rd of November, of a body difinterred from its Grave and coffin. This most peculiar occurrence was undertaken at the beheft of the father of the deceafed young woman therein buried, a circumftance making the affair even ftranger ftill." What follows is a description of a ritual which will be familiar to anyone who has read of the 1892 Mercy Brown case from Exeter, or the much earlier exhumation of Nancy Young (summer of 1827), or other purported New England "vampires."

In September, Abby Gladding's body was discovered in Newport Harbor by a local fisherman, and it was determined that she had drowned. The body was in an advanced state of decay, leading me to wonder if the date of the headstone is meant to be the date the body was found, not the date of her death. There were persistent rumors that the daughter of Samuel Gladding, a local merchant, had taken her own life. She is said to have been a "child of singular and morbid temperament," who had recently refused a marriage proposal by the eldest son of another Newport merchant, Ebenezer Burrill.

There was also back-fence talk that Abby had practiced witchcraft in the woods bordering the town, and that she would play her violin (a gift from her mother) to summon "voracious wolves and other such dæmons to do her bidding."

Very shortly after her death, her youngest sister, Susan, suddenly fell ill. This was in October, and the girl was dead before the end of the month. Her symptoms, like those of Mercy Brown's stricken family members, can readily be identified as late-stage tuberculosis. What is peculiar here is that Abby doesn't appear to have suffered any such wasting disease herself, and the speed with which Susan became ill and died is also atypical of consumption. Even as Susan fought for her life, Abby's mother, Mary, fell ill, and it was in hope of saving his wife that Solomon Gladding agreed to the exhumation of his daughter's body. The article in the *Newport Mercury* speculates that he'd learned of this ritual and folk remedy from a Jamaican slave woman.

At sunrise, with the aid of several other men, some apparently family members, the grave was opened, and all present were horrified to see "the body fresh as the day it was configned to God," her cheeks "flufhed with colour and lufterous." The liver and heart were duly cut out, and both were discovered to contain clotted blood, which Solomon had been told would prove that Abby was rising from her grave each night to steal the blood of her mother and sister. The heart was burned in a fire kindled in the cemetery, the ashes mixed with water, and the mother drank the mixture. The body of Abby was turned facedown in her casket, and an iron stake was driven through her chest, to insure that the restless spirit would be unable to find its way out of the grave. Nonetheless, according to parish records from Trinity Church, Mary Gladding died before Christmas. Her father fell ill a few months later, and died in August of 1786.

And I find one more thing that I will put down here. Scribbled in sepia ink, in the left-hand margin of the newspaper page containing the account of the exhumation of Abby Gladding is the phrase *Jé-rouge*, or "red eyes," which I've learned is a Haitian term denoting werewolfery and cannibalism. Below that word, in the same spidery hand, is written "As white as snow, as red as red, as green as briers, as black as coal." There is no date or signature accompanying these notations.

And now it is almost Friday night, and I sit alone on a wooden bench at Bowen's Wharf, not too far from the kiosk advertising daily boat tours to view fat, doe-eyed seals sunning themselves on the rocky beaches ringing Narragansett Bay. I sit here and watch the sun going down, shivering because I left home this morning without my coat. I do not expect to see

Abby Gladding, tonight or ever again. But I've come here, anyway, and I may come again tomorrow evening.

I will not include the 1785 disinterment in my thesis, no matter how many feathers it might earn for my cap. I mean never to speak of it again. What I have written here, I suspect I'll destroy it later on. It has only been written for me, and for me alone. If Abby was trying to speak *through* me, to find a larger audience, she'll have to find another mouthpiece. I watch a lobster boat heading out for the night. I light a cigarette, and eye the herring gulls wheeling above the marina.

Come up with a convincing character and no one will ask: Is it true or is it make-believe? For the period of reading, it will necessarily be true. How eagerly we collaborate in our own hoodwinking. All an author has to do is say: Listen. This is what happened . . .

TRAGIC LIFE STORIES

STEVE DUFFY

Eidetic, a. (Psychol.) Applied to an image that creates an optical impression with hallucinatory clearness, or to the faculty of seeing such images, or to a person having this faculty. Also *n.*, one who sees eidetic images.

"The inability to discriminate between hallucinations and normal mental imagery and the mental confusion thereby entailed is responsible for a psychological abortion called the *eidetic image.*"

—C. Fox, *Educational Psychology*

It was an attritional season, the spring of slow destruction. In the space of four months beginning in January, Dan had managed to lose both his life partner and his book deal. He'd seen the first one coming: things between him and Angie had been getting bad for quite some time, and when she finally said, Look, there's this man at work, he'd accepted it pretty much without protesting. She'd fallen out of love with him, was all. What else could he do? He was fine with it, really, so long as he didn't stop to think about the two of them together, Angie and Malcolm. So long as he didn't ever do that, it was fine. Because if he did, it was like a hook in his guts, like being caught on barbed wire while the rats gnawed your heart out. Whenever he thought about that, or about the times they'd had, or about the bitter hopelessness of the Ange-subtracted future, then it was pretty bad, and so he tried not to, inasmuch as that was possible.

The business with the book deal, on the other hand, had come out of nowhere. He'd had an invitation to lunch in town, to talk over the options—that's what they'd said, those were exactly the words they'd used, he remembered it perfectly—and before the dessert trolley had come round, he'd been dumped. "Taking a hard look at the fiction end of the operation." "Revising our strategies." "Great opportunities to explore new partnerships." *Bullshit*. He'd been given the heave-ho. You get to recognize the signs, after a while. When enough people take it in turns to crap on you, you either get an umbrella or you put up a notice saying Town Dump. He barely heard the bleated goodbyes from the insultingly young suit they'd sent to do the dirty deed. Mechanically, he shook hands and stumbled off into the gray afternoon, on the verge of a major panic attack.

An hour of aimless rambling round the streets of Chester brought him back to himself, more or less, stabilized him without even beginning to cheer him up. He might have gone home then, back to his rented flat across the railway tracks—but to what? Instead, he made the great mistake of going into WHSmith's, just for a look, just to prove something to himself, that's all. It was a large branch with an extensive book section, and he made a beeline for FANTASY.

There they were, the bastards—all the usual suspects, smug and secure in their shiny bastard jackets. This one: he couldn't write two grammatical sentences in a row, his sub-editor spent upwards of six months on each MS, Dan knew that for a fact. Not so much editing it, as translating it into English. *This* one next to him: been ripping off Tolkien for how long now? Surprised she hadn't grown a beard and changed her name to Gandalf. And this one? This one was very, very lucky the girl's parents had decided not to bring charges—and no one was taking a hard look at the fiction end of *his* operation, were they? *Bastards*. At least he'd never have to share a panel with them at some godawful convention in Leicester or Ashton-under-Lyne ever again. It was the small presses for him now—if he could even be bothered.

Really, though: could he? Go the small press route? Right now, he suspected not. Chronicling the lives and times of Nevernesse was onerous enough at the best of times, when you knew the results would enjoy a guaranteed appearance between elegantly foil-embossed covers on the shelves of bookshop and library, with a print run firmly into four figures. Was he really going to go back to desktop-publishing layouts and editions of two hundred and fifty? *Could* he?

It was that or get a proper job, though. That, or stop to take stock of the world without Ange—and there it was, jabbing right into the heart of him again. A gangling young pair of Goths with big hair and multi-buckled garments crowded him out of the way of the Fantasy shelves, where they immediately honed in on . . . who else but the biggest bastard of the lot? Mister fucking Peter Perfect, darling of the convention, Angie's favorite author—she's actually told him that much, in Dan's own hearing, that time in Nottingham. He had to get away. Eyes swimming, overcome all at once with a sour uprush of exquisite self-pity, he wandered off to an adjacent section.

"Excuse me? Are you okay?" There was genuine solicitude in the voice of the well-dressed woman who touched his elbow. "Is everything all right?"

Trying very hard not to break down and weep aloud in the middle of WHSmith (there would be a time and a place, but not here, not now, please god), Dan bit down on his lip. What might be a good enough reason to be blubbing in a bookshop? He was about to invent a wholly spurious bereavement, and was casting about for the right degree of relationship to the beloved departed, when the woman said sympathetically, "Is it to do with the book? It's nothing to be ashamed of, you know."

Bloody hell, word traveled fast, didn't it? "I'm sorry?"

"It *is* very moving. I cried myself." She was holding on to his elbow, standing very close by his side. Her voice, pitched conspiratorially low, sounded in his ear like the sea inside a shell. He hadn't been so close to a woman in months. Now she was whispering a secret: "I actually think it's rather lovely, that you're so connected with your feelings. Most men aren't. Like my ex. Or poor Ando's father."

"Sorry?" Was she actually insane, though? There were lots of walking wounded on the streets these days. They got thrown out of their bed-and-breakfasts at ten, and couldn't go back till teatime. This one was far more presentable than any of those, and not so patently damaged as the majority of them. . . . but she *was* holding his elbow quite tightly, and she *did* have a slightly despondent kind of look about her, some fundamental neediness chronically unassuaged. Maybe money couldn't buy you happiness after all. Dan tried to concentrate on the conversation at hand. "Ando?"

"Ando, in the book." She picked up a hardback from the display stand in front of them. Dan hadn't noticed it was even there. "Ando McElwee? *I Won't Do It Any More, Daddy?*"

That was the title, all right. Dan rubbed his eyes with the end of his sleeve, got a grip of himself, and focused on the book. The words were spelled out in a child's crayon scrawl over a photograph of a little boy hiding under a table, fists screwed into his weeping eyes. He looked just about how Dan felt, in fact. Why hadn't he thought to hide under a table? Mechanically, Dan flipped the book open, looking for a synopsis of the plot.

The inside cover blurb told a story of familial horror even Virginia Andrews would have thought twice before using. Apparently the young man on the front cover had been raised by the chickens on his family farm, his operatically dysfunctional family (father, stepmother, sundry half-brothers and -sisters) having obliged him to live in the shed since his fifth birthday. From then until adulthood, they'd more or less left him to the roosters, except to look in on him once every week or so and subject him to Wagnerian passages of escalating abuse, group and solo, all conducted by Daddy—hence the title. This until he escaped, and moved to California to write his memoirs, described by *Marie-Claire* as "heart-rending" and by *Cosmopolitan* as, bizarrely enough, "uplifting and inspiring".

"I tell myself: if you only had a fraction of his courage, Molly." The woman was gripping his elbow still, patting his forearm with her free hand in reassurance. As if replacing an unexploded hand grenade, Dan set the book back on the shelf and looked at her more closely. She was thin, painfully so, with a figure that complemented the expensive designer clothes she was wearing. Her hair was possibly not quite the rich shade of auburn under which it advertised itself, and repeated shots of Botox had smoothed ten years' worth of lines from her face without touching the underlying worries that had caused them. Still, you know what they say about beggars. Dan, who in his best suit looked like a named and shamed Fred Flintstone dragged before the magistrate's court, swallowed hard and chose anyway. "You're very kind," he told her, engulfing her birdlike hand in his hot bear's paw and returning her friendly squeeze. "Look, there's a Costa over there. Can I get you a coffee or something to say thank you?"

Molly, it turned out, was absolutely thrilled to be sharing a cappuccino with a real live writer. Dan, only too aware that this flattering description was now obsolete in several respects, did his best to appear modest. Yes, he'd had five books out. Yes, they'd done pretty well. Yes, he was working on something at the moment.

Well, that last was stretching it a bit, maybe. For over a year now he'd been trying to breathe life into the flatlined, faintly odorous corpse of *Storm's Doom: The Sixth Chronicle of Nevernesse*. He'd finally given up on it soon after Christmas, round about the same time Angie had served notice on their relationship. Now, he found it impossible to return to the wreckage of one without being confronted with the shambles of the other. They were inextricably linked in his mind, twin aspects of his general uselessness, guarantors of his indignity. Still, the file did actually exist on his hard drive, so there you were. "Trying to knock it into shape, you know," he explained, and Molly gazed at him with wholly unfeigned admiration, as she might have gazed on Michelangelo finding David inside the obdurate lump of marble. There was one question yet to come, though—

"Where do you get your ideas from?"

That's the one. Like a number ten bus rolling up to the stop. "Well, there's this site on the Internet," he said, and Molly snorted with laughter, in a way she clearly felt unbecoming—she covered her mouth with a hand—but which Dan actually found rather cute. She was quite pretty when she laughed. Vivacious, even. It took years off her. "No, seriously: ideas dot com, slash, better-ideas-than-yours, all one word. Absolute godsend. They take all major credit cards." She was laughing again. God, this was going well. *Still got it*, he told himself hollowly.

"But you're interested in tragic life stories too," she said, regaining her composure.

"I'm sorry?" *Tragic what?*

"Like Ando McElwee. Tragic life stories?"

Oh, Christ. Misery-lit. *A Child Called Shit*. That balloon juice she'd been going on about in the bookshop. "Well," he began, playing for time, "well, yeah, I suppose I do find that sort of thing, you know, quite, um, interesting . . . " Interesting. Right. *Cheap holidays in other people's misery*, was what he'd actually said: at the last Nevercon, it was, a bunch of them propping up the bar, Dan holding boozily forth while Angie sat abandoned at their table, the only sane woman in a room full of geeks and blowhards.

"I think it goes beyond interesting," Molly said. It was one of the things he found attractive about her: she didn't waste time with the commonplaces. "I actually find it quite humbling, to read about these people's struggles. Uplifting, too, in a way. I mean, it gives me such a perspective on my own life."

Yeah, but that was part of the problem, wasn't it? They were suffering to make you feel good about yourself, then, these poor sods? It was almost like the old argument against fox hunting: one was against it not only because of the discomfort suffered by the fox, but because of the enjoyment derived by the spectators. After a while, misery must surely become as addictive, not to say as formulaic, as pornography—two subjects on which Dan felt supremely well qualified to comment. When you slurped down shelf after shelf of this stuff, what did it say about your discernment? If you started to empathize with it, what did it say about your self-image?

Of course, he said none of these things, not wanting the doe-eyed and frankly doting expression on Molly's face to cloud over. Instead, he said: "I saw the film of *Angela's Ashes*. Do you go to the cinema much, at all?"

By the time they'd finished their coffees, there existed a more-or-less definite commitment to a film, perhaps a meal as well, or a drink, or both. The Cheshire Oaks had been mentioned, a retail village complete with multiplex just up the M53. Molly lived in Mickle Trafford, not ten minutes away from the misery hutch in Hoole that Dan called a bachelor flat. He could pick her up, no trouble: Pizza Hut and a movie, then let's see what happens. That was the plan, to be enacted sometime in the very near future. Not right away, though, since the Easter holidays would make the multiplex all but unbearable for a week or so. This led to a question, which Dan hesitantly pitched . . .

And received the expected answer. Though divorced, Molly had no children: imagine, all those nurturing instincts, and no kids on which to squander them. Dan used to dream about that sort of thing.

He was under no illusions as to the long-term prospects of their dating. He was aware, after all, of the neon sign that flashed on and off above his head, spelling out the salient points of his situation to potential partners: HUNGUP, SELF-CENTERED AND WORRYINGLY INFANTILE—PLEASE PASS. The wise ones did, and as for the rest of them? At least when it all went tits-up in the end, they couldn't say they hadn't been warned.

In the meantime, though, Molly should be just the job. It was fair to say she was the first good thing that had happened to him all year—and after the time he'd had, he needed several very good things indeed, coming one after another. Stroke after stroke of luck, good fortune stacked up in wedding-cake layers, just to tempt him out from under the table, away from the lugubrious company of Ando McElwee and his brothers in pain.

Like giggly adolescents, the two of them exchanged contact details outside on the street. Dan gallantly punched his number into the memory of her Blackberry (which she clearly had no idea how to use) and stored her own on his Samsung—work phone, home landline, *and* mobile, just to be on the safe side. Her words, not his. He remembered just in time the photo of Angie that was still set to display as the wallpaper on his phone's screen, and managed to shield it off without making it look too obvious.

Having seen Molly off along the Rows—she kept turning round for one last wave, which he found slightly needy yet undeniably appealing—Dan set out for "home" with a strange mixture of emotions. On the one hand, he'd lost his deal. Crap, crap, crap: that was the deal gone, unbelievable. His *deal*, his precious seven-booker. On the other, a well-off, presentable woman who was neither his dentist nor his bank manager had shared his company for just over an hour, and showed every sign of wanting to repeat the experience, pretty much as soon as possible. True, said woman *was* heavily into misery-lit—not to mention angel-lit, a swoony sub-genre of inspirational New Age which Dan viewed with the utmost foreboding. Still, sensitive souls like that could occasionally surprise you with a startlingly uninhibited attitude in the sack. Low self-esteem, he supposed, coupled with a tendency to the histrionic. Swings and roundabouts, then.

Looked at objectively, of course, and with a proper sense of proportion, losing his book deal was bad, very bad. However, the events of the afternoon had given him an idea. Maybe all was not lost after all. First, though, there was the rest of the day to get through.

The evening fizzled out to nothing, like a bullet fired into a water tank for forensics. After forking down his singleton's microwave slop-pail and flicking through the electronic programme guide for the least annoying channels of distraction, Dan spent the hours before sleep downing can after can of Stella, going over his cunning new plan, and most importantly of all, not calling his old number to talk to Angie. Definitely not doing that. Malcolm had a habit of picking up first, for all the world as if he lived there—which, of course, he did. Damn. Dan slept the sleep of the inexpertly anesthetized, and woke some time before six the next morning, feeling pretty much the way you might expect.

He put the coffee on to drip while he attended to the most pressing of his hygienic requirements. Taking his brimming mug of Colombian roast through to the back room, he powered up the computer, before abandoning it on a whim for his Powerbook. He wrote Nevernesse on the desktop machine, and this would be something different, after all.

Sitting at the desk like a diner who isn't particularly hungry and who sees nothing on the menu to tempt him, Dan eyed the white screen of a blank new Word file with bleary distaste. Experimentally he clicked on the Open File icon: there they were, seven directories' worth of Nevernesse. Drafts, revisions, fair copies, PDF proofs. How many words? How many million billion characters tapped out in his stiff four-finger typing? How much of his precious time on this earth?

Well, that last one was easy enough to work out. Nevernesse spanned with pretty fair exactitude the duration of his relationship with Angie: from the first short tales of Hawkheart in Galibion, round about the time they'd met, to the wreck of the sixth chronicle, when she'd moved Malcolm in to their fatally compromised wedding bed. *Fuck it, anyway. Fuck Nevernesse, and fuck Angie. Fuck the lot of you, actually.* Crabbily, Dan clicked on the red X at the corner of the window to make it go away.

Back on the blank white page, the cursor blinked on and off like a metronome. Dan fiddled with the blink rate in the Control Panel for a while before catching himself. No more diversionary tactics. He'd be changing his default font next.

Almost without thinking, he typed "My uncle used to burn the soles of my feet." It had been running through his head since yesterday, ever since he'd looked at the Ando McElwee book. He read the sentence back, then pressed Home and amended its beginning. "When I was a little boy, my uncle used to burn the soles of my feet." The End key took him back to the end of the line, where he added "with cigarettes" to give the line a better balance. "When I was a little boy, my uncle used to burn the soles of my feet with cigarettes."

There was a voice in there, he thought: simple, declarative, with a naïve kind of narrative authority. This, you felt, was what had happened. You were buying it from the off. You wanted to find out more.

So let's see what comes next. Kindling the narrative spark, urging the fire to catch a hold, he typed on. "He used to come back from the pub and come into my bedroom . . . " No. Two *comes* in the one sentence, that wasn't good. Make that "*barge* into my bedroom, smelling of beer." Smelling of *ale*. Better. Gives it a geographical reality. He had in mind the north country, where he was born, and he wanted to get the phrasing right. Nobody spoke like this in Nevernesse; but then, nobody there had bad uncles barging into their bedrooms all aled up, either. Also, in Nevernesse everyone tended to be either hero or villain, and this new protagonist was neither—he was a victim, possibly *the* victim, the all-time award winning injured party. For Dan, it was a total departure from the known: his first work of misery-lit.

He'd always found the start of a new project an exciting, even a magical thing. He'd tried to capture a flavor of it in the very first Chronicle, in the opening scenes where young Berain stands on the hilltop of fair counsel and gazes over the long marches of Nevernesse receding into hazy distance, the towers of far Indricium rearing up in the spring sunshine many leagues to the West. Etcetera, etcetera. And yet that was how Dan always felt, starting a story: as if he were standing on a hilltop, surveying the spread of possibilities ranged below. Truly surveying them: the eidetic image is really nothing like the image produced by mental recollection. Dan knew not all writers shared this gift, but privately he didn't reckon much to the work of those who hadn't got it. You could always tell.

So you beheld your creation, unfolded as if by magic before you. There were landmarks by which to navigate: plot points you'd thought out beforehand, action you needed to incorporate, but all the rest was up for grabs. There might be anything out there in those misty golden reaches—anything at all! —and discovering it would be like a great adventure, a journey for both the hero and the child popularly held to cohabit inside us all.

Why did people knock escapism in literature? he'd once asked the audience at a convention. Why, when you spend thousands of pounds on a holiday where everything goes wrong and you spend the first three nights stuck at the airport and they lose your bags, and the hotel's appalling when you get there and the sandflies buzz you all the while and you come back with the squirting shits and a bank balance that could crawl underneath a settee, and you swear you'll never go back *there* again . . . why, when you were prepared to go through all that twice a year, would you want to knock the greatest escape of all, the one you made simply by opening the cover of a book? He'd actually got a round of applause for that, though to be fair he had been preaching to the converted, not to say borderline obsessive. Most people—most *normal* people, the ones who watched the soaps where narrative was brought to your plate ready pureed, all the meat cut up for you in case you choked on an uncomfortably chewy plot development—they would still have dismissed him as an irredeemable saddo. A book-owl, a weirdo, a wimp. Fuck them, anyway (as previously noted). Fuck the lot of them. He was breaking through now. Going mainstream with a vengeance.

The plan, as he'd envisaged it the night before, was to spend no more than a couple of months knocking out an unbelievably harrowing yet totally spurious work of misery-lit, the completed MS to be hawked round the publishers under a nom-de-plume, as was standard practice to protect the innocent. Specifically, him. In the absence of any childhood trauma—no uncles, drunk or sober, had ever burned the soles of his feet—he would fall back on his powers of invention. If he could conjure all the complicated grandeur of Nevernesse into being, he ought to be able to manage the tale of one child's formative years among the cigarette-ends. Sell one of these babies, and he'd never have to work again. How many lustrals since Gorlain was regent in Indricium? Who gave a flying toss?

And it was coming together, that was the great thing. It was coming to life. He had a handle on it. There was the child cowering in his bed; there, the bad uncle looming in the lighted doorway. Now he had to find the surroundings. What sort of place was it all happening in? The easiest thing to do was to use this very room as his template, of course. The back room of this flat, which had obviously been a bedroom once upon a time. So: out with all these books, move that filing-cabinet, shift those shelves. Let's have . . . a wardrobe in the recess there, a knocked-around wardrobe with mirrors in the doors and model airplanes on the top. Model tanks? No, airplanes. They'd signify his desire to escape, later on. And there was the bed, against that wall. Single bed, with an old-fashioned coverlet, sheets and blankets. And on the other side, the fitted cupboards; they could stay. Maybe the young lad would hide in there from time to time. Yes, the young lad. What was his name, now?

That was a tough one, for some reason or other. Dan auditioned a whole litany of boys' forenames, none of which seemed right somehow, before shaking his head and typing in X. X was fine for now—in a way, X might even do as a permanent solution. Like those black activists in the 1960s trading in their slave names. So, there's X in the bed, with a picture on the wall, a picture of . . . *The Light of the World*? Creepy Jesus, looming in the gloaming? Religious was good. If abusers were the worst kind of hypocrites, then the subset of the religious hypocritical had to be worse still—they were the ones all the other nonces looked down on, surely. The Light of the World, then? Maybe. Wasn't sure. But leave it there for the time being. Flying fingers, flying fingers.

Curtains at the window. The sort of house where the curtains would often stay closed in the daytime, he thought. Stuffy. Secretive. House of secrets. Neighbors never guessed a thing. And outside? Dan glanced through his own window, over the rooftops of Hoole at the railway lines receding into the distance. That would do. Again, might be used later: symbol of child's wish to escape. He could bring all that out in the second draft, where you picked out the symbolism and polished it to best effect. First draft, you followed the seam of the narrative, knocked in the pit-props of plot, and let the symbols look after themselves.

This was good, it was actually working. He knew where he was now; he had his bearings, his handle on the reality of things. The eidetic image was strong in his head, alive already. Onward, ever onward. He typed quickly, as if taking dictation, "Afterwards, I used to look out of my window at the railway lines and wish I was somewhere far away." Judiciously, he arrow-keyed back to the space before "away," to add a comma and another "far." Outside, the sun rose over the Chester suburbs. Dan, oblivious to everything but the story, typed on.

It was knocking midday when he pushed away from the desk and stretched his legs. He'd gone through three pots of coffee, and managed over three thousand words. Good work, too: surprisingly good, considering he'd never done this sort of thing before. Good purely as in "wouldn't need much editing," mind you; as to the ultimate literary worth of his MS, Dan was under no illusions whatsoever. This was not the place to prove himself worthy of the awards currently gathering dust on his shelves (Most Promising Work of Short Fantasy, 1994; Best Character in an Ongoing Saga, 1999). Here, two things were necessary, and two things only: the outward appearance of realism, and the jarring dissonance between horror and the everyday. Piece of cake. It was oddly liberating to work in such narrowly circumscribed circumstances. Once your characters were properly established, you could turn out something approaching pure narrative, page after page of what happened next.

Dan crossed the room to the window and lifted the sash, letting the warm fresh morning air flow in on the stale west-facing room. On the wall to his left was the fitted cupboard, a plasterboard relic of indifferent DIY from the '60s. It filled up the alcove to the right of the chimney-breast: there was a corresponding recess to the left where Dan had put his bookcases. The cupboard boards were warping now, and had Dan owned the place, rather than rented, he'd have torn the lot out and cleared the alcove without a second thought.

Inside the cupboard, behind all the junk left by a previous tenant (mildewed suits, old vinyl albums by Wishbone Ash and Camel) there was a door in the wall, blocked off at the sill with a length of two-by-four nailed to the bare floorboards like a brutalist draft excluder. Dan had seen this sort of thing many times in semis and terraces, back when he was a student in Liverpool. This was what landlords used to do before building regs clamped down on them and emphasized the need for proper fire escapes. It was a fire door: it would open on to a narrow space and then another, exactly similar door which gave access to the adjacent property. In the event of a fire you were supposed to pile through to next door's bedroom—that is, assuming some previous tenant afraid of burglars (or worse) hadn't nailed the door shut.

With a grimace—it was horribly musty in there, that was where the stink came from in this room, clearly—Dan peered inside the cupboard door. Next time someone had a skip on the street, he'd chuck the lot out. For now, he was thinking it would do very well as a place for X to hide in. That space in between the two doors. "The smell of old clothes and damp used to make me feel sick," murmured Dan aloud. "Or maybe it was just the fear—the fear of what would happen when he found me." Sort of thing.

He was peckish after a hard morning's work, and thought he'd go into town for a cooked meal in his favorite bistro down by the river. It remained only to name his file. After rejecting, with whimsical regret, *Cigarettes Are Harmful to Your Health* and *A Boy Called X*, he typed into the Save As dialogue box the words *SAY UNCLE*. He could see it now, in messy crayon over a photo of a child hiding in a cupboard. It had a ring to it.

By the end of the week, Dan had almost twelve thousand words of fair copy. It was the sort of work rate he used to reach once he was well embarked on a Nevernesse project, where he knew inside-out the characters and the universe they inhabited. Working in the dark with X and his ne'er-do-well family, twelve thousand inside a week was little short of miraculous. He'd impressed himself.

He had an excellent working image of the house and its inhabitants in his head. There was Liza the gymslip mother, easily cowed, too easily led astray. Jack, the dad, was away with the Merchant Marine eleven months out of twelve. Something very bad was going to happen to him in Manila, thought Dan. *He* wouldn't be seeing Newcastle again. And of course there was Bob, Liza's fancy man, the gruesome alpha male who ruled the roost in Jack's absence—"Uncle" Bob, that was. Say Uncle. And the lad X, cowering there in his cupboard; mustn't forget him. Our special little fella; our tiny gold mine.

Actually, that wasn't the whole truth, not any more. It might have been at the start of the project, when Dan was still envisaging the whole thing purely as a quick, vaguely satirical way to turn a cynical profit. But you can't stay around people for hours at a time and not become a little sensitized to their suffering, not unless you're a total pig. Even kidnappers must fall prey to some Stockholm syndrome-in-reverse, and start to feel a kind of responsibility towards their abductees. If you weren't emotionally engaged with a writing project, then the characters would never come to life—that was Dan's experience. So while maintaining a healthy perspective on X's Byzantine travails, he did at least feel a modicum of sympathy towards the poor mite shivering behind the fire door in the cupboard.

Apart from anything else, it helped Dan get inside his head, and that was the key to making the finished manuscript halfway readable, he thought. Get the little details right, and you'd smuggle the rest through unnoticed. Come up with a convincingly wounded child, and no one would think to ask, *Is it true or is it make-believe?* For the period of reading, it would necessarily be true. That was the trick, after all. How eagerly we collaborate in our own hoodwinking. All an author has to do is say: *Listen. This is what happened.* And we can't get enough: like fledglings we strain wide our beaks for another mess of regurgitated worms. Not one of the more elegant metaphors for the writer's craft, but in this case it seemed only too appropriate.

As he hammered out the paragraphs on his humming Powerbook, Dan cast many a glance at the back cupboard, visualizing the tight restricted space between the fire doors, between this flat and the one next door. Having decided that's where X would hide, he'd tried to work out the internal logic of it, just to see if it was worth persevering with. Perhaps the main feature was an all-pervasive threat, a hazard from either side. X was stuck between two doors, one which opened on a known and terrifying situation, the other on a peril unknown, yet no less scary. Maybe. He might be able to do something with that, when the time came. Symbolism in the second draft, and not before. In the meantime, it felt right, which was good enough for the time being.

He'd gone so far as to remove the piece of wood that blocked the fire door on his side, so he could have a look at the gap in between. A small space, all cobwebs and builder's dust: big enough for a skinny kid to squeeze inside with both doors shut, but no larger than that. Opening up the fire door might not have been the best idea so far as his own comfort went, though. It seemed to have let a draft through from somewhere, and now the room was not only colder then before, but the cupboard door rattled from time to time, just the wrong side of annoyingly.

The weekend passed as weekends will for men in Dan's position: indistinguishable from the week preceding it, and from the week still to come. He wrote; he watched TV; he drank slightly more than was good for him, because no one told him not to. On Sunday night, he managed (after several pints of Stella) to screw up his courage and ring the number—Molly's home phone. She was letting the machine pick up until she heard Dan's introductory stammer, then all of a sudden she cut through her own voice on the line, gushing in relief. Apparently she'd been scared he wouldn't ring. *She* was scared? Clearly this was worth going through with after all. Nobody had been this pleased to hear from him in years.

They arranged a get-together: that was what they were calling it still, just to be on the safe side. Get-together rather than date, no pressure, no sweat. He'd pick her up at her place on Thursday evening, and they'd go to the Cheshire Oaks as agreed for a pizza and a film. As soon as she said yes—which she did immediately, as if she'd been waiting all week just for him to ask—Dan suddenly had a debilitating attack of should-I. He was obliged to counterfeit an incoming call on his other line, just so he could get off the phone and take stock.

Unless he was misreading the situation with an emotional illiteracy bordering on the remedial, he'd cracked it with Molly. But was it the right thing for him at this specific moment? Was it really what he wanted? He lit a Marlboro—and *that* was something odd, right there. After giving up smoking for five years he'd suddenly gone out and bought a pack that morning after writing. What was that about? He decided it was the absence of Angie, as much as anything. He liked cigarettes, after all, he craved the clarity and the focus they gave him, and the only reason he'd given up in the first place was because she'd wanted him to. Now, he could do whatever he wanted. Smoke. Drink. Date other women. Prostitute his talent. Whatever. Anyway, smoking helped him think, so shut up.

This business, now: this thing with Angie. *Molly!* Molly. (Had to stop doing that: suppose it happened on their date? Dan grimaced reflexively, caught himself doing it in the mirror, and mentally slapped the other side of his face. *If the wind changes, you'll be stuck like that*, Angie used to say.) What was so bad about Molly, anyway? She was highly presentable, in that Cheshire commuter-belt style he'd always assumed was outside his range; she was kind and thoughtful, and she wore her heart pinned bravely on her sleeve. Any other problems? *Well, she's not* Angie, *is she*, pointed out a small mutinous voice from some reactive cranny of his mind.

Oh, excuse me? he wanted to say. Not *who* again? Angie who dumped me? Angie who lobbed the ten years we spent together right down the fucking pan? Angie who moved another bloke in on the exact same weekend *I* packed up and moved out? To show the voice exactly what he thought of that argument, he redialed Molly's number on the spot, apologized for the hiatus ("Nothing important") and firmed up the details of their get-together, specifying time and place. Thursday, then, and he'd be at hers for seven: fine. She seemed genuinely glad he'd rung back—absurdly so, in fact. It was remarkable.

In the end it seemed easier to drink a few more cans of Stella Artois than to analyze matters. Action first, as with writing. Think about it later. He'd got lucky for once, that was all—don't start picking holes in it, not yet for God's sake. Nodding to himself with the lumbering owlishness of the drunk, he fell asleep on the sofa, and woke up around three with a crick in his neck, an urgent need to pee, and a dismal suspicion he wouldn't be able to get back to sleep. And lo, it came to pass.

Submitting around four a.m. to the inevitable, he shuffled yawning into the back room, dressed for bed still in tracksuit bottoms and T-shirt. In one hand he clutched a carton of orange juice, in the other a monster mug of coffee. The juice helped stave off dehydration, and cut the stale nasty taste in his mouth, while the coffee helped him form legible sentences—or so he hoped. He lit up a cigarette (ash, he noticed with a throb of shame, was already accumulating between the keys of his Powerbook) and flipped open the lid.

By now, rather than sitting at the desk, he'd taken to propping his laptop on a padded tray, like an invalid's dinner, and making himself comfortable in the recliner by the window. This arrangement allowed him not to turn his back on the room, which was handy if he needed to check some feature or other, and it was much more comfortable. Now, with the *Say Uncle* file open on screen, he leaned back, narrowed his eyes, and did some more visualizing. The eideteker's gift requires mental space, and a sensitivity to nuance not everyone possesses, but once the connection is established it's surprising—alarming, to some—how real everything will seem.

Here was X with the cupboard door closed, in the space between the fire doors. The business with the cupboard being his place of escape: he was happy with that, wasn't he, by the way? Easy enough to write it out at the first draft, otherwise. It wasn't too *The Lion, the Witch and the Wardrobe*, for instance, was it?

"I read *The Lion, the Witch and the Wardrobe* books," he told himself in X's reedy voice, like a bad ventriloquist—his lips moved on the *W*s, but everybody's did, a bit. "I used to imagine that, if I could make myself very small and very thin, I wouldn't have to go through either door—I could squeeze through the space in between, and come out somewhere else entirely." That was good. That wasn't a bad angle, actually. One door, in this reading, would symbolize his current plight: his blighted childhood, his bad uncle. The other would symbolize, er, something else—his future, probably, adulthood yet to come, as represented by the normal people next door who didn't know anything about what was going on (wasn't too sure about that, exactly, just yet. Did he want to get the neighbors involved? On the whole, Dan's instinct was rather against bringing the neighbors into it). The space between, now: that was actually quite interesting. Child's flight into something or other. The crack in between. Escape.

"Escape," he said aloud, and heard X repeat it, lisping slightly on the sibilants in that childish way of his. His voice was muffled, barely audible from his hiding place. But the cupboard door was open—had he left it open? He'd thought it was shut. No wonder the room smelt so fusty. And the fire door, he'd opened that up days ago, hadn't he? Poor old X, there in the cobwebs. Cobwebs on his striped pyjamas. "Help, Danny." He looked like a little murder victim, bless him, crouching in the confined space, trying to flatten himself into the crack between the houses, the damp-course in the brickwork. Like one of Christie's lodgers, wrapped up in a blanket and forgotten. Like a little Belsen horror. Look at him, his granny in Ponteland used to say, *He's so pale and thin. Like a little Belsen horror, aren't you?* And a pinch of his cheek. If only she'd known.

"Help, Granny," pleaded X. That was what he *meant* to say, thought Dan dreamily, firming up the connections in his mind. He wanted to ask her for help, but he couldn't. Uncle Bob would kill him. "He'd kill me," amplified X, bruised eyes saucer-wide in his drawn white face, following Dan's train of thought exactly. "He'd kill me mam first, then he'd start on me. There'd be no one left to protect me then, he says. He'd have me all to hisself, he could take as long as he wants, and afterwards he'd put me down a hole. Please help."

"Help," echoed Dan, nodding with satisfaction. It was there. It had long since stopped being words on screen; now, it was coming to life. Slowly, warily, X emerged from the cupboard, brushing the cobwebs from his hair with a sleeve caught up in his fist. Turn him around, view him in 3D like one of Spielberg's CGI dinosaurs. Real as you like. "Help me," he begged distressingly. Across the keys Dan's fingers danced to life. "But there was no one there to help me. I was on my own. I had to keep on hiding, and hope he wouldn't find me. But he always would." "He always would," agreed Dan, out loud.

Slowly, almost reproachfully, the little figure shuffled back into its hiding place. Dan, never once looking up from the screen, never needing to now, typed on. Make that "throw me down a well", he thought, erasing "put me down a hole" with the backspace key. Glumly, obediently, the little boy mouthed the words with him. Another couple of thousand, before they called it a day.

Into the second week of his new project, Dan realized he was going to bed earlier and earlier, and getting up for work while it was still dark. He seemed to do his best work in the hush before dawn, sitting in the recliner with an unobstructed view of X's hiding place. The doors were open all the time now: he hoped it would help air the cupboard out, get rid of the moldy smell. It was taking a while to shift, and he had to keep the study door shut in case the stink permeated the whole flat. Not so much for his sake—he'd got used to it—but in case anyone came round. Molly, for instance. But let's not get ahead of ourselves. Haven't even had that first date yet. *Get-together.*

The great day was approaching. On Thursday morning Dan woke at some absurd time, four o'clock, it was dark still outside, rain against the window. He made coffee and fetched it through to the study, where its aromatic steam helped cut the must from the cupboard. X was in his usual place, peering out fearfully from his dusty recess, arms hugging his bony knees. Casting a perfunctory glance his way for reassurance, Dan set to work.

Liza was on her way out—the beehive freshly cemented with Elnett, the lashes stuck into place, the strappy microdress barely hiding the bruises on her thighs. Liza was about as hard to pull as a cistern chain: Dan had to admit there was something about her slutty availability that was perilously tempting. You could see why Bob would be sniffing around like a farmyard dog. Occasionally, when she got sloshed and demonstrative and gave X tearful hugs after falling in late from the pub, it was enough to make Dan slightly jealous. In fact, he was half-wondering whether there might not be some way of writing in a surreptitious yet lingeringly explicit love scene between Liza and Bob, pretty much entirely for the fun of it. It could be witnessed, he grudgingly conceded in the name of the plot, by a hiding X:

some squalid encounter on X's bed while the tot squirmed uncomfortably in his cupboard, peering through a crack in the door at the funny funny wrestling match between Mummy and the nasty man. Not now, anyway; Liza was on her way out, and Bob had volunteered to babysit. Just X and Uncle Bob, then (and Dan watching, of course).

"Don't go out. Stay in with us." He sounded frightened. Surely Liza was getting that? She was his mother, wasn't she?

"Divven be soft," mouthed Dan, lips moving unconsciously. "It's bingo the neet up the Mecca, and us gorls are gannin oot afta." He'd decided quite early on not to transcribe all the dialogue in cod Geordie—thank God. It was hard work on him and the reader both, and ran the risk of being irrevocably comic where comedy was least of all required. Anyway, it made it more universal in a way if he didn't. "Don't be soft," he typed. "It's bingo tonight up the Mecca, and us girls are goin' out after." Clipping her speech was okay; that suggested the looseness of the idiom, its laxity. *Lax* was the word, above all others, he associated most with Liza: she was undeniably lax around the fellers, treacherously so. Her mouth, he knew, would feel so soft and lax as it opened, yielding helplessly to a rough and tonguing kiss . . .

"Don't go out. Stay with me. I'll be scared . . . " X was getting fretful, poor lad. You could see a tear running down his dirty cheek. "Say home tonight, please."

"Rubbish," typed Dan decisively. "I don't get no fun in life hardly at all, me—and no wonder. You're like a bloody drag anchor, you are. You can watch telly with your Uncle Bob till nine, and then it's off to bed." Off (ta-ta-tat, space), to (ta-*tap* and space), bed (ra-ta-*tat*, full *stop*, space, space). He was quite unaware he was saying it out loud.

In his dingy cupboard, X shrank back into a fetal tuck. "But I want you to stay with me!" A more attentive ear might have responded to the pleading—to the neediness that accented the word *you* at the heart of the sentence.

"Shurrup." She *would* say that. It was just like her. She listened only when she chose to, when insecurity and sentimentality coincided for a while in her fickle heart, and she needed to play the loving mother, needed to feel needed. Anyway. Back in your cupboard, little feller. None of your old harry. Doing Liza now, shush.

"I'll hide! I'll run away!"

"Do what you bloody want, then, only quit pesterin' me, willyer? Little bastard." Nice way to treat a kiddie, that. And your own boy, too. She was a piece of work, that Liza—talk about hard! Still . . . Dan settled back into the comfy chair, and allowed his eyelids to close for a moment. He was concentrating on the image of Liza, posed like a model with braced extended leg, adjusting her garter belt, tugging up her stocking-tops—never know what you might pick up down the town, eh, Lize? Not a night for tights, man pet.

In the cupboard, X pressed himself even more tightly into the crack between the walls, out of sight for the moment and consequently out of mind. Under his breath he was muttering, choked and wretched, "I will, too. I will, you'll see. Just see if I don't."

But no one saw, no one at all. Even as he squeezed all the way through, passed beyond the bounds of imagination, no one suspected. Everyone was looking the other way at the time: Bob with his Party Seven in front of the telly, Liza shouting House down the bingo, Dan lost in lubricious daydreams as the Powerbook teetered dangerously on his sharply steepling lap.

When he awoke from his reverie, just in time to catch the Powerbook as it started to slide, the cupboard was empty. No X. *Well, what did you expect? It was only a story, after all. Downstairs with Bob watching telly, wasn't he?* He blinked, took a swig of cold coffee, and got back to work.

He wrote on till well past nine, stopping only when his stomach creased up with a huge refractory gurgle. Breakfast, then. He splashed some water on his face before dressing and the walk into town. A baguette at the chi-chi little bistro off Leadworks Lane ought to hold him for the time being. He was just beginning to get nervous about his da—his *get-together*, but it was a *good* nervous, he told himself. Roll with it, relax. Remember, you're a published author. Show her your awards.

In this respect, it was a trifle unfortunate that he walked on into town after breakfast, stopping at the Texas Cool Book Depository on Foregate Street. Among the cheerfully indiscriminate piles of remaindered stock in which they dealt, it came as something of a slap in the face to discover Volumes One, Two and Three of the Chronicles of Nevernesse going for £1.99 each, three for a fiver all marked stock. Wahey. Published author, there you go. Coming to a high street clearance store near you.

"Bollocks," he said aloud, grinding the three fat paperbacks in his hands. For the second time in the space of a week, he was making a spectacle of himself in a bookshop—only this time there was no Molly to the rescue. An elderly customer glared at him, and the young student-looking lad on his other side said, "Yeah, they've got all sorts in the back, though, Matrix novels and that. It's not just that Bilbo shit."

The erstwhile purveyor of Bilbo shit, overcome of a sudden with a weariness nigh on inexpressible, retreated to the counter, where he handed over five pounds in return for five years' worth of his authorial blood, sweat and tears. The books would do as a slightly showboaty present for Molly, he supposed, once he'd peeled the Final Reduction stickers off.

Behind him as he paid up, wholly unnoticed by Dan, a small boy stood and watched, rubbing his eyes with his sleeve.

Later that evening, parking up outside Molly's place in Mickle Trafford, Dan's nervousness was mounting. There was room on the herringbone brick driveway for a fleet of limos, let alone Dan's clapped-out Cavalier, and the house, good god the *house*: prime stockbroker belt four-bedroom detached, conservatory round the back, room for an orangery.

Ringing the doorbell he felt grubby and disheveled, like a miner coming off shift. He was trying to catch his reflection in the faux-leaded double glazing when Molly opened the door on him craning his neck like an imbecile. Just as well she chose not to notice.

"Hello!" A brilliant smile; that hand on his arm again. In an instant, Dan straightened his posture by several degrees, a trained ape who could just about pass for human. "You found it, then!"

Dan tried to think of something suave and soignée to say instead of "Yeah," but it wasn't coming. In the end, his unique spin on the casual affirmative was to leave an embarrassing pause beforehand, then elongate the word itself like a village idiot, grinning foolishly all the while: " . . . Yeeeeh." But no crassness he could commit seemed to tell against him. He was still invited in for five minutes while Molly finished getting ready. Damn, she was so *into* him. It was great.

The house was . . . it was the sort of house that Dan always felt wary of entering, in case he broke anything or left stains on the fabrics and fittings. The sort of house you saw in advertisements for pension policies, the gray-haired hunk embracing the glamorous granny in the warm glow of financial independence and good double glazing. No one he knew socially lived in a house like this: there were Angie's parents, of course, in Alderley Edge, but he doubted they'd let him in the front door these days. They weren't like Molly, who was tripping back down the stairs with a brilliant smile on her face. Helplessly, he held out the books he'd bought at the Depository. He ought really to have had them leather-bound, to fit in with the décor.

"Is that a present? Oh, how *lovely*! Have you signed them?"

It honestly hadn't occurred to Dan to sign them. They were remaindered paperbacks, for god's sake. It'd be like monogramming toilet tissue. "Sorry, no, I will if you want . . . " He took her pen, and scrawled across the title page of each volume.

As had always been the case at conventions and long ago in-store P.A.s, none of the signatures really resembled the others. They looked like a forger having three goes before kiting a cheque. Angie always said it was a confidence thing. Well, obviously she'd know; what remained of his confidence had been blasted away the minute she'd said "There's this guy at work called Malcolm . . . " *Anyway.*

"There you go," he said, handing her back the last paperback. Never mind Malcolm just now. This was miles out of Malcolm's league. Dan had moved up a division.

"Brilliant," she said, crossing to the bookshelves. "Now I can take these spare ones to the charity shop." Dan goggled. She'd bought the lot. All five volumes of Nevernesse, plus the anthos and the *Year's Best Fantasy & Horror of 1995.*

"Good God, where on earth did you get those?"

"I tried in Borders, but they didn't have them in stock," she said, and Dan did his best not to grimace. "So I put your name into Amazon, and got the lot. I haven't started them yet, though—I hope you're not put out?" She said it as if she was actually concerned—as if what Dan thought about anything could possibly make a difference.

"No, no. I'm just surprised you bothered, that's all." Which he was, genuinely.

Molly made a little *moue.* "My first author? I should think not. I'll read them all, of course. What a lot of work! You must be very dedicated."

"Well, you keep reading them, and I'll keep writing," said Dan. He thought Say Uncle might be more up her street, though. He could visualize it on the shelf, in between *Berain's Dawn: The First Chronicle of Nevernesse* and *Mummy Did a Bad Thing*, by Chastity Bobs. Chastity *Bobs*?

"So tell me about your new thing, the one you're writing now," she said, slipping a light jacket over her shoulders, and Dan was obliged to make up a new rule on the spot.

"You never do that with work in progress," he said, as if it was something he, John Grisham and Stephen King would chant to each other over cocktails in the green room when doing Letterman or Leno. "Breaks the spell."

"Well, we wouldn't want to do that, would we?" said Molly with great seriousness. "Ready, then?

"As I'll ever be," Dan said gamely.

On the drive up the M53, Dan dreamed in vain of charming country pubs run by retired majors in cravats serving gourmet bar meals to the Cheshire set—somewhere Molly might feel at home. But nowhere they passed seemed even halfway acceptable: nary a single home-made sausage on a bed of caramelized-onion mash. As they got out of the car at the retail park, he was framing his brief yet heartfelt apology for even mentioning the words *Pizza Hut,* when she surprised him yet again by racing him to the doors and, once inside, whispering her top tips for the salad bar into his ear while the waiter seated them. Once again, Dan had read a woman all wrong. Surprise, surprise, hold the front page.

Gradually, over the course of the meal (a twelve-inch skinny margherita, olives, no anchovies, they shared it slice for slice), he began to get her measure, together with something of her backstory. She'd been divorced just three years now: her husband, a corporate pensions manager, had run off with his secretary, which would have been pretty unremarkable in their social circle had not the secretary's name been Brian. She'd got the house (with mortgage long since paid off) and a comfortable settlement, which she augmented with some bookkeeping on a freelance basis for a big firm of solicitors in town. She was on the local board of magistrates, she belonged to a book club at Borders, just across the car park (they came here after the meetings for pizza and further discussion), and she had (as previously advertised) no children. And—hey, even Dan could pick *this* much up—she was very lonely, very tired of being alone.

The other thing? The really rather amazing thing? She seemed, even on this briefest of acquaintances, to like him very much. Dan liked her, too, come to that: it's hard not to think fondly of those who think fondly of us. So, what were the two of them going to do about it? That was the question.

Pizza cleared away, they crossed the car park to the multiplex, where Guillermo del Toro's new film was showing, his Oscar-tipped remake of *The Innocents*. Less than half-an-hour in, Molly was clutching Dan's arm in fright, and when the fear subsided, what do you know? She didn't pull away. Experimentally, Dan slipped his hand into hers. A squeeze and a stroke told him all he needed to know. It was like being sixteen again.

The next ten minutes or so were largely lost on Dan, who if truth be told had expected little from the evening beyond yet more chances to embarrass himself round the ladies—pizza cheese down his shirt front, misunderstandings in the back row, noisy mortification and the manager called. Instead, he sat there not quite able to believe his luck, super-sensitive to the utterly comfortable touch of Molly's hand in his own, running through a host of pleasurable scenarios for the remainder of the evening. It was all too much. He had to go for a cigarette.

Excusing himself *sotto voce*, he slipped out into the foyer and explained his craving—the cigarette part of it at least—to the bored teen at the ticket check. She nodded in the direction of the doors in a way that suggested he could pretty much please himself, short of leaping from roof to roof of the cars outside with no clothes on—actually, just do what you want, yeah? Another hour-and-a-half and she was out of here, see ya.

"Thanks," he said, heading for outside without waiting for the automatic

"Yeah, wh'evah" that followed him through the automatic doors. He was fumbling his Marlboros out along the way.

As the doors slid shut behind him he was already sucking down his first drag. Oooh, good. The idea was that if you smoked it very fast, the smell wouldn't have time to settle in your clothing, and you could eat a handful of those breath mints on the way back in. Fresh breath might be useful *later on*, or so he hoped.

He'd smoked the cigarette halfway down in three prodigious gulps when he became aware he was not alone. Of course, you always got gangs of kids hanging round outside the movies: clearly the next best thing to actually watching the film was leaning on the poster while swapping grubbily pornographic assessments of its leading lady. Except . . .

Except this wasn't a gang of kids. It was one kid, and a very small one at that, standing just behind the poster for *Holiday in Guantánamo*. Outside the multiplex it was already getting dark, and the light streaming out from the foyer silhouetted a pair of thin legs, shuffling together in that want-a-wee way small children have when they're anxious. Obscurely apprehensive, Dan made no move to investigate. None of his concern.

Two more monster drags took him most of the way down to the filter. Hurriedly, Dan ground the butt out, filled his mouth with mini-mints and made to go back inside. Just as he'd reached the sliding doors a voice came from behind him: "Mister?"

He knew that voice. Except, of course, he didn't, because this couldn't be—it just couldn't, that's all. So imagine Dan's discomfiture when the small voice came again: "Mister, me feet hurt." *Hort*, that dopey North-East vowel sound that gave the game away. "Mister?"

Dan stepped back, out of the sensor's range. The automatic doors slid shut. The small figure came out from behind the poster stand.

It was X.

Take as read for the time being Dan's gobsmacked response: the gaping, the eyes standing out on stalks, the involuntary swallowing of breath mints and the coughing fit that followed. The hand disbelievingly extended, is-he-real? Real as he ever was, eidetically speaking; but solid to the touch? Apparently, yes—and cold, very cold, shivering slightly in the mean April wind. Bloody hell. He'd no idea it could work that way, that a character sufficiently fleshed out could become . . . well, *fleshed out*. It never used to. Seeing was believing, before this, when it had all been in his control. But now . . .

What did this fresh development signify? What the hell was happening? Specifically, what was happening *to him*? He'd known he was under a certain amount of strain, what with the separation and everything else, but he'd thought he was coping. Really he had. And now, this. The boy gazed up at him through eyes swollen from too many tears, and Dan just stood there, unwilling to believe the evidence of his own senses.

A couple on their way out of the cinema glanced in his direction—in *their* direction, Dan supposed, X's and his. Reflexively, Dan moved closer to the boy, the better to shield him from prying eyes. No one else must see this thing, not least because it was the easiest way of believing that no one else *could* see it.

As soon as he got within range, the child clutched at him. Hung on for grim death and would not let go, no matter what. Amazing, how real it felt, how exactly like the real thing. Dan, whether sane or otherwise, would back his powers of imagination against anyone's, but this was as if X was actually standing right in front of him—a condition which every faculty he possessed assured him was most certainly the case. He had to promise to put him in the car before the kid would so much as give an inch.

"Can't I come back in the fillums with you?" pleaded the boy, his unhappy face pressed against Dan's fiercely churning stomach. "Please? I'll be dead quiet an' that."

"No, you can't," hissed Dan, bewildered by the sheer irreducible *wrongness* of what was happening here—plea-bargaining with a character he'd made up. "It's a fifteen certificate, the usher'll tell us off." Even as he said it he was thinking, *What the hell sort of an excuse was that? Why not go hog wild*, he reproached himself: *Why not write yourself into the story and give yourself superhero superpowers? Then if the usher does say anything you can zap her into cinders. So long as we're making stuff* up, *I mean.*

"But it's dark out here." There was a whiny, fearful edge to the small boy's voice that played terribly on Dan's twanging nerves. It was as if, any time now, he might just burst into tears and start wailing, and that would definitely not do. No scene, not here, not now. *Just do something*, he told himself in blank panic—*just get this, this* situation *dealt with here. After that you can spend all evening analyzing yourself. You unbelievable fucking nut-job, you.*

And then, flooding back into his mind, came the other main business of the evening. Molly. Oh god. What was he going to do about Molly?

First things first, though. "In the car—now," he hissed, manhandling the boy off his feet—his bare feet, for god's sake—and jogging towards the car park. Again; so convincing to the touch. Weight and texture, unbelievable.

How did he *do* that? What combination of misfiring neurons and wild creativity had conspired to create this implausible thing he held? Either he was the number-one prize eideteker of all time, or he ought to be sectioned, there on the spot. He'd often wondered what it would be like, if he were actually to go crazy in the end, proper raving mad. Now he knew. It would be like sprinting across tarmac late at night with an imaginary seven-year-old in your arms, telling him lies preparatory to cramming him into the boot of your car.

"It'll be fine," gasped Dan as he ran, "all nice and snug, you can lie down in the back and go to sleep. I won't be long. I think there's a rug."

Lies, all lies—but it didn't matter, because by then all this would be over, wouldn't it? The hallucination, or whatever it was, would dwindle into insignificance as soon as the boot slammed shut, and he was back holding Molly's hand. Actually—yes. That would do it. Once he was back with Molly, all this would be a dream. Surely. And afterwards, first thing tomorrow, he could look it all up in a book, *T* for *tulpas*, *S* for *schizophrenia*, *N* for *nut-job*. Get help, see someone. Right now, this was just imagining things, no big deal, it was what he did for a living, but it had to stop. He had to get a grip. It didn't matter that he could actually feel the weight of the boy in his arms, or hear his tremulous protestations of fear all hot and panting in his ear. It didn't matter, because it was all in his *imagination*, from working too hard and not eating at proper hours. The stress of the separation from Angie. Those magic mushrooms he took, just the once, all those years ago. Whatever.

It's all in your mind, he told himself as he set the boy down by the car, batting off his panicky clutching hands while he got the boot open. "In you jump, nice and cosy," he heard himself saying. He hadn't thought it possible, to despise himself any more than he already did. One last despairing cry from X: "It's all dark!" Then, down with the boot, *clunk*, and Dan was standing on his own in the car park next to his solidly familiar, unambiguously real Cavalier. Nobody there. He'd just come back to the car for cigarettes, or a coat, or whatever. If anyone was looking.

Guiltily he looked around. All clear, it seemed. Breathing heavily, he rested his ample backside against the boot till the panic subsided and his legs felt like teaming up with the rest of the gang again. Then the thought of Molly sitting in the movie wondering where he'd got to hit him like a slap in the face, and he got all out of breath again jogging back over to the multiplex.

"Gosh that was a long one," whispered Molly as he slid back shamefacedly into his seat. "Thought you'd gone down the plughole." He could feel her quivering with suppressed laughter; she felt no more and no less real than had X.

"Sorry," he whispered. Eloquence is the proud preserve of all the top writers.

"I used to smoke myself," she told him, pinching his Pinocchio nose between two bony knuckles. "Don't worry." Despite the extremity of his plight, Dan still found the time to appreciate this. Silently, he offered thanks to whatever gods looked after these things. Like, how brilliant a date was Molly—I mean, really? *Look, Molly, it's like this. I'm a walking disaster area, my wife chucked me out, I can't get a book published to save my life, and I think—it's a strong supposition, mind you—I* think *I might be going crackers, because I'm starting to hallucinate and shit.* Yeah, never mind, big hug, don't worry.

And maybe that was the answer, platitudinous as it seemed: not to worry. Maybe, if he'd worried a bit less in the first place—if he hadn't spent the last few months ripping himself so methodically into shreds—then he might not have ended up in quite such a state as he was clearly in right now. So, probably good advice then, if only he could take it. Under the circumstances, it might be a little difficult; but then Molly took his hand again, and that helped more than anything possibly could have.

In the movie, eeriness proliferated. The children were playing by the lake under the watchful eye of their governess, the by now comprehensively frazzled Naomi Watts. As Dan tried to slip back into the screen world, Molly sighed happily, shifted in her seat and cuddled up against him. With a relief so complete you could almost cast it in plaster, Dan slipped his arm around her shoulders. One hand went somewhere extremely naughty, just for a playful little second, then scurried for cover like cheeky cartoon mice.

Molly gave a rich chuckle, and tilted up her face to be kissed . . . and temporarily at least, Dan's qualms about the unsettling episode outside—the *hallucination*, as he'd decided to think of it—slid into the background. On screen, the jittery governess screamed at the sight of her dead predecessor, reflected in the waters of the lake. In their seats, Dan and Molly didn't even notice.

A mutually gratifying regression to the teenage ensued, with both partners left feeling slightly dazed and confused when the auditorium lights went up and people started walking past them. Snogger's cramp, at their age? Unbelievable. Walking as if on a dance floor sprung with air, Dan left the cinema hand in hand with Molly.

Outside, the *hallucination* began to play on his mind once more, especially as they approached the Cavalier parked away from the other cars in the rapidly emptying lot. For an instant he was convinced that, when he put his key in the door and deactivated the central locking, the boot would spring open and his dirty little secret would come to light. He would stand revealed—in front of a Molly whose outrage could be taken as read—with a strange kid locked in the boot, a kid for whom there was absolutely no accounting.

But no, that wasn't going to happen, because this was a *hallucination*, wasn't it? As in, *an idea or belief to which nothing real corresponds. The apparent perception of an external object when no such object is actually present.* So he would be fine; so get on with it. Mental breakdown is often characterised by a withdrawal from social activity and the occurrence of delusions and halluci-nations—so there you were. He needed to get out more.

As things turned out, it *was* fine. He unlocked the Cavalier and opened the passenger door for Molly, then took a last quick look around the empty car park. All clear. And nothing whatsoever from the boot. *Where there was nothing in the first place, remember?*

Back at Molly's he could very easily have accepted her invitation to come in for coffee and other, unspecified indulgences. That he didn't was a matter of no little chagrin, but on reflection, driving back the few miles home after a prolonged and thoroughly engaged goodnight kiss with the promise to return the very next evening, he knew it was impossible. It was all to do with the boy. What he needed to do, first of all, was this: he needed to get back home, spark up the Powerbook and see whether the boy X was where he ought to be. Though obviously he would be. How could he not, when that thing earlier on was just, you know, an hallucination? But still, it would be nice to see it happen: to demonstrate to himself who held the whip hand in this relationship. With relief, he turned on to the Hoole Road. Almost home now. Half a mile.

Then, out of nowhere, the knocking started to come from the boot.

Dan's involuntary swerve almost ran him into the side of the road. It was a dull muffled thumping, and it called into question every rationalization of the last hour or so, blew them effortlessly out of the water. There *was* something in his boot. That there couldn't be, because there wasn't anything there in the first place, didn't matter, because he knew, because he'd put it there himself. At the first opportunity he pulled over, got out of the car with the engine still running and approached, with a stomach-churning mixture of disbelief and irrational conviction, the rear of the car.

Flashing lights and a siren stab made him catch his breath and straighten up just in time, shielding his eyes from the oncoming headlights. A police car had pulled in behind him, and its occupants, two constables, male and female, were getting out. "Everything all right, sir?" inquired the woman, with what seemed to Dan unnecessarily heavy sarcasm.

"Noticed you seemed to pull over a bit sharpish just now," said the other one, taking his cue from his colleague. "We were just wondering, what was the matter?"

The WPC was not to be outdone. "It's gone twelve. Bit late for practicing your emergency stops, eh, sir?" Dan smiled weakly. *Yeah, hilarious. What do you want, bitch?* Aloud, he said:

"Yes—I, er, I thought I might have run something over. I thought I felt a thump. Just now, while I was turning on to Hoole Road." *Talk normal*, the voice in his ear was hissing. *Act natural. Proper dialogue. You sound like a right shifty sod*. With a mighty act of will, Dan refrained from telling it to shut up.

"Run something over, sir?" Why couldn't *they* talk proper? Why, in the twenty-first century, did all policemen and women still think they had to carry on like something out of sodding *Z-Cars*? "What sort of thing?"

"A . . . cat? I don't know. A small dog? Maybe a squirrel. I didn't see."

"You didn't see?" As if they were all foreigners talking some mutually understood *lingua franca*, and they had to keep checking they'd got the vocabulary right. Now the woman was chipping in again.

"So: you thought you'd run something over, a small dog or a squirrel—but you were going to the back of the car? Not to the front, to see if there was any damage . . . ?"

Well done, Juliet Bravo. "I thought I might be able to see it on the road. See if it was badly hurt."

The woman made a great show of looking out across the empty tarmac, while the man picked up where she'd left off: "But you seemed to be going to open your boot, sir, when we stopped . . . ?"

Dan was on the end of a snide cop/smart-arse cop routine, and he wanted very badly to be out of there. Specifically, he very badly *didn't* want to hear the words that came next, from the WPC. "I wonder would you mind just going ahead and popping the boot open, sir, so's we can all have a little look inside?

Oh, shit. Oh Christ, no. "Er . . . the boot?"

"Yes sir," patiently, as if to a congenital imbecile, "the boot. If you'd just pop it open for us, sir."

"Just now," confirmed the policeman, moving to the back of Dan's car. "If you wouldn't mind, then we could have a quick shufti, make sure everything's in its right place."

Understanding that some definite action was required of him, Dan managed to fight off the temptation simply to repeat, ad infinitum, "The boot?" As if underwater, he fumbled the locking mechanism open. As the boot swung up, he turned to the police, his face a white mask. "There you go," he said, like a trunk murderer exhibiting his handiwork. He didn't dare look inside, waiting instead for the expression on the faces of the constables to change. Registering after a few seconds their habitual deadpan, he risked a glance.

Of course, it was empty.

They breathalyzed him, naturally, and checked his registration on their handheld data gadget; then, having nothing on which to hold him further, they let him go with a lecture about his driving and an admonition, implied rather than stated, as to his future conduct and general standards of behavior (so just watch it, all right?). To Dan, punchy still from the succession of unexpected events, pleasant and otherwise, over the course of the evening, it was all water off a duck's back. He drove the remaining few hundred yards home under the baleful eyes of the constabulary, who tailed him back to the flat and didn't drive off till he'd shut the front door with a guilty little wave and beneath his breath a muttered "Fuck *off*."

The boot, of course, had always been empty. Nothing in there, ha-ha, no sir, no indeedy. Ask the police. Under the circumstances it would have been totally unnecessary to have taken a look inside just now when he was parking up, to see what was making that frantic knocking noise he'd heard all the way down the road. For one thing it would have given entirely the wrong idea to the watching plod, and for another, *the boot was empty.* Had he mentioned that? Nothing knocking, because nothing *to* knock, nothing there.

The corollary of this, though, was that his hallucinations were clearly no longer confined to the visual, or indeed the tactile. Pouring himself a drink, Dan collapsed on to the sofa and tried to sort out what was going so spectacularly awry in his head. He was way too freaked to even consider writing—not tonight, not even to see if his Prospero grasp on his characters was holding under the strain.

You read about cases like this, he knew. At one time, soon after discovering his particular eidetic gift, he'd been quite interested in the topic. (Privately, he'd always worried that there was something not quite right about it—and, by extension, about him). He was aware that some of these threshhold experiences could tip over into out-and-out hallucinations. Stress, they said, could do it—it didn't have to be anything more organic than that. So, hey, stress? Bleakly and without enthusiasm Dan picked over the succession of wrecks and forced reverses in his life over the last few months. First Angie, then the house, then the book deal, gone, gone, gone: where did you want to start?

If hallucinations *were* a denial, willed or otherwise, of objective reality, then just at present Dan found it hard to argue with their basic underlying premise. Denial was only natural, because really, what was there to affirm?

He hated his life: he hated this flat, he hated being on his own, he hated losing love when love was all that had bound him to the world in the first place, he hated the publishers who'd dumped him in favor of the sort of idiot spit and dribble that actively devalued the nature of existence on this earth. What was there in this abject perversion of existence to justify him spending any more time there than he had to? Very little. Molly, maybe. Argh. *Molly.*

He rang her straight away, while he was still slightly breathless from the shock, and had to explain he'd just run up two flights of stairs. When she asked him what the rush had been, he improvised with the fluent desperation of the practiced liar or storyteller and said he couldn't wait to hear her voice again. This seemed to go down rather well.

"You should have come inside," she said, "and I'd have whispered sweet nothings in your ear." It was a lifebelt thrown from the dry land of sanity, and Dan grabbed for it with both hands. He arranged to meet her the following night; she would cook him a meal, and they'd take it from there. On the verge of putting the phone down, all that *you first, no you* business, he thought he heard her saying "Love you." But how could he be sure? He couldn't even trust his own ears any more.

Too many drinks and no significant conclusions later, Dan hit the sack, falling almost immediately into a nauseating, exhaustingly realistic loop-dream in which he ran over a collie dog, again and again. Expiring on the verge in a shatter of blood and fur, the collie would lift its Lassie head to lick his hand, and he'd see etched on its collar the words *Bad Dog Dan.* Getting to his feet, he'd turn around and there would be Angie, watching from behind the wheel of a fast car with Malcolm in the passenger seat. Before he could explain, they were gone, and he was left with the image of Angie's well-remembered face, all twisted in loathing and repugnance.

The last time round, the collie bit him, and he woke in a thrashing panic. The alarm clock showed four-fifteen, the very worst time at which to wake. No real chance of getting off again; and why would he want to? Enough trauma for one night, thank you very much.

Instead he hauled his aching middle-aged frame out of bed and through to the kitchen. Black coffee. Pasteurized orange juice. These things would help, presumably. Cigarettes—now you're talking. Ohh, the first of the day, how it rasped and solaced all together. Fag dangling from his lips, coffee steaming in his big black mug, Dan lumbered through to the study, a grizzly roused from hibernation before the spring thaw.

Opening his Powerbook, it hit him: crunch time. The confrontation he'd ducked last night was now back on, for better or worse. Bringing up the

Say Uncle file he quickly read over the last few paras to bring him up to speed, and then typed the words "I stayed in the cupboard the whole night." Involuntarily he glanced up. Nothing there.

Okay, don't panic. What, now? Let's see. "It was so dark in there. No one could see me, and I couldn't see anything, but that was fine by me."

But even when it's pitch dark you know if someone's there, and he wasn't, X, not any more. Dan wasn't seeing it, he wasn't feeling it.

"I came out around half four." Except he didn't; that was Dan saying it, not him actually doing it. Just words, dead words crawling on a screen. He might as well have typed in *adlg jt'wegjj*. How could you believe what you didn't see? And why couldn't he *see* him any more?

"Mister." Over by the hall door. Dan had to grab hold of the Powerbook on its cushioned tray: the whole lot almost went over. "Hey, mister."

There he was at the door, faint light from the hallway spilling around his silhouette: the original eidetic boy wonder. X from the story; X the child whose uncle did him bad. Whose mummy didn't love him enough. Whose biographer tried to keep him in a cupboard, then locked him in the boot of the car. X, who'd finally made his move.

"It was horrible in that boot." So matter-of-fact, yet infinitely reproachful. It was all Dan could do to type it without wincing. "I felt sick, it stank of petrol. Why did you put me in there?"

"You weren't in there! I looked!" *You don't have to take that sort of guff from a kid. Where would it end up, if you let them get the whip-hand?*

"I was too. You put me in there. You locked me in the boot."

"I had to!" The golden rule with children is, assume superiority. Don't let then sense your vulnerability. Dan, who'd never had children of his own, was losing this one already. "You didn't belong there in the first place—it was a grown-up's night, it wasn't for little boys. How did you get there, anyway?"

"I followed you out. I was in the car all along." Of course. So X was following him outside now.

"Listen." Dan struggled to find the right tone. "Listen. You can't go around the place tagging after me. You belong in here. In there," as one might indicate a favorite playpen, gesturing towards the cupboard.

"But I don't *like* it in there." That quaver in his voice again, precursor to hot tears and adult panics. "There's spiders."

"Spiders are all right!" Yeah. Even Dan didn't think he'd fall for that one. "Sammy Spider!"

"I *don't* like it." Something new: a mutinous edge to the voice, now. Something Dan hadn't bargained for. "I'm not going back."

"Well, you've got to, and that's that." When reason is a bust, there's always because-I-said-so. And when authority fails, you have to back up words with deeds.

"No I don't," insisted X stubbornly. "I found the way out. In between the middle." He still said "miggle". He was only seven, remember. "When you come out, it's different outside to when you went in. Uncle Bob can't get me, here. He can't get through. He doesn't know how stories work."

Was that it, by God? Escaped? Run away from his bad uncle? Well then, there was nothing for it but to play his trump card. "What about your mummy? She must be frantic, wondering where you've gone . . . " He did his best to make it sound genuinely concerned, poor mummy, poor X.

"You sent her to the bingo, and I wanted her to stay and read me a story!" Jesus, he could turn at the drop of a hat, this one. "She *always* does what a man wants her to, *any* man, and she *never* does what I want. Uncle Bob tells her what to do, and you tell her what to do, and she always does what you want, and she doesn't love me, not really, and—" not even pausing to draw breath "—I don't love her any more, and I don't care, I won't go back, and *she* started it, anyway, leaving me on my own!"

"But you can't stay here with me!" *Let's just make that perfectly clear, shall we, before this all gets out of hand?* "I can't look after you, do you understand? I've . . . I've got to go out to work, daddies have to go to the office and that, and what would you do all day, stuck in here on your own?"

"I could go to school. You could take me to school in the morning, and pick me up from after-school club like all the other kids."

"Hang on!" Errors in internal logic always rankled with Dan. "They didn't have after-school club in your day! It's 1972 when you go to school!"

"That was back then." X was having none of it. "It's not *then* any more, not here. They've got after-school club. And there's telly just for kids. Cartoons and that."

Yes, and they've got Wii and PlayStation too. God, if he got a sniff of all that he was never going back, was he? Newcastle in the seventies would feel like the Gulag by comparison. Think. What would have made *him* do what he was told, at that age? Well, obviously one thing.

"Look, I'm not messing around now. Get back." His voice roughened, took on an admonitory edge. No more Mister Nice Guy. Where most parents go wrong is, they haven't got any idea when it comes to discipline.

"No!" With a stamp of his foot, if you please.

"Don't make me put down this laptop. Don't interrupt my work." He sounded convincing enough. *All you have to do is act the part, and authority comes to you. Bluff your way through it. Remember: he's only seven.*

"I don't want to go back in there!" The waterworks, now. Might have known. With a horrible frown, Dan set the Powerbook aside and got up from his chair.

"Right. I'm angry now. Stop that."

But X continued to grizzle. Every time Dan said "Stop it," he shook his head and blubbed a little more loudly, and every time it pushed Dan's button a little more energetically. In the end it was loud enough to wake the neighbors, and that's when Dan lost it. That's when something happened: something not good.

The first time you hit a child will always be in anger, and Dan was certainly angry enough; scared, too, caught up in X's own childish panic. What he couldn't have known—what he couldn't have anticipated, because nobody ever knows until it's happened—was how very natural it would be. How easy it would be to do the thing, the bad thing.

Understand: it doesn't actually solve the problem, inasmuch as we define the problem in its narrowest sense as *stopping this bloody kid from crying.* Yes, it may surprise the child temporarily: it might shock him quiet, the way X was shocked just for a little while when Dan . . . when he did what he did (the *bad thing*). But that's not an end to tears and tantrums; it's just one stop further down the line. It doesn't give you peace. What it does give you is control, just for a second, or the illusion at least of control—and let's face it, the illusion is all that most of us ever get. Only you can't keep doing it, that's the thing; you just can't. Such exchanges are necessarily thermonuclear in their severity, precisely because they split apart the family nucleus, releasing huge amounts of bad, unclean energy, poisoning the atmosphere, blowing down the structures. They're first strikes with no possibility of response: the very definition of hemispheric brutality.

Stand well clear now, because this is toxic stuff; radioactive, as already established. But ask the question anyway, even if it hurts: admit the possibility. Suppose that when you do it that first time—the *bad thing*—suppose it's easier than you thought it would be. So easy, in fact, that you do it again, and again. And carry on doing it, even after the first flush of panic-anger fades.

I know, I know: not you, not me, not anyone we'd have round to dinner. But there are such people, they do exist, and not all of them are slavering Nazis in black leather. And we're not even talking about what you go on to do once you've made the discovery, even though such moral choices are both necessary and inescapable—forming, in fact, the only basis on which we may ultimately be judged. Even before you get into the realm of judgement and morality, there's the unslippable, unevadable question, waiting patiently while you get to the end of your prevarication, why? What was working inside you, when you raised your hand to a little child?

Dan couldn't say—or wouldn't. It all happened too fast for him to understand; that was what he told himself. Hustling X back into the cupboard, jamming home the bolts at top and bottom of the door, he wanted only to get him out of the way, to shut his noise, as Bob might have put it. The comparison with Bob was not exactly to his credit, he knew that, but he needed space to think. Maybe he actually did want to ask himself that question, the one we talked about just now. It was always the question that had scared him most of all, on the deepest, most basic level: suppose you could be a bad man all the while, and only find out once it was too late?

As the muffled sobs wore down to silence and the bangs on the cupboard door grew weaker and weaker, Dan sat as if stunned. As if he was the one who'd been hit. He cast his mind back over his forty-odd years, looking for anything that might prefigure his sudden giving way to the basest of instincts. Well—it was disturbing, in retrospect, how quickly the memory came to mind—well, there had been Rachel, hadn't there?

Rachel his girlfriend in university, his bit of high-class damaged goods; Rachel who used to get him to smack her bottom before they did the business. Had that ever been anything other than embarrassing, though? Had it ever really been about *him*, even? It was hard to say: when there's a plummy-voiced eighteen-year-old posh bird sprawled across your lap, grinding away in lascivious desperation, calling you Daddy and purring seductively about what a bad girl she's been, your responses will necessarily be somewhat compromised. Especially if you're a sex-starved lump of Northern discomfiture, thinking all his Christmases have come at once. Under the circumstances, it would take a saint to resist giving such a forward minx a *little* bit of a tap—and not every saint would have been proof against the temptation, Dan suspected. Rachel, then: not proven. And Angie had never gone in for that sort of thing, had she?

You're forgetting that time, the unstillable voice in his head piped up, *you know, when you couldn't*—Okay. Yes. It had been something they'd tried, just the once, when he was working long hours at the tech and doing Nevernesse in the evenings, and the physical side of the relationship was going through a fallow patch. Dan had read something in a magazine, and Angie was willing to go along with it for his sake, for the sake of their relationship. Had it clicked, though? Had it actually done the trick? Dan thought not: he remembered it mostly as a long, wearying and ultimately futile night, the bedroom floor littered with risibly unconvincing props like the backstage area of some provincial pantomime, and they'd never tried it again.

Only: looking at things more closely now, free from the obligation to take both sides of the equation into account . . . hadn't it been more a case of Angie pulling the plug than of his own failure to rise to the occasion? Ange, the great deflater. And—why not follow this particular squirrel up its tree, after all?—and, wasn't that just typical of the way their relationship had been deteriorating, even then? Dan couldn't manage it, and Angie couldn't be bothered. Cue lots of Penguin Classics in bed and hot milky drinks for one, till the baleful advent of rough priapic Malcolm, the Mellors to her Lady Chatterley. He taught amenity horticulture, for God's sake, at the sixth-form college in Hawarden. Gagging painfully on his bitter cuckold's cud, Dan wondered whether Angie was getting through quite so much Ovaltine with *him* forking over her plot.

So, not proven was the best verdict he could come up with—which, let's face it, was no sort of a distraction, and was no use whatsoever in letting him off the hook. It meant he still had to evaluate what had happened on its own phenomenological merits. Which was not in itself a piece of cake, because for a start, you had to deal with the fact that X was . . . well, what he was. A head-birth, a figment, a spirit called from the vasty deep or whatever. Through the medium of fiction, Dan had been brutalizing him for days now, from the soles of his feet to his pudding-bowl home haircut. It was the thing about misery lit: someone had to get hurt. Moodily, as if tonguing a rotten tooth, Dan rubbed his tingling palm. *Something* had been slapped. Something was sniveling in the cupboard still. So much for empirical analysis.

And would it even make any difference whether X was real or not, in the moral sense? On this topic, President Jimmy Carter and the late Pope John Paul were in censorious accord: sins committed in the secret chambers of the heart weigh every bit as heavy as dirty deeds done in public, once placed in the critical balance. Lust, wrath, whatever: all equally mortal. On the other hand, Jimmy Carter and the Pope? Par-tay, dude. What did they know about life as she was lived? Both of them could stand to lighten up a bit.

But it wasn't just the guilt he had to deal with, or even the self-loathing. In a way, more worrying still—of devastating, overpowering concern to Dan as he sat slumped in his chair, too traumatised by panic and the horrors of self-realization to even realize the Powerbook was humming still by his side, the ticking cursor waiting to be pushed along the page by whatever came next—more worrying still was what was happening in his head. What was happening to his *mind*, which just now felt about as compromised as seemed humanly possible. Whichever way he turned, there was horror of one kind or another. It was like trying to follow a long and complicated sentence—a sentence in some foreign language, where you have to wait till the end for the verb to make sense of it—a sentence with two independent clauses, each of which contains shatteringly bad news. The ability to entertain two separate and contradictory concepts at the same time is held by some to be the true definition of "genius"; for Dan, it felt as if it were fracturing his brain, right down the corpus callosum, a cracked and shrivelled walnut split in two.

Thoughts came buzzing at him like wasps around a lolly. He'd hit a child. He'd imagined a child. An imaginary child was crouching, beaten, in the cupboard. Only he wouldn't be there when he looked, because he wasn't in the boot before. Only he had to be, because he'd put him there himself. It was no good, he had to look. No, he couldn't look. Instead, he cast around for something to hang on to (almost literally—he felt like a man stumbling through the false-perspective corridors of a funhouse filled with bad mirrors) before settling as a last resort on the Powerbook. Clutching it to his lap like a lost child, he jammed down the Page Up key till he arrived at the top of the file, SAY UNCLE in eighteen-point caps. Beneath this title he typed the words *A Novel by Dan Trehearne*. For the moment, it seemed the best thing he could do, perhaps the only thing. Call it a novel, say it's not real life.

The night passed, without ever really ending. Morning found Dan slumped in his easy chair, snoring with a dogged persistence. Probably the Powerbook had been sliding gently off his knees throughout his nap; only with the sunup, when gravity (or mischief) gave that last imperceptible tug, did the whole shebang, tray and all, land with a nasty-sounding thump on the threadbare carpet at his feet.

Shitshitshit. . . . Dan woke, wrenched with painful suddenness into consciousness, looking first of all for the cupboard door—still shut, thank god, still locked. Like a man who can't find the alarm clock to turn it off he looked around in a daze, before noticing the foundered Powerbook at his feet.

At first sight it didn't seem that bad. Nothing was obviously shattered. The power-save function had come on, and he had to hold down the On switch until the screen hummed back to life, thus revealing the true extent of the damage.

On the screen, rather than the sixteen-odd thousand neatly justified words he'd produced over the course of the last few days, there was only a gray dialogue box with the message *Some of your file was not saved, and therefore may not be recoverable. Would you like to go ahead anyway?* Helplessly Dan pressed OK; no other option was offered him.

It was a file of bits and scraps, tildes and pilcrows, diacritics and gibberish. A typical section read: `h _ snos' _ brôt,' _ twil _ t, ¶§ □□□□ wanted to run away, but å□ go ej∑ß _ miserable küld □□□□□□µ±™ □□ and I cry a lot.` Rarely, if ever, did it get any more legible. So much for *Say Uncle*.

Dan, ready to cry a lot himself, page-downed disbelievingly through reams of this junk, fragments from a damaged mind, the pleas of a broken machine. Somewhere the story would begin again, whole and uncorrupted. This gibberish would begin to make sense. But it never did: it carried on garbage all the way through to the final para, the cursor trapped against the right-hand margin no matter how often he pressed the arrow key. Time's arrow, nudging an immovable barrier: the unalterable, read-only end of things.

When, overwhelmed by the sheer idiot futility of it all, he went to close the file and the computer asked him whether he wanted to save changes, he clicked No. No, don't save changes. Put everything back as it was. Put me in my proper bed in my proper house, with my proper wife, writing my proper books. Put an end to all this, because I'm sick of it.

The corrupted file vanished, and the screen went gray, waiting to see what he might do next.

With a convulsive fury sufficient to pull half the muscles in his shoulder, Dan hurled the Powerbook straight at the cupboard door. Though it had managed to survive its tumble from his lap with only minor loss of data, this was definitely its point of no return. The screen came off entirely, the black plastic casing split open; the whole thing landed at the foot of the splintered door like a roadkill crow. If only X had been there, thought Dan crazily. If only he'd been standing there in his fucking pajamas to take the brunt of it, then so much the better. He'd spoiled everything—Dan realized it through his weeping, through the paroxysm of tears that choked him up almost immediately after. He'd ruined it. It was all his fault. Not playing right, then whining like a little brat afterwards. He asked for it, you see, that was his problem. He asked for it.

"You stupid bastard," sobbed Dan aloud, hitting himself quite painfully on the thigh with his clenched fist. "You stupid, stupid bastard . . . " A punch on each beat, *stupid*, *stupid*, *stupid*, till it hurt so much he had to stop. Only when he stopped punching, it didn't stop hurting.

After a while he had to get out. Out of the back room and all its hateful associations; out of the flat, which he loathed no less. While the world bolted breakfast and went to work he roamed, in no particular direction, down a suburban perplex of dead ends and culs-de-sac, hemmed in on all sides, the path he'd walked only a moment before vanishing behind him, unretrace-able. Mummy bears and daddy bears strapped baby bears into the backs of people-carriers, remote as tiny popes inside their Popemobiles. Playgroup leaders received their charges with wide artificial smiles. Teenagers and their social networks clogged the pavements around schools, forming shoving, jostling mobs around the matchbook screens of mobile phones to bray at the filmed humiliations of the night before. Through it all pushed Dan, sealed in his misery, wholly unaware of his companion trailing after.

Those who noticed assumed the boy was off school. He did look poorly, pale and thin, as if he didn't get out much. Scruffy, unwashed. And that lout of a bloke was no better. Why didn't he slow down and wait for the lad, hold his hand on busy crossings? Poor little mite wasn't even dressed for going outside, hadn't got a coat on or anything. Some people, they've got no idea. So disapproval followed Dan like a bad smell, with sympathy for X its residual afterscent. If only they knew. If only he'd known himself.

Along the surly streets they trudged, Dan and his shadow. When Dan stopped, more or less at random, for greasy coffee in a greasy spoon, his companion hung around outside the greasy window, half-hidden behind the hulking frame of a greasy customer hunched over sausage, egg and greasy beans. Pay the greasy man and be on your way. Onward, with a sour belch and the taste of defeat in your mouth. The boy watches. He follows after, determinedly.

In the precinct, they pegged Dan for a troublemaker and tried to move him on. He wasn't causing any trouble, he protested; but his head was filled with trouble, they must have known, they must have seen it on his face, his unshaved mug deformed with an awful agitation. He couldn't explain without starting to shout, and a security guard clamped him by the arm and hustled him out on to the pavement. As he stood in the gutter and lit with trembling hands his umpteenth cigarette of the awful morning, he glared at the figure that had caused his agitation, there in the window of Smith's. His shouting turned half the heads on Foregate Street, but even as a space opened up on the busy pavement for the mad yelling smackhead, the care-in-the-community, the unwashed nutter, he realized, too late, the mistake he'd made. It was an advertising display, was all: a cardboard child in two dimensions gazing piteously out at the shoppers, please buy my book, it's really really sad. *The Things He Made Me Do* by Conor Newlove.

The things he made me do, thought Dan bleakly. *You have no idea*. From behind the display a peeping head emerged, bruised black eyes fixed on Dan through the window, but he never saw it, he was gone into the crowd and the past was the past and nothing mattered.

Because we all have to go home sooner or later, or else abandon ourselves wholly to the space between things, Dan trailed back across town to the flat sometime in the afternoon. He let himself in the front door, then spent a long time crouched in the hallway, listening at the keyhole for any hint of movement inside his apartment. Nothing. A builder's radio out in the street; the sound of distant traffic on the Hoole Road. Maybe it was safe. He decided to risk it.

He conducted an FBI-style shakedown of the flat, pausing at each door before kicking it open, sizing up the corners while keeping an eye on any suspicious movement behind him. Nothing. Not even in the back room, which he thought he'd left locked up. All clear. He retreated to the lounge, where he collapsed on the sofa and tried to make his mind go empty. A woman kept ringing him from Calcutta to ask about car insurance, till he disconnected the phone. Blank, empty, think of nothing. Thinking instead of everything, every hurtful, shameful thing, he eventually beat himself down into sleep, till a knocking woke him up. A knocking at the door to the flat.

Outside it was almost dusk, sun dipping beneath a banked mass of gray cloud, turning the end of a leaden day to gold. Dan came upright all in one at the sound of the knock, a dreadful tic pulling one side of his stubbly face into a remarkable grimace. "Who is it?" he croaked, without stopping to ask himself how they were going to hear him out there at the top of the stairs. Unsurprisingly, then, no answer. He crept into the hallway and tried again, a little louder. This time, he heard something.

"Dan?" A woman. "Dan, is that you? Are you okay?"

For a giddy moment he thought it might be Angie. Then, more fully awake, he recognized Molly's voice, and remembered, several hours too late, their date for after work this evening, dinner at hers.

He was all apologies opening the door, gabbling before he'd turned the knob. Molly had to beat aside a gush of guilt and contrition even to get inside the flat. And the first thing she said? Not where do you think you've been, or dinner's ruined now, hope you're happy, you bastard. No. "Are you all right? Oh, sweetheart, look at you, you look so poorly. Come in and sit down. Poor Dan. There we go, ups-a-daisy. Come on. Sit down. You look dreadful. When did this come on?"

"When I was going home last night," admitted Dan weakly, allowing her to reinstall him on the sofa. He slid all in a heap at the touch of her hand, and buried his mashed-up head in the soft upholstered sanity of her lap. "It's . . . I'm not well."

"And you've been trying to sleep it off. That's why you took your phone off the hook." Things that would make other women throw plates at him, Molly recognized as both necessary and practical. Dan wondered whether he could keep her forever. Maybe she'd fit into the cupboard, he thought, with a self-accusatory wince. Wait, she was talking, listen now. "I tried your mobile, but it was off too. I wondered whether everything was okay, or maybe you were just, you know, busy writing . . . ?"

"No," Dan said truthfully. "No, I've not been writing, not today. . . . . I just haven't felt too hot, that's all. Look, I'm really, really sorry I forgot to ring—I've been flat out on the settee here, I didn't know what time it was. Now I've missed dinner, messed it all up—I really am so sorry, An—" that was a close one, he'd been just about to say Ange, but caught it in time so it just sounded like a bit of a gawp "—and, and, you must be hungry, what time is it, I don't know if there's anything in the house, I could ring for a pizza, no, we had pizza last night, didn't we . . . " *Rambling.* Stop it.

Molly smiled. "You wait there," she said, and got up. And like a good boy Dan did just that, till she reappeared from her short dash out to the car and back, holding aloft a tin-foiled dish of moussaka in her oven-gloved hands.

At least there was some wine in the house: incredible, what were the odds? So they ate Molly's warmed-up moussaka from trays balanced on their knees, and toasted each other with discount Shiraz, and decided between them that Dan's ailment must have been one of those twenty-four hour bug things that go away as quickly as they come on, and he was probably over the worst of it. After the meal they piled up the unwashed crocks in the sink and retreated, first of all to the sofa, where multiple passages of mutual contentment ensued; and then, later on, when there became little point in delaying the inevitable any longer, to the bedroom, where Dan had fortunately remembered to change the sheets earlier in the week.

Later on, freed from care and blessed with pleasure, snuggled tight against Molly's flawless back like spoons stored away in a drawer, Dan felt every bit as purely, elementally happy as he'd been miserable only hours before. As happy as he'd been since Angie, since before it all went wrong—let alone the fall of Nevernesse and the business with X. This, he told himself, was the real world, and he'd connected with it once more; a man and a woman in bed together, no thinking, only doing, nothing else to it but a long, smooth slide into pleasure. That had been *great.* Soon, it would happen again; and again and again, as often as could feasibly be achieved. Even the thought of it . . . Almost (but not quite) involuntarily, Dan waxed improper, just an inch or so.

"Hello?" Bleary confusion in Molly's waking murmur. "Who are you then, little chap?"

"Not so much of the little," murmured Dan into the hot rushing depth of her ear, before seeing what she'd seen and turning to ice-water jelly right there in the bed, shrinking away from her like a salted slug.

Standing by the bedside, rubbing his nose with a dirty sleeve, was X in his pajamas. "I'm scared," was all he said. Before Dan could get to him, before he could throw him back into the cupboard or out of a window or down a well, whatever it would take to be rid of him, once and for all: "I'm scared, missus."

"Love?" Molly struggling up on one elbow, reaching for her clothes. "What's the matter? Why are you scared?"

"I'm frightened." A gulp. "He shouted at me. He made me go in the cupboard."

"No!" Dan was trying to hold it together, but already he could feel it slipping out from under him. Not so much a moodswing as a tectonic shift, a geological catastrophe. "Get out! Get out of here!"

"Don't let him hurt me again, missus!" X shrank back, and instinctively Molly reached for him, the way she'd reached out to Dan in the bookshop. Dan, meanwhile, was frantically trying to free himself from the duvet, get around the bed to shut X up before it was too late.

"It's all right, no one's going to hurt you." Molly had him now, both hands on his trembling shoulders. "Tell me what happened."

Just then, Dan caught his foot in the flex of the bedside lamp and tipped the lot over, table, lamp and all. Molly started at the crash; X gave a high-pitched, unearthly scream and flung himself into her arms.

"He's horrible to me!" he sobbed. "He makes me go in the cupboard, and he threw me in the boot of his car, and he hurt me, I've got bruises, and I'm hungry, and he shouted, and I hate him!"

"Dan?" Molly turned to Dan, X clasped tight against her as Dan himself had been only minutes ago. It was all going wrong. It was too late, it was ending before it had really begun. "Dan, what's going on? Who's this boy? Where does he come from? Who's been hurting him?"

"He's . . . he's from next door," Dan improvised frantically. "He comes through the fire door, I unblocked it, I was looking where it went, and he comes through all the time now." Gabbling, no time to think, making stuff up on the spot. "They're, they're like this problem family, you know, single parent, there's a social worker comes round, social services? I'll take him back where he belongs," hopping on the spot, trying to get both legs down one side of his jogging pants, before overbalancing on to the bed. The dream of too-late, the dream of disaster in slow motion, and there's nothing you can do. And you don't even have any trousers on.

"*Nooo!*" The child was shrieking now, and Molly clung to him more tightly, trying to calm him. "No! Don't let him put me back in there!"

"Love, you've got to go back," she tried to tell him, and Dan for a moment glimpsed a speck of hope. "Your mummy'll be looking for you, she'll be worried—"

"I don't live with me mam any more," sobbed X. "I live here, and he's horrible to me all the time. He brought me here to live with him, and he shouts at me and hurts me—"

"Hurts you?" Molly looked from X to Dan disbelievingly. Dan couldn't meet her eyes; he just couldn't do it. Afraid of what he might see. "Dan, what's he saying? Who hurts him? Is it the father?"

"He's lying," protested Dan, oblivious in his panic to the implications of what he was saying. "I've never touched him." Walking right into it. But Molly was already running her hands over X, checking for damage. She caught sight of something, bent to examine it more closely, and gasped.

"Oh my God . . . " She swung to face Dan. "His feet! What's happened to the soles of his *feet*?"

"He burned them!" X's wail cut through the humming panic in Dan's head: it filled the room, it filled everything Dan knew or was aware of. "With a cigarette! He said I hadn't to tell!"

"Who? Who did?" Molly held his face in both her hands, looked straight into his eyes. "Tell me who did this to you?"

"HE DID!" Hand outstretched, pointing straight at Dan. The tiny traitor, Judas in his stained pajamas. "HE DID! IT WAS HIM! HE DID!" Till Molly hushed him, clutched him to her bosom so his thin high screams were muffled between her breasts, her breasts so lately cupped by Dan's guilty hands in post-coital serenity. She tried to hug him, to hang on to him and calm him down, but the boy twisted away, he couldn't be held, couldn't be contained that way. With one last accusation—"It was HIM!"—he was gone, out of the bedroom to who knew where, to whatever reality he now inhabited. And Dan, stuck inconveniently in this worst of all worlds, stayed slumped against the wall, ruined and abandoned, hardly hearing a thing, aware only peripherally of Molly's disbelieving accusations, her mounting anger. The noise in his head swelled to drown it out, so that each time she tried to get an explanation, each fresh accusation she flung at him in her mounting anger, all he heard was a harsh and monstrous buzzing, the feedback whine of metal stressed on metal, the sound of an engine wrecking itself.

In the end, her parting words cut through. "I'm getting out of here. And I'm calling the police." He looked up, just in time to receive her slap full in the face. She was fully dressed now, glaring at him with pure repugnance. He turned away, unable to bear the loathing in her eyes.

After the door slammed shut behind her, Dan half-hoped the noise in his head might abate a little. It didn't, though; not even when he slammed his ringing head against the loathsome, hopeless reflection that mocked him in the mirror. Neither pain nor blood nor destruction could touch it. It was his new condition, the scornful complement to the loss of everything else. Welcome, stranger, to the world of the insane.

In a childish attempt to get away from it—as if he could escape from the inside of his own head—he even crawled into the cupboard, X's special place, tugged the door shut behind him and flattened himself against the cobwebbed brickwork. The feel of the rough edges grinding against his face brought him a temporary measure of relief at least; though the noise never went away, he felt that here he could bear it better, or could try to at least. When the knocking came at the door to the flat, harsh and relentless, he pressed himself still further against the gap, willing it to stretch open and receive him entire, translate him to some other world, some other mode of being; a kinder fiction, a life story somehow less tragic.

How do you deal with a zombie apocalypse? Make Cleveland, Ohio, a zombie preserve/penal colony, of course . . .

THE NATURALIST

MAUREEN MCHUGH

Cahill lived in the Flats with about twenty other guys in a place that used to be an Irish bar called Fado. At the back of the bar was the Cuyahoga River, good for protection since zombies didn't cross the river. They didn't crumble into dust, they were just stupid as bricks and they never built a boat or a bridge or built anything. Zombies were the ultimate trash. Worse than the guys who cooked meth in trailers. Worse than the fat women on WIC. Zombies were just useless dumbfucks.

"They're too dumb to find enough food to keep a stray cat going," Duck said.

Cahill was talking to a guy called Duck. Well, really, Duck was talking and Cahill was mostly listening. Duck had been speculating on the biology of zombies. He thought that the whole zombie thing was a virus, like Mad Cow Disease. A lot of the guys thought that. A lot of them mentioned that movie, *28 Days* where everybody but a few people had been driven crazy by a virus.

"But they gotta find something," Duck said. Duck had a prison tattoo of a mallard on his arm. Cahill wouldn't have known it was a mallard if Duck hadn't told him. He could just about tell it was a bird. Duck was over six feet tall and Cahill would have hated to have been the guy who gave Duck such a shitty tattoo cause Duck probably beat him senseless when he finally got a look at the thing. "Maybe," Duck mused, "maybe they're solar powered. And eating us is just a bonus."

"I think they go dormant when they don't smell us around," Cahill said.

Cahill didn't really like talking to Duck, but Duck often found Cahill and started talking to him. Cahill didn't know why. Most of the guys gave Duck a wide berth. Cahill figured it was probably easier to just talk to Duck when Duck wanted to talk.

Almost all of the guys at Fado were white. There was a Filipino guy, but he pretty much counted as white. As far as Cahill could tell there were two kinds of black guys, regular black guys and Nation of Islam. The Nation of Islam had gotten organized and turned a place across the street—a club called Heaven—into their headquarters. Most of the regular black guys lived below Heaven and in the building next door.

This whole area of the Flats had been bars and restaurants and clubs. Now it was a kind of compound with a wall of rubbish and dead cars forming a perimeter. Duck said that during the winter they had regular patrols organized by Whittaker and the Nation. Cold as shit standing behind a junked car on its side, watching for zombies. But they had killed off most of the zombies off in this area and now they didn't bother keeping watch. Occasionally a zombie wandered across the bridge and they had to take care of it, but in the time Cahill had been in Cleveland, he had seen exactly four zombies. One had been a woman.

Life in the zombie preserve really wasn't as bad as Cahill had expected. He'd been dumped off the bus and then spent a day skulking around expecting zombies to come boiling out of the floor like rats and eat him alive. He'd heard that the life expectancy of a guy in a preserve was something like two and a half days. But he'd only been here about a day and a half when he found a cache of liquor in the trunk of a car and then some guys scavenging. He'd shown them where the liquor was and they'd taken him back to the Flats.

Whittaker was a white guy who was sort of in charge. He'd had made a big speech about how they were all more free here in the preserve than they'd ever been in a society that had no place for them, about how there used to be spaces for men with big appetites like the wild west and Alaska—and how that was all gone now but they were making a great space for themselves here in Cleveland where they could live true to their own nature.

Cahill didn't think it was so great, and glancing around he was pretty sure that he wasn't the only one who wouldn't chuck the whole thing for a chance to sit and watch the Sox on TV. Bullshitting was what the Whittakers of the world did. It was part of running other people's lives. Cahill had dragged in a futon and made himself a little room. It had no windows and only one way in, which was good in case of attack. But he found most of the time he couldn't sleep there. A lot of time he slept outside on a picnic table someone had dragged out into the middle of the street.

What he really missed was carpet. He wanted to take a shower and then walk on carpet in a bedroom and get dressed in clean clothes.

A guy named Riley walked over to Cahill and Duck and said, "Hey, Cahill. Whittaker wants you to go scavenge."

Cahill hated to scavenge. It was nerve-wracking. It wasn't hard; there was a surprising amount left in the city, even after the groceries had been looted. He shrugged and thought about it and decided it was better not to say no to Whittaker. And it gave him an excuse to stop talking to Duck about zombies. He followed Riley and left Duck sitting looking at the water, enjoying the May sun.

"I think it's a government thing," Riley said. Riley was black but just regular black, not Nation of Islam. "I think it's a mutation of the AIDs virus."

Jesus Christ. "Yeah," Cahill said, hoping Riley would drop it.

"You know the whole AIDs thing was from the CIA, don't you? It was supposed to wipe out black people," Riley said.

"Then how come fags got it first?" Cahill asked.

He thought that might piss Riley off but Riley seemed pleased to be able to explain how gay guys were the perfect way to introduce the disease because nobody cared fuckall what happened to them. But that really, fags getting it was an accident because it was supposed to wipe out all the black people in Africa and then the whites could just move into a whole new continent. Some queer stewardess got it in Africa and then brought it back here. It would kill white people but it killed black people faster. And now if you were rich they could cure you or at least give you drugs for your whole life so you wouldn't get sick and die which was the same thing, but they were still letting black people and Africans die.

Cahill tuned Riley out. They collected two other guys. Riley was in charge. Cahill didn't know the names of the two other guys—a scrawny, white-trash looking guy and a light-skinned black guy.

Riley quit talking once they had crossed the bridge and were in Cleveland.

On the blind, windowless side of a warehouse the wall had been painted white, and in huge letters it said:

Hell from beneath is moved for thee to meet thee at thy coming.
—Isaiah (ch. XIV, v. 9)

This same quote was painted at the gate where the bus had dumped Cahill off.

There were crows gathering at Euclid, and, Riley guessed, maybe around East Ninth, so they headed north towards the lake. Zombies stank and the crows tended to hang around them. Behind them the burned ruins of the Renaissance Hotel were still black and wet from the rain a couple of days ago.

When they saw the zombie there were no crows but that may have been because there was only one. Crows often meant a number of zombies. The zombie fixed on them, turning her face towards them despite the blank whiteness of her eyes. She was black and her hair had once been in cornrows, though now half of it was loose and tangled. They all stopped and stood stock still. No one knew how zombies "saw" people. Maybe infrared like pit vipers. Maybe smell. Cahill could not tell from this far if she was sniffing. Or listening. Or maybe even tasting the air. Taste was one of the most primitive senses. Primitive as smell. Smelling with the tongue.

She went from standing there to loping towards them. That was one of the things about zombies. They didn't lean. They didn't anticipate. One minute they were standing there, the next minute they were running towards you. They didn't lead with their eyes or their chins. They were never surprised. They just were. As inexorable as rain. She didn't look as she ran, even though she was running through debris and rubble, placing her feet and sometimes barely leaping.

"Fuck," someone said.

"Pipes! Who's got pipes!" Riley shouted.

They all had pipes and they all got them ready. Cahill wished he had a gun but Whittaker confiscated guns. Hell, he wished he had an MK19, a grenade launcher. And a Humvee and some support, maybe with mortars while he was at it.

Then she was on them and they were all swinging like mad because if she got her teeth into any of them, it was all over for that guy. The best thing to do was to keep up a goddamn flurry of swinging pipes so she couldn't get to anyone. Cahill hit other pipe mostly, the impact clanging through his wrist bones, but sometimes when he hit the zombie he felt the melon thunk. She made no noise. No moaning, no hissing, no movie zombie noises, but even as they crushed her head and knocked her down (her eye socket gone soft and one eye a loose silken white sack) she kept moving and reaching. She didn't try to grab the pipes, she just reached for them until they had pounded her into broken bits.

She stank like old meat.

No blood. Which was strangely creepy. Cahill knew from experience that people had a lot more blood in them than you ever would have thought based on TV shows. Blood and blood and more blood. But this zombie didn't seem to have any blood.

Finally Riley yelled, "Get back, get back!" and they all stepped back.

All the bones in her arms and legs were broken and her head was smashed to nothing. It was hard to tell she had ever looked like a person. The torso hitched its hips, raising its belly, trying to inchworm towards them, its broken limbs moving and shuddering like a seizure.

Riley shook his head and then said to them. "Anybody got any marks? Everybody strip."

Everybody stood there for a moment, ignoring him, watching the thing on the broken sidewalk.

Riley snarled, "I said strip, motherfuckers. Or nobody goes back to the compound."

"Fuck," one of the guys said, but they all did and, balls shriveled in the spring cold, paired off and checked each other for marks. When they each announced the other was clear, they all put their clothes back on and piled rubble on top of the twitching thing until they'd made a mound, while Riley kept an eye out for any others.

After that, everyone was pretty tense. They broke into an apartment complex above a storefront. The storefront had been looted and the windows looked empty as the socket of a pulled tooth, but the door to the apartments above was still locked which meant that they might find stuff untouched. Cahill wondered: If zombies did go dormant without food, what if someone had gotten bit and went back to this place, to their apartment? Could they be waiting for someone to enter the dark foyer, for the warmth and smell and the low steady big drum beat of the human heart to bring them back?

They went up the dark stairwell and busted open the door of the first apartment. It smelled closed, cold and dank. The furniture looked like it had been furnished from the curb, but it had a huge honking television. Which said everything about the guy who had lived here.

They ignored the TV. What they were looking for was canned goods. Chef Boyardee. Cans of beef stew. Beer. They all headed for the kitchen and guys started flipping open cabinets.

Then, like a dumbshit, Cahill opened the refrigerator door. Even as he did it, he thought, "Dumbass."

The refrigerator had been full of food, and then had sat, sealed and without power, while that food all rotted into a seething, shit-stinking mess. The smell was like a bomb. The inside was greenish black.

"Fuck!" someone said and then they all got out of the kitchen. Cahill opened a window and stepped out onto the fire escape. It was closest and everyone else was headed out into the living room where someone would probably take a swing at him for being an asshole. The fire escape was in an alley and he figured that he could probably get to the street and meet them in front, although he wasn't exactly sure how fire escapes worked.

Instead he froze. Below him, in the alley, there was one of those big dumpsters, painted green. The top was off the dumpster and inside it, curled up, was a zombie. Because it was curled up, he couldn't tell much about it—whether it was male or female, black or white. It looked small and it was wearing a striped shirt.

The weird thing was that the entire inside of the dumpster had been covered in aluminum foil. There wasn't any sun yet in the alley but the dumpster was still a dull and crinkly mirror. As best he could tell, every bit was covered.

What the fuck was that about?

He waited for the zombie to sense him and raise its sightless face but it didn't move. It was in one corner, like a gerbil or something in an aquarium. And all that freaking tinfoil. Had it gone into apartments and searched for aluminum foil? What for? To trap sunlight? Maybe Duck was right, they were solar powered. Or maybe it just liked shiny stuff.

The window had been hard to open and it had been loud. He could still smell the reek of the kitchen. The sound and the stink should have alerted the zombie.

Maybe it was dead. Whatever that meant to a zombie.

He heard a distant *whump*. And then a couple more, with a dull rumble of explosion. It sounded like an air strike. The zombie stirred a little, not even raising its head. More like an animal disturbed in its sleep.

The hair was standing up on the back of Cahill's neck. From the zombie or the air strike, he couldn't tell. He didn't hear helicopters. He didn't hear anything. He stamped on the metal fire escape. It rang dully. The zombie didn't move.

He went back inside, through the kitchen and the now empty apartment, down the dark stairwell. The other guys were standing around in the street, talking about the sounds they'd heard. Cahill didn't say anything, didn't say they were probably Hellfire missiles although they sure as hell sounded like them, and he didn't say there was a zombie in the alley. Nobody said anything to him about opening the refrigerator, which was fine by him.

Riley ordered them to head back to see what was up in the Flats.

While they were walking, the skinny little guy said, "Maybe one of those big cranes fell. You know, those big fuckers by the lake that they use for ore ships and shit."

Nobody answered.

"It could happen," the little guy insisted.

"Shut up," Riley said.

Cahill glanced behind them, unable to keep from checking his back. He'd been watching since they started moving, but the little zombie didn't seem to have woken up and followed them.

When they got to Public Square they could see the smoke rising, black and ugly, from the Flats.

"Fuck," Cahill said.

"What is that?" Riley said.

"Is that the camp?" "Fuck is right." "One of the buildings is on fire?" Cahill wished they would shut the fuck up because he was listening for helicopters.

They headed for Main Avenue. By the time they got to West 10th, there was a lot more smoke and they could see some of it was rising from what used to be Shooters. They had to pick their way across debris. Fado and Heaven were gutted, the buildings blown out. Maybe someone was still alive. There were bodies. Cahill could see one in what looked like Whittaker's usual uniform of orange football jersey and black athletic shorts. Most of the head was missing.

"What the fuck?" Riley said.

"Air strike," Cahill said.

"Fuck that," Riley said. "Why would anyone do that?"

Because we weren't dying, Cahill thought. We weren't supposed to figure out how to stay alive. We certainly weren't supposed to establish some sort of base. Hell, the rats might get out of the cage.

The little guy who thought it might have been a crane walked up behind Riley and swung his pipe into the back of Riley's head. Riley staggered and the little guy swung again, and Riley's skull cracked audibly. They little guy hit a third time as Riley went down.

The little guy was breathing heavy. "Fucking bastard," he said, holding the pipe, glaring at them. "Whittaker's bitch."

Cahill glanced at the fourth guy with them. He looked as surprised as Cahill.

"You got a problem with this?" the little guy said.

Cahill wondered if the little guy had gotten scratched by the first zombie and they had missed it. Or if he was just bugfuck. Didn't matter. Cahill took a careful step back, holding his own pipe. And then another. The little guy didn't try to stop him.

He thought about waiting for a moment to see what the fourth guy would do. Two people would probably have a better chance than one. Someone to watch while the other slept. But the fourth guy was staring at the little guy and at Riley, who was laid out on the road, and he didn't seem to be able to wrap his head around the idea that their base was destroyed and Riley was dead.

Too stupid to live, and probably a liability. Cahill decided he was better off alone. Besides, Cahill had never really liked other people much anyway.

He found an expensive loft with a big white leather couch and a kitchen full of granite and stainless steel and a bed the size of a football field and he stayed there for a couple of days, eating pouches of tuna he found next door but it was too big and in a couple of days, the liquor cabinet was empty. By that time he had developed a deep and abiding hatred for the couple who had lived here. He had found pictures of them. A dark haired forty-ish guy with a kayak and a shit-eating grin. He had owned some kind of construction business. She was a toothy blonde with a big forehead who he mentally fucked every night in the big bed. It only made him crazy horny for actual sex.

He imagined they'd been evacuated. People like them didn't get killed, even when the zombies came. Even in the first panicked days when they were in dozens of cities and it seemed like the end of the world, before they'd gotten them under control. Somewhere they were sitting around in their new, lovely loft with working plumbing, telling their friends about how horrible it had been.

Finally, he dragged the big mattress to the freight elevator and then to the middle of the street out front. Long before he got it to the freight elevator, he had completely lost the righteous anger that had possessed him when he thought of the plan, but by then he was just pissed at everything. He considered torching the building but in the end he got the mattress down to the street, along with some pillows and cushions and magazines and kitchen chairs and set fire to the pile, then retreated to the third floor of the building across the way. Word was that zombies came for fire. Cahill was buzzing with a kind of suicidal craziness by this point, simultaneously terrified and elated. He settled in with a bottle of cranberry vodka, the last of the liquor from the loft, and a fancy martini glass, and waited. The vodka was not as awful as it sounded. The fire burned, almost transparent at first, and then orange and smoky.

After an hour he was bored and antsy. He jacked off with the picture of the toothy blonde. He drank more of the cranberry vodka. He glanced down at the fire and they were there.

There were three of them, one standing by a light pole at the end of the street, one standing in the middle of the street, one almost directly below him. He grabbed his length of pipe and the baseball bat he'd found. He had been looking for a gun but hadn't found one. He wasn't sure that a gun would make much difference anyway. They were all unnaturally still. None of them had turned their blind faces towards him. They didn't seem to look at anything—not him, not the fire, not each other. They just stood there.

All of the shortcomings of this presented themselves. He had only one way out of the building, as far as he knew, and that was the door to the street where the zombies were. There was a back door but someone had driven a UPS truck into it and it was impassable. He didn't have any food. He didn't have much in the way of defense—he could have made traps. Found bedsprings and rigged up spikes so that if a zombie came in the hall and tripped it, it would slam the thing against the wall and shred it. Not that he had ever been particularly mechanical. He didn't really know how such a thing would work.

Lighter fluid. He could douse an area in lighter fluid or gasoline or something, and if a zombie came towards him, set fire to the fucker. Hell, even an idiot could make a Molotov cocktail.

All three of the zombies had once been men. One of them was so short he thought it was a child. Then he thought maybe it was a dwarf. One of them was wearing what might have once been a suit, which was a nice thing. Zombie businessmen struck Cahill as appropriate. The problem was that he didn't dare leave until they did, and the mattress looked ready to smolder for a good long time.

It did smolder for a good long time. The zombies just stood there, not looking at the fire, not looking at each other, not looking at anything. The zombie girl, the one they'd killed with Riley, she had turned her face in their direction. That was so far the most human thing he had seen a zombie do. He tried to see if their noses twitched or if they sniffed but they were too far away. He added binoculars to his mental list of shit he hoped to find.

Eventually he went and explored some of the building he was in. It was offices and the candy machine had been turned over and emptied. He worried when he prowled the darkened halls that the zombies had somehow sensed him, so he could only bring himself to explore for a few minutes at a time before he went back to his original window and checked. But they were just standing there. When it got dark, he wondered if they would lie down, maybe sleep like the one in the dumpster but they didn't.

The night was horrible. There was no light in the city, of course. The street was dark enough that he couldn't see the short zombie. Where it was standing was a shadow and a pretty much impenetrable one. The smoldering fire cast no real light at all. It was just an ashen heap that sometimes glowed red when a breeze picked up. Cahill nodded off and jerked awake, counting the zombies, wondering if the little one had moved in on him. If the short one sensed him, wouldn't they all sense him? Didn't the fact that two of them were still there mean that it was still there, too? It was hard to make out any of them, and sometimes he thought maybe they had all moved.

At dawn they were all three still there. All three still standing. Crows had gathered on the edge of the roof of a building down the street, probably drawn by the smell.

It sucked.

They stood there for that whole day, the night, and part of the next day before one of them turned and loped away, smooth as glass. The other two stood there for a while longer—an hour? He had no sense of time anymore. Then they moved off at the same time, not exactly together but apparently triggered by the same strange signal. He watched them lope off.

He made himself count slowly to one thousand. Then he did it again. Then finally he left the building.

For days the city was alive with zombies for him although he didn't see any. He saw crows and avoided wherever he saw them. He headed for the lake and found a place not far from the Flats, an apartment over shops, with windows that opened. It wasn't near as swanky as the loft. He rigged up an alarm system that involved a bunch of thread crossing the open doorway to the stairwell and a bunch of wind chimes. Anything hit the thread and it would release the wind chimes, which would fall and make enough noise to wake the fucking dead.

For the first time since he left the loft, he slept that night.

The next day he sat at the little kitchen table by the open window and wrote down everything he knew about zombies:

they stink

they can sense people

they didn't sense me because I was up above them? they couldn't smell me? they couldn't see me?

sometimes they sleep or something sick? worn down? used up charge?

they like fire

they don't necessarily sleep

they like tinfoil ???

Things he didn't know but wanted to:

do they eat animals

how do they sense people

how many are there

do they eventually die? fall apart? Use up their energy?

It was somehow satisfying to have a list.

He decided to check out the zombie he had seen in the dumpster. He had a backpack now with water, a couple of cans of Campbell's Chunky soups—including his favorite, chicken and sausage gumbo, because if he got stuck somewhere like the last time, he figured he'd need something to look forward to—a tub of Duncan Hines Creamy Homestyle Chocolate Buttercream frosting for dessert, a can opener, a flashlight with batteries that worked, and his prize find, binoculars. Besides his length of pipe, he carried a Molotov cocktail; a wine bottle three-fourths filled with gasoline mixed with sugar, corked, with a gasoline soaked rag rubber-banded to the top and covered with a sandwich bag so it wouldn't dry out.

He thought about cars as he walked. The trip he was making would take him an hour and it would have been five minutes in a car. People in cars had no fucking appreciation for how big places were. Nobody would be fat if there weren't any cars. Far down the street, someone came out of a looted store carrying a cardboard box.

Cahill stopped and then dropped behind a pile of debris from a sandwich shop. If it was a zombie, he wasn't sure hiding wouldn't make any difference, and he pulled his lighter out of his pocket, ready to throw the bottle. But it wasn't a zombie. Zombies, as far as he knew, didn't carry boxes of loot around. The guy with the box must have seen Cahill moving because he dropped the box and ran.

Cahill occasionally saw other convicts, but he avoided them, and so far, they avoided him. There was a one dude who Cahill was pretty sure lived somewhere around the wreckage of the Renaissance Hotel. He didn't seem to want any company, either. Cahill followed to where this new guy had disappeared around a corner. The guy was watching and when he saw Cahill, he jogged away, watching over his shoulder to see if Cahill would follow. Cahill stood until the guy had turned the corner.

By the time Cahill got to the apartment where he'd seen the zombie in the dumpster, he was pretty sure that the other guy had gotten behind him and was following him. It irritated him. Dickweed. He thought about not going upstairs, but decided that since the guy wasn't in sight at the moment, it would give Cahill a chance to disappear. Besides, they hadn't actually checked out the apartment and there might be something worth scavenging. In Cahill's months of scavenging, he had never seen a zombie in an apartment, or even any evidence of one, but he always checked carefully. The place was empty, still stinking a little of the contents of the fridge, but the smell was no worse than a lot of places and a lot better than some. Rain had come in where he'd left the kitchen window open, warping the linoleum. He climbed out onto the fire escape and looked down. The dumpster was empty, although still lined with some tattered aluminum foil. He pulled out his binoculars and checked carefully, but he couldn't really see anything.

He stood for a long time. Truthfully he couldn't be a hundred percent sure it was a zombie. Maybe it had been a child, some sort of refugee? Hard to imagine any child surviving in the city. No, it had to be a zombie. He considered lighting and tossing the Molotov cocktail and seeing if the zombie came to the alley, but didn't want to wait it out in this apartment building. Something about this place made him feel vulnerable.

Eventually he rummaged through the apartment. The bedside table held neither handgun nor D batteries, two things high on his scavenger list. He went back down the dark stairwell and stopped well back from the doorway. Out in the middle of the street, in front of the building to his left but visible from where he stood, was an offering. A box with a bottle of whiskey set on it. Like some kind of perverse lemonade stand.

Fucking dickweed.

If the guy had found a handgun, he could be waiting in ambush. Cahill figured there was a good chance he could outlast the guy but he hated waiting in the stairwell. There were no apartments on the first level, just a hallway between two storefronts. Cahill headed back upstairs. The apartment he'd been in before didn't look out the front of the building. The one that did was locked.

Fuck.

Breaking open the lock would undoubtedly make a hell of a lot of racket. He went back to the first apartment, checked one more time for the zombie, and peed in the empty toilet. He grabbed a pillow from the bed.

Cahill went back downstairs and sat down on the bottom step and wedged the pillow in behind his back. He set up his bottle and his lighter beside him on the step, and his pipe on the other side and settled in to watch. He could at least wait until dark although it wasn't even mid-morning yet. After awhile he ate his soup—the can opener sounded louder than it probably was.

It was warm midday and Cahill was drowsy warm when the guy finally, nervously, walked out to the box and picked up the whiskey. Cahill sat still in the shadow of the stairwell with his hand on his pipe. As best as he could tell, he was unnoticed. The guy was a tall, skinny black man wearing a brown Cleveland football jersey and a pair of expensive looking, olive-green suit pants. Cahill looked out and watched the guy walk back up the street. After a minute, Cahill followed.

When Cahill got out to the main drag, the guy was walking up Superior towards the center of downtown. Cahill took a firm hold of his pipe.

"Hey," he said. His voice carried well in the silence.

The guy started and whirled around.

"What the fuck you want?" Cahill asked.

"Bro," the man said. "Hey, were you hiding back there?" He laughed nervously and held up the bottle. "Peace offering, bro. Just looking to make some peace."

"What do you want?" Cahill asked.

"Just, you know, wanna talk. Talk to someone who knows the ropes, you know? I just got here and I don't know what the fuck is going on, bro."

"This is a fucking penal colony," Cahill said.

"Yeah," the guy laughed. "A fucking zombie preserve. I been watching out for them zombies. You look like you been here awhile."

Cahill hadn't bothered to shave and last time he'd glanced in a mirror he'd looked like Charles Manson, only bearded and taller. "Lie down with your hands away from your body," Cahill said.

The black guy squinted at Cahill. "You shittin' me."

"How do I know you don't have a gun?" Cahill asked.

"Bro, I don't got no gun. I don't got nothin' but what you see."

Cahill waited.

"Listen, I'm just trying to be friendly," the guy said. "I swear to God, I don't have anything. How do I know *you're* not going to do something to me? You're a freaky dude—you know that?"

The guy talked for about five minutes, finally talking himself into lying down on his stomach with his arms out. Cahill moved fast, patting him down. The guy wasn't lying, he didn't have anything on him.

"Fuck man," the guy said. "I told you that." Once he was sure Cahill wasn't going to do anything to him he talked even more. His name was LaJon Watson and his lawyer had told him there was no way they were going to drop him in the Cleveland Zombie Preserve because the Supreme Court was going to declare it unconstitutional. His lawyer had been saying that right up until the day they put LaJon on the bus, which was when LaJon realized that his lawyer knew shit. LaJon wanted to know if Cahill had seen any zombies and what they were like and how Cahill had stayed alive.

Cahill found it hard to talk. He hadn't talked to anyone in weeks. Usually someone like LaJon Watson would have driven him nuts, but it was nice to let the tide of talk wash over him while they walked. He wasn't sure that he wouldn't regret it, but he took LaJon back to his place. LaJon admired his alarm system. "You gotta show me how to unhook it and hook it back up. Don't they see it? I mean, has one of them ever hit it?"

"No," Cahill said. "I don't think they can see."

There were scientists studying zombies and sometimes there was zombie stuff on Fox News, but LaJon said he hadn't paid much attention to all that. He really hadn't expected to need to know about zombies. In fact, he hadn't been sure at first that Cahill wasn't a zombie. Cahill opened cans of Campbell's Chunky Chicken and Dumplings. LaJon asked if Cahill warmed them over a fire or what. Cahill handed him a can and a spoon.

LaJon wolfed down the soup. LaJon wouldn't shut up, even while eating. He told Cahill how he'd looked in a bunch of shops, but most of them had been pretty thoroughly looted. He'd looked in an apartment, but the only thing on the shelves in a can was tomato paste and evaporated milk. Although now that he thought about it, maybe he could have made some sort of tomato soup or something. He hadn't slept in the two days he'd been here and he was going crazy and it was a great fucking thing to have found somebody who could show him the ropes.

LaJon was from Cincinnati. Did Cahill know anybody from Cincinnati? Where had Cahill been doing time? (Auburn.) LaJon didn't know anybody at Auburn, wasn't that New York? LaJon had been at Lebanon Correctional. Cahill was a nice dude, if quiet. Who else was around, and was there anyone LaJon could score from? (Cahill said he didn't know.) What did people use for money here anyway?

"I been thinking," LaJon said, "about the zombies. I think it's pollution that's mutating them like the Teenage Mutant Ninja Turtles."

Cahill decided it had been a mistake to bring LaJon. He picked up the bottle of whiskey and opened it. He didn't usually use glasses but got two out of the cupboard and poured them each some whiskey.

LaJon apologized, "I don't usually talk this much," he said. "I guess I just fucking figured I was dead when they dropped me here." He took a big drink of whiskey. "It's like my mouth can't stop."

Cahill poured LaJon more to drink and nursed his own whiskey. Exhaustion and nerves were telling, LaJon was finally slowing down. "You want some frosting?" Cahill asked.

Frosting and whiskey was a better combination than it had any right to be. Particularly for a man who'd thought himself dead. LaJon nodded off.

"Come on," Cahill said. "It's going to get stuffy in here." He got the sleepy drunk up on his feet.

"What?" LaJon said.

"I sleep outside, where it's cooler." It was true that the apartment got hot during the day.

"Bro, there's zombies out there," LaJon mumbled.

"It's okay, I've got a system," Cahill said. "I'll get you downstairs and then I'll bring down something to sleep on."

LaJon wanted to sleep where he was and, for a moment, his eyes narrowed to slits and something scary was in his face.

"I'm going to be there, too," Cahill said. "I wouldn't do anything to put myself in danger."

LaJon allowed himself to be half-carried downstairs. Cahill was worried when he had to unhook the alarm system. He propped LaJon up against the wall and told him. "Just a moment." If LaJon slid down the wall and passed out, he'd be hell to get downstairs. But the lanky black guy stood there long enough for Cahill to get the alarm stuff out of the way. He was starting to sober up a little. Cahill got him down to the street.

"I'll get the rest of the whiskey," Cahill said.

"What the fuck you playing at?" LaJon muttered.

Cahill took the stairs two at a time in the dark. He grabbed pillows, blankets, and the whiskey bottle and went back down to the sidewalk. He handed LaJon the whiskey bottle. "It's not so hot out here," he said, although it was on the sidewalk with the sunlight.

LaJon eyed him drunkenly.

Cahill went back upstairs and came down with a bunch of couch cushions. He made a kind of bed and got LaJon to sit on it. "We're okay in the day," he said. "Zombies don't like the light. I sleep in the day. I'll get us upstairs before night."

LaJon shook his head, took another slug of whiskey, and lay back on the cushions. "I feel sick," he said.

Cahill thought the motherfucker was going to throw up, but instead LaJon was snoring.

Cahill sat for a bit, planning and watching the street. After a bit, he went back to his apartment. When he found something good scavenging, he squirreled it away. He came downstairs with duct tape. He taped LaJon's ankles together. Then his wrists. Then he sat LaJon up. LaJon opened his eyes, said, "What the fuck?" drunkenly. Cahill taped LaJon's arms to his sides, right at his elbows, running the tape all the way around his torso. LaJon started to struggle, but Cahill was methodical and patient, and he used the whole roll of tape to secure LaJon's arms. From shoulders to waist, LaJon was a duct tape mummy.

LaJon swore at him, colorfully then monotonously.

Cahill left him there and went looking. He found an upright dolly at a bar, and brought it back. It didn't do so well where the pavement was uneven, but he didn't think he could carry LaJon far and if he was going to build a fire, he didn't want it to be close to his place, where zombies could pin him in his apartment. LaJon was still where he left him, although when he saw Cahill, he went into a frenzy of struggling. Cahill let him struggle. He lay the dolly down and rolled LaJon onto it. LaJon fought like anything, so in the end, Cahill went back upstairs and got another roll of duck tape and duck taped LaJon to the dolly. That was harder than duct taping LaJon the first time, because LaJon was scared and pissed now. When Cahill finally pulled the dolly up LaJon struggled so hard that the dolly was unmanageable, which pissed Cahill off so much he just let go.

LaJon went over, and without hands to stop himself, face planted on the sidewalk. That stilled him. Cahill pulled the dolly upright then. LaJon's face was a bloody mess and it looked like he might have broken a couple of teeth. He was conscious, but stunned. Cahill started pushing the dolly and LaJon threw up.

It took a couple of hours to get six blocks. LaJon was sober and silent by the time Cahill decided he'd gone far enough.

Cahill sat down, sweating, and used his T-shirt to wipe his face.

"You a bug," LaJon said.

Bug was prison slang for someone crazy. LaJon said it with certainty.

"Just my fucking luck. Kind of luck I had all my life. I find one guy alive in this fucking place and he a bug." LaJon spat. "What are you gonna do to me?"

Cahill was so tired of LaJon that he considered going back to his place and leaving LaJon here. Instead, he found a door and pried it open with a tire iron. It had been an office building and the second floor was fronted with glass. He had a hell of a time finding a set of service stairs that opened from the outside on the first floor. He found some chairs and dragged them downstairs. Then he emptied file cabinets, piling the papers around the chairs. LaJon watched him, getting more anxious.

When it looked like he'd get a decent fire going, he put LaJon next to it. The blood had dried on LaJon's face and he'd bruised up a bit. It was evening.

Cahill set fire to the papers and stood, waiting for them to catch. Burnt paper drifted up, raised by the fire.

LaJon squinted at the fire, then at Cahill. "You gonna burn me?"

Cahill went in the building and settled upstairs where he could watch.

LaJon must have figured that Cahill wasn't going to burn him. Then he began to worry about zombies. Cahill watched him start twisting around, trying to look around. The dolly rocked and LaJon realized that if he wasn't careful, the dolly would go over again and he'd faceplant and not be able to see.

Cahill gambled that the zombies wouldn't be there right away, and found a soda machine in the hallway. He broke it open with his tire iron and got himself a couple of Cokes and then went back to watch it get dark. The zombies weren't there yet. He opened a warm Coke and settled in a desk chair from one of the offices—much more comfortable than the cubicle chairs. He opened a jar of peanut butter and ate it with a spoon.

It came so fast that he didn't see it until it was at the fire. LaJon saw it before he did and went rigid with fear. The fire was between LaJon and the zombie.

It just stood there, not watching the fire, but standing there. Not "looking" at LaJon, either. Cahill leaned forward. He tried to read its body language. It had been a man, overweight, maybe middle-aged, but now it was predatory and gracile. It didn't seem to do any normal things. It was moving and it stopped. Once stopped, it was still. An object rather than an animal. Like the ones that had come to the mattress fire, it didn't seem to need to shift its weight. After a few minutes, another one came from the same direction and stopped, looking at the fire. It had once been a man, too. It still wore glasses. Would there be a third? Did they come in threes? Cahill imagined a zombie family. Little triplets of zombies, all apparently oblivious of each other. Maybe the zombie he'd seen was still in the zombie den? He had never figured out where the zombies stayed.

LaJon was still and silent with terror, but the zombies didn't seem to know or care that he was there. They just stood, slightly askew and indifferent. Was it the fire? Would they notice LaJon when the fire died down?

Then there was a third one, but it came from the other side of the fire, the same side LaJon was on so there was no fire between it and LaJon. Cahill saw it before LaJon did, and from its directed lope he was sure it was aware of LaJon. LaJon saw it just before it got to him. His mouth opened wide and it was on him, hands and teeth. LaJon was clearly screaming, although behind the glass of the office building, Cahill couldn't hear him.

Cahill was watching the other zombies. They didn't react to the noise at all. Even when there was blood all over, they didn't seem to sense anything. Cahill reflected, not for the first time, that it actually took people a lot longer to die than it did on television or in the movies. He noted that the one that had mauled and eventually killed LaJon did not seem to prefer brains. Sometime in the night, the fire died down enough that the zombies on the wrong side of the fire seemed to sense the body of LaJon, and in an instant, they were feeding. The first one, apparently sated, just stood, indifferent. Two more showed up in the hours before dawn and fed in the dim red of the embers of the fire. When they finally left, almost two days later, there was nothing but broken bones and scattered teeth.

Cahill lay low for a while after that, feeling exhausted. It was hot during the day and the empty city baked. But after a few days, he went out and found another perch and lit another fire. Four zombies came to that fire, despite the fact it was smaller than his first two. They had all been women. He still had his picture of the toothy blonde from the loft, and after masturbating, he looked out at the zombie women, blank-white eyes and indifferent bodies, and wondered if the toothy blonde had been evacuated or if she might show up at one of his fires. None of the women at the fire appeared to be her, although it wasn't always easy to tell. One was clearly wearing the remnants of office clothes, but the other three were blue jean types and all four had such rat's nests of hair that he wasn't sure if their hair was short or long.

A couple of times he encountered zombies while scavenging. Both times his Molotov cocktails worked, catching fire. He didn't set the zombies on fire, just threw the bottle so that the fire was between him and the zombie. He watched them stop, then he backed away, fast. He set up another blind in an apartment and, over the course of a week, built a scaffolding and a kind of block and tackle arrangement. Then he started hanging around where the bus dropped people off, far enough back that the guys patrolling the gate didn't start shooting or something. He'd scoured up some bottles of water and used them to shave and clean up a bit.

When they dropped a new guy off, Cahill trailed him for half a day, and then called out and introduced himself. The new guy was an Aryan Nation asshole named Jordan Schmidtzinsky who was distrustful, but willing to be led back to Cahill's blind. He wouldn't get drunk, though, and in the end, Cahill had to brain him with a pipe. Still, it was easier to tape up the unconscious Schmidtzinsky than it had been the conscious LaJon. Cahill hoisted him into the air, put a chair underneath him so a zombie could reach him, and then set the fire.

Zombies did not look up. Schmidtzinsky dangled above the zombies for two whole days. Sometime in there he died. They left without ever noticing him. Cahill cut him down and lit another fire and discovered that zombies were willing to eat the dead, although they had to practically fall over the body to find it.

Cahill changed his rig so he could lower the bait. The third guy was almost Cahill's undoing. Cahill let him wander for two days in the early autumn chill before appearing and offering to help. This guy, a black city kid from Nashville who for some reason wouldn't say his name, evidently didn't like the scaffolding outside. He wouldn't take any of Cahill's whiskey, and as when Cahill pretended to sleep, the guy made the first move. Cahill was lucky not to get killed, managing again to brain the guy with his pipe.

But it was worth it, because when he suspended the guy and lit the fire, one of the four zombies that showed up was the skinny guy who'd killed Riley back the day the air strike had wiped out the camp.

He was white-eyed like the other zombies, but still recognizable. It made Cahill feel even more that the toothy blonde might be out there, unlikely as that actually was. Cahill watched for a couple of hours before he lowered Nashville. The semiconscious Nashville started thrashing and making weird coughing choking noises as soon as Cahill pulled on the rope, but the zombies were oblivious. Cahill was gratified to see that once the semiconscious Nashville got about so his shoes were about four feet above the ground, three of four zombies around the fire (the ones for whom the fire was not between them and Nashville) turned as one and swarmed up the chair.

He was a little nervous that they would look up—he had a whole plan for how he would get out of the building—but he didn't have to use it.

The three zombies ate, indifferent to each other and the fourth zombie, and then stood.

Cahill entertained himself with thoughts of the toothy blonde and then dozed. The air was crisp, but Cahill was warm in an overcoat. The fire smelled good. He was going to have to think about how he was going to get through the winter without a fire—unless he could figure out a way to keep a fire going well above the street and above zombie attention but right now things were going okay.

He opened his eyes and saw one of the zombies bob its head.

He'd never seen that before. Jesus, did that mean it was aware? That it might come upstairs? He had his length of pipe in one hand and a Molotov in the other. The zombies were all still. A long five minutes later, the zombie did it again, a quick, birdlike head bob. Then, bob-bob, twice more, and on the second bob, the other two that had fed did it too. They were still standing there, faces turned just slightly different directions as if they were unaware of each other, but he had seen it.

Bob-bob-bob. They all three did it. All at the same time.

Every couple of minutes they'd do it again. It was—communal. Animallike. They did it for a couple of hours and then they stopped. The one on the other side of the fire never did it at all. The fire burned low enough that the fourth one came over and worked on the remnants of the corpse and the first three just stood there.

Cahill didn't know what the fuck they were doing, but it made him strangely happy.

When they came to evacuate him, Cahill thought at first it was another air strike operation—a mopping up. He'd been sick for a few days, throwing up, something he ate, he figured. He was scavenging in a looted drug store, hoping for something to take—although everything was gone or ruined—when he heard the patrol coming. They weren't loud, but in the silent city noise was exaggerated. He had looked out of the shop, seen the patrol of soldiers and tried to hide in the dark ruins of the pharmacy.

"Come on out," the patrol leader said. "We're here to get you out of this place."

Bullshit, Cahill thought. He stayed put.

"I don't want to smoke you out, and I don't want to send guys in there after you," the patrol leader said. "I've got tear gas but I really don't want to use it."

Cahill weighed his options. He was fucked either way. He tried to go out the back of the pharmacy, but they had already sent someone around and he was met by two scared nineteen-year-olds with guns. He figured the writing was on the wall and put his hands up.

But the weird twist was that they *were* evacuating him. There'd been some big government scandal. The Supreme Court had closed the reserves, the president had been impeached, elections were coming. He wouldn't find that out for days. What he found out right then was that they hustled him back to the gate and he walked out past rows of soldiers into a wall of noise and light. Television cameras showed him lost and blinking in the glare.

"What's your name?"

"Gerrold Cahill," he said.

"Hey Gerrold! Look over here!" a hundred voices called.

It was overwhelming. They all called out at the same time, and it was mostly just noise to him, but if he could understand a question, he tried to answer it. "How's it feel to be out of there?"

"Loud," he said. "And bright."

"What do you want to do?"

"Take a hot shower and eat some hot food."

There was a row of sawhorses and the cameras and lights were all behind them. A guy with corporal's stripes was trying to urge him towards a trailer, but Cahill was like someone knocked down by a wave who tries to get to their feet only to be knocked down again.

"Where are you from?" Tell us what it was like!"

"What was it like?" Cahill said. Dumbshit question. What was he supposed to say to that? But his response had had the marvelous effect of quieting them for a moment, which allowed him to maybe get his bearings a little. "It wasn't so bad."

The barrage started again but he picked out "Were you alone?"

"Except for the zombies."

They liked that and the surge was almost animalistic. Had he seen zombies? How had he survived? He shrugged and grinned.

"Are you glad to be going back to prison?"

He had an answer for that, one he didn't even know was in him. He would repeat it in the interview he gave to *The Today Show* and again in the interview for *20/20*. "Cleveland was better than prison," he said. "No alliances, no gangs, just zombies."

Someone called, "Are you glad they're going to eradicate the zombies?"

"They're going to what?" he asked.

The barrage started again, but he said, "What are they going to do to the zombies?"

"They're going to eradicate them, like they did everywhere else."

"Why?" he asked.

This puzzled the mob. "Don't you think they should be?"

He shook his head. "Gerrold! Why not?"

Why not indeed? "Because," he said, slowly, and the silence came down, except for the clicking of cameras and the hum of the news vans idling, "because they're just . . . like animals. They're just doing what's in their nature to be doing." He shrugged.

Then the barrage started again. *Gerrold! Gerrold! Do you think people are evil?* But by then he was on his way to a military trailer, an examination by an army doctor, a cup of hot coffee and a meal and a long hot shower.

Behind him the city was dark. At the moment, it felt cold behind him, but safe, too, in its quiet. He didn't really want to go back there. Not yet. He wished he'd had time to set them one last fire before he'd left.

After the whispers begin—but before the sugar in the glass bowl glows and dims and brightens, like a pulse—Pershing considers it might be time, after twenty years, to move from the Broadsword. Yet in his heart he despairs of escaping; he is a part of the hotel . . . perhaps Mr. Pershing should have reconsidered . . .

THE BROADSWORD

LAIRD BARRON

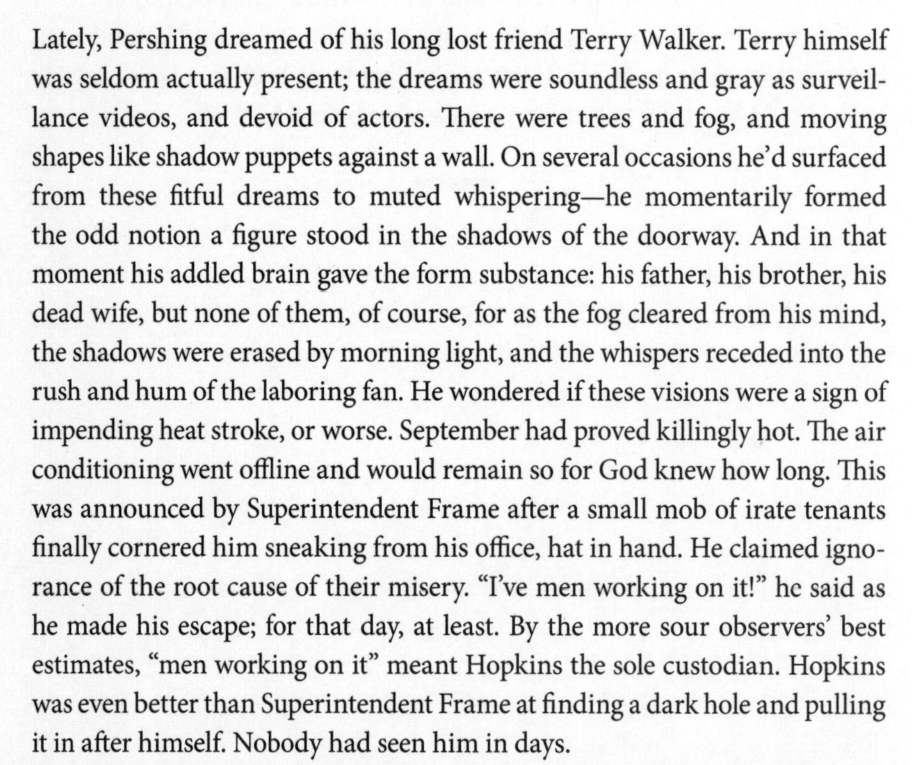

Lately, Pershing dreamed of his long lost friend Terry Walker. Terry himself was seldom actually present; the dreams were soundless and gray as surveillance videos, and devoid of actors. There were trees and fog, and moving shapes like shadow puppets against a wall. On several occasions he'd surfaced from these fitful dreams to muted whispering—he momentarily formed the odd notion a figure stood in the shadows of the doorway. And in that moment his addled brain gave the form substance: his father, his brother, his dead wife, but none of them, of course, for as the fog cleared from his mind, the shadows were erased by morning light, and the whispers receded into the rush and hum of the laboring fan. He wondered if these visions were a sign of impending heat stroke, or worse. September had proved killingly hot. The air conditioning went offline and would remain so for God knew how long. This was announced by Superintendent Frame after a small mob of irate tenants finally cornered him sneaking from his office, hat in hand. He claimed ignorance of the root cause of their misery. "I've men working on it!" he said as he made his escape; for that day, at least. By the more sour observers' best estimates, "men working on it" meant Hopkins the sole custodian. Hopkins was even better than Superintendent Frame at finding a dark hole and pulling it in after himself. Nobody had seen him in days.

Pershing Dennard did what all veteran tenants of the Broadsword Hotel had done over the years to survive these too frequent travails: he effected emergency adaptations to his habitat. Out came the made-in-China box fan across which he draped damp wash cloths. He shuttered the windows and snugged heavy drapes to keep his apartment dim. Of course he maintained a ready supply of vodka in the freezer. The sweltering hours of daylight were for hibernation; dozing on the sofa, a chilled pitcher of lemonade and booze at his elbow. These maneuvers rendered the insufferable slightly bearable, but only by inches.

He wilted in his recliner and stared at the blades of the ceiling fan cutting through the blue-streaked shadows while television static beamed between the toes of his propped-up feet. He listened. Mice scratched behind plaster. Water knocked through the pipes with deep-sea groans and soundings. Vents whistled, transferring dim clangs and screeches from the lower floors, the basement, and lower still, the subterranean depths beneath the building itself.

The hissing ducts occasionally lulled him into a state of semi-hypnosis. He imagined lost caverns and inverted forests of roosting bats, a primordial river that tumbled through midnight grottos until it plunged so deep the stygian black acquired a red nimbus, a vast throbbing heart of brimstone and magma. Beyond the falls, abyssal winds howled and shrieked and called his name. Such images inevitably gave him more of a chill than he preferred and he shook them off, concentrated on baseball scores, the creak and grind of his joints. He'd shoveled plenty of dirt and jogged over many a hill in his career as a state surveyor. Every swing of the spade, every machete chop through temperate jungle had left its mark on muscle and bone.

Mostly, and with an intensity of grief he'd not felt in thirty-six years, more than half his lifetime, he thought about Terry Walker. It probably wasn't healthy to brood. That's what the grief counselor had said. The books said that, too. Yet how could a man not gnaw on that bone sometimes?

Anyone who's lived beyond the walls of a cloister has had at least one bad moment, an experience that becomes the proverbial dark secret. In this Pershing was the same as everyone. His own dark moment had occurred many years prior; a tragic event he'd dwelled upon for weeks and months with manic obsession, until he learned to let go, to acknowledge his survivor's guilt and move on with his life. He'd done well to box the memory, to shove it in a dusty corner of his subconscious. He distanced himself from the event until it seemed like a cautionary tale based on a stranger's experiences.

He was an aging agnostic and it occurred to him that, as he marched ever closer to his personal gloaming, the ghosts of Christmases Past had queued up to take him to task, that this heat wave had fostered a delirium appropriate to second-guessing his dismissal of ecclesiastical concerns, and penitence.

In 1973 he and Walker got lost during a remote surveying operation and wound up spending thirty-six hours wandering the wilderness. He'd been doing fieldwork for six or seven years and should have known better than to hike away from the base camp that morning.

At first they'd only gone far enough to relieve themselves. Then, he'd seen something—someone—watching him from the shadow of a tree and thought it was one of the guys screwing around. This was an isolated stretch of high country in the wilds of the Olympic Peninsula. There were homesteads and ranches along its fringes, but not within ten miles. The person, apparently a man, judging from his build, was halfcrouched, studying the ground. He waved to Pershing; a casual, friendly gesture. The man's features were indistinct, but at that moment Pershing convinced himself it was Morris Miller or Pete Cabellos, both of whom were rabid outdoorsmen and constantly nattering on about the ecological wonderland in which the crew currently labored. The man straightened and beckoned, sweeping his hand in a come-on gesture. He walked into the trees.

Terry zipped up, shook his head and trudged that direction. Pershing thought nothing of it and tagged along. They went to where the man had stood and discovered what he'd been staring at—an expensive backpack of the variety popular with suburbanite campers. The pack was battered, its shiny yellow and green material shredded. Pershing got the bad feeling it was brand new.

Oh, shit, Terry said. *Maybe a bear got somebody.* We better get back to camp and tell Higgins. Higgins was the crew leader; surely he'd put together a search and rescue operation to find the missing owner of the pack. That would have been the sensible course, except, exactly as they turned to go, Pete Cabellos called to them from the woods. His voice echoed and bounced from the cliffs and boulders. Immediately, the men headed in the direction of the yell.

They soon got thoroughly lost. Every tree is the same tree in a forest. Clouds rolled in and it became impossible to navigate by sun or stars. Pershing's compass was back at camp with the rest of his gear, and Terry's was malfunctioning—condensation clouded the glass internally, rendered the needle useless. After a few hours of stumbling around yelling for their colleagues, they decided to follow the downhill slope of the land and promptly found themselves in mysterious hollows and thickets. It was a grave situation, although, that evening as the two camped in a steady downpour, embarrassment figured more prominently than fear of imminent peril.

Terry brought out some jerky and Pershing always carried waterproof matches in his vest pocket, so they got a fire going from the dried moss and dead twigs beneath the boughs of a massive old fir, munched on jerky, and lamented their predicament. The two argued halfheartedly about whether they'd actually heard Pete or Morris calling that morning, or a mysterious third party.

Pershing fell asleep with his back against the mossy bole and was plunged into nightmares of stumbling through the foggy woods. A malevolent presence lurked in the mist and shadows. Figures emerged from behind trees and stood silently. Their wickedness and malice were palpable. He knew with the inexplicable logic of dreams that these phantoms delighted in his terror, that they were eager to inflict unimaginable torments upon him.

Terry woke him and said he'd seen someone moving around just beyond the light of the dying fire. Rain pattering on the leaves made it impossible to hear if anyone was moving around in the bushes, so Terry threw more branches on the fire and they warmed their hands and theorized that the person who'd beckoned them into the woods was the owner of the pack. Terry, ever the pragmatist, suspected the man had struck his head and was now in a raving delirium, possibly even circling their camp.

Meanwhile, Pershing was preoccupied with more unpleasant possibilities. Suppose the person they'd seen had actually killed a hiker and successfully lured them into the wild? Another thought insinuated itself; his grandmother had belonged to a long line of superstitious Appalachian folk. She'd told him and his brother ghost stories and of legends such as the Manitou, and lesser-known tales about creatures who haunted the woods and spied on men and disappeared when a person spun to catch them. He'd thrilled to her stories while snug before the family hearth with a mug of cocoa and the company of loved ones. The stories took on a different note here in the tall trees.

It rained hard all the next day and the clouds descended into the forest. Emergency protocol dictated staying put and awaiting the inevitable rescue, rather than blindly groping in circles through the fog. About midday, Terry went to get a drink from a spring roughly fifty feet from their campsite. Pershing never saw him again. Well, not quite true: he saw him twice more.

Pershing moved into the Broadsword Hotel in 1979, a few months after his first wife, Ethel, unexpectedly passed away. He met second wife, Constance, at a hotel mixer. They were married in 1983, had Lisa Anne and Jimmy within two years, and were divorced by 1989. She said the relationship was been doomed from the start because he'd never really finished mourning Ethel. Connie grew impatient of his mooning over old dusty photo albums and playing old moldy tunes on the antique record player he stashed in the closet along with several ill-concealed bottles of scotch. Despite his fondness for liquor, Pershing didn't consider himself a heavy drinker, but rather a steady one. During their courtship, Pershing talked often of leaving the Broadsword. Oh, she was queenly in her time, a seven-floor art deco complex on the West Side of Olympia on a wooded hill with a view of the water, the marina, and downtown. No one living knew how she'd acquired her bellicose name. She was built in 1918 as a posh hotel, complete with a four-star restaurant, swanky nightclub-cum-gambling hall, and a grand ballroom; the kind of place that attracted not only the local gentry, but visiting Hollywood celebrities, sports figures, and politicians. After passing through the hands of several owners, the Broadsword was purchased by a Midwest corporation and converted to a middle-income apartment complex in 1958. The old girl suffered a number of renovations to wedge in more rooms, but she maintained a fair bit of charm and historical gravitas even five decades and several face lifts later. Nonetheless, Pershing and Connie had always agreed the cramped quarters were no substitute for a real house with a yard and a fence. Definitely a tough place to raise children—unfortunately, the recession had killed the geophysical company he'd worked for in those days and money was tight.

Connie was the one who eventually got out—she moved to Cleveland and married a banker. The last Pershing heard, she lived in a three-story mansion and had metamorphosed into a white-gloved, garden party-throwing socialite who routinely got her name in the lifestyle section of the papers. He was happy for her and the kids, and a little relieved for himself. That tiny single bedroom flat had been crowded!

He moved up as well. Up to the sixth floor into 119; what the old superintendent (in those days it was Anderson Heck) sardonically referred to as an executive suite. According to the super, only two other people had ever occupied the apartment—the so-called executive suites were spacious enough that tenants held onto them until they died. The previous resident was a bibliophile who'd retired from a post at the Smithsonian. The fellow left many books and photographs when he died and his heirs hadn't seen fit to come around and pack up his estate. As it happened, the freight elevator was usually on the fritz in those days and the regular elevator wasn't particularly reliable either. So the superintendent offered Pershing three months' free rent if he personally dealt with the daunting task of organizing and then lugging crates of books and assorted memorabilia down six steep flights to the curb.

Pershing put his muscles to good use. It took him three days' hard labor to clear out the apartment and roughly three hours to move his embarrassingly meager belongings in. The rest, as they say, was history.

Pershing would turn sixty-seven in October. Wanda Blankenship, his current girlfriend of nine months and counting, was fortysomething—she played it coy, careful not to say, and he hadn't managed a peek at her driver license. He guessed she was pushing fifty, although she took care of herself, hit the Pilates circuit with her chums, and thus passed for a few years on the uphill side. "Grave robber!" he said when she goosed him, or made a halfhearted swipe at his testicles, which was often, and usually in public. She was a librarian too; a fantasy cliché ironically fulfilled during this, his second or third boyhood when he needed regular doses of the little blue pill to do either of them any justice.

Nine months meant their relationship had edged from the danger zone and perilously near the edge of no return. He'd gotten comfortable with her sleeping over a couple of nights a week, like a lobster getting cozy in a kettle of warm water. He'd casually mentioned her to Lisa Anne and Jimmy during one of their monthly phone conferences, which was information he usually kept close to his vest. More danger signals: she installed a toothbrush in the medicine cabinet and shampoo in the bath. He couldn't find his extra key one night after coming home late from the Red Room and realized he'd given it to her weeks before in a moment of weakness. As the robot used to say, *Danger, Will Robinson! Danger! Danger!* He was cooked, all right, which was apropos, considering the weather.

"Oh, ye gods! Like hell I'm coming up there!" she said during their latest phone conversation. "My air conditioner is tip top. *You* come over here." She paused to snicker. "Where I can get my hands on you!"

He wanted to argue, to resist, but was too busy melting into the couch, and knew if he refused she'd come flying on her broom to chivvy him away most unceremoniously. Defeated, he put on one of his classier ties, all of which Constance had chosen, and made the pilgrimage—on foot in the savage glare of late afternoon because he walked everywhere, hadn't owned a car since he sold his El Camino in 1982. Walking generally suited him; he'd acquired a taste for it during his years of toil in the wilderness. He took a meager bit of pride in noting that his comfortable "traveling" pace left most men a quarter his age gasping and winded after a short distance.

He disliked visiting her place, a small cottage-style house in a quiet neighborhood near downtown. Not that there was anything wrong with the house itself, aside from the fact it was too tidy, too orderly, and she insisted on china dishes for breakfast, lunch, supper, and tea. He lived in constant fear of dropping something, spilling something, breaking something with his large, clumsy hands. She cheerily dismissed such concerns, remarking that her cups and dishes were relics passed down through the generations—"They gotta go sometime. Don't be so uptight." Obviously, this served to heighten his paranoia.

Wanda made dinner; fried chicken and honeydew, and wine for dessert. Wine disagreed with his insides and gave him a headache. When she broke out the after-dinner merlot, he smiled and drank up like a good soldier. It was the gentlemanly course—also, he was loath to give her any inkling regarding his penchant for the hard stuff. Her husband had drunk himself to death. Pershing figured he could save his own incipient alcoholism as an escape route. If things got too heavy, he could simply crack a bottle of Absolut and guzzle it like soda pop, which would doubtless give him a heart attack. Freedom either way! Meanwhile, the deceit must perforce continue.

They were snuggling on the loveseat, buzzed by wine and luxuriating in the blessed coolness of her living room, when she casually said, "So, who's the girl?"

Pershing's heart fluttered, his skin went clammy. Such questions never boded well. He affected nonchalance. "Ah, sweetie, I'm a dashing fellow. Which girl are you talking about?" That heart attack he sometimes dreamt of seemed a real possibility.

Wanda smiled. "The girl I saw leaving your apartment the other morning, silly."

The fact he didn't know any girls besides a few cocktail waitresses didn't make him feel any better. He certainly was guilty of looking at lots of girls and couldn't help but wonder if that was enough to bury him. Then, instead of reassuring her that no such person existed, or that there must be some innocent mistake, he idiotically said, "Oh. What were you doing coming over in the morning?" In short order, he found himself on the porch. The sky was purple and orange with sunset. It was a long, sticky walk back to the hotel.

The next day he asked around the Broadsword. Nobody had seen a girl and nobody cared. Nobody had seen Hopkins either. *Him* they cared about. Even Bobby Silver—Sly to his friends—didn't seem interested in the girl, and Sly was the worst lecher Pershing had ever met. Sly managed a dry cackle and a nudge to the ribs when Pershing described the mystery girl who'd allegedly come from his apartment. Young (relatively speaking), dark-haired, voluptuous, short black dress, lipstick. "Heard anything about when they're gonna fix the cooling system? It's hotter than the hobs of Hell in here!" Sly sprawled on a bench just off the columned hotel entrance. He fanned himself with a crinkled Panama hat. Mark Ordbecker, a high school math teacher who lived in the apartment directly below Pershing's with his wife Harriet and two children, suggested a call to the police. "Maybe one of them should come over and look around." They made this exchange at Ordbecker's door. The teacher leaned against the doorframe, trying in vain to feed the shrieking baby a bottle of milk. His face was red and sweaty. He remarked that the start of the school year would actually be a relief from acting as a househusband. His wife had gone east for a funeral. "The wife flies out and all hell breaks loose. She's going to come home to my funeral if the weather doesn't change."

Ordbecker's other child, a five-year-old boy named Eric, stood behind his father. His hair was matted with sweat and his face gleamed, but it was too pale.

"Hi, Eric," Pershing said. "I didn't see you there. How you doing, kiddo?"

Little Eric was normally rambunctious or, as Wanda put it, obstreperous, as in *an obstreperous hellion*. Today he shrank farther back and wrapped an arm around his father's leg.

"Don't mind him. Misses his mom." Mark leaned closer and murmured, "Separation anxiety. He won't sleep by himself while she's gone. You know how kids are." He reached down awkwardly and ruffled the boy's hair. "About your weirdo visitor—call the cops. At least file a report so if this woman's crazy and she comes at you with a pair of shears in the middle of the night and you clock her with a golf club, there's a prior record."

Pershing thanked him. He remained unconvinced this was anything other than a coincidence or possibly Wanda's imagination, what with her sudden attack of jealousy. He almost knocked on Phil Wesley's door across the hall. The fellow moved in a few years back; a former stage magician, or so went the tales, and a decade Pershing's senior. Well-dressed and amiable, Wesley nonetheless possessed a certain aloofness; also, he conducted a psychic medium service out of his apartment. Tarot readings, hypnosis, séances, all kinds of crackpot business. They said hello in passing, had waited outside Superintendent Frame's office, and that was the extent of their relationship. Pershing preferred the status quo in this case.

"Cripes, this is all nonsense anyway." He always locked his apartment with a deadbolt; he'd become security conscious in his advancing years, not at all sure he could handle a robber, what with his bad knees and weak back. Thankfully, there'd been no sign of forced entry, no one other than his girlfriend had seen anything, thus he suspected his time schlepping about the hotel in this beastly heat playing amateur investigator was a colossal waste of energy.

Wanda didn't call, which wasn't surprising considering her stubbornness. Dignity prohibited *him* ringing her. Nonetheless, her silence rankled; his constant clock watching annoyed him, too. It wasn't like him to fret over a woman, which meant he missed her more than he'd have guessed.

As the sun became an orange blob in the west, the temperature peaked. The apartment was suffocating. He dragged himself to the refrigerator and stood before its open door, straddle-legged in his boxers, bathed in the stark white glow. Tepid relief was better than nothing.

Someone whispered behind him and giggled. He turned quickly. The laughter originated in the living area, between the coffee table and a bookshelf. Because the curtains were tightly closed the room lay in a blue-tinged gloom that played tricks on his eyes. He sidled to the sink and swept his arm around until he flicked the switch for the overhead light. This illuminated a sufficient area that he felt confident to venture forth. Frankie Walton's suite abutted his own—and old Frankie's hearing was shot. He had to crank the volume on his radio for the ball games. Once in a while Pershing heard the tinny exclamations of the play-by-play guys, the roar of the crowd. This, however, sounded like a person was almost on top of him, sneering behind his back.

What, you think someone's hiding under the table? Don't be a fool, Percy. Good thing your girl isn't here to see you shaking in the knees like a wimp.

Closer inspection revealed the sounds had emanated from a vent near the window. He chuckled ruefully as his muscles relaxed. Ordbecker was talking to the baby and the sound carried upstairs. Not unusual; the hotel's acoustics were peculiar, as he well knew. He knelt and cocked his head toward the vent, slightly guilty at eavesdropping, yet in the full grip of curiosity. People were definitely in conversation, yet, he gradually realized, not the Ordbeckers. These voices were strange and breathy, and came from farther off, fading in and out with a static susurration.

Intestines. Kidneys.

Ohh, either is delectable.

And sweetbreads. As long as they're from a young one.

Ganglia, for me. Or brain. Scoop it out quivering.

Enough! Let's start tonight. We'll take one from—

They tittered and their words degenerated into garble, then stopped.

Shh, shh! Wait! . . . Someone's listening.

Don't be foolish.

They are. There's a spy hanging on our every word.

How can you tell?

I can hear them breathing.

He clapped his hand over his mouth. His hair stood on end.

I hear you, spy. Which room could you be in? First floor? No, no. The fifth or the sixth.

His heart labored. What was this?

We'll figure it out where you are, dear listener. Pay you a visit. While you sleep. Whoever it was laughed like a child, or someone pretending to be one. *You could always come down here where the mome wraths outgrabe. . . .* Deep in the bowels of the building, the furnace rumbled to life as it did every four hours to push air circulation through the vents. The hiss muffled the crooning threats, which ceased altogether a few minutes later when the system shut down.

Pershing was stunned and nauseated. Kidneys? Sweetbreads? He picked up the phone to punch in 911 before he got hold of his senses. What on earth would he say to the dispatcher? He could guess what they'd tell him: *Stop watching so many late night thrillers, Mr. Dennard.* He waited, eyeing the vent as if a snake might slither forth, but nothing happened. First the phantom girl, now this. Pretty soon he'd be jumping at his own shadow. *First stage dementia, just like dear old Dad.* Mom and Uncle Mike put Ernest Dennard in a home for his seventieth birthday. He'd become paranoid and delusional prior to that step. At the home Pop's faculties degenerated until he didn't know if he was coming or going. He hallucinated his sons were the ghosts of war buddies and screamed and tried to leap through his window when they visited. Thankfully, long before this turn of events Mom had the foresight to hide the forty-five caliber pistol he kept in the dresser drawer. Allegedly Grandma went through a similar experience with Gramps. Pershing didn't find his own prospects very cheery.

But you don't have dementia yet, and you don't knock back enough booze to be hallucinating. You heard them, clear as day. Jeezus C., who are they?

Pershing walked around the apartment and flicked on some lights; he checked his watch and decided getting the hell out for a few hours might be the best remedy for his jangled nerves. He put on a suit—nothing fancy, just a habit he'd acquired from his uncle who'd worked as a professor—and felt hat and left. He managed to catch the last bus going downtown. The bus was an oven; empty except for himself, a pair of teens, and the driver. Even so, it reeked from the day's accumulation; a miasma of sweat and armpit stench.

The depot had attracted its customary throng of weary seniors and the younger working poor, and a smattering of fancifully coiffed, tattooed, and pierced students from Evergreen; the former headed home or to the late shift, the latter off to house parties, or bonfires along the inlet beaches. Then there were the human barnacles—a half-dozen toughs decked out in parkas and baggy sports warm-up suits despite the crushing heat; the hard, edgy kind who watched everyone else, who appraised the herd. Olympia was by no means a big town, but it hosted more than its share of beatings and stabbings, especially in the northerly quarter inward from the marina and docks. One didn't hang around the old cannery district at night unless one wanted to get mugged.

Tonight none of the ruffians paid him any heed. From the depot he quickly walked through several blocks of semi-deserted industrial buildings and warehouses, made a right and continued past darkened sporting good stores, bookshops, and tattoo parlors until he hooked onto a narrow side lane and reached the subtly lighted wooden shingle of the Manticore Lounge. The Manticore was a hole in the wall that catered to a slightly more reserved set of clientele than was typical of the nightclubs and sports bars on the main thoroughfares. Inside was an oasis of coolness, scents of lemon and beer.

Weeknights were slow—two young couples occupied tables near the darkened dais that served as a stage for the four-piece bands that played on weekends; two beefy gentlemen in tailored suits sat at the bar. Lobbyists in town to siege the legislature; one could tell by their Rolexes and how the soft lighting from the bar made their power haircuts glisten.

Mel Clayton and Elgin Bane waved him over to their window booth. Mel, an engineering consultant who favored blue button-up shirts, heavy on the starch, and Elgin, a social worker who dressed in black turtlenecks and wore Buddy Holly-style glasses and sometimes lied to women at parties by pretending to be a beat poet; he even stashed a ratty pack of cloves in his pocket for such occasions. He quoted Kerouac and Ginsberg chapter and verse regardless how many rounds of Johnny Walker he'd put away. Pershing figured his friend's jaded posturing, his affected cynicism, was influenced by the depressing nature of his job: he dealt with emotional basket cases, battered wives, and abused children sixty to seventy hours a week. What did they say? At the heart of every cynic lurked an idealist. That fit Elgin quite neatly.

Elgin owned a house in Yelm, and Mel lived on the second floor of the Broadsword—they and Pershing and three or four other guys from the neighborhood got together for drinks at the Manticore or The Red Room at least once a month; more frequently now as the others slipped closer to retirement and their kids graduated college. Truth be told, he was much closer to these two than he was to his younger brother Carl, who lived in Denver and whom he hadn't spoken with in several months.

Every autumn, the three of them, sometimes with their significant others, drove up into the Black Hills outside Olympia to a hunting cabin Elgin's grandfather owned. None of them hunted; they enjoyed lounging on the rustic porch, roasting marshmallows, and sipping hot rum around the campfire. Pershing enjoyed these excursions—no one ever wanted to go hiking or wander far from the cabin, and thus his suppressed dread of wilderness perils remained quiescent, except for the occasional stab of nervousness when the coyotes barked, or the wind crashed in the trees, or his unease at how perfectly dark the woods became at night.

Mel bought him a whiskey sour—Mel invariably insisted on covering the tab. *It's you boys or my ex-wife, so drink up!* Pershing had never met the infamous Nancy Clayton; she was the inimitable force behind Mel's unceremonious arrival at the Broadsword fifteen years back, although judging from his flirtatious behavior with the ladies, his ouster was doubtless warranted. Nancy lived in Seattle with her new husband in the Lake Washington townhouse Mel toiled through many a late night and weekend to secure. He'd done better with Regina, his second wife. Regina owned a bakery in Tumwater and she routinely made cookies for Pershing and company. A kindly woman and large-hearted; she'd immediately adopted Mel's cast of misfit friends and associates.

After the trio had chatted for a few minutes, griping about the "damnable" weather, mainly, Elgin said, "What's eating you? You haven't touched your drink."

Pershing winced at eating. He hesitated, then chided himself. What sense to play coy? Obviously he wished to talk about what happened. Why else had he come scuttling in from the dark, tail between his legs? "I . . . heard something at home earlier tonight. People whispering in the vent. Weird, I know. But it really scared me. The stuff they said . . . "

Mel and Elgin exchanged glances. Elgin said, "Like what?"

Pershing told them. Then he briefly described what Wanda said about the mystery girl. "The other thing that bothers me is . . . this isn't the first time. The last couple of weeks I've been hearing stuff. Whispers. I wrote those off. Now, I'm not so sure."

Mel stared into his glass. Elgin frowned and set his palm against his chin in apparently unconscious imitation of *The Thinker*. He said, "Hmm. That's bizarre. Kinda screwed up, in fact. It almost makes me wonder—"

"—if your place is bugged," Mel said.

"Bugged?"

"This from the man with a lifetime subscription to the *Fortean Times*," Elgin said. "Damn, but sometimes I think you and Freeman would make a great couple." Randy Freeman being an old school radical who'd done too much Purple Haze in the '60s and dialed into the diatribes of a few too many Che Guevara-loving hippie chicks for his own good. He was another of The Red Room set.

Mel took Elgin's needling in stride. "Hey, I'm dead serious. Two and two, baby. I'll lay odds somebody miked Percy's apartment."

"For the love of—" Elgin waved him off, settling into his mode of dismissive impatience. "Who on God's green earth would do something crazy like that? No-freaking-body, that's who."

"It is a bit farfetched," Pershing said. "On the other hand, if you'd heard this crap. I dunno."

"Oh, hell." Elgin took a sip of his drink, patently incredulous.

"Jeez, guys—I'm not saying Homeland Security wired it for sound . . . maybe another tenant is playing games. People do wacko things."

"No forced entry." Pershing pointed at Mel. "And don't even say it might be Wanda. I'll have to slug you."

"Nah, Wanda's not sneaky. Who else has got a key?"

Elgin said, "The super would have one. I mean, if you're determined to go there, then that's the most reasonable suspect. Gotta tell you, though—you're going to feel like how Mel looks when it turns out to be television noise—which is to say, an idiot."

"Ha, ha. Question is, what to do?"

"Elgin's right. Let's not make a bigger deal of this than it is . . . I got spooked."

"And the light of reason shines through. I'm going to the head." Elgin stood and made his way across the room and disappeared around a big potted fern.

Pershing said, "Do you mind if I sleep on your couch? If I'm not intruding, that is."

Mel smiled. "No problem. Gina doesn't care. Just be warned she goes to work at four in the morning, so she'll be stumbling around the apartment." He glanced over to make certain Elgin was still safely out of sight. "Tomorrow I'll come up and help you scope your pad. A while back Freeman introduced me to a guy in Tacoma who runs one of those spy shops with the minicameras and microphones. I'll get some tools and we'll see what's what."

After another round Elgin drove them back to the Broadsword. Just before he pulled away, he stuck his head out the window and called, "Don't do anything crazy."

"Which one of us is he talking to?" Mel said, glaring over his shoulder.

"I'm talking to both of you," Elgin said. He gunned the engine and zipped into the night.

Regina had already gone to bed. Mel tiptoed around his darkened apartment getting a blanket and a pillow for Pershing, cursing softly as he bumped into furniture. Two box fans blasted, but the room was muggy as a greenhouse. Once the sleeping arrangements were made, he got a six-pack of Heineken from the refrigerator and handed one to Pershing. They kicked back and watched a repeat of the Mariners game with the volume turned most of the way down. The seventh-inning stretch did Mel in. His face had a droopy, hangdog quality that meant he was loaded and ready to crash. He said goodnight and sneaked unsteadily toward the bedroom.

Pershing watched the rest of the game, too lethargic to reach for the remote. Eventually he killed the television and lay on the coach, sweat molding his clothes to him like a second skin. His heart felt sluggish. A night light in the kitchen cast ghostly radiance upon the wall, illuminating bits of Regina's Ansel Adams prints, the glittery mica eyes of her menagerie of animal figurines on the mantel. Despite his misery, he fell asleep right away.

A woman gasped in pleasure. That brought him up from the depths. The cry repeated, muffled by the wall of Mel and Gina's bedroom. He stared at the ceiling, mortified, thinking that Mel certainly was one hell of a randy bastard after he got a few drinks under his belt. Then someone whispered, perhaps five feet to his left where the light didn't penetrate. *The voice chanted: This old man, this old man . . .*

The syrupy tone wicked away the heat as if he'd fallen into a cold, black lake. He sat upright so quickly pains sparked in his neck and back. His only consolation lay in the recognition of the slight echoing quality, which suggested the person was elsewhere. Whistling emanated from the shadows, its falsetto muted by the background noise. He clumsily sprang from the couch, his fear transformed to a more useful sense of anger, and crabwalked until he reached the proper vent. "Hey, jerk!" he said, placing his face within kissing distance of the grill. "I'm gonna break your knees with my baseball bat if you don't shut your damn mouth!" His bravado was thin—he did keep a Louisville slugger, signed by Ken Griffey Jr., no less, in the bedroom closet in case a burglar broke in at night. Whether he'd be able to break anyone's knees was open to question.

The whistling broke off mid-tune. Silence followed. Pershing listened so hard his skull ached. He said to himself with grudging satisfaction, "That's right, creepos, you *better* stuff a sock in it." His sense of accomplishment was marred by the creeping dread that the reason his tormentors (or were they Mel's since this was his place?) had desisted was because they even now prowled the stairwells and halls of the old building, patiently searching for him.

He finally went and poured a glass of water and huddled at the kitchen table until dawn lighted the windows and Gina stumbled in to make coffee.

The temperature spiked to one hundred and three degrees by two p.m. the following afternoon. He bought Wanda two dozen roses with a card and chocolates, and arranged to have them delivered to her house. Mission accomplished, he went directly to an air-conditioned coffee shop, found a dark corner, and ordered half a dozen consecutive frozen Frappucinos. That killed time until his rendezvous with Mel at the Broadsword.

Mel grinned like a mischievous schoolboy when he showed off his fiber-optic snooper cable, a meter for measuring electromagnetic fluctuations, and his battered steel toolbox. Pershing asked if he'd done this before and Mel replied that he'd learned a trick or two in the Navy. "Just don't destroy anything," Pershing said. At least a dozen times he'd started to tell Mel about the previous night's visitation, the laughter; after all, if this was occurring in different apartments on separate floors, the scope of such a prank would be improbable. He couldn't devise a way to break it to his friend and still remain credible, and so kept his peace, miserably observing the operation unfold. After lugging the equipment upstairs, Mel spread a drop cloth to protect the hardwood floor and arrayed his various tools with the affected studiousness of a surgeon preparing to perform open-heart surgery. Within five minutes he'd unscrewed the antique brass grillwork plate and was rooting around inside the guts of the duct with a flashlight and a big screwdriver. Next, he took a reading with the voltmeter, then, finding nothing suspicious, made a laborious circuit of the entire apartment, running the meter over the other vents, the molding, and outlets. Pershing supplied him with glasses of lemonade to diffuse his own sense of helplessness.

Mel switched off the meter, wiping his face and neck with a damp cloth. He gulped the remainder of the pitcher of lemonade and shook his head with disappointment. "Damn. Place is clean. Well, except for some roaches."

"I'll make Frame gas them later. So, nothing, eh? It's funny acoustics. Or my imagination."

"Yeah, could be. Ask your neighbors if they heard anything odd lately."

"I dunno. They already gave me the fishy eye after I made the rounds checking on Wanda's girl. Maybe I should leave it alone for now. See what happens."

"That's fine as long as whatever happens isn't bad." Mel packed his tools with a disconsolate expression.

The phone rang. "I love you, baby," Wanda said on the other end.

"Me too," Pershing said. "I hope you liked the flowers." Meanwhile, Mel gave him a thumbs up and let himself out. Wanda asked if he wanted to come over and it was all Pershing could do to sound composed. "It's a date. I'll stop and grab a bottle of vino."

"No way, Jose; you don't know Jack about wine. I'll take care of that—you just bring yourself on over."

After they disconnected he said, "Thank God." Partly because a peace treaty with Wanda was a relief. The other portion, the much larger portion, frankly, was that he could spend the night well away from the Broadsword. *Yeah, that's fine, girly man. How about tomorrow night? How about the one after that?*

For twenty years he'd chewed on the idea of moving; every time the furnace broke in the winter, the cooling system died in the summer, or when the elevators went offline sans explanation from management for weeks on end, he'd joined the crowd of malcontents who wrote letters to the absentee landlord, threatened to call the state, to sue, to breach the rental contract and disappear. Maybe the moment had come to make good on that. Yet in his heart he despaired of escaping; he was a part of the hotel now. It surrounded him like a living tomb.

He dreamed that he woke and dressed and returned to the Broadsword. In this dream he was a passenger inside his own body, an automaton following its clockwork track. The apartment smelled stale from days of neglect. Something was wrong, however; off kilter, almost as if it wasn't his home at all, but a clever recreation, a stage set. Certain objects assumed hyperreality, while others submerged into a murky background. The sugar in the glass bowl glowed and dimmed and brightened, like a pulse. Through the window, leaden clouds scraped the tops of buildings and radio antennas vibrated, transmitting a signal that he felt in his skull, his teeth fillings, as a squeal of metal on metal. His nose bled. He opened the bathroom door and stopped, confronted by a cavern. The darkness roiled humid and rank, as if the cave was an abscess in the heart of some organic mass. Waves of purple radiation undulated at a distance of feet, or miles, and from those depths resonated the metallic clash of titanic ice flows colliding. "It's not a cave," Bobby Silver said. He stood inside the door, surrounded by shadows so that his wrinkled face shone like the sugar bowl. It was suspended in the blackness. "This is the surface. And it's around noon, local time. We do, however, spend most of our lives underground. We like the dark."

"Where?" He couldn't manage more than a dry whisper.

"Oh, you *know*," Sly said, and laughed. "C'mon, bucko—we've been beaming this into your brain for months—"

"No. Not possible. I've worn my tinfoil hat every day."

"—our system orbits a brown star, and it's cold, so we nestle in heaps and mounds that rise in ziggurats and pyramids. We swim in blood to stay warm, wring it from the weak the way you might squeeze juice from an orange."

Pershing recognized the voice from the vent. "You're a fake. Why are you pretending to be Bobby Silver?"

"Oh. If I didn't wear this, you wouldn't comprehend me. Should I remove it?" Sly grinned, seized his own cheek, and pulled. His flesh stretched like taffy accompanied by a squelching sound. He winked and allowed it to deform to a human shape. "It's what's underneath that counts. You'll see. When we come to stay with you."

Pershing said, "I don't want to see anything." He tried to flee, to run shrieking, but this being a dream, he was rooted, trapped, unable to do more than mumble protestations.

"Yes, Percy, you do," Ethel said from behind him. "We love you." As he twisted his head to gape at her, she gave him the soft, tender smile he remembered, the one that haunted his waking dreams, and then put her hand against his face and shoved him into the dark.

He stayed over at her place for a week—hid out, like a criminal seeking sanctuary from the Church. Unhappily, this doubtless gave Wanda the wrong impression (although at this point even Pershing wasn't certain what impression she should have), but at all costs he needed a vacation from his suddenly creep-infested heat trap of an apartment. Prior to this he'd stayed overnight fewer than a dozen times. His encampment at her house was noted without comment.

Jimmy's twenty-sixth birthday fell on a Sunday. After morning services at Wanda's Lutheran church, a handsome brick building only five minutes from the Broadsword, Pershing went outside to the quiet employee parking lot and called him. Jimmy had wanted to be an architect since elementary school. He went into construction, which Pershing thought was close enough despite the nagging suspicion his son wouldn't agree. Jimmy lived in California at the moment—he migrated seasonally along the West Coast, chasing jobs. Pershing wished him a happy birthday and explained a card was in the mail. He hoped the kid wouldn't check the postmark as he'd only remembered yesterday and rushed to get it sent before the post office closed.

Normally he was on top of the family things: the cards, the phone calls, the occasional visit to Lisa Anne when she attended Berkeley. Her stepfather, Barton Ingles III, funded college, which simultaneously indebted and infuriated Pershing, whose fixed income allowed little more than his periodic visits and a small check here and there. Now graduated, she worked for a temp agency in San Francisco and, embarrassingly, her meager base salary surpassed his retirement.

Toward the end of their conversation, after Pershing's best wishes and obligatory questions about the fine California weather and the job, Jimmy said, "Well, Pop, I hate to ask this . . . "

"Uh, oh. What have I done now? Don't tell me you need money."

Jimmy chuckled uneasily. "Nah, if I needed cash I'd ask Bart. He's a tightwad, but he'll do anything to impress Mom, you know? No, it's . . . how do I put this? Are you, um, drinking? Or smoking the ganja, or something? I hate to be rude, but I gotta ask."

"Are you kidding?"

There was a long, long pause. "Okay. Maybe I'm . . . Pop, you called me at like two in the morning. Wednesday. You tried to disguise your voice—"

"*Wha-a-t?*" Pershing couldn't wrap his mind around what he was hearing. "I did no such thing, James." He breathed heavily, perspiring more than even the weather called for.

"Pop, calm down, you're hyperventilating. Look, I'm not pissed—I just figured you got hammered and hit the speed dial. It would've been kinda funny if it hadn't been so creepy. Singing, no less."

"But it wasn't me! I've been with Wanda all week. She sure as hell would've noticed if I got drunk and started prank calling my family. I'll get her on the phone—"

"Really? Then is somebody sharing your pad? This is the twenty-first century, Pop. I got star sixty-nine. Your number."

"Oh." Pershing's blood drained into his belly. He covered his eyes with his free hand because the glare from the sidewalk made him dizzy. "What did I—this person—sing, exactly?"

"'This Old Man,' or whatever it's called. Although you, or they, added some unpleasant lyrics. They slurred . . . falsetto. When I called back, whoever it was answered. I asked what gave and they laughed. Pretty nasty laugh, too. I admit, I can't recall you ever making that kinda sound."

"It wasn't me. Sober, drunk, whatever. Better believe I'm going to find the bastard. There's been an incident or three around here. Wanda saw a prowler."

"All right, all right. If that's true, then maybe you should get the cops involved."

"Yeah."

"And Pop—let me explain it to Mom and Lisa before you get on the horn with them. Better yet, don't even bother with Mom. She's pretty much freaked outta her mind."

"They were called."

"Yeah. Same night. A real spree."

Pershing could only stammer and mumble when his son said he had to run, and then the line was dead. Wanda appeared from nowhere and touched his arm and he nearly swung on her. She looked shocked and her gaze fastened on his fist. He said, "Jesus, honey, you scared me."

"I noticed," she said. She remained stiff when he hugged her. The tension was purely reflexive, or so he hoped. His batting average with her just kept sinking. He couldn't do a much better job of damaging their relationship if he tried.

"I am so, so sorry," he said, and it was true. He hadn't told her about the trouble at the Broadsword. It was one thing to confide in his male friends, and quite another to reveal the source of his anxiety to a girlfriend, or any vulnerability for that matter. He'd inherited his secretiveness from Pop who in turn had hidden his own fears behind a mask of stoicism; this personality trait was simply a fact of life for Dennard men.

She relented and kissed his cheek. "You're jumpy. Is everything all right?"

"Sure, sure. I saw a couple of the choir kids flashing gang signs and thought one of the little jerks was sneaking up on me to go for my wallet."

Thankfully, she accepted this and held his hand as they walked to her car.

A storm rolled in. He and Wanda sat on her back porch, which commanded a view of the distant Black Hills. Clouds swallowed the mountains. A damp breeze fluttered the cocktail napkins under their half-empty Corona bottles, rattled the burnt yellow leaves of the maple tree branches overhead. "Oh, my," Wanda said. "There goes the drought." "We better hurry and clear the table." Pershing estimated at the rate the front was coming they'd be slammed inside of five minutes. He helped her grab the dishes and table settings. Between trips the breeze stiffened dramatically. Leaves tore from the maple, from trees in neighboring yards, went swirling in small Technicolor cyclones. He dashed in with the salad bowl as the vanguard of rain pelted the deck. Lightning flared somewhere over the Waddell Valley; the boom came eight seconds later. The next thunderclap was five seconds. They stood in her window, watching the show until he snapped out his daze and suggested they retreat to the middle of the living room to be safe.

They cuddled on the sofa, half watching the news while the lights flickered. Wind roared around the house and shook its frame as if a freight train slammed along tracks within spitting distance of the window, or a passengerjet winding its turbines for takeoff. The weather signaled a change in their static routine of the past week. Each knew without saying it that Pershing would return to the Broadsword in the morning, and their relationship would revert to its more nebulous aspect. Pershing also understood from her melancholy glance, the measured casualness in her acceptance, that matters between them would remain undefined, that a line had been crossed.

He thought about this in the deepest, blackest hours of night while they lay in bed, she lying gently snoring, her arm draped across his chest. How much easier his life would be if his mock comment to Elgin and Mel proved true—that Wanda was a lunatic; a split personality type who was behind the stalking incidents. *God, I miss you, Ethel.*

"Houston, we have a problem," Mel said. He'd brought ham sandwiches and coffee to Pershing's apartment for an early supper. He was rattled. "I checked around. Not just you hearing things. Odd, odd stuff going on, man."

Pershing didn't want to hear, not after the normalcy of staying with Wanda. And the dreams. . . . "You don't say." He really wished Mel wouldn't.

"The cops have been by a couple of times. Turns out other tenants have seen that chick prowling the halls, trying doorknobs. There's a strange dude, as well—dresses in a robe, like a priest. Betsy Tremblay says the pair knocked on her door one night. The man asked if he could borrow a cup of sugar. Betsy was watching them through the peephole—she says the lady snickered and the man grinned and shushed her by putting his finger over his lips. Scared the hell out of Betsy; she told them to scram and called the cops."

"A cup of sugar," Pershing said. He glanced out at the clouds. It was raining.

"Yeah, the old meet-your-cute-neighbor standby. Then I was talking to Fred Nilson; he's pissed because somebody below him is talking all night. 'Whispering,' he said. Only problem is, the apartment below his belongs to a guy named Brad Cox. Cox is overseas. His kids come by every few days to water the plants and feed the guppies. Anyway, no matter how you slice it, something peculiar is going on around here. Doncha feel better?"

"I never thought I was insane."

Mel chuckled uneasily. "I was chatting with Gina about the whole thing, and she said she'd heard someone singing while she was in the bath. It came up through the vent. Another time, somebody giggled in the closet while she dressed. She screamed and threw her shoe. This was broad daylight, mind you—no one in there, of course."

"Why would there be?"

"Right. Gina thought she was imagining things; she didn't want to tell me in case I decided she was a nut. Makes me wonder how many other people are having these . . . experiences and just keeping it to themselves."

The thought should have given Pershing comfort, but it didn't. His feelings of dread only intensified. *I'm almost seventy, damn it. I've lived in the woods, surrounded by grizzlies and wolves; spent months hiking the ass end of nowhere with a compass and an entrenchment spade. What the hell do I have to be scared of after all that?* And the little voice in the back of his mind was quick to supply Sly's answer from the nightmare, *Oh, you know.* He said, "Food for thought. I guess the police will sort through it."

"Sure they will. Maybe if somebody gets their throat slashed, or is beaten to death in a home invasion. Otherwise, I bet they just write us off as a bunch of kooks and go back to staking out the doughnut shop. Looks like a police convention some mornings at Gina's store."

"Wanda wants me to move in with her. I mean, I think she does."

"That's a sign. You should get while the getting's good."

They finished the sandwiches and the beer. Mel left to meet Gina when she got home from work. Pershing shut the door and slipped the bolt. The story about the strange couple had gotten to him. He needed a stiff drink.

The lights blinked rapidly and failed. The room darkened to a cloudy twilight and the windows became opaque smudges. Sounds of rain and wind dwindled and ceased. "Gracious, I thought he'd *never* leave." Terry Walker peeked at him from the upper jamb of the bedroom door, attached by unknown means, neck extended with a contortionist's ease so his body remained obscured. His face was very white. He slurred as if he hadn't used his vocal chords in a while, as if he spoke through a mouthful of mush. Then Pershing saw why. Black yolks of blood spooled from his lips in strands and splattered on the carpet. "Hello, Percy."

"You're alive," Pershing said, amazed at the calmness of his own voice. Meanwhile, his brain churned with full-blown panic, reminding him he was talking to an apparition or an imposter.

"So it seems." Terry was unchanged from youth—clean-shaven, red hair curling below his ears, and impressive mutton chop sideburns in the style that had been vogue during the '70s.

"It was you in the vents?" Then, as an afterthought, "How could you terrorize my family?"

"I got bored waiting all week for you to come back. Don't be mad—none of them ever cared for you anyway. Who knows—perhaps we'll get a chance to visit each and every one; make them understand what a special person you are." Terry grinned an unpleasant, puckered grin and dropped to the floor, limber as an eel. He dressed in a cassock the color of blackened rust.

"Holy crap. You look like you've come from a black mass." He chuckled nervously, skating along the fine line of hysteria. There was something wrong with his friend's appearance—his fingers and wrists had too many joints and his neck was slightly overlong by a vertebra or two. This wasn't quite the Terry Walker he knew, and yet, to some degree it was, and thus intensified Pershing's fear, his sense of utter dislocation from reality. "Why are you here? Why have you come back?" he said, and regretted it when Terry's smile bloomed with Satanic joy.

"Surveying."

"Surveying?" Pershing felt a new appreciation for the depths of meaning in that word, the inherent coldness. Surveying preceded the destruction of one order to make way for another, stronger, more adaptable order.

"What else would I do? A man's got to have a niche in the universe."

"Who are you working for?" Oh *Lord, let it be the FBI, Homeland Security, anybody.* Still trying for levity, he said, "Fairly sure I paid my taxes, and I don't subscribe to *American Jihadist.* You're not here to ship me to Guantánamo, or wherever, are you? Trust me, I don't know jack squat about anything."

"There's a migration in progress. A diaspora, if you will. It's been going on . . . well, when numbers grow to a certain proportion, they lose relevance. We creep like mold." Terry's grin showed that the inside of his mouth was composed of blackened ridges, and indeed toothless. His tongue pulsed; a sundew expanding and contracting in its puddle of gore. "Don't worry, though, Earthman. We come in peace." He laughed and his timbre ascended to the sickly sweet tones of a demented child. "Besides, we're happy to live in the cracks; your sun is too bright for now. Maybe after it burns down a bit . . . "

The bathroom door creaked open and the woman in the black dress emerged. She said, "Hullo there, love. I'm Gloria. A pleasure to meet you." Her flesh glowed like milk in a glass, like the sugar bowl in his visions. To Terry, she said, "He's older than I thought."

"But younger than he appears." Terry studied Pershing, his eyes inscrutable. "City life hasn't softened you, has it, pal?" He nodded at the woman. "I'm going to take him. It's my turn to choose."

"Okay, dear." The woman leaned her hip against the counter. She appeared exquisitely bored. "At least there'll be screaming."

"Isn't there always?"

Pershing said, "Terry . . . I'm sorry. There was a massive search. I spent two weeks scouring the hills. Two hundred men and dogs. You should've seen it." The secret wound opened in him and all the buried guilt and shame spilled forth. "Man, I wanted to save you. It destroyed me."

"You think I'm a ghost? That's depressingly provincial of you, friend."

"I don't know what to think. Maybe I'm not even awake." He was nearly in tears.

"Rest assured, you will soon make amazing discoveries," Terry said. "Your mind will shatter if we aren't careful. In any event, I haven't come to exact vengeance upon you for abandoning me in the mountains."

The woman smirked. "He'll wish you were here for that, won't he?"

"Damn you, you're not my friend," Pershing said. "And lady, you aren't Gloria, whoever she was—poor girl's probably on a milk carton. You wear faces so we will understand, so you can blend in, isn't that right? Who are you people, really?"

"*Who are you people?*" Gloria mimicked. "The Children of Old Leech. Your betters."

"Us?" Terry said. "Why, we're kin. Older and wiser, of course. Our tastes are more refined. We prefer the dark, but you will too. I promise." He moved to a shelf of Pershing's keepsakes—snapshots from the field, family photos in silver frames, and odd pieces of bric-a-brac—and picked up Ethel's rosary and rattled it. "As I recall, you weren't a man of any particular faith. I don't blame you, really. The New Testament God is so nebulous, so much of the ether. You'll find my civilization's gods to be quite tangible. One of them, a minor deity, dwells in this very system in the caverns of an outer moon. Spiritual life is infinitely more satisfying when you can meet the great ones, touch them, and, if you're fortunate, be touched. . . . "

Pershing decided to go through the woman and get a knife from the butcher block. He didn't relish the notion of punching a girl, but Terry was bigger than him, had played safety for his high school football team. He gathered himself to move—

Gloria said, "Percy, want me to show you something? You should see what Terry saw . . . when you left him alone with us." She bowed her neck and cupped her face. There came the cracking as of an eggshell; blood oozed through her fingers as she lifted the hemisphere of her face away from its bed. It made a viscid, sucking sound; the sound of bones scraping together through jelly. Something writhed in the hollow. While Pershing was transfixed in sublime horror, Terry slid over and patted his shoulder.

"She's got a cruel sense of humor. Maybe you better not watch the rest." He smiled paternally and raised what appeared to be a bouquet of mushrooms, except these were crystalline and twinkled like Christmas lights.

Violet fire lashed Pershing.

In UFO abduction stories, hapless victims are usually paralyzed and then sucked up in a beam of bright light. Pershing was taken through a hole in the subbasement foundation into darkness so thick and sticky it flowed across his skin. They did use tools on him, and, as the woman predicted, he screamed, although not much came through his lips, which had been sealed with epoxy. An eternal purple-black night ruled the fleshy coomb of an alien realm. Gargantuan tendrils slithered in the dark, coiling and uncoiling, and the denizens of the underworld arrived in an interminable procession through vermiculate tubes and tunnels, and gathered, chuckling and sighing, in appreciation of his agonies. In the great and abiding darkness, a sea of dead white faces brightened and glimmered like porcelain masks at a grotesque ball. He couldn't discern their forms, only the luminescent faces, their plastic, drooling joy. We love you, Percy, the Terry-creature whispered right before he rammed a needle into Pershing's left eye.

His captors dug in his brain for memories and made him relive them. The one they enjoyed best was the day of Pershing's greatest anguish: When Terry hadn't returned to their impromptu campsite after ten minutes, Pershing went looking for him. The rain slashed through the woods, accompanied by gusts that snapped the foliage, caused treetops to clash. He tramped around the spring and saw Terry's hat pinned and flapping in some bushes. Pershing began to panic. Night came early in the mountains, and if sundown found him alone and isolated . . . Now he was drenched as well. Hypothermia was a real danger. He caught movement from the corner of his eye. A figure walked across a small clearing a few yards away and vanished into the underbrush. Pershing's heart thrilled and he shouted Terry's name, actually took several steps toward the clearing, then stopped. What if it wasn't his friend? The gait had seemed wrong. Cripes, what if, what if? What if someone truly was stalking them? Farfetched; the stuff of latenight fright movies. But the primeval ruled in this place. His senses were tuned to a much older frequency than he'd ever encountered. The ape in him, the lizard, hissed warnings until his hackles rose. He lifted a stone from the muck and hefted it, and moved forward.

He tracked a set of muddy footprints into a narrow ravine. Rock outcroppings and brush interlaced to give the ravine a roof. Toadstools and fungi grew in clusters among beds of moss and mold. Water dripped steadily and formed shallow pools of primordial slime. There was Terry's jacket in a wad; and ten yards further in, his pants and shirt hanging from a dead tree that had uprooted and tumbled down into the gulley. A left hiking shoe had been dropped nearby. The trail ended in a jumble of rocks piled some four or five yards high. A stream, orange and alkaline, dribbled over shale and granite. There was something about this wall of stone that accentuated his fear; this was a timeless grotto, and it radiated an ineffable aura of wickedness, of malign sentience. Pershing stood there in its presence, feeling like a Neanderthal with a torch in hand, trembling at the threshold of the lair of a nameless beast.

Two figures in filthy robes stood over a third, mostly naked man, his body caked in mud and leaves. The moment elongated, stretched from its bloom in September 1973 across three and a half decades, embedded like a cyst in Pershing's brain. The strangers grasped Terry's ankles with hands so pale they shone in the gloom. They wore deep cowls that hid their faces . . . yet, in Pershing's nightmares, that inner darkness squirmed with vile intent.

The robed figures regarded him; one crooked a long, oddly jointed finger and beckoned him. Then the strangers laughed—that sickening, diabolic laughter of a man mimicking a child—and dragged Terry away. Terry lay supine, eyes open, mouth slack, head softly bumping over the slimy rocks, arms trailing, limp, an inverted Jesus hauled toward his gruesome fate. They walked into the shadows, through a sudden fissure in the rocks, and were gone forever.

The one that imitated Terry released him from the rack and carried him, drifting with the ungainly coordination of a punctured float, through a stygian wasteland. This one murmured to him in the fashion of a physician, a historian, a tour guide, the histories and customs of its race. His captor tittered, hideously amused at Pershing's perception of having been cast into a subterranean hell.

Not hell or any of its pits. You have crossed the axis of time and space by means of technologies that were old when your kind yet oozed in brine. You, sweet man, are in the black forest of cosmic night.

Pershing imagined passing over a colossal reef of flesh and bone, its coils and ridges populated by incalculable numbers of horridly intelligent beings that had flown from their original planets, long since gone cold and dead, and spread implacably across the infinite cosmos. This people traveled in a cloud of seeping darkness. Their living darkness was a cancerous thing, a mindless, organic suspension fluid that protected them from the noxious light of foreign stars and magnified their psychic screams of murder and lust. It was their oxygen and their blood. They suckled upon it, and in turn, it fed upon them.

We eat our children, Terry had said. *Immortals have no need for offspring. We're gourmands, you see; and we do love our sport. We devour the children of every sentient race we metastasize to . . . we've quite enjoyed our visit here. The amenities are exquisite.*

He also learned their true forms, while humanoid, were soft and wet and squirming. The human physiognomies they preferred for brief field excursions were organic shells grown in vats, exoskeletons that served as temporary camouflage and insulation from the hostile environments of terrestrial worlds. In their own starless demesne they hopped and crawled and slithered as was traditional.

Without warning, he was dropped from a great height into a body of water that bore him to its surface and buoyed him with its density, its syrupy thickness. He was overcome with the searing stench of rot and sewage. From above, someone grasped his hair and dragged him to an invisible shore.

There came a long, blind crawl through what felt like a tunnel of raw meat, an endless loop of intestine that squeezed him along its tract. He went forward, chivvied by unseen devils who whispered obscenities in his ear and caressed him with pincers and stinging tendrils, who dripped acid on the back of his neck and laughed as he screamed and thrashed in the amniotic soup, the quaking entrails. Eventually, a light appeared and he wormed his way to it, gibbering mindless prayers to whatever gods might be interested.

"It is always hot as hell down here," Hopkins the custodian said. He perched on a tall box, his grimy coveralls and grimy face lighted by the red glow that flared from the furnace window. "There's a metaphor for ya. Me stoking the boiler in Hell."

Pershing realized the custodian had been chatting at him for a while. He was wedged in the corner of the concrete wall. His clothes stuck to him with sweat, the drying juices of a slaughterhouse. He smelled his own rank ammonia odor. Hopkins grinned and struck a match and lighted a cigarette. The brief illumination revealed a nearly done in bottle of Wild Turkey leaning against his thigh. Pershing croaked and held out his hand. Hopkins chuckled. He jumped down and gave Pershing the bottle.

"Finish it off. I've got three more hid in my crib, yonder." He gestured into the gloom. "Mr. 119, isn't it? Yeah, Mr. 119. You been to hell, now ain't you? You're hurtin' for certain."

Pershing drank, choking as the liquor burned away the rust and foulness. He gasped and managed to ask, "What day is it?"

Hopkins held his arm near the furnace grate and checked his watch. "Thursday, 2:15 p.m., and all is well. Not really, but nobody knows the trouble we see, do they?"

Thursday afternoon? He'd been with *them* for seventy-two hours, give or take. Had anyone noticed? He dropped the bottle and it clinked and rolled away. He gained his feet and followed the sooty wall toward the stairs. Behind him, Hopkins started singing "Black Hole Sun."

As it happened, he spent the rest of the afternoon and much of the evening in an interrogation room at the police station on Perry Street. When he reached his apartment, he found Superintendent Frame had left a note on the door saying he was to contact the authorities immediately. There were frantic messages from Mel and Wanda on the answering machine wondering where he'd gone, and one from an Officer Klecko politely asking that he report to the precinct as soon as possible. He stripped his ruined clothes and stared at his soft, wrinkled body in the mirror. There were no marks, but the memory of unspeakable indignities caused his hands to shake, his gorge to rise. Recalling the savagery and pain visited upon him, it was inconceivable his skin, albeit soiled with dirt and unidentifiable stains, showed no bruises or blemishes. He showered in water so hot it nearly scalded him. Finally, he dressed in a fresh suit and fixed a drink. Halfway through the glass he dialed the police and told his name to the lady who answered and that he'd be coming in shortly. He called Wanda's house and left a message informing her of his situation.

The station was largely deserted. An officer on the opposite side of bullet-proof glass recorded his information and asked him to take a seat. Pershing slumped in a plastic chair near a pair of soda machines. There were a few empty desks and cubicles in a large room to his left. Periodically a uniformed officer passed by and gave him an uninterested glance.

Eventually, Detective Klecko appeared and shook his hand and ushered him into a small office. The office was papered with memos and photographs of wanted criminals. Brown water stains marred the ceiling tiles and the room smelled moldy. Detective Klecko poured orange soda into a Styrofoam cup and gave it to Pershing and left the can on the edge of the desk. The detective was a large man, with a bushy mustache and powerful hands. He dressed in a white shirt and black suspenders, and his bulk caused the swivel chair to wobble precariously. He smiled broadly and asked if it was all right to turn on a tape recorder—Pershing wasn't being charged, wasn't a suspect, this was just department policy.

They exchanged pleasantries regarding the cooler weather, the Seattle Mariners' disappointing season, and how the city police department was woefully understaffed due to the recession, and segued right into questions about Pershing's tenancy at the Broadsword. How long had he lived there? Who did he know? Who were his friends? Was he friendly with the Ordbeckers, their children? Especially little Eric. Eric was missing, and Mr. Dennard could you please tell me where you've been the last three days?

Pershing couldn't. He sat across from the detective and stared at the recorder and sweated. At last he said, "I drink. I blacked out."

Detective Klecko said, "Really? That might come as a surprise to your friends. They described you as a moderate drinker."

"I'm not saying I'm a lush, only that I down a bit more in private than anybody knows. I hit it pretty hard Monday night and sort of recovered this afternoon."

"That happen often?"

"No."

Detective Klecko nodded and scribbled on a notepad. "Did you happen to see Eric Ordbecker on Monday . . . before you became inebriated?"

"No, sir. I spent the day in my apartment. You can talk to Melvin Clayton. He lives in 93. We had dinner about five p.m. or so."

The phone on the desk rang. Detective Klecko shut off the recorder and listened, then told whoever was on the other end the interview was almost concluded. "Your wife, Wanda. She's waiting outside. We'll be done in a minute."

"Oh, she's not my wife—"

Detective Klecko started the recorder again. "Continuing interview with Mr. Pershing Dennard. . . . So, Mr. Dennard, you claim not to have seen Eric Ordbecker on Monday, September 24? When was the last time you did see Eric?"

"I'm not claiming anything. I didn't see the kid that day. Last time I saw him? I don't know—two weeks ago, maybe. I was talking to his dad. Let me tell you, you're questioning the wrong person. Don't you have the reports we've made about weirdos sneaking around the building? You should be chatting them up. The weirdos, I mean."

"Well, let's not worry about them. Let's talk about you a bit more, shall we?"

And so it went for another two hours. Finally, the detective killed the recorder and thanked him for his cooperation. He didn't think there would be any more questions. Wanda met Pershing in the reception area. She wore one of her serious work dresses and no glasses; her eyes were puffy from crying. Wrestling with his irritation at seeing her before he'd prepared his explanations, he hugged her and inhaled the perfume in her hair. He noted how dark the station had become. Illumination came from the vending machines and a reading lamp at the desk sergeant's post. The sergeant himself was absent.

"Mr. Dennard?" Detective Klecko stood silhouetted in the office doorway, backlit by his flickering computer monitor.

"Yes, Detective?" *What now? Here come the cuffs, I bet.*

"Thank you again. Don't worry yourself over . . . what we discussed. We'll take care of everything." His face was hidden, but his eyes gleamed.

The detective's words didn't fully hit Pershing until he'd climbed into Wanda's car and they were driving to Anthony's, an expensive restaurant near the marina. She declared a couple of glasses of wine and a fancy lobster dinner were called for. Not to celebrate, but to restore some semblance of order, some measure of normalcy. She seemed equally, if not more, shaken than he was. That she hadn't summoned the courage to demand where he'd been for three days told him everything about her state of mind.

We'll take care of everything.

Wanda parked in the side lot of a darkened bank and went to withdraw cash from the ATM. Pershing watched her from the car, keeping an eye out for lurking muggers. The thought of dinner made his stomach tighten. He didn't feel well. His head ached and chills knotted the muscles along his spine. Exhaustion caused his eyelids to droop.

"Know what I ask myself?" Terry whispered from the vent under the dash. "I ask myself why you never told the cops about the two 'men' who took me away. In all these years, you've not told the whole truth to anyone."

Pershing put his hand over his mouth. "Jesus!"

"Don't weasel. *Answer the question.*"

In a gesture he dimly acknowledged as absurd, he almost broke the lever in his haste to close the vent. "Because they didn't exist," he said, more to convince himself. "When the search parties got to me, I was half dead from exposure, ranting and raving. You got lost. You just got lost and we couldn't find you." He wiped his eyes and breathed heavily.

"You think your visit with us was unpleasant? It was a gift. Pull yourself together. We kept the bad parts from you, Percy my boy. For now, at least. No sniveling; it's unbecoming in a man your age."

Pershing composed himself sufficiently to say, "That kid! What did you bastards do? Are you trying to hang me? Haven't I suffered enough to please you sickos?"

"Like I said; you don't know the first thing about suffering. Your little friend Eric does, though."

Wanda faced the car, folding money into her wallet. A shadow detached from the bushes at the edge of the building. Terry rose behind her, his bone-white hand spread like a catcher's mitt above her head. His fingers tapered to needles. He grinned evilly at Pershing, and made a shushing gesture. >From the vent by some diabolical ventriloquism: "We'll be around. If you need us. Be good."

Wanda slung open the door and climbed in. She started the engine and kissed Pershing's cheek. He scarcely noticed; his attention was riveted upon Terry waving as he melted into the shrubbery.

He didn't touch a thing at dinner. His nerves were shot—a child cried, a couple bickered with a waiter, and boisterous laughter from a neighboring table set his teeth on edge. The dim lighting was provided by candles in bowls and lamps in sconces. He couldn't even see his own feet through the shadows when he glanced under the table while Wanda had her head turned. The bottle of wine came in handy. She watched in wordless amazement as he downed several consecutive glasses.

That night his dreams were smooth and black as the void.

The calendar ticked over into October. Elgin proposed a long weekend at his grandfather's cabin. He'd bring his latest girlfriend, an Evergreen graduate student named Sarah; Mel and Gina, and Pershing and Wanda would round out the expedition. "We all could use a day or two away from the bright lights," Elgin said. "Drink some booze, play some cards, tell a few tales around the bonfire. It'll be a hoot."

Pershing would have happily begged off. He was irritable as a badger. More than ever he wanted to curl into a ball and make his apartment a den, no trespassers allowed. On the other hand, he'd grown twitchier by the day. Shadows spooked him. Being alone spooked him. There'd been no news about the missing child and he constantly waited for the other shoe to drop. The idea of running into Mark Ordbecker gave him acid. He prayed the Ordbeckers had focused their suspicion on the real culprits and would continue to leave him in peace.

Ultimately he consented to the getaway for Wanda's sake. She'd lit up at the mention of being included on this most sacred of annual events. It made her feel that she'd been accepted as a member of the inner circle.

Late Friday afternoon, the six of them loaded food, extra clothes, and sleeping bags into two cars and headed for the hills. It was an hour's drive that wound from Olympia through the nearby pastureland of the Waddell Valley toward the Black Hills. Elgin paced them as they climbed a series of gravel and dirt access roads into the high country. Even after all these years, Pershing was impressed how quickly the trappings of civilization were erased as the forest closed in. Few people came this far—mainly hunters and hikers passing through. Several logging camps were located in the region, but none within earshot.

Elgin's cabin lay at the end of an overgrown track atop a ridge. Below, the valley spread in a misty gulf. At night, Olympia's skyline burned orange in the middle distance. No phone, no television, no electricity. Water came from a hand pump. There was an outhouse in the woods behind the cabin. While everyone else unpacked the cars, Pershing and Mel fetched wood from the shed and made a big fire in the pit near the porch, and a second fire in the massive stone hearth inside the cabin. By then it was dark.

Wanda and Gina turned the tables on the men and demonstrated their superior barbequing skills. Everyone ate hot dogs and drank Löwenbräu and avoided gloomy conversation until Elgin's girlfriend Sarah commented that his cabin would be "a great place to wait out the apocalypse" and received nervous chuckles in response.

Pershing smiled to cover the prickle along the back of his neck. He stared into the night and wondered what kind of apocalypse a kid like Sarah imagined when she used that word. Probably she visualized the polar icecaps melting, or the world as a desert. Pershing's generation had lived in fear of the Reds, nuclear holocaust, and being invaded by little green men from Mars.

Wind sighed in the trees and sent a swirl of sparks tumbling skyward. He trembled. *God, I hate the woods. Who thought the day would come?* Star fields twinkled across the millions of light years. He didn't like the looks of them either. Wanda patted his arm and laid her head against his shoulder while Elgin told an old story about the time he and his college dorm mates replaced the school flag with a pair of giant pink bloomers.

Pershing didn't find the story amusing this time. The laughter sounded canned and made him consider the artificiality of the entire situation, man's supposed mastery of nature and darkness. Beyond this feeble bubble of light yawned a chasm. He'd drunk more than his share these past few days; had helped himself to Wanda's Valium. None of these measures did the trick of allowing him to forget where he'd gone or what he'd seen; it hadn't convinced him that his worst memories were the products of nightmare. Wanda's touch repulsed him, confined him. He wanted nothing more than to crawl into bed and hide beneath the covers until everything bad went away.

It grew chilly and the bonfire died to coals. The others drifted off to sleep. The cabin had two bedrooms—Elgin claimed one, and as the other married couple, Mel and Gina were awarded the second. Pershing and Wanda settled for an air mattress near the fireplace. When the last of the beer was gone, he extricated himself from her and rose to stretch. "I'm going inside," he said. She smiled and said she'd be along soon. She wanted to watch the stars a bit longer.

Pershing stripped to his boxers and lay on the air mattress. He pulled the blanket to his chin and stared blankly at the rafters. His skin was clammy and it itched fiercely. Sharp, throbbing pains radiated from his knees and shoulders. Tears formed in the corners of his eyes. He remembered the day he'd talked to Mark Ordbecker, the incredible heat, young Eric's terrified expression as he skulked behind his father. Little pitchers and big ears. The boy heard the voices crooning from below, hadn't he?

A purple ring of light flickered on the roughhewn beam directly overhead. It pulsed and blurred with each thud of his heart. The ring shivered like water and changed. His face was damp, but not from tears, not from sweat. He felt his knuckle joints split, the skin and meat popping and peeling like an overripe banana. What had Terry said about eating the young and immortality?

How does our species propagate, you may ask. Cultural assimilation, my friend. We chop out the things that make you lesser life forms weak and then pump you full of love. You'll be part of the family soon; you'll understand everything.

A mental switch clicked and he smiled at the memory of creeping into Eric's room and plucking him from his bed; later, the child's hands fluttering, nerveless, the approving croaks and cries of his new kin. He shuddered in ecstasy and burst crude seams in a dozen places. He threw off the blanket and stood, swaying, drunk with revelation. His flesh was a chrysalis, leaking gore.

Terry and Gloria watched him from the doorways of the bedrooms—naked and ghostly, and smiling like devils. Behind them, the rooms were silent. He looked at their bodies, contemptuous that anyone could be fooled for two seconds by these distorted forms, or by his own.

Then he was outside under the cold, cold stars.

Wanda huddled in her shawl, wan and small in the firelight. Finally she noticed him, tilting her head so she could meet his eyes. "Sweetie, are you waiting for me?" She gave him a concerned smile. The recent days of worry and doubt had deepened the lines of her brow.

He regarded her from the shadows, speechless as his mouth filled with blood. He touched his face, probing a moist delineation just beneath the hairline; a fissure, a fleshy zipper. Near his elbow, Terry said, "The first time, it's easier if you just snatch it off."

Pershing gripped a flap of skin. He swept his hand down and ripped away all the frailties of humanity.

Herein we witness magic and marvels and discover (again) that the world is, indeed, a vaster and much mysteriouser place than queens and god-men would have us believe . . .

A THOUSAND FLOWERS

MARGO LANAGAN

I walked away from the fire, in among the trees. I was looking for somewhere to relieve myself of all the ale I'd drunk, and I had told myself, goodness knows why, in my drunkenness, that I must piss where there were no flowers.

And this, in the late-spring forest, was proving impossible, for whatever did not froth or bow with its weight of blossoms was patterned or punctuated so by their fresh little faces, clustered or sweetly solitary, that a man could not find any place where one of them—some daisy closed against the darkness, some spray of maiden-breath testing the evening air—did not insist, or respectfully request, or only lean in the gloaming and hope, that he not stain and spoil it with his leavings.

"Damn you all," I muttered, and stumbled on, and lurched on. The fire and the carousing were now quite a distance behind me, no more than a bar or two of golden light among the tree-trunks, crossed with cavorting dancers, lengthened and shortened by the swaying of storytellers. The laughter itself and the music were becoming part of the night-forest noise, a kind of wind, several kinds of bird-cry. My bladder was *paining* me, it was so full. Look, I could trample flower after flower underfoot in my lurching—I could *kill* plant after plant that way! Why could I not stop, and piss on one, from which my liquids would surely drip and even be washed clean again, almost directly, by a rain shower, or even a drop of dew plashing from the bush, the tree, above?

It became a nightmare of flowers, and I was alone in it, my filth dammed up inside me and a pure world outside offering only innocents' faces, pale, fresh, unknowing of drunkenness and body dirt, for a man to piss on—which, had he any manners in him at all, he could not do.

But don't these flowers grow from dirt themselves? I thought desperately. Aren't they rooted in all kinds of rot and excrements, of worm and bird and deer, hedgehog and who knows what else? I scrabbled to unbutton my trousers, my mind holding to this scrap of sense, but fear also clutched in me, and flowers crowded my eyes, and breathed sweetness up my nose. I could have wept.

It is all the drink, I told myself, that makes me bother this way, makes me mind. *Have another swig, Manny!* Roste shouted in my memory, thumping me in the back, thrusting the pot at me with such vigor, two drops of ale flew out, catching my cheek and my lip two cool tiny blows. I gasped and flailed among the thickening trees. They wanted to fight me, to wrestle me down, I was sure.

I made myself stop; I made myself laugh at myself. "Who do you think you are, Manny Foyer," I said, "to take on the whole forest? There, that oak. That's clear enough, the base of it. Stop this foolishness, now. Do you want to piss yourself? Do you want to go back to the fire piss-panted? And spend tomorrow's hunt in the smell of yourself?"

I propped myself against the oak trunk with one hand. I relieved myself most carefully against the wood. And a good long wash and lacquering I gave it—aah, is there any better feeling? I stood and stood, and the piss poured and poured. Where I had been keeping it all? Had it pressed all my organs out to the sides of me while it was in there? I had not been much more than a piss-flask—no wonder I could scarce think straight! Without all this in me, I would be so light, so shrunken, so comfortable, it might only require a breath of the evening breeze to blow me like a leaf back to my fellows.

As I shook the very last droplets into the night, I saw that the moon was rising beyond the oak, low, in quite the wrong place. Had I wandered farther than I thought, as far as Artor's Outlook? I looked over my shoulder. No, there still was firelight back there, as if a house-door stood open a crack, showing the hearth within.

The moon was not the moon, I saw. It gave a nicker; it moved. I sidled round the tree very quietly, and there in the clearing beyond, the creature glowed in the starlight.

Imagine a pure white stallion, the finest conformed you have ever seen, so balanced, so smooth, so long-necked, you could picture how he would gallop, easy-curved and rippling as water, with the main and tail foaming on him. He was muscled for swiftness, he was *big* around the heart, and his legs were straight and sound, firm and fine. He'd a grand head, a king's among horses, such as is stitched upon banners, or painted on shields in a baron's banquet hall. The finest pale velvet upholstered it, with the veins tracing their paths beneath, running his good blood about, warming and enlivening every neat-made corner of him.

Now imagine that out of that fine forehead, just as on a shield, spears a battle-spike—of narwhal-horn, say, spiraling like that. Then take away the spike's straps and buckles, so that the tusk grows straight from the horse's brow—*grows*, yes, from the skull, sprouts from the velvet brow as if naturally, like a stag-antler, like the horn of a rhinockerous.

Then . . .

Then add magic. I don't know how you will do this if you have not seen it; I myself only saw it the once and bugger me if I can describe it, the quality that tells you a thing is bespelled, or sorcerous itself. It is luminosity of a kind, cool but strong. All-encompassing and yet very delicate, it trickles in your bones; slowly it lifts the hairs on your legs, your arms, your chest, in waves like fields of high-grown grass under a gentle wind. And it thins and hollows the sounds of the world, owl hoots and rabbit scutters, and beyond them it rumors of vast rustlings and seethings, the tangling and untangling of the workings of the universe, this giant nest of interminable snakes.

When something like this appears before you, let me tell you, you must look at it; you must look at nothing else; your eyes are pulled to it like a falcon to the lure. Twinned to that compulsion is a terror, swimming with the magic up and down your bones, of being seen yourself, of having the creature turn and lock you to its slavery forever, or freeze you with its gaze; whatever it wishes, it might do. It has the power, and you yourself have nothing, and *are* nothing.

It did not look at me. It turned its fine white head just a touch my way, then tossed its mane, as if to say, *How foolish of me, even to notice such a drab being!* And then it moved off, into the trees at the far side of the clearing.

The rhythm of its walking beat in my muscles, and I followed; the sight of it drew me like pennants and tent-tops on a tourney-field, and I could not but go after. Its tail, at times, braided flowers into itself, then plaited silver threads down its strands, then lost those also and streamed out like weed in brook-water. Its haunches were pearly and moony and muscular. I wanted to catch up to its head and ask it, ask it . . . What impossible thing could I ask? And what if it should turn and answer—how terrible would that be? So all confusion I stumbled after, between the flowers of the forest, across their carpet and among their curtains and beneath their ribbons and festoons.

We came to a streamside; the creature led me into the water, stirring the stars on the surface. And while I watched a trail of them spin around a dimple left by his passing, he vanished—whether by walking away, or by leaping up and becoming stars himself, or by melting into the air, I could not say, but I was standing alone, in only starlight, my feet numb and my ankles aching with the water's snow-melt cold.

I stepped out onto the muddy bank; it was churned with many hoofprints, all unshod that I could distinguish. There was no magic anywhere, only the smell of the mud and of wet rock, and behind that, like a tapestry behind a table, of the forest and its flowers.

Something lay higher up the bank, which the horse had fetched me to see. It was a person's body; I thought it must be dead, so still did it lie.

Another smell warned me as I walked closer on my un-numbing feet, on the warm-seeming mud, where the trampled grass lay bruised and tangled. It was not the smell of death, though. It was a wild smell, exciting, something like the sea and something like . . . I don't know, the first breath of spring, perhaps, of new-grown greenness somewhere, beckoning you across snow.

It was a woman—no more than a girl—and indecent. Lace, she wore, lace under-things only, and the lace was torn so badly about her throat that it draggled, muddily, aside and showed me her breast, that gleamed white as that horse's flank, with the bud upon it a soft round stain, a dim round eye.

Where do I begin with the rest of her? I stood there stupidly and stared and stared. Her storm-tossed petticoats were the finest weavings, broiderings, laces I had seen so close. Her muddied feet were the finest formed, softest, whitest, pitifullest feet I had laid eyes on in my life. The skirts of the underclothes were wrenched aside from her legs, but not from her thatch and privates, only as far as the thigh, and there was blood up there, at the highest place I could see, some dried and some shining fresher.

Her hair, my God! A great pillow of it, a great swag like cloth, torn at the edges, ran its shreds and frayings out into the mud. It was dark, but not black; I thought in proper light it might show reddish lights. Her face, white as milk, the features delicate as a faery's, was cheek-pillowed on this hair, the open lips resting against the knuckle and nail of one thumb; in her other hand, as if she were in the act of flinging it away, a coronet shone gold, and with it were snarled a few strands of the hair, that had come away when she tore the crown from her head.

I crouched a little way from this princess, hissing to myself in awe and fright. I could not see whether she breathed; I could not feel from here whether she was warm.

I stood and tiptoed around her, and crouched again, next to the crown. What a creation! I had never seen such smithing or such gems. You could not have paid me enough to touch the thing, it gave off such an atmosphere of power.

I was agitated to make the girl decent. I have sisters; I have a mother. They would not want such fellows as those back at the fire to happen on them in such a state. I reached across the body and lifted the lace, and the breast's small weight fell obedient into the pocket and hid itself. Then, being crouched, I waddled most carefully down and tried to make sense of the lace and linen there, not wanting to expose the poor girl further with any mistaken movement of the wrong hem or tatter. I decided which petticoat-piece would restore her modesty. I reached out to take it up with the very tips of my fingers.

A faint step sounded on the mudded grass behind me. I had not time to turn. Four hands, strong hands, the strongest I had ever felt, caught me by my upper arms, and lifted me as you lift a kitten, so that its paws stiffen out into the air searching for something to grasp.

"We have you." They were soldiers, with helmets, with those sinister clipped beards. They threw me hard to the ground away from the princess, and the fence they formed around me bristled with blades. Horror and hatred of me bent every back, deformed every face.

"You will die, and slowly," said one, in deepest disgust, "for what you done to our Lady."

They took me to the queen's castle, and put me in a dungeon there. Several days, they kept me, on water-soup and rock-bread, and I was near despair, for they would not tell me my fate nor allow me to send word to any family, and I could well imagine I was to spend the rest of my days pacing the rough cell, my brief time in the colorful out-world replaying itself to madness in my head.

Guards came for me, though, the third day. "Where are you taking me?" I said.

"To the block, man," said one.

My knees went to lily-stalks. The other guard hauled me up and swore. "Don't make trouble, Kettle," he told his fellow. "We don't want to bring him before them having shitted himself."

The other chuckled high, and slapped my face in what he doubtless thought a friendly way. "Oh no, lad, 'tis only a little conference with Her Majesty for you. A little confabulation regarding your misadventures." Which was scarcely less frightening than the block.

From the stony under-rooms of the castle, up we went. The floor flattened and the walls dried out and we passed the occasional terrifying thing: a suit of armor from the Elder Days; a portrait of a royal personage in silks bright as sunlit water, in lace collars like insect wings; a servant with a tray with goblets and decanter so knobbed and bejeweled you could scarce tell what they were.

"Here's the place," said the humorous guard, as we arrived at a doorway where people were waiting, gentlemen hosed and ruffed and cloaked, with shining-dressed hair, and two abject men about to collapse off that bench, they leaned so spineless and humiliated.

The guards let us straight in, to a room so splendid, I came very close to filling my pants. It was all hushed with the richest tapis, and ablaze with candles, and God help me, there was a throne, and the queen sat upon it, and at the pinnacle of all her clothing, all her posture, above her bright, severe eyes and her high forehead filled with brains, a fearsome crown nestled so close in her silvering reddish hair, it might have grown into place there. Under her gaze, my very bones froze within me.

"Give your name and origins," said the guard, nudging me.

"My name is Manny Foyer, of Piggott's Leap, Your Majesty."

"Now bow," the guard muttered.

I bowed. Oh, my filthy boots were sad on that bright carpet! But I would rather look on them than on that royal face.

"Daughter?" The queen did not take her attention from my face.

I gaped. Was she were asking me if I *had* a daughter? Why would she care? Had she confused me with some other offender?

But a voice came from the shadows, beside, behind the throne. "I have never seen him in my life. I don't know why he has been brought here."

The queen spoke very slowly and bitterly. "Take a close look, daughter."

Out of the shadows walked the princess, tall and splendidly attired, her magnificent hair taken up into braids and knots and paddings so elaborate, they almost overwhelmed her little crown. Her every movement, and her white, fine-modelled face, spoke disdain—for me, for her mother, for the dignitaries and notables grouped about in their bright or sober costumes, in their medals and accoutrements or the plainer cloaks of their own authority.

She circled me. Her gown's heavy fabrics rustled and swung and shushed across the carpet. Then she looked to her mother, and shrugged. "He is entirely a stranger to me, Madam."

"Is it possible he rendered you insensible with a blow to your head, so that you did not see his face?"

The princess regarded me, over her shoulder. She was the taller of us, but I was built stockier than her, though almost transparent with hunger at this moment.

"Where is my constable? Where is Constable Barry?" said the queen impatiently, and when he was rattled forth behind me, "Tell me the circumstances of this man's arrest."

Which he did. I had my chance to protest, when he traduced me, that I had not touched the lady, that I had only been adjusting her clothing so that my fellows would not see her so exposed. I thought I sounded most breathless and feeble, but while the constable continued with his story I caught a glance from the princess, that was very considering of me, and contained some amusement, I thought.

There was a silence when he finished. The queen dandled my life in her hands. I was near to fainting; a thickness filled my ears and spots of light danced at the edges of my sight.

"He does not alter your story, daughter?" said the queen.

"I maintain," said the magnificent girl, "that I am pure. That no man has ever touched me, and certainly not this man."

The two of them glared at each other, the coldest, most rigid-faced, civilized glare that ever passed between two people.

"Free him," said the queen, with a tiny movement of her finger.

Constable Barry clicked his tongue, and there was a general movement and clank of arms and breastplates. They removed me from that room—I dare say I walked, but truly it was more that they wafted me, like a cloud of smoke that you fan and persuade towards a chimney.

They put me out the front of the castle, with half a pound-loaf of hard bread to see me home. It was raining, and cold, and I did not know my way, so I had quite a time of it, but eventually I did find my road home to Piggott's, and into the village I tottered late next day.

My mam welcomed me with relief. My dad wanted my word I had done no wrong before he would let me in the house. My fellows, farm men and hunters both, greeted me with such ribaldry I scarce knew where to look. "I never touched her!" I protested, but however hard I did, still they drank to me and clapped my back and winked at me and made unwholesome reference. "White as princess-skin, eh, Manny?" they would say, or, "Oh, he's not up for cherry-picking with us, this one as has wooed royalty!"

"Take no notice, son," Mam advised. "The more you fuss, the longer they will plague you."

And so I tried only to endure it, though I would not smile and join in their jesting. They had not seen her, that fine girl in her a-mussment; they had not been led to her through the flowering forest by a magical horse with a horn in its head; they had not quailed under her disdain, or plumped up again with hope when she had looked more kindly on them. They had not been in that dungeon facing their death, nor higher in the palace watching the queen's finger restore them to life. They did not know what they spoke of, so lightly.

I thought it all had ended. I was begun to relax and think life might return to being more comfortable, the night Johnny Blackbird took it into his head to goad me. He was a man of the lowest type; I knew even as I swung at him that Mam would be disgusted—Dad also—by my having let such an earwig annoy me with his crawlings. But he had gone on and on, pursuing me and insisting, full of rude questions and implications, and I was worn out with being so fecking noble about the whole business, when I had never asked to be led away and put beside a princess; I had never wanted picking up by queen-people and bringing into royal presences; most of all I had not wanted, not for a moment, to touch even as much of her clothing as I touched, of that young lady, let alone her flesh. I had never thought a smutty thought about her, for though she were a beauty she were much too imposing for a man like me to do more than bow down before, to slink away from.

Anyway, once I had landed my first thump, to the side of Blackbird's head, the relief of it was so great, I began to deliver on him all the blows and curses I had stored up till that moment. And hard blows they were, and well calculated, and curses that surged like vomit from my depths, so sincere I hardly recognized my own voice. He called pax almost straight away, the little dung-piece, but I kept into him until the Pershron twins pulled me off, by which time his face was well colored and pushed out of shape, the punishment I'd given him.

After that night people left me alone, and rather more than I wanted. They respected me, though there was the smell of fear, or maybe embarrassment—bad feeling, anyhow—in their respect. And I could not jolly them out of it, having never been that specimen of a jolly fellow. So I tended then to gloom off by myself, to work when asked and well, but less often to join the lads at the spring for a swim, or at the Brindle for a pot or two.

We were stooking early hay when the soldiers came again. One moment I was easy in the sunshine, watching how each forkful propped and fell; the next I came aware of a crowding down on the road like ants at jam, and someone running up the field—Cal Devonish it was, his shirt frantic around him. As soon as he was within the distance of me he cried, "They are come for you, Manny!" And I saw my death in his face, and I ran too.

The chase was messy and short. I achieved the forest, but I was not long running there before my foot slipped on a root, then between two roots, and the rest of my body fled over it and the bone snapped, above my ankle. I sat up and extricated myself, and I was sitting there holding my own foot like a broken baby in both my hands, knowing I would never run again, when the soldiers—how had they crossed the hayfield so fast?—came thundering at me out of the trees.

"What have I done?" I cried piteously. They wrenched me up. The leg-pain shouted up me, and flared off the top of my head as screams. " 'Tis no less true now, what I said, than it was in the spring!"

"Why did you run, then," said one of them, "if you are so innocent?" And he kicked my broken leg, then slapped me awake when I swooned from the pain.

Up came Constable Barry, his face a creased mess of disgust and delight. "You *filth*." He spat in my face; he struck me to the ground. "You animal." He kicked me in my side, and I was sure he broke something there. "Getting your spawn upon our princess, spoiling and soiling the purest creature ever was."

"But I never!"

But he kicked me in the mouth, then, and thank God the pain of that shatterment washed straight back into my head, and wiped his ugly spittle-face from my sight, and the trees and the white sky behind it.

Straight up to the foot of the tower he rode, the guard. He dismounted jingling and untied a sacking bag from his saddle. It was stained at the bottom, dark and plentifully.

"You have someone in that tower, I think, miss," he says to me. "A lady?"

"We do." I could not tear my gaze from the sack.

"I'm charged to show her something, and take her response to the Majesty."

"Very well," I said.

He followed me in; I conveyed his purpose to Joan Vinegar.

"Oh yes? And what is the thing you're to show?" And she stared at the bag just as I had, knowing it were some horror.

"I'm to show the leddy. I've no instructions to let anyone else see."

"I'll take you up." Joan was hoping for a look anyway. So was I. He was mad if he thought we would consent to not see. Nothing ever happened here; we were hungry for events, however grim.

Up they went, and I walked back outside, glanced to my gardening and considered it, then followed my musings around to the far side of the tower, under the arrow-slit that let out of the lady's room.

It was a windless day, and thus I heard clearly her first cry. If you had cared about her at all, it would have broke your heart, and now I discovered that despite the girl's general lifelessness, and her clear stupidity in getting herself childered when some lord needed her purity to bargain with, I did care. She was miserable enough already—what had he brought to make her miserabler?

Well, I knew, I knew. But there are some things you know but will not admit until you have seen them yourself. The bag swung black-stained before my mind's eye, a certain shape, a certain weight, and the lady cried on up there, not in words but in wild, unconnected noises, and there were thuds, too, of furniture, a crash of pottery. I drew in a sharp breath; we did not have pots to spare here, and the lady knew it.

I hurried back to the under-room. Her shrieks sounded down the stairs, and then the door slammed on them, and the man's boots hurried down, and there he was in the doorway, a blank, determined look on his face, the bag still in his hand, but looser, only held closed, not tied.

He thrust it at Joan as she arrived white-faced behind him. "Bury this," he said.

She held it away from her skirts.

"I'll be off," he said.

"You'll not sleep, sir, or take a bite?" said I.

"Not with that over me." He looked at the ceiling. We could hear the lady, but not down the stairs; her noise poured out the arrow-slit of her room, and bounced off the rocks outside, and in at the tower door. "I would sooner eat on a battlefield, with cavalry coming on, both sides."

And he was gone. Joan and I could not move, transfixed by the repellent bag.

"She has gone mad," I said.

"For the moment, yes," said Joan, as if she could keep things ordinary with her matter-of-fact tone.

We exchanged a long look. She read my question and my fear; she was not stupid. "Outside," she said. "We don't want to sully our living-place wi' this. Fetch the spade."

We stepped out in time for a last sight of the horseman a-gallop away into the trees. The gray light flared and fluttered unevenly, like my heartbeats. Joan bore the bag across the yellow grass, and I followed her into the edge of the forest, where we had raised the stone for old Cowlin. Joan sat on Cowlin's stone. She leaned out and laid the bag on the grass. "Dig," she said, pointing. "Right there."

She did not often order me about, only when she was very tired or annoyed, but I did not think to question her. I dug most efficiently, against the resistance of that bastard mountain soil, quite different from what we had managed to rot and soften into the vegetable garden. The last time I had dug this was for Cowlin's grave, and the same sense of death was closed in around us, and of the smallness of our activity among the endless pines, among the endless mountains.

While I dug, Joan sat recovering, her fingers over her mouth as if she would not let words out until she had ordered them better in her head. Every time I glanced at her she looked a different age, glistening a wide-eyed baby the once, then crumpled to a crone, then a fierce matron in her full strength. And she would not meet my eye.

"There," I said eventually. "'Tis done." The mistress's wails in the tower were weakening now; you might imagine them whistles of wind among the rocks, had your very spine not attuned itself to them like a dowser's hazel-rod bowing towards groundwater.

Joan sprang up. She brought the bag. She plunked it in my digging. Then she cast me a look. "You'll not be content 'til you see, will you."

"No."

"It will haunt your dreams, girl."

"I don't care," I said. "I will *die* if you don't show me."

"I will show you, then." And with her gaze fixed brutal on my face she flicked back the corner of the sacking.

I looked a long time; I truly looked my fill. Joan had thought I would squirm and weep, maybe be sick, but I did not. I'd seen dead things before, and beaten things.

"It is her lover," I said. "The father of her bab," I added after some more of looking.

Joan did not answer. Who else would he be?

I touched him, his hair, his cold skin; I closed the eyelid that was making him look out so frightening. I pressed one of the bruises at his jaw. I could not hurt him; I could push as hard as I liked. But I was gentle. I felt gentle; there is nothing like the spectacle of savagery to bring on a girl's gentleness.

"I am astounded she recognized him," I said.

"Oh, she did," said Joan. "In an instant."

I looked a little longer, turned the head to both sides and made sure I saw all there was to see. "Well, for certain he don't look very lovable now."

"Well, he was once. Listen to her noise, would you?"

I glanced behind me, as if I might be able to see the thin skein of it winding from the window. One last glance at the beaten head, at the mouth—that had been done with a boot-toe, that had—to fix the two of them together in my mind, and then I laid him in the sacking in the ground, and I put the cloth over his face and then some of the poor soil on top of that, and proceeded to hide him away.

Joan Vinegar woke me, deep that night. "Come, girl, it is time for midwifery."

"What?" Muzzily I swam up from my dream. "There are months to go yet."

"Oh no there ain't," she said. "Today has brought it on, the sight of her man. She is in the throes now."

"What should I do?" I said frightened. "You have not had time to show me."

"Assist, is all. Just do as I tell. I must get back to her. Bring all the cloths you can find, and a bowl and jug of water." And she was gone.

I rose and dressed and ran barefoot across the grass and rocks to the tower. The silence in the night, the smaller silence in the tower; the parcels of herbs opened on the table; the bowl and jug there, ready for me to fill; the stove a crack open, with the fire just woken inside—all of a sudden I was awake, with the eeriness of it, with the unusualness, with the imminence of a bab's arriving

Up I went with my bringings, into the prison-room. It was all cloth and candlelight up there, the lady curled around herself on the creased bed. She looked asleep, or dead, as far as I could see from my fearful glances. The fire was built up big, and it was hotter in here than I had ever known it, hotter than it ought to be, for the lady was supposed to enjoy no comforts, but find every aspect of her life here a punishment.

Joan took the cloths from me, took the jug and bowl. "Make up a tea," she said, "of just the chamomile, for now. Lots of blooms, lots of leaves, about a fifth what is in my parcel there, in the middling pot."

"No," murmured the lady, steeling herself for a pain, and Joan almost pushed me outside. I hurried away. I had only heard screams and dire stories of childbed, and the many babs brought healthy from its trials had done nothing to counter my terror of it.

Down in the lower room I went to work, with Joan's transmitted voice murmuring in the stairway door, wordless, like a low wind in a chimney. I tidied the fire and put the pot on, then sat with the stove open and my face almost in the flames, drinking of their orange-ness and stinging heat, listening for a sound from the lady above, which did not come; she must noise loudly for her dead man, but stay stalwart for babbing, it seemed. They are a weird folk, the nobility; they do nothing commonsensically.

I took up the tea, and Joan told me the next thing to prepare, and so began the strange time, that seemed to belong neither to night nor to day, but to happen as an extremely slow and vivid dream. Each time I glanced in at the door the lady would be somewhere else, but motionless—on the bed, crouched beside it, bracing herself against the chimney-breast, her hair fallen around her like a cloak, full of snarls and tangles. Joan would hurry at me, as if I must not be seeing even as much as I saw. She would take what I had brought, and instruct me what next she needed. Downstairs was all smells and preparations—barley mush with honey and medicine-seeds crushed into it, this tea and that, from Joan's store of evil-smelling weeds, warmed-over soup for all of us, to sustain us in our various labors.

The fear came and went. Had I a task to do, I was better off, for it took my whole mind to ensure in my tiredness that I performed it right. When I was idle by the stove with Joan murmuring in the stairs, that was worse, when I could not envisage what awfulness might be happening up there, when only the lady's occasional gasp or word, pushed out of her on the force of a birth pain, stoked up my horrors. "Girl?" Joan would come to the door and say down the stairs, not needing to raise her voice. And then my fear would flare worst, at what I might glimpse when I went up, at what I might hear.

Then a new time began, and I could avoid the room no longer. Joan made me bring up the chair from the kitchen, and sit on it, and become a chair of sorts myself, with the lady's arms hooked over my thighs, my lap full of her hair. "Give her a sip," Joan would say, or, "Lift the hair off her neck and fan her there; she is hot as Hades." And in between she would be talking up into the lady's face, crouched before us, and though she was tired and old and aproned, I could see how she once must have been, and how her man might still desire her even now, her kind, fierce face, her living, watching eyes, her knowing what to do, after child after child after child of her own. She knew how to look after all of us, the laboring lady and the terrified girl assisting; she knew how to damp those two great forest fires, grief and fear, contain them and stop them taking over the world; she was in her element, doing what she was meant to do.

In the middle of one of the pains the lady reared, and there was a rush and a gush, and Joan exchanged sodden cloth for dry, out of sight there, under the lady's nightgown. She looked up exultant, over the bump of the baby. "That's your waters popped," she said. "Not long now, love-a-do."

I was almost in a faint, such a strong scent billowed out from the soaked cloth beside us, from the lady herself. Jessamine, I thought. No, elderflower. No—But as fast as I could name the flowers, the scent grew past them and encompassed others, sweet and sharp, so different and so strong my mind was painted now with scattered pinks, now with blood-black roses and with white daphne.

"Oh," I whispered, and drank another deep breath of it, "I can almost *taste* the sweetness!"

The lady's head lolled to the side; released from the pain, she faded into momentary sleep, her face almost rapturous with the relief. Beyond her Joan held the nightgown out, and watched below, shaking her head. "What is coming?" she said softly. "What is coming out of you, lovely girl?"

"A little horse," said the lady in her sleep. "A little white horse."

"Well, that will be a sight." Joan laughed gently, and arranged her cloths beneath.

What came, four pains and pushes later, was of course not a horse, but a child—but a child so strange, a horse might almost have been less so. For the child was white—not white in contrast to Moorish or Mongol or African prince, but white like a lily, white like the snow, like the moon, entirely without color, except . . . He was a boy-child, and the boy spout on him was tipped with wrinkled green like a bud, and the boy-sacks on him—a good size for one so small—were also green, and darker, like some kind of fruiting, or vegetable.

He was small, he was unfinished, he did not live long. Joan gave him into the lady's arms, and I sat behind her on the floor and supported her, and over her shoulder I watched as he took a few pained breaths of the sweet, heated air, and then took no more, but lay serene. He was barely human, barely arrived; he was an idea of a person that had not got quite properly uttered, not properly formed out of slippery white clay; and yet a significance hovered all round him quite disproportionate to his size. He smelled divine, and he looked it, a tiny godlet, precise in all his features, delicate, pale, powerful like nothing I had seen before, like nothing I have seen since.

"What is that on his forehead?" I said. Perhaps all newborns had it, and I was ignorant.

Joan shrugged, touched the crown of his tiny head. "Some kind of carbuncle?"

The lady held him better to the light.

"It looks like a great pearl there," I said. "Set in his skin. It has a gleam."

"Yes, a pearl," said the lady distantly, as if she had expected no less, and she kissed the bump of it.

Joan gave her a cloth, and she wrapped him, her hands steady, though I had begun to cry behind her, and were dripping onto her shoulder.

There was business to deal with—a body that has birthed needs to rid itself of all sorts of muck, and be washed, and dressed cleanly, and laid in a clean bed to rest, and it can only move slowly through these things. We proceeded calmly, Joan saying what I should do, task after simple task, and always I was aware of the little master, in his wrappings there, by the fire as if to keep his small deadness warm, and the dance we were doing around him, in his sweet air, in the atmosphere of him.

When she was abed the lady asked for him, and the three of us sat there in a row very quiet, and she held him, unwrapped, lying along her up-propped thighs. Quite lifeless, he was, quite bloodless, with the scrap of green cord hanging from his narrow belly; he ought to have looked pitiful, but I could feel through the lady's arm against mine, through the room's air, through the *world*, that none of us pitied him.

"He looks so wise," I whispered. "Like a wise little old man."

"Wise and wizened," said the lady. I have never known anyone so tranquil and strong as this lady, I thought. Whoever she was, all I wanted that night was to serve her forever, me and Joan together in that tower, bonded till death by this night's adventure, by the bringing of this tiny lad to the world, and the losing of him from it.

In the morning the flower-scent was gone; the fire had died, the tower was cold, and the air felt rotten with grief. *He will haunt your dreams*, Joan had told me, of that lover's head, but in fact he filled my waking mind, so well remembered in all his details that it was as if a picture of him—his ragged neck-flesh, the turned-up eye—went before me, painted on a cloth, wherever I went, to the well or the woods or wherever. And when he was not there, his son, pale as a corpse-candle, floated before me instead.

The lady gave the bab into Joan's hands, a tight-wrapped, tiny parcel, banded and knotted with lengths of her own hair. "Oh, of course!" I said when Joan brought it down the stair. "So that he always has his mam around him! And such a color, so warm!"

She laid him on the table. "So we've more digging to do, for him and the other birth-leavings. It is best to bury those, with proper wordage and herbery."

"How is she?" I said timidly. I was unnerved that our bond was gone, that we were three separate people again.

"Resting," said Joan. "Peaceful."

Then I must have looked very lost and useless, because she came to where I sat on the bench, and stood behind me with her hands on my shoulders, and she held me together while I cried into my apron, and "There, there," she said, and "There, there," but calmly, and patiently, as if she did not expect me ever to stop, but would stand quiet and radiant behind me, however long I took to weep myself dry.

I sent the girl home. She was in too much distress to be much use to me, and I could not let her near the lady. I thought it odd—she had hardly been squeamish at all when that head was brought in. I had had hopes for her. But the bab undid her, whether its birth or its death or its strangeness, or the fact that its mam shed no tears over it, but sank straight back away into the stupor we were used to, as if she had never been childered, as if she had never raved and suffered over her man's death.

With the rider who brought supplies and took the girl away, I sent a message to Lord Hawley, that the mistress was delivered of a dead child, and what were we to do now? For my contract with him had only specified up to the birth, but now that the bab was gone, could not some other woman, without midwifing skills, be brought to the task of guarding my lady? For though I could use the good money he was paying, I felt a fraud here now, when there were plenty of childered women in my own village to whom I could be truly useful, rather than playing nursemaid here.

For answer he sent money, money extra upon what he had promised, as if the death of the bab had been my doing and he wanted to show me favor for it. And he bid me stay on, while they sorted themselves out at court about this state of affairs. I could see them there in their ruffs and robes, around their glasses of foreign wine, discussing: ought they to humiliate the lady with further exile, or ought they allow her back, instead to be constantly reminded of her sullied state by the faces and gestures of others?

And so I stayed nursemaid. Although there were only the two of us now, I kept to my contracted behavior and did not keep company with my prisoner, but only attended her health as long as that was necessary, and made and brought her meals, emptied her chamber pot, and tended her small fire. I was under orders to speak to her only when spoken to, and to resist any attempt she might make to engage me in conversation, but had I obeyed them we would have passed our days entirely in silence, so to save my own sanity I kept to my practice after the birth of greeting the lady when I entered, and she would always greet me back, so that we began each day with my asserting that she was a lady and hers that I was Joan Vinegar, which otherwise we might well have forgot, there being nothing much else to remind us.

A month and a half we lived together, the lady and me in our silences, the mountain wastes around us. The lord's man came with his foodstuffs and more money, with no accompanying message. He told me all the gossip of court, sitting there eating bread and some of the cheese and wine that he himself had supplied, and truly it was as if he spoke of animals in a menagerie, so strange were their behaviors, so high-colored and passionate. He filled the tower-room with his noise and his uniform. I was so glad when he went and left us in peace again that I worried for myself, that I was turning like that one upstairs, entirely satisfied with nothing, with watching the endless parade of my own thoughts through my head.

I stood, with the man's meal-crumbs at the far end of the table, and a cabbage like a great pale-green head at the near, and the gold scattered beside it that I could not spend, for how much longer yet he had not said. She was silent upstairs. She had maintained her silence so thoroughly while the man was here, he might have thought me a hermit, hired only to do my prayers and observances for sake of the queen's health, not to attend any other human business. And none of this made sense, not the gold, or the cabbage, or the smell of the wine-dregs from the cup, or the disturbance his cheerful voice had wrought on the air of the usually silent room, but all flew apart in my senses like sparrows shooed from a seeded field, in all directions, to all quite different refuges.

My lady's womb ceased its emissions from the birth, and paused awhile dry. Then came a day when she requested cloths for her monthly blood. I wondered, as I brought them, then later as I washed them, whether this was good or bad, this return to normal health. Would Hawley have preferred—would he have showered me with yet more gold?—if she had died in expelling her child, or thereafter from some fever of childbed? Had I been supposed to understand that she was not to return alive from this exile? Had I failed in an unstated duty?

"Well, she is as *good* as dead," I said to myself, rinsing the scrubbed cloth and watching the pink cloud dissipate down the stream. "If you ask me."

Dreams began to trouble me. Often I dreamed of the dead child. Sometimes he lived, and made wise dreamish utterance that carried no sense when I repeated it to myself in the morning. Sometimes he died, or fell to pieces as he came out of his mother, or changed to a plant or a fleeing animal on emerging, but always these dreams were filled with the scent of him, maddening, unplaceable, all flowers and fruits combining, so strong it seemed still to linger in the room even after I woke, and slept again, and woke again in the morning, so tantalizing that several times I hunted on my hands and knees in the meadow around the cottage for the blossom that might be the source, that I might carry it about with me and tantalize myself further with the scent.

I woke very suddenly from one of these dreams, and lay frightened in the night, washes of color flowering forth onto the darkness with the surprise of the wakening to my heart and blood. My hearing was gone so sensitive, if one of my grandchildren had turned over in his sleep back home, I think I would have heard it. Outside a thud sounded, and another, earthen, and then another; a horse was about, not ridden by anyone, but perhaps it had pulled itself loose when tied to browse, and now wandered this unfruitful forest and had come upon our meadow in its hunger.

When I had tamed my heart and breath, I left my bed and quietly opened the cottage door, to see whether the animal was wild or of some worth. I dare say I had it in mind how useful a horse would be, if it were broken and not too grand, how I might add interest to my dreary life here with excursions, with discoveries of towns within a day's ride of the tower. I might spend a little of my gold there; I might converse with sellers and wives. Figures and goods and landscapes flowed across my imaginings, as I stepped out into the cold night, into the glare of the stars, the staring of the moon.

The air was thick with the flower-scent of the dead boy-child—such a warm, summery smell, here in autumn's chills and dyings! The horse stood white—a stallion, he was—against the dark forest. He was down the slope from the tower. He had raised his head and seemed to gaze at the upper window.

"Perhaps you are too splendid," I whispered, but I fetched the rope anyway, and tied a slip-loop. Then across the meadow I crept, stepping not much faster than a tree steps, so as not to frighten the horse away.

At a certain point my breathing quieted and the night breeze eased to where the low noise issuing from my lady's window reached me. That rooted me to the meadow-ground more firmly, her near-inhuman singing, her crooning, broken now and then with grunts and gutturals, something like triumphant laughter.

I have often been thought a witch myself, with my ugly looks and my childbedding, but I tell you, I have never evoked any such magic as shivered under that fine horse's moonlit hide, as streamed off it in the night, fainting me with its scent and eluding my eye with its blown blooms and shining threads. And I have never cast such a spell as trailed out that window on my mistress's, my charge's, song, if song it were. It turned my bones to sugar ice, I tell you, my mind to sweet syrup and my breath to perfume.

And then among her singing another sound intruded, with no voice to it, no magic, no song. It was an earthly sound and an earthy: stone scraped on stone, heavily, and surreptitious somehow.

Then I knew what she was about, with her mad singing, with her green-tipped baby, with her caring so little for the shame of the queen's name and family. And I ran—more, I *flew*—across the meadow grasses and around to the tower door. I must be quiet, or she would hurry and be gone before I reached her; I must be quick!

I took the prison-room key from under its stone and managed to open the tower door silently. I sped up the stairs, put the key in the lock and turned it, with its usual squeaks and resistance. From inside, loud now, undisguised, came the grinding, the push, of stone on stone.

"My lady!" I forced the stiff key around.

More grinding. Then, and as I flung myself into the room, the stone the girl had loosened from the arrow-slot—months of labor in the night, it would have taken her!—thudded down into the meadow at the foot of the tower.

"My lady, no!"

She darkened the hole with her body, for the moments it took me to cross the room. My fingertip brushed the hem of her nightgown. Then moonlight and starlight whitened my reaching hand.

"Madam!" I screamed to the waiting horse, but through my scream I heard the impact of the lady below, the crack of breaking bone.

"Madam, no! What have you done?"

I pressed myself to the arrow-slot, peering down. The horse stepped up the grass, and I gasped. He bore a fine long spiraling horn on his brow, like some animals of Africa, anteloupes and such. I could smell him, the sweet ferocious flower-and-fruitishness of him, so powerfully that I was not surprised—I did not gasp again—when my lady appeared, walking across the meadow, not limping as she ought, or nursing any injury that I could see. And when she embraced him, he bowing his head to hold her slight body against his breast, and crooking his knee to further enclose her, the rightness and the joy of it caught me in belly and groin, like a birth-pain and a love pang together, and I drank of the sight as they each seemed to be drinking of the other, through their skins, through his coat and her clothing, from the warmth they pressed into being between them.

She held and held him, around his great neck, her fingers in his mane; she murmured into him, and rubbed her cheek on the nap of him and kissed him; she reached along his shoulder and the muscles there, holding him to her, and no further proof was needed than that embrace, and the sight of her lifted face, and the scent in my nostrils of all that lived and burgeoned, that the two of them were lovers and had loved, that the little green-tipped boy had been issue of this animal and this maiden, that the carbuncle on the boy's brow had been the first formings towards his own horn, that I had been witness to magic and marvels. The world, indeed, was a vaster and much mysteriouser place than queens and god-men would have us believe.

My mistress led the horse to the tree-stump I used for chopping kindling on. She mounted him from there, and rode him away. I shook my head and clutched my breast to see them, so nobly did he move, and so balanced was her seat to his movement—they were almost the one creature, it was clear to me.

And then they were gone. There was nothing below but night-lit meadow, giving onto black forest. Above, stars sang out blindly in the square of air where my lady had removed the stone. The prison-room was empty; the door yawned; the window gaped. Everything felt loose, or broken. The sweetness slipped out of the air, leaving only the smell of the dead fire, and of cold stone.

I left the door ajar, from some strange notion that my lady might return, and require to imprison herself again. I walked down the stairs I had so lately flown up. Slowly I crossed the lower room to the other gaping door, and stepped out into the meadow. Brightly colorless, it was, under the moonlight, the grass like gray straw, the few late flowers leaning or drooping asleep.

I rounded the tower. There she was, her head broken on the fallen stone. I scarce could believe my eyes. I scarce could propel myself forward, surprise had frozen so thickly around the base of my spine, where all the impulses to walk begin, all the volitions.

"My lady, my lady!" I *fell* to my knees rather than knelt to them. How little she was, and fine, and pale! How much more delicate-crafted are noble ladies, aren't they?, than us countrywomen all muscled for fieldwork and family life! But even my thick skull could not have prevailed against that stone, and from that height. Blood had trickled from her eye-corner, and her nose and mouth, and poured through her hair; now she seemed glued blackly to the stone, staring to the forest, watching herself ride away.

This is the end of my story. I told a different one to Lord Hawley when I walked out of the mountains, and bought myself a strong little bay mare to ride to the palace and give my information. My lord—I had not seen him in person before—was small, and his furs and silks and chains and puffed-out sleeves made him seem as wide as he was tall. He listened to my tale most interestedly, and then he released me from my contract, paying it out in full though I had four months to serve yet, and adding to that amount the sum I had paid for the mare, and double the sum I had outlaid for bed and food to visit him, so that I should not arrive home at all out of pocket. He gave me a guard to protect me and my moneys all the way to Steeping Dingle; that guard, in time, was to marry my youngest, little Ruth, and sire me four grandsons and three granddaughters.

I had no reason to complain of my treatment by the queen's house; every royal man gave me full courtesy and respect. And though I was sworn to secrecy over the whole affair, the fact that I had had royal dealings, as evidenced by my return with the guard, did much for my standing, and from that time on I made a tidier living bringing out babies than all the other good-women combined, in my village and throughout the surrounding country.

The book never existed and yet Bethany remembered it, which was good for a gasp or two and certainly pertained to the matter at hand—but its real function was to propel her headlong into a thrilling and probably life-threatening adventure . . .

FRUMPY LITTLE BEAT GIRL

PETER ATKINS

"They don't make hats like that anymore," says Mr. Slater.

Jesus. Five minutes in and first thing out of his mouth. Bethany looks up from her book and through the windshield to see what the hell he's talking about.

There's a pedestrian, a Hispanic guy, crossing in front of the Lexus. He's in no particular hurry about it, and he doesn't need to be. The light they're stuck at, the one at San Fernando and Brand, can take three minutes even in a good mood and, at eight-thirty in the morning, you can usually count on it being pissy.

"Sure they do," Bethany says, meaning the hat.

"No," Mr. Slater says, his head moving to watch the man reach the sidewalk and turn to wait, like them, for the northbound green. Bethany hears the pleasure, the admiration, in his voice. "They make things that *look* like it, maybe," he says. "But that's *period*."

He has a point. It's not only the gray fedora. The pedestrian—elderly but vigorous, his body lean and compact, face like leather but like, you know, *good* leather—is dressed in a subtly pinstriped black suit that could be new or that could have been really well looked after for decades. There's a tight quarter-inch of white handkerchief showing above the suit's breast pocket, and the man wears opinionated shoes.

"Cool," Bethany says. "*Buena Vista Social Club*."

"You think he's Cuban?" Mr. Slater asks, as if she was being literal. "I mean, like, not Mexican?"

Bethany, no idea, shrugs and smiles. The light changes and Mr. Slater—*you know, you really can start calling me David*, he's said more than once but she's been babysitting for him and his wife since she was fourteen and just can't get her head around it—moves through the intersection and takes one last look back at the guy. "Check him out," he says, happy and impressed. "It's 1958. And it's never not going to be."

Gay Michael's on with a customer when Bethany comes into the bookstore but he takes the time to cover the phone's mouthpiece and stare pointedly out the plate-glass window as Mr. Slater's Lexus pulls away into the Glendale traffic. He gives her an eyebrow. "Bethany Lake," he says, delighted. "You appalling little slut."

"My neighbor," she starts to tell him, ready to add that she'd needed a ride because her piece-of-shit Dodge is in the shop again but he's already back on the phone giving directions.

"Yes, ma'am," he's saying, "Michael & Michael. On Brand. Between Wilson and California." Listens for a moment. "Of course. Consider it held. And it really is in lovely condition. The website pictures don't do it justice." Bethany watches him run his hand over the tooled leather binding of the book on the counter in front of him as if he can send the seductive feel of it down the line. It's an 1827 *Paradise Lost*, the famous one with the John Martin mezzotints. Bethany catches his eye, points to the curtained annex at the rear of the store, mimes a coffee-cup at her mouth.

She'd figured she'd have to brew a fresh pot but Fat Michael's already on it; three mugs waiting, OCD-ed into a handle-matching line atop a napkin that's folded in geometric precision. On a shelf above the coffee-maker, his iPod is nestled in its cradle-and-mini-speakers set-up and its random shuffle—which Bethany pretends is a radio station with the call-sign K-FMO, for Fat Michael's Oddities—is playing "Jack the Ripper" by Screaming Lord Sutch. "*Is your name Mary Blood?*" his Lordship is currently screaming, albeit at low volume; Fat Michael would like to pipe K-FMO through to the store, but Gay Michael's foot is firmly down on that one. "What are we, fucking Wal-Mart?" is about as far as the conversation ever gets.

"He's really got a bite on that Milton?" Bethany says, knowing the guys have been asking high four figures. The coffee-maker pings.

"Some sitcom star's trophy wife," Fat Michael says, filling Bethany's mug first and handing it to her, no milk no sugar, just right. "She's shopping for his birthday. You know, like he can read."

"None of your customers read, Michael," she says. "They *collect*."

"Hmph," he says, because he doesn't like to be reminded, and then, as the next selection comes up on K-FMO, "Oh, listen. It's your song."

It so is *not* her song. It's a bad novelty record called "Kinky Boots" about how everybody's wearing, you know, kinky boots. The only boots Bethany owns are a pair of Doc Martens but it wasn't footwear that had made the boys declare it her song. Couple of months earlier, Gay Michael, bored on a customerless afternoon, had treated her to an appraising look as she was leaning on the counter reading.

"Look at you," he'd said. "With your jean jacket and your ironic T-shirts." The one she'd been wearing that day had read *Talk Nerdy to Me*. "With your Aimee Bender paperbacks and your rah-rah skirts and leggings. You know what you are, Bethany? You're a frumpy little beat girl."

Fat Michael had clapped his hands in delight. Sometimes Bethany wondered which of the partners was actually the gay one. "*Sweet girls, Street girls, Frumpy little beat girls*," he'd recited, just in case Bethany had missed the reference to the stupid song's lyrics. She couldn't be mad at either of them—it was all so obviously coming from a place of affection—but, you know, Jesus Christ. Frumpy little beat girl.

She takes a sip of her coffee. "Not my song," she reminds Fat Michael, even though she knows it's like trying to lose a high school nickname.

Gay Michael pulls the annex curtain aside. "I have to drive it over at lunchtime," he says, meaning the Milton.

"She won't come here?" says Fat Michael.

"What, and leave the 'two-one-oh?" Gay Michael says. "She'd melt like Margaret Hamilton." He raises a pre-emptive hand before Fat Michael can object further. "I am not risking losing this sale, Michael," he says. "It's two months' rent."

"It's just that I have that, you know, that thing," says Fat Michael.

"I'll mind the store," Bethany says. She knows that "that thing" means a lunch date with a woman from whatever dating service he's currently using. She also knows it won't work out, they never do, but Fat Michael is a trier and Bethany sort of loves him for it.

She's never been left alone in charge of the store because the Michaels always stagger their lunch-hours, so her offer to tend it for a couple of hours without adult supervision prompts, big surprise, a discussion. But they do their best not to make a drama out of it—which Bethany appreciates 'cause God knows it's an effort for both of them—and it boils down to her receiving several over-cautious instructions, all of which pretty much translate as *don't do anything stupid*. After she promises that she'll do her best not to, they take her up on it and Gay Michael's gone by 11:45 to beat traffic and Fat Michael's out of there by noon.

Which is how Bethany comes to be alone when the man in the Chinese laundry initiates the Apocalypse.

Bethany's lost in her Kelly Link collection when the old-school bell tinkles on the entrance door. She looks up to see the door swinging shut behind a new customer as he walks in, holding a hardcover book in one gloved hand.

Huh, Bethany thinks. Gloves.

They're tight-fitting gray leather and, given that it's spring in California, would look even odder than they do were it not that the man's pretty overdressed anyway. His suit is a three-piece and its vest sports a chain that dangles in a generous curve from a button and leads, Bethany presumes, to a pocket-watch that is currently, well, pocketed.

He's not in *costume* exactly, Bethany realizes—the suit is of modern cut and fit—but he's hardly inconspicuous. She flashes on the elderly Hispanic guy she and Mr. Slater had seen at the light earlier and wonders if she somehow missed the memo about this being Sharp-Dressed-Man Day in Glendale. ZZ Top start riffing in her head but the accompanying mind-video is a spontaneous mash-up with Robert Palmer and his fuck-me mascarenes and Bethany makes a note to self that she needs to start spending a little less time watching *I Love the 80s.*

"I wonder if you can help me?" the customer says, coming to the counter. Cute accent. Like the guy from *House* when he's not being the guy from *House.*

"Almost certainly not," she says. "But I'll be real nice about it."

"Ah," he says, not put out at all. Far from. "I take it, then, that you are neither Michael nor, indeed, Michael?" Now he's doing the other Hugh—Grant, not Laurie—and Bethany thinks he's laying it on a bit thick but decides to gives him the benefit of the doubt.

"Just Bethany," she says.

"Exactly who I was looking for," he says, laying the book he's carrying onto the counter. "I wanted to ask you about this."

There's no such thing as a book you never see again, Fat Michael had told her, a little booksellers' secret, shortly after she started working here. *Sooner or later, no matter how rare it is, another copy comes across the counter.* He'd been trying to make her feel better because she'd fallen in love with a UK first of Kenneth Grahame's *The Golden Age* and had been heartbroken when it left the store with somebody who could afford it. He'd been right, too; in her time with the Michaels, Bethany had seen many a mourned book wander back to their inventory, including the Grahame; one of the store's free-lance scouts had scored another copy at an estate sale just a few weeks ago.

And now here comes this customer with another book, another blast from Bethany's past, from long before she worked here, but just as she remembers it; rich green cloth boards with a stylized Nouveau orchid on the front panel, its petals cupping the blood-red letters of the title.

"You do recognize it, don't you?" the man says.

"Sure," Bethany says, because she does. "*The Memory Pool.* 1917. First and only edition."

When she looks up from the book she sees that the customer is staring at her with an expression that she finds confusing, one of well-intentioned but distant sympathy, the kind of expression you might give to a recently bereaved stranger. He touches the book's front panel lightly and briefly. "Mmm," he says. "And quite rare, wouldn't you say?"

"Extremely rare," Bethany says, and immediately wants to slap her stupid mouth. *Curse me for a novice*, she thinks, a mantra of Gay Michael's whenever he's made a rare misstep in a negotiation. She's only been at the store a year, really is a novice still, but tipping a customer off that they've got something of real value *is* like entry-level dumb.

"Oh, don't worry. I'm not actually looking to sell it," he says, as if reading her dismay. "Just wanted to see if you knew it."

"Huh," says Bethany because, you know, Huh.

The customer looks at her again, cocking his head as if intrigued. He extends his gloved hand across the counter. "James Arcadia," he says, as Bethany shakes it. "I think, Just Bethany, we'd best have lunch."

"Why?" she asks, and she's smiling. Not too much, though; he's cute and all but, c'mon, he has to be forty at least. Still, she's flattered. Feels like she should conference-text the Michaels. *Not so frumpy.*

Arcadia returns the smile and she's glad that his eyes are kind because it softens the blow of his reply. "We need to discuss exactly how we're going to save the world," he says.

Well, Bethany thinks, that *was dramatic*, and, as if on cue, a woman screams from somewhere beyond the store. By the time a man's voice, equally horrified, hollers *My God, look at that!* Bethany and Arcadia have already turned to look through the window.

On the street outside, a man is melting.

He'd presumably been walking, but he's not walking anymore. He's rooted to the sidewalk, his legs already a fused and formless mass, his flesh and his clothes running in multicolored ripples of dissolution down what used to be his body as if he was some life-size religious candle burning in fast-forward.

Other people on Brand Boulevard are screaming now, some running away, some gathering to see, one idiot on his cell-phone like he could actually fetch help, another using hers to snap a little souvenir of the atrocity. A group forms around the vanishing man, circling him but not going near, as if instinctively establishing a perimeter from which to bear witness but to keep themselves safe.

From what's left of the man's face—now liquidly elongated into a vile burlesque that puts Bethany briefly and horribly in mind of Munch's screamer—he appears to be, have been, a middle-aged white guy. *He has a life*, Bethany thinks, *he has a story, has people who love him*. But he's featureless in little more than a second. One of his arms has already disappeared into the oozing chaos of the meltdown but the other is waving grotesquely free, fingers twitching either in agony or, as Bethany wonders with a devastating stab of pity, as if he just wants someone to hold his hand in farewell as he slides helplessly from life.

When there's finally nothing about it to suggest it had ever been human, the roiling mass begins to shrink in on itself, disappearing into a vanishing center as if hungry for its own destruction, growing smaller and smaller until, at last, it shivers itself into nothingness. There's not even a stain on the sidewalk. It's taken maybe seven seconds.

"Oh my God," says Bethany.

Arcadia is keeping his eyes on the window. "Watch what happens next," he says. And when Bethany does, she decides that it's even more appalling than what came before.

Everybody walks away.

There's a blink or two from one or more of them, and one older woman in a blue pantsuit looks to her left as if she thought her peripheral vision may have just registered something, but there's no screaming, no outrage, no appeals to heaven or cries of *what-just-happened*? Everybody on the street quietly moves on about their day, neither their manner nor their expressions suggesting that anything out of the ordinary had occurred.

"What's *wrong* with them?" says Bethany. "They're all acting like it never happened."

"Don't be cross with them," Arcadia tells her. "It sort of *didn't* happen."

"But it did."

"I don't want to get too abstract about it," he says, "but it's a sort of tree falling in the forest question, isn't it? Can something actually be said to have happened if it's something nobody in the world remembers?"

"*I* remember," Bethany says.

Arcadia holds her gaze for a second or two, his face expressionless. "A-ha," he says quietly.

Bethany's still trying to think about that when he pulls his watch from his vest pocket and checks it. "Hmm," he says. "Only eleven minutes in and already a serious anomaly. That's a bit worrying."

"What?" says Bethany, horrified as much at his calmness as at the idea that this nightmare is on some kind of a schedule.

"Clock's a-ticking," he says. "Lunch will have to wait. Come on."

Bethany's surprised to see that she's following him as he moves to the door and opens it. Perhaps it's the tinkling of the bell, perhaps just a desire to remember what she was doing the last time the world made sense, but something makes her look back at the counter.

"Wait," she says. "What about your book?"

Arcadia throws it an unconcerned glance. "Do you know what a MacGuffin is, Bethany?" he says.

"Yes," she says, because she does. She watches her fair share of Turner Classic Movies and she briefly dated a guy who once had an actual name but whom she's long decided will be known to her memoirs only as The Boy Who Loved Hitchcock.

"Well, the book's a MacGuffin," Arcadia says. "It's not *irrelevant*—I mean, it never existed and yet you remember it, which is good for a gasp or two and certainly pertains to the matter at hand—but its real function is this: To propel us headlong into a thrilling and probably life-threatening adventure. You good to go?"

He waves her through the door with a hurrying motion and they're on the street and walking south before Bethany can get her question out.

"What do you mean, 'it never existed'?" she says.

"Well, not in this particular strand of the multiverse. It's a crossover, like the unfortunate gentleman outside your shop. Do you have a car, by the way?"

"No," she says. "I mean, not here."

"Oh," he says, stopping in front of a green Mercedes. "Let's take this one, then." He opens the passenger door for her, apparently without needing a key. Bethany doesn't ask. Nor does she look too closely at how he starts it up before making an illegal U-turn and heading down Brand towards Atwater Village.

"What are we *doing*?" she asks, because she figures it's about time.

"Well, we're fixing a hole—"

"Where the rain gets in?" she says, flashing absurdly on the Beatles vinyl she'd rescued from her dad's stuff.

"Would that it were merely rain," he says. He nods toward the sidewalk they're speeding past, and Bethany looks to see a small boy turning to green smoke while pedestrians stare open-mouthed and his screaming mother tries to grab him, her desperate fingers clawing only at his absence. By the time Bethany has swung in her seat to look out the rear window, the smoke has vanished and the crowd, including the mother, has forgotten it was ever there.

Bethany's eyes are wet with pity as she turns back to Arcadia. "Tell me what's happening!" she almost shouts.

Arcadia swings the car into the right lane as they pass under the railroad bridge. "I'll try to make this as quick as I can," he says, and takes a preparatory breath. "The spaces between the worlds have been breached. Realities are bleeding through to each other. People who took one step in their own dimension took their next in another. What you've witnessed is the multiverse trying to correct itself by erasing the anomalies. Problem is it's happening in each reality and the incidents will increase exponentially until there's nothing left in any of them." He turns to look at her. "With me so far?"

Bethany unfortunately *is* with him so far, though she wishes she'd heeded those schoolyard theories that comic books weren't really for girls. "Collapse of the space-time continuum," she says in a surprisingly steady voice.

"Precisely," says Arcadia, pleased that this is going so well. "A return to a timeless shining singularity without form, thought, or feeling."

"But how?" she says. "And why?"

Arcadia has started to slow the car down now, scanning the storefronts of Atwater Village's main drag. "Because about seventeen minutes ago, something that's lived all its life as a man remembered what it really is and spoke certain words of power."

Bethany doesn't like the sound of that at all and, as Arcadia pulls up outside one of the few remaining un-gentrified stores on a strip that is mostly hipper new businesses and milk-it-quick franchises, she stays silent, feeling the sadness and fear tightening in her stomach like cancer, thinking of people vanishing from the world like a billion lights blinking out one by one.

"Is this where we're going?" she finally says, nodding at the store as they get out of the car.

"Yes," Arcadia says. "Have you seen it before?"

Bethany nods, because she has. It could have been here since 1933, she's always thought; peeling red paint on aged wood; plate-glass window whitewashed from the inside to keep its secrets; and a single hanging sign with the hand-painted phrase, *Chinese Laundry.* She doesn't think she's ever seen it open for business. "I always figured it was a front for the Tongs," she says as if she was kidding, but realizes as she says it that that actually is what she's always thought.

"You're such a romantic," Arcadia says, and he sounds delighted with her. He opens the door to the laundry and leads her inside.

Its interior is as weathered and as free of decoration as the outside. A hardwood floor that hasn't seen varnish for decades and utterly plain walls painted long ago in the kind of institutionally vile colors usually reserved for state hospitals in the poorest neighborhoods. Bethany is surprised, though, to smell the heavy detergent and feel the clammy humidity of what is clearly a working laundry. There's even the slow hissing, from behind the screen space-divider, of a heavy-duty steam press. The place isn't menacing, merely nondescript. The fifty-year-old man behind the bare wood counter would be nondescript too, were it not for the subtle phosphorescent glow of his flesh.

Arcadia makes the introductions. "Bethany Lake," he says—and Bethany registers the use of the surname she hadn't told him—"meet the entity formerly known as Jerry Harrington."

Bethany gasps a little as the man fixes his eyes on her because they are the almost solid black of a tweaker on an overdose about to kill him.

Not Chinese at all, a part of her brain wastes its time thinking, and wonders if it's entirely PC of him not to have changed the name, however generic, of the business he bought.

"What do you want?" Harrington says. His tone is hardly gracious, but at least it still sounds human, for which Bethany is grateful.

"What *do* we want?" she says to Arcadia.

"Well, I want him to stop destroying reality," Arcadia says. "Don't you?"

"Yes," Bethany says. "Of course."

Arcadia turns back to Harrington. "There you go," he says. "Two votes to one. Majority rules. What do you say?"

Harrington laughs, but there's little humor in it.

"What *is* he?" Bethany asks Arcadia quietly. She's turned her head away from Harrington because his face seems to be constantly coming in and out of focus in a way that she finds not just frightening but physically disturbing.

"A being from a time outside time," Arcadia says. "There's several of them around, hidden in the flesh since the Fall. Most of them don't remember themselves, but occasionally there's a problem."

The Fall? Bethany hesitates to ask, because she doesn't want to say something that sounds so ridiculous but she supposes she has to. "Are you talking about angels?" she says. "Fallen Angels?"

"Well, you needn't be so Judeo-Christian specific about it," he says, a little sniffily. "But, yes."

"What do you want?" Harrington says again, exactly as he'd said it before. So exactly that it creeps Bethany out. Less like a person repeating themselves and more like someone just rewound the tape.

"We're here to make you reconsider," Arcadia says. "We can do it the hard way, if you want, but I'd prefer to talk you out of it."

Again, the laugh. But there's little human in it.

Arcadia moves closer to the counter, which Bethany finds almost indescribably brave. "Look, I get it," he says. "You're homesick. You want a return to the *tabula rasa*, the blank page, the white light, the glorious absence. You yearn for it like a sailor for the sea or a child for its mother. You're disgusted by all this . . . this . . . " he waves his hands, searching for the words ". . . . all this multiplicity, this variousness, this detail and color and noise and *stuff*."

"You talk too much," Harrington says, and Bethany, though shocked at her treachery, thinks he's got a point.

"But isn't there another way to look at it?" Arcadia says. "We're all going back to the white light eventually, so what does it matter? Couldn't we imagine looking at these people amongst whom your kind has fallen not with contempt but with delight? Isn't it possible that an angel could embrace the flesh rather than loathe it? Could choose to be humanity's protector rather than its scourge?"

"You can imagine whatever you like if it makes you feel better," Harrington says, and his voice is confident and contemptuous. "But you won't imagine it for very long. Because that's not the path I've chosen."

Arcadia smiles, like there's been some misunderstanding. "Oh, I wasn't talking about you," he says.

Bethany is wondering just who the hell he *is* talking about when the pores of her flesh erupt and the light starts to stream from her body. The rush of release almost drowns out the beating of her terrible wings and the sweet music of Harrington's scream.

Arcadia picks up the small pitted cinder-like object from the laundry counter with a pair of tweezers. It's still smoking slightly and he blows on it to cool it before dropping it into a thin test tube which he slips back into an inside pocket of his suit.

"I'll put it with the others," he says to Bethany. She wonders where the *if that's all right with you* tone has come from, like he's her Beautiful Assistant rather than vice-versa, but she nods anyway. She and he are the only people in the place and she's sort of grateful that she has no memory of the last few minutes. She feels quite tired and is glad of Arcadia's arm when he walks her to the car.

Bethany's relieved that she's back in the store before either of the Michaels. As ever, there are several out-of-shelf books lying around here and there and she decides to do a little housekeeping to assuage her guilt for playing hooky. She shelves most of them in the regular stacks, some in the high-end display cases, and one in the spaces between the worlds, though she doesn't really notice that because she's thinking about her crappy Dodge and how much the shop is going to charge her to fix it this time.

Gay Michael gets back first. Maybe Fat Michael's date is going better than expected. Bethany hopes so.

"Anything happen?" Gay Michael says.

"Not so you'd notice," Bethany tells him.

This quiet story is stark and true and all the more horrific for it: "Ants and man make war 'cause they can. . . . Man ain't happy till he kills everything in his path and cuts down everything that grows. He sees something wild and beautiful and wants to hold it down and stab it, punish it 'cause it's wild. Beauty draws him to it, and then he kills it."

THE STARS ARE FALLING

JOE R. LANSDALE

Before Deel Arrowsmith came back from the dead, he was crossing a field by late moonlight in search of his home. His surroundings were familiar, but at the same time different. It was as if he had left as a child and returned as an adult to examine old property only to find the tree swing gone, the apple tree cut down, the grass grown high, and an outhouse erected over the mound where his best dog was buried.

As he crossed, the dropping moon turned thin, like cheap candy licked too long, and the sun bled through the trees. There were spots of frost on the drooping green grass and on the taller weeds, yellow as ripe corn. In his mind's eye he saw not the East Texas field before him or the dark rows of oaks and pines beyond it, or even the clay path that twisted across the field toward the trees like a ribbon of blood.

He saw a field in France where there was a long, deep trench, and in the trench were bloodied bodies, some of them missing limbs and with bits of brains scattered about like spilled oatmeal. The air filled with the stinging stench of rotting meat and wafting gun smoke, the residue of poison gas, and the buzz of flies. The back of his throat tasted of burning copper. His stomach was a knot. The trees were like the shadowy shades of soldiers charging toward him, and for a moment, he thought to meet their charge, even though he no longer carried a gun.

He closed his eyes, breathed deeply, shook his head. When he opened them the stench had passed and his nostrils filled with the nip of early morning. The last of the moon faded like a melting snowflake. Puffy white clouds sailed along the heavens and light tripped across the tops of the trees, fell between them, made shadows run low along the trunks and across the ground. The sky turned light blue and the frost dried off the drooping grass and it sprang to attention. Birds began to sing. Grasshoppers began to jump.

He continued down the path that crossed the field and split the trees. As he went, he tried to remember exactly where his house was and how it looked and how it smelled, and most important, how he felt when he was inside it. He tried to remember his wife and how she looked and how he felt when he was inside her, and all he could find in the back of his mind was a cipher of a woman younger than he was in a long, colorless dress in a house with three rooms. He couldn't even remember her nakedness, the shape of her breasts and the length of her legs. It was as if they had met only once, and in passing.

When he came through the trees and out on the other side, the field was there as it should be, and it was full of bright blue and yellow flowers. Once it had been filled with tall corn and green bursts of beans and peas. It hadn't been plowed now in years, most likely since he left. He followed the trail and trudged toward his house. It stood where he had left it. It had not improved with age. The chimney was black at the top and the unpainted lumber was stripping like shedding snakeskin. He had cut the trees and split them and made the lumber for the house, and like everything else he had seen since he had returned, it was smaller than he remembered. Behind it was the smokehouse he had made of logs, and far out to the left was the outhouse he had built. He had read many a magazine there while having his morning constitutional.

Out front, near the well, which had been built up with stones and now had a roof over it supported on four stout poles, was a young boy. He knew immediately it was his son. The boy was probably eight. He had been four years old when Deel had left to fight in the Great War, sailed across the vast dark ocean. The boy had a bucket in his hand, held by the handle. He set it down and raced toward the house, yelling something Deel couldn't define.

A moment later she came out of the house and his memory filled up. He kept walking, and the closer he came to her, standing framed in the doorway, the tighter his heart felt. She was blond and tall and lean and dressed in a light-colored dress on which were printed flowers much duller than those in the field. But her face was brighter than the sun, and he knew now how she looked naked and in bed, and all that had been lost came back to him, and he knew he was home again.

When he was ten feet away the boy, frightened, grabbed his mother and held her, and she said, "Deel, is that you?"

He stopped and stood, and said nothing. He just looked at her, drinking her in like a cool beer. Finally he said, "Worn and tired, but me."

"I thought . . . "

"I didn't write cause I can't."

"I know . . . but . . . "

"I'm back, Mary Lou."

They sat stiffly at the kitchen table. Deel had a plate in front of him and he had eaten the beans that had been on it. The front door was open and they could see out and past the well and into the flower-covered field. The window across the way was open too, and there was a light breeze ruffling the edges of the pulled-back curtains framing it. Deel had the sensation he'd had before when crossing the field and passing through the trees, and when he had first seen the outside of the house. And now, inside, the roof felt too low and the room was too small and the walls were too close. It was all too small.

But there was Mary Lou. She sat across the table from him. Her face was clean of lines and her shoulders were as narrow as the boy's. Her eyes were bright, like the blue flowers in the field.

The boy, Winston, was to his left, but he had pulled his chair close to his mother. The boy studied him carefully, and in turn, Deel studied the boy. Deel could see Mary Lou in him, and nothing of himself.

"Have I changed that much?" Deel said, in response to the way they were looking at him. Both of them had their hands in their laps, as if he might leap across the table at any moment and bite them.

"You're very thin," Mary Lou said.

"I was too heavy when I left. I'm too skinny now. Soon I hope to be just right." He tried to smile, but the smile dripped off. He took a deep breath. "So, how you been?"

"Been?"

"Yeah. You know. How you been?"

"Oh. Fine," she said. "Good. I been good."

"The boy?"

"He's fine."

"Does he talk?"

"Sure he talks. Say hello to your daddy, Winston."

The boy didn't speak.

"Say hello," his mother said.

The boy didn't respond.

"That's all right," Deel said. "It's been a while. He doesn't remember me. It's only natural."

"You joined up through Canada?"

"Like I said I would."

"I couldn't be sure," she said.

"I know. I got in with the Americans, a year or so back. It didn't matter who I was with. It was bad."

"I see," she said, but Deel could tell she didn't see at all. And he didn't blame her. He had been caught up in the enthusiasm of war and adventure, gone up to Canada and got in on it, left his family in the lurch, thinking life was passing him by and he was missing out. Life had been right here and he hadn't even recognized it.

Mary Lou stood up and shuffled around the table and heaped fresh beans onto his plate and went to the oven and brought back cornbread and put it next to the beans. He watched her every move. Her hair was a little sweaty on her forehead and it clung there, like wet hay.

"How old are you now?" he asked her. "How old?" she said, returning to her spot at the table. "Deel, you know how old I am. I'm twenty-eight, older than when you left."

"I'm ashamed to say it, but I've forgotten your birthday. I've forgotten his. I don't hardly know how old I am."

She told him the dates of their births.

"I'll be," he said. "I don't remember any of that."

"I . . . I thought you were dead."

She had said it several times since he had come home. He said, "I'm still not dead, Mary Lou. I'm in the flesh."

"You are. You certainly are."

She didn't eat what was on her plate. She just sat there looking at it, as if it might transform.

Deel said, "Who fixed the well, built the roof over it?"

"Tom Smites," she said.

"Tom? He's a kid."

"Not anymore," she said. "He was eighteen when you left. He wasn't any kid then, not really."

"I reckon not," Deel said.

After dinner, she gave him his pipe the way she used to, and he found a cane rocker that he didn't remember being there before, took it outside and sat and looked toward the trees and smoked his pipe and rocked.

He was thinking of then and he was thinking of now and he was thinking of later, when it would be nighttime and he would go to bed, and he wasn't certain how to approach the matter. She was his wife, but he hadn't been with her for years, and now he was home, and he wanted it to be like before, but he didn't really remember how it was before. He knew how to do what he wanted to do, but he didn't know how to make it love. He feared she would feel that he was like a mangy cat that had come in through the window to lie there and expected petting.

He sat and smoked and thought and rocked.

The boy came out of the house and stood to the side and watched him.

The boy had the gold hair of his mother and he was built sturdy for a boy so young. He had a bit of a birthmark in front of his right ear, on the jawline, like a little strawberry. Deel didn't remember that. The boy had been a baby, of course, but he didn't remember that at all. Then again, he couldn't remember a lot of things, except for the things he didn't want to remember. Those things he remembered. And Mary Lou's skin. That he remembered. How soft it was to the touch, like butter.

"Do you remember me, boy?" Deel asked.

"No."

"Not at all?"

"No."

"'Course not. You were very young. Has your mother told you about me?"

"Not really."

"Nothing."

"She said you got killed in the war."

"I see . . . Well, I didn't."

Deel turned and looked back through the open door. He could see Mary Lou at the washbasin pouring water into the wash pan, water she had heated on the stove. It steamed as she poured. He thought then he should have brought wood for her to make the fire. He should have helped make the fire and heat the water. But being close to her made him nervous. The boy made him nervous.

"You going to school?" he asked the boy.

"School burned down. Tom teaches me some readin' and writin' and cipherin'. He went eight years to school."

"You ever go fishin'?"

"Just with Tom. He takes me fishin' and huntin' now and then."

"He ever show you how to make a bow and arrow?"

"No."

"No, sir," Deel said. "You say, no, sir."

"What's that?"

"Say yes, sir or no, sir. Not yes and no. It's rude."

The boy dipped his head and moved a foot along the ground, piling up dirt.

"I ain't gettin' on you none," Deel said. "I'm just tellin' you that's how it's done. That's how I do if it's someone older than me. I say no, sir and yes, sir. Understand, son?"

The boy nodded.

"And what do you say?"

"Yes, sir."

"Good. Manners are important. You got to have manners. A boy can't go through life without manners. You can read and write some, and you got to cipher to protect your money. But you got to have manners too."

"Yes, sir."

"There you go . . . About that bow and arrow. He never taught you that, huh?"

"No, sir."

"Well, that will be our plan. I'll show you how to do it. An old Cherokee taught me how. It ain't as easy as it might sound, not to make a good one. And then to be good enough to hit somethin' with it, that's a whole nuther story."

"Why would you do all that when you got a gun?"

"I guess you wouldn't need to. It's just fun, and huntin' with one is real sportin', compared to a gun. And right now, I ain't all that fond of guns."

"I like guns."

"Nothin' wrong with that. But a gun don't like you, and it don't love you back. Never give too much attention or affection to somethin' that can't return it."

"Yes, sir."

The boy, of course, had no idea what he was talking about. Deel was uncertain he knew himself what he was talking about. He turned and looked back through the door. Mary Lou was at the pan, washing the dishes; when she scrubbed, her ass shook a little, and in that moment, Deel felt, for the first time, like a man alive.

That night the bed seemed small. He lay on his back with his hands crossed across his lower stomach, wearing his faded red union suit, which had been ragged when he left, and had in his absence been attacked by moths. It was ready to come apart. The window next to the bed was open and the breeze that came through was cool. Mary Lou lay beside him. She wore a long white nightgown that had been patched with a variety of colored cloth patches. Her hair was undone and it was long. It had been long when he left. He wondered how often she had cut it, and how much time it had taken each time to grow back.

"I reckon it's been a while," he said.

"That's all right," she said.

"I'm not sayin' I can't, or I won't, just sayin' I don't know I'm ready."

"It's okay."

"You been lonely?"

"I have Winston."

"He's grown a lot. He must be company."

"He is."

"He looks some like you."

"Some."

Deel stretched out his hand without looking at her and laid it across her stomach. "You're still like a girl," he said. "Had a child, and you're still like a girl . . . you know why I asked how old you was?"

" 'Cause you didn't remember."

"Well, yeah, there was that. But on account of you don't look none different at all."

"I got a mirror. It ain't much of one, but it don't make me look younger."

"You look just the same."

"Right now, any woman might look good to you." After she said it, she caught herself. "I didn't mean it that way. I just meant you been gone a long time . . . in Europe, they got pretty women, I hear."

"Some are, some ain't. Ain't none of them pretty as you."

"You ever . . . you know?"

"What?"

"You know . . . While you was over there."

"Oh . . . reckon I did. Couple of times. I didn't know for sure I was comin' home. There wasn't nothin' to it. I didn't mean nothin' by it. It was like filling a hungry belly, nothin' more."

She was quiet for a long time. Then she said, "It's okay."

He thought to ask her a similar question, but couldn't. He eased over to her. She remained still. She was as stiff as a corpse. He knew. He had been forced at times to lie down among them. Once, moving through a town in France with his fellow soldiers, he had come upon a woman lying dead between two trees. There wasn't a wound on her. She was young. Dark haired. She looked as if she had lain down for a nap. He reached down and touched her. She was still warm.

One of his comrades, a soldier, had suggested they all take turns mounting her before she got cold. It was a joke, but Deel had pointed his rifle at him and run him off. Later, in the trenches he had been side by side with the same man, a fellow from Wisconsin, who like him had joined the Great War by means of Canada. They had made their peace, and the Wisconsin fellow told him it was a poor joke he'd made, and not to hold it against him, and Deel said it was all right, and then they took positions next to each other and talked a bit about home and waited for the war to come. During the battle, wearing gas masks and firing rifles, the fellow from Wisconsin had caught a round and it had knocked him down. A moment later the battle had ceased, at least for the moment.

Deel bent over him, lifted his mask, and then the man's head. The man said, "My mama won't never see me again."

"You're gonna be okay," Deel said, but saw that half the man's head was missing. How in hell was he talking? Why wasn't he dead? His brain was leaking out.

"I got a letter inside my shirt. Tell Mama I love her . . . oh, my god, look there. The stars are falling."

Deel, responding to the distant gaze of his downed companion, turned and looked up. The stars were bright and stuck in place. There was an explosion of cannon fire and the ground shook and the sky lit up bright red; the redness clung to the air like a veil. When Deel looked back at the fellow, the man's eyes were still open, but he was gone.

Deel reached inside the man's jacket and found the letter. He realized then that the man had also taken a round in the chest, because the letter was dark with blood. Deel tried to unfold it, but it was so damp with gore it fell apart. There was nothing to deliver to anyone. Deel couldn't even remember the man's name. It had gone in one ear and out the other. And now he was gone, his last words being, "The stars are falling."

While he was holding the boy's head, an officer came walking down the trench holding a pistol. His face was darkened with gunpowder and his eyes were bright in the night and he looked at Deel, said, "There's got to be some purpose to all of it, son. Some purpose," and then he walked on down the line.

Deel thought of that night and that death, and then he thought of the dead woman again. He wondered what had happened to her body. They had had to leave her there, between the two trees. Had someone buried her? Had she rotted there? Had the ants and the elements taken her away? He had dreams of lying down beside her, there in the field. Just lying there, drifting away with her into the void.

Deel felt now as if he were lying beside that dead woman, blond instead of dark haired, but no more alive than the woman between the trees.

"Maybe we ought to just sleep tonight," Mary Lou said, startling him. "We can let things take their course. It ain't nothin' to make nothin' out of."

He moved his hand away from her. He said, "That'll be all right. Of course." She rolled on her side, away from him. He lay on top of the covers with his hands against his lower belly and looked at the log rafters.

A couple of days and nights went by without her warming to him, but he found sleeping with her to be the best part of his life. He liked her sweet smell and he liked to listen to her breathe. When she was deep asleep, he would turn slightly, and carefully, and rise up on one elbow and look at her shape in the dark. His homecoming had not been what he had hoped for or expected, but in those moments when he looked at her in the dark, he was certain it was better than what had gone before for nearly four horrible years.

The next few days led to him taking the boy into the woods and finding the right wood for a bow. He chopped down a bois d'arc tree and showed the boy how to trim it with an axe, how to cut the wood out of it for a bow, how to cure it with a fire that was mostly smoke. They spent a long time at it, but if the boy enjoyed what he was learning, he never let on. He kept his feelings close to the heart and talked less than his mother. The boy always seemed some yards away, even when standing right next to him.

Deel built the bow for the boy and strung it with strong cord and showed him how to find the right wood for arrows and how to collect feathers from a bird's nest and how to feather the shafts. It took almost a week to make the bow, and another week to dry it and to make the arrows. The rest of the time Deel looked out at what had once been a plowed field and was now twenty-five acres of flowers with a few little trees beginning to grow, twisting up among the flowers. He tried to imagine the field covered in corn.

Deel used an axe to clear the new trees, and that afternoon, at the dinner table, he asked Mary Lou what had happened to the mule.

"Died," Mary Lou said. "She was old when you left, and she just got older. We ate it when it died."

"Waste not, want not," Deel said.

"Way we saw it," she said.

"You ain't been farmin'. How'd you make it?"

"Tom brought us some goods now and then, fish he caught, vegetables from his place. A squirrel or two. We raised a hog and smoked the meat, had our own garden."

"How are Tom's parents?"

"His father drank himself to death and his mother just up and died."

Deel nodded. "She was always sickly, and her husband was a lot older than her . . . I'm older than you. But not by that much. He was what? Fifteen years? I'm . . . Well, let me see. I'm ten."

She didn't respond. He had hoped for some kind of confirmation that his ten-year gap was nothing, that it was okay. But she said nothing.

"I'm glad Tom was around," Deel said.

"He was a help," she said.

After a while, Deel said, "Things are gonna change. You ain't got to take no one's charity no more. Tomorrow, I'm gonna go into town, see I can buy some seed, and find a mule. I got some muster-out pay. It ain't much, but it's enough to get us started. Winston here goes in with me, we might see we can get him some candy of some sort."

"I like peppermint," the boy said.

"There you go," Deel said.

"You ought not do that so soon back," Mary Lou said. "There's still time before the fall plantin'. You should hunt like you used to, or fish for a few days . . . you could take Winston here with you. You deserve time off."

"Guess another couple of days ain't gonna hurt nothin'. We could all use some time gettin' reacquainted."

Next afternoon when Deel came back from the creek with Winston, they had a couple of fish on a wet cord, and Winston carried them slung over his back so that they dangled down like ornaments and made his shirt damp. They were small but good perch and the boy had caught them, and in the process, shown the first real excitement Deel had seen from him. the sunlight played over their scales as they bounced against Winston's back. Deel, walking slightly behind Winston, watched the fish carefully. He watched them slowly dying, out of the water, gasping for air. He couldn't help but want to take them back to the creek and let them go. He had seen injured men gasp like that, on the field, in the trenches. They had seemed like fish that only needed to be put in water.

As they neared the house, Deel saw a rider coming their way, and he saw Mary Lou walking out from the house to meet him.

Mary Lou went up to the man and the man leaned out of the saddle, and they spoke, and then Mary Lou took hold of the saddle with one hand and walked with the horse toward the house. When she saw Deel and Winston coming, she let go of the saddle and walked beside the horse. The man on the horse was tall and lean with black hair that hung down to his shoulders. It was like a waterfall of ink tumbling out from under his slouched, gray hat.

As they came closer together, the man on the horse raised his hand in greeting. At that moment the boy yelled out, "Tom!" and darted across the field toward the horse, the fish flapping.

They sat at the kitchen table. Deel and Mary Lou and Winston and Tom Smites. Tom's mother had been half Chickasaw, and he seemed to have gathered up all her coloring, along with his Swedish father's great height and broad build. He looked like some kind of forest god. His hair hung over the sides of his face, and his skin was walnut colored and smooth and he had balanced features and big hands and feet. He had his hat on his knee.

The boy sat very close to Tom. Mary Lou sat at the table, her hands out in front of her, resting on the planks. She had her head turned toward Tom.

Deel said, "I got to thank you for helpin' my family out."

"Ain't nothin' to thank. You used to take me huntin' and fishin' all the time. My daddy didn't do that sort of thing. He was a farmer and a hog raiser and a drunk. You done good by me."

"Thanks again for helpin'."

"I wanted to help out. Didn't have no trouble doin' it."

"You got a family of your own now, I reckon."

"Not yet. I break horses and run me a few cows and hogs and chickens, grow me a pretty good-size garden, but I ain't growin' a family. Not yet. I hear from Mary Lou you need a plow mule and some seed."

Deel looked at her. She had told him all that in the short time she had walked beside his horse. He wasn't sure how he felt about that. He wasn't sure he wanted anyone to know what he needed or didn't need.

"Yeah. I want to buy a mule and some seed."

"Well, now. I got a horse that's broke to plow. He ain't as good as a mule, but I could let him go cheap, real cheap. And I got more seed than I know what to do with. It would save you a trip into town."

"I sort of thought I might like to go to town," Deel said.

"Yeah, well, sure. But I can get those things for you."

"I wanted to take Winston here to the store and get him some candy."

Tom grinned. "Now, that is a good idea, but so happens, I was in town this mornin', and—"

Tom produced a brown paper from his shirt pocket and laid it out on the table and carefully pulled the paper loose, revealing two short pieces of peppermint.

Winston looked at Tom. "Is that for me?"

"It is."

"You just take one now, Winston, and have it after dinner," Mary Lou said. "You save that other piece for tomorrow. It'll give you somethin' to look forward to."

"That was mighty nice of you, Tom," Deel said.

"You should stay for lunch," Mary Lou said. "Deel and Winston caught a couple of fish, and I got some potatoes. I can fry them up."

"Why that's a nice offer," Tom said. "And on account of it, I'll clean the fish."

The next few days passed with Tom coming out to bring the horse and the seed, and coming back the next day with some plow parts Deel needed. Deel began to think he would never get to town, and now he wasn't so sure he wanted to go. Tom was far more comfortable with his family than he was and he was jealous of that and wanted to stay with them and find his place. Tom and Mary Lou talked about all manner of things, and quite comfortably, and the boy had lost all interest in the bow. In fact, Deel had found it and the arrows out under a tree near where the woods firmed up. He took it and put it in the smokehouse. The air was dry in there and it would cure better, though he was uncertain the boy would ever have anything to do with it.

Deel plowed a half-dozen acres of the flowers under, and the next day Tom came out with a wagonload of cured chicken shit, and helped him shovel it across the broken ground. Deel plowed it under and Tom helped Deel plant peas and beans for the fall crop, some hills of yellow crookneck squash, and a few mounds of watermelon and cantaloupe seed.

That evening they were sitting out in front of the house, Deel in the cane rocker and Tom in a kitchen chair. The boy sat on the ground near Tom and twisted a stick in the dirt. The only light came from the open door of the house, from the lamp inside. When Deel looked over his shoulder, he saw Mary Lou at the washbasin again, doing the dishes, wiggling her ass. Tom looked in that direction once, then looked at Deel, then looked away at the sky, as if memorizing the positions of the stars.

Tom said, "You and me ain't been huntin' since well before you left."

"You came around a lot then, didn't you?" Deel said.

Tom nodded. "I always felt better here than at home. Mama and Daddy fought all the time."

"I'm sorry about your parents."

"Well," Tom said, "everyone's got a time to die, you know. It can be in all kinds of ways, but sometimes it's just time and you just got to embrace it."

"I reckon that's true."

"What say you and me go huntin'?" Tom said, "I ain't had any possum meat in ages."

"I never did like possum," Deel said. "Too greasy."

"You ain't fixed 'em right. That's one thing I can do, fix up a possum good. 'Course, best way is catch one and pen it and feed it corn for a week or so, then kill it. Meat's better that way, firmer. But I'd settle for shootin' one, showin' you how to get rid of that gamey taste with some vinegar and such, cook it up with some sweet potatoes. I got more sweet potatoes than I know what to do with."

"Deel likes sweet potatoes," Mary Lou said.

Deel turned. She stood in the doorway drying her hands on a dishtowel. She said, "That ought to be a good idea, Deel. Goin' huntin'. I wouldn't mind learnin' how to cook up a possum right. You and Tom ought to go, like the old days."

"I ain't had no sweet potatoes in years," Deel said.

"All the more reason," Tom said.

The boy said, "I want to go."

"That'd be all right," Tom said, "but you know, I think this time I'd like for just me and Deel to go. When I was a kid, he taught me about them woods, and I'd like to go with him, for old time's sake. That all right with you, Winston?"

Winston didn't act like it was all right, but he said, "I guess."

That night Deel lay beside Mary Lou and said, "I like Tom, but I was thinkin' maybe we could somehow get it so he don't come around so much."

"Oh?"

"I know Winston looks up to him, and I don't mind that, but I need to get to know Winston again . . . Hell, I didn't ever know him. And I need to get to know you . . . I owe you some time, Mary Lou, the right kind of time."

"I don't know what you're talkin' about, Deel. The right kind of time?" Deel thought for a while, tried to find the right phrasing. He knew what he felt, but saying it was a different matter. "I know you ended up with me because I seemed better than some was askin'. Turned out I wasn't quite the catch you thought. But we got to find what we need, Mary Lou."

"What we need?"

"Love. We ain't never found love."

She lay silent.

"I just think," Deel said, "we ought to have our own time together before we start havin' Tom around so much. You understand what I'm sayin', right?"

"I guess so."

"I don't even feel like I'm proper home yet. I ain't been to town or told nobody I'm back."

"Who you missin'?"

Deel thought about that for a long time. "Ain't nobody but you and Winston that I missed, but I need to get some things back to normal . . . I need to make connections so I can set up some credit at the store, maybe some farm trade for things we need next year. But mostly, I just want to be here with you so we can talk. You and Tom talk a lot. I wish we could talk like that. We need to learn how to talk."

"Tom's easy to talk to. He's a talker. He can talk about anything and make it seem like somethin', but when he's through, he ain't said nothin' . . . You never was a talker before, Deel, so why now?"

"I want to hear what you got to say, and I want you to hear what I got to say, even if we ain't talkin' about nothin' but seed catalogs or pass the beans, or I need some more firewood or stop snoring. Most anything that's got normal about it. So, thing is, I don't want Tom around so much. I want us to have some time with just you and me and Winston, that's all I'm sayin'."

Deel felt the bed move. He turned to look, and in the dark he saw that Mary Lou was pulling her gown up above her breasts. Her pubic hair looked thick in the dark and her breasts were full and round and inviting.

She said, "Maybe tonight we could get started on knowing each other better."

His mouth was dry. All he could say was, "All right."

His hands trembled as he unbuttoned his union suit at the crotch and she spread her legs and he climbed on top of her. It only took a moment before he exploded.

"Oh, God," he said, and collapsed on her, trying to support his weight on his elbows.

"How was that?" she said. "I feel all right?"

"Fine, but I got done too quick. Oh, girl, it's been so long. I'm sorry."

"That's all right. It don't mean nothin'." She patted him stiffly on the back and then twisted a little so that he'd know she wanted him off her.

"I could do better," he said.

"Tomorrow night."

"Me and Tom, we're huntin' tomorrow night. He's bringin' a dog, and we're gettin' a possum."

"That's right . . . Night after."

"All right, then," Deel said. "All right, then."

He lay back on the bed and buttoned himself up and tried to decide if he felt better or worse. There had been relief, but no fire. She might as well have been a hole in the mattress.

Tom brought a bitch dog with him and a .22 rifle and a croaker sack. Deel gathered up his double barrel from out of the closet and took it out of its leather sheath coated in oil and found it to be in very good condition. He brought it and a sling bag of shells outside. The shells were old, but he had no cause to doubt their ability. They had been stored along with the gun, dry and contained.

The sky was clear and the stars were out and the moon looked like a carved chunk of fresh lye soap, but it was bright, so bright you could see the ground clearly. The boy was in bed, and Deel and Tom and Mary Lou stood out in front of the house and looked at the night.

Mary Lou said to Tom, "You watch after him, Tom."

"I will," Tom said.

"Make sure he's taken care of," she said.

"I'll take care of him."

Deel and Tom had just started walking toward the woods when they were distracted by a shadow. An owl came diving down toward the field. They saw the bird scoop up a fat mouse and fly away with it. The dog chased the owl's shadow as it cruised along the ground.

As they watched the owl climb into the bright sky and fly toward the woods, Tom said, "Ain't nothin' certain in life, is it?"

"Especially if you're a mouse," Deel said.

"Life can be cruel," Tom said. "Wasn't no cruelty in that," Deel said. "That was survival. The owl was hungry. Men ain't like that. They ain't like other things, 'cept maybe ants."

"Ants?"

"Ants and man make war 'cause they can. Man makes all kinds of proclamations and speeches and gives reasons and such, but at the bottom of it, we just do it 'cause we want to and can."

"That's a hard way to talk," Tom said.

"Man ain't happy till he kills everything in his path and cuts down everything that grows. He sees something wild and beautiful and wants to hold it down and stab it, punish it 'cause it's wild. Beauty draws him to it, and then he kills it."

"Deel, you got some strange thinkin'," Tom said.

"Reckon I do."

"We're gonna kill so as to have somethin' to eat, but unlike the owl, we ain't eatin' no mouse. We're having us a big, fat possum and we're gonna cook it with sweet potatoes."

They watched as the dog ran on ahead of them, into the dark line of the trees.

When they got to the edge of the woods the shadows of the trees fell over them, and then they were inside the woods, and it was dark in places with gaps of light where the limbs were thin. They moved toward the gaps and found a trail and walked down it. As they went, the light faded, and Deel looked up. A dark cloud had blown in.

Tom said, "Hell, looks like it's gonna rain. That came out of nowhere."

"It's a runnin' rain," Deel said. "It'll blow in and spit water and blow out before you can find a place to get dry."

"Think so?"

"Yeah. I seen rain aplenty, and one comes up like this, it's traveling through. That cloud will cry its eyes out and move on, promise you. It ain't even got no lightnin' with it."

As if in response to Deel's words it began to rain. No lightning and no thunder, but the wind picked up and the rain was thick and cold.

"I know a good place ahead," Tom said. "We can get under a tree there, and there's a log to sit on. I even killed a couple possums there."

They found the log under the tree, sat down and waited. The tree was an oak and it was old and big and had broad limbs and thick leaves that spread out like a canvas. The leaves kept Deel and Tom almost dry.

"That dog's done gone off deep in the woods," Deel said, and laid the shotgun against the log and put his hands on his knees.

"He gets a possum, you'll hear him. He sounds like a trumpet."

Tom shifted the .22 across his lap and looked at Deel, who was lost in thought. "Sometimes," Deel said, "when we was over there, it would rain, and we'd be in trenches, waiting for somethin' to happen, and the trenches would flood with water, and there was big ole rats that would swim in it, and we was so hungry from time to time, we killed them and ate them."

"Rats?"

"They're same as squirrels. They don't taste as good, though. But a squirrel ain't nothin' but a tree rat."

"Yeah? You sure?"

"I am."

Tom shifted on the log, and when he did Deel turned toward him. Tom still had the .22 lying across his lap, but when Deel looked, the barrel was raised in his direction. Deel started to say somethin', like, "Hey, watch what you're doin'," but in that instant he knew what he should have known all along. Tom was going to kill him. He had always planned to kill him. From the day Mary Lou had met him in the field on horseback, they were anticipating the rattle of his dead bones. It's why they had kept him from town. He was already thought dead, and if no one thought different, there was no crime to consider.

"I knew and I didn't know," Deel said.

"I got to, Deel. It ain't nothin' personal. I like you fine. You been good to me. But I got to do it. She's worth me doin' somethin' like this . . . Ain't no use reaching for that shotgun, I got you sighted; twenty-two ain't much, but it's enough."

"Winston," Deel said, "he ain't my boy, is he?"

"No."

"He's got a birthmark on his face, and I remember now when you was younger, I seen that same birthmark. I forgot but now I remember. It's under your hair, ain't it?"

Tom didn't say anything. He had scooted back on the log. This put him out from under the edge of the oak canopy, and the rain was washing over his hat and plastering his long hair to the sides of his face.

"You was with my wife back then, when you was eighteen, and I didn't even suspect it," Deel said, and smiled as if he thought there was humor in it. "I figured you for a big kid and nothin' more."

"You're too old for her," Tom said, sighting down the rifle. "And you didn't never give her no real attention. I been with her mostly since you left. I just happened to be gone when you come home. Hell, Deel, I got clothes in the trunk there, and you didn't even see 'em. You might know the weather, but you damn sure don't know women, and you don't know men."

"I don't want to know them, so sometimes I don't know what I know. And men and women, they ain't all that different . . . You ever killed a man, Tom?"

"You'll be my first."

Deel looked at Tom, who was looking at him along the length of the .22.

"It ain't no easy thing to live with, even if you don't know the man," Deel said. "Me, I killed plenty. They come to see me when I close my eyes. Them I actually seen die, and them I imagined died."

"Don't give me no booger stories. I don't reckon you're gonna come see me when you're dead. I don't reckon that at all."

It had grown dark because of the rain, and Tom's shape was just a shape. Deel couldn't see his features.

"Tom—"

The .22 barked. The bullet struck Deel in the head. He tumbled over the log and fell where there was rain in his face. He thought just before he dropped down into darkness: It's so cool and clean.

Deel looked over the edge of the trench where there was a slab of metal with a slot to look through. All he could see was darkness except when the lightning ripped a strip in the sky and the countryside lit up. Thunder banged so loudly he couldn't tell the difference between it and cannon fire, which was also banging away, dropping great explosions near the breastworks and into the zigzagging trench, throwing men left and right like dolls.

Then he saw shapes. They moved across the field like a column of ghosts. In one great run they came, closer and closer. He poked his rifle through the slot and took half-ass aim and then the command came and he fired. Machine guns began to burp. The field lit up with their constant red pops. The shapes began to fall. The faces of those in front of the rushing line brightened when the machine guns snapped, making their features devil red. When the lightning flashed they seemed to vibrate across the field. The cannons roared and thunder rumbled and the machine guns coughed and the rifles cracked and men screamed.

Then the remainder of the Germans were across the field and over the trench ramifications and down into the trenches themselves. Hand-to-hand fighting began. Deel fought with his bayonet. He jabbed at a German soldier so small his shoulders failed to fill out his uniform. As the German hung on the thrust of Deel's blade, clutched at the rifle barrel, flares blazed along the length of the trench, and in that moment Deel saw the soldier's chin had bits of blond fuzz on it. The expression the kid wore was that of someone who had just realized this was not a glorious game after all.

And then Deel coughed.

He coughed and began to choke. He tried to lift up, but couldn't, at first. Then he sat up and the mud dripped off him and the rain pounded him. He spat dirt from his mouth and gasped at the air. The rain washed his face clean and pushed his hair down over his forehead. He was uncertain how long he sat there in the rain, but in time, the rain stopped. His head hurt. He lifted his hand to it and came away with his fingers covered in blood. He felt again, pushing his hair aside. There was a groove across his forehead. The shot hadn't hit him solid; it had cut a path across the front of his head. He had bled a lot, but now the bleeding had stopped. The mud in the grave had filled the wound and plugged it. The shallow grave had most likely been dug earlier in the day. It had all been planned out, but the rain was unexpected. The rain made the dirt damp, and in the dark Tom had not covered him well enough. Not deep enough. Not firm enough. And his nose was free. He could breathe. The ground was soft and it couldn't hold him. He had merely sat up and the dirt had fallen aside.

Deel tried to pull himself out of the grave, but was too weak, so he twisted in the loose dirt and lay with his face against the ground. When he was strong enough to lift his head, the rain had passed, the clouds had sailed away, and the moon was bright.

Deel worked himself out of the grave and crawled across the ground toward the log where he and Tom had sat. His shotgun was lying behind the log where it had fallen. Tom had either forgotten the gun or didn't care. Deel was too weak to pick it up.

Deel managed himself onto the log and sat there, his head held down, watching the ground. As he did, a snake crawled over his boots and twisted its way into the darkness of the woods. Deel reached down and picked up the shotgun. It was damp and cold. He opened it and the shells popped out. He didn't try to find them in the dark. He lifted the barrel, poked it toward the moonlight, and looked through it. Clear. No dirt in the barrels. He didn't try to find the two shells. He loaded two fresh ones from his ammo bag. He took a deep breath. He picked up some damp leaves and pressed them against the wound and they stuck. He stood up. He staggered toward his house, the blood-stuck leaves decorating his forehead as if he were some kind of forest god.

It was not long before the stagger became a walk. Deel broke free of the woods and onto the path that crossed the field. With the rain gone it was bright again and a light wind had begun to blow. The earth smelled rich, the way it had that night in France when it rained and the lightning flashed and the soldiers came and the damp smell of the earth blended with the biting smell of gunpowder and the odor of death.

He walked until he could see the house, dark like blight in the center of the field. The house appeared extremely small then, smaller than before; it was as if all that had ever mattered to him continued to shrink. The bitch dog came out to meet him but he ignored her. She slunk off and trotted toward the trees he had left behind.

He came to the door, and then his foot was kicking against it. The door cracked and creaked and slammed loudly backward. Then Deel was inside, walking fast. He came to the bedroom door, and it was open. He went through. The window was up and the room was full of moonlight, so brilliant he could see clearly, and what he saw was Tom and Mary Lou lying together in mid-act, and in that moment he thought of his brief time with her and how she had let him have her so as not to talk about Tom anymore. He thought about how she had given herself to protect what she had with Tom. Something moved inside Deel and he recognized it as the core of what man was. He stared at them and they saw him and froze in action. Mary Lou said, "No," and Tom leaped up from between her legs, all the way to his feet. Naked as nature, he stood for a moment in the middle of the bed, and then plunged through the open window like a fox down a hole. Deel raised the shotgun and fired and took out part of the windowsill, but Tom was out and away. Mary Lou screamed. She threw her legs to the side of the bed and made as if to stand, but couldn't. Her legs were too weak. She sat back down and started yelling his name. Something called from deep inside Deel, a long call, deep and dark and certain. A bloody leaf dripped off his forehead. He raised the shotgun and fired. The shot tore into her breast and knocked her sliding across the bed, pushing the back of her head against the wall beneath the window.

Deel stood looking at her. Her eyes were open, her mouth slightly parted. He watched her hair and the sheets turn dark.

He broke open the shotgun and reloaded the double barrel from his ammo sack and went to the door across the way, the door to the small room that was the boy's. He kicked it open. When he came in, the boy, wearing his nightshirt, was crawling through the window. He shot at him, but the best he might have done was riddle the bottom of his feet with pellets. Like his father, Winston was quick through a hole.

Deel stepped briskly to the open window and looked out. The boy was crossing the moonlit field like a jackrabbit, running toward a dark stretch of woods in the direction of town. Deel climbed through the window and began to stride after the boy. And then he saw Tom. Tom was off to the right, running toward where there used to be a deep ravine and a blackberry growth. Deel went after him. He began to trot. He could imagine himself with the other soldiers crossing a field, waiting for a bullet to end it all.

Deel began to close in. Being barefoot was working against Tom. He was limping. Deel thought that Tom's feet were most likely full of grass burrs and were wounded by stones. Tom's moon shadow stumbled and rose, as if it were his soul trying to separate itself from its host.

The ravine and the blackberry bushes were still there. Tom came to the ravine, found a break in the vines, and went over the side of it and down. Deel came shortly after, dropped into the ravine. it was damp there and smelled fresh from the recent rain. Deel saw Tom scrambling up the other side of the ravine, into the dark rise of blackberry bushes on the far side. He strode after him, and when he came to the spot where Tom had gone, he saw Tom was hung in the berry vines. The vines had twisted around his arms and head and they held him as surely as if he were nailed there. The more Tom struggled, the harder the thorns bit and the better the vines held him. Tom twisted and rolled and soon he was facing in the direction of Deel, hanging just above him on the bank of the ravine, supported by the blackberry vines, one arm outstretched, the other pinned against his abdomen, wrapped up like a Christmas present from nature, a gift to what man and the ants liked to do best. He was breathing heavily.

Deel turned his head slightly, like a dog trying to distinguish what it sees. "You're a bad shot."

"Ain't no cause to do this, Deel."

"It's not a matter of cause. It's the way of man," Deel said.

"What in hell you talkin' about, Deel? I'm askin' you, I'm beggin' you, don't kill me. She was the one talked me into it. She thought you were dead, long dead. She wanted it like it was when it was just me and her."

Deel took a deep breath and tried to taste the air. It had tasted so clean a moment ago, but now it was bitter.

"The boy got away," Deel said.

"Go after him, you want, but don't kill me."

A smile moved across Deel's face. "Even the little ones grow up to be men."

"You ain't makin' no sense, Deel. You ain't right."

"Ain't none of us right," Deel said.

Deel raised the shotgun and fired. Tom's head went away and the body drooped in the clutch of the vines and hung over the edge of the ravine.

The boy was quick, much faster than his father. Deel had covered a lot of ground in search of him, and he could read the boy's sign in the moonlight, see where the grass was pushed down, see bare footprints in the damp dirt, but the boy had long reached the woods, and maybe the town beyond. He knew that. It didn't matter anymore.

He moved away from the woods and back to the field until he came to Pancake Rocks. They were flat, round chunks of sandstone piled on top of one another and they looked like a huge stack of pancakes. He had forgotten all about them. He went to them and stopped and looked at the top edge of the pancake stones. It was twenty feet from ground to top.

He remembered that from when he was a boy. His daddy told him, "That there is twenty feet from top to bottom. A Spartan boy could climb that and reach the top in three minutes. I can climb it and reach the top in three minutes. Let's see what you can do."

He had never reached the top in three minutes, though he had tried time after time. It had been important to his father for some reason, some human reason, and he had forgotten all about it until now.

Deel leaned the shotgun against the stones and slipped off his boots and took off his clothes. He tore his shirt and made a strap for the gun, and slung it over his bare shoulder and took up the ammo bag and tossed it over his other shoulder, and began to climb. He made it to the top. He didn't know how long it had taken him, but he guessed it had been only about three minutes. He stood on top of Pancake Rocks and looked out at the night. He could see his house from there. He sat cross-legged on the rocks and stretched the shotgun over his thighs. He looked up at the sky. The stars were bright and the space between them was as deep as forever. If man could, he would tear the stars down, thought Deel.

Deel sat and wondered how late it was. The moon had moved, but not so much as to pull up the sun. Deel felt as if he had been sitting there for days. He nodded off now and then, and in the dream he was an ant, one of many ants, and he was moving toward a hole in the ground from which came smoke and sparks of fire. He marched with the ants toward the hole, and then into the hole they went, one at a time. Just before it was his turn, he saw the ants in front of him turn to black crisps in the fire, and he marched after them, hurrying for his turn, then he awoke and looked across the moonlit field.

He saw, coming from the direction of his house, a rider. The horse looked like a large dog because the rider was so big. He hadn't seen the man in years, but he knew who he was immediately. Lobo Collins. He had been sheriff of the county when he had left for war. He watched as Lobo rode toward him. He had no thoughts about it. He just watched.

Well out of range of Deel's shotgun, Lobo stopped and got off his horse and pulled a rifle out of the saddle boot.

"Deel," Lobo called. "It's Sheriff Lobo Collins."

Lobo's voice moved across the field loud and clear. It was as if they were sitting beside each other. The light was so good he could see Lobo's mustache clearly, drooping over the corners of his mouth.

"Your boy come told me what happened."

"He ain't my boy, Lobo."

"Everybody knowed that but you, but wasn't no cause to do what you did. I been up to the house, and I found Tom in the ravine."

"They're still dead, I assume."

"You ought not done it, but she was your wife, and he was messin' with her, so you got some cause, and a jury might see it that way. That's something to think about, Deel. It could work out for you."

"He shot me," Deel said.

"Well now, that makes it even more different. Why don't you put down that gun, and you and me go back to town and see how we can work things out."

"I was dead before he shot me."

"What?" Lobo said. Lobo had dropped down on one knee. He had the Winchester across that knee and with his other hand he held the bridle of his horse. Deel raised the shotgun and set the stock firmly against the stone, the barrel pointing skyward.

"You're way out of range up there," Lobo said. "That shotgun ain't gonna reach me, but I can reach you, and I can put one in a fly's asshole from here to the moon."

Deel stood up. "I can't reach you, then I reckon I got to get me a wee bit closer."

Lobo stood up and dropped the horse's reins. The horse didn't move. "Now don't be a damn fool, Deel."

Deel slung the shotgun's makeshift strap over his shoulder and started climbing down the back of the stones, where Lobo couldn't see him. He came down quicker than he had gone up, and he didn't even feel where the stones had torn his naked knees and feet.

When Deel came around the side of the stone, Lobo had moved only slightly, away from his horse, and he was standing with the Winchester held down by his side. He was watching as Deel advanced, naked and committed. Lobo said, "Ain't no sense in this, Deel. I ain't seen you in years, and now I'm gonna get my best look at you down the length of a Winchester. Ain't no sense in it."

"There ain't no sense to nothin'," Deel said, and walked faster, pulling the strapped shotgun off his shoulder.

Lobo backed up a little, then raised the Winchester to his shoulder, said, "Last warnin', Deel."

Deel didn't stop. He pulled the shotgun stock to his hip and let it rip. The shot went wide and fell across the grass like hail, some twenty feet in front of Lobo. And then Lobo fired.

Deel thought someone had shoved him. It felt that way. That someone had walked up unseen beside him and had shoved him on the shoulder. Next thing he knew he was lying on the ground looking up at the stars. He felt pain, but not like the pain he had felt when he realized what he was.

A moment later the shotgun was pulled from his hand, and then Lobo was kneeling down next to him with the Winchester in one hand and the shotgun in the other.

"I done killed you, Deel."

"No," Deel said, spitting up blood. "I ain't alive to kill."

"I think I clipped a lung," Lobo said, as if proud of his marksmanship. "You ought not done what you done. It's good that boy got away. He ain't no cause of nothin'."

"He just ain't had his turn."

Deel's chest was filling up with blood. It was as if someone had put a funnel in his mouth and poured it into him. He tried to say something more, but it wouldn't come out. There was only a cough and some blood; it splattered warm on his chest. Lobo put the weapons down and picked up Deel's head and laid it across one of his thighs so he wasn't choking so much.

"You got any last words, Deel?"

"Look there," Deel said.

Deel's eyes had lifted to the heavens, and Lobo looked. What he saw was the night and the moon and the stars. "Look there. You see it?" Deel said. "The stars are fallin'."

Lobo said, "Ain't nothin' fallin', Deel," but when he looked back down, Deel was gone.

There are restless spirits in "Hurt Me" and—like many traditional ghost stories—they are fueled by obsession, guilt, malice, anger, and revenge . . . but perhaps not in the way you might expect.

HURT ME

M.L.N. HANOVER

There weren't many three-bedroom houses that a single woman could afford; 1532 Lachmont Drive was an exception. Built in the 1930s from masonry block, it sat in the middle of a line of houses that had once been very similar to it. Decades of use and modification had added character: basement added in the 1950s, called "finished" only because the floor was concrete rather than dirt; garage tacked on to the north side that pressed its outer wall almost to the property line; artificial pond in the back yard that had held nothing but silt since the 1980s. The air smelled close and musty, the kitchen vent cover banged in the wind, and the Air Force base three miles to the north meant occasional jet noise loud enough to shake the earth. But the floors were hardwood, the windows recently replaced, and the interiors a uniform white that made the most of the hazy autumn light.

The realtor watched the woman—Corrie Morales was her name—nervously. He didn't like the way she homed in on the house's subtle defects. Yes, there had been some water damage in the bathroom once. Yes, the plaster in the master bedroom was cracking, just a little. The washer/dryer in the basement seemed to please her, though. And the bathtub was an old iron claw-footed number, the enamel barely chipped, and she smiled as soon as she saw it.

She wasn't the sort of client he usually aimed for. He was better with new families, either just-marrieds or first-kid types. With them, he could talk about building a life, and how the house had room to grow in. A sewing room for the woman, an office for the man, though God knew these days it seemed to go the other direction often as not. New families would come in, live for a few years, and trade up. Or traffic from the base; military people with enough money to build up equity and flip the house when they got re-assigned rather than lose money by paying rent. He had a different set of patter for those, but he could work with them. New families and military folks. Let the other realtors sell the big mansions in the foothills. Maybe he didn't make as much on each sale, but there were places in his territory he'd sold three or four times in the last ten years.

This woman, though, was hard to read: in her late thirties and seeing the place by herself; no wedding ring. Her face had been pretty once, not too long ago. Might still be, if she wore her hair a little longer or pulled it back in a ponytail. Maybe she was a lesbian. Not that it mattered to him, as long as her money spent.

"It's a good, solid house," he said, nodding as a trick to make her nod along with him.

"It is," she said. "The price seems low."

"Motivated seller," he said with a wink.

"By what?" She opened and closed the kitchen cabinets.

"Excuse me?"

"Motivated by what?" she said.

"Well, you know how it is," he said, grinning. "Kids grow up, move on. Families change. A place maybe fits in one part of your life, and then you move on."

She smiled as if he'd said something funny.

"I don't know how it is, actually," she said. "The seller moved out because she got tired of the place?"

The realtor shrugged expansively, his mental gears whirring. The question felt like a trap. He wondered how much the woman had heard about the house. He couldn't afford to get caught in an outright lie.

"Well, they were young," he said. "Just got hitched, and they had all these ideas and plans. I don't like selling to newlyweds. Especially young ones. Too young to know what they're getting into. Better to go rent a few places, move around. Find out what you like, what you don't like."

"Bought it and didn't like it?"

"Didn't know quite what they were getting into," he said.

The sudden weariness around the woman's eyes was like a tell at a poker table. The realtor felt himself relax. Divorced, this one. Maybe more than once. Alone now, and getting older. Maybe she was looking for someplace cheap, or maybe it was just the allure of new beginnings. That he was wrong in almost every detail didn't keep him from playing that hand.

"My wife was just the same, God rest her," he said. "When we were kids, she'd hop into any old project like she was killing snakes. Got in over her head. Hell, she probably wouldn't have said yes to me if she'd thought it through. You get older, you know better. Don't get in so many messes. They were good kids, just no judgment."

She walked across the living room. It looked big, empty like this. Add a couch, a couple chairs, a coffee table, and it would get cramped fast. But right now, the woman walked across it like it was a field. Like she was that twenty-year-old girl with her new husband outside getting the baggage or off to work on the base. Like the world hadn't cut her down a couple times.

He could smell the sale. He could taste it.

"Lot of rentals in the neighborhood," she said, looking out the front window. He knew from her voice that her heart wasn't in the dickering. "Hard to build up much of a community when you're getting new neighbors all the time."

"You see that with anything near the base," he said, like they were talking about the weather. "People don't have the money for a down payment. Or some just prefer renting."

"I can't rent anymore."

"No?"

"I smoke," she said.

"That's a problem these days. Unless you've got your own house, of course."

She took a deep breath and let it out slowly. The realtor had to fight himself not to grin. Here we go.

"Wrap it up," she said. "I'll take it."

Mr. And Mrs. Kleinfeld had lived at 1530 Lachmont Drive for eight years, making them the longest-standing residents of the block. To them, the U-Haul that pulled up on Sunday morning was almost unremarkable. They ate their toast and jam, listened to the preacher on the radio, and watched the new neighbor start unloading boxes. She wore a pair of old blue jeans, a dark T-shirt with the logo of a long-canceled television show across the front, and a pale green bandana. When the breakfast was over, Mrs. Kleinfeld turned off the radio and cleaned the plates while Mr. Kleinfeld ambled out to the front yard.

"Morning," he said as the new woman stepped down from the back of the truck, a box of under-packed drinking glasses jingling in her hand.

"Hi," she said with a grin.

"Moving day," Mr. Kleinfeld said.

"It is," she said.

"You need a hand with any of that?"

"I think I'm good. Thanks, though. If it turns out I do . . . ?"

"Me and the Missus are here all day," he said. "Come over any time. And welcome to the neighborhood."

"Thanks."

He nodded amiably and went back inside. Mrs. Kleinfeld was sitting at the computer, entering the week's expenses. A trapped housefly was beating itself to death against the window, angry buzzing interrupted by hard taps.

"It's happening again," Mrs. Kleifeld said.

"It is."

It took her the better part of the day to put together the basics. Just assembling the new bed had taken over an hour and left her wrist sore. The refrigerator wouldn't be delivered until the next day. The back bedroom, now a staging area, was thigh-deep in packed one-thing-and-another. There was no phone service except her cell. The electricity wasn't in her name yet. But by nightfall, there were clothes in the closet, towels in the bathroom, and her old leather couch in the living room by the television. She needed to take the U-Haul back, but it could wait for morning.

She walked briskly through the house—*her* house—and closed all the blinds. The slick white plastic was thick enough to kill all the light from the street. The new double-glazed windows cut out the sounds of traffic. It was like the walls had been suddenly, silently, transported someplace else. Like it was a space capsule, a million miles from anything human, cut off from the world.

She turned on the water in the tub. It ran red for a moment, rust in the pipes, and then clear, and then scalding hot. She stripped as the steam rose. Naked in front of the full-length mirror, she watched the scars on her legs and elbows—the tiny circles no bigger than the tip of a lit cigarette; the longer, thinner ones where a blade had marred the skin—blur and fade and vanish. Her reflected body softened, and the glass began to weep. She turned off the water and eased herself into the bath slowly. The heat of it brought the blood to her skin like a slap. She laid her head against the iron tub's sloping back, fidgeting to find the perfect angle. She had soap, a washcloth, shampoo, the almond-scented conditioner that her boyfriend David liked. She didn't use any of them. After about ten minutes, she turned, leaning over the edge to reach for the puddle of blue cloth that was her jeans. A pack of cigarettes. A Zippo lighter with its worn Pink Martini logo. The slick and hiss of the flame. The first long drag of smoke curling through the back of her throat. She tossed cigarette pack and lighter onto the floor, and lay back again. The tension in her back and legs and belly started to lose its grip.

Around her, the house made small sounds: the ticking of the walls as they cooled, the hum of her computer's cooling fan, the soft clinking of the water that lapped her knees and breasts. Smoke rose from her cigarette, lost almost instantly in the steam. The first stirrings of hunger had just touched her belly when the screaming started, jet engines ramping up from nothing to an inhuman shriek between one breath and the next. Something fluttered in her peripheral vision, and she scrambled around, dropping her cigarette in the tub and soaking the floor with water.

Something moved in the mirror. Something that wasn't her. The condensation made it impossible to see him clearly. He might have had pale hair or he might have been bald. He might have jeans or dark slacks. The shirt was white where it wasn't red. The movement of balled fists was clearer than the hands themselves, and somewhere deep in the airplane's roar, there were words. Angry ones. Corrie yelped, her feet slipping under her as she tried to jump clear.

The noise began to fade as suddenly as it had come. The rumbling echoes batting at the walls more and more weakly. The mirror was empty again, except for her. She took a towel, wrapping herself quickly. Her blood felt bright and quick, her heart fluttering like a bird, her breath fast and panic-shallow. Her mouth tasted like metal.

"Hello?" she said. "Is someone in here?"

The floor creaked under her weight. She stood still, waiting for an answering footstep. The water pooled around her feet, and she began to shiver. The house had grown viciously cold.

"Is anyone here?" she said again, her voice small and shaking.

Nothing answered her but the smell of her spent cigarette.

"All right, then," she said, hugging her arms tight around herself. "Okay."

"Mom. *Listen* to me. Everything's fine. We're not breaking up," she said, willing her voice to be more certain than she was.

"Well, you move out like this," her mother said, voice pressed small and tinny by the cell connection. "And *that* house? I think it's perfectly reasonable of me to be concerned."

Corrie lay back on the couch, pressing the tips of her fingers to her eyes. Sleeplessness left her skin waxy and pale, her movements slow. She had taken the day off work, thinking she would finish unpacking, but the boxes were still where they had been the day before. Afternoon sun spilled in through the windows, making the small living room glow. The refrigerator had arrived an hour before and hummed to itself from the kitchen, still empty.

"It's just something I need to do," Corrie said.

"Is he beating you?"

"Who? David? *My* David?"

"People have habits," her mother said. She raised her voice when she lectured. "They imprint. I did the same thing when I was young. All my husbands were alcoholics, just like my father was. I like David very much. He's always been very pleasant. But you have a type."

"I haven't dated anyone seriously since Nash. I don't have a type."

"What about that Hebrew boy? Nathaniel?"

"I saw him a total of eight times. He got drunk, broke a window, and I never talked to him again."

"Don't turn into a lawyer with me. You know exactly what I mean. There's a kind of man that excites you, and so of course you might find yourself involved with that kind of man. If David's another one like Nash, I think I have a right to—"

Corrie sat up, pressing her hand at the empty air as if her mother could see the gesture for *stop*. The distant music of an ice-cream truck came from a different world, the jaunty electronic tune insincere and ominous.

"Mother. I don't feel comfortable talking about the kind of man that does or doesn't excite me, all right? David is absolutely unlike Nash in every possible way. He wouldn't hurt me if I asked him to."

"Did you?" her mother snapped.

"Did I what?"

"Did you ask him to hurt you?"

The pause hung in the air, equal parts storm and silence.

"Okay, we're finished," Corrie said. "I love you, Mom, and I really appreciate that you're concerned, but I am *not* talking about—"

"You are!" her mother shouted. "You are talking about *everything* with me! I have spent too much time and money making sure that you are all right to pretend that there are *boundaries*. Maybe for other people, but not for us, *mija*. Never for us."

Corrie groaned. The quiet on the end of her cell phone managed to be hurt and accusing.

"I'm sorry," she said. "I understand that you're scared about this. And really, I understand why you're scared. But you have to trust that I know what I'm doing. I'm not twenty anymore."

"Did you or did you not ask David to hurt you?"

"My sex life with David has been very respectful and loving," Corrie said through gritted teeth. "He is always a perfect gentleman. The few times that we've talked—just talked—about anything even a little kinky, he's been very uncomfortable with including even simulated violence in our relationship. Okay? Now can we please drop—"

"Is that why you left him?"

"We're not breaking up."

"Because that's the other side, isn't it?" her mother said, talking fast. "You find someone who isn't your type, and you put yourself with him because he's good and clean and healthy, and then there you are being good and clean and healthy. Like eating wheat germ every meal when you really want a steak."

"All right, I'm lost now," she said, her voice taking on a dangerous buzz. "Are you saying that David's an abusive shit, or that he's too good for me? What's your argument?"

She could hear her mother crying now. Not sobs. Nothing more than the little waver in tone that meant tears were in her eyes.

"I don't know why you're doing this," her mother said. "Why you moved out of David's apartment. Why you're in that house. I'm afraid you've gone to a very dark place." The last words were so thin and airless, Corrie had to take a deep breath.

"Maybe I have," she said, drawing the words out. "But it's all right. I'm not scared anymore."

"Shouldn't you be? Is there nothing to be frightened of?"

Corrie stood. It was only four steps to the bathroom door. With the lights off, the full-length mirror showed her in silhouette, the brightness of day behind her, and her features lost in shadow. There was no other shape, no man with balled fists or knives. No promises that the damage was a sign of love. No cigarette burns or dislocated fingers or weekends of sex she was afraid to refuse. It was just a mirror. She was the only thing in it.

Is there nothing to be frightened of?

"Don't know," Corrie said. "I'm finding out."

"Oh," Mr. Kleinfeld said, suddenly off his stride. "So you knew it was . . . "

"Haunted?" the new neighbor—Corrie, her name was—said. "Sure. I mean, just in general terms."

Mr. Kleinfeld smiled, but his eyebrows were crawling up his forehead. Across the table, his wife poured out cups of tea for the three of them; her smile might have meant anything.

"Is that how you heard about it?" Mrs. Kleinfeld asked. "You're one of those 'ghost hunters?' "

Sunlight pressed through the still air along with the distant chop of a helicopter formation. The new neighbor took the proffered cup and sipped at it. His wife put two small silver spoonfuls of sugar into his, stirred it twice neatly, and handed him his cup.

"Not really," the new neighbor said. "It was just one of those things you hear about, you know? In the air. I don't even know where I stumbled onto it the first time, but the realtor was pretty up-front."

"Was he?" Mr. Kleinfeld said. That had never happened before either.

"Sure. I mean, there weren't a lot of gory details. I asked about why the price was low, and he said something about ghost stories and the old tenants getting freaked out and leaving."

"The women," Mrs. Kleinfeld said. "It doesn't seem to care about men, but it *hates* women."

"It?" the new neighbor said, and Mr. Kleinfeld watched his wife settle back into her chair. The first part of the meeting might not have gone along its usual path, but they were back in familiar territory now.

"There is a restless spirit in that house," Mrs. Kleinfeld said. "Has been since before we came. It never bothers the men. They never see it."

"The girls, though," Mr. Kleinfeld said, shaking his head the way he always did. "I could make a list of the young women we've had banging on our door in the middle of the night, scared out of their wits. It's not a fit house for a girl to live in. Especially alone."

He sipped his tea, but it was still scalding. He blew across its surface.

"Weird," the new neighbor said. "Any particular reason anyone knows about? Ancient Indian burial ground?"

His wife nodded slowly, the steam rising from her teacup swirling around her face. The chop of the helicopters grew gradually louder. Mr. Kleinfeld shifted back a degree in his chair. His part was done for now, and just as well. The Missus was better at getting through to people than he was. She always had been.

"There's a story," she said. "I don't know how much of it's true and how much of it's fancied up, but I've never heard or seen anything to contradict it. Twenty years ago, there was a couple of young people moved into that house you're in today. Young man and his wife. Well, it wasn't long before the wife started showing up at the grocery store in big sunglasses. Wearing long sleeves in the middle of the summer. That sort of thing."

"Lots of domestic abuse in the world," the new neighbor said. "Doesn't make for a million haunted houses." Her tone was light, but Mr. Kleinfeld heard something strong under it. Maybe skepticism. Maybe something else.

"He was an *evil* man," Mrs. Kleinfeld said. "People used to hear them fighting. They say he used to try to hide the worst of the screaming under the jet noise, but the whole neighborhood knew. One fellow who lived on the other side, where that nice Asian family is now, tried to make an issue of it, and the man threatened to cut his nose off. And then one night they were gone. Man and wife both, vanished from the face of the earth like they'd never been. A few months later, her people came and packed up all the furniture, and put the place up for sale. Rumor was that the wife was in some sort of asylum out west, with her mind all gone to putty, talking about demons and Satan. She never did get out of that place."

The new neighbor was caught now, her expression sharp as a pencil point. Mrs. Kleinfeld had to stop for a moment while the helicopters passed overhead, the blades cutting through the high air with enough violence to drown out their words. Or their screams, for that matter.

"Next people who moved in were an older couple with a girl just in high school," she said, her voice loud enough to carry over the falling racket as the copters flew on. "Six months they were there. Not more. The mother said she'd have tried to stand it, but the spirit started coming after the daughter too, and that was that. Sold the place at a loss and moved across to the other side of the base. Only time the place has had the same owner for more than a year since then was five years back when there were four young men sharing the place, and even then, I saw their girlfriends leaving in the middle of the night, crying too hard to stop."

"What does it do to them?" the new neighbor asked. The hardness was still there, but it wasn't skepticism. Something more immediate, more demanding. Something like hunger.

"It *comes* for them," Mrs. Kleinfeld said, "and thank God they can feel it. No one's ever stayed long enough to know what it would do if it caught them, but there are nights I can feel it hating all the way over here. I'm in my bed at night saying my prayers, and it's like someone put ice against the wall. You couldn't pay me to stay a night in that place. Not for a million dollars. Something lives in that house, and it hates women."

The new neighbor nodded, more, Mr. Kleinfeld thought, to herself than to him or his wife. There was a brightness in her eyes. Not fear. Maybe even pleasure. The new neighbor's smile disturbed him more than his wife's story ever did. He cleared his throat, and she seemed to wake up a little. Her smile widened and became less authentic.

"Have you seen anything yet," he asked. "Anything out of the ordinary?"

"Me? No," she said. "Not a thing."

The cold front came on Friday, almost a week later; vicious winds blasting down from a cloudless sky. Gritty air ripped at the trees, stripping off leaves that were still turning from green to yellow and red and gold; the glories of autumn cut short and shredded. The low Western sun turned bloody as it fell, and Corrie wheeled her car into the undersized garage like a child pulling up a blanket. The thin walls were less protection than the idea of them. Every new gust battering against the house made the garage creak. Dust settled from the frame roof. She scurried from car to kitchen, hunched against the sound of the wind.

Once she got into the house itself, she unfurled. The wind still threw handfuls of dirt against the windows, the thick plastic blinds shuffled and clicked in the drafts, but the masonry walls seemed beyond any violence nature could contrive, solid and sober as a prison. Corrie turned on every light as she walked through the house. She examined each room in turn;the broken-down boxes in the spare bedroom, the legal pads and laptop docking station in her makeshift office, the sheets and blankets in the linen closet. In the kitchen, she counted the knives on the magnetic rack and checked the oven. In her bedroom, she squatted, her eye on a level with the unmarked bedspread. She took her shotgun from its place under the bed, counting out the shells under her breath as she unloaded it and loaded it again. In the bathroom, she lingered in front of the mirror for over a minute, her fingertips on the glass, eyes unfocused and attention turned inward. Nothing had moved. Nothing was missing. Even the raging wind hadn't so much as rolled a pencil.

She microwaved a plate of lasagna, poured herself a glass of wine, and sat down on the couch. A few bites, and she was up again, pacing. Restless. Frustrated. Outside, the sun slipped lower.

"I know you're here," she said to the empty air. "I know you can hear me."

The wind shrieked and murmured. The window blinds shuddered. The air smelled of tomato sauce a little, but burned at the edges; acid with a touch of smoke. She stood in the middle of the room, jaw clenched. Silent.

The moment lasted years before the hint of a smile touched her mouth and a mad, reckless light came into her eyes. She walked back to the couch, picked up her plate, and took it to the kitchen. She ate two more bites standing at the sink, and then dropped the plate onto the brushed steel with a clatter. The faucet swung easily, cold water drowning the food. Reddened bits of meat and pale sheets of pasta swum in a cold, ugly soup and then settled, clogging the drain. She looked at the mess and deliberately stepped back, leaving it there. Her chin rose, daring the emptiness around her.

Something within the house shifted. Walls that had been only block and plaster and paint turned their attention to her. The windows hid behind their blinds like closed eyes. She kicked off her shoes, chuckling to herself. The floor felt colder than it should have. The glass of wine still rested on the coffee table; she scooped it up, taking her purse in the other hand. The furnace kicked on, blowers roaring a thousand miles away.

In the kitchen, she leaned against the counter beside the sink. Goosebumps covered her arms and thighs. Her breath was coming fast and shallow and shaking a little. She lit a cigarette and then sipped the cool, astringent wine, rolling it in her mouth, feeling the alcohol pressing through the soft, permeable membranes of her flesh. When she swallowed, her throat went a degree warmer. She set the cigarette between her lips and stretched out a hand, lifting the half-full glass. Red trembled for a moment, as she slowly, deliberately, poured it out, the wine spilling over the floor and staining the tiles. She dropped the glass into the sink with her ruined dinner and stepped forward, grinding the soles of her feet into the puddle.

The storm outside sounded like a warning. She shifted her hips, twisted at the waist, dancing in the mess. She rolled her weight back and forth, humming to herself, and raised her arms over her head. Her joints loosened, her belly grew warm and heavy. Her nipples hardened and her breath became visible and feather-white in the sudden arctic chill. Voices came from somewhere nearby, raised in anger, but distant.

Still dancing, she pressed one hand to her belly, took the cigarette between her fingers, and drew the smoke back into her. The taste of it was like drinking fire. She flicked the ash, watching the soft gray fall down, down, down into the wide, red puddle at her feet.

Not wine.

Blood.

He stood framed by the basement door. A young man, and ageless. His shoulders were broad as a bull, his pale hair cut close to the skull. The dark slacks she'd seen in the mirror were tight and strained across the hip, as if designed to point out the thing's barely-restrained erection. With every deep, heaving breath, blood sheeted down his body from the hole where his heart should have been. She had the impression of corrupted meat beneath that pale skin. His lips curled back in wordless rage, baring teeth too sharp to be human.

The warmth within her was gone. Her face was pale, and the electric shock of fear turned her dance to stillness. The man shook his head at her once, slow back and forth. When he opened his mouth and howled, she retreated two quick involuntary steps, the countertop digging at the small of her back. Hatred radiated from him. Hatred and malice and the promise of violence. The tiles between them were the slick red of fresh slaughter.

When she spoke, her voice trembled. It sounded very small, even to her.

"Don't like it, huh?"

The ghost shifted his head side-to-side, neither nod nor shake, but stretching. Like an athlete preparing for some terrible effort. A clearer threat than balled fists.

"W-what," she tried to say, then crossed her arms and took a fast, nervous drag on the cigarette. She lifted her chin in defiance. "What're you gonna do about it?"

His eyes moved across her body like she was something he owned. The hissing sound of his breath came from everywhere.

"So, what? You want to hurt me? Come on, then," she said, her voice taking on a little strength. "If you're gonna do it, *do* it!"

He stepped into the room, filling the doorway. The death-blood, slick on his belly, glittered. He bared his teeth, growling like a dog.

"You want to hurt me? Then hurt me," she yelled. "*Hurt me!*"

The ghost screamed and rushed across the room toward her. She felt its rage and hatred surrounding her, swallowing her. She saw its hand rising to slap her down, and she flinched back, her eyes closed, and braced for the blow. Every scar on her skin tingled like someone had touched them with ice. Filthy water poured into her mouth, her nose, corrupted and sour with decay. She felt the spirit pressing against her, pushing into her skin. Its rage lifted her like a wave.

And then it was gone.

She stood in the kitchen, her body shaking and her ragged breath coming in sobs. She was terribly cold. The wine on her toes—only wine—was half-dried and sticky. Storm wind battered at the windows, the walls. The furnace rumbled, fighting against the frigid air. She sank slowly, her back against the cabinet, and hugged her knees. A stray tear fell down her cheek and she shuddered uncontrollably twice.

Then, between one breath and the next, her mouth relaxed. Her body released. The breaking tension was more than sexual.

She started laughing: a deep, satisfied sound, like the aftermath of orgasm.

Sunday morning brought the first snow of the season. The thick, wet flakes appeared just before dawn, dark against the bright city backsplash of the clouds, and transformed to a prefect white once they had fallen. After the morning's toast and tea and sermon, Mr. Kleinfeld, wrapped in his good wool overcoat, lumbered out after breakfast, snow shovel over his shoulder. He cleared his walkway and his drive, then the stretch of sidewalk in front of his house. The trees all around were black-barked and frosted with snow, and very few cars passed, the tracks of their tires leaving white furrows and never digging so deep as the asphalt.

Finished with his own house, he made his way through the ankle-high snow to his neighbor's. No lights glowed in the house, no tracks marked her walk. Her driveway hadn't been used. He hesitated, not wanting to wake her, but it was almost midday. He rang the bell, and when no answer came, mittened manfully on the door. No one came. He shook his head and put himself to work. The clouds above were bright as the snow when he finished, the air not yet above the freezing point, but warmer all the same.

His wife met him at the door with a cup of hot cocoa, just as he'd known she would. He leaned the snow shovel by the door, took the warm mug, and kissed his wife's dry cheek.

"I don't think our new neighbor made it home last night," he said. He sat in his chair. "I figure she's seen it. Won't be long now before she moves on."

It was a conversation they'd had before, and he waited now for his wife's agreement, her prediction: two more months, another month, a week. The Missus was better at judging these things than he was. So he was surprised when she stood silent for a long moment, shaking her head.

"I don't know," she said. "I just do not know . . . "

David's apartment still showed the gaps where she had been. His clothes still hung in only half of the bedroom closet, the hangers moving into the emptiness she had left only slowly, as if hoping that her blouses and slacks and dresses might come back. The corner where her desk had once been was still vacant, the four hard circles that the legs had pressed into the carpet relaxed out a little, but not gone. The kid upstairs was practicing his guitar again, working on power chords that had driven her half-crazy when she'd lived there. They seemed sort of cute now.

"He's getting better," David said.

She rolled over, stuffing the pillow under her head and neck as she did. A thin line of snow ran along the window sill; the first of the season. David, beside her, nodded toward the ceiling.

"He made it all the way through "Jesus of Suburbia" last week," he said.

"All five parts?"

"Yep."

"Kid's going places," she said.

"Please God that it's places out of earshot."

She brushed her fingertips across his chest. His skin was several tones darker than hers, and the contrast made her hand seem paler than she was, and her scars as white as the snow. He had his first gray hair in among the black, just over his ear. His dark eyes shifted over to her, his smile riding the line between post-coital exhaustion and melancholy. Quick as the impulse, she rolled the few more inches toward him and kissed his shoulder. He raised his eyebrows the way he always did when he knew that she was nervous.

"What's your plan for the day?" he asked.

"Housework," she said. "You?"

"Get up early and hit the Laundromat," he said.

She nodded.

"And since that didn't work?"

"Do an emergency load in the sink to get through work tomorrow," he said. "I've got to meet up with Gemma at three to get back my scanner."

"You'll need to get hopping. It's past noon now."

"Another few minutes won't make a difference," he said, putting his hand over hers. He wasn't pretty; his face too wide, his nose bent where it had broken as a child and never been put right, his jaw touched by the presentiment of jowls. Handsome, maybe, in an off-putting way. "Is there something to talk about?"

"Is," she said.

He took a long, slow breath and let it out slowly. Not a sigh so much as the preparatory breath of a high diver. Or a man steeling himself for bad news.

"I think you should come over tonight," she said. "Take a look at the place. Bring your laundry, too."

He sat up. The blankets dropped to his lap. She looked at him, unable to read his expression.

"You're changing the rules?" he said. Each word was as gentle as picking up eggs.

"No, I'm not. I always said that the not coming over part was temporary. It's just . . . time. That's all."

"So. You really *aren't* breaking up with me?"

"Jesus," she said. She took the pillow from under her head and hit him with it lightly. Then she did it again.

"It is traditional," he said. "Girl gets a house without consulting her boyfriend, moves all her stuff out, tells him he can't come over. Says she's 'working through something' but won't say what exactly it is? It's hard not to connect those dots."

"And the part where I tell you in simple declarative sentences that I'm not breaking up with you?"

"Goes under mixed signals," he said.

She took a deep breath. On the street, a siren rose and fell.

"Sorry," she said. She got up from the bed, pulling one of the sheets with her and wrapping it around her hips. "Look, I understand that this has been hard. I've asked for a lot of faith."

"You really have."

"And given that I don't have an entirely uncheckered past, and all," she said. "I see why you would freak. You and my mother both."

"Your mother?"

"She's been reading me the riot act ever since she heard about it. She really likes you."

He leaned back, surprise and pleasure in his expression.

"Your mother *likes* me?"

"Focus, sweetheart. I'm apologizing here."

"And I don't mean to interrupt," he said.

Relief had left him giddy. Between his brave face and her attention being elsewhere, she'd managed to ignore the sadness and dread that had been seeping into him. Now that it was lifting a little, she saw how deep it had gone. She found her pants in a heap on the floor, sat down at the dressing table and lit a cigarette. The taste of the smoke helped her to think. When she spoke, her voice was lower.

"I've had a rough ride this life, you know? I used to be ashamed of that. I used to think that after Nash I was . . . Broken. Damaged goods. Like that. And feeling like that has . . . "

She stopped, shook herself, laughed at something, and took another drag.

"Feeling like that has *haunted* me," she said, with an odd smile.

"And this house is part of not feeling that way?"

"It is."

"Then I already like it," he said. "Sight unseen. If it helps you see yourself the way I see you, then it's on my side."

Corrie chuckled and shook her head.

"That might be going a little far," she said. "But anyway. I want you to come over. I want you to see it. You should bring a sweater. It gets kind of cold sometimes."

"I'm there."

"*And* I want you to think about whether you'd like to move in."

"Corrie?"

"There's enough room. The neighborhood's a little sketchy, and the jet noise sucks, but not worse than the juke box hero practicing all the time."

"Corrie, are you saying you still want to live with me?"

Her smile was tight and nervous.

"Not asking for a decision," she said. "But I'm opening negotiations."

He slipped to the side of the bed, slid to the floor at her feet, and laid his head in her lap. For a long moment, neither of them moved or spoke, then Corrie wiped her eyes with the back of her hand.

"Come on, silly," she said. "You've got to get ready for Gemma. Go get that scanner back."

"I do," he said with a sigh. "Come shower with me?"

"Not today," she said. And when he raised his eyebrows, "I want to smell like you when I get home."

1532 Lachmont Drive seethed around her. Every noise—the hum of the refrigerator, the distant roar of the furnace, the ticking of the wooden floors as the push-pull of heat and cold adjusted the boards—had voices behind them, screaming. The faintest smell of hair and skin burning touched the air. She knew they were meant to be hers.

Corrie hung her coat in the closet. A shape flickered in the basement doorway, dark eyes and inhuman teeth. She set a kettle on the stove top and smoked a cigarette while it heated. When the clouds outside broke, the doubled light of sky and snow pressed in at the blinds. The kettle whistled. She took a mug out of the cupboard, put in a bag of chamomile tea, and poured the steaming water in. When she sat down, there was blood on the floor. A bright puddle, almost too red to be real, and then a trail wide as a man's hips where the still-living man had been dragged across to the basement door. When she looked up, the air had a layer of smoke haze a foot below the ceiling. It might have been her cigarette. It might have been gun smoke. She sipped her tea, savoring the heat and the faint sweetness.

"Fine," she said.

She stood up slowly, stretching. The stairs down to the basement were planks of wood painted a dark, chipping green. The years had softened the edges. The basement had none of the brightness of the day above it. Even with the single bare bulb glowing, the shadows were thick. The furnace roar was louder here, and the voice behind it spat rage and hatred. She followed the trail of blood to the corner of the basement, where washer and dryer sat sullen in the gloom. She leaned down, put her shoulder to the corner of the dryer, and shifted it.

The metal feet shrieked against the concrete. The scar under it was almost three feet wide, a lighter place where the floor had been broken, taken up, and then filled in with a patch of almost-matching cement. She sat down on the dusty floor. There was blood on her hands now, black and sticky and copper-smelling. A spot of white appeared on the odd concrete and began to spread: frost. She put her hand on it like she was caressing a pet.

"We should probably talk," she said. "And when I say that, I mean that I should talk, and you, for once, should listen."

Something growled from the corner by the furnace. A shadow detached from the gloom and began pacing like a tiger in its cage. She sipped her tea and looked around the darkness, her gaze calm and proprietary.

"It's funny the things they get wrong, you know? They remember that you threatened Joe Arrison, but instead of his nose, you were going to cut off his cock. They know I went to the Laughing Academy, but they don't remember that I got out. Apparently, I was going on about Satan or something. 'Mind gone to putty.' "

She stroked the concrete. The frost was spreading. A dot of red smeared it at the center, blood welling up from the artificial stone.

"And you really screwed me up, you know?" she said. "Shooting you really was worse than I thought it would be. I was so scared that someone would find you. I had nightmares all the time. I'd see someone who looked a little like you or I'd smell that cheap-ass cologne you liked, and I'd start panicking. I even tried to kill myself once. Didn't do a very good job of it.

"I was one messed up chica. Every couple weeks, I'd do a search online. I just knew that there was going to be something. Bones found at 1532 Lachmont Drive. So what do I find instead? Ghost stories. There was one that even had a drawing of you. And so, I knew, right?"

The shadow shrieked at her, its mouth glowing like there was something burning inside it. The blood at the center of the frost became a trickle. Corrie let the icy flow stain her fingers.

"I was so freaked out," she said, laughing. "I spent years putting myself back together, and here you still were. I don't think I slept right for a month. And then one day, something just clicked, you know? I've got a job. I can buy a house if I want."

She sipped at her tea, but it had gone cold. She was sitting in a spreading pool of gore now, the blood spilling out to the corners of the room. More blood than a real body could contain. It soaked her pants and wicked up her shirt, chilling her, but not badly. The shadow hunched forward, ready to leap.

"David's coming over tonight," she said. "I wasn't going to let him until I was sure it was safe. But tonight, I'm going to make him dinner, and we're probably going to get a little high, watch a DVD, something like that. And then I'm going to fuck him in your bedroom. And you? You're going to watch."

The blood rushed up. It was almost ankle-deep now, tiny waves of red rising up through the basement. Corrie smiled.

"You'll really hate him," she said. "He is everything you could never be, and he really, really loves me. And you know what? I love him too. And we're going to be here, maybe for years. Maybe forever. And we're going to do everything you couldn't. And we're going to do it right. So, seriously. How's that for revenge?"

The shadow screamed, rising up above her, blotting out the light. She could almost feel its teeth at her neck. She scratched.

"You're dead, fucker," she whispered to the darkness. "You can't hurt me."

Blood-soaked, she picked up her teacup and walked to the stairs. The ghost whipped at her with cold, insubstantial fingers. It screamed in her ears, battering her with anger and hatred. Corrie grinned, a sense of peace and calm radiating from her. The voice grew thinner, more distant, richer with despair. With each step she took, the visions of blood faded a little more, and by the time she stepped into the winter light, she was clean.

It is the nature of parents to give and children to take. Despite the pain children can inflict, good parents try to protect them, keep promises to them, do what's best for them . . . even when the world is full of monsters . . .

ARE YOU TRYING TO TELL ME THIS IS HEAVEN?

SARAH LANGAN

I.
He Gets Bit

The midday sun slaps Conrad Wilcox's shoulders and softens the blacktop highway so that his shoes sink just slightly. It's a wide road with a middle island upon which Magnolias bloom. Along the sides of the street are parked or crashed cars, most of them rusted. He's got three more miles to go, and then, if his map is correct, a left on Emancipation Place. Two more miles after that, and he'll reach whatever's left of the Louisiana State Correctional Facility for women. He'll reach Delia.

Along the highway-side grass embankment lies a green traffic sign that has broken free from its metal post. It reads:

WELCOME TO BATON ROUGE—AUTHENTIC LOUISIANA AT EVERY TURN!

And under that, in scripted spray-paint:

PLAGUE ZONE—KEEP OUT!

Conrad wipes his brow with the back of an age-spot-dappled hand and keeps walking. He's come nearly two thousand miles, and he buried his fear back in Tom's River, along with the bodies. In fear's place came hysteria, followed by paralysis, depression, the urge to do self-harm, and, finally, the enduring numbness with which he has sustained his survival. But so close to the end, his numbness cracks like an external skeleton. His chest and groin feel exposed, as if they've loosened from their bony cradles, and are about to fall out.

"I'm almost there, Gladdy," he says. "You'd better be watching. You'd better help me figure out what to do when the time comes, you old cow."

"I am." He answers himself in a fussy, high-pitched voice, then adds, "Don't call me a cow."

Another quarter-mile past the city limits brings him to a kudzu-covered 7-Eleven. It's the first shop since the Hess Station in Howell that doesn't look bombed out or looted. "Water. Here we go, Connie," he mumbles in that same, wrong-sounding voice. "See? It's all going to turn out great!"

He shuffles toward the storefront on a bent back and spry, skinny limbs, so that the overhead view of him appears crablike. He is sixty-two years old, but could pass for eighty.

His reflection, a grizzled wretch with a concave chest and hollowed eyes, moves slowly in the jagged storefront glass, but everything else is still. No crickets chirp. No children scream. It's too quiet. He grabs his holster—empty—and remembers that he lost his gun to the bottom of the Mississippi River two days ago, and has been without water and food ever since.

"This looks like Capital-T trouble. Right here in River City," he says in the high-pitched voice. It belongs to his wife Gladys. He's so lonely out here that he's invented her ghost. "Keep walking, Connie."

He knows she's right, but he's so thirsty that his tongue has swollen inside his mouth, and if he doesn't find water soon, he'll collapse. So he sighs, angles himself between the shards of broken doorway glass, and enters the 7-Eleven.

It's small—two narrow aisles flanked by an enclosed counter up front. Dust blankets the stock like pristine brown snow. A morbidly obese woman with a balding black widow's peak and chipped purple nail polish stands behind the counter, holding a bloodied issue of *The Enquirer*. "Zombies rise up from Baton Rouge Ghetto!" the lead article screams.

"Hi," Connie says.

The woman drops the magazine and bobbles in his direction. Something has eaten most of her abdomen and in the weeks or months since her death, the wet climate has not dried her out, but instead made a moldy home of her. He pictures lizards, crickets, even unborn children flying out from her gaping hole. Her apron, which presumably once read, *Thank Heaven for 7-Eleven!* now reads: *Heaven-Eleven!*

"Are you trying to tell me this is heaven?" Conrad asks.

She lunges at him and the force of her weight against the three-foot-high counter opens her stomach, spraying the shrunken Big Bite Hot Dogs' spit glass and *Enquirer* with gangrenous green fluid.

"Sorry. I didn't mean to tease you," he grunts as he wipes his face and pitches toward the darkened glass refrigerators in the back.

Behind him, Heaven figures it out and climbs the counter, then falls to the floor and crawls after him on a leaking stomach.

Conrad tries to pick up his pace, but he's so dehydrated that his heart is a trapped bird in his chest, fluttering and in pain.

Do zombies eat cold meat? Do they dream of electric sheep?

"Shut up about the poor, innocent zombies and find the water, Con!" he hisses, only he's too tired to use Gladys' voice, so now it's just him, talking to himself, which strikes him as sort of sad.

Behind, Heaven pushes herself to her feet. Her lips spread into a grin, and then keep spreading until they split open. The heat has turned her blood to thick soup that doesn't run.

He hurries, but his heart's not in it. Literally. It's pumping spastically, as if to Muzak—his wedding song forty years ago:

With all of your faults, I love you still. It had to be you!

Lovely young Heaven lunges and swipes at him. He reaches the refrigerator, whose shelves are lined with new world gold, and lifts a gallon-sized container of Poland Spring Water. Though Heaven's gaining, he chugs for one second . . . two . . . three . . . as he rounds the second aisle and doubles back toward the exit.

Just then, something cracks. "What the—?" he asks.

Glass skids like sand under Heaven's feet. To his shock, she isn't shambling anymore; she's running. Bad luck. Runners are rare.

"Hurry up, Con," he pants, but he's rooted there for a second, water in hand, as her voluminous flesh bounces and thuds. He's wondering if maybe this is the second coming and he got left behind, because Heaven's lips have split length-wise like a hag's clit, and inside, all her teeth are gold.

She dives, fast this time. He doesn't know she's got hold of his denim jacket until she reels him into a festering embrace. She's strong and tall—his toes don't even touch the floor, so he uses her body as a hinge and kicks up as hard as he can. His knees slop against her chest, hooking gristle as something cracks (her ribs? her hardened kidneys?), and she drops him.

Back muscles screaming like cop sirens, he dives over the counter. His hands find the twelve-gauge on the shelf beneath the cash register, and he reaches over and presses it against Heaven's ugly face before his physical mind ever recognizes that it's a gun.

"I'm sorry, Heaven" he intends to say as he squeezes the trigger. But instead, Freudian slip: "I'm sorry, Delia."

The mention of his daughter's name trips him up. He hesitates as he shoots, and by luck or intention, she knocks the gun out of the way. He hears the sound of shattering glass, but doesn't see what the slug hit. All he can see is Heaven as she sinks her gold teeth into his shoulder, down to the bone.

There's no time to think. He reaches inside her open belly with both hands and pulls her spine until it cracks. She hugs him tighter and then lets go, falling backward and in half.

"I loved you where the ocean met the sky," he tells the thing named Heaven, though he does not hear himself say those strange words. She blinks, only her eyelids aren't long enough to cover her rot-bloated eyes. So she watches him, perhaps seeing nothing, perhaps seeing everything, as he pulls the trigger and her head explodes.

When he's finished, he stands over her remains while his shoulder bleeds and infection worms its way through his heart and into his frontal lobe. "I'm sorry, Delia," he tells her, "for that bloodlust. For Adam, and not testifying. For not believing you that time you called. Especially for that. I'm sorry for everything," he says. Then he staggers out, a damned man down a long, lonely road that is almost over, toward Delia.

II.
How Rosie Perez Foretold the End

Some blamed cockroach feces. Others, the hand of God. Whatever it was, nobody who got the virus survived. It attacked the immune system first, then it devoured the entire frontal lobe. The sick forgot who they were or how to walk, and eventually, how to breathe. After they died, the virus worked its way into the hindbrain's instinct center, and kept eating. Then something funny happened. They woke up, only this time, the virus was in charge, and it was hungry.

Fox News broke the story on April 1, 2020. At first, everybody thought it was a joke: the dead rising from embalming and autopsy tables, sick beds, basement bedrooms. They spread the blood-borne disease with their bites. It started in Baton Rouge, but quickly spread to all of Louisiana. Overnight, hospitals throughout the south were full. A week later, national radio signals and satellites were offline. Two weeks after that, the army disbanded and went rogue. By Easter, America had dissolved.

Conrad had only been walking for three months since the world ended, but it felt like years. He didn't like to think about the old days. They were bittersweet.

When his wife got pregnant with Delia more than twenty years ago, Gladys had called the child a gift from God. After three miscarriages, two years of fertility treatments, and, finally, experimental blood transfusions, they'd almost given up hope. "She's the best thing we could have hoped for," Gladys said the day she arrived at the hospital, and for once, cynical Conrad had agreed: Delia Christen Wilcox was perfect.

Smart, pretty, full of giggles. They'd doted, indulged, hugged, and kissed until their hearts had overfilled, broken, and grown back larger and more accommodating. And she'd taken. And kept taking. It had started at her mother's tit, which she'd suckled too hard and drawn blood. Then the bigger things: backyard swing-set, horseback riding lessons, her own room, a lock on her door, hand-sewn boutique clothes, ski vacations, all-night curfews, and finally, the silver and crystal, and even their flat screen television.

Drugs, they'd guessed, though they'd never known for sure. After their dog Barkley went missing, Conrad had imagined it was something much worse. Bloodier. Probably, one of them should have asked.

She moved out at sixteen and began couch surfing at boyfriends' houses. "Back surfing," he'd once called it, for which the kid had slapped him. He'd slapped her right back. Then she'd bit his arm hard enough to draw blood.

There were more shenanigans. The house got broken into. The Dodge stolen. Some fool named Butter had called them at all hours, asking for his "Sweet Momma." They instituted a curfew when the high school kids at Tom's River started turning up dead, but she'd still climbed out the window and come waltzing back at dawn. Then she went missing entirely, and though both of them had imagined this absence in their darkest moments and assumed it would bring relief, it only ushered more misery. Was she cold, frightened, alone? Did she need them, only she was ashamed to ask?

Two years later, they got the call from a special victims unit detective in Louisiana—Delia had been arrested for the human trafficking of her own child.

He'd learned but had promptly forgotten the particulars: A son named Adam born a year after she left home, a kiddie-porn ring, a trannie boyfriend who'd kept her high and happy, a $1000 payoff for her infant son. It amounted to less than the going rate for any of the boy's individual organs on the black market, as if the living child as a whole was worth less than the sum of his parts.

Though he considered it, in the end Conrad decided not to testify in his daughter's defense. She was sentenced to eight years at the Louisiana Women's Correctional Facility. He never visited. She never wrote. He and Gladys legally adopted Adam. They gave away Delia's pretty things and painted her old room blue. Adam never learned to attach significance to the word mother, and for this they considered themselves lucky.

"It's like she's dead," Gladys once said. Behind her, the section of wall where Delia's picture once hung had appeared especially white.

"It's not like she's dead," Conrad replied. "It's like she was never born."

After some time, they got used to the boy. They cherished his coos, and the way he cried out with glee when he woke from naps, so happy, once again, to find them waiting. This second time around the scale tilted in the opposite direction, and they did not spare the rod. For this they were rewarded with an obedient, if less spirited child.

Trouble came when the boy turned five. It started with the fevers. When the welts appeared, the specialists diagnosed him with viral meningitis. He'd gotten it, the best anyone could figure, from an act of sodomy while under his mother's care. This was also how he'd gotten the syphilis.

Conrad and Gladys sold everything Delia had not stolen, from the diamond ring to the Belgian lace linens. When insurance wouldn't cover the experimental spinal filtration, they mortgaged their house. Little Adam lived in the Columbia-Presbyterian Intensive Care Unit, and as much as they could, they lived there, too.

Two months later, they saw firsthand in the hospital what the virus did to its victims. They survived somehow, in the way that people meant to live through every kind of misery always do. To his own surprise, Conrad got cold blooded. He bashed two infecteds' heads with an IV pole while Gladys pulled the tubing from Adam's wrists, and together they ran. Most others, from the administrators to the doctors, surrendered with open hands and horrified expressions. Fighting meant believing, and they hadn't been ready for that. But by then Conrad's daughter was a jailbird junkie, his grandson's skin too tender to touch, and his wife a new-age Jesus freak, praying for the health of her lost family, so what the fuck did a few zombies matter?

He and Gladys took the boy back home to Tom's River, where he wheezed his final breaths in their arms. Throughout, Adam wore this betrayed expression on his face, like he'd died under the misapprehension that Conrad was God and could have cured him, but had chosen otherwise, to teach him a lesson.

Outside their manicured split-level ranch, sirens blasted. Carnage littered the streets. Inexplicably, his walking buddy Dale Crowther, slick with soap, ran naked down Princeton Road. But the animated dead stuck to old routines, and in the suburbs nobody visits their neighbors, so Conrad dug the shallow grave in the backyard next to the family dog's bones unperturbed.

On the television the next night, they learned that the research institutes were close to a cure. With Martial Law declared and Civil Rights rescinded, the CDC had turned the southern prisons into laboratories, and begun experimenting on convicts. In thick Brooklyn-ese, Rosie Perez, the fill-in WPIX news anchor, announced that the government had discovered a twenty-three-year-old convict who was immune.

"Isn't that the lady from the lottery movie?" Gladys asked. Conrad shushed her by putting his hand over her mouth, and they'd sat erect and tense as metal tuning forks while a still photo of their daughter had illuminated the television. She'd looked younger and more pissed off than he'd expected.

"They shot her full of the virus and she's not sick?" Gladys whispered. "Thank the Great Buddha. My baby, I love you so much. Momma loves you," she told the angry woman on the glowing screen while Conrad inspected his hands, because the sight of his wife's tears, when he was helpless to console her, was intolerable.

Then Rosie returned, and spoke off teleprompter. "So, basically, we're killing a buncha prisoners even though there's like, a million zombies out there we could capture and test instead. So if this Delia Wilcox winds up curing everybody, then I guess it was worth it. But if she doesn't . . . " Rosie had looked directly into the camera, through the screen, at Conrad, and he'd felt like someone who's done wrong, and been caught.

"Think about it, people! They can't see and they can't hear but they'll still chase you twenty miles, 'cause it's not your skin these fuckin' things want. This virus eats souls. That's not gonna be me. Is it gonna be you?"

Rosie glared. Connie thought about Delia, and the dog Barkley, and that day the ocean met the sky. Then Rosie produced a gun, pressed it to the side of her head while the cameraman shouted, thought better of her strategy, placed the gun in her mouth, and fired. The program went offline.

Conrad and Gladys got close enough to press their faces to the snowy screen, just in case Delia came back. She didn't. After a half-hour, a rerun of *America's Funniest Home Videos* played. Somebody's cheeky monkey stole a bunch of bananas from a grocery store. Then the signal went out, the television was gone, and America died, just like that.

That night, Gladys shook him awake. The bed was just a mattress on the floor—he'd broken apart the cedar frame, along with the rest of the wood furniture, and nailed it against the windows and doors. They were living on saltines and defrosted vegetables. Some days it felt like camp, but mostly it didn't.

"I'm dying, Connie," Gladys said.

His belly filled with cold and his heart slowed as it pumped. "You're healthy as a cow, Gladys," he told her, though in fact she was sweating now, her breath shallow, and he understood with increasing alarm that there was something he'd forgotten.

"It's my heart. We're out of the digitalis."

"I'll get it right now," he answered. The digitalis—why hadn't she reminded him?

"It's no good, Connie," she said, and he realized then that she hadn't been too *upset* to help dig Adam's plot: she'd been too *sick*. "I didn't tell you because I didn't want you to risk it."

"Stop this talk," he answered, standing now, in the dark. Orange light played through the cracks in the windows, because something out there was on fire. "I know a little high school chemistry. We'll cook it on the kitchen stove. What's digitalis made of?"

"No, Con. I'm on my way, and you've got to promise me something."

He ran his hands along the sheets, and found that they were wet with her sweat. "I won't promise you anything. You tricked me, you coward."

Gladys shook her head. "Stop that, Connie. Now promise. I won't rest peacefully knowing she's alone. Locked up, even, with no one to remember to feed her. Remember the time with the blood? She drank it all straight out of the freezer bag. Maybe there's a reason she ran off and it wasn't just the drugs. We were wrong to give up on her like that. You've got to promise to see what's become of her."

He looked at his wife, whose complexion had turned orange with the fire. Over these last thirty-nine years, she'd grown wrinkled and fat and timid. He hated her whiny voice, and her old lady stink, and her sagging tits. Mostly, he hated her worthless ticker. "I'm empty, Gladys. I don't love anything anymore. Not even you."

She shook her head in what he would later remember as amusement. You're married to somebody that long, you know better than to pretend like love is a fish. "Oh shut up and find her, you big baby!"

In the morning he dressed her in her comfy bathrobe and plastic-soled slippers, then cut off her head just in case, and buried her next to the boy and the dog. By noon he was gone. Walking south, toward Delia.

III.
He Finds the Dog

It's only been two hours since he left the 7-Eleven, but his water is gone and he's thirsty again. Dusk has settled like a tall man's shadow, and though the prison is still two miles of dark, broken road to go, he doesn't have time to set up camp for the night, so will instead persevere.

His back went out during that last fight, so his crab-walk is exaggerated, but at least his shoulder has stopped hurting and become numb. Veins along his neck shine bright blue and green with infection, and he wonders what those little virions are eating. His defenses probably, then his memories.

That's when he hears the howl carrying across the broken blacktop. It sounds human—a soulful lament. He thinks it must be the thrumping bass of old world music since he can't imagine there are any survivors left who'd be so incautious as to wail.

Then again, maybe it's his imagination. Since he got bit, he's been hearing voices. They don't belong to Gladys.

—*Sorry I bit you, mister.*

—*Could you help an old altar boy, Father?*

—*I saw the multitudes to every side of me, and their howls were loud.*

He thinks it might be a disorder of the brain. He hopes so, at least.

"Maybe you didn't even get bit, Con," he says in the wrong voice. Gladys' voice. "Maybe you just imagined it, and you're totally fine."

"No, Gladdy. I'm losing it," he says as a second howl interrupts him. He spots the thing in the middle of the magnolia-strewn street. A black Lab retriever. A dog! It cowers with its head between its paws.

He can't help it. He smiles and comes to life a little. A dog! He thought they all were dead—eaten up first by the infected, and then by the survivors. He shambles faster. Grinning like an idiot. Remembers games he taught his old mutt Barkley—*fetch my beer* and *lift Gladys' skirt.*

As he crab-walks, he passes a crawling zombie without legs, that is chewing its own flesh—

I like it because it is bitter, and because it is my heart.

—but is too decomposed to chase him.

When he gets to the pup he offers it his closed fist. Out of habit, he pulls back when he sees the thing's chewed-up snout and bloated, white eyes. It doesn't try to bite him, and he's confused until he realizes that it smells his infection and knows they are kindred. So he does the dog a favor. With one hand, he takes it by the chin, and with the other he draws the butt of his shotgun and smashes it over the mutt's skull. It whines, just like a real dog.

I loved you where the ocean met the sky, he thinks, *even though your mouth was bloody.* Then he keeps walking, toward Delia. By his map, he's almost there.

IV.
Bestial Creatures

He's seen a lot of things, none of them good. In Tupelo he met a band of lunatics who sacrificed their healthiest to the infected in the hopes of pleasing God. Still, they'd been company. In Delaware he met a couple who traveled with him until they got botulism from canned Spam. How can you taste the difference? In Asheville he took pity on an old shut-in and stole a kitchen's worth of food for her before leaving. On his way out she said, "Stay. Take care of me. You can't really think your daughter's still alive." She wept as he shut the door to her small, airless basement, and it occurred to him that in the old days, he might have wasted more time trying to comfort her.

When Delia was small, he'd carried her on his shoulders from place to place, and pitied his bosses at the accounting firm, who'd considered their children's rearing the domain of women. Now that seemed smug. Who had he been, to judge? Shit happens. You can blame yourself and God and everybody around you, but sometimes shit just happens.

Like when they went fishing, and the trout flopped in the plastic bucket filled with water. The stillness of the ocean had mesmerized him, and for a moment, he mistook nine-year-old Delia's bloody mouth for a fever dream. But then he heard the slurping. The sun began to rise, and its color married the water to the sky. Maybe it was the blood treatments, or bad genes, or bad rearing. Maybe some people are just born wrong, and there is nothing you can do. "I love you," he told her as he'd dumped the dead bluefish back into the water.

A few years later, Barkley turned up drained and hanging from the roof like a Christmas suckling pig. He buried the dog before Gladys ever saw how badly it was mangled.

Once, a long time ago, he got a phone call. Gladys slept through, even while he spoke in hushed tones next to her. The voice on the other line came reluctantly, " . . . . Dad?"

"Yeah?" It had been months by then. She'd left on a Sunday afternoon while they were at church, and had taken her mother's heirloom pearls with her.

" . . . I need help," she said. "Money. I'm in trouble."

He looked at the phone a long while, thinking. "Did you hurt somebody?"

"It's not about that. It's a debt. About five thousand."

"We're out, D. You robbed us blind and I'm not working full-time like I used to."

"They'll make me pay for it with my body," she said. "And I'm pregnant, Dad." She'd been crying, but that hadn't meant it was true. He'd been so angry, or maybe so shocked, that he'd hung up.

Next time they heard from her was two years later, in Baton Rouge. His heart swelled like a leaking sponge when he found out she'd been telling the truth.

"Did you ever imagine she had a baby?" Gladys asked as they sat on the plane headed south, their IRAs cashed in for bail. "It's a blessing, maybe," she said with tearful eyes. "Little feet running around. Burping and pooping. God, I've missed that."

Connie looked out the window at the clouds as they'd kissed the ocean.

He thought about how, in purgatory, you relive your life over and over without ever finding resolution or redemption. The colors outside the plane had been blue ocean on blue sky, and, in between, the red of a sunset. "I had no idea," he'd said.

V.
Delia and the Start of It All

The prison is an ordinary building. The cast-iron gate surrounding it is open and rusted. It's dark out, but with the infection threading his veins, Connie can see. He can hear, too. Already, he knows that the prison is lousy with the dead. They're looking for things they've lost. Children. Love. Ambitions. Their souls.

"*Maybe she wasn't immune, and they only told people that to keep hope alive*," he says in Gladys' voice as he comes to the end of Emancipation Place. "*It's a lie, just like everything else. Maybe she wasn't the cure; she was the cause.*"

"You're the optimist, Glady. Not me."

"You should shoot yourself now while you still can. I hate the idea of you turning into one of them. What if there's a heaven, and you're not allowed because your soul is gone?"

He stops and looks up at the vast, brick prison whose windows are all barred. "I've come this far, Glady. We both know she was never right, but I can't chicken out now," he says, then climbs the steps to the entrance.

The lobby inside is small and long, with reception stations down the entire length of the building. He wanders first the east wing, then the west, where he passes a slender child who sways to the rhythm of the vents that pump hot, wet air. Her eyes are bloody, and out of habit, he kicks her so that she lands against the tiled hall wall. Something cracks (her femur?) but she doesn't come after him. Only lies against the cafeteria wall like a fractured doll.

"Sorry," he mumbles, then keeps walking.

It's okay, she answers in his mind. *Have you seen my daddy? He abandoned me.*

"That's a low blow," he mumbles back, only maybe he doesn't say the words. Maybe now, he and the dead understand each other.

She grins.

The holding cells are in the back of the building. About thirty in all, they border the periphery of a large, two-story room. Connie walks from cell to cell. Half are empty, the other half singly occupied by emaciated, uninfected women lying mostly in their beds. None bear Delia's face. It seems a waste to Conrad that no one thought to set them free or feed them. In cell nine, a woman clings to the bars with locked fingers. Her front teeth are worn down to the gums from where she tried to bite her way out.

There are zombies, too, of course. They walk in aimless circles, and have spread nearly equidistant—about one per every ten square feet—like air molecules in stasis, mindless and inanimate. For the most part, they don't notice him, though he can hear their thoughts:

I'm hungry.

I'm thirsty.

I'm lonely.

It's so dark in here, and my love is so dry.

In the basement of the west wing, he finds the makeshift laboratory where it looks like surgeries happened in the hallways. He sees the IV trees, monitors, and needles that remind him of Adam. It occurs to him that he and Gladys never asked Delia if she wanted the child. Instead they took him, then abandoned her as if she were junk. In admitting his own fault, it's easier to admit the greater truth: she murdered the fish, and Barkley, and those high school kids, too. She was born with a bloodlust.

In the basement, he finds the rest of the prisoners chained to gurneys. They must have been injected with the virus, because their heads are cleanly sawed away.

A doctor and nurse, both infected, wander the aisles, forever trapped in their roles of sick and, well, prisoner and captive. They seem to believe they are ministering comfort as they check lifeless wrists for pulses.

"Delia!" he shouts. They look at him for a moment, then return to their work. *If she is alive, and I find her, I will be happy,* he thinks. *Even if she has not changed, I will take comfort from finishing this journey, and be fulfilled.*

"Delia!" he cries. Like his joints, his throat is beginning to lock.

Just then, a tiny, faraway voice shouts back: "Here!"

It's been years since he's seen her, but her voice transcends time. It is imprinted upon him and dwells in the reptile part of his brain that even the virus cannot devour. His body moves, almost of its own volition. Not even his back hurts anymore. He is entirely numb.

"Delia!"

In reply is that same hesitation from years ago, when she called late at night while Gladys slept. He's run that moment over in his mind every day since, and recognizes now that her hesitation was shame. It was always shame.

" . . . Dad?"

He's racing on stiff, rigor mortis legs while his favorite memories, long forgotten, surface: the night she stayed home from a party to play chess with him; the poster of dogs playing poker in her bedroom that he never took down, even after Adam moved in; the color red, that he has forever associated with Delia, his perfect child, who was born with a taste for blood. These memories surface like exploding stars, and then just as quickly, disappear. He tries to catch them, but they are mist. By the time he reaches the lower level of the basement, he is aware only of their loss, and not what they contained.

"Delia!" He cries, and now he can't remember—is he chasing her ghost, or the actual girl?

"Dad, I'm here. In the bomb shelter!" she answers.

He shambles, standing tall now, past the walking dead National Guard and orderlies and reporters, through the second examination room, where the rest of the headless prisoners lay, and toward the back stairs that lead farther down. His muscles tear and creak as he descends. He unlocks another door to another wide room, where there are no zombies. Just a single cell in the center of the room. Several bodies lay half inside the bars, their legs and chests chewed down to the bones. He looks up, and there is Delia, red-cheeked and glowing, peering out from her cage.

"Dad," she says.

He doesn't remember her name, and her young, vigorous face doesn't look familiar, but he knows her, and he loves her like red dawn. He walks stiff-legged to the bars. She's crying. The sound is both terrible and beauteous.

There are voices, many voices, whispering words of nonsense.

I'm hungry.

I'm lonely.

It's so dark.

Nine hundred ninety-nine times out of a thousand, my master will lie.

And then, through all that, so softly he can barely hear it: *Connie, promise me. She's all we've got.*

The woman is small and sharp-featured. Though he has no evidence or memory, he knows she is his daughter. "You're immune?" he asks.

"Sort of," she says. She can't look him in the eyes.

"Why didn't they make a vaccine?"

She shakes her head. He waits for more. She doesn't ask about the boy, Adam. He doesn't remember the name or what the word represents. He only knows he's disappointed, like always. And she's ashamed, like always. And the chasm between their two distinct natures is red.

"I got bit," he tells her. "Where are the keys? I better get you out so you can run away."

She nods her head at the key ring about twenty feet away and he retrieves it. There is only one key, and it occurs to him that to put her here, they must have thought she was very dangerous.

"Don't worry about me," she says. "I can't get what you have."

Something clicks inside him. The part that knew this all along. The part that came all this way because it knew, and needed to finish what it had started.

He comes closer. In one hand, he's got the shotgun. In the other, the key. He feels himself nodding off. He thinks about the ocean and the sky, and the time they went fishing at dawn, and how she told him she loved him, too.

And then there is Gladys, looking down on them both with the baby in her arms like the Virgin Mary.

"Why are you immune?" he asks.

She points to the back of her cell. He notices that the structures he'd first imagined as furniture are bones. She has fashioned a chair, a bed. The rest are piled and polished like shiny rocks. He realizes why this room is free of zombies. Little is left, save their bones. "I feed on their blood. Any blood. It keeps me young. But you knew that."

He nods, but doesn't answer, because he has lost the words. He is losing himself, one brain cell at a time.

She licks her lips, and he sees that she's less happy to see him than hungry. But this is the nature of parents and children. The former give, the latter take. "The key, Dad?" she asks.

It feels sharp in his hand. He remembers those missing high school kids, and after that, the junkies' bodies he read about in the paper that had been drained of blood. No wonder she developed a taste for heroin.

"The virus came from me," she says. "I bit someone and they lived. It mutated inside them and spread."

"I'm dying," he says.

Her orange jumpsuit is slack in the hips and waist. It's probably been a while since she fed. If he opens the door for her, she'll make a meal of him. But what are fathers for, if not sustenance? "Fuck you, Dad. You never understood it was a gift. You made me ashamed."

He shakes his head. Feels his heart slowing in his chest. It doesn't remember how to pump, so he hits it, hard. "I love you," he says.

Her eyes water. He thinks that means she's sad, but he can't really tell. Monsters don't act like normal people. "I love you, too," she answers. "Now give me the key."

Are you lonesome, just like me?

Connie, did you know? Gladys asks. Maybe it's coming from him. Maybe it's her ghost.

"Yes, I knew," he whispers. "So did you."

Behind the bars, Delia licks her lips. "The key."

He doesn't remember his name anymore, or this woman before him. All that is left is the emotion underneath it, and instinct.

"Now, Dad."

He fires the shotgun. His aim is true.

Then he turns the shotgun on himself, but it is too long and his fingers won't obey him, so he drops it.

The young woman lies motionless while blood pools around her. He thinks about the color blue as he reaches through the bars that will now separate them for an eternity, and squeezes her fingers. She squeezes back as if she is relieved, and then lets go.

In sadness he can no longer comprehend, his heart tears itself into wings and flaps blood. It is a caged bird in there, that has shred itself inside-out but still can't get free.

We live in the Age of Solipsism. You care only for yourself and that which is yours. The agony of another—or even the existence of monstrosity—goes almost unnoticed unless viewed on film or video or in pixels . . .

SEA WARG

TANITH LEE

1.

One dull red star was sinking through the air into the sea. It was the sun. But eastward the October night had already commenced. There the water was dark green and the air purple, and the old ruinous pier stood between like a burnt spider.

Under the pier was a ghostly blackness, holed by mysterious luminous apertures. Ancient weeds and shreds of nets dripped. The insectile, leprous, wooden legs of the pier seemed to ripple, just as their drowning reflections did. The tide would be high.

The sea pushed softly against the land. It was destroying the land. The cliffs, eaten alive by the sea (smelling of antique metal, fish odor of Leviathan, depth, death), were crumbling in little pieces and large slabs, and the promenade, where sea-siders had strolled not more than thirty years ago, rotted and grew rank. Even the DANGER notices had faded and in the dark were only pale splashes, daubed with words that might have been printed in Russian.

But the sea-influencing moon would rise in a while.

Almost full tonight.

Under the pier the water twitched. Something moved through it. Perhaps a late swimmer who was indifferent to the cold evening or the warning danger—keep out. Or nothing at all maybe, just some rogue current, for the currents were temperamental all along this stretch of coast.

A small rock fell from above and clove the water, copying the sound of a rising fish.

The sun had been squashed from view. Half a mile westward the lights of hotels and restaurants shone upward, like the rays of another world, another planet.

When the man had stabbed him in the groin, Johnson had not really believed it. Hadn't *understood* the fountain of blood. When the next moment two security guards burst in and threw the weeping man onto the fitted carpet, Johnson simply sat there. "Are you okay? *Fuck.* You're not," said the first security guard. "Oh. I'm—" said Johnson. The next thing he recalled, subsequently, was the hospital.

The compensation had been generous. And a partial pension, too, until in eighteen years' time he came of age to draw it in full. The matter was hushed up otherwise, obliterated. Office bullying by the venomous Mr. Haine had driven a single employee—not to the usual nervous breakdown or mere resignation—but to stab reliable Mr. Johnson, leaving him with a permanent limp and some slight but ineradicable impairments both of a digestive and a sexual nature. "I hope you won't think of us too badly," said old Mr. Birch, gentle as an Alzheimer's lamb. "Not at all, sir," replied Johnson in his normal, quiet, pragmatic way.

Sandbourne was his choice for the bungalow with the view of the sea—what his own dead father had always wanted, and never achieved.

Johnson wasn't quite certain why he fitted himself, so seamlessly, into that redundant role.

Probably the run-down nature of the seaside town provided inducement. House prices were much lower than elsewhere in the southeast. And he had always liked the sea. Besides, there were endless opportunities in Sandbourne for the long, tough walks he must now take, every day of his life if possible, to keep the spoilt muscles in his left leg in working order.

But he didn't mind walking. It gave extra scope for the other thing he liked, which had originally furnished his job in staff liaison at Haine and Birch. Johnson was fascinated by people. He never tired of the study he gave them. A literate and practiced reader, he found they provided him with animated books. His perceptions had, he was aware, cost him his five-year marriage: he had seen too well what Susan, clever though she had been, was up to. But then, Susan wouldn't have wanted him now anyway, with his limp and the bungalow, forty-two years of age, and two months into the town and walking everywhere, staring at the wet wilderness of waters.

"I see that dog again, up by the old pier."

"Yeah?" asked the man behind the counter. "What dog's that, then?"

"I tol' yer. Didn' I? I was up there shrimping. An' I looks an' it's swimming aroun' out there, great big fucker, too. Don' like the looks of it, mate. I can tell yer."

"Right."

"Think I oughta call the RSPCee like?"

"What, the Animal Rights people?" chipped in the other man.

"Nah. He means the RSPCA, don't ya, Benny?"

"'S right. RSPCee. Only it shouldn' be out there like that on its own. No one about. Just druggies and pushers."

The man behind the counter filled Benny's mug with a brown foam of coffee and slapped a bacon sandwich down before the other man at the counter. Johnson, sitting back by the café wall, his breakfast finished, watched them closely in the way he had perfected, seeming not to, seeming miles off.

"An' it's allus this time of the month."

"Didn't know you still had them, Benny, times of the month."

Benny shook his head, dismissing—or just missing—the joke. "I don' mean that."

"What *do* ya mean then, pal?"

"I don' like it. Great big bloody dog like that, out there in the water when it starts ter get dark and just that big moon ter show it."

"Sure it weren't a shark?"

"Dog. It was a dog."

"Live and let live," said the counter man.

Benny slouched to a table. "You ain't seen it."

After breakfast Johnson had meant to walk up steep Hill Road and take the rocky path along the cliff top and inland, to the supermarket at Crakes Bay.

Now he decided to go eastwards along the beach, following the cliff line, to the place where the warning notices were. There had been a few major rockfalls in the 1990s, so he had heard; less now, they said. People were always getting over the council barricade. A haunt of drug addicts, too, that area, "down-and-outs holing up like rats" among the boarded-up shops and drown-foundationed houses farther up. Johnson wasn't afraid of any of that. He didn't look either well-off or so impoverished as to be desperate. Besides, he'd been mugged in London once or twice. As a general rule, if you kept calm and gave them what they wanted without fuss, no harm befell you. No, it was in a smart office with a weakened man in tears that harm had happened.

The beach was an easy walk. Have to do something more arduous later.

The sand was still damp, the low October sun reflecting in smooth, mirrored strafes where the sea had decided to remain until the next incoming tide fetched it. A faintly hazy morning, salt-smelling and chilly and fresh.

Johnson thought about the dog. Poor animal, no doubt belonging to one of the drugged outcasts. He wondered if, neglected and famished, it had learned to swim out to sea, catching the fish that a full moon lured to the water's surface.

There were quite a few other people walking on the beach, but after the half mile it took to come around to the pier-end, none at all. There was a dismal beauty to the scene. The steely sea and soft gray-blue sky featuring its sun. The derelict promenade, much of which had collapsed. Behind these the defunct shops with their look of broken toy models, and then the long, helpless arm of the pier, with the hulks of its arcades and tea-rooms, and the ballroom, now mostly a skeleton, where had hung, so books on Sandbourne's history told one, sixteen crystal chandeliers.

Johnson climbed the rocks and rubbish—soggy pizza boxes, orange peels, beer cans—and stood up against the creviced pavement of the esplanade. It looked as if bombs had exploded there.

Out at sea nothing moved, but for the eternal sideways running of the waves.

At the beginning of the previous century, a steamboat had sailed across regularly from France, putting in by the pier, then a white confection like a bridal cake. The strange currents that beset this coast had made that the only safe spot. The fishing fleet had gone out from here too, this old part of the city-town, the roots of which had been there, it seemed, since Saxon times. Now the boats put off from the west end of Sandbourne, or at least they did so when the rest of Europe allowed it.

Johnson wondered whether it was worth the climb, awkward now with his leg, over the boarding and notices. By day there were no movements, no people. They were night dwellers very likely, eyes sore from skunk, skins scabrous from crack.

And by night, of course, this place would indeed be dangerous.

As he turned and started back along the shore, Johnson's eye was attracted by something not the cloud-and-sea shades of the morning, lying at the very edge of the land. He took it at first for some unusual shell or sea-life washed ashore. Then decided it must be something manufactured, some gruesome modern fancy for Halloween, perhaps.

In fact, when he went down the beach and saw it clearly, lying there as if it had tried to clutch at the coast, kept its grip but let go of all else, he found it wasn't plastic or rubber but quite real. A man's hand, torn off raggedly just behind the wrist bone, a little of which stuck out from the bloated and discoloring skin.

Naturally he thought about it, the severed hand.

He had never, even in London, come across such an item. But then, probably, he'd never been in the right (wrong) place to do so.

Johnson imagined that one of the down-and-outs had killed another, for drugs or cash. Maybe even for a burger from the Alnite Caff.

He did wonder, briefly, if the near-starving dog might have liked to eat the hand. But there wasn't much meat on a hand, was there?

That evening, after he had gone to the supermarket and walked all the way back along Bourne Road, he poured himself a Guinness and sat at his table in the little "study" of the bungalow and wrote up his find in his journal. He had kept a journal ever since he started work in Staff Liaison. Case-notes, histories . . . *people*—cameos, whole bios sometimes.

Later he fried a couple of chops and ate them with a green salad.

Nothing on TV. He read Trollope until 11:36, then went to bed.

He dreamed of being in the sea, swimming with great strength and ability, although in reality he had always been an inadequate swimmer. In the dream he was aware of a dog nearby, but was not made afraid by this. Instead he felt a vague exhilaration, which on waking he labeled as a sort of puerile pleasure in unsafety. Physically he had long outgrown it. But there, deep in his own mind, perhaps not so?

2.

The young man was leaning over his motorbike, adjusting something apparently. The action was reminiscent of a rider with his favorite steed, checking the animal for discomfort.

Johnson thought he had seen him before. He was what? Twenty-five, thirty? He had a thick shock of darkish fair hair, cut short the way they did now, and a lean face from which the summer tan was fading. In the sickly glare under the streetlight his clothes were good but ordinary. He had, Johnson thought, very long fingers, and his body was tall and almost athletic in build.

This was outside the pub they called in Sandbourne the "Biker Inn."

Johnson didn't know the make of the bike, but it was a powerful model, elegant.

Turning off Ship Street, Johnson went into the Cat In Clover. He wasn't yet curious as to why he had noted the man with the bike. Johnson noted virtually everyone. An hour into the evening he did, however, recall where he had twice seen him before, which was in the same launderette Johnson himself frequented. Nice and clean then. Also perhaps, like Johnson, more interested in coming out to do the wash than in buying a machine.

During the rest of the week Johnson found he kept seeing the man he then named, for the convenience of the journal, *Biker*. Johnson believed that in fact he wasn't coincidentally and now constantly "bumping into" Biker, but that he had become *aware* of Biker. Therefore he noticed him now each time he saw him, whereas formerly he had frequently seen him without noticing, therefore *without* consciously *seeing*.

This kind of thing had happened before.

In the beginning, when in his teens, Johnson had thought it meant something profoundly important, particularly when it was a girl he abruptly kept on seeing—that was, noticing. Even in his thirties he had been misled by that idea, with Susan. He had realized, after their separation, that what had drawn him to her at first wasn't love or sex but her own quirkiness and his observation of it. She had worked it out herself, eventually. In the final year of their life together she came to call those he especially studied (including those at Haine and Birch) his "prey." "Which of your prey are you seeing tomorrow?" she would ask playfully.

Now grasping that it was some type of acuity in him that latched on to certain others in this fashion, Johnson had not an instant's doubt that he had reacted differently to Biker.

So what was it then, with Biker? *What* had alerted Johnson there under the street lamp on that moonless night?

During the next week, Johnson took his washing to the launderette about six p.m., and there Biker sat.

Biker was unloading his wash, but raised his eyes. They were very long eyes, extraordinarily clear, a pale, gleaming gray.

"Cold out," said Johnson, dumping the washing.

"Yeah," said Biker.

"Damn it, this machine isn't working."

"Yeah," said Biker. He looked up again. "Try kicking it."

"You're joking," said Johnson placidly.

"No," said Biker, and he came over quite calmly, and did something astonishing. Which was he jumped straight upward with enormous agility and power, and fetched the washer the lightest but most expressive slap with his left foot. Landing, he was like a lion—totally coordinated, unfazed. While the machine, which had let out a rattling roar, now gulped straight into its cycle. Biker nodded and returned to his wash.

"Wow," said Johnson. "Thanks."

"Don't mention it."

"I owe you a drink. The girlfriend's refused to come round till I get these bloody sheets done."

Biker glanced at him.

Johnson saw there was neither reluctance nor interest in the smooth, lean face, hardly any expression at all. The eyes were only mercury and white china.

"I'll be in the Victory," he said.

Once Biker left, Johnson, not to seem too eager, stayed ten minutes with his washing. He had chosen the crank machine on purpose. And what a response he had got! Biker must be an acrobat. At the very least a trained dancer.

Perhaps, Johnson thought, he shouldn't indulge this. Perhaps it was unwise. But then, he usually did indulge his observation. It had never led to anything bad. Except once.

Had being stabbed and disabled made him reckless? He thought not. Johnson *wasn't* reckless. And he could afford the price of a couple of drinks.

When he got into the pub, the place was already full. The music machine filled the air with huge thuddings, while on every side other machines for gambling flashed like a firework display.

He looked round, then went to the bar and ordered a drink, whisky for the cold. He could already see Biker wasn't there.

Which might mean *he* had distrusted Johnson, or that something else had called him away. Or anything, really.

Johnson was not unduly disappointed. Sometimes *not* knowing was the more intriguing state. Besides, going out of the door he heard a man say, as if signaling to him, "Yeah, there's something out by the old pier sometimes. I seen it too. Big animal. Dolphin p'rhaps. But it was dark."

Yet another week after the exchange with Biker, Johnson was in the smaller supermarket, near the cinema, when he glimpsed his quarry, bikeless, driving by in a dark blue BMW.

Johnson knew he would thereafter keep his eyes open also for the car, whose number-plate he had at once memorized. He was sure, inevitably, that he had often seen the car as well. He was struck by an idea, too, that Biker, in some strange, low-key way, wished to be visible—the bike itself, the car, the habit of the launderette. And that in turn implied (perhaps) a wish to be less visible, or non-visible, on other occasions.

With his groceries Johnson picked up one of the local papers. He liked to glance at it; the doings of Sandbourne amused and puzzled him. Accordingly he presently read in it that another late-season holiday maker had gone missing. There had apparently been two the previous summer, who vanished without a trace. Keen swimmers, they were thought to have fallen foul of the wild currents east of the town. The new case, however, one Alice Minerva McClunes, had been a talented lady from New York. On the southeast coast to visit a niece, she had gone out with her camera and sketch pad and failed to return. "She wanted to stay on the beach," the presumably woebegone niece reported, "till moonrise. It was the full moon." Alice was, it seemed, known for her photography of moonlight on various things.

This small article stayed intransigently with Johnson for the rest of the evening. He reread it twice, not knowing quite why.

Johnson the observer had made no friendships in Sandbourne, but he had by now gained a few acquaintances to say "hello" to.

He went to the local library the next day, then to the fishmarket above the beach. There, in between the little shops, he met the man he knew as Reg. And then Biker appeared walking along from the east end of the town, from the direction actually of the eldritch pier. And Reg called out to him, "Hi, mate. Okay?" and Biker smiled and was gone.

As one might, Johnson said, "You know him? I've seen him around—nice bike. Drives a car, too, doesn't he?"

"Yes, that's Jason. Don't know his other name. Lives in one of the rock-houses. Got a posh IT job in London—only goes up a couple of times a week. Oh, and once a month, three days and nights in Nores." Reg pronounced this neighboring, still parochial, town in the proper local way as Nor-ez. "Bit of money, yes."

"A rock-house? They're the ones built into the cliff, aren't they?"

"Yep. Caves in back with pools of seawater. Pretty trendy now. Not so good when we get a freak high tide. Flooded out last year, all of 'em. Only, he was off at Nores—three days every time. Thought he might come back to see the damage but he never did. When I saw him he just says, 'I'll just buy a new carpet.' Okay for some."

"Yes," said Johnson regretfully.

But his mind was busy springing off along the last stretch of habitable Sandbourne, mentally inspecting the houses set back into the cliffs. Smugglers had put them to good use in the 1800s. Now renovated and "smart," they engaged the wealthy and artistic. He was curious (*of course* he was) as to which house was Jason's—Jason, who, after all, must be rich. He thought of the pools of sea that lay behind the facades, and the great stoops of bending cliff that overhung them. Johnson had seen photographs of these structures in *History of Sandbourne.*

He visualized acrobatic Jason leaping straight down into a glimmering, glittery, nocturnal pool, descending like a spear, wriggling effortless and subtle as an eel out through some pipe or fissure, and so into the black-emerald bowel of the sea. He pictured those cold silver eyes under the glazes of blind green water, and the whip of the two legs, working as one, like a merman's tail. But somehow, too, Johnson pictured Jason as a sort of dog—hairy, unrecognizable, though swimming—as if there had been a dream of this, and now he, Johnson, recalled. As gradually he had remembered, was remembering all the rest, the sightings in launderette, car—all, everything.

3.

Turquoise, blood-orange, daylight snagged the drips of nets under the skeletal arm of the pier. Bottle-green light gloomed through rotted struts, shining up the mud, debris, the crinkle of water like pleated glass . . .

And the day lifted to its zenith, and folded away. It was November now. Behind the west end, the sky bled through paintwork themes of amber and golden sienna. The sea blued. Sidelit, long tidal runners, like snakes with triangular pale indigo heads, swarmed inward on the land. Darkness began to stir in the east.

They forgot, people, how the dark began there, eastward, just as light did. The sun, the moon, rose always from the east. But so did night.

Never mind that. Soon the moon would be full again.

Under the pier, the mind was lying in its shell of skull. As dark filled in on dark, dark was in the brain, smooth and spontaneously ambient as the ink of a squid.

Under the pier.

Overhead the ruin, and the ancient ballroom, which a full moon might light better than sixteen chandeliers.

Something not a wave moved through the water.

Perhaps a late swimmer, indifferent to the cold.

Jason lived in the house behind the courtyard. It had high gates that were, most of the time, kept shut and presumably locked. A craning tree of a type unknown to Johnson grew up the wall, partly hiding with its bare, twisted slender branches an upper-storey window. Johnson discovered the correct house by knocking at another in the group, asking innocently for Jason, the man with the bike. An uninterested young woman said the man with the bike lived at the one with the courtyard. She didn't want to know Johnson's business. Johnson guessed the BMW would be parked in one of the garages above that corresponded with the rock terrace. The bike, according to the woman, was kept in the yard.

Having walked past the relevant house, he walked back and up Pelling Road to the cliff top. He sat on a bench there, looking down at the winter shore and the grayling sea. From here, away along the saucer curve of the earth, he could make out the pier like a thing of matchsticks. They said any storm destroyed always another piece of it. And yet there it still was, incredibly enduring.

He had visited the library again, looking at back numbers of the local papers. There had been a few disappearances mentioned in those past years he had viewed. But he supposed only tax-paying citizens or visitors would be counted. The coast's flotsam might well vanish without a trace.

That night the moon came up like a white plate in the tree at the end of the bungalow's small fenced garden.

The disk wasn't yet full, but filling out; in another couple of nights it would be perfect.

Johnson put down the Graham Greene novel he was reading and went out into the dusk.

Sea-influencing, blood-influencing, mind-influencing moon.

He thought of Jason, perhaps in his rich-man's house just above the beach, behind the high gates and the yard, inside stone walls with the sea in the back of them.

By midnight Johnson was in bed asleep. He dreamed clearly and concisely of standing inside the cliffs, in a huge cave that was pearl white, lit by a great flush of brilliance at either end. And the far end opened to the sea, long thick rollers combering in, and where they struck the inner floor of the cave, white chalk sprayed up in the surf. But then out of the sea a figure came, riding fast on a motorbike. He was clad in denim and had short andlustrous hair, but as he burst through the cave, brushing Johnson with the rush of his passage, anyone would have noticed that the biker had the face of a dog, and in his parted jaws, rather delicately, he held a man's severed hand.

Waking from this, Johnson found he had sat bolt upright.

There was a dull, groaning ache in his lower gut and back, which he experienced off and on since the stabbing. He was barely aware of it.

Johnson was thinking of the changes the moon brought. And how something so affected might well share an affinity with the lunar-tidal sea. But also Johnson thought of an old acquaintance of his, fussy Geoffry Prentiss, who had been fascinated by the sightings, detailed in papers, of strange fauna, such as the Beast of Bodmin. He'd coined a term for such a phenomenon: *warg.* An acronym, WARG stood for Weird Animal Reported Generally.

With a slow, inevitable movement, not really disturbing, Johnson got up, went into the bathroom, and presently returned to put on his clothes and boots.

By the time he reached the town center, the clock showed ten minutes to three a.m. There had been almost no one on the upper streets, just a young couple kissing. Soon though, a surreal distant pounding revealed the area of the nearest nightclubs, and outside the Jester a trio of youths were holding up another, who was being impressively sick. Compared to London, Sandbourne was a mild place. Or so it had seemed.

He wondered, when he turned east along the promenade, under the high lamps already strung with their Christmas neons of holly and stars, if he were sleepwalking. He considered this with complete calm, analytically. Never before had he taken his study of others to such an extremity. Had he in fact had a breakdown, or in more honest words, gone mad?

But the night was keen. He felt and smelled and saw and *experienced* the night. This was not a dream. He walked in the world.

The moon had vanished westward in cloud, as if in pretense of modesty. Beyond the line of land, the sea was jet-black under jet-black sky, yet the pale fringes of wavelets came in and in. Constant renewal. Repetition of the most elaborate and harmonious kind. Or the most *relentless* kind.

In the end, the seas would devour all the landmasses of the earth. The waters would cover them.

Several elderly men, drunk or drugged, sprawled on a bench and swore at him as he passed, less maliciously than in a sort of greeting for which, by now, they lacked other words.

Gulls, which never slept, circled high above the town, lit underneath translucently by the lamps.

Johnson went down the steps and into the area where the fishing fleet left its boats and sheds. The sand, the sheds, the boats, were sleeping. Only a tiny glow of fire about fifty feet away showed someone there keeping watch, or dossing.

The shadows clung as he passed the fish shops and turned into the terraced street above the shore. The lamps by the rock-houses were greenish and less powerful. They threw a stark quarter-glow on the stone walls, then on the many-armed tree, the two high gates. One of which stood ajar.

Jason, the acrobat with metallic eyes. And the gate was open.

Inside, the yard had been paved, but the bike wasn't to be seen. Instead a single window burned yellow in the lower storey, casting a reflected oblong, vivid and unreal as if painted there, on the ground.

Johnson accepted that it was impossible not to equate this with a trap, or an invitation, and that it was probably neither.

He hesitated with only the utter silence, the silence of the sea, which was a sound, to guide him. Such an ancient noise, the clockwork rhythm of an immortal god that could never cease. No wonder it was cruel, implacable.

He went through the gate and stepped softly over the yard until he reached the window's edge.

The bright room was lit by a powerful overhead source. It showed banks of computers, mechanical accessories, a twenty-first-century nerd's paradise. And there in the middle of it Jason kneeled on the uncarpeted floor. He was dressed in jeans, shirt, and jumper. He was eating a late supper.

A shock passed through Johnson, quite a violent one.

Afterwards, he was slightly amazed at his own reaction.

For Jason was not dining on a severed hand, not on anything human at all, and yet—Yet the way he ate and what he ate—a fish, evidently raw and very fresh, head and scales and fins and tail and eyes and bones all there, tearing at them with his opened jaws, eating, gnawing, swallowing all, those metal eyes glazed like those of a lion, a *dragon*—This alone. It was enough.

Not since London had Johnson driven, but his license was current and immaculate. Even his ironic leg, driving, gave him no problems.

He hired the red Skoda in town. It wasn't bad, easy to handle.

On the afternoon of the almost full moon, having waited on the Nores Road for six and three-quarter hours, he spotted Jason's blue BMW instantly. Johnson followed it on through forty minutes of country lanes, between winter fields and tall, bare trees, all the way to a small village known as Stacklebridge. Here, at a roundabout, the BMW turned around and drove straight back the way it had come.

Johnson, however, drove on to Newsham and spent an hour admiring the Saxon church, sheep, and rush-hour traffic going north and south. He had not risked the obvious move of also turning and tracking the other car homeward. Near Sandbourne, he was sure, Jason would park his vehicle in concealment off the road, perhaps in a derelict barn. Then walk, maybe even sprint the last distance, to reach his house or the pier before moonrise.

The nature of his studies had often meant Johnson must be patient. He had realized, even before following the blue car, that he could do nothing now, that was, nothing this month; it was already too late. But waiting was always part of watching, wasn't it? And he had been stupidly inattentive and over-confident only once, and so received the corrective punishment of a knife. He would be careful this time.

4.

He didn't need to dream about it now. He was forewarned, forearmed.

But the dream still occurred.

He was in the pier ballroom, and it was years ago because the ballroom was almost intact, just some broken windows and holes in the floor and walls, where brickwork and struts and darkness and black water showed. But the chandeliers burned with a cold, sparkling lemon glory overhead. All about were heaps of dancers, lying in their dancing clothes, black and white and rainbow. They were all dead and mutilated, torn, bitten, and rotted almost to unrecognizability.

Jason came up from under the pier, directly through the floor, already eating, with a savage hunger that was more like rage, a long white arm with ringed fingers.

But his eyes weren't glazed now. They were fixed on Johnson. They *knew* Johnson. And in ten seconds more Jason would spring, and as he sprang, would become what he truly was, even if only for three nights of every month. The nights he had made sure everyone who knew of him here also thought he spent in Nores.

Johnson reacted prudently. He woke himself up.

He had had dreams about other people, too, which had indicated to him some psychological key to what was troubling them, far beyond anything they had been able to say. Johnson had normally trusted the dreams, reckoning they were his own mechanism of analysis, explaining to him. And he had been very accurate. Then Johnson had dreamed that gentle, tearful Mark Cruikshank from Publicity had come up to him on the carpark roof at Haine and Birch and stuck a long, pointed fingernail through his heart. The dream was so absurd, so out of character, so overdramatic that Johnson dismissed it as indigestion. But a couple of days later Mark stabbed him in the groin, with the kind of knife you could now buy anywhere in the backways of London. For this reason Johnson did not think to discount the dreams of Jason. And for this reason, too, Johnson had known, almost at once, exactly what he was dealing with.

Christmas, personally irrelevant to Johnson for years, was much more important this year. Just as December was, with its crowds of frantic shoppers—not only in the festive, noisy shops, but in their cars racing up to London and back, or to Nores and back.

Moonrise on the first of the three nights (waxing full, full declining to gibbous) was earlier in the day, according to the calendar Johnson had bought. It was due at 5:33 p.m.

Not knowing, therefore, if Jason would set out earlier than he had the previous month in order to beat the rush-hour traffic after four, Johnson parked the hired Skoda in a lay-by just clear of the suburbs, where the Nores Road began.

In fact the BMW didn't appear until three-thirty. Perhaps Jason had been delayed. Or perhaps, as Johnson suspected, a frisson of excitement always ruled the man's life at this time, adding pleasure to the danger of cutting things fine. For, once the moon was up, visible to Jason and to others; the change must happen. (There were plenty of books, fiction and non, to apprise any researcher of this point.)

On this occasion, Johnson only followed the blue car far enough to get out into the hump-backed country lanes. Then he pulled off the road and parked on a narrow, pebbly shoulder.

He had himself to judge everything to within a hair's breadth.

To begin the maneuver too soon would be to call attention, and therefore assistance and so *dispersal*. Indeed, the local radio station would doubtless report it, and so might warn Jason off. There were other places after all that Jason, or what Jason became, could seek refuge in.

Probably Jason always turned round at the Stacklebridge roundabout, however. It was the easiest spot to do so.

Johnson kept his eye on his watch. He had made the trip twice more in the interim, and it took consistently roughly eighty minutes to the village and back. But already there was a steady increase in cars buzzing, and frequently too quickly, along the sea-bound lane.

At ten to four the sun went. The sky stayed a fiery lavender for another thirteen minutes.

At four twenty-five Johnson, using a brief gap in traffic, started the Skoda and drove it back fast onto and across the narrow road, simultaneously slamming into reverse. A horrible crunching. The car juddered to a permanent halt.

He had judged it on his last trip: stalled and slanted sidelong across the lane, the Skoda blocked the thoroughfare entirely for anything—save a supermodel on a bicycle.

Johnson got out of the car and locked the doors. He made no attempt to warn the next car whose headlamps he could see blooming. It came bounding over the crest of the lane, registered it had about twenty yards to brake, almost managed it, and tapped into the Skoda with a bump and screech. Belted in, the driver didn't come to much harm. But he had buckled a headlight, and the Skoda's bodywork would need some repairs, aside from its gearbox. The driver scrambled out and began to swear at Johnson, who was most apologetic, describing how his vehicle had gone out of control. They exchanged details. Johnson's were the real ones; he saw no need to disguise them.

As they communicated, three more cars flowed over the crest and, not going quite so fast, pulled to a halt without mishap. Meanwhile two other cars coming from the direction of Sandbourne were also forced to stop.

Soon there was quite a crowd.

The police must be called, and the AA, plus partners and others waiting. Lights from headlamps and digital gadgets flickered and blazed. Mobiles were out all along the verges, chattering and chiming and playing silly tunes under the darkling winter trees.

All the while, the back-up of trapped cars on either side was growing.

Covered by this group event, Johnson absented himself carefully, slipping off along the tree-walled hem of the fields, making his way back up the static vehicular line towards Stacklebridge.

People asked him if he knew what had happened, how long help would be in coming. He said some idiot had crashed his gears. He said the police were on their way.

It was full dark, five-fifteen, eighteen minutes to moonrise, when he noted Jason's BMW. It was boxed in on all sides, and people were out of their cars here, too, shouting, making calls, angry, frustrated, and only Jason still there, poised over the wheel, staring out blankly like something caught in a cage. *He* didn't look angry. He wasn't making a call. Standing back in darkness under the leafless boughs, Johnson observed Jason and timed the moon on his luminous watch.

In fact, the disk didn't come up over the slope to the left until the dial showed 5:41. By then the changes were well advanced.

Afterward, Johnson guessed no one else had noticed much what happened *inside* the BMW. It was the Age of Solipsism. You cared only for yourself and what was yours. The agony of another, unless presented on celluloid, was missed.

But Johnson saw.

He saw the flurry and then the frenzy, planes of half light and deep darkness fighting with each other like two vultures over a corpse. And he heard the screams.

And when the creature—and by then this was all one could call it—burst out, straight out the side of the BMW, none of them could ignore that they might have to deal with it.

Jason had become his true self. He—it—was about seven feet tall and solidly built, but as fluid in movement as an eel. The head and face, chest and back and arms were heavily hairy, covered in a sort of pelt through which two pale, fishlike eyes and a row of icy teeth glared and flamed. The genital area was also sheathed in fur, but under that the legs were scaled like those of a giant snake or fish. When the huge clawed hands rose up, they, too, had scales, very pallid in the blaze of headlights. It snarled, and it stank, rank, stale, fishy. This anomalous thing, with the face of a dog and the eyes of a cod, sprang directly against the crowd.

Johnson, cool, calculating, lonely Johnson (to whom every human was a type of study animal), had deemed casualties inevitable, and certainly there were a few. But then, as he, student of humanity, had predicted, they *turned.*

Subsequent news broadcasts spared no one who heard, saw, or read them the account of how a mob of already outraged people had ripped the monstrous beast apart. Questioned later they had been nauseous, shivering, crying, but at the hour, Johnson himself had seen what they did, and how they stood there after, looking down at the mess smeared and trampled on the roadway. Jason of course, given half a chance, would have and had done the same to them. And contrary to the myth, he did not alter back in death to human form, to lie there, defenseless and accusing. No, he, it, had retained the metamorphosis, to puzzle everyone for months, perhaps years, to come. Naturally, too, it hadn't needed a silver bullet, either. Silver bullets were the product of legends where the only strong metal, church candlesticks, was melted down to make suitable ammunition. If Johnson had had any doubt, Jason's own silvery eyes would have removed it.

That night, when the howling tumult and the flying sprays of blood had ceased, Johnson had stood there under the trees. He had felt quite collected. Self-aware, he was thinking of Mark Cruikshank, who had stabbed him, and that finally he, Johnson, for once in his bleak and manacled life, had got his own back on this bloody and insane world of aliens—werewolves, *human beings.*

There are tragedies we never get over, but we are, as a character in "Crawlspace" relates, supposed to grow enough scar tissue over the wounds to continue to function. But does every injury heal? And when truth is also pain, should it be told?

CRAWLSPACE

STEPHEN GRAHAM JONES

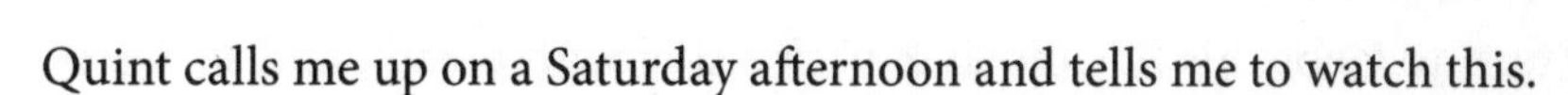

Quint calls me up on a Saturday afternoon and tells me to watch this.

I stand in my kitchen and study the stove I put in last Christmas, all my tools on the counter, and all the ones I'd borrowed from Quint. It's still crooked.

"What channel?" I say.

This is different, though.

Twenty minutes later, Sherry at home with my promise to be back before ten, I've eased down to Quint's, a broken six-pack on the seat beside me, the sole of my boot skimming the loose asphalt gravel between his house and mine.

He's waiting for me on the porch, smoking like he's twelve years old again and we only have five minutes before his aunt comes home.

"What?" I say, arcing a beer across the yard to him in a spiral so perfect it should be in a commercial.

He takes it, doesn't crack it open. That more than anything tells me something's up.

"Is it Tanya?" I say, looking behind me for some reason.

Tanya's Quint's wife. Sunday nights she's usually on-shift at the hospital.

"Inside," Quint says, and holds the screen door open, ushers me in.

I shrug, duck into the cat smell of his house and run my finger under my nose.

Quint places his hand on my shoulder like a priest and guides me past his television through the dead part of the kitchen to the hall, then down the hall. The only room this deep into his house is Gabe's. He's six months old, maybe. Born just before Christmas. The twin that lived, big tragedy, all that. One that's supposed to be already over, that Quint's supposed have dealt with. Not so much gotten out of his system—Sherry says things like that never get out of your system—but at least grown enough scar tissue over it to function.

Until now, too, I'd assumed that was the case. That Quint was functioning.

But now. Being led back to Gabe's room.

None of the pictures I have in my head are good. Better than half of them involve me lying to the police. Or, worse, to Tanya. So, when Quint palms Gabe's door open, spilling a wedge of light across his stained crib, Gabe just sleeping there, his thumb cocked in his mouth, I relax a bit.

"Say his name," Quint says.

"What?"

"Try to wake him up. Just not very hard."

"Quint, man—"

"My responsibility."

I turn to Gabe, his lips moving, back rising with breath, and shrug, fill my mouth with beer, do what I know's an annoying-as-hell little gargle.

Gabe shifts position but doesn't wake.

"What?" I say. "You gave him some Benadryl?"

My voice makes Gabe roll over, his head screwing around on his pudgy neck, his shoulder blades drawing together.

Quint crosses the room, places a hand on Gabe's side until his breathing's even again. Before he leaves he angles the baby monitor a little bit closer to the crib.

We walk back to the kitchen.

"Sherry put you up to this?" I ask.

Quint laughs without any sound, tells me to wait.

Again I look over my shoulder, for Tanya maybe, coming home early in her nurse whites, or for Sherry, waiting for me see how cute Gabe was. How we need one.

It's just us, though.

I push off the counter with my butt, follow where Quint leads.

It's to the garage, the old recliner Tanya told him he couldn't keep in the house even one day longer. Even one minute. It's in the corner by his toolcart, surrounded by the ashes of ten thousand cigarettes.

"Real nest you got here," I say, drawing my lips back from my teeth, not in appreciation.

Quint doesn't say anything, just settles down into it.

On the makeshift table beside his recliner is the listening end of the baby monitor. Gabe's breathing comes through it like he's right here with us.

I settle back against the Chevelle Quint still hasn't fixed up.

"Just watch," he says again, and takes a paperback from the stack by his chair. It's a horror novel, like all of them. I can tell by the full moon on the front, the red lettering on the spine. And because I've known Quint for nearly eighteen years now.

He settles back into what must be reading position #1, starts reading.

I lean forward, look side to side again, this time for candid cameras, then come back to him.

"Quint, dude—"

He never looks up from the book, just holds his finger up for quiet.

I shake my head—*this* is what I had to talk my way out of the house for, what I'm going to be paying for for the rest of the week—dig through the bottom drawer of Quint's toolcart for the magazines he's always kept there. They're legal, I'm pretty sure, but still, you wouldn't want the cops stumbling onto them.

For maybe four minutes I lean against the Chevelle, study the girls in the classifieds ads after I've studied all the girls in the main part of the magazine, and Quint just sits there, hunched over his damn book.

Finally I hiss a laugh through my front teeth, roll the magazine into a tube to hammer down through my fist, and am already pushing off the Chevelle to make for the door and whatever I can scrounge from his fridge when the monitor's lights pulse red, from left to right. Like a tachometer, I think, Gabe really winding up.

"Shhh," Quint says, still reading the book, his eyes narrow from the effort.

Gabe's voice comes through the monitor. A moan, I'd call it.

"Listen," I say, "this has been exciting and all, and it's not that I'm not thankful, but—"

Gabe interrupts, screaming, all the monitor's lights flashing red now.

Quint stands, his bottom lip between his teeth. He's nodding, as if waiting for me to agree that it was worth coming over here.

I just stand there.

"Like clockwork," he says, then passes his little horror novel over to me, his index finger holding his place. Without even meaning to, I put my finger there too, and then he's gone, to Gabe.

The monitor's close enough to the crib that I hear the springs in the miniature mattress when Quint picks him up, hear what he's saying, that's it's all right, buddy. That it's not real, it's not real. Daddy just had to show his friend.

I study the red lights on the monitor, then the book in my hands. Read where Gabe must have been.

It's scene where a guy's sleeping in a bed with his wife, and this guy, he's watching his doorway like it's the most important thing in the world. But still, he's not watching close enough. He blinks once, twice, and then on the third blink—ten, twelve minutes of sleep—he wakes to a dead little kid tugging on the covers, then trying to crawl in. Then crawling in anyway.

Quint says it again to Gabe: "It's not real, buddy. It's just nothing, man. Nothing at all . . . "

I put the book down, open to the place he was, and make it back to Sherry fifteen minutes before I'd promised.

On Wednesday I meet Tanya at the regular place, the usual time. Gabe's with Sherry on our living room floor. As far as Sherry knows, Tanya's sitting with her pregnant sister at the doctor's office. Wednesdays are when he sees expectant mothers. It's a weekly appointment.

As far as where I am, it's work. The only thing different from every other day is I'm taking my lunch an hour and a half early.

The lie I tell myself in the trailer I have a key to is that the reason I'm not telling Tanya about Quint, reading to Gabe from across the house, without words, is that on Wednesdays we never have time to talk, really. It's just unbutton, unbutton, lock the door twice then test the knob to be sure.

The truth of it of course is that I don't have the words to tell her, and that it's stupid anyway.

A few nights later, Quint's at my door, baby monitor in hand.

"You didn't leave him there," I say, leaning to the side to look past him, for the stroller.

"He's safe," Quint says, insulted, eyeballing all my baseboards for an outlet.

I shake my head no, tell him not in here.

On the way to the shed in back, where the light socket doubles as a plug, where Sherry'll never come because there's spiders, Quint fills me in on Gabe. It's been a week of testing. He's been reading all different kinds of novels, from all different rooms of the house, at all times of the day and night, with all different clothes and jewelry on. What he's found is that it works best when he's lying down, the book propped on his stomach. And the book, it has to be bloody of some kind. Haunted houses, werewolves, serial killers, whatever. Nothing sappy or consoling.

"Why?" I say, holding the shed door open against the wind.

Quint shrugs, steps up onto the plywood floor, says like it's obvious, "It puts him to sleep, man. Keeps him there, I mean."

I follow him in, nod.

It makes sense is the thing.

"What about science fiction?"

"He likes it."

"Sex stuff?"

"He's nine months old."

I clean a space on the bench for the baby monitor.

"He doesn't understand the war stuff, either," Quint adds, tuning Gabe's distant breathing in. "And . . . I don't know how to explain it. I think—I think it's not so much like he's seeing the words or anything. It's like he's seeing flashes of the pictures the books put in my head, yeah?"

"No," I tell him. "I don't."

Quint pulls a thin paperback up from his back pocket.

"This'll be the farthest away I've tried," he says.

I nod—what am I supposed to say, here?—and he slips into his book, his eyes narrowing with gore, maybe, or a vampire swooping down, and then, just when I think he's forgetting this is all a big experiment, Gabe lets loose through the static.

Quint looks up, momentarily lost. "Think you can stop now," I say, pushing the book down so he can't read it anymore. Gabe stands, the realization washing over him, and then's gone, sprinting the quarter mile between my house and his. By the time he gets there, he's breathing hard. He rips Gabe up from the crib, holds him close. "You there?" he says when he can, through the monitor. I nod, walk the monitor down to him.

Over enchiladas Sherry tells me that Tanya's messing around on Quint. I chew, chew, swallow. "What?" I say, my face poker-straight, another bite ready on my fork, in case I need a stall. "On Wednesdays she drops Gabriel off here, y'know?" I shrug, fork the bite in. "Well," Sherry says, looking out the kitchen window, I think, "this last

Wednesday, her sister started having contractions, she thought."

"Her *sister*?"

"Ronnie—you don't remember her. She's having twins too."

"Ronnie," I say, swirling the bean juice and cheese on my plate. "But Tanya just had Gabe."

"You know what I mean."

She doesn't know I'm stalling here. Spinning out.

"It was a false alarm," she goes on. "But Tanya was supposed to be with her's the thing. As far as anybody knew."

I nod, chew some more, trying each word out fifty times before I actually say it out loud.

"Does Quint know?"

"He's your friend."

I agree with her about that, study the kitchen window too. Through it there's the aluminum pole of a streetlight. It doesn't shimmer or tremble or do anything to warrant my interest in it. Still, without it to lock onto, I'd probably be throwing up.

The next week, a Monday, I'm standing on Quint's porch, synchronizing my watch with his. What he's paying me with is two beers. Where he's going is somewhere past the range of the baby monitor. My job is to record when and if Gabe wakes up, scared, and to somehow pat him back to sleep, or at least hold him until Quint gets back.

Written on the back of my arm, upside down to me, is the payphone number of wherever he's going. Because he's trying to follow the scientific method, he says, I don't need to know where he's going. It might influence the experiment in some way neither of us could anticipate.

"Okay then?" he says from the farthest part of his lawn.

I nod, tongue my lip out some. Can see the tree in front of my house from here.

Before Quint's to the end of the block, I've got the payphone number dialed in. A kid answers. In answer to my questions the kid says he's a bagboy, that the phone is by the ice machine, not quite to the firewood—why?

"Where in the larger sense, I mean," I tell him.

The grocery store.

It's two miles away.

I thank him, hang up, check on Gabe, finally turn away from him to close the door then come back again, looking at him the way I used to, those first months before his hair came in just like Quint's. It's something I can't bring up when Sherry's wanting a baby: that I've already been through it once. From a distance. That that was why I lost twelve pounds last Christmas, even with all the Thanksgiving leftovers. Praying and praying, and hating myself for each prayer, that the one that was stillborn was the one that could have given us away. Because I saw on the news that it can work like that, each twin being from a different dad. I saw it on the news and knew that we'd been lucky enough so far that this one-in-a-million shot had to be a sure thing, to make up for everything having been so good so far.

Gabe, though, his red hair, it's a gift. Everything I could have asked for. But still. I stand in Tanya's kitchen and hold one of Quint's beers to my forehead like the hero does in the movie he's trying to get out of.

On the refrigerator is a list of each thing Quint's eaten over the last ten days. Tanya thinks he's on a diet he saw on TV. She laughed into my chest when she told me, and I smoothed the hair down on the back of her head, closed my eyes.

The first time with her had been an accident, sure. But not the second, or all the rest. And now this, Quint going telepathic or whatever. Or—or not Quint, maybe, but Gabe. Maybe Quint just has a leaky mind, is one of those people my parents wouldn't ever play Spades with, and Gabe, because they have the same blood, can tune him in better than anybody.

"Bullshit," I say out loud, alone in Quint and Tanya's hall, and peel the tab off the second beer.

Except that when I was twelve, for about six weeks I'd always been able to tell when the phone was going to ring. I didn't hear it exactly, just kind of felt it in the bone behind my ear. It was just those six weeks though, and I never went to Vegas like my dad kept saying, and some things, if you just ignore them hard enough, they go away.

Like this.

What I could do here, I know, is not write anything down for Quint. Even if Gabe does wake up screaming, pictures of zombies in his head. It'd probably be best for him, even, save him from a childhood stocked with every bloody image Quint can find on the paperback rack. Because, it's not like they're going to take this on the road or anything. You don't get rich off your father's dreams seeping into your head. Parlor tricks are supposed to be neat, small. What Quint's doing requires way too much setup, and looks fake anyway.

I sit down at the table, push the notebook into the napkin dispenser we'd stole one night from some bar, years ago. Tanya still likes to make a show of checking her lipstick in it when we're over, like this is all a game—the house, marriage, kids. I have to look away when she's like that, because Sherry's smart, too smart.

And then I think the thing I always think, when I'm not with Tanya: that this has to end. Not because it's wrong, but because we're going to get caught, and then have to live down the road from each other for the rest of our lives.

I shake my head no, that this *isn't* what I wanted, and realize at the same time that what I'm doing is trying to talk myself into doing the right thing.

I drink off all of the beer I can. See that Quint's last meal was sloppy joe mix on tortilla chips, with three jalapeños, sliced.

Right about now, he's down in the parking lot of the grocery store, oblivious, a few pages into his book, his window down to hear the phone ring. Sherry's at the garage, punching holes in people's tickets. Tanya on-shift, covering for somebody, and, for me, it's just another lunch.

While Quint reads, I make a sandwich from his deli drawer, eat it standing up, and am like that—sandwich in one hand, third beer in the other—when Gabe starts screaming like he's just seen right into the black heart of evil. Like somebody's holding his head there, making him look.

I drop my sandwich, try to pick it up before it's dirty, end up tipping beer onto it instead.

"Okay, okay," I call to Gabe, and then, just as I'm standing, I feel something in my head. It stops me, cranks my head over to the phone. Seconds later, it rings.

By the third ring I manage to draw the receiver to my ear.

It's Tanya.

When I don't say anything, she asks if I'm going to get the baby or not. I look through the doorway to the hall, can almost feel the telepathy popping in the air.

"*Q?*" Tanya says then, quieter, urgent-like, and there's a ball in my throat I can't explain—like I'm betraying her, standing in her kitchen, collecting her kid from his crib. Letting her think I'm Quint.

I hang up softly, call Quint, get the bagboy, hear Tanya ringing back on the other line.

"What do you want me to tell him?" the bagboy asks, his voice hushed like he knows more about what's going on here than he should.

Behind him is the sound of cars rattling, women talking, doors swishing open and shut.

Gabe nestles his head into the hollow of my shoulder, gathers the fabric of my shirt in his right hand.

"Tell him I've got to get back to work," I say, then hold the phone in place long after I've hung up.

It's a form of prayer.

As apology or something, I finally take one of the books Quint's always trying to get me to read.

"You know why he likes that stuff, right?" Sherry asks.

We're in bed, the television on but muted, so we can hear the new squirrels pad around above us.

"Why he likes scary shit, you mean?" I say.

"Because it's at his level."

"Hm," I say, and turn the page.

The book is that first one I watched him read to Gabe. I spend equal time on the page and television, and fall asleep somewhere in-between, wake deep in the morning, the sheets twisted under my fingers.

"Hun?" Sherry says, from her side of the bed. For a long time I don't answer, then, once she's breathing even again, I tell her I'm sorry too, the same way I'm telling Quint: where they can't hear.

The talk I have with Quint that Friday night over beers in my garage is stumbling and ridiculous, and I'm embarrassed for him, almost. For both of us.

It starts with me, explaining that this trick him and Gabe have, it probably isn't what he thinks.

What I'm doing is being a good friend. Saving him from himself. Saving Gabe.

"Then what is it?" Quint says, eyeing me over his beer.

"You want it to be ESP."

"What else could it be?"

I shrug, rub a spot on my chin that doesn't itch.

What I can't say is what Sherry said, when I explained all this to her: that if she'd been fired from *her* job, was sponging off her wife's double shifts, spending all day every day with her infant son, then yeah, she might invent some special powers too. Just to cope.

What I really can't say is that maybe the twin that died's involved in all this somehow. A door I can't open around Quint, because he'd fall through.

"It's like—like those people you see on *That's Incredible*, with dogs and horses, y'know?" I tell him instead. "They want so bad for it to be real that they don't even realize they're tapping their toe on the ground seven times, after asking what's four plus three."

Quint tips some more beer down the hatch.

"I'm not saying you're tapping your foot," I add.

His eyes are red around the rims.

"Then what?" he finally says, for the second time.

I shrug, open my mouth like I have something ready, but don't, finally fall back on a half-baked version of Sherry's explanation: that Quint's spent so much time at home lately that he's cued into Gabe's sleeping patterns. That sometimes Gabe wakes up when Quint's *not* reading, right?

"He's a baby," Quint shrugs. "That doesn't mean it's not . . . extra-sensory."

I swish some spit back and forth between my front teeth.

"If it is," I finally say, "it's not like you think."

This gets Quint's attention. The way he smiles a little, too, I can tell that he can hear Sherry's voice in mine, knows I'm her sock puppet here.

"When you read," I go on, closing my eyes to try to sound only like myself, "I don't think—I mean, Gabe can't read, right? Even if he were hearing your little reading voice in your head, the way you say it to yourself, all spooky or whatever, it would just be your voice, not really words. Because he doesn't understand words yet."

"That we know of."

"He's a baby."

Quint shrugs, says where I can barely hear, "I did it in Spanish too."

I stare at the floor, finally close my eyes.

"And it worked?"

"Scientific method," Quint says, crunching his can against his thigh.

"Then that proves it," I say. "Gabe doesn't know Spanish."

"Maybe there's a language under words? One that we think in or something. A telepathic society might not have any reason to ever evolve more than one language, did you think about that?"

"*Aliens*, you mean?"

"I'm just saying." Quint shrugs, comes back. "He still woke up. When I did it in Spanish. That means something."

"Because he . . . because it's not thoughts you're shooting out of your head, or even pictures, that's what it means. It's feelings, the shapes of things. Like, however reading about a dumbass zombie book makes you feel—scared, grossed-out, whatever—Gabe's feeling that."

Quint pulls his top lip in for a long time, finally nods whatever, takes another beer.

"So you calling Child Services on me, or what?" he says.

I look away, and then he says it: "You were right, though. This does prove it."

"ESP?"

"That he's mine."

What my heart does right then is stop, cave in on itself some.

"That he's yours?" I hear myself saying, my voice wooden, hollow.

In answer, Quint pushes up from the trash can he's been leaning on, then hooks his head to the door that leads into the house. It's still closed, Sherry and Tanya in there walking on dynamite.

"I wasn't sure," Quint says, not using his lips at all. My heart flushes itself, heats up the back of my eyes.

"What do you mean?" I say just as quietly. "*Tanya?*"

The disbelief in my voice is so real.

Quint purses his lips out, shrugs once.

"Been going on for a while, I think," he says. "If I hadn't got laid off . . . I don't know. I never would have figured it out, probably."

My mouth is moving to form questions, but I can't think of the right ones, don't have time to test them from each angle before throwing them into the ring.

"She—she couldn't," I try.

"I think that's what you always think," Quint says. "What I'm supposed to think, right?"

"Then . . . what—?"

"Just little stuff," Quint shrugs. "Like, the other day. She says she called the house, but I wouldn't talk to her or something. She asked if I still trusted her, if I was just waiting to see who she was going to ask for."

"Who else could it have been?"

Quint shakes his head no, says I'm not getting it: if she thought the guy was there, then that meant that he *had* been there, right?

I just stare at him.

He shrugs, chews the inside of his right cheek the way he's always done. His mother used to spank him for it in elementary.

"I was there," I say, weakly, the blood surging in my neck now, at the chance I'm taking.

"You would have talked to her though," Gabe shrugs, not even slowing down. "I told her it was me anyway, yeah?" Then he smiles, covers it with his hand. "She's acting guilty," he says between his fingers. "It's getting to her, I mean. Building up inside her."

"What about Gabe?"

Quint does his eyebrows, bites his lower lip now.

"He's mine," he says, "right? I mean, if he wasn't, we wouldn't be able to—we wouldn't have this connection."

I nod, try to blink in a normal fashion.

"So now I know whose side he's on," Quint adds, raising his beer to me, holding it up like that so it's the only thing in the world I can see, that I can allow myself to see.

Five days from then, it's Wednesday.

What I say into the damp hair close to Tanya's scalp is that he knows, Quint. That he knows, and it's over now, it has to be.

What she says back isn't in words, so much, but it's not ESP either. The opposite, really.

We hide in each other.

The mask I wear for the next two weeks is just like my face, only it doesn't give anything away, is always ready to smile, to take part in a shrug then look away.

The reason for the mask is that Tanya and Quint are talking to a counselor down at Tanya's hospital.

Sherry watches Gabe while they're there.

It makes me so tired, controlling my thoughts around him for those hour-and-a-halfs.

One night I finally break down, go to the store for milk we don't need, and call Quint's house from the grocery store. The bagboy watches me, his lower lip pulled between his teeth like he knows too much.

"You haven't told him, have you?" I say to Tanya when she picks up.

I've got the phone cupped in both hands, am pressing it into the side of my head.

"Trevor?" Tanya says back, a note of something bad in her voice.

Trevor is her brother. The last any of us knew, he was in Maine.

A muscle at the base of my jaw quivers.

In the background of her kitchen, I hear Quint asking her something.

"Tell me you haven't," I whisper.

"Of course not," she says, distant—to Quint, or me?—"I don't know who it is."

I hang up gently, hold the phone there with my eyes closed, then nod, go in for the milk, park in front of my house minutes later, make myself drink the whole half gallon, tell myself that if I can do it, and keep it down, then Tanya won't tell, no matter how honest their next session at the hospital gets.

Halfway to the door, though, I throw it all up, and Sherry finds me like that, starts breathing too hard herself, the phone already in her hands. Ninety seconds later Tanya is leaning over me, hugging me, helping me to stand, long strings of bubbly white leaking down from the corners of my mouth, from my nose. She breaks them off with the side of her hand, guides them away, slings them towards the street.

" . . . must have been bad," I tell her and Sherry, when I can.

At first they don't respond, and then Sherry laughs a single laugh through her nose—disgust—says, "The *gallon* of milk, you mean?"

I shrug, caught. Stare at the grass for a lie, finally find one: "That new guy at work."

"The one from prison?" Sherry whispers.

"He said milk—he drinks it for his stomach ulcer."

Sherry shakes her head at this.

"And you think you have a stomach ulcer now, right?"

When I don't answer, she apologizes to Tanya with her eyes. Because I'm one of those people who can get sick from talking to somebody on the phone. It's a joke, has been for years.

"I think you're going to be all right," Tanya says, smiling.

Her hand is on my knee.

I smile, shrug one shoulder, no eye contact.

It makes them comfortable, lets them be moms, me the little boy.

To keep them from digging my hole any deeper, I point to the kitchen to show them where I'm going, then go there, run water over my hands. I can still hear them, though. "So how's it going?" Sherry asks Tanya, in a way that I can see the parentheses Sherry's holding around her eyes, like a Sunday morning cartoon. I turn off the water. "Good," Tanya says, her hands surely in her lap, innocent. I reach for the dishtowel, draw it to my chin.

Good.

I want to laugh. Want my fingers to stop trembling.

I wind them up tight in the dishtowel, follow Sherry and Tanya to the door.

"So where's the good knight tonight?" I say from behind Sherry.

It's what we used to call Quint back in high school. From some song.

Walking backwards into the darkness, barefoot, Tanya exaggerates her shrug, says he was going down to the store or something. He didn't say.

I feel my mask smile, lift the dishtowel in farewell, and, because the kind of telepathy *I* have makes me see Quint down at the grocery store, offering a cigarette to the bagboy, the bagboy in return pointing to the pay phone, to the redial button, I hear Tanya start running through the wet grass home. To catch the phone or Gabe, I don't know.

"What?" Sherry says, holding the screen open for me.

I shake my head no, nothing. Duck back through the door.

Three days later my phone rings, and I beat Sherry to it. It's nobody. My lips are shaped around the sound of a whispered, desperate T? when Quint says something into his end. I can't make it out.

"What?" Sherry says, stepping half out of the bedroom, her work shirt most of the way on.

"Quint," I say, then pull the phone deeper into the kitchen. Quint's not saying anything else. But he's not hanging up either. Finally I thumb the dial tone button, say, loud enough for Sherry, "It's in the shed, I think. Want me to walk it down?"

When I step into the bedroom then, to say it—*Quint needs his quarter-inch ratchet back, that one that's spray-painted blue so nobody'll steal it*—Sherry's buttoning her shirt, her eyes already settled on me.

I tilt my head up to tell her where I'm going but then see how close she is to the nightstand. Where the other phone is.

"Quint," she says, her voice artificially light, I think. Maybe.

I tell her to have a good day at the garage, then hold her side as we touch lips, and talk to myself the whole way down to Quint's. How the only part of the conversation Sherry could have heard was me, saying that about the shed. But—would it sound different to her if the line was dead? Would it have been louder in her ear, my voice closer, because half of it wasn't getting sucked down the line?

Partway to Quint's, I remember the blue ratchet, go back for it, find it on the coffee table, Sherry already gone.

I reach for it like maybe it's hot, or electric, and, when I have it, it's light like old, dry paper. What I do with it is sit, and hold it hard to my forehead, my eyes closed, and make myself breathe, breathe. Tell myself that, whatever else, Sherry can't know anything for sure, and that Tanya's not going to tell. That Quint's not waiting in his own living room down the street, a pistol in his lap, Gabe crying in the other room.

I'm half-right: Quint is in his chair, just not the new one Tanya financed for him two birthdays ago. Instead it's the ratty one, out in the garage.

He looks up at me when I step down onto the stained concrete.

His eyes are red around the rims, and the hand he has wrapped around his paperback, the knuckles are scraped raw. The kind of rash you get from punching sheetrock, over and over.

I feel along the side of the Chevelle, lift my chin to him.

"I thought you were choking or something," I say, "on the phone, I mean."

He smiles without looking at me, says, "So you brought my ratchet down to work on me?"

I look at it blue in my hand, and see it in an evidence bag.

It makes a solid *thunk* when I toss it into his tool drawer. With the wrenches instead of the sockets, but Quint doesn't notice, is staring at something I can't see.

"What'd you want, then?" I say.

Quint laughs as if just now returning to the garage, shrugs, throws me the magazine I was looking at last time I was here.

I unroll it, study it too long, come back to him.

"Thanks, I guess," I tell him. "I can't take it home, though, y'know?"

Quint smiles, shakes his head no, says, "You're an antenna, I think."

"A what?"

"It works best when—I don't know. When you're around. Involved."

"With you and Gabe?"

Quint nods, his eyes suddenly glossy wet.

"What's going on?" I say.

Quint doesn't answer, just shakes his head no, brings his paperback horror novel up to his face, starts reading hard enough that his lips move.

"I've already seen this—" I start, but Quint interrupts by holding his hand up. I stare at him like that for maybe four seconds, then lean back against the Chevelle again, open the mag, see the same barely-legal girls in the same unlikely positions. Soon enough I'm watching the tiny bulbs on the baby monitor. They're black, don't even remember red.

Quint swallows loud, pulls the book closer to his face, reading as hard as he knows how, then finally closes his eyes, slings the book past me.

It brings something down from the shelf, something that falls for a long time. Snow chains, I'm thinking, or one of those hanging lamps like old ladies have, with all the stained glass. I don't look around to see. Just at Quint. He's crying, trying not to. Not wiping his face, because that would be admitting that there were tears.

"He grew out of it," I say, in explanation.

Quint shakes his head no, settles his eyes on what looks like the Chevelle's front tire.

"It's not him," he says, then looks up at me. "It's not him."

"Then—what?"

"You said he was . . . that he was picking up on how this shit made me feel."

"The books, yeah."

"They just, they don't scare me anymore, I guess."

I smile, cross my arms.

"Then *you* grew out of it," I say. "Sherry always said you would."

Quint smiles, rubs it into his face. "Sherry," he says. "You're lucky. To have her, I mean."

"So are you."

"What?"

"Lucky. Tanya."

Quint keeps the same expression on his face, but changes gears in his head. I can tell.

"So find something scarier," I say. "Romance. Algebra."

Quint doesn't laugh.

Instead, he pulls a chain up from his shirt. A necklace, like dogtags, except, instead of a little nameplate on the end, it's a silver key.

"What?" I say.

"In the . . . in the books, it's all fake. I know that now."

"What do you mean?"

"This is real," he says, holding the key up before his face.

I don't have anything to say to this.

"Dr. Jak—our therapist," Quint goes on. "He says it's Tanya's symbol that she's with me again. All the way. Like before."

"A *key*?"

"She used to it to—to meet her . . . To meet him."

And then I get it: the key he's wearing, it's the one I had cut for Tanya. It fits the trailer, has unlocked more Wednesdays than I can count.

He looks up, nods.

"Yeah," he says. "I was right. She's been screwing around."

"How long?"

"Two years."

"Who?"

Quint shrugs one shoulder, looks away. "It's not supposed to be important who," he says. "Just that it's"—he holds the key up, to show—"that it's over. A name isn't going to help me move on."

"Shit." It's the only word in my head. In my whole *life.*

Quint nods, does his eyebrows up in agreement.

"Then . . . Gabe?" I finally manage.

Quint stands, runs his fingers through his hair, dislodging his cap. It falls down his back. His fingers stay in his hair, his elbows out like stunted wings.

"Either I'm not—can't get scared like I used to," Quint says, his tone all about matter-of-factness, "or . . . or the other guy, he had red hair too."

I swallow. My hair is black.

"So you're saying she—Tanya—that she was stepping out on you with somebody who looks just like you?"

Quint doesn't turn back around to me.

"It's my fault," he says. "If I would have, y'know. Not been out here all the time, I guess. Maybe she was, like, looking for me all over again, yeah? Like, how I used to be?"

"You still are like that," I try. "We all are."

Quint laughs about this. The kind of laugh you manage when your doctor tells you you have six weeks left to live.

"You know he's yours," I say then, "Gabe. You wouldn't have been able to do—that ESP shit. It wouldn't have worked."

Quint turns around, his face slack. "How do we know his father isn't the telepathic one?"

"His *red-headed* father?"

"The one Tanya's been seeing," Quint says, holding the key up again, his eyes flashing behind it, "yeah." I stare at him until he shrugs, slams his fist down to the face of his rolling toolbox.

"You want to go somewhere?" I say. "I can call in."

Quint just closes his eyes tight. "How about we go to two years ago? You manage that, you think?"

"You want to hit somebody then?" I say, stepping forward. Quint looks up at me and for a long moment I think he's going to do it, and that, if there's any justice in the world, my jaw will crack down some important line, or a sinus cavity will collapse, or a vertebra will snap in my neck.

Instead, he just hugs me for the first time since elementary, then holds onto me, his face warm on my chest. The spot I stare at on the wall is where a nail is buried all the way to the head, so it's just a little metal dot. On my way out minutes later, I pass Gabe's room. He's sleeping, unaware. Perfect.

I am not an antenna. In the breakroom a week after the talk with Quint in the garage, I write this onto the top of the table until it's a mat of words: *I am not an antenna.*

The next day it's just a blue stain that smells like citrus.

Instead of the regulation white hose all the other nurses wear, Tanya wears thigh-highs with a lace band at top. They stop just after her skirt starts. The number of people I can tell this to is zero. The number of people Quint told it to two years ago was one.

When she steps off the elevator into the garage the following Wednesday, I'm waiting for her.

She smiles, looks away. Never stops walking towards me.

After myself, the person I hate most in the world is Dr. Jakobi. In addition to a marriage counselor, he's a preacher. I tell Sherry that this is a conflict of interest for him, but then can't stuff it into words, exactly why. It has something to do with his stake in other people's marriages. Like, if he'd been the one to marry Tanya and Quint nine years ago, then, now, he'd be doing anything he could to keep them together, right? Just to keep his average up.

Sherry says preachers don't compare averages and percentiles.

"Sometimes you should just give up, though," I say.

This gets Sherry looking at me harder than I want.

"You want her to leave him?" she finally says.

I smile, shake my head no, like she's talking particulars, friends, where I'm more in a hypothetical mode.

I don't want them to break up, no.

But I don't sleep so much either. And it's not just the squirrels.

Under Quint's couch now is a slender little fire safe. It has a handle like a briefcase.

He calls me up on a Tuesday to see it.

"You're wanting to test it?" I say from his doorway. I haven't carried a lighter now for years.

Quint laughs through his nose some.

"It's in there," he says.

"What?"

He chews his tongue, squinches one side of his face up.

"With the doctor the other day. I wouldn't drop it, the, y'know. Whoever it was. That's not supposed to matter."

"The other guy."

Yes.

"So?" I say.

Where I'm standing is half in, half out his screen door. My fingertips holding it open. In any television show or movie, this would be a definite sign of guilt. The audience would be howling with laughter.

"So we had to move on," Quint says, the box in his lap now. "Dr. Jakobi said I didn't really want to know. Who."

Because I don't trust my voice, I don't say anything. Either that or I can't.

"It was her idea," Quint says. "She wrote it on a piece of paper, folded it up, then Dr. J held it until I came back with a safe to lock it in."

He pats the fire safe, the slap of his hand soft, almost loving.

I swallow.

"To make it mean something, though, I had it keyed for this," Quint says, holding the key up from around his neck.

"And you haven't looked?" I say.

"It's not moving on if I do. This way, it's . . . what? An artifact, like. An old thing. Part of the past." He pauses, studies a commercial on TV. "All that matters now is what's ahead."

These aren't his words.

I don't tell them they're lies, though, and I don't ask Tanya whose name is written on that piece of paper.

It's not because I don't want to know, but more because knowing will mean a hundred other things, none of which I can face.

So I walk through my shifts in a trance, and the next Wednesday is just another day, and if I have an extra beer after work, nobody notices, and one night, desperate, I even read Quint's little horror novel cover to cover, drinking cup after cup of coffee.

It's stupid, not scary at all, but still, Tanya calls down to ask if we have any clothes that need drying. Because she's out of laundry but still needs to run the dryer. It's where they sit Gabe's car seat when he won't sleep. When he can't.

I walk down a load of wet colors, pass them through the door to Quint. His eyes are dancing.

"What?" I say.

"It's working again," he whispers, then hooks his chin inside, like I should come see Gabe crying.

"Maybe he's sick," I offer.

"C'mon," Quint says, and jabs the screen door more open for me, turns before it can swing shut.

I don't follow.

Their lights are on until two, when I stop looking.

"What?" Sherry says, passing through the living room, on a cleaning jag.

I don't answer. My mind is shaped like a fire safe, though. One of the letter-sized ones, just for documents.

There are no people with red hair in my family.

I've even called my mom to be sure.

She thought I was joking, and we laughed fake laughs together, and then I asked again.

The only thing that consoles me anymore is the blue ratchet that made its way back to my porch somehow.

I hold it by the quarter inch bolt, spin it around seven times to the left, then reverse the head, spin it back the other way seven times.

The sound is like one click, then a series of perfectly-spaced echoes.

In the other room now, Sherry, scrubbing, smart and oblivious.

I spin the ratchet louder.

Because Quint thinks he has telepathy again, he buys a high dollar baby monitor. His old one makes its way down to our house. Like the blue ratchet—holding it in one hand, the monitor in the other, I finally make the association I'm supposed to here: the ratchet, it sounds like a rattle.

The way the monitor made it down is that Sherry asked for it. She thinks we're going to be needing it.

This makes my face warm, then cold.

Two nights later, snugged in with the groceries I'm carrying in, I see a flat box of lace-top, thigh-high hose. They're black, not white, and make my heart just thump the wall of my chest. Not because I want them on her, then off her, but because—are they a test? If I like them, will it confirm what Sherry's maybe suspecting? Or, is this how Tanya reaches me, after a week without a Wednesday: dressing Sherry up in her hose, telling her how guys love those? And, *guys*, or me in particular?

It's too much for one three-dollar pack of hose.

That night, the hose thankfully in Sherry's top drawer, I try to just read a car magazine, so Quint and Tanya can sleep—because what if I'm the one waking him with what I think?—but every caption and every tooltip cuts right to the center of me, until Tanya's calling again, and I'm walking a load of Sherry's uniforms down, passing them across to Quint.

"What?" he says, when I just stand there.

Not on purpose, I looked at his couch, at the firesafe tucked under it, and it shut me down some.

I shake my head no, nothing.

"You should see," he says, trying to lure me in again.

His eyes are bloodshot, his beard growing in scraggly.

"He's scared of *you*," I say. "Fucking zombie."

Quint laughs, rubs his dry bottom lip with the back of his hand, and joke-punches me on the shoulder, and for a moment it feels like I actually wasn't lying the other week—that we are all still the same. That our kids are still going to be born the same year, to grow up together like we did. That our wives are going to sit in the kitchen with weak margaritas while we burn things on the grill, one of us always running down to the store for ice and beer. Taking just whichever truck's parked closest to the road.

Sherry finds me on our porch an hour later.

Instead of asking anything or even saying my name, she just hangs up the phone—Tanya, like always when Gabe's having nightmares—and sits by me.

When her robe parts over her thigh, I see the silky black hose she's got rolled up her legs, and Tanya flashes in my head, her white nurse's shoe pushing hard into the headliner of her car.

I take the corner of Sherry's robe, pull it back into place.

That weekend, when Tanya won't, I pick Quint up from the county lock-up.

What he's in for isn't owning the kind of pornography he's been using to try to scare himself, to connect with Gabe, but for getting caught buying it downtown.

Sherry says no wonder Tanya's been stepping out, right?

I'm at the door, about to leave.

"She told you with who yet?" I say, real casual, no eye contact.

"You asking for you or for him?" she snaps back, smiling behind it so I have no idea what she might be really saying.

I pull the door to, back out of the driveway slowly, obeying every law I can remember.

Two nights ago, waking all at once from a dream, the patter of squirrel feet in my head, the first thing I saw was the baby monitor on our dresser. It was on, the red lights amping up, like someone was running the pad of their finger over the microphone on the other end.

It wasn't plugged in, but did have a nine-volt battery inside, one that had leaked, scabbed over.

For the rest of the night I stared at it, the monitor, until I could make out some breathing. Gabe's? This monitor was tuned to the same band or frequency or whatever as the new one, the one that was powerful enough to push the signal all the way down here. That had to be it.

So it would wear out during the day, and because I wasn't going to be there, I left it on.

Or, really, because I didn't want to touch it.

The dream I was waking from wasn't a dream either, really. More like a nightmare. It involved the Wednesday trailer somehow, but our stubby attic too, and Gabe at twelve years old, his hair dyed black to match his clothes, chains and anger seeping off every angle of his body. The only chain that mattered was the one around his neck, though. The one Tanya's Wednesday key was hanging from.

And maybe it wasn't a dream, even.

When I woke, anyway, it wasn't like I opened my eyes to the baby monitor. More like I realized I'd been staring at it.

Getting into my truck in the parking lot of lock-up, all his possessions in a manila envelope, Quint asks what's wrong?

I just look over at him.

He's still smiling. How he lived through booking and sixteen hours in lock-up is a complete mystery. That's the kind of oblivious he can be, though. The kind of focus he's always had.

Instead of going back to our houses, he directs me downtown. Because they confiscated his cardboard box of illegal porn, wouldn't even let him tear any of the pages out.

Because his cash is all in the form of a city-issued check, I have to give him the thirty-two dollars it costs for the cigar-box of photographs he buys from a guy I try hard not to be remembering.

"Don't," I say, holding the lid of the box down when he starts to open it.

He hisses a laugh through his teeth, pours his possessions out from his manila envelope. Last, because it sticks on the brad, is Tanya's key to Wednesday.

"You should chuck it," I say as he's ducking into the chain. "Temptation, all that."

"I get points for it," he says, pulling the chest of his shirt out to drop the key down.

"Points?"

"Dr. J. It's one of the things I have to show each week. Whoever has the most points gets to go first."

"So show him a different one," I say, my arms draped over the steering wheel so I'm driving with my forearms and elbows. So it would be awkward to look directly sideways anymore.

Quint considers this.

"What if I want to know someday?" he says.

"You don't," I tell him, wincing inside because I'm agreeing with Jakobi. "I mean, what would you do, if you knew?"

Quint stares at my dashboard. "Something bad," he finally says.

I pooch my lips out, nod. "Leaving Gabe where?" I tack on.

Quint nods, keeps nodding, then reaches over to my keys, thumbing through for one that's properly silver, and small enough that it could fool Jakobi.

The first thing I think, his finger suddenly on the key to the trailer, about to hold it up to his, to compare, is to haul the wheel over, like his hand at the ignition's scared me somehow.

We might crash into a bridge abutment or concrete pylon, yeah.

But he wouldn't find the key.

He sees it all coming though, nods ahead to the wreck I'm about to involve us in, and I veer back to my side of the road, a film of sweat breaking out all over, the cigar box of illegal porn spilling down from the dash so that I have to see splashes of skin I could probably go to jail for transporting.

What I tell Quint as he's trying to collect all his porn is that I need all my keys for work, then, after I drop him off, I vacuum the floorboard on his side for three seventy-five cent cycles. The sound of the vacuum is strong and institutional, and I think I could do this for a job, maybe. A career.

With that kind of sound in your ears, it's hard to think, I mean.

I finally come home at dark.

Sherry's waiting for me on the porch, and it's good at least not to have to make some excuse to take a shower. Instead of Tanya, I just smell like the carwash.

We eat lasagna again, forking in bite after perfect bite. Somewhere in there Sherry informs me that we're watching Gabe tomorrow night.

"Tanya's sister finally pop?" I say, chewing.

"Emergency therapy," Sherry says, stabbing through another layer of pasta. "Dr. Jakobi."

My keys are in their tin dog bowl on the table by the back door.

I go to sleep thinking of them, waiting for the red lights of the monitor to wrap around again, and try hard not to think of Tanya's nurse shoe pressing against any headliner. Because my head's leaky, I know, and that's not the kind of thing a son should have to know about his mom.

In trade for us giving up our Friday night, Tanya leaves a hot meatloaf on their kitchen table for us, and two rented movies on top of the TV, a twelve-pack dead center on the bottom shelf of the fridge.

Quint mopes out after her, his eyes trying to tell me something. I can't make it out, though. Maybe I'm supposed to be making some excuse for him, saving him from Jakobi. Or maybe I'm supposed to call the hospital if Quint gets scared enough in therapy that Gabe wakes up screaming. Or maybe I'm supposed to be handing him his blue ratchet now, instead of leaving it in my pocket.

I don't know.

The movies are an even split: one romance, one action.

As soon as Quint's truck is gone, Sherry has Gabe up from his crib, is cooing to him, pretending. Practicing.

I sit at the table alone, scraping off the ketchup baked onto the top of the meatloaf, listening to this wonderful absence of squirrels, and find myself four beers into the twelve-pack by the time Sherry sits down across from me, Gabe on her knee.

"He's the one I feel sorry for, really," she says, halving the piece of meatloaf I saved for her.

"He doesn't know," I say, flicking my eyes to Gabe then away.

Hanging from the rusted shower rod in the bathroom, where they don't have to be, is one of Tanya's lace-top pairs of hose.

I stand there, stand there, finally have to shut my eyes to pee. Aim by echo location.

In their dryer, still, are half of Sherry's work shirts.

After dinner I stand in the utility doorway with a beer, watch Sherry fold them into a paper bag, one after the other, Gabe undoing one for every two she can get done.

She's so patient with him, is making it all into a game.

"You should watch your movie," she says. "I'll keep him in here."

"What about yours?" I say.

"Just go," she says, already half into some peek-a-boo game with Gabe.

By the time she's through, she'll have folded everything in the utility, I know.

I collect another beer on the way to the living room, push my movie into the player, settle back into the couch, and am twenty minutes into it—eight people dead already—when the beer I'm trying to settle into the carpet dings on the firesafe.

It's like a gong in my head.

And it doesn't draw Sherry.

Using more beer as an excuse, I get up, deposit my two empties in the trash, carry the last of the twelve-pack back to the living room, and study the street through the gauzy front curtain. It's empty. Nobody watching, no Quint-truck idling in the drive, him and Tanya talking about their marriage. To be sure, I lock the door, then, to be even more sure, ease down the hall. Sherry's in the bedroom with Gabe now, dressing him in outfit after outfit. "We can watch your movie," I offer. She looks up to me, her eyebrows drawing together in what I register as earnest consternation—something I don't think I've ever registered before, from anybody—then reaches forward to keep Gabe from overbalancing off the edge of the bed.

"I hope she doesn't move," she says.

"Tanya?"

"If they split up, I mean."

"It's her parent's house."

"I know. It's just—"

"They won't."

"Would you?" she asks.

"Would I what?" I say back.

"If I was, y'know. Like Tanya."

If she were like Tanya. If I'd been meeting her each Wednesday for two years. If somebody like me had. If I were Quint. "Trying to tell me something?" I say, smiling around my beer. This is as serious as we ever talk. As serious as I can ever let it get, anyway.

It's like walking through a field of bear traps. I tilt my beer to her, a toast, and back out, leave the hall light on behind me so I'll be able to see her shadow if she's walking towards the living room.

Still, sitting in front of my movie, the sound turned up as cover, the firesafe in my lap—I don't know. Is this a trap too? Has Quint spit-glued hairs around the edges, so if I open it they'll break?

Was that whole thing about an artifact of Tanya's affair just something he made up, when what's really in the box is a picture of me and him, from ten years ago? Did Jakobi slip something therapeutic in there while he wasn't looking, which'll get ruined if I see it?

The box is so heavy with all this that I'm surprised I'm even able to lift it. That it's not already crushing me.

Six times, then, the movie blaring, I count to ten, waiting for truck headlights—any headlights—to wash over the curtains, and six times they don't. So I ease my key into the lock, twist. The top sighs open.

Inside is a folded piece of paper. It's been ripped from a small notebook, the kind any good therapist is going to keep handy. My lips are trembling, inside. Not where anybody would be able to see. Written in Tanya's hand, in pencil, a name, not mine, just somebody she made up on the spot, because she's not stupid. I close my eyes in thanks, maybe even smile, and when I open them again

Sherry's standing there, Gabe on her hip.

She's just staring at me. No expression on her face at all.

"He—he gave you the key," she says, her eyes boring right into me now, and—it's my only choice, really—I nod, once. Leave my head down.

She knows about the firesafe, the name, the special key. All of it.

"And?" she says.

"What?" My voice is weak. I'm not built for this. "Are you going to tell him now?"

I look down to the paper again, then back up to her.

"I don't want to know," she says. "It's none of our business, right?" Beside her, Gabe is staring at me too. His eyes seeing I-don't-know-how deep Behind them, guns and a car exploding.

"He's my best friend," I say, trying to watch the movie now. Again. Still.

"And you think it'll be good for him, to know?"

What I'm supposed to say is built into her question, how she asks it. It usually is.

I shake my head no, it wouldn't be good for him. That, because he's my friend, I won't tell, will keep it inside, hold it forever, even if it gives me cancer.

Sherry shakes her head at me, turns on her heel, goes back to whatever she has going on in the other part of the house. I relock the firesafe, push it back under the couch, and watch the movie without seeing any of it. At some point the name Tanya wrote on the paper hits me—Was it a *real* name, some *other* other guy?—and then a tank blows up on-screen and Gabe cries in the other room. I turn the movie down, and the next time I move my head, I think, is when Quint's truck door shuts outside. Just one door. It means Tanya sat beside him for the drive home. A good session, then.

When they come through the screen, they're holding hands. Or, Tanya's holding Quint's. What he is is limp, like he's being dragged. But that's better than a lot of the ways he could be. You don't go to emergency therapy for illegal porn then come home happy, I don't guess.

Sherry appears in the door, Gabe in outfit number 435, or somewhere up there.

Tanya crosses the room to him, leading with the heels of her hands the ways moms do, and Sherry's watching me close, I know. Waiting for me to nod or not nod to Quint.

Instead, I just try to avoid his eyes altogether. Throw him the second-to-last beer, another impossible spiral.

"He was an angel," Sherry's saying above me, on her way to the turn the movie off.

"You like it?" Quint says, unloading his wallet onto the speaker by the door, nodding to the paused movie.

"Which one?" I say, and he laughs in his way, looks into the kitchen for some reason—it's dark in there—then does the thing that almost makes me forget how to breathe: ducks out of the chain around his neck.

He hangs it from the upslanted peg just under his hat.

Sherry sees this, I know, even directs a question down to me, her eyes hot and sad both, but doesn't say anything, and, either because she's smart or by chance—but it can't be chance—when she comes to bed later that night she's got those lace-topped hose on, and makes sure I see.

"You like?" she says, and I nod, pull her close, wonder the whole way through if the noises she's making are hers or what she imagines Tanya might sound like, and then I think that maybe, if she *can* be Tanya, *like* Tanya, then maybe she'll get pregnant like she wants, like she deserves, and then none of this will matter, and to try to make it stick, to make it take, I even whisper Tanya's name into the pillow at the end, instantly hate myself. And then we roll away to our sides of the bed.

"Gabe?" Sherry says after a few minutes of fake breathing.

"Share," I say.

There's nothing to say, though.

It took, I know. She's pregnant now, has to be. It's the only thing that can stop me from being me, the only thing that can turn me into something else, something better. A dad.

For a few tense moments there's a tremble in the bed, and I think she's crying but lie to myself that she doesn't want me to reach across, touch her thigh, her hip, her hand.

And then nothing. Sleep. Me fixed on those dead lights of the baby monitor on the dresser, waiting for them to wind up.

They do.

Just a weak glow at first, but then that first bulb's on, and the red's climbing, wrapping, opening some connection, a conduit, a fissure.

I shake my head no, please. No no no.

But then there's a touch on my thigh, my hip, my hand.

I look over, am thinking of my old German shepherd growing up, how he'd always nose me in the morning, just nudge me awake.

This isn't my dog, though.

It's a boy, maybe three years old already—time moves different over there—his hair long and wild on his shoulders, glinting with fiberglass. Too dark to see his face, quite, but his mouth, the lower jaw, it's just hanging, so there's just this black oval. A void.

And he's tugging at my hand, like he should be.

It's Tanya's other twin. The one she buried. Mine.

He pulls on the side of my hand and I let him, stand, follow. He looks back once to be sure and I'm reaching ahead, for his tiny shoulder.

I lose him in the hallway, though, step into the kitchen where a little black body would be stark against all the white cabinets.

I open my mouth to shape his name, whatever I would have named him, but look to the phone instead.

The bone behind my ear, it's alive again.

My hand stabs out, pulls the receiver to the side of my head before it can ring.

It's Quint. He's breathing heavy, guilty, wrong.

"Hey," he says, his whole body cupped around his phone, I can tell, so Tanya won't hear, "hey, yeah, you've got to come down, man, see this. It's, it's—"

I balance the receiver on top of its cradle without hanging up, so that the connection's still there.

I came the wrong way, that's it.

There was fiberglass in his matted hair. *Fiberglass.*

From the attic, the crawlspace. Insulation.

Of course. Footsteps in the attic, not on the roof.

I feel my back into the hallway, see the silhouette of Sherry sitting up in the bed, and she sees me too, I think, but I'm just a shadow, less. I open my mouth to apologize to her, for everything, but all that comes out is the blue ratchet sound. One click, a thousand identical ones tumbling into place behind it.

It's better this way.

At the other end of the hallway is the only ceiling vent in the house. So the attic can breathe. It's ten inches by six inches, and just a cut-out in the sheetrock now, the vent already pulled up, balanced on two rafters.

Ten inches by six inches.

Just enough for me to reach up, grab onto each side, try to force my head in.

In a rush of shadow, my son pulls me the rest of the way through.

Danny knows you can never tell which compromises the gods will understand—for the sake of a good effort—and which ones bring down their wrath. He learns you can work most arcane rituals with nothing more than a sharpened paper clip and grass cuttings . . .

MOTHER URBAN'S BOOKE OF DAYES

JAY LAKE

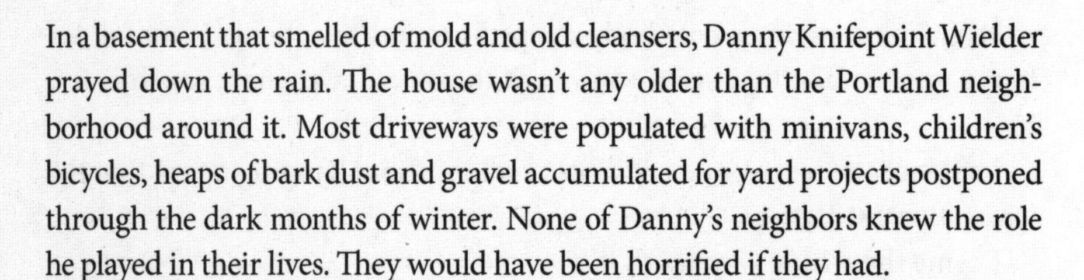

In a basement that smelled of mold and old cleansers, Danny Knifepoint Wielder prayed down the rain. The house wasn't any older than the Portland neighborhood around it. Most driveways were populated with minivans, children's bicycles, heaps of bark dust and gravel accumulated for yard projects postponed through the dark months of winter. None of Danny's neighbors knew the role he played in their lives. They would have been horrified if they had.

Not making it to church on time carried scarcely a ripple of consequence compared to what would happen if Danny didn't pray the world forward. Lawn sprinklers chittering, children screeching at their play—these were the liturgical music of his rite.

"Heed me, Sky."

Danny circled the altar in his basement.

"Hear my pleas, freely given from a free soul."

Green shag carpeting was no decent replacement for the unbending grass of the plains on which the Corn Kings had once vomited out their lives to ensure the harvest.

"I have bowed to the four winds and the eight points of the rose."

Wood-grain paneling echoed memories of the sanctifying rituals that had first blessed this workroom.

"Heed me now, that your blessing may fall upon the fields and farms." With a burst of innate honesty he added: ". . . . and gardens and patios and window boxes of this land."

"Daniel Pierpont Wilder!" his mother yelled down the stairs. "Are you talking to a girl down there?"

"Mooooom," Danny wailed. "I'm buuuusy!"

"Well, come be busy at the table. I'm not keeping your lunch warm so you can play World of Warships."

"War*craft*, Mom," he muttered under his breath. But he put away his knife, then raced up the steps two at a time.

Behind him, on the altar, his wilting holly rustled as if a breeze tossed the crown of an ancient oak tree deep within an untouched forest. Oil smoldered and rippled within the beaten brass bowl. Rain, wherever it had gotten to, did not fall.

That night Danny climbed up the Japanese maple in the side yard and scooted onto the roof. He'd been doing that since he was a little kid. Mom said he was still kid, and always would be, but at twenty-two Danny had long been big enough to have to mind the branches carefully. If he waited until after Mom went to her room to watch TiVoed soap operas through the bottom of a bottle of Bombay Sapphire, she didn't seem to notice. The roofing composite was gritty and oddly slick, still warm with the trapped heat of the day, and smelled faintly of tar and mold.

The gutters, as always, were a mess. Something was nesting in the chimney again. The streetlight he'd shot out with his BB gun remained dark, meaning that the rooftop stayed in much deeper shadow than otherwise.

Sister Moon rising in the east was neither new, nor old, but halfway in between. Untrustworthy, that was, Danny knew. If Sister Moon couldn't make up her mind, how was Sky to know which way to pass, let alone the world as a whole to understand how to turn? This was the most dangerous time in the circle of days.

He had his emergency kit with him. Danny spent a lot of time on his emergency kit, making and remaking lists.

- Nalgene bottle of boiled tap water
- *The Old Farmer's Almanac*
- *Mother Urban's Booke of Dayes*
- ~~Silver~~ Stainless steel knife
- Paper clips
- Sisal twine
- Spare retainer
- Bic lighter (currently a lime green one)
- Beeswax candles (black and white)

That last was what he spent most of his allowance on. Beeswax candles, and sometimes the right herbs or incense. That and new copies of the

Almanac every year. The *Booke of Dayes* he'd found at a church rummage sale—it was one of those big square paperback books, like his *The Complete Idiot's Guide to Magic*, with a cover that pretended to look like some oldtimey tome or grimoire. The entire kit fit into a Transformers knapsack so dorky looking he wasn't in any danger of losing it on the bus or having it taken from him, except maybe by some really methed-out homeless guy or something.

Danny had figured out a long time ago that he'd get further in life if he didn't spend time worrying about being embarrassed about stuff.

This night he lay back on the roof, one foot braced on the plumbing vent stack in case he fell asleep and rolled off again. The black eye he'd gotten that time had taken some real explaining.

It hadn't rained in Portland for sixty days now, which was very weird for the Pacific Northwest, and even the news was talking about the weather a lot more. Danny knew it was his fault, that he'd messed up the Divination of Irrigon specified in The *Booke of Dayes* to shelter the summer growing season from Father Sun's baleful eye. That had been back in June, and he'd gotten widdershins and deosil mixed up, then snapped the Rod of Seasons by stepping on it, which was really just a dowel from Lowe's painted with the Testor's model paints he'd found at a rummage sale.

You could never tell which compromises the gods would understand about, for the sake of a good effort, and which ones brought down their wrath. Kind of like back in school, with his counselors and his tutors, before he'd quit because it was stupid and hard and too easy all at the same time.

Anyway, he'd gone the wrong way around the altar, then broken the Rod, and the rain had dried up to where Mom's tomatoes were coming in nicely but everything else in the yard was in trouble.

Since then, Danny had been studying the *Almanac* and the *Booke of Dayes*, trying to find a way to repair his error. He was considering the Pennyroyal Rite, but hadn't yet figured out where to find the herb. The guy at the Lowe's garden center claimed he'd never heard of it.

He'd finally realized that having offended Sky, he would have to ask Sky how best to apologize. And so the rooftop at night. Sky during the day was single-minded, the bright servant of Father Sun. Sky in darkness served as a couch for Sister Moon, but also the tiny voices of the Ten Thousand Stars sang in their sparkling choir. Sometimes a star broke loose and wrote its name across heaven in a long, swift stroke that Danny had tried again and again to master in his own shaky penmanship.

Tonight, as every night for the past week, he hoped for the stars to tell him how to make things right.

A siren wailed nearby. *Fire engine*, Danny thought, and wondered if the flames had been sanctified, or were a vengeance. More likely someone had simply dropped a pan of bacon, but you could never tell what was of mystic import. Mother Urban was very clear on that, in her *Booke of Dayes*. Even the way the last few squares of toilet paper were stuck to the roll could tell you much about the hours to come. Or at least the state of your tummy.

He listened to the trains rumble on the Union Pacific mainline a few blocks away. Something peeped as it flew overhead in the darkness. The air smelled dry, and almost tired, with a mix of lawn and car and cooking odors. The night was peaceful. If not for the scratchiness of the roof under his back, he might have relaxed.

A star hissed across the sky, drawing its name in a pulsing white line. Danny sat up suddenly, startled and thrilled, but his foot slipped off the vent pipe, so that he slid down the roof and right over the edge, catching his right wrist painfully on the gutter before crashing into the rhododendron.

He sat up gasping in pain, left hand clutching the wound.

"That was not so well done," said a girl.

Danny's breath stopped, leaving his mouth to gape and pop. He tried to talk, but only managed to squeak out an "I—"

Then his Transformers knapsack dropped off the roof and landed on his head. The girl—for surely she was a girl—leaned over and grabbed it before Danny could sort out what had just happened.

"Nice pack," she said dryly. He was mortified. Then she opened it and began pulling his emergency kit out, piece by piece.

Miserable, Danny sat in the rhododendron where he had fallen and looked at his tormentor. She was skinny and small, maybe five feet tall. Hard to tell in the dark, but she looked Asian. Korean? Though sometimes Mexicans looked Asian to him, which Danny knew was stupid. She wore scuff-kneed jeans and a knit top with ragged sleeves.

He had no idea if she was twelve or twenty-two. Of course, Danny mostly wasn't sure about himself. He knew what his ID card said, the stupid fake driver's license they gave to people who couldn't drive so those people who were completely undeserving of pity or scorn could get a bus pass or cash an SSI check. His ID card said he was twenty-two, but lots of times Danny felt twelve.

Almost never in a good way.

"This your stuff?" She turned the retainer over in her fingers as if she'd never seen one.

"Nah." Danny stared at the broken branches sticking out from under his thighs. "They belonged to some other guy I met up on the roof."

She laughed, her voice soft as Sister Moon's light. "You should tell that other guy he'd get farther with a silver athame that with a stainless steel butter knife."

"It's the edge that counts," Danny said through his pout.

The girl bent close. He could almost hear the smile in her voice, though he wouldn't meet her eye. "You'd be surprised how many people don't know that," she said, so near to him that her breath was warm on his face. "A sharpened paper clip and grass cuttings will serve for most rituals, if the will is strong enough and the need is great."

Now he looked up. She was smiling at him, and not in the let's-smack-the-stupid-kid-around way he'd grown used to over the years. Then she reached into her sleeve and pulled out a short, slightly curved blade that gleamed dully under the gaze of Sister Moon. "Try this one," she said, handing it to him, "and look on page two-thirty-eight of the Booke of Dayes."

Danny stared at the knife a moment, then glanced up again. She was gone. Not mysteriously, magically vanished—he could hear the girl singing in the street as she picked up a bicycle and pedaled away with the faint clatter of chain and spokes. But still gone.

The knife, though. . . . Touching it, he drew blood from his fingertip. Wow, he thought, then raced inside to read page 238 by flashlight under the covers.

Reversal of Indifference

Betimes the Practitioner hath wrought some error of ritual, perhaps through inattention, or even a fault of the Web of the world in disturbance about zir sacred space, and so the Practitioner hath lost the full faith and credit of the kindlier spirits as well as the older, quieter Forces in the World.

Zie may in such moments of tribulation turn to the Reversal of Indifference, which shalleth remake the rent asundered in the fabric of the Practitioner's practice, and so invite the beneficent forces once more within zir circle of influence. Thus order may be restored to the business of the World, and the Practitioner rest easier in zir just reward.

Zie should gather three mice, material with which to bind their Worldly selves, and all the tools of the Third Supplicative Form before attempting the exercise in the workbook for this section.

Danny didn't have the workbook—he'd only found *Mother Urban's Booke of Dayes* by accident in the first place. He'd checked, though; the workbook wasn't available on Amazon or anywhere. So he'd done without. Most of the time he'd been able to sort out the needed ritual, trusting in his own good faith to bridge any gaps. This was not so different. He understood the Third Supplicative Form well enough. Still, he'd never noticed the Reversal of Indifference before.

It was such a big book, with so many pages.

Mice, and binding, though. There were mice in the basement, in the heater room and sometimes in the laundry closet. He went to set out peanut butter in the bottom of a tall trash bucket, built a sort of ramp up to the lip of the bucket out of a stack of dog-eared Piers Anthony novels, then considered how to bind the sacrificial animals once they were his.

The answer, as it so often seemed to be, was duct tape. Danny was excited enough to want to try the Reversal of Indifference that same night. He had his new athame, and the star had certainly sent him a detailed message in the mouth of that strange Asian girl. A practitioner could only be so lucky, and he aimed to use his luck for all it was worth.

Danny had harvested four mice within the hour, so he left one inside the trash bucket for a spare in case he made a mistake. One by one, he took the other three and wrapped them in duct tape. They were trembling, terrified little silver mummies, only their shifting black eyes and quivering noses protruding.

"Sorry, little guys," he whispered, feeling a bit sick. But magic was serious business, the lifeblood of the world, and he had failed to call down the rain.

No one would miss a few mice.

Then Danny made himself sicker wondering if one of the mice was a mother, and would little mouse babies starve in some nest behind the walls.

He shifted his thoughts away with the heft of the athame in his hand. The knife was tiny, but nothing felt like silver. The Third Supplicative Form—as best as Danny understood without the workbook available—was a long chant followed by the delivery of the sacrifice. Usually he sacrificed a candy bar, or maybe a dollar bill. In tonight's case, the sacrifice was obvious.

This time Danny remembered to take the battery out of the smoke alarm. Then he lit his candles, purified his hands in the bowl of Costco olive oil, and began the chant. The mice shivered on the altar, one little mummy actually managing to roll over and almost fall off onto the green shag. He nudged it back into place and tried to concentrate on magical thoughts instead of what he was about to do.

When the moment came, the mice bled more than he thought they could. One managed to bite his finger before dying. Still, he laid them in the hibachi, squirted Ronson lighter fluid on them, and flicked them with the Bic. The duct tape burned with a weird, sticky kind of smell, while the mice were like tiny roasts.

Guilt-ridden, Danny grabbed the trash bucket to go free the last mouse into the yard, but halfway up the basement stairs he had to throw up. By the time he got outside, the last mouse had drowned in the pool of vomit, floating inert with the potato chunks and parsley flecks from dinner.

He washed his mouth and hands for a long time, but still went to bed feeling grubby and ill.

Morning brought rain.

Danny lay in his little bed—he had to curl up to even lie in the blue race car, but Mom kept insisting how much he'd loved the thing when he was seven—and listened to water patter on the roof. Portland rain, like taking a shower with the tap on low. It didn't rain so much in August, but it was never this dry either.

He'd done it.

Sky had heard him, and returned blessings to the land.

Danny didn't know if it was the girl's athame, or the mice, or just more careful attention to the *Booke of Dayes*. He wanted to bounce out of bed and write Mother Urban another letter to her post office box in New Jersey, but he wanted more to run outside and play in the rain.

Then he thought some more about the mice, and looked at the red spot on his finger where one of them had bitten him, and wept a while into his pillow.

It rained for days, as if this were February and the Pacific storms were pouring over the Coastal Mountains one after another. Danny performed the Daily Observances and leafed through the *Booke of Dayes* in his quiet moments to see what else he'd missed besides the Reversal of Indifference. Mostly he let Sky take care of the land and wondered when he'd see Father Sun again.

Mom seemed distracted, too. Danny knew she loved him, but she was so busy with her work and taking care of the house, she didn't always remember to hug him like their therapist said to, or feed him like their doctor said to.

That was okay. He could hug himself when he needed, and there was always something to eat in the kitchen.

So mostly Danny mooned around the house, watched the rain fall, and wished he could take the bus to Lowe's to look for new magical herbs in the garden center. He wasn't allowed TV, and there wasn't much else to do except read *Mother Urban* or one of his fantasy novels.

Except as the days went by, the rain did not let up. First Mom became angry about her tomatoes. Then he saw a dead puppy bumping down the gutter out front, drowned and washing away in a Viking funeral without the burning boat. The news kept talking about the water, and how the East Side Sewer Project wasn't ready for the overflow, and whether the Willamette River would reach flood stage, and which parks had been closed because the creeks were too swollen to be safe.

Danny watched outside to see if the Asian girl came by again on her bike. He wanted to ask her what to do now, what to do next. There was no point in climbing the roof to ask Sky—the only answer he would get there was a faceful of water and Oregon's endless, featureless dirty cotton flannel rain clouds.

If anything, Sky was even less informative in such a rain than when Father Sun shouted the heat of his love for the world.

So Danny sat by the dining room window looking out on the street and leafed through *Mother Urban's Booke of Dayes* for anything he could find about rain, about water, about asking the sun to return once more.

He read all about the *Spelle for a Seizure of the Bladder*, but realized after a while that wasn't the right kind of water. *Maidens' Tears & the Love of Zir Hearte* had seemed promising, but even from the first words, Danny knew better. Still, he'd studied the lists of rose hips and the blood of doves and binding cords braided from zir hair. Closer, in a way, was the *Drain Cantrip*, though that seemed more straightforward, being a spell of baking soda and vinegar and gravity.

Danny tried to imagine how much baking soda and vinegar it would take to open up the world to swallow all this rain.

The news talked about people packing sandbags along the waterfront downtown. All the floodgates were open in the dam at Oregon City. A girl drowned in the Clackamas River at Gladstone, trying to feed bedraggled ducks. A grain barge slipped its tow and hit a pillar of the Interstate Bridge, shutting down the Washington-bound traffic for days.

All his fault. All this water.

He prayed. He stood before his altar and begged. He even tried the roof one night, but only managed to sprain his ankle slipping—again—on the way down. And he read the Booke of Dayes. Studying it so closely, Danny realized that Mother Urban must have been a very strange author, because often he could not find the same spell twice, yet would locate spells he'd never seen before in all his flipping through the book.

Meanwhile, his own mother complained about the weather, set buckets in the living room and bathroom under the leaks, and sent Danny to the basement or his bedroom more often than not. Something had happened to her job—too wet to work outdoors at the Parks Department—and she stopped using the TiVo, just watching TV through the filter of gin all day and all night. He wasn't sure she slept anymore.

Danny was miserable. This was all his fault. He never should have listened to the Asian girl, never should have killed those mice, not even for a ritual. If only he could bring them back to life, or set that stupid, fateful star back into the sky.

He couldn't undo what was done, but maybe he could do something else. That was when he had his big idea. It couldn't rain everywhere, right? If he worked the ritual again, somewhere else, the rain would leave Oregon behind to move on. Things would be better again, for Mom, for his neighbors, for the people fighting the flood. For everyone!

Excited but reluctant, Danny caught five more mice. He put them in a Little Oscar cooler with some newspaper, along with cheese and bread to eat, and pounded holes in the lid with a hammer and a screwdriver so they could breathe. He gathered the rest of his materials—the silver athame, duct tape, the brass bowl, the bottle of Costco olive oil, the Ronson lighter fluid—and stuffed all of it in his dorky Transformers knapsack.

All he needed was money for a bus ticket to Seattle. They wouldn't even notice the extra rain there. Mom never really slept, but she was full of gin all the time now, and spent a lot of her day breathing through her mouth and staring at nothing. Danny waited for her noises to get small and regular, then crept into her room.

"Mom," he said quietly.

She lay in her four-poster bed, the quilted coverlet spotted with gin and ketchup. Her housedress hung open, so Danny could see her boobs flopping, even the pink pointy nipples, which made him feel weird in a sick-but-warm way. Her head didn't turn at the sound of his voice.

"Momma, I'm hungry." That wasn't a lie, though mostly he'd been eating the strange old canned food at the back of the pantry for days.

She snorted, then slumped.

"Momma, I'm taking some money from your purse to go buy food." There was the lie, the one he'd get whipped for, and have to pray forgiveness at the altar later on. *Mother Urban's Booke of Dayes* was very clear on the penalties for a Practitioner's lying to the Spirit Worlde.

But without the money, he could not move the rain. Besides, surely he'd buy food on the way to Seattle. So it wasn't *really* a lie.

He reached into her purse, pushed aside the pill bottles and lipsticks and doctor's shots to find her little ladybug money purse. Too scared to count it out, Danny took the whole thing and fled without kissing his mother goodbye or tucking her boobs back in her dress or even locking the front door.

Danny's pass got him on the number 33 bus downtown. Even in the floods, Tri-Met kept running. The bus's enormous wheels seemed to be able to splash through deep puddles where cars were stuck. The rain had soaked him on the way to the bus stop, and at the bus shelter, and even now its clear fingers were clawing at the window to drag him out. Danny clutched his Little Oscar cooler and his Transformers knapsack and stared out, daring the rain to do its worst.

If he made the rain mad enough, and Sky who was both mother and father of the rain, maybe it would follow him to Seattle even without the *Reversal of Indifference.*

The Greyhound station downtown had a sign on the door that said NO SERVICE TODAY DUE TO INCLEMENT WEATHER. Danny wasn't sure exactly what "inclement" meant, but he understood the sign.

He sat out front and stared at the train station down the street, crying. It was in the rain, no one would notice him in tears. The Little Oscar emitted scratching noises as the mice did whatever it was mice did in the dark. He knew he should draw out *Mother Urban's Booke of Dayes* and try to work out what to do next.

Then the girl on the bike showed up again. She came splashing through puddles with a big smile on her face, as though this flood were a sprinkler on a summer lawn. The bike skidded sideways in front of him, splashing Danny with grimy water. She leapt off like she was performing some great trick, and let her bicycle fall over into the flooded gutter.

"So how's your edge, Danny?" she asked brightly.

He couldn't remember that he'd ever told the girl his name. It wasn't like he knew hers. "Th-this is all your fault!" he blurted.

Somewhere out in the rain a ship's horn bellowed, long and slow. The bus station was near the waterfront, Danny knew.

The girl's grin expanded. "Somebody's going to hit the Broadway Bridge."

"*You* s-set me up."

"No, Danny." She leaned close, her hands on her knees. "I just told you how to do what you wanted. You set you up. A Practitioner must know zir Practice."

He was startled out of his growing pout. "You know everything about the *Booke of Dayes*, don't you? Tell me, how do I fix this?"

Another laugh. "Think," she said. "Smart kid like you doesn't have to go to Seattle to stop the rain."

"I been doing nothing but think for days!" The tears started up. "People been drowning, that p-puppy, Mom's got no w-work, the tomatoes are rotting . . . " Danny screwed his eyes shut to shut the tears off, just like Mom always made him do.

When the girl's voice spoke hot-breathed in his ear, he squeaked like a duct-taped mouse. "What's the name of the ritual, Practitioner?"

"*R-reversal of Indifference.*"

"What does that *mean?*"

He wasn't stupid! Danny concentrated, like they'd always tried to make him do in school. Reversal . . . reversal. . . . The meaning hit him suddenly. "You can turn something around from either direction," he said with a gasp.

She clapped her hands with glee. "And so . . . ?"

"And so . . . " Danny let his thoughts catch up with his words. He could see this thread, like a silver trail in the sky, tying a star back into place. "And so I can make Sky stop thinking about rain on Portland, make Sky take the rain back."

"Bravo!" Her eyes sparkled with pure delight.

"Wh-what's your n-name?" he asked, completely taken in by the girl's expression.

"Geneva," she said, serious but still amused. "Geneva Fairweather."

He squatted on the bench in front the Greyhound station and opened the Little Oscar. Five sets of beady eyes looked from a reek of piss and damp animal. Danny already had his duct tape out, but when he reached for the first mouse, he remembered that it was the edge that counted. Geneva Fairweather had said you could work most rituals with a sharpened paper clip and grass cuttings.

So maybe he didn't need to kill three mice. Or even tape them into tiny mummies to bind them. His fist would hold the mouse. The athame was sharp enough to prick three drops of blood from the mouse's back. The poor animal squirmed and squealed, but it was not dead. He folded the blood into a corner of paper torn from *Mother Urban's Booke of Dayes*, and followed the ritual from there.

Within moments, the rain slackened and Father Sun peeked down for the first time in three weeks. Danny turned to Geneva. "See? I could do it!"

A distant bicycle splashed through the puddles. She was gone.

Still, it didn't matter. Danny knew he'd done something important. Real important. And Geneva Fairweather would be back, he was sure of it.

As for Danny, if he could do this, how much more could he do?

What effect would a Reversal of Indifference have on his mom?

Clutching his bus pass, Danny walked back toward the Tri-Met stop. He would study *Mother Urban's Booke of Dayes* all the way home.

On the bus, he noticed for the first time the tiny illustration of a girl on a bicycle that appeared somewhere on every page of *Booke of Dayes.* Sometimes inside another illustration, sometimes tucked within the words, sometimes on the edge.

Had she been there before?

Did it matter?

The mice rustled in his jacket pocket. A pungent odor told Danny they were already making themselves at home there. That was fine with him. Smiling, he pricked his finger with the athame, right there on the bus, and watched the blood well like a fat-bellied ruby. Once he got home, some things would begin to change.

You take children's tears and you rob them of all the tears they might ever cry. You steal their ability to feel joy, compassion, pain. You remove what makes them human. You take their lives . . . Most folk, Normal or Weyrd, are law-abiding, but there's a market for everything . . .

BRISNEYLAND BY NIGHT

ANGELA SLATTER

"How many kids now?" I asked.

"Twenty-five we can identify for sure. But that's out of a couple of hundred a week. Not all those are ours."

"Don't say *ours*, Bela. They're nothing to do with me." I looked out the window. My reflection stared back. Beyond that I watched the night speed past. I should have been at my next-door neighbor's eighth birthday party, pretending I didn't like children; I shouldn't have been here.

It was a gypsy cab in every sense of the word: battered and beaten, any white surface reduced to gray, the vinyl of the seat a little sticky. The rubber mats on the floor were so thin as to be almost transparent. I imagined they were the only thing stopping me from seeing Wynnum Road's bitumen beneath us. Instead of an air freshener, a gris-gris hung from the rear view mirror. It wasn't minty fresh, but then again it didn't smell bad; cinnamon-y if anything. Scratched along the inside of the doors were protective symbols and sigils even I couldn't read. I did the dumb thing and looked a bit closer. Some of them were actually fingernail marks. I didn't want to think about that too much. Bernard Fanning howled out of the speakers behind my head, wanting to wish everyone well yet wondering why someone gave up on him too soon. There weren't too many cabs like this in Brisbane, although as the population grew, so did the demand. The general clientele covered Weyrd, wandering Goth, and too-drunk-to-notice Normal. Most times even the drunks thought twice about getting into this kind of vehicle, snapped out of their stupor by the strangeness it exuded.

The eye in the back of the driver's head examined me through thin ginger hair, while the two on his face dealt with the nighttime traffic. Ziggi and I knew each other, kind of; nodding acquaintances. He and Bela had taken me to hospital a few months back. He'd help save my life and I guessed I should be a bit more gracious. The pain in my leg didn't make me feel gracious. It made me feel grumpy that I couldn't drive myself anywhere anymore; at least not for a long while.

So I was a regular victim of public transport. Buses and trains might have been environmentally friendly, but sometimes my fellow commuters were creepier than the Weyrd drivers. Instead of being independent, I was now a chauffeured invalid with a foul temper. Some might argue that my temper wasn't so sweet beforehand.

I wanted to think this wasn't my usual kind of job; Bela assured me it was, really. There was a time, not so long ago, when I swore I wouldn't work for him again, but then again once upon a time I didn't ache inside and walk with a limp. I didn't wake up sweating, thinking something was at my window, and I didn't dream of claws reaching through the gaps in the stairs of that house and tearing so much flesh from my leg that I looked like I'd been ringbarked.

I needed money. Not for rent or anything because the house, at least, was mine, but I still needed to eat and pay for the electricity and phone. Maybe Bela felt guilty although it wasn't an emotion I associated with him. It was just another job to him. But I wouldn't have been there if he hadn't asked me to be—I kept wondering when the "ex" part of ex-boyfriend would kick in.

Bernard changed tack, wishing for buttons to push.

"I should be eating ice cream cake," I announced to no one in particular. "I should be watching Lizzie open her presents. I really should."

"What did you get her?" asked Ziggi, which elicited an annoyed noise from Bela.

"A book of fairy tales. The proper ones."

"Good choice."

"Verity, if it's—" interrupted Bela.

"It's not," I said shortly.

"If it is, then maybe it's like your dad."

He waited for me to speak, to defend myself. I rewarded him with silence, so he went on. "If it's a *kinderfresser* like your father, then we need to get him quickly. He won't stop by himself. I can't keep this out of the papers for too long, even if they're only street kids going missing."

"Do you really think I don't know that?"

My glare was enough to make him look away. He cleared his throat. "Where are you going to start?"

"I've got some ideas," I said, refusing to give him anything more. I could feel his gaze, even though I was looking out the window again. I thought he might be staring at my neck, at the pale curve, at the spot where the vein beat blue close to the surface. I thought he might be remembering what I tasted like.

"Ziggi," he said abruptly, "keep an eye on her."

And he was gone, just like that. I turned and the seat beside me was empty, smelling vaguely of his expensive aftershave. Things were quiet, except for Bernard's strumming, for a few beats.

"I hate it when he does that. Freaks me out," said Ziggi.

Bela made even other Weyrd uncomfortable. I felt kind of proud.

"It is a bit creepy," I admitted. "He used to do that in the kitchen all the time. I dropped a lot of dishes."

I bit down on my lip. Hadn't meant that to slip out. Ziggi was polite enough to ignore it.

"So, where to? You said you got some ideas."

"I may have exaggerated. I have one idea. Let's start with Little Venice."

"Probably should have told me that three seconds ago when I could have taken the turnoff," he said mildly. He cut off a dully gleaming four-wheel drive to change lanes. As we drove onto the Story Bridge I glanced out. The lights of the city, down and to the left, and those of New Farm, down and to the right, swam in the blackness.

"It's okay. We got nothing but time," I lied and hunched into the upholstery.

West End's filled with Weyrd. Everyone thinks it's just students, drunks, artists, writers, a few yuppies waiting for an upgrade, junkies and the Saturday markets for cheap fruit and veggies. There's also a metric buttload of Weyrd, who do their best to blend in, generally successfully. They fit in fine in suburbs that already have a pretty bizarre human population—places where it's difficult to distinguish the wondrous-strange from the nut jobs. The old guy who yells at the trees on the corner of Boundary Street and Montague Road? Weyrd. The kid who keeps peeing on the front steps of the Gun Shoppe? Weyrd. The woman who asks people in the street if they can spare some dirty washing? You get the picture. The smart ones use glamours to hide what they are. There are a few spots, though, where they can go and just be themselves. Little Venice is one of them.

The place *looks* ordinary enough. It's cute: dingy little entryway lapping the street, long thin corridor that's dim and cool leading into four big rooms filled with shadows and incense. Out the back is a walled, stone paved courtyard that's generally not used during the daylight hours except by stray Normals. Above is a tightly-twined roof of leaves and vines, enough to keep the sun and rain out, but not quite enough to hide the snakes that lurk there. I could see through the wide archway: the space was packed in the bruised evening. A man with a sitar was accompanied by another playing a theremin and the seated crowd swayed along contentedly. Two emo-Weyrd waitresses sloped between tables delivering drinks and finger food.

Little Venice does good coffee and amazing cakes (fat moist chocolate, rich bitter citrus and a caramel marshmallow log that will stop your heart). The three sisters who own the place, the Misses Norn, take turns reading palms, cards and tea leaves—each has her preferred method and each tells a different thing: one genuinely lays out your choices, one will make your future with her words, and the third simply lies. Problem is this: you can't really tell which does which. They're not malicious; just Weyrd. It's what they do.

Aspasia was working the counter in the main room, which wasn't too full, but the low hum coming from the other rooms told me they might be a different matter. Behind her was a mirror that looked like lace made of snowflakes. She gave me a smile as I limped in. Ziggi was driving around and around—it's easier to find a good park in Hell. This sister was all dark serpentine curls, obsidian eyes and red, red smile. When her lips opened I could see how sharp her teeth were.

"Verity, my sweet. Come to hear your future?" Her smile widened and I re-thought my malice assessment. She gave a shimmy and gracefully extended her hand. "Cross my palm with silver, girly."

I shook my head. "My answer's the same as it's been for the past ten years. But I will take a long black, some information and a slice of that caramel marshmallow log. And a latte and a piece of mud cake to go. Make the latte super-sweet."

She raised her eyebrows. "You got a new boyfriend?"

"Hardly." I shook my head at the idea of Ziggi-as-boyfriend and sat carefully on one of the tall stools, rested my elbows on the fossilized countertop and smiled. It's a good smile, nice and bright, disarming. "Kids are going missing."

"So sad." She wasn't fooled and began to make the coffee, caressing the machine into doing her bidding. There was the bubble and spit of it all, a comforting buzz that made me salivate like one of Pavlov's dogs. Efficiently she sliced away a chunk of the deadly dessert and plated it in front of me. I took a glutton's bite then had to wash it down with the coffee. So much sugar my heart did a little jig. She started making Ziggi's takeaway, slower this time.

"Street kids thus far, so under the radar pretty much. Still," I said, "it's only a matter of time before some little Normal goes astray and people in high places start looking at our kind. Well," I paused, "your kind."

"Half-breed," she hissed before she could stop herself. I watch the hair on her head curl and twist, vipers forming there and writhing until she got herself under control.

I gave a cold smile around another mouthful of caramel mush. "All I'm saying, Aspasia, is if you know anything now would be the time to share. And I would be the person to share it with. You know me: I'll do things quietly. Do you really want Brisneyland's Keystone Cops traipsing through your place? If word of this gets out, not even your connections will stop them from coming down here. Then where will all the Weyrd go?"

Her shoulders shook with the effort of not hitting me. She didn't like being threatened and truth be told, I didn't like threatening—it was cheap and easy. But I didn't stop. "Although, I'm sure Shaky Jakes would pick up the slack, were Little Venice no longer able to guarantee its clients refuge from the ordinary."

"It's not about flesh. We haven't seen a *kinderfresser* since . . . " she said, which was what I'd figured. "But I've been offered—wine."

That sat me back on my arse. Wine? My confusion must have shown because she leaned forward. I did the same and felt one of the hair-snakes brush my left ear, soft as a kiss. It was kind of nice.

Aspasia spoke low. "Kids cry, right? I mean, they're kids, there's always something to cry over. But enough to fill two, three, four wine bottles? Like, wouldn't that be a lifetime of tears?"

I stared at her.

"I was offered a case. A case, Fassbinder. That's a lot of kids, a lot of tears. You take that . . . "

You take their tears and you rob them of all the tears they might ever cry. You steal their ability to feel joy, compassion, pain. You remove what makes them human. You take their lives. Not a *kinderfresser*, no, but something somehow worse.

"Who?" I asked. "Who's been offering?"

She jerked her head towards a table in the corner. I didn't turn around but watched in the mirror. A thin young girl sat there, badly made-up, her pale floss hair twisted back in a clip, her limbs so sharp they looked like they might make a break for it, given half a chance. She wore a gray singlet top with an irregular pattern on the front—whatever the design had been was gone along with the sequins. Beneath the table I could see stick legs and a far-too-short denim skirt.

"Why is she here?"

"She pays," said Aspasia flatly.

"When did she offer you the case?"

"Two, maybe three weeks ago." She shrugged.

"You didn't think to tell anyone about this?" How many lives lost in that time?

"You think a couple of the Weyrd Council haven't taken her up on the offer?"

"The Council hired me."

"No, princess, Tepes hired you. He's only one of them."

Again, I sat back, digested that. The problem was bigger than we thought. I wouldn't be reporting back too soon. I needed to finish this off-radar and it needed to be fast; then the Council could get purged, weeded, whatever Bela thought appropriate. I flicked my eyes to the girl in the corner; she was looking at me. We stared at each other for maybe five seconds but that's all it took. She was up and out of her chair and haring down the long corridor before I could so much as turn around. There was no way I was running after her; no way I'd even bother to try.

"What's her name and where do I find her?" I asked Aspasia who was casually putting the lid on Ziggi's takeaway latte and sliding the chunk of cake into a paper coffin. She pushed them towards me and I handed over a twenty. I had the feeling she didn't want to tell me any more and just as her hand retracted clutching the cash I grabbed at her and held on tight. I felt her wrist bones grind against each other beneath my grip. I may look Normal, I may be a half-breed, but it doesn't mean I've got nothing of the Weyrd about me. I thought about wrapping the other hand around her throat and risking a few nips from the snakes, but decided she might find it hard to talk.

"Sally Crown. Lives on the streets. Sometimes she sleeps behind the West End Library. Sometimes in the derelict flats on Hardgrave Road. Now let me go and get the fuck out."

"You need to work on your customer service skills, Aspasia. Keep the change."

The whole way down the corridor I could feel her eyes boring into the back of my neck. Verity Fassbinder in action: winning friends and influencing people.

"I'll see you tonight."

Ziggi waved a hand in my general direction as he drove off; it was probably a "yes." Those drivers play hard to get. Dawn had crept over the horizon about an hour ago and we'd given up watching the West End Library for any sign of Sally Crown. Admittedly, in the first place we tried—Hardgrave Road—I'd nearly been spitted on the umbrella of an especially grumpy old lady whose wings unfurled in shock when she found me in the flat she was using as a squat.

I made my way up the cracked path to my ramshackle cottage. The jasmine was thick on the front fence, lushly green with white-star flowers like icing. The scent was heady. I felt for my keys in the pockets of my jeans.

"Verity? Verity! Can you get my ball?" High and fluting, the voice came over the side fence. Between the palings was a small face, sharp-chinned, snub-nosed, wide-eyed, with a shock of mousey hair even messier than mine. A little hand pushed through the gap and pointed to a soccer ball lying under my front steps. Lizzie wasn't allowed out of her yard without a parent in tow. She hated it, but I thought it a good idea and told her so at every opportunity—those were the days she decided not to talk to me.

I limped over and picked up the ball. It was really, really new. "Birthday present? Sorry I couldn't come."

"Uh huh. I like the book best." She smiled and the edges of the crescent went so high that the break in the fence wasn't wide enough to display them. The book of real fairy tales, the ones with little girls who were eaten by wolves and bears with no rescue; boys who got lost in the forest and weren't found again ever; where your brother is a danger to you and your sister cannot be trusted; children whose greatest enemies were their own parents. Lizzie's mother had frowned, but I told her that forewarned was forearmed. Lizzie loved the books in my house, so I knew I was on a winner.

I reached up and dropped the ball over.

"Thanks, Verity. Can I come and read later?"

"Not today, my friend. I've had a very long night. Maybe on the weekend?"

"Mmmmm-huh." The tone told me she wasn't impressed.

"Have a good day, sweetheart," I said and headed to the door.

Inside, the hot air was smothering, so I opened all the windows and the double doors onto the back verandah. The breeze did its thing and soon the place was bearable. I carried a glass of cold water and a collection of painkillers out and sat in one of the faded green deck chairs.

I stretched my leg out and rested it on the top of the table. The pain eased. In the gigantic jacaranda tree that took up most of the back yard an extremely fat kookaburra perched. I gave him a nod; he stared, unmoved.

I needed a nap. I needed to do some research. But most of all, I needed the nap. Just a few hours.

I had to dig up the past; exhume my father. I didn't want to, I really didn't, but I had no choice. I closed my eyes, dropped my head back until there was a satisfying crack and things sat a little more comfortably.

My father. His murders.

My mother was Normal and gone before I knew her. The everyday things of my childhood were salt in the corners of a room to soak up the curses that might come our way; to keep away the worst of the shades blood was baked into the bread and left as an offering once a week; dust was swept from the footpath towards the house as we chanted "for all the wealth of the city to come home to us." Took me a long time to work out there were two cultures and I could walk between them. That I could fool the Normals. And I could step into the Weyrd—they'd talk to me, but were wary.

Truth was, with one foot in each world I didn't belong anywhere.

Twenty years ago my father was jailed as a pedophile and child killer, but that didn't even begin to touch the skin of what he was.

Most folk, Normal or Weyrd, are law-abiding. But there's a market for everything, and the law of supply and demand, and some tables demanded the most tender of flesh. Small groups, private parties—it was a particular taste indulged in by the very few, a leftover from the past, when stealing children was an accepted practice; a hobby and a habit. Someone had to source and butcher that flesh.

My father. *Kinderfresser.* Child eater. Butcher to the Weyrd.

He never touched me—that needs to be clear—and he got caught like so many of them do. He got sloppy. He got lazy. He didn't take the hunt far enough away from his home. All those fairy tales and my father was the monster.

Grigor lasted precisely how long you'd think a child killer would last in prison. He was a big man, but no match for the six prisoners who held him down. With him gone, my maternal grandparents brought me up; I learned "normal" from them. They loved me, cared for me, left me the house. Some days, though, I'd catch them looking at me as if I were something awful and fascinating, a cuckoo in the nest. It hurt at first, but in the end I accepted it. I let my father fade from my memory as much as I could.

The people Grigor had been supplying just faded into the background—that part never came out, that he was a *kinderfresser* and that his employers had disappeared without a trace, although the flow of child disappearances seemed to stop for a long, long time—at least, those connected to Brisneyland's Weyrd. The Normal justice system isn't really designed to cope with stuff like that. Hell, it can't cope with its own mundane crimes.

Now, though, something had changed. Something new was on the market.

The State Library was cold, the air-conditioning set to *arctic breeze*. The microfiche reader made a slight buzz and gave off a lot of heat. I was tempted to rub my hands in front of it and maybe try to toast a marshmallow or two.

There was surprisingly little about Grigor's murders; Weyrd influence in the corridors of power, I supposed, keeping things on the lowdown. But there were pictures of him being taken to and from the Supreme Court; a large handsome man in a bad suit, with hangdog eyes and a loose-lipped grin that showed off sharp teeth.

I hadn't looked at these things before; hadn't wanted to, had chosen not to, as if none of it had happened. But I think some days, when my thoughts turn that way, that everything I've done as an adult has been a kind of penance for what my father did. I try to be an atonement for him.

Where Grigor went wrong was to take a cared-for child, one from a happy home, a rich neighborhood; a child loved and for whom someone would look. Had he stuck to the guttersnipes, the unwanted children, who knows how long he might have continued undetected?

I kept scrolling through the black and white projections of words and pictures: glamorous women smiled out from the social pages, their shoulder pads taking up much of the space; school kids celebrated as dux of their school; public outcry over the knocking down of yet another historic building; rubber duck races on the river of brown; writers and film festivals. Other crimes just as awful but not linked to me. Ah, Brisneyland.

When my fingers went numb, I gave up. Nothing there, a wasted afternoon. The need for more sleep buzzed in my head like a determined fly. And I was meeting Ziggi at my place at six. Sure, he could have picked me up from the library, but I was independent and didn't plan to rely on anyone. My leg told me I was an idiot. I had to agree as I hobbled out the sliding doors and into the last of the stinking summer heat.

Lizzie's mother stood on the patio of my house, pale and shaking in the late afternoon, knocking hard on the door.

"Hey, Mel."

She turned and looked at me with desperate hope. I just knew I was going to disappoint her.

"Is Lizzie here? She said she was coming over to read with you."

Little bugger.

"No, Mel, she's not. When did she leave?" My heart thumped. No! I told myself, wrong neighborhood. A cared-for child. Another part of my brain chimed in with, *Grigor did it.*

"Have you checked the tree?" Lizzie liked to hide in the hollow of the jacaranda tree in my back yard. She had comic books in sealed plastic bags, a blanket, and a couple of dolls.

Her mother and I pretended we didn't know about it—every kid needs a secret spot.

She shook her head. "Not there—it was the first place I looked."

"Okay, playing with friends in the street? You've called school friends?" She nodded, trying not to cry. "Okay, don't mess around. Call the cops."

"I don't want to overreact . . . " she said, but I knew that's exactly what she wanted to do, like any mother. She wanted to scream until her baby came back. She wanted to kill the person who'd caused her this tearing fear. I pushed her gently away from my door.

"Go. Call. Better to be safe than sorry. I've got to go out," I said, eyeing the gypsy cab as it pulled up. "But you've got my mobile number if you find anything, if you need anything, okay? I can't avoid this appointment, but I will be back later this evening, I promise."

She nodded again and the movement was enough to spill the tears over. I hugged her hard and gave her a nudge in the right direction. I stumbled as I headed towards Ziggi and his chariot. Bernard was keeping him company again and at volume, worrying about paper cuts or something. How many times was he going to play that CD? I'm a big Bernard fan, but everyone has their limit.

If it had been me, I wouldn't have gone back to my usual haunts, at least not that soon. I'd have waited maybe a week for interested parties to give up. Maybe I'm smarter than most people.

But Sally Crown—now Sally Crown was young and dumb.

Ziggi killed the engine and we rolled to a stop outside the West End Library. Out the front was a community noticeboard covered with flyers for self-help groups, book clubs, writers groups, sewing circles, and one enlargement of a newspaper article. A perfectly coiffed matron's smiling face gleamed out from a photocopied feature about her handing over a substantial cheque to some charity or other. Someone had drawn a mustache across her top lip.

"You okay on your own?" Ziggi asked around a mouthful of day-old chocolate cake.

"Yep."

"Only Bela said . . . "

"Fuck Bela."

"He's not my type."

"If I yell then you come running, okay? Otherwise, finish your cake—it was expensive and I may not be able to go back there again for some time. And I cannot believe you still have some left."

I got out and made my way around the back, surprisingly quietly, all things considered. I was tired enough to cry tears of self-pity and my leg ached so much it felt like the wounds might have opened again, even though they were well-scarred over. There she was, tucked up like a dirty angel on a clapped-out sofa, a grubby old chequered picnic blanket pulled up to her chin. Mozzies buzzed enthusiastically, but wisely left me alone.

I gently lowered myself to sit beside her and cooed her name. She came awake with a start and slashed at me. Luckily, I was ready for that, suspicious type that I am.

"Okay, unfriendly and counterproductive," I told her, snatching away the blade and tossing it over the fence. "So, Sally, tell me everything you know."

"Fuck you, bitch."

"You kiss your mother with that mouth?"

She let loose with a few more choice profanities and in the end I lost patience, grabbing at her face and squeezing the corners of her jaw so she whimpered.

"Now, you will notice that I am freakishly strong, Sally. I can and will pop your head if you don't tell me what I want to know."

She tried to say something. It sounded like *half-breed*, so I squeezed a little tighter. Tears trickled down her cheeks. I felt bad and let her go. I stroked her hair and that made her flinch.

"Okay, let's try again. Sally, I'm looking for a friend of mine. She's young and she's innocent and if anything happens to her I swear I'll be back for you and you will not enjoy our reunion. Now, I suspect you've been leading children astray. No, don't say anything—if I only suspect things, you're safe." I waved a finger at her. "If I know for certain then I will not be able to turn a blind eye. I will tell Tepes." The fear in her eyes told me she knew about Bela. "But I am willing to ignore all the other things you've done if you tell me where I can find my friend."

"She'll kill me," the child whined.

Beneath the rat-like demeanor I could see a little girl who'd been ill-used; who did what she could to survive; whose humanity had been stripped away until she thought of no one but herself. I felt sorry for her, but it didn't stop me from saying, "And if you don't tell me, I'll kill you."

She whimpered.

"Sally, tell me and I will stop her. She won't hurt anyone again. She won't be a danger to you. I promise."

She seemed to weigh the odds and the scales dropped in my favor. "House at Ascot."

She reeled off the address and I stood up, anxious. I pulled whatever notes I had in my pocket out and gave them to her, thinking they might keep her from doing anything awful for a night or two at least. "If you've lied to me . . . "

She nodded *I know, I know.*

And then I had a thought. "Did you take her?" Lizzie wouldn't have gone to an adult. She would have gone to another child, though, she would have wanted to play.

The hesitation was enough. I felt sick but I turned and walked away.

"Aw, Ziggi. How did we not know about this place?"

The house in Ascot was a big, old architectural layer cake. I didn't remember seeing it before and looked askance at my sidekick. I mean, I like old houses, I spend a lot of time in them, and I know Brisneyland pretty damned well.

He shrugged. "Glamoured."

He was right—it was kind of hard to look at. My eyes kept sliding to the side and I had to concentrate for the first few minutes we sat and watched. It got easier after a while, but still the building seemed, well, slippery. I leaned against the body of the cab while Ziggi hung out the window. "Right. Big trees, too."

The block of land was huge (even for this area) and the house was set far back from the road, in the middle of an overgrown garden. Camphor laurels led up the driveway and grew so tall and close that they formed a canopy above the gravel path on which the taxi was parked. Flying foxes squeaked overhead, heading off for an evening of stripping people's fruit trees and crapping on their laundry. They were darker patches against the moonlit sky, like shadow puppets.

"Aw, Ziggi," I repeated. "Shit."

"What? You don't think it looks right?"

"I think it looks too damned right." I pushed myself away from the grimy duco. "You're not going anywhere?"

"I ain't going nowhere," he said, then added hopefully, "Hey, if anyone comes you got a secret signal you want me to give?"

"Fuck no. I want you to make a really big noise so I hear you. Who knows, maybe you'll scare them away. And I want you to listen out in case I start yelling for help. Help would be good. You know, cavalry, etcetera."

"I got it. Big fuckin' noise."

I gave him a thumbs-up and walked down the drive.

This would have made sense in West End, but this . . . this was Ascot. Home to the important people; property prices so high they could give you a nosebleed. If the car in the drive wasn't a Jag or a Merc, then you knew it belonged to the cleaning woman. And here was this house, gigantic, glamoured, and seemingly empty.

The wood creaked under my feet as I went up the five steps to the verandah. A swing-chair sat beside the double front doors. There was a doorbell. I pushed it, hard, swung on it for a long while. What if Sally lied? Hell, what if Sally had told the truth? If anyone answered I'd ask if they were interested in a pyramid selling scheme. That ruse had gotten me out of trouble more than once. People tended to back away, like you had a spare eye or a secondary nose. Of course, it had also gotten me into trouble once or twice.

No one came. I tried the handle—no joy. I peered in through the windows. They were clean, as was the upholstery on the swing-chair. So. Not deserted, and someone was concerned enough to keep the place spick and span.

I tapped my foot. Maybe Sally had lied and this was just a normal house. Then, why the glamour? I might have given up but that was the kicker; that and the sick feeling in my gut. Something was off. Where do you hide a whole bunch of kids? How do you make them disappear without a trace? Take them somewhere no one would look. Hide them away.

I couldn't see too much further inside: dark tidy rooms, some expensive pieces of furniture, a chandelier catching stray streaks of moonlight, thick curtains on most of the other windows. I listened hard for the sound of someone moving about inside. Nothing.

I broke a panel of the frosted glass in the front door, then reached through and let myself in. Ziggi studiously ignored my break and enter. I wasn't too worried about making noise. The cops I could deal with. Dead kids, I couldn't.

The long hallway had a thin Persian carpet running its length and that muffled my footsteps. I didn't know what I was looking for, not exactly, but something like a door to a basement would be a good start. Eventually, I found it in the kitchen; in the pantry to be exact, right next to a shelf stacked with salt, sugar and water crackers. Plain as day. I guess when you've got a glamour around your house and you live in Ascot you think you're bulletproof.

The door wasn't locked and the stairway that led down was brightly lit. My sneakers were soft on the steps, but not quite silent because the ache in my leg meant I brought one foot down harder than the other.

At the bottom of the stairs I found a large white room, the floor dark gray polished concrete. The house was old and the basement must have been dug at the same time as the foundations were laid, but it wasn't some dingy old cellar; it was pristine, industrial. One wall was lined with wine racks, half of them full. There was a row of steel tables, a large furnace in the back corner, a round vat with a screw-down lid and pipes running into and out of it like a moonshine still. Stark against the floor next to the furnace was a tumbling stack of small shoes and the air ached with a faint smell of cooked flesh.

In the middle of this stood a woman.

For all intents and purposes, she looked like an Ascot matron; in fact, she was the Ascot matron who'd smiled out at me from the community noticeboard. She didn't look much different. Maybe in her sixties, but her true age was concealed by a combination of expensive cosmetics, a little glamour and a lot of Botox. Not overly tall, but with a good figure; a little thick around the waist. Her pale blue dress was impeccable and her hair an elegant mix of gray and blond. The ensemble was completed by an expensive gold watch, pearl earrings and knuckle-duster rings probably worth more than my house.

"Yes?" she said. Didn't say, *What are you doing in my house, peasant? I'm calling the police.* She was holding a pair of thick black gloves maybe made out of that same stuff they're using to make muffin trays nowadays. They were at odds with the rest of her outfit.

I must have looked dumbly at her when I said, "You're not eating them."

"Oh, no. If you take their tears," she told me quite tenderly, "you can't use the meat afterwards. It's too dry, tough. Really, it's either wine or veal." She smiled. "You're Grigor's daughter, aren't you?"

I swallowed and peered around, noticing at last that on one of the tables lay a child. She was still dressed; her chest rose and fell. The woman nodded toward her. "Isn't she lovely? I was very happy with Sally for this one—it's much nicer when they're clean and content." She smiled. "She smells a little like you, you know—my, what a vintage you would have made, my girl, when you were young! What grief, what unadulterated heartache! Oh, what wouldn't I have done to take the tears from you? The wine tastes so much sweeter when it's born of sorrow."

"Lizzie," I said. She didn't stir. Louder: "Lizzie!"

"She can't hear you, dear. I keep them under, just a little sleeping spell, right up until I'm ready to put them in the press. You don't want too much panic; that sours things. It's the grief you want, the pain. Best taken fresh; giving them time to worry just makes things, well, stale."

"Wake her up," I said. "Wake her up and give her to me and we walk out of here. I tell no one about you. Just give her to me." I wondered how many deals like this I'd try to make.

"I knew your father. Wonderful butcher. Reliable business partner. Talented *kinderfresser*, but sometimes so stupid, so rash." She shook her head.

"Bela Tepes knows I'm here," I lied. "You mess with me, you mess with him. You mess with him, you mess with the Weyrd Council."

"I can handle them. Two of my best customers are on the board, lovey," she confided.

On the table, Lizzie moved. The woman tut-tutted. "Oh, look you've broken my concentration. She's waking up."

And she came at me so quickly I didn't have time to think. In my head, she was still the sort of woman who was only dangerous if you took the last friand at her favorite coffee shop. But she was older than that, infinitely stranger, and stronger. She punched me in the chest with both fists. I felt her rings rip the thin cotton of my overwashed T-shirt and pierce my skin, into the flesh. I fell straight backward. She cackled like a fairy tale witch. I hit my head on the concrete and black welled across my eyes.

Next thing I knew I could feel myself being dragged along the smooth cold floor. She had hold of my ankles, the agony of her pulling on my bad leg having woken me; that and the pain in my lacerated chest and my aching skull. She reached the furnace and let go—that hurt too—and I lay there trying to get my brain in order, trying to make my body work, trying to get to my damned feet and fight. I turned my head and looked into Lizzie's open, terrified eyes.

I heard the door of the furnace clank open and felt the heat whoosh out. I raised my gaze and saw the old woman had finally put her gloves on, and yes, they did indeed clash with her outfit.

"Now," she said, tilting her head to consider me, "you're quite tall. How am I going to fit you in? Might be a bit of a squeeze."

She leaned down to grab my hands so she could pull me forward. She was hideously strong; she was Baba Yaga, the witch in the forest, the stepmother with a poisoned apple in her hand. She hauled my top half up and for a moment our faces almost touched. She smiled and laughed and her breath was like rotten meat. I got my hand around her throat and she laughed again, kept laughing until she felt my grip tighten.

Then she was gasping and taking me seriously. I felt her nails against my back as they burst through the heatproof gloves and tore into me. I screamed and kept squeezing, watching her face turn purple. Her nails slid further in, closer to organs that would not react well to puncturing.

And then she was gone; the talons tore bigger holes in me as she was pushed aside and I fell to my knees.

Lizzie and my attacker fell back against the open maw of the furnace. I heaved myself up and pushed Lizzie out of the way. The old woman, smoke already rising from behind her head, started to scream. I punched at her torso just as she had done to me and she overbalanced, silver-gray hair becoming red and gold with flame. I grabbed at her ankles and lifted—the top half of her disappeared into the furnace and Lizzie and I jammed the rest of her in after. We pushed the door shut and locked it.

Welcome to the Gingerbread House.

The cab rolled across the Story Bridge in the soft darkness. I felt every bump and dip in the road, a regular rolling rhythm of *thud thud thud*. My T-shirt was sticky with blood; my wounds ached and itched. I wanted to get Lizzie home to her mother before I went to hospital. Sleep called but I fought it. Ziggi looked at me, the back eye intent and the two at the front flicking to my image in the rear view mirror. I gave him a weak grin and a wave.

"You okay?" he asked.

"I'm a human pincushion."

"When are you gonna tell Bela?"

"When I stop bleeding."

"Kid okay?"

I looked down at Lizzie. Her little body was curled on the seat beside me and her head was in my lap. She sucked her thumb. My hand was on her shoulder and I could feel the occasional tremor running through her, like a dog that dreamed it was chasing a rabbit.

"Yeah," I said, thinking of all the kids who weren't. "She's okay." Ziggi pushed a CD into the player. Softly, Bernard sang about being washed clean. The sun came up.

Can you ever rely on your memories of love—lost or otherwise? How powerful is the imagination? Neil Gaiman makes us consider such questions with this haunting tale . . .

THE THING ABOUT CASSANDRA

NEIL GAIMAN

So there's Scallie and me wearing Starsky-and-Hutch wigs, complete with sideburns, at five o'clock in the morning by the side of a canal in Amsterdam. There had been ten of us that night, including Rob, the groom, last seen handcuffed to a bed in the Red Light district with shaving foam covering his nether regions and his brother-in-law giggling and patting the hooker holding the straight razor on the arse, which was the point I looked at Scallie and he looked at me, and he said, "Maximum deniability?" And I nodded, because there are some questions you don't want to be able to answer when a bride starts asking pointed questions about the stag weekend, so we slipped off for a drink, leaving eight men in Starsky-and-Hutch wigs (one of whom was mostly naked, attached to a bed by fluffy pink handcuffs, and seemed to be starting to think that this adventure wasn't such a good idea after all) behind us, in a room that smelled of disinfectant and cheap incense, and we went and sat by a canal and drank cans of Danish lager and talked about the old days.

Scallie—whose real name is Jeremy Porter, and these days people call him Jeremy, but he had been Scallie when we were eleven—and the groom-to-be, Rob Cunningham, had been at school with me. We had drifted out of touch, more or less, had found each other the lazy way you do these days, through Friends Reunited and Facebook and such, and now Scallie and I were together for the first time since we were nineteen. The Starsky-and-Hutch wigs, which had been Scallie's idea, made us look like we were playing brothers in some made-for-TV movie—Scallie the short, stocky brother with the thick mustache, me, the tall one. Given that I've made a significant part of my income since leaving school modeling, I'd add the tall good-looking-one, but nobody looks good in a Starsky-and-Hutch wig, complete with sideburns.

Also, the wig itched.

We sat by the canal, and when the lager had all gone we kept talking and we watched the sun come up.

Last time I saw Scallie he was nineteen and filled with big plans. He had just joined the RAF as a cadet. He was going to fly planes, and do double duty using the flights to smuggle drugs, and so get incredibly rich while helping his country. It was the kind of mad idea he used to have all the way through school. Usually the whole thing would fall apart. Sometimes he'd get the rest of us into trouble on the way.

Now, twelve years later, his six months in the RAF ended early because of an unspecified problem with his right knee, he was a senior executive in a firm that manufactured double-glazed windows, he told me, with, since the divorce, a smaller house than he felt that he deserved and only a golden retriever for company.

He was sleeping with a woman in the double-glazing firm, but had no expectations of her leaving her boyfriend for him, seemed to find it easier that way. "Of course, I wake up crying sometimes, since the divorce. Well, you do," he said at one point. I could not imagine him crying, and anyway he said it with a huge, Scallie grin.

I told him about me: still modeling, helping out in a friend's antique shop to keep busy, more and more painting. I was lucky; people bought my paintings. Every year I would have a small gallery show at the Little Gallery in Chelsea, and while initially the only people to buy anything had been people I knew—photographers, old girlfriends, and the like—these days I have actual collectors. We talked about the days that only Scallie seemed to remember, when he and Rob and I had been a team of three, inviolable, unbreakable. We talked about teenage heartbreak, about Caroline Minton (who was now Caroline Keen, and married to a vicar), about the first time we brazened our way into an 18 film, although neither of us could remember what the film actually was.

Then Scallie said, "I heard from Cassandra the other day."

"Cassandra?"

"Your old girlfriend. Cassandra. Remember?"

". . . No."

"The one from Reigate. You had her name written on all your books."

I must have looked particularly dense or drunk or sleepy, because he said, "You met her on a skiiing holiday. Oh, for heaven's sake. *Your first shag.* Cassandra."

"Oh," I said, remembering, remembering everything. "Cassandra."

And I did remember.

"Yeah," said Scallie. "She dropped me a line on Facebook. She's running a community theatre in East London. You should talk to her."

"Really?"

"I think, well, I mean, reading between the lines of her message, she may still have a thing for you. She asked after you."

I wondered how drunk he was, how drunk I was, staring at the canal in the early light. I said something, I forget what, then I asked whether Scallie remembered where our hotel was, because I had forgotten, and he said he had forgotten too, and that Rob had all the hotel details and really we should go and find him and rescue him from the clutches of the nice hooker with the handcuffs and the shaving kit, which, we realized, would be easier if we knew how to get back to where we'd left him, and looking for some clue to where we had left Rob, I found a card with the hotel's address on it in my back pocket, so we headed back there and the last thing we did before I walked away from the canal and that whole strange evening was to pull the itchy Starsky-and-Hutch wig off my head and throw it into the canal.

It floated.

Scallie said, "There was a deposit on that, you know. If you didn't want to wear it, I'd've carried it." Then he said, "You should drop Cassandra a line."

I shook my head. I wondered who he had been talking to online, who he had confused for her, knowing it definitely wasn't Cassandra.

The thing about Cassandra is this: I'd made her up.

I was fifteen, almost sixteen. I was awkward. I had just experienced my teenage growth-spurt and was suddenly taller than most of my friends, self-conscious about my height. My mother owned and ran a small riding stables, and I helped out there, but the girls—competent, horsey, sensible types—intimidated me. At home I wrote bad poetry and painted watercolors, mostly of ponies in fields; at school—there were only boys at my school—I played cricket competently, acted a little, hung around with my friends playing records (the CD was around, but they were expensive and rare, and we had all inherited record players and hi-fis from parents or older siblings). When we didn't talk about music, or sports, we talked about girls.

Scallie was older than me. So was Rob. They liked having me as part of their gang, but they liked teasing me, too. They acted like I was a kid, and I wasn't. They had both done it with girls. Actually, that's not entirely true. They had both done it with the same girl, Caroline Minton, famously free with he favors and always up for it once, as long as the person she was with had a moped.

I did not have a moped. I was not old enough to get one, my mother could not afford one (my father had died when I was small, of an accidental overdose of anaesthetic, when he was in hospital to have a minor operation on an infected toe. To this day, I avoid hospitals). I had seen Caroline Minton at parties, but she terrified me and even had I owned a moped, I would not have wanted my first sexual experience to be with her.

Scallie and Rob also had girlfriends. Scallie's girlfriend was taller than he was, had huge breasts, and was interested in football, which meant that Scallie had to feign an interest in football, Crystal Palace, while Rob's girlfriend thought that Rob and she should have things in common, which meant that Rob stopped listening to the mid-80s electropop the rest of us liked and started listening to hippy bands from before we were born, which was bad, and that Rob got to raid her dad's amazing collection of old TV series on video, which was good.

I had no girlfriend.

Even my mother began to comment on it.

There must have been a place where it came from, the name, the idea: I don't remember though. I just remember writing "Cassandra" on my exercise books. Then, carefully, not saying anything.

"Who's Cassandra?" asked Scallie.

"Nobody," I said.

"She must be somebody. You wrote her name on your maths exercise book."

"She's just a girl I met on the skiing holiday." My mother and I had gone skiing, with my aunt and cousins, the month before, in Austria.

"Are we going to meet her?"

"She's from Reigate. I expect so. Eventually."

"Well, I hope so. And you *like* her?"

I paused, for what I hoped was the right amount of time, and said, "She's a really good kisser," then Scallie laughed and Rob wanted to know if this was French kissing, with tongues and everything, and I said, "What do you think?" and by the end of the day, they both believed in her.

My mum was pleased to hear I'd met someone. Her questions—what Cassandra's parents did, for example—I simply shrugged away.

I went on three "dates" with Cassandra. On each of our dates, I took the train up to London, and took myself to the cinema. It was exciting, in its own way.

I returned from the first trip with more stories of kissing, and of breast-feeling.

Our second date (in reality, spent watching *Weird Science* on my own in Leicester Square) was, as told to my mum, holding hands together at what she still called "the pictures," but as told to Rob and Scallie (and over that week, to several other school friends who had heard rumors from sworn-to-secrecy Rob and Scallie, and now needed to find out if it was true), the day I lost my virginity, in Cassandra's aunt's flat in London: the aunt was away, Cassandra had a key. I had (for proof) a packet of three condoms missing the one I had thrown away and a strip of four black-and-white photographs I had found on my first trip to London, abandoned in the basket of a photobooth on Victoria Station. The photostrip showed a girl about my age with long straight hair (I could not be certain of the color. Dark blonde? Red? Light brown?) and a friendly, freckly, not unpretty, face. I pocketed it. In art class I did a pencil sketch of the third of the pictures, the one I liked the best, her head half-turned as if calling out to an unseen friend beyond the tiny curtain. She looked sweet, and charming.

I put the drawing up on my bedroom wall, where I could see it from my bed.

After our third date (it was *Who Framed Roger Rabbit?*) I came back to school with bad news: Cassandra's family was going to Canada (a place that sounded more convincing to my ears than America), something to do with her father's job, and I would not see her for a long time. We hadn't really broken up, but we were being practical: those were the days when transatlantic phone calls were too expensive for teenagers. It was over.

I was sad. Everyone noticed how sad I was. They said they would have loved to have met her, and maybe when she comes back at Christmas? I was confident that by Christmas, she would be forgotten.

She was. By Christmas I was going out with Nikki Blevins and the only evidence that Cassandra had ever been a part of my life was her name, written on a couple of my exercise books, and the pencil drawing of her on my bedroom wall, with *Cassandra, February 19th, 1985* written underneath it.

When my mother sold the riding stable in 1989, the drawing was lost in the move. I was at art college at the time, considered my old pencil-drawings as embarrassing as the fact that I had once invented a girlfriend, and did not care.

I do not believe I had thought of Cassandra for twenty years.

My mother sold the riding stables, the attached house, and the meadows to a property developer, who built a housing estate where it had once been, and, as part of the deal, gave her a small, detached house at the end of Seton Close. I visit her at least once a fortnight, arriving on Friday night, leaving Sunday morning, a routine as regular as the grandmother clock in the hall.

Mother is concerned that I am happy in life. She has started to mention that various of her friends have eligible daughters. This trip we had an extremely embarrassing conversation that began with her asking if I would like to meet the church organist, a very nice young man of about my age.

"Mother. I'm not gay."

"There's nothing wrong with it, dear. All sorts of people do it. They even get married. Well, not proper marriage, but it's the same thing."

"I'm still not gay."

"I just thought, still not married, and the painting, and the modeling."

"I've had girlfriends, Mummy. You've even met some of them."

"Nothing that ever stuck, dear. I just thought there might be something you wanted to tell me."

"I'm not gay, Mother. I would tell you if I were." And then I said, "I snogged Tim Carter at a party when I was at art college but we were drunk and it never went beyond that."

She pursed her lips. "That's quite enough of that, young man." And then, changing the subject, as if to get rid of an unpleasant taste in her mouth, she said, "You'll never guess who I bumped into in Tesco's last week."

"No, I won't. Who?"

"Your old girlfriend. Your first girlfriend, I should say."

"Nikki Blevins? Hang on, she's married, isn't she? Nikki Woodbridge?"

"The one before her, dear. Cassandra. I was behind her, in the line. I would have been ahead of her, but I forgot that I needed cream for the berries today, so I went back to get it, and she was in front of me, and I knew her face was familiar. At first, I thought she was Joanie Simmond's youngest, the one with the speech disorder, what we used to call a stammer but apparently you can't say that anymore, but then I thought, I know where I know that face, it was over your bed for five years, of course I said, 'It's not Cassandra, is it?' and she said, 'It is,' and I said, 'You'll laugh when I say this, but I'm Stuart Innes's mum.' She says, 'Stuart Innes?' and her face lit up. Well, she hung around while I was putting my groceries in my shopping bag, and she said she'd already been in touch with your friend Jeremy Porter on Bookface, and they'd been talking about you—"

"You mean Facebook? She was talking to Scallie on Facebook?"

"Yes, dear."

I drank my tea and wondered who my mother had actually been talking to. I said, "You're quite sure this was the Cassandra from over my bed?"

"Oh yes, dear. She told me about how you took her to Leicester Square, and how sad she was when they had to move to Canada. They went to Vancouver. I asked her if she ever met my cousin Leslie, he went to Vancouver after the war, but she said she didn't believe so, and it turns out it's actually a big sort of a place. I told her about the pencil drawing you did, and she seemed very up-to-date on your activities. She was thrilled when I told her that you were having a gallery opening this week."

"You *told* her that?"

"Yes, dear. I thought she'd like to know." Then my mother said, almost wistfully "She's very pretty, dear. I think she's doing something in community theatre." Then the conversation went over to the retirement of Dr. Dunnings, who had been our GP since before I was born, and how he was the only non-Indian doctor left in his practice and how my mother felt about this.

I lay in bed that night in my small bedroom at my mother's house and turned over the conversation in my head. I am no longer on Facebook and thought about re-joining to see who Scullie's friends were, and if this psuedo-Cassandra was one of them, but there were too many people I was happy not to see again, and I let it be, certain that when there was an explanation, it would prove to be a simple one, and I slept.

I have been showing in the Little Gallery in Chelsea for over a decade now. In the old days, I had a quarter of a wall and nothing priced at more than three hundred pounds. Now I get my own show, every October for a month, and it would be fair to say that I only have to sell a dozen paintings to know that my needs, rent, and life are covered for another year. The unsold paintings remain on the gallery walls until they are gone and they are always gone by Christmas.

The couple who own the gallery, Paul and Barry, still call me "the beautiful boy" as they did twelve years ago, which I first exhibited with them, when it might actually have been true. Back then, they wore flowery, open-necked shirts and gold chains; now, in middle age, they wear expensive suits and talk too much for my liking about the stock exchange. Still, I enjoy their company. I see them three times a year in September when they come to my studio to see what I've been working on, and select the paintings for the show, at the gallery, hanging and opening in October, and in February, when we settle up.

Barry runs the gallery. Paul co-owns it, comes out for the parties, but also works in the wardrobe department of the Royal Opera House. The preview party for this year's show was on a Friday night. I had spent a nervous couple of days hanging the paintings. Now, my part was done, and there was nothing to do but wait, and hope people liked my art, and not to make a fool of myself. I did as I had done for the previous twelve years, on Barry's instructions, "Nurse the champagne. Fill up on water. There's nothing worse for the collector than encountering a drunk artist, unless he's a famous drunk, and you are not, dear. Be amiable but enigmatic, and when people ask for the story behind the painting, say "my lips are sealed". But for god's sake, imply there is one. It's the story they're buying."

I rarely invite people to the preview any longer; some artists do, regarding it as a social event. I do not. While I take my art seriously, as art, and am proud of my work (the latest exhibition was called "People In Landscapes," which pretty much says it all about my work anyway) I understand that the party exists solely as a commercial event, a come-on for eventual buyers and those who might say the right thing to other eventual buyers. I tell you all this so that you will not be surprised that Barry and Paul manage the guest list to the preview, not I.

The preview begins at 6:30 p.m. I had spent the afternoon hanging paintings, making sure everything looked as good as it could. The only thing that was different about this particular event was how excited Paul looked, like a small boy struggling with the urge to tell you what he had bought you for a birthday present. That, and Barry, who said, while we were hanging, "I think tonight's show will put you on the map."

I said, "I think there's a typo on the Lake District one." An oversized painting of Windemere at sunset, with two children staring lostly at the viewer from the banks. "It should say three thousand pounds. It says three hundred thousand."

"Does it?" said Barry, blandly. "My, my."

It was perplexing, but the first guests had arrived, a little early, and the mystery could wait. A young man invited me to eat a mushroom puff from a silver tray. Then I took my glass of nurse-this-slowly champagne and I prepared to mingle.

All the prices were high, and I doubted that the Little Gallery would be able to sell them at those prices, and I worried about the year ahead.

Barry and Paul took responsibility for moving me around the room, saying, "This is the artist, the beautiful boy who makes all these beautiful things, Stuart Innes," and I would shake hands, and smile. By the end of the evening I will have met everyone, and Paul and Barry are very good about saying, "Stuart, you remember David, he writes about art for the *Telegraph* . . . " and I for my part am good about saying, "Of course, how are you? So glad you could come."

The room was at its most crowded when a striking red-haired woman to whom I had not yet been introduced began shouting. "Representational bullshit!"

I was in conversation with *The Daily Telegraph* art critic and we turned. He said, "Friend of yours?" I said, "I don't think so."

She was still shouting, although the sounds of the party had now quieted. She shouted, "Nobody's interested in this shit! Nobody!" Then she reached her hand in to her coat pocket and pulled out a bottle of ink, shouted, "Try selling this now!" and threw ink at *Windemere Sunset.* It was blue-black ink.

Paul was by her side then, pulling the ink bottle away from her, saying, "That was a three hundred thousand pound painting, young lady." Barry took her arm, said, "I think the police will want a word with you," and walked her back in to his office.

She shouted at us as she went, "I'm not afraid! I'm proud! Artists like him, just feeding off you gullible art buyers. You're all sheep! Representational crap!"

And then she was gone, and the party people were buzzing, and inspecting the ink-fouled painting and looking at me, and the Telegraph man was asking if I would like to comment and how I felt about seeing a three hundred thousand pound painting destroyed, and I mumbled about how I was proud to be a painter, and said something about the transient nature of art, and he said that he supposed that tonight's event was an artistic happening in its own right, and we agreed that, artistic happening or not, the woman was not quite right in the head.

Barry reappeared, moving from group to group, explaining that Paul was dealing with the young lady, and that her eventual disposition would be up to me. The guests were still buzzing excitedly as he was ushering people out of the door, apologizing as he did so, agreeing that we lived in exciting times, explaining that he would be open at the regular time tomorrow.

"That went well," he said, when we were alone in the gallery.

"*Well?* That was a disaster!"

"Mmm. 'Stuart Innes, the one who had the three hundred thousand pound painting destroyed.' I think you need to be forgiving, don't you? She was a fellow artist, even one with different goals. Sometimes you need a little something to kick you up to the next level."

We went into the back room.

I said, "Whose idea was this?"

"Ours," said Paul. He was drinking white wine in the back room with the red-haired woman. "Well, Barry's mostly. But it needed a good little actress to pull it off, and I found her." She grinned, modestly: managed to look both abashed and pleased with herself.

"If this doesn't get you the attention you deserve, beautiful boy," said Barry, smiling at me, "nothing will. Now you're important enough to be attacked."

"The Windemere painting's ruined," I pointed out.

Barry glanced at Paul, and they giggled. "It's already sold, ink-splatters and all, for seventy five thousand pounds," he said. "It's like I always say, people think they are buying the art, but really, they're buying the story."

Paul filled our glasses: "And we owe it all to you," he said to the woman. "Stuart, Barry, I'd like to propose a toast. To Cassandra."

"Cassandra," we repeated, and we drank. This time I did not nurse my drink. I needed it.

Then, as the name was still sinking in, Paul said, "Cassandra, this ridiculously attractive and talented young man is, as I am sure you know, Stuart Innes."

"I know," she said. "Actually, we're very old friends."

"Do tell," said Barry.

"Well," said Cassandra, "twenty years ago, Stuart wrote my name on his maths exercise notebook."

She looked like the girl in my drawing, yes. Or like the girl in the photographs, all grown up. Sharp-faced. Intelligent. Assured.

I had never seen her before in my life.

"Hello Cassandra," I said. I couldn't think of anything else to say.

We were in the wine bar beneath my flat. They serve food there, too. It's more than just a wine bar.

I found myself talking to her as if she was someone I had known since childhood. And, I reminded myself, she wasn't. I had only met her that evening. She still had ink-stains on her hands.

We had glanced at the menu, ordered the same thing—the vegetarian mezze—and when it had arrived, both started with the Dolmades, then moved on to the hummus.

"I made you up," I told her.

It was not the first thing I had said; first we had talked about her community theatre, how she had become friends with Paul, his offer to her—a thousand pounds for this evening's show—and how she had needed the money, but mostly said yes because it sounded like a fun adventure. Anyway, she said, she couldn't say no when she heard my name mentioned. She thought it was fate.

That was when I said it. I was scared she would think I was mad, but I said it. "I made you up."

"No," she said. "You didn't. I mean, obviously you didn't. I'm really here." Then she said, "Would you like to touch me?"

I looked at her. At her face, and her posture, at her eyes. She was everything I had ever dreamed of in a woman. Everything I had been missing in other women. "Yes," I said. "Very much."

"Let's eat our dinner first," she said. Then she said, "How long has it been since you were with a woman?"

"I'm not gay," I protested. "I have girlfriends."

"I know," she said. "When was the last one?"

I tried to remember. Was it Brigitte? Or the stylist the ad agency had sent me to Iceland with? I was not certain. "Two years," I said. "Perhaps three. I just haven't met the right person yet."

"You did once," she said. She opened her handbag then, a big floppy purple thing, pulled out a cardboard folder, opened it, removed a piece of paper, tape-browned at the corners. "See?"

I remembered it. How could I not? It had hung above my bed for years. She was looking around, as if talking to someone beyond the curtain. *Cassandra*, it said, *February 19th, 1985*. And it was signed, *Stuart Innes*. There is something at the same time both embarrassing and heartwarming about seeing your handwriting from when you were fifteen.

"I came back from Canada in '89," she said. "My parents' marriage fell apart, and Mum wanted to come home. I wondered about you, what you were doing, so I went to your old address. The house was empty. Windows were broken. It was obvious nobody lived there anymore. They'd knocked down the riding stables already—that made me so sad, I'd loved horses as a girl, obviously, but I walked through the house until I found your bedroom. It was obviously your bedroom, although all the furniture was gone. It still smelled like you. And this was still pinned to the wall. I didn't think anyone would miss it."

She smiled.

"Who *are* you?"

"Cassandra Carlisle. Aged 34. Former actress. Failed playwright. Now running a community theatre in Norwood. Drama therapy. Hall for rent. Four plays a year, plus workshops, and a local panto. Who are you, Stuart?"

"You know who I am." Then, "You know I've never met you before, don't you?"

She nodded. She said, "Poor Stuart. You live just above here, don't you?"

"Yes. It's a bit loud sometimes. But it's handy for the tube. And the rent isn't painful."

"Let's pay, and go upstairs."

I reached out to touch the back of her hand. "Not yet," she said, moving her hand away before I could touch her. "We should talk first."

So we went upstairs.

"I like your flat," she said. "It looks exactly like the kind of place I imagine you being."

"It's probably time to start thinking about getting something a bit bigger," I told her, "But it does me fine. There's good light out the back for my studio—you can't get the effect now, at night. But it's great for painting."

It's strange, bringing someone home. It makes you see the place you live as if you've not been there before. There are two oil paintings of me in the lounge, from my short-lived career as an artists' model (I did not have the patience to stand and wait), blown-up advertising photos of me in the little kitchen and the loo, book covers with me on—romance covers, mostly, over the stairs.

I showed her the studio, and then the bedroom. She examined the Edwardian barber's chair I had rescued from an ancient barbers' that closed down in Shoreditch. She sat down on the chair, pulled off her shoes.

"Who was the first grown-up you liked?" she asked.

"Odd question. My mother, I suspect. Don't know. Why?"

"I was three, perhaps four. He was a postman called Mister Postie. He'd come in his little post-van and bring me lovely things. Not every day. Just sometimes. Brown paper packages with my name on, and inside would be toys or sweets or something He had a funny, friendly face with a knobby nose."

"And he was real? He sounds like somebody a kid would make up."

"He drove a post-van inside the house. It wasn't very big."

She began to unbutton her blouse. It was cream-colored, still flecked with splatters of ink. "What's the first thing you actually remember? Not something you were told you did. That you really remember?"

"Going to the seaside when I was three, with my mum and my dad." "Do you remember it? Or do you remember being told about it?" "I don't see what the point of this is . . . ?" She stood up, wiggled, stepped out of their skirt. She wore a white bra, dark green panties, frayed. Very human: not something you would wear to impress a new lover. I wondered what her breasts would look like, when the bra came off. I wanted to stroke them, to touch them to my lips.

She walked from the chair to the bed, where I was sitting. "Lie down, now. On that side of the bed. I'll be next to you. Don't touch me."

I lay down, my hands at my sides. She said, "You're so beautiful. I'm not honestly sure whether you're my type. You would have been when I was fifteen, though. Nice and sweet and unthreatening. Artistic. Ponies. A riding stable. And I bet you never make a move on a girl unless you're sure she's ready, do you?"

"No," I said. "I don't suppose that I do."

She lay down beside me.

"You can touch me now," said Cassandra.

I had started thinking about Stuart again late last year. Stress, I think. Work was going well, up to a point, but I'd broken up with Pavel, who may or may not have been an actual bad hat although he certainly had his finger in many dodgy East European pies, and I was thinking about Internet dating. I had spent a stupid week joining the kind of websites that link you to old friends, and from there it was no distance to Jeremy "Scallie" Porter, and to Stuart Innes.

I don't think I could do it anymore. I lack the single-mindedness. The attention to detail. Something else you lose when you get older.

Mister Postie used to come in his van when my parents had no time for me. He would smile his big gnomey smile, wink an eye at me, hand me a brown-paper parcel with Cassandra written on in big block letters, and inside would be a chocolate, or a doll, or a book. His final present was a pink plastic microphone, and I would walk around the house singing or pretending to be on TV. It was the best present I had ever been given.

My parents did not ask about the gifts. I did not wonder who was actually sending them. They came with Mister Postie, who drove his little van down the hall and up to my bedroom door, and who always knocked three times. I was a demonstrative girl, and the next time I saw him, after the plastic microphone, I ran to him and threw my arms around his legs.

It's hard to describe what happened then. He fell like snow, or like ash. For a moment I had been holding someone, then there was just powdery white stuff, and nothing.

I used to wish that Mr. Postie would come back, after that, but he never did. He was over. After a while, he became embarrassing to remember: I had fallen for *that*.

So strange. this room.

I wonder why I could ever have thought that somebody who made me happy when I was fifteen would make me happy now. But Stuart was perfect: the riding stables (with ponies), and the painting (which showed me he was sensitive), and the inexperience with girls (so I could be his first) and how very, very tall, dark and handsome he would be. I liked the name, too: it was vaguely Scottish and (to my mind) like the hero of a novel.

I wrote Stuart's name on my exercise books.

I did not tell my friends the most important thing about Stuart: that I had made him up.

And now I'm getting up off the bed and looking down at the outline of a man, a silhouette in flour or ash or dust on the black satin bedspread, and I am getting into my clothes.

The photographs on the wall are fading too. I didn't expect that. I wonder what will be left of his world in a few hours, wonder if I should have left well enough alone, a masturbatory fantasy, something reassuring and comforting. He would have gone through his life without ever really touching anyone, just a picture and a painting and a half-memory for a handful of people who barely ever thought of him anymore.

I leave the flat. There are still people at the wine bar downstairs. They are sitting at the table, in the corner, where Stuart and I had been sitting. The candle has burned way down but I imagine that it could almost be us. A man and a woman, in conversation. And soon enough, they will get up from their table and walk away, and the candle will be snuffed and the lights turned off, and that will be that for another night.

I hail a taxi. Climb in. For a moment—for, I hope, the last time—I find myself missing Stuart Innes.

Then I sit back in the seat of the taxi, and I let him go. I hope I can afford the taxi fare, and find myself wondering whether there will be a cheque in my bag in the morning, or just another blank sheet of paper. Then, more satisfied than not, I close my eyes, and I wait to be home.

Monsters don't just happen. We make them, day by day, choice by choice. Francis Ford Coppola adapted Joseph Conrad's 1902 novella Heart of Darkness *and re-set it from the Congo Free State at the turn of the century to 1968-1969 Viet Nam and Cambodia for his 1979 movie* Apocalypse Now. *Neither included zombies. Simon Green does.*

HE SAID, LAUGHING

SIMON R. GREEN

Saigon. 1969. It isn't Hell; but you can see Hell from here.

Viet Nam is another world; they do things differently here. It's like going back into the Past, into the deep Past—into a primitive, even primordial place. Back to when we all lived in the jungle, because that was all there was. But it isn't just the jungle that turns men into beasts; it's being so far away from anything you can recognize as human, or humane. There is no law here, no morality, none of the old certainties. Or at least, not in any form we know, or can embrace.

Why cling to the rules of engagement, to honorable behavior, to civilized limits; when the enemy so clearly doesn't? Why hide behind the discipline of being a soldier, when the enemy is willing to do anything, anything at all, to win? Why struggle to stay a man, when it's so much easier to just let go, and be just another beast in the jungle?

Because if you can hang on long enough . . . you get to go home. Being sent to Viet Nam is like being thrown down into Hell, while knowing all the time that Heaven is just a short flight away. But even Heaven and Hell can get strangely mixed up, in a distant place like this. There are pleasures and satisfactions to be found in Hell, that are never even dreamed of in Heaven. And after a while, you have to wonder if the person you've become can ever go home. Can ever go back, to the person he was.

Monsters don't just happen. We make them, day by day, choice by choice.

I was waiting for my court-martial, and they were taking their own sweet time about it. I knew they were planning something special for me. The first clue came when they put me up in this rat-infested hotel, rather than the cell where I belonged. The door wasn't even locked. After all, where could I go? I was famous now. Everyone knew my face. Where could I go, who would have me, who would hide me, after the awful thing I'd done? I was told to wait, so I waited. The Army wasn't finished with me yet. I wasn't surprised. The Army could always find work for a monster, in Viet Nam.

They finally came for me in the early hours of the morning. It's an old trick. Catch a man off guard, while he's still half-drugged with sleep, and his physical and mental defenses are at their dimmest. Except I was up and out of bed and on my feet the moment I heard footsteps outside my door, hands reaching for weapons I wasn't allowed any more. It's the first thing you learn in country, if you want to stay alive in country. So when the two armed guards kicked my door in, I was waiting for them. I smiled at them, showing my teeth, because I knew that upset people. Apparently I don't smile like a person any more.

The guards didn't react. Just gestured for me to leave the room and walk ahead of them. I made a point of gathering up a few things I didn't need, just to show I wasn't going to be hurried; but I was more eager to get going than they were. Finally, someone had made a decision. The Army was either going to give me a mission, or put me up against a wall and shoot me. And I really wasn't sure which I wanted most.

I ended up in a cramped little room, far away from anything like official channels. My armed guard closed the door carefully behind me, and locked it from the outside. There was a chair facing a desk, and a man sitting behind the desk. I sat down in the chair without waiting to be asked, and the man smiled. He was big, bulk rather than fat, and his chair made quiet sounds of protest whenever he shifted his weight. He had a wide happy face under a shaven head, and he wasn't wearing a uniform. He could have been a civilian contractor, or any of a dozen kinds of businessman, but he wasn't. I knew who he was, what he had to be. Perhaps because one monster can always recognize another.

"You're CIA," I said, and he nodded quickly, smiling delightedly.

"And people say you're crazy. How little they know, Captain Marlowe."

I studied him thoughtfully. Despite myself, I was intrigued. It had been a long time since I met anyone who wasn't afraid of me. The CIA man had a slim gray folder set out on the desk before him. Couldn't have had more than half a dozen pages in it, but then, I'd only done one thing that mattered since they dropped me off here and bet me I couldn't survive. Well, I showed them.

"You know my name," I said. "What do I call you?"

"You call me 'Sir.' " He laughed silently, enjoying the old joke. "People like me don't have names. You should know that. Most of the time we're lucky if we have job descriptions. Names come and go, but the work goes on. And you know what kind of work I'm talking about. All the nasty, necessary things that the Government, and the People, don't need to know about. I operate without restrictions, without orders, and a lot of the time I make use of people like you, Captain Marlowe, because no one's more expendable than a man with a death sentence hanging over him. I can do anything I want with you; and no one will give a damn."

"Situation entirely normal, then," I said. "Sir."

He flashed me another of his wide, meaningless smiles, and leafed quickly through the papers in my file. There were photos too, and he took his time going through them. He didn't flinch once. He finally closed the file, tapped the blank cover with a heavy finger a few times, and then met my gaze squarely.

"You have been a bad boy, haven't you, Captain? One hundred and seventeen men, women, and children, including babes in arms, all wiped out, slaughtered, on one very busy afternoon, deep in country. You shot them until you ran out of bullets, you bayoneted them until the blade broke, and then you finished the rest off with the butt of your rifle, your bare hands, and a series of improvised blunt instruments. You broke in skulls, you tore out throats, you ripped out organs and you ate them. When your company finally caught up with you, you were sitting soaking your bare feet in the river, surrounded by the dead, soaked in their blood, calmly smoking a cigarette. Was it an enemy village, Captain?"

"No."

"Did anyone attack you, threaten you?"

"No."

"So why did you butcher an entire village of civilians, Captain Marlowe?"

I showed him my smile again. "Because it was there. Because I didn't like the way they looked at me. Does it matter?"

"Not particularly, no." The CIA man leaned forward across the desk, fixing me with his unblinking happy gaze. "You're not here to be court-martialed, Captain. It has already been decided, at extremely high levels, that none of this ever happened. There never was any massacre; there never was any crazy captain. Far too upsetting, for the folks at home. Instead, I have been empowered to offer you a very special, very important, very . . . sensitive mission. Carry it out successfully, and this file will disappear. You will be given an honorable discharge, and allowed to go home."

"First thing you learn in the army," I said, "is never volunteer. Especially not for very special, important, and sensitive missions."

"Should you decline this opportunity, I am also empowered to take you out the back of this building and put two bullets in your head," said the CIA man, still smiling.

I surprised him by actually taking a moment to think about it. If this mission was too important for the Army, and too dangerous for the CIA, and they needed a monster like me to carry it out successfully . . . it had to involve something even worse than wiping out a whole village of noncombatants. And, I wasn't sure I wanted to go home. After everything I'd seen, and done. I still loved the memories I had, of family and friends. I didn't like to think of their faces, when they realized what had come home to them. I didn't like to think of them with a monster in their midst, walking around, hidden behind my old face.

I didn't want to stay in Hell, but there was enough of a man left in me that I knew I had no business contaminating the streets of Heaven with my bloody presence.

So I nodded to the CIA man, and he sank back into his chair, which made piteous sounds of protest as his weight settled heavily again. He opened a drawer in his desk, put away my file, and took out another. It was much thicker than mine. The cover was still blank. Not even a file number. Just like mine. The CIA man opened it, took out a glossy eight-by-ten, and skimmed it across the desk to me. I looked at the photo, not touching it. The officer looking back at me had all the right stripes and all the right medal ribbons, and a bland, impassive face with no obvious signs of character or authority.

"That is Major Kraus," said the CIA man. "Excellent record, distinguished career. Wrote a good many important papers. Had a great career ahead of him, Stateside. But he wanted to be here, where the action was . . . where he could be a real soldier. Somehow he persuaded his superiors to allow him to go deep in country, where he could try out some special new theories of his own. The first reports indicated that he was achieving some measure of success. Later reports were more . . . ambiguous. And then the reports stopped. We haven't heard anything from Major Kraus in over a year.

"The army sent troops in after him. They never reported back. We sent some of our people in—good men, experienced men. We never heard from them again. And now reports have begun trickling out of that area, mostly from fleeing native villagers. They say Kraus has assembled his own private army, and turned them loose on everything that moves. They're moving inexorably through the jungle, killing everything in their path. It isn't enemy territory any more, but it isn't ours, either. Major Kraus seems intent on carving out his own little kingdom in the jungle, and we can't have that."

"Of course not," I said. "The army's never approved of individual ambition."

"Don't push your luck, Captain. Your mission is to go up river, all the way into the jungle to the major's last reported position, evaluate the situation, and then put an end to his little experiment."

I smiled. "I get to kill a major?"

The CIA man smiled back at me. "Thought you'd like that. If the major cannot be persuaded to rein himself in, and follow orders, you are empowered to execute him. If the situation can be brought back under control, do so. If not, just present us with the exact coordinates, and we'll send the fly boys in to wipe the whole mess right off the map. Any questions?"

"Why me?"

"Because you are completely and utterly expendable, Captain. If you should fail, we'll just find another psycho and send him up the river. It's not like there's a shortage, these days. We'll just keep sending people like you, until one of you finally gets the job done. We're not in any hurry. If nothing else, Major Kraus is at least keeping the enemy occupied."

"If I do this, and come back," I said. "Do I have to go home? Or could there be more sensitive missions for me?"

"Why not?" said the CIA man, smiling his crocodile smile. "We're always looking for a few good psychos."

The patrol boat they gave me was a broken-down piece of shit called the *Suzie Q*. The crew of three that came with her weren't much better. I gave the pilot what maps I had, and then retired to the cabin, to be alone. I didn't ask their names. I didn't want to know. They didn't matter to me, except to get me where I was going. They didn't know it, but they were even more expendable than I was.

They didn't want to talk to me. Someone had told them who I was, and what I'd done. They maintained a safe, respectful distance at all times, and their hands never moved far from their weapons. I smiled at them, now and again, just to keep them on their toes.

I watched them die, one by one, as we headed up the winding river and deep into the dark and savage jungle. It doesn't matter how they died. The jungle just reached out and took them, in its various bloody ways. I waited for the darkness to strike me down too, but somehow its aim was always that little bit off. So when the long and twisting river finally came to its end, I was the only one left to guide the *Suzie Q* through the narrowing channels to its dark and awful source.

The jungle pressed in close around me, trees and vegetation crowding right up to the river's edge, a harsh green world impenetrable to merely human gaze. Huge gnarled trees reached out over the water, tall branches thrusting forward to meet each other, and form a thick canopy that blocked out the sky. Light had to shoulder its way in, heavy golden shafts punching through the canopy like spotlights. The air was heavy with the thick green scents of growing things, interlaced with the sickly sweet smells of death and corruption. Great clouds of insects rose up from the river to break against the boat's prow, and then reform again behind her.

The darker it got, the more at home I felt. The other three died because they were still men, while I had left that state behind long ago. In the jungle, in all the places of the world where man is never meant to live, you cannot hope to survive if you insist on remaining a man. This is a place for beasts, for nature, red in tooth and claw, for animal instincts and brutal drives. The jungle knows nothing of human limitations like honor and sentiment, compassion and sanity.

There were still some people in the jungle. I saw them, passing by. Grim gray silent ghosts, who had made their own bargain with the jungle. Black-pajama men and women, slipping along concealed trails, their supplies balanced on carts and bicycles. Peasant villagers, carrying their life's possessions, retreating in the face of something that could not be stopped, or bargained with, or survived. I let them go. Partly because my mission was too important to risk revealing myself, but mostly because I knew that if I started shooting, started killing, I might not be able to stop. I'd made a cage inside me to hold my beast, but the door was only closed, not locked.

I kept the beast quiet, traveling up the river, by considering all the awful things I was going to do to Major Kraus, before I finally let him die.

When the maps ran out, I just pointed the *Suzie Q* forward and kept going. The river narrowed steadily, closing remorselessly in from both sides, the crowded vegetation creeping right up to the edges of both banks to get a good look at me. I passed the time studying the major's CIA file. There were reports of burned out and deserted villages, and wide swathes of devastated land, radiating out from Kraus' compound at the end of the river. Whole populations slaughtered, and the bodies . . . just gone. Taken? Nobody knew. Kraus' private army ranged far and wide, butchering every living thing in its path, but not one dead body was ever seen afterwards, anywhere. Cannibalism, perhaps? The file had theories, ideas, guesses, but no one knew anything, where Kraus was concerned. Someone had written the words *Psychological warfare?* across the bottom of one page, but that was all.

The river finally ran out, ending in a wide natural harbor deep in the dark green heart of the jungle. The thick crumbling river banks were so close now I could reach out from the *Suzie Q* and trail my fingertips along the turgid vegetation and creepers as they drooped down into the dark waters. The thick canopy overhead blocked out the sun, plunging the river into an endless twilight, like the end of the world. I had left the world behind, to come to a place man should have left behind, long ago. We have no business here. We cannot be man, in a place like this.

The river banks came together, closing in like living gates, so close now I could barely squeeze the *Suzie Q* through, and then they opened out abruptly, revealing the wide calm waters of the natural harbor where Major Kraus had established his compound. It was very dark now, almost night, and at first all I could see were the lights up ahead. They jumped and flared, a sickly yellow, like so many will-o'-the-wisps.

The river banks rose sharply up around me, great clay and earth walls rising twenty, thirty feet above my head. Roots burst out of the wet earth here and there, curling around great open mouths, dark caves and caverns peering at me from the river banks. Huge centipedes crawled in and out of the openings, slow ripples moving up and down their unnaturally long bodies. The waters ahead of me were flat and still, disturbed only by the slow sullen waves preceding the boat's prow. The steady chugging of the boat's engine was disturbingly loud in the quiet, so I turned it off, allowing the boat to glide the rest of the way in. There were hundreds of lights now, blazing atop the tall river banks like so many watchful eyes.

There was no dock, as such. Just a natural protrusion of dull gray earth, thrusting out into the water. I eased the *Suzie Q* in beside it, and she lurched fitfully to a halt as her prow slammed against the earth dock in a series of slow, slowing bumps. I left the boat and stepped cautiously out onto dry land. It felt like stepping out onto an alien planet and leaving my spaceship behind. The tall earth banks were lined from end to end with flaring lights now. I craned my head back, and dozens of natives looked down at me, holding crude flaring torches. None of them moved, or spoke. They just looked.

A set of rough steps had been cut into the tall earth wall beside me, curving slowly upwards. They didn't look in any way safe or dependable, but I hadn't come this far to be put off by anything less than a gun in my face. I started up the steps, pressing my left shoulder hard against the yielding clay and earth of the river bank, careful not to look anywhere but straight in front of me. The steps squelched loudly beneath my boots, and my arm and shoulder were soon soaked with slime and seepage from the earth wall.

I paused beside the first great opening, peering into the dark tunnel beyond. I seemed to sense as much as hear movement within, of something much larger and heavier than a centipede. I pressed on, stamping my boots heavily into the slippery steps to keep my balance. The natives were still looking down at me, saying nothing.

I was out of breath and aching in every limb when I finally reached the top. I took a moment to get my breath back, and coughed harshly on the rank air. The usual jungle stench of living and dying things pressed close together was overwhelmed here by a heavy stench of death and decay, close up and personal. It was like breathing in rotting flesh, like sticking your face into the opened belly of a corpse. It was a smell I knew all too well. For a moment I wondered whether all of this had been nothing but a dream, and I was still back in my village, cooling my bare feet in the river and smoking a cigarette, as I waited for them to come and find me, and all the awful things I'd done. . . . But this stench, this place, was too vile to be anything but real.

The natives stood before me, holding their torches, and every single one of them was dead. I only had to look at them to know. They stood in endless ranks, unnaturally still, their eyes not moving and their chests neither rising nor falling; flies buzzed and swarmed and crawled all over them. Some were older than others, their flesh desiccated and mummified. Others were so recent they still bore the dark sticky blood of the wounds that had killed them. Some had no eyes, or great holes in their torsos, packed with squirming maggots. Everywhere I looked there was some new horror, of missing limbs, or dropped off lower jaws, or pale gray and purple strings of intestines spilling out of opened-up bellies. They carried knives and machetes and vicious clubs, all of them thickly crusted with dried blood. They wore rags and tatters, almost as decayed as their bodies. Some wore what was left of army uniforms, north and south.

And then it got worse, as two of the dead men dropped their torches uncaringly onto the wet ground, and moved towards me. They did not move as living things move; there was nothing of grace or connection in their movements. They moved as though movement had been imposed upon them. It was horrible to look at; an alien, utterly unnatural thing, as though a tree had ripped up its roots and lurched forward. I started to back away, and then remembered there was nothing behind me but the earth steps, and a long drop. I wanted to scream and run and hide.

But I didn't. This was what I had come here for: to learn Major Kraus' awful secret.

The two dead men took me by the arms and hauled me forward. I didn't try to fight them. Their hands were horribly cold on my bare skin. They didn't look at me, or try to speak to me, for which I was grateful. I didn't think even I could have stood to learn what a dead man's voice sounded like.

They led me through the army of the dead, across an uneven ground soaked with blood and littered with discarded body parts. There were great piles of organs, torn away or fallen out, revealed suddenly as great clouds of flies sprang into the air at our approach. There were hacked off hands, and broken heads, faces rotted away to reveal wide smiles of perfect teeth. My dead guards walked right over them, and did not allow me time to be fastidious. By the time we got where I was going, my boots and trousers were soaked in blood and gore.

I should never have taken this mission. I only thought I knew what Hell was.

I'd never felt so scared, or so alive. After the village, after what I did there, I didn't feel much of anything. But now, surrounded by death, and the fear of something worse than death, I felt alive again. My heart hammered in my chest, and every breath was a glorious thing, despite the stench. I was here among things that couldn't be, shouldn't be . . . and I wanted to know more.

The men I killed never got up again. That would be awful, if they should rise up again and look at me with knowing, accusing eyes. The men who served beside me, who were cut down by an often unseen enemy—they never rose up again either. In Viet Nam, death was the one thing you could depend on. Except . . . not here. What had Major Kraus done, here, so far from civilization and sanity? Who knew what might be possible here, so far from science and logic and all the other things man depends on to make sense of his world? Perhaps . . . if you went back far enough, into the past, into the jungle, you could leave reality behind in favor of a whole new world where anything, anything at all, was possible.

My dead guards brought me to a great hole in the ground and stopped. They let go of me, and just stood there, looking at nothing. I rubbed my arms hard, where their cold flesh had touched mine, without menace or care or any feeling at all. I looked down into the hole. It seemed to fall away deep into the blood-soaked earth, but there was light at the bottom. A metal ladder had been roughly attached to one side of the wet earth. I started down it. I wanted, needed answers; if answers there were to be had.

The ladder went down and down, a descent long enough to raise fierce cramps in my arms and legs. It ended in a tunnel, dug deep into the earth of the tall river bank, lit by oil lamps set in niches in the earth walls. The red clay in the walls gave them a disturbingly organic quality, as though I was invited to go stumbling through the guts of some long-dead colossus, buried ages ago.

The tunnels were a maze, a warren of narrow inter-connecting passageways, and I soon lost all sense of place, or direction. I just lurched along, following the lit tunnels, sweating profusely in the close hot air. The lamps had to be for my benefit; dead men wouldn't need them. It was no wonder the CIA man's maps had been so vague about Major Kraus' secret compound. He'd hidden it underground, to conceal just how big it was—hidden it underground, where only the dead men go. If the CIA had even suspected how big Kraus' base was, how extensive his army, they would have sent the fly boys in long ago to burn the whole place back to bare unliving stone.

Clever Kraus.

Finally I came to the heart of the labyrinth, to the place of the monster, to the awful court of Major Kraus. There was no sign, no warning, no preparation. I just rounded a corner and found myself standing in a clean, brightly lit earth chamber. There were rushes on the floor, shelves on the walls holding books and oil lamps and an assortment of presumably precious objects. There was a table, covered in maps and papers, and two surprisingly comfortable-looking chairs. But there was no clock anywhere, or even a calendar; nothing to tell you what time it might be, as though time had no meaning here, as though it had become irrelevant in this old, old place where the dead walked. I was in the Past now, in the deep Past, in the ancient primordial jungle, and that was all that mattered.

Kraus sat in a chair behind his table, hands clasped lightly on the tabletop before him, and he watched me with calm, amused eyes. He was alive. His chest rose and fell easily as he breathed, and his smile was real if thin. His simple vitality was like a shock of cold water in the face, breaking me out of the nightmare I'd been wandering through.

I studied the man I'd come so far to find. He was stick thin, without a spare ounce of fat on him, as though all such physical weakness has been burned away in some spiritual kiln. He had sharp, aesthetic features under close-cropped hair, and even though he was sitting perfectly still and at ease, he blazed with barely suppressed nervous energy. His spotlessly clean Army uniform hung loosely about him, as though it had once fitted a much larger man. His smile was slight but genuine, and his eyes were disturbingly sane.

I nodded slowly, to the man I'd been sent to kill. I never know what to say, on occasions like this. All my old certainties had been thrown down and trampled into the dirt, but still some small spark of stubborn pride wouldn't allow me to blurt out the obvious question. Major Kraus just smiled and nodded back at me, as though he quite understood. I had no gun or knife. Dead hands had taken all my weapons from me, before I was allowed down the ladder into the underworld. I could still kill him with my bare hands. I'd been trained. But if I should fail . . . I didn't want to die here. Not in this awful place, where the dead didn't stay dead.

That would be terrible: to die, and still not know peace.

Kraus gestured easily for me to sit down. A calm, casual gesture, from a man who knew he held all the power in the room. Just for a moment, the major reminded me of the CIA man, back in Saigon. I sat down. Kraus smiled again, just a brief movement of the lips, revealing stained yellow teeth.

"Yes," he said. "They're dead. They're all dead. The ones who brought you here, the ones who stand guard, and the ones I send out to kill my enemies. Dead men walking, every single one of them, torn from their rest, raised up out of their graves, and set to work by me. Everyone's dead here, except me. And now, you. Tell me your name, soldier."

"Captain Marlowe," I said. "Torn from my cell, raised up from my court-martial, and sent here by the CIA to kill you, Major Kraus. They're frightened of you. Of course, if they knew what you were really doing here . . . "

"There's nothing they can do to stop me. My army is made up of men who are beyond fear, or suffering, who cannot be stopped by bullets or bombs or napalm. Zombies, Captain Marlowe. Old voodoo magic, from the deep south of America, where the really old ways are not forgotten. You needn't worry, Captain, they won't attack you. And they certainly won't try and eat you, as they did in a cheap horror movie I saw, before I came out here. Into the real horror show, that never ends. . . . My men have no need to eat, any more than they need to drink, or piss, or sweat. They are beyond such human weaknesses now. They have no appetites, no desires, and the only will that moves them is mine. I give them purpose, for as long as they last. They are my warriors of the night, my weapons cast against an uncaring world, my horror to set against the horror men have made of this place.

"War . . . is too important to be left to the living."

"Of course," I said numbly. "The perfect soldiers. The dead don't get tired, don't get stopped by injuries, and will follow any order you give them, without question. Because nothing matters to them any more."

"Exactly," said Kraus, favoring me with another brief smile. "I just point them in the right direction, and let them roll right over whatever lies in their path. They destroy everything and everyone, like army ants on the march. Most people won't even stand against them any more; they just turn and flee, as they would in the face of any other natural disaster. And if I should lose some men, through too much damage, I can always make up the numbers again, by raising up the fallen enemy dead.

"You're not shocked, Captain Marlowe. How very refreshing."

"'Why this is Hell, nor am I out of it,' " I murmured. "I have seen worse things than this, Major. Done worse things than this, in my time."

He leaned forward across his desk, fixing me with his terribly sane, compassionate gaze. "Yes . . . I can see the darkness in you, Captain. Tell what you saw, and what you did."

"I have been here before," I said. "In country, in the dark and terrible place where the old rules mean nothing, and so you can do anything, anything at all. Because no matter how bad we are, the enemy is always worse. I've seen much scarier things than zombies, in country."

"I'm sure you have," said Kraus. "They have no idea what it's like here—the real people back in their real world. Where there are laws and conventions, right and wrong, and everything makes sense. They can't know what it's like here, or why would fathers and mothers allow their sons to be sent into Hell . . . and then act all surprised when the command structure breaks down, army discipline breaks down, and their sons have to do awful, unforgivable things just to stay alive? What did you do, Captain, to earn a mission like this?"

"I wiped out a whole village," I said. "Killed them all: men, women and children. And then refused to say sorry."

"Why, Captain? Why would you do such a thing?"

For the first time, I was being asked the question by someone who sounded like he actually wanted to hear the truth. So I considered my answer seriously. "Why? Because I wanted to. Because I could. No matter what you do here, the jungle always throws back something worse . . . I don't see the enemy as people any more, just so many beasts in the jungle. The things they've done . . . they give the jungle's dark savagery a face, that's all. And after a while, after you've done awful, terrible things in your turn, and it hasn't made a damned bit of difference . . . you feel the need to do more and more, just to get a response from that bland, indifferent, jungle face. You want to see it flinch, make it hurt, the way it's hurt you. That need drives you on, to greater and greater acts of savagery . . . until finally, you look into the face of the jungle . . . and see your own face looking back at you."

"I know," said Major Kraus. "I understand."

I sat slumped in my chair, exhausted by the force of my words. And Kraus smiled on me, like a father with a prodigal son.

"It's the curse of this country, this war, Captain. This isn't like any other war we ever fought. There are no real battle lines, no clear disputed territories, no obvious or lasting victories. Only a faceless enemy, an opposing army and a hateful population, prepared to do anything, anything at all, to drive us out. Any atrocity, any crime against nature or civilization, is justified to them because we are outsiders, and therefore by definition not human.

"There is only one way to win this war, Captain, and that is to be ready and willing to do even worse things to them. To embrace the darkness of the jungle in our hearts, and in our souls, and throw it in their faces. We tried to raise a light in the darkness, when we should have eaten the darkness up with spoons and made it ours—given it shape and purpose and meaning. I have done an awful and unforgivable thing here, Captain, but for the first time I am making progress. I am taking and holding territory, and I am forcing the enemy back.

"I will win this war, which my own superiors are saying cannot be won. I will win it because I am ready and willing to do the one thing the enemy is not willing to do. They are ready to fight us to the death, but I have made death a weapon I can turn against them. And after my dead warriors have subjugated this entire country, North and South, and I have won because not one living soul remains to stand against me. . . . Then, *then*, I will take the war home. I will cross the great waters with a dead army millions strong, and I will turn them loose on the streets of America, turn them loose on all those uncaring people who sent their children into Hell.

"I will make our country a charnel house, and then a cemetery, and then, finally, the war will be over. And I can rest."

He looked at me for a long time, and his smile and his eyes were kind. "They sent you here to kill me, Captain Marlowe, those cold and uncaring men. But you won't. Because that's not what you really want. Stay here, with me, and be my Boswell; write the record of what I am doing. And then I will send it home, ahead of the army that's coming, as a warning. It's only right they should understand their crime, before they are punished for it. Tell my story, Captain Marlowe, and when I don't need you any more . . . I promise I will kill you, and let you stay dead. No more bad thoughts, no more bad dreams, no more darkness in the heart. You will rest easy, sleep without dreams, and feel nothing, nothing at all. Isn't that what you really want, Captain Marlowe?"

"Yes," I said. "Oh, yes."

Major Kraus smiled happily. "I shall put an end to all wars, and death shall have dominion, when Johnny comes marching home.

" 'The horror! The horror!' " he said, laughing.

Valorius awakes from a dream with his father's words ringing through his thoughts, and he never forgets them. Whether they are as false as most words, he cannot say, for it is only those words that hold power over the thing they represent that are not false, and they are few and seldom found. . . .

BLOODSPORT

GENE WOLFE

Sit down and I'll tell you.

I was but a youth when I was offered for the Game. I would have refused had that been possible; it was not—those offered were made to play. As I was already large and strong, I became a knight. Our training was arduous; two of my fellows died as a result, and one was crippled for life. I had known and liked him, drank with him, and fought him once. Seeing him leave the school in a little cart drawn by his brothers, I did not envy him.

After two years, I was knighted. I had feared that I would rank no higher than bowman; so it was a glad day for me. Later that same day I was given three stallions, the finest horses ever seen—swift golden chargers with manes and tails dark as the darkest shadows. Many an hour I spent tending and training them; and I stalled them apart, never letting them graze in the same meadow or even an adjoining meadow, lest they war. If I were refused that many meadows on a given day, one remained in his stall while the other two grazed; but I was never refused after my first Game.

Now the Game is no longer played. Perhaps you have forgotten it, or perhaps you never had the ill fortune to see it. The rules are complex—I shall not explain them.

But I shall say here and say plainly that it was never my intention to slay my opponent. Never, or at least very seldom. It was my task to defeat my opponent—if I could. And his to defeat me. Well do I recall my first fight. It was with another knight, and those engagements are rarest of all. I had been ordered to a position in which a moon knight might attack me. It seemed safe enough, since our own dear queen would be sure to attack him if he triumphed. Yet attack he did.

Under the rules, the attacker runs or rides to the defender's position, a great advantage. I had been taught that; but never so well as I learned it then, when I did not know I was to be attacked until I heard the thunder of his charger's hooves. That white charger cleared the lists with a leap that might have made mock of two, and he was upon me. The axe was his weapon, mine the mace. We fought furiously until some blow of mine struck the helm from his head and left him-still in the saddle—half-stunned. To yield, one must drop one's weapon; so long as the weapon remains in hand, the fight continues. His eyes were empty, his flaccid hand scarce able to grasp his axe.

Yet he did not drop it. I might have slain him then and there; I struck his gauntlet instead. A spike breached the steel, nailing his hand-for a moment only-to the haft of his axe. I jerked my mace away and watched him fall slowly from his game saddle. His head struck the wretched stony soil of the black square first, and I feared a broken neck. Yet he lived, and was mewing and moving when they bore him away. The spectators were not pleased with me, but I was pleased with myself; it is winning that matters, not slaying.

My next was with a pawn. She was huge, as they all are; bred like chargers, some say. Others declare that it is only a thing the mages do to baby girls. As you are doubtless aware, pawn's arms are the simplest of all: a long sword and a shield nearly as tall as the pawn herself, and wider. Other than those, sandals and a loincloth, for pawns wear no armor. I thought to ride her down, or else to slay her readily with my sword. One always employs the sword against pawns.

It was not to be. She sprang to my left, my stroke came too late, and she stripped me from the saddle. A moment more and I lay upon the fair green grass of a sun square, with her sword's point tickling my throat. "I yield!" I cried, and she grinned her triumph.

I was taken from the game, and Dhorie, my trainer, found me sitting alone, my head in my hands. He slapped my back and told me he was proud of me.

"I charged a pawn," I mumbled.

"Who bested you."

I nodded.

"Could happen to anybody. Lurn is the best of the moon pawns, and you had been charged by a knight scarcely a hundred breaths before." (This last was an exaggeration.) "You had given mighty blows and received them. Two moves and you were sent again. Do you know how often a knight is charged by another, but defeats him? The stands are still abuzz with your name."

I did not believe him but was comforted nonetheless. Soon I learned that he had been correct, for my bruises had not yet faded when I was put forward in a new game. That game I shall not describe. Nor the others.

We do not mix, yet I saw the pawn who had bested me twice more. Once we occupied adjacent squares, and though speaking is forbidden, her face told me she knew me just as I knew her. She spun her sword, grinning, and I raised my own and pointed at the sun. Her hair was black as night, her shoulders broad, and her waist small. Her muscles slid beneath her moon-white skin like so many dragons, and I knew I could scarcely have lifted the crescent moon-sword that danced for her.

The Hunas swept down upon us, and the games were ended. There was talk of employing us in battle; and I believe—yes, I believe still—that we might have turned them back. Before it could be done, they rushed upon the city by night. We fought and fled as best we could, I on Flare, my finest charger. For four days and three nights he and I hid in the hills, where I bandaged our wounds and applied poultices of borage and the purple-flowered high-heal that none but a seventh son may find.

The city had been put to the torch, but we returned to it. My father had been a mage of power, I knew, and I felt that his house might somehow have survived. In that I was mistaken; yet it had not been destroyed wholly. The south wing stood whole, and thus I was able to return to the very chamber I had called my own as a boy. My bed was there and waiting, and I felt an attraction to it by no means strange in a weary, wounded man. I saw to Flare as well as I could—water, a roof, and a little stale bread I found in the larder—and slept where I had slept for nights that had seemed endless so long ago. In the hills I had not dreamt; the imps and fiends that sought me out there had been those of waking. Returned to my own bed in the bedchamber that had been my own, I dreamt indeed.

In dream, my father sat before me, his head cloven to the jaw. He could not speak, but wrote upon the ground for me to read: *I blessed and I cursed you, Valorius, and my blessing and my curse are the same. You will inherit.*

I woke with his words ringing in through my thoughts, and I have never forgotten them. Whether they be so or no, who is to say? Perhaps I have inherited already, and know not of it. Perhaps they are as false as most dreams—false as most words, I ought to have said. For it is only those words that hold power over the thing they represent that are not false, and they are few and seldom found.

A league beyond the Gate of Exile, I saw Lurn sleeping in the shade of a spreading chestnut. Dismounting, I went to her; I cannot say why. Seeing that she slept soundly and was not liable to waken soon, I unsaddled Flare and let him graze, which he was eager to do. After that I sat near her, my back propped by the bole of the tree, and thought upon many things.

"What puzzles you so?"

Hearing her voice for the first time, I knew it was hers, deeper than my own yet a woman's. I smiled, I hope not impudently, and said, "Gaining your friendship. I fear that you will wish to engage, and that would be but folly as the world stands today."

"Folly indeed, for it stands not but circles the moon as both swim among stars." She laughed like a river over stones. "As for engaging, Valorius, why, I bested you. I choose to stand upon my victory, for you might die were we to engage again."

"You would not see me dead."

"No," she said; and when I did not speak, she said, "Would you see me so? You might have killed me while I slept."

"You would have sprung up and wrested the sword from my hand."

"Yes! Let us say that." The river flowed again. "Let us say it, that I may be joyful."

"You would not see me dead," I repeated, "and you troubled to learn my name, Lurn."

"And you mine." She sat up.

"I have seen sun and moon in the same sky," I told her. "They did not engage."

"They do but rarely." She smiled as she spoke, and there was something in her smile of the maid no man has bussed. "When they do she bests him, as is only to be expected. Bests him, and brings darkness over the earth."

"Is that true?"

"It is. She bests him, but having bested him she bids him rise. Someday—do you credit prophesy?"

I do not, but said I did.

"Someday he will best her and, besting her, take her life. So is it written. When the evil day comes, you men will walk in blind dark from twilight to dawn and much harm come of it."

"And what of women?"

"Women will have no warning, so that they bleed in the market. Will you come and sit by me, Valorius?"

"Gladly," I said. I rose and did so.

"Have the Hunas killed everyone save you and me?"

"They have slain many," I said, "but they can scarcely have slain everyone."

"When they have looted the towns and burned them, not many will remain. Those of our people who can still hold the hilt might be rallied to resist."

"Are they really our people?" I inquired.

"I was born among them. So were you, I think. I took shelter in this deep shade because my skin can't bear your noonday sun. When your sun is low, I'll walk again. Then we'll see what a lone woman can accomplish."

I shrugged. "Much, perhaps, with a knight to assist her. We must get you a wide hat, however, and a gown with long sleeves."

When the sun declined, we journeyed on together, and very pleasant journeying it was, for her head was level with my own when I rode Flare. We chattered and joked, and in time—not that day, I think, but the next—I beheld something in Lurn's eyes that I had never seen in the eyes of any woman.

That day we discovered a crone who knew the weaving of hats; she made such hat as Lurn required, a hat woven of straw, with a crown like a sugar loaf and brim wide as a shield. She sent us to a little man with a crooked back, who for a silver piece made Lurn not one long gown but three, all of coarse white cloth. Of our rallying of the people, I shall say little or nothing. We armed them with whatever could be made or found, and ere long enlisted a forester. Bradan knew the longbow, and taught some youths how to make and use war-arrows, bows, bowcases, bracers, quivers, and all such things—a great blessing.

The Hunas fight on horseback, and are quick to flee when they fear they may lose the light. To defeat them, one lays an ambush that shall catch them as they flee. Or else one must block the point of flight; we did both at one time or another. It is not the Game, yet it is a game of the same sort. We played it well, Lurn and I.

A mountain town called Scarp was besieged, and we marched to its relief. It lay in the valley of the Bright, and while one may go up that valley, or down it, a mounted man may not leave it for many a long league. Lurn and I flipped a crown; I lost and took two hundred or so of the rabble we tried to make foot soldiers, seventeen archers, and twenty-five horsemen upstream, skirting the town by night. Ere the sun was high, we found a place where the mountains pressed in on either side and the land on both sides of the road was rough and thickly wooded. I set out sentries, stationed my horsemen a thousand paces higher to prevent desertion, ordered the rest to get some sleep, and led by example.

Flare stamped to wake me. When I sat up, I could hear, though but faintly, the sounds he had heard more clearly—our trumpets, the drums of the Hunas, and the shouts, clashing blades, and screams of war. Then I could picture Lurn as I had seen her so often, leading the half-armed men she alone made bold. She had held her attack until the sun declined. Now her wide hat and white gown had been laid aside, and she would be fighting in sandals and a loincloth as she had as a pawn, a woman who towered above every man as those men towered above children, and the target of every Hunas horse-bow.

I knew the Hunas had broken when their drums fell silent. Lurn's trumpets shrilled orders, call after call: "Form up!" "Give way for the horse!" "Canter!" And again, "Canter!"

The Hunas had turned and fled. Our archers had the best of targets then, the riders' backs. We wanted to capture uninjured horses almost as much as we wanted to slay Hunas. And that moment—the moment when they turned and fled—would be the best of all moments to do it. If our horsemen galloped after them, they would flee the faster, which we did not want. Besides, our horsemen would soon break up, the best mounted outdistancing the rest. Then the Hunas might rally and charge, and our best mounted would go down. We did not want that, either.

"Here they come!"

It was a sentry upon a rocky outcrop. He waved and yelled, and soon another was waving and yelling, too. I formed up my men, halberds in front and pikes behind the halberds. Archers on the flanks, half-protected by trees and stones.

"I'll be in front. Stand firm behind me when I stand. Advance behind me when I advance. I'll not retreat. Come forward to take the place of those who fall. If the Hunas get past us, we've lost. If they don't, we've won. Do we mean to win?"

They shouted their determination; and not long after, when the first Hunas rode into sight, someone struck up the battle hymn. They were farmers and farriers, tinkers, tailors, and tradesmen, not soldiers and certainly not Game pieces. Would they run? They will not run, I told myself, if I do not run.

Not all the Hunas carry lances, but a good many do. Their lances are shorter than ours, thus easier to control. Lighter, too, and thus quick to aim. Now they positioned five lancers in front—enough to fill the road side-to-side. There were more behind, and I was glad to see them there, sensing that if the first were stopped (and I meant to stop them) they might be ridden down by those pressing forward.

The drums boomed like thunder, and the first five clapped spurs to their chargers.

My shield slipped the too-high lance-head, sending it over my left shoulder, and my point took his knee. Perhaps he yowled; if so, it could not be heard above the thudding drums and thundering hooves.

No more could the singing of our bows, but I saw the lancer next to him fall with an arrow in his throat. I had warned our pikemen to spare the horses. A horse screamed nonetheless, screamed and reared with the pike still in his vitals.

Then all was silence.

Though I did not dare look behind me, I glanced to right and left and counted the five—five lancers and one charger. Four lay still. One lancer writhed until a halberd-blade split his skull. The charger struggled to regain its feet; it would never succeed, but it would not cease to try until it died.

I waited for the next five lancers, but they did not charge. They must have known, as I did, that Lurn was behind them, strengthened by whatever troops had joined her from the town. And knowing that, known that they were caught between jaws. But they did not charge. We received a shower of arrows from their horse-bows; a few men cried out, and it may be that some died. Still, they did not charge.

Our battle hymn had ceased. I waved my sword above my head and began the hymn again myself. When I advanced, I heard the rest behind me, advancing as I did.

The road was no wider here, but its shoulders were clearer.

More Hunas could front us now. They were more likely to attack, and we more likely to scatter. I wanted the first, and felt sure the last was little risk enough. They dismounted and came for us on foot; I knew the gods fought beside us then.

They had light horse-axes and serpent swords. Both were more dangerous than they appeared. They had helmets, too, and seeing them I hoped my own men would have sense enough to strip them from the dead Hunas—and wear them. There were pikes to either side of me; those Hunas who came straight at me died, unable to parry my thrusts. Again and again I stepped forward over the bodies of our foes. In a hundred Games, no knight would ever slay half so many. It ought to have sickened me. It did not because I thought only of Lurn; each Hunas who fell to me was one who would never shed her blood.

I have never liked slaying men, and slaying women—I have done that, too—is worse. No doubt slaying children would be worse still. I have never done it and am glad, though I have met children who should be slain. Slaying animals is, for me, the worst of all. A stag fell to my bow yesterday; and I was glad, for I (I had almost said "we") needed the meat. That stag has haunted me ever since. What a fine, bold beast he was! It was not until now, when I have already told so much, that I kenned why I feel as I do.

Animals have no evil in them. Men have much, women (I think) half as much or less. Children have still less. Yet all humanity is touched by evil. Possibly there are men who have never been cruel. I have tried to be such a man, but is there a man above grass who would say I have succeeded? Certainly I will not say it.

Yonder stands my stag. I see him each time I look up, standing motionless where the shadows are thickest. He watches me with innocent eyes. There are always ghosts in a forest. My father taught me that a year, perhaps, before he gave me over to the games. Ghosts in forests, and few demons. In a desert, he said, that situation is reversed. Deserts call to demons and not to ghosts. (Yet not to demons only.) Among hills and mountains, their numbers are about equal—but who shall count them?

Can you see my stag? He is there beside Lurn, who stands beside him as a woman of ordinary size may stand beside a dog.

Let me gather more wood.

When we were no longer wanted, Lurn and I passed through this forest, which covers the hills at the feet of the mountains. She pressed forward eagerly and I hurried because she did. It was no easy thing for me to keep pace with her long strides, though most of my armor had been cast away.

It was these mountains, she assured me, that had given rise to the Game. The little mounds upon which we stand at the beginning of each playing of the Game are but the toys men have fashioned in imitation of these works of the gods. "It will mean nothing to you," she told me, "but it will mean the world and more to me." As I have said, I do not credit prophesy. Gods can prophesy, perhaps. No woman can, and no man.

If I recalled more of our journey, I would tell it now. I remember only hunger and cold, for it grew colder and colder as the land rose. There was less game, too. The mountain sheep are very wise, dwelling where the land lies open to their gaze. To hunt them, one must climb behind them, disturbing not one stone. They leap at the sound of the bow, though by then it is too late-leap and fall, always breaking the arrow and too often falling into bottomless clefts where they are devoured by demons.

Oh, yes! They eat as men do, and more. They cannot starve, though they grow lean; yet they eat nevertheless. The flesh of infants is what they like best. Witches offer it to them to gain their favor. We do not do that.

In time, I gave up all hope of finding one of the forty palaces of which she spoke. I only knew that if we went far enough, the mountains would cease their climb to the clouds and diminish again. Lurn would want to turn back; I would insist that we press forward, and we would see who would prevail.

It rained and we took shelter. A day exhausted the little food we had. Famished, we waited for a second day. On the third we went forth to hunt, knowing that we must hunt or starve. I knowing, too, that I dared not use my bow lest the string be wetted. Toward afternoon we flushed a flight of deer. Lurn could run more swiftly than they, they turn more sharply than she. She turned them and turned them until at last I was able to dash among them like a wolf, stabbing and slashing. I have no doubt that some escaped us, and that some of those who thus escaped soon perished of their wounds. We got three, even so, and chewed raw meat that night, and roasted meat the night following when we were able at last to kindle a fire, and so hungry as to abide the smoke of the twigs and fallen branches we collected.

We slept long that night. Day had come when we awoke, the clouds had lifted, and far away-yet not so distant as to be beyond our sight-we beheld a white palace on the side of the mountain looming before us. "There will be a garden!" Lurn's left hand closed on my shoulder with such strength that I nearly cried out.

"I see none," I told her.

"That green . . . "

"A mountain meadow. We've seen many."

"There must be a garden!" She spun me around. "A coronation garden for me. There must be!"

There was none, but we went there even so, a half-starved journey of two days through a forest filled with birdsong. There had been a wall about the palace, a low stone wall that might readily have been stormed. In many places it had fallen, and the gate of twisted bars had fallen into rust.

The rich chambers of centuries past had been looted, and here and there defiled. Their carpets were gone, and their hangings likewise. In many chambers we saw where fires of broken furniture had once blazed. Their ashes had been cold for heaped years no man could count, and their half-burned ends of wood, their strong square nails, and their skillfully wrought bronze screws had been scattered long ago, perhaps by the feet of the great-grandsons of those who had kindled them.

"This is a palace of ghosts," I told Lurn.

"I see none."

"I have seen many, and heard them, too. If we stay the night here . . . " I let the matter drop.

"Then we will go." She shrugged. "This was an error, and an error of my doing. We must first find food, and afterward another."

"No. We must go into the vaults." My own words surprised me.

She looked incredulous, but the ghost in the dark passage ahead nodded and smiled; it seemed almost a living man, though its eyes were the eyes of death.

"What's gotten into you?"

"I must go, and you with me," I told her. "I must go and bring you. You are afraid. I—"

"You lie!"

"Fear better suits a woman than a man. Even so, I am the more frightened. Yet I will go, and you will come with me." I set off, following the ghost, and very soon I heard Lurn's heavy tread behind me.

The corridor we traversed was dark as pitch. I slung my shield over my back, traced the damp stone walls with my left hand, and groped the dark before me with my sword point, testing the flagstones with every step. None of which mattered in the least. The ghost led me, and there was no treachery.

We descended a stair, narrow and steep, and I saw light below. Here was a cresset, filled with blazing wood and dripping embers. The ghost, which ought to have dimmed in the firelight, seemed almost a living man, a man young and nearly as tall as I, in livery of gray and crimson.

"Who is that?" Lurn's voice came from behind me, but not far behind.

I did not speak, but followed our guide.

He led us to a second stair, a winding stair that seemed at first to plunge into darkness. We had descended this for many steps when I took notice of a faint, pale light below.

"Where are we going?" Lurn asked.

I was harkening to a nightingale. It was our guide who answered her: "Where you wished to go, O pawn."

"Why are you talking to me like that, Valorius?"

I shrugged, and followed our guide into a garden lit by stars and the waning moon. He led us over smooth lawns and past tinkling fountains. The statues we saw were of pieces, of kings and queens, of slingers and spearmen, of knights such as I and pawns like Lurn. Winged figures stood among them, figures whiter than they and equally motionless; though these did not move or appear to breathe, it seemed to me they were not statues. They might have moved, I thought, this though they did not live.

"There can be no such place underground!" Lurn exclaimed.

I turned to face her. "We are not there. Surely you can see that. We entered into the stone of the mountain, and emerged here."

"It was broad day!"

"And is now night. Be silent."

That last I said because our guide stood behind her, his finger to his lips. He pointed, but I saw only a thick growth of cypress. I went to it, nonetheless; and when I stood before it I heard a muted creaking and squeaking, as though some portal long closed were opening. I pushed aside the boughs to look. There my eyes saw nothing. My father (who seemed to sit before me, his head cloven by the axe) had entered my mind and let me see him there.

I knelt.

He took his mantle from his shoulders and fastened it about mine. For a moment only I knew the freezing cold of the gold brooch that had held it. I reached for it. My fingers found nothing, yet I knew then (as I know now) where that mantle rests.

"What's in there?" Lurn asked.

"A tomb," I told her. "You did not come here to see a tomb, but to become a queen. See you the moon?"

"My lady? Yes, of course I see her."

"She rises to behold your coronation, and is already near the zenith. There is a circle of white stones, just there." I pointed. "Do you see it?"

It appeared as I spoke.

"No—yes. Yes, I see it now."

"Stand there—and wait. When the moon-shadows are short and every copse and course is bathed in moonlight, you will become a queen."

She went gladly. I stood before her; the distance was half as far, perhaps, as a boy might fling a stone.

I recall that she said this: "Won't you sit, Valorius? You must be tired."

"Are you not?"

"I? When I am to become a queen? No, never!"

That was all. That, and this: "Why do you rub your head?"

"It is where the axe went in. I rub it because the place is healed and my father at rest."

The moon rose higher yet, and one of the white figures came to kneel before me. She held a pillow of white silk; upon it lay a great visored helm white as any pearl, and upon that a silver crown.

I accepted it and rose. Six more were arming Lurn, armor of proof that no sword could cleave: breastplate and gorget, tasset and race. As earth circles moon, I circled her; and when her arming was complete save for the helm, poised that as high as I might. "From the goddess whom you serve, receive the crown that is your due." Standing, her head was higher than my upstretched arms; but she knelt before me to receive helm and crown, and I set them upon her head. They felt no heavier than their own pale plumes.

Rising, she pulled down the visor to try it; and I saw that there was a white face graven upon the visor now—and that white face was her own.

"I am a queen!" It might have been ten-score trumpets speaking.

I nodded.

"We will restore the kingdom, Valorius!"

I nodded as before. It had been my own thought.

"I shall restore the kingdom, and the Game will be played again. The Game, Valorius, and I a queen!"

I knew then that she whom I had kissed so often must die. Men have said my sword springs to my hand. That is not so, yet few draw more swiftly. She parried my first thrust with her gauntlet and sought to seize the blade; it escaped her—thus I lived.

Of our fight in that moonlit garden I will say little. She could parry my blows, and did. I could not parry hers; she was too strong for it. I dodged and ducked and was knocked sprawling again and again. I hoped for help, and received none. If longing could foal a horse from air, I would have had two score. No horse appeared.

What came at last was Our Lord the Sun, and that was better. I turned her until she faced it and put my point through her eyeslot. The steel that went in was not so long as my hand and less wide than two fingers together, yet it was enough. It sufficed.

Now?

Now I wander the land. Asked to prophesy, I say we shall overthrow the tyrants and make a new nation for ourselves and our children. Should our folk require a sword, I am the sword that springs to their hands. Asked to heal, I cure their sick—when I can. If they bring food, I eat it. If they do not, I fast or find my own. And that is all, save that from time to time I entertain a lost traveler, such as yourself. East lies the past, west the future. Go north to find the gods, south to find the blessed. Above stands the All High, and below lies Pandemonium. Choose your road and keep to it, for if you stray from it, you may encounter such as I. Fare you well! We shall not meet again.

You can find ghosts anywhere, even amusement parks. (Yes, there really is an Oaks Amusement Park near Portland, Oregon.) Of course, ghosts are often much closer than you might want to think . . .

OAKS PARK

M.K. HOBSON

You are thirty-nine years old and you are a woman and a mother, and you've just avoided saying something to your husband that would cause a fight. Summer is almost over, though the days are still long and the evening still warm and heavy with the sound of insects, and this makes you feel desperate, but you don't know why. You have a daughter who you already don't understand even though she is only twelve. Even your own life is puzzling to you, you move in a fog of mild discontent, whatever ability you ever had to make a decision or form an opinion lost to the endless consensus of family, the compromises of marriage, every day covering you like a sheet with holes cut out.

Your daughter has friends all over the neighborhood, tanned scuffed elastic creatures, each as wild and improbable as she. They are like another species. They come from nowhere, they come up from behind you and you never hear them coming. They all look alike. They lounge on couches inside dark cool houses hiding from daylight's glare, watching Nick for Teens and sipping Capri Suns, crushing packages of ramen and eating the crumbled noodles raw. They leave a trail of wrappers and crumbs. One day your daughter is prompted by her best girlfriend, a girl who looks exactly like your daughter, to ask "Can you take us to Oaks Park?" and you say "If you clean your room," knowing that she will never clean her room so you will never have to take her to Oaks Park.

Later, you hear your daughter talking to two more of her friends, a boy and a girl who look exactly like her, scraped knees and dark tanned skin and cornsilk hair and T-shirts that assert their unswerving allegiance to an anime show. They are all sitting in the shade of the porch, eating popsicles, dripping bright colored sugarwater on the worn treads.

"Oaks Park is haunted," one of them says. "Someone died there and the ghost wanders around."

You listen closely. You haven't heard this story before. You want to ask, *Who died there? Is there really a ghost? What does it look like?* But none of the kids on the porch have these questions, so they are not asked and not answered. The kids run into the streets and seize their bikes, leaving behind wrappers and sticks and puddles of sugary sweetness for ants to swarm over.

You turn to the Internet.

Oaks Park is a modest amusement park located 3.5 miles (6 km) south of downtown Portland, Oregon in the United States.

The park was built by the Oregon Water Power and Railway Company and opened in 1905, when trolley parks were often constructed along streetcar lines.

The large wooden roller skating rink is open year-round. The centerpiece is the largest remaining pipe organ installed in a skating rink in the world.

As of December 2005, Keith Fortune is at the organ's console providing music for skaters on Thursdays and Sundays.

It's all ragtimey, bandstands and box lunches, women in gored skirts and men in straw boater hats. You find bits of information about the flyscreened dance-hall and how the floor of the roller skating rink is on floating pontoons so it can stay above water when the Willamette River floods. There is nothing about a dead child or a ghost. The absence of such information makes you feel better. The vague anxiety you have been feeling eases. Your husband comes home, and you avoid talking about something that would upset you both, and you make dinner and eat it in front of the television, closing the curtains against the summer sunlight that blazes long into the night.

The next day, you receive an email from a young man named Chuck. He works at Oaks Park. You've already forgotten that you emailed him—Internet time works like that. But when the message pops into your email box you suddenly remember filling out a web form marked "history questions. Your message was brief.

Is there a ghost that haunts Oaks Park?

Chuck's emailed reply is just as brief.

Some people have reported seeing the ghost of a girl, about 12 years old. She's dressed in seventies-era clothing. She steals cotton candy from the snack bar and rides the rides. The Octopus is her favorite.

Your fingers type a furious question in response:

Is she happy?

But you don't hit "send," because you know that Chuck won't know the answer and you already do.

The last time you went to Oaks Park you were twelve and it was 1977.

You remember riding in the back seat of the Dodge Dart, American steel bullying across the narrow Sellwood Bridge, sweltering heat pouring in through all four open windows.

Your hands are sticky and you are wearing Haggar shorts and a Garanimals T-shirt from the Sears Surplus over by Lloyd Center. Your hair is cornsilk blond and your skin is brown and scratched, scabs everywhere like a map of stars.

Your parents are brittle, recovering from a night-long fight. This is your reward, your battle pay, your assurance that everything in the world is perfect.

Your dad's profile is sleek and handsome and brutal. Your mom's face is soft and young beneath a smooth Dorothy Hamill cut, her eyes watchful behind huge amber sunglasses. Your legs stick to the vinyl. "Hotel California" plays on the radio.

Your parents park the car under knobby, diseased trees. The small parking lot seems like it's in the wrong place; you get to it by driving past a caretaker's shack and a shop with old ride parts jumbled before it. You approach the park from behind, like you're sneaking up on it, stepping carefully over cracked mounds where tree roots have broken the asphalt. You leave your parents behind to mutter between themselves. That's the only time they talk, these days—when they think you can't hear.

To get to the new rides you have to pass the old midway, abandoned attractions that have been shut down for years. The old buildings are regal in their decay, silvered wood and peeling paint, bulb-broken light fixtures clotted with nests and twigs, cottonwood fluff piled in unswept corners.

One tilting building has a gigantic round doorway, like a giant storm drain, all boarded up. You run up to it, peek through the boards, peer into the darkness. The cool air coming from inside smells of mold. Your parents call you away, to where the new rides are—the steel-spiderweb Ferris wheel, the carousel with its cracked menagerie of dragons and rabbits, the Erector Set roller-coaster of rusted bolts and oil-smeared wood. A vast go-kart track sprawls to the north, belching gas fumes and the smell of baking rubber; beyond it, a fetid river lowland, a swamp filled with abandoned cars and frayed tires. There's a neon sign for a ride called the Fly-O but the ride that's actually there is the Octopus, spinning arms swinging bulbous black seats like fists.

While you are standing in line to ride the Octopus, you see a boy and girl in the shade of the snack bar. She is wearing a halter-top and baby-blue shorts, and she has long smooth hair that gleams down her back. She has one thumb hooked in the top of her shorts, and a velour prize monkey under her arm. The boy has tight curly hair, and he is leaning against her, his thumbs stroking the sides of her ribs. You are eating popcorn. You don't understand them and you know, suddenly, that you don't want to understand them. You never want to understand them. Your father has gone off somewhere, and you are alone with your mother. You watch her watch them. She understands them. There is betrayal and regret on her face.

The sun is still beating down but you feel cold. The line is moving, and it is almost your turn to get on the Octopus, but you know that there are clouds coming in, and you know that it will rain, and it will get cold. Your parents will fight again and again and again. And school will start and you will have a new teacher in a room with waxed floors, and you will wear new clothes and then it will be Christmas and then spring and then summer again, and then high school and then college and then you will be far far away from here, far from where old wise buildings keep the order of time. You will be the girl with the straight shiny hair or you will be the curly haired boy in cutoffs, betrayed. You will be your parents. You will be thirty-nine years old, and a woman, and a mother, and nothing will make any sense but it will all hurt. You see it all in one shambling terrifying moment, you see that everything will go on and on, spinning.

You ride the Octopus with your mother. Then you run away.

You find a deserted place, trash-strewn nook behind the bumper cars near the old line of bathrooms. You hide there, legs drawn up to your chest. You rest your forehead on your knees, and you close your eyes.

You imagine a ghost, a shell, a hollow creature that can be buffeted and molded, pliant as your mother when your father's bulbous fists swing around and around, yielding as the girl with long smooth hair, the curly-haired boy looming over her like a cloud over the sun. You pretend someone else out into the world. You send her in your place.

You can't ever come back, you whisper to her. You tell yourself it's like a game. A game of hide and seek. You will hide from time and fear and betrayal and regret.

Someone else goes home in the car with your parents, someone new and formless, someone who feels no fear because she feels nothing. As insubstantial as mist, as air under a sheet. You will stay at Oaks Park. You will sleep during the hottest part of the day and at night, when the lights come on, the buildings will whisper their secrets to you and they will keep you safe forever.

You are thirty-nine years old and you are a woman and a mother.

You wake up after a night of unsettling dreams, whirling spinning dreams full of screaming and blurred lights and the smell of burnt sugar, and you have a fight with your husband. You tell him he's the worst decision you ever made. You tell him you wish you'd never married him. You tell him you never loved him. You tell him you hate him, and when you tell him this, you feel the sickening truth of it. You scream at each other for hours, and you're both late for work, and your daughter is late for school.

You drive her, and she cowers in the back seat and you feel, rather than see, the anxiety on her face. You understand it completely. You remember it, the fear of everything falling apart. The memory is strange and alien. It is a fear that is supposed to belong to someone else, someone like you.

You don't go in to work. You come home and sit on the couch in your front room, heat beating against the walls of the house. You draw curtains against it, you move the air with fans, but it's so terribly hot. You drowse, but every time you nod off you dream of boarded up buildings and peeling paint. The buildings are empty. You thought they held secrets, you thought they were wise. But they contain nothing. They are as empty as you are. You wake screaming.

Late in the afternoon, you drive to Oaks Park.

The air is still and sunny. You make the turn off the Sellwood Bridge at sunset, the dazzling light making your eyes tear. You drive along the road that leads to the park, fluff from the cottonwood trees glistening in the golden air. A stiff breeze from the Willamette makes faded nylon pennants ripple. The lights have been turned on, but you can't see them, not yet.

Everything has changed. The big flat expanse of cracked blacktop where the go-karts used to be is now acres of smoothly paved parking. The swamp is now wetland and there are multi-use trails and urban hiking areas threaded throughout it. Everything is smaller. Most of the rides you remember are gone, even the Tilt-o-Whirl with its evil clown faces—you never liked it, it gave you a headache and made you feel sick and it smelled like diesel. The Erector Set roller-coaster has been replaced by something plastic and candy-colored that has a loop-de-loop. You pass what used to be the Haunted Mine, and remember that it used to scare you, but now it is called The Lewis and Clark Adventure and beavers jump out at you instead of skeletons. It's all bad hand-me-down Funtastic carnival rides with cheap graphics of secondhand superheroes. Alternative rock spews from the speakers.

All the old boarded up rides are gone, razed. Where they once stood, picnic space has been cleared for corporate picnics and soccer team parties.

You buy popcorn from the snack bar. Made in China, it comes in a foil bag and is very stale. You sit on one of the old green wooden benches and wait for it to get dark.

You see her before she sees you. She's wearing Haggar shorts and a Garanimals shirt from Sears Surplus. She has a chunk of cotton candy in her hand. She's all eyes, wandering through the crowd in the watchful way of lost children, her brow creased with anxiety. You watch her until she sees you, watch her face light with perfect joy and relief. Feelings wrap around you like a winter coat. Anger. Resentment. Bitterness. Regret.

She runs to you, clutching grubby hands at your clothing. She buries a dirty face in your stomach and breaks, brave wary watchfulness dissolving into sobs. She wails and moans, a lost child found, and you pet her back and say soft soothing things to her. She clings to you, and people are watching, making sympathetic clucking sounds. You savor this moment. You hold onto it for as long as you can. You think of your daughter and you remember a million looks on her face that you couldn't interpret. You understand them all now. You remember a hundred times you hated your husband, your life, your job . . . even your own child.

I want to go home, she sobs into your stomach, against your shirt. I want to go home.

You want to take her home. You want to put her in the back seat of your car, and let her fall asleep, exhausted by her ordeal. You would drive home, and when you got there, she would be gone, melted into the car, melted back into you. You would be whole again. Oaks Park would have one less ghost, and you would have one more.

And there would be another fight and another and another, and you would see the infinity of days stretch before you again, and you would see the looks your daughter gives you, and understand them for what they are—disgust, pity, shame. And maybe you would hurt her, hurt her so much that she would make her own ghost, and this whole terrible wheel would turn again, this carnival wheel, this gut-wrenching loop-de-loop.

You can't take her home.

Dread of what you will have to do makes all the small muscles in your body ache. You can't think about it. You will have to just do it. Your hands will have to rescue you.

You take her hand and walk. She is content to be pulled along, compliant and humbled, nose running. You are walking in the direction of the old parking lot at the back of the park. But you are really walking to the place behind the bumpercars, behind the bathrooms. It is the same as it was twenty-seven years ago, trash-strewn with the same trash, the same cottonwoodfluff.

You pull her down beside you and you take her in your arms and hold her tight, cradling her for a few minutes more, telling her how brave she's been. She talks fast, sentences like broken sticks: she didn't mean to, it was just a game, she didn't mean to get lost, she was scared, she was looking for you.

You murmur *shh, shh* in her ear as your fingers find the kitchen knife you have brought from home.

You pull the knife across her smooth brown throat. She gushes, but it is not blood. She bleeds time, a million golden sunsets and white illuminated nights, and she bleeds fear, the shambling shadow of the eternal, dark and molasses-like. She bleeds regret. She thrashes in your arms, making betrayed noises, animal noises. She deflates. She melts. Then she is nothing but a pile of dirty old clothes from Sears Surplus. You hide these beneath the trash.

Walking back to your car, you are trembling, but it is only a physical thing. Your mind is calm, and everything feels vague and unknowable again. Your accustomed numbness returns, and you know that everything will be all right.

She will stay at Oaks Park. She will ride the rides and steal cotton candy. But she will be someone else, someone new and formless, someone who feels all the terror that you should share. As insubstantial as mist, as air under a sheet. She will sleep during the hottest part of the day and at night, when the lights come on, she search watchfully through crowds for the mother she didn't mean to lose and a life she didn't mean to surrender.

You leave her to her haunts.

You return to yours.

Inspired by the ballet Swan Lake, *the author revisits the character of Odile, the Black Swan, while keeping in mind that not every girl wants a prince or even a crown . . .*

THIMBLERIGGERY AND FLEDGLINGS

STEVE BERMAN

The Sorcerer Bernhard von Rothbart scratched at a sore on his chin with a snow-white feather, then hurled it as a dart at the chart hanging above the bookshelves. The quill's sharp end stabbed through the buried feet of the dunghill cock, *Gallus gallus faecis,* drawn with a scarab clutched in its beak.

"A noble bird," von Rothbart muttered as he bit clean his fingernails, "begins base and eats noble things."

He expected his daughter to look up from a book and answer "Yes, Papa," but there was only silence. Above him, in the massive wrought iron cage, the wappentier shifted its dark wings. One beak yawned while the other preened. A musky odor drifted down.

Why wasn't Odile studying the remarkable lineage of doves?

Von Rothbart climbed down the stairs. Peered into room after room of the tower. A sullen chanticleer pecked near the coat rack. Von Rothbart paused a moment to recall whether the red-combed bird had been the gardener who had abandoned his sprouts or the glazier who'd installed murky glass.

He hoped to find her in the kitchen and guilty of only brushing crumbs from the pages of his priceless books. But he saw only the new cook, who shied away. Von Rothbart reached above a simmering cauldron to run his fingers along the hot stones until they came back charred black.

Out the main doors, the sorcerer looked out at the wide and tranquil moat encircling his home, and at the swans drifting over its surface. He knew them to be the most indolent birds. So much so they barely left the water.

He brushed his fingers together. Ash fell to the earth and the feathers of one gliding swan turned soot-dark and its beak shone like blood.

"Odile," he called. "Come here!"

The black swan swam to shore and slowly waddled over to stand before von Rothbart. Her neck, as sinuous as any serpent's, bent low until she touched her head to his boots.

The Black Swan

Odile felt more defeated than annoyed at being discovered. Despite the principle that, while also a swan, she should be able to tell one of the bevy from the other, Odile had been floating much of the afternoon without finding Elster. Or, if she had, the maiden—Odile refused to think of them as pens, despite Papa insisting that was the proper terminology—had remained mute.

"What toad would want this swan's flesh?" her papa muttered. "I want to look upon the face of my daughter."

In her head, she spoke a phrase of *rara lingua* that shed the albumen granting her form. The transformation left her weak and famished; while she had seen her papa as a pother owl devour a hare in one swallow, Odile as a swan could not stomach moat grass and cloying water roots. No longer the tips of great wings, her fingers dug at the moss between flagstones.

"There's my plain girl." Smiling, he gently lifted her by the arms. "So plain, so sweet." He stroked her cheek with a thumb.

She could hear the love in his voice, but his familiar cooing over her rough-as-vinegar face and gangly limbs still hurt. A tear escaped along the edge of her nose.

"Why you persist in playing amongst the bevy. . . . " He stroked her cheek with a thumb. "Come inside." He guided her towards the door. "There won't only be lessons today. I'll bring a Vorspiel of songbirds to the window to make you smile."

Odile nodded and walked with him back into the tower. But she would rather Papa teach her more of *rara lingua*. Ever since her sixteenth birthday, he had grown reluctant to share invocations. At first, Odile thought she had done something wrong and was being punished, but she now she suspected that Papa felt magic, like color, belonged to males. The books he let her read dealt with nesting rather than sorcery.

From his stories, Odile knew he had been only a few years older when he left his village, adopted a more impressive name, and traveled the world. He had stepped where the ancient augers had read entrails. He had spoken with a cartouche of ibises along the Nile and fended off the copper claws of the gagana on a lost island in the Caspian Sea.

But he never would reveal the true mark of a great sorcerer: how he captured a the wappantier. His secrets both annoyed Odile and made her proud.

The Wappentier

As the sole-surviving offspring of the fabled ziz of the Hebrews, the wappentier is the rarest of raptors. Having never known another of its ilk, the wappentier cannot speak out of loneliness and rarely preens its dark feathers. Some say the beast's wings can stretch from one horizon to the other, but then it could not find room in the sky to fly. Instead, this lusus naturae *perches atop desolate crags and ruins.*

The Rashi claimed that the wappentier possesses the attributes of both the male and female. It has the desire to nest and yet the urge to kill. As soon as gore is taken to its gullet, the wappentier lays an egg that will never hatch. Instead, these rudiments are prized by theurgists for their arcane properties. Once cracked, the egg, its gilded shell inscribed with the Tetragrammaton, reveals not a yolk but a quintessence of mutable form, reflected in the disparate nature of the beast. A man may change his physique. A woman may change her fate. But buried, the eggs become foul and blacken like abandoned iron.

This Swan May

When Elster was nine, her grandmother brought her to the fairgrounds. The little girl clutched a ten-pfenning tight in her palm. A gift from her papa, a sour-smelling man who brewed gose beer all day long. "To buy candy. Or a flower," said her grandmother.

The mayhem called to Elster, who tugged at her grandmother's grip wanting to fly free. She broke loose and ran into the midst of the first crowd she came upon. Pushing her way to the center, she found there a gaunt man dressed in shades of red. He moved tarnished thimbles about a table covered in a faded swatch of silk.

The man's hands, with thick yellowed warts at every bend and crease, moved with a nimble grace. He lifted up one thimble to reveal a florin. A flip and a swirl and the thimble at his right offered a corroded haller. The coins were presented long enough to draw sighs and gasps from the crowd before disappearing under tin shells.

"I can taste that ten-bit you're palming," said the gaunt man. Thick lips hid his teeth. How Elster heard him over the shouts of the crowd—"Die linke Hand"—she could not guess. "Wager for a new life? Iron to gold?" His right hand tipped over a thimble to show a shining mark, bit of minted sunlight stamped with a young woman's face. Little Elster stood on her toes, nearly tipping over the table, to see the coin's features. Not her mother or her grandmother. Not anyone she knew yet. But the coin itself was the most beautiful of sights; the gold glittered and promised her anything.

Everything. Her mouth watered and she wanted the odd man in red's coin so badly that spittle leaked past her lips.

When she let go of the table, the iron pfenning rolled from her sweaty fingers. The gaunt man captured it with a dropped thimble.

"Now which one, magpie? You want the shiny one, true? Left or right or middle or none at all?"

Elster watched his hands. She could not be sure and so closed her eyes and reached out. She clamped her hand over the gaunt man's grip. His skin felt slick and hard like polished horn. "This one," she said. When she looked, his palm held an empty thimble.

"Maybe later you'll find the prize." When he smiled she saw that his front teeth were metal: the left a dull iron, the right gleamed gold.

A strong arm pulled her away from the table. "Stupid child." Her grandmother cuffed her face. "From now on, a thimble will be your keep."

The Message

Down in the cellar, the stones seeped with moisture. Odile sneezed from the stink of mould. She could see how her papa trembled at the chill. The floor was fresh-turned earth. Crates filled niches in the walls. In the tower's other cage, a weeping man sat on a stool. The king's livery, stained, bunched about his shoulders.

"The prince's latest messenger." Papa gestured at a bejeweled necklace glittering at the man's feet. "Bearing a bribe to end the engagement."

Papa followed this with a grunt as he stooped down and began digging in the dirt with his fingers. Odile helped him brush away what covered a dull, gray egg. "Papa, he's innocent."

He gently pulled the egg loose of the earth. "Dear, there's a tradition of blame. Sophocles wrote that 'No man loves the messenger of ill.' "

He took a pin from his cloak and punched a hole into the ends of the egg while intoning *rara lingua*. Then he approached the captive man, who collapsed, shaking, to his knees. Papa blew into one hole and a vapor reeking of sulfur drifted out to surround the messenger. Screams turned into the frantic call of a songbird.

"We'll send him back to the prince in a gilded cage with a message. 'We delightfully accept your offer of an engagement ball.' Perhaps I should have turned him into a parrot and he could have spoken that."

"Papa," Odile chided.

"I'll return his form after the wedding. I promise." He carried the egg to one shelf and pulled out the crate of curse eggs nestled in soil. "What king more wisely cares for his subjects?"

The Prince

The prince would have rather mucked out every filthy stall in every stable of the kingdom than announce his engagement to the sorcerer's daughter at the ball. His father must have schemed his downfall; why else condemn him to marry a harpy?

"Father, be reasonable. Why not the Duke of Bremen's daughter?" The prince glanced up at the fake sky the guildsmen were painting on the ballroom's ceiling. A cloud appeared with a brushstroke.

"The one so lovely that her parents keep her at a cloister?" asked the king. "Boy, your wife should be faithful only to you. Should she look higher to God, she'll never pay you any respect."

"Then that Countess from Schaumberg—"

The king sighed. "Son, there are many fine lands with many fine daughters but none of them have magic."

"Parlor tricks!"

"Being turned into a turkey is not a trick. Besides, von Rothbart is the most learned man I have ever met. If his daughter has half the mind, half the talent . . . "

"Speaking dead languages and reciting dusty verse won't keep a kingdom."

The king laughed. "Don't tell that to Cardinal Passerine."

The Fledgling

In the silence, Odile looked up from yellowed pages that told how a pelican's brood are stillborn until the mother pecks its chest and resurrects them with her own blood. Odile had no memory of her own mother. Papa would never answer any question she asked about her.

She pinched the flame out in the sconce's candle and opened the shutters. The outside night had so many intriguing sounds. Even if she only listened to the breeze it would be enough to entice her from her room.

She went to her dresser, opened the last drawer, and found underneath old mohair sweaters the last of the golden wappentier eggs she had taken. She could break it now, turn herself into a night bird and fly free. The thought tempted her as she stared at her own weak reflection on the shell. She polished it for a moment against her dressing gown.

But the need to see Elster's face overpowered her.

So, as she had done so many nights, Odile gathered and tied bed sheets and old clothes together as a makeshift rope to climb down the outer walls of her papa's tower.

As she descended, guided only by moonlight, something large flew near her head. Odile became still, with the egg safe in a makeshift sling around her chest, her toes squeezing past crumbling mortar. A fledermaus? Her papa called them vermin; he hunted them as the pother owl. If he should spot her. . . . But no, she did not hear his voice demand she return to her room. Perhaps it was the wappentier. Still clinging to the wall, she waited for the world to end, as her papa had said would happen if the great bird ever escaped from its cage. But her heartbeat slowly calmed and she became embarrassed by all her fears. The elder von Rothbart would have fallen asleep at his desk, cheek smearing ink on the page. The sad wappentier would be huddled behind strong bars. Perhaps it also dreamed of freedom.

Once on the ground, Odile walked towards the moat. Sleeping swans rested on the bank. Their long necks twisted back and their bills tucked into pristine feathers.

She held up the wappentier egg. Words of *rara lingua* altered her fingernail, making it sharp as a knife. She punctured the two holes, and as she blew into the first, her thoughts were full of incantations and her love's name. She had trouble holding the words in her head; as if alive and caged, they wanted release on the tongue. Maybe Papa could not stop from turning men into birds, though Odile suspected he truly enjoyed doing so.

She never tired of watching the albumen sputter out of the shell and drift over the quiet swans like marsh fire before falling like gold rain onto one in their midst.

Elster stretched pale limbs. Odile thought the maid looked like some unearthly flower slipping through the damp bank, unfurling slender arms and long blonde hair. Then she stumbled until Odile took her by the hand and offered calm words while the shock of the transformation diminished.

They fled into the woods. Elster laughed to run again. She stopped to reach for fallen leaves, touch bark, then pull at a loose thread of Odile's dressing gown and smile.

Elster had been brought to the tower to fashion Odile a dress for court. Odile could remember that first afternoon, when she had been standing on a chair while the most beautiful girl she'd ever seen stretched and knelt below her measuring. Odile had never felt so awkward, sure that she'd topple at any moment, yet so ethereal, confidant that had she slipped, she would glide to the floor.

Papa instructed Elster that Odile's gown was to be fashioned from sticks and string, like a proper bird's nest. But, alone together, Elster showed Odile bolts of silk and linen, guiding her hand along the cloth to feel its softness. She would reveal strands of chocolate-colored ribbon and thread them through Odile's hair while whispering how pretty she could be. Her lips had lightly brushed Odile's ears.

When Papa barged into Odile's room and found the rushes and leaves abandoned at their feet and a luxurious gown in Elster's lap, he dragged Elster down to the cellar. A tearful Odile followed, but she could not find the voice to beg him not to use a rotten wappentier egg.

In the woods, they stopped, breathless, against a tree trunk. "I brought you a present," Odile said.

"A coach that will carry us far away from your father?"

Odile shook her head. She unlaced the high top of her dressing gown and allowed the neckline to slip down inches. She wore the prince's bribe but now lifted it off her neck. The thick gold links, the amethysts like frozen drops of wine, seemed to catch the moon's fancy as much as their own.

"This must be worth a fortune." Elster stroked the necklace Odile draped over her long, smooth neck.

"Perhaps. Come morning, I would like to know which swan is you by this."

Elster took a step away from Odile. Then another until the tree was between them. "Another day trapped. And another. And when you marry the prince, what of me? No one will come for me then."

"Papa says he will release all of you. Besides, I don't want to marry the prince."

"No. I see every morning as a swan. You can't—won't—refuse your father."

Odile sighed. Lately, she found herself daydreaming that Papa had found her as a chick, fallen from the nest, and turned her into a child. "I've never seen the prince," Odile said as she began climbing the tree.

"He'll be handsome. An expensive uniform with shining medals and epaulets. That will make him handsome."

"I heard his father and mother are siblings. He probably has six fingers on a hand." Odile reached down from the fat branch she sat upon to pull Elster up beside her.

"Better to hold you with."

"The ball is tomorrow night."

"What did he do with the gown I made you?"

"He told me to burn it. I showed him the ashes of an apron. It's hidden beneath my bed."

"Let me wear it. Let me come along to the ball with you."

"You would want to see me dance with him?"

Elster threaded her fingers through Odile's hair, sweeping a twig from the ends. "Wouldn't you rather I be there than your father?"

Odile leaned close to Elster and marveled at how soft her skin felt. Her pale cheeks. Her arms, her thighs. Odile wanted music then, for them to dance together dangerously on the branches. Balls and courts and gowns seemed destined for other girls.

The Coach

On the night of the ball, von Rothbart surprised Odile with a coach and driver. "I returned some lost sons and daughters we had around the tower for the reward." He patted the rosewood sides of the coach. "I imagine you'll be traveling to and from the palace in the days to come. A princess shouldn't be flying."

Odile opened the door and looked inside. The seats were plush and satin.

"You wear the same expression as the last man I put in the cellar cage." He kissed her cheek. "Would a life of means and comfort be so horrible?"

The words in her head failed Odile. They wouldn't arrange themselves in an explanation, in the right order to convey to Papa her worries about leaving the tower, her disgust at having to marry a man she didn't know and could never care for. Instead she pressed herself against him. The bound twigs at her bosom stabbed her chest. The only thing that kept her from crying was the golden egg she secreted in the nest gown she wore.

When the coach reached the woods, Odile shouted for the driver to stop. He looked nervous when she opened the door and stepped out on to the road.

"Fraulein, your father insisted you arrive tonight. He said I'd be eatin' worms for the rest of my days."

"A moment." She had difficulty running, because of the rigid gown. She knew her knees would be scratched raw by the time she reached the swans. Odile guided a transformed Elster to the road. The sight of the magnificent coach roused her from the change's fugue.

"Finally I ride with style." Elster waited for the driver to help her climb the small steps into the coach. "But I have no dress to wear tonight."

Odile sat down beside her and stroked the curtains and the cushions. "There is fabric wasted here to make ten gowns."

When Odile transformed her fingernails to sharp points to rip free satin and gauze, she noticed Elster inch away. The magic frightened her. Odile offered a smile and her hand to use as needles. Elster took hold of her wrist with an almost cautious touch.

The bodice took shape in Elster's lap. "We could stay on the road. Not even go to the ball. You could turn the driver into a red-breasted robin and we could go wherever we want."

"I've never been this far away from home." Odile wondered why she hadn't considered such an escape. But all her thoughts had been filled with the dreaded ball, as if she had no choice but to accept the prince's hand. She glanced out the tiny window at the world rushing past. But Papa would be waiting for her tonight. There would be studies tomorrow and feeding the wappentier, and she couldn't abandon Papa.

It was a relief that she had no black egg with her, that she had no means to turn a man into fowl. She had never done so, could not imagine the need. So she shook her head.

Elster frowned. "Always your father's girl." She reached down and bit free the thread linking Odile's fingers and her gown. "Remember that I offered you a choice."

The Ball

The palace ballroom had been transformed into an enchanting wood. The rugs from distant Persia rolled up to allow space for hundreds of fallen leaves fashioned from silk. The noble attendees slipped on the leaves often. A white-bearded ambassador from Lombardy fell and broke his hip; when carried off he claimed it was no accident but an *atto di guerra*.

Trees, fashioned by carpenters and blacksmiths, spread along the walls. The head cook had sculpted dough songbirds encrusted them with dyed sugars and marzipan beaks.

The orchestra was instructed not to play any tune not found in nature. This left them perplexed and often silent.

"Fraulein Odile von Rothbart and her guest Fraulein Elster Schwanensee." The herald standing on the landing had an oiled, thick mustache.

Odile cringed beneath the layers of twigs and parchment that covered her torso and trailed off to sweep the floor. How they all stared at her. She wanted to squeeze Elster's hand for strength but found nothing in her grasp; she paused halfway down the staircase, perplexed by her empty hand. She turned back to the crowd of courtiers but saw no sign of her swan maid.

The courtiers flocked around her. They chattered, so many voices that she had trouble understanding anything they said.

"That frock is so . . . unusual." The elderly man who spoke wore a cardinal's red robes. "How very bold to be so . . . indigenous."

A sharp-nosed matron held a silken pomander beneath her nostrils. "I hope that is imported mud binding those sticks," she muttered.

The Lovebirds

Elster picked up a crystal glass of chilled Silvaner from a servant's platter. She held the dry wine long in her mouth, wanting to remember its taste when she had to plunge a beak into moat water.

"Fraulein von Rothbart. Our fathers would have us dance."

Elster turned around. She had been right about the uniform. Her heart ached to touch the dark blue-like-evening wool, the gilded buttons, the medals at the chest, and the thick gold braid on the shoulders. A uniform like that would only be at home in a wardrobe filled with fur-lined coats, jodhpurs for riding with leather boots, silken smoking jackets that smelled of Turkish tobacco. The man who owned such clothes would only be satisfied if his darling matched him in taste.

She lowered her gaze with much flutter and curtsied low.

"I am pleased you wore my gift." The prince had trimmed fingernails that looked so pink as to possibly be polished. He lifted up one section of the necklace she wore. The tip of his pinky slid into the crease between her breasts. "How else would I know you?"

She offered a promissory smile.

He led her near where the musicians sought to emulate the chirp of crickets at dusk.

"So, I must remember to commend your father on his most successful enchantment."

"Your Imperial and Royal Highness is too kind."

Three other couples, lavish in expensive fabric and pearls and silver, joined them in a quadrille. As the pairs moved, their feet kicked up plumes of silk leaves. Despite the gold she wore around her neck, Elster felt as if she were a tarnished coin thimblerigged along the dance floor.

"I have an admission to make," she whispered in the prince's ear when next she passed him. "I'm not the sorcerer's daughter."

The prince took hold of her arm, not in a rough grasp, but as if afraid she would vanish. "If this is a trick—"

"Once I shared your life of comfort. Sheets as soft as a sigh. Banquet halls filled with drink and laughter. Never the need for a seamstress as I never wore a dress twice.

"My parents were vassals in Saxony. Long dead now." She slipped free of his hold and went to the nearest window. She waited for his footsteps, waited to feel him press against her. "Am I looking East? To a lost home?"

She turned around. Her eyes lingered a moment on the plum-colored ribbon sewn to one medal on his chest. "So many years ago—I have lost count—a demonic bird flew into my bedchamber."

"Von Rothbart."

Elster nodded at his disgust. "He stole me away, back to his lonely tower. Every morning I woke to find myself trapped as a swan. Every night he demands I become his bride. I have always refused."

"I have never stood before such virtue." The prince began to tear as he stepped back and then fell to one knee. "Though I can see why even the Devil would promise himself to you."

His eyes looked too shiny, as if he might start crying or raving like a madman. Elster had seen the same sheen in Odile's eyes. Elster squeezed the prince's hand but looked over her shoulder at where she had parted with the sorcerer's daughter. The art of turning someone into a bird would never dress her in cashmere or damask. Feathers were only so soft and comforting.

The Lost

When Odile was a young girl, her father told her terrible tales every *Abend vor Allerheiligen*. One had been about an insane cook who had trapped over twenty blackbirds and half-cooked them as part of a pie. All for the delight of a royal court. Odile had nightmares about being trapped with screeching chicks, all cramped in the dark, the stink of dough, the rising heat. She would not eat any pastry for years.

Watching Elster dance with the prince filled Odile with pain. She didn't know whether such hurt needed tears or screams to be freed. She approached them. The pair stopped turning.

"Your warning in the coach? Is this your choice?" asked Odile.

Elster nodded though her hands released the prince's neck.

The *rara lingua* to tear the swan maid's humanity from her slipped between Odile's lips with one long gasp. Her face felt feverish and damp. Perhaps tears. She called for Papa to take the swan by the legs into the kitchen and return carrying a bulging strudel for the prince.

The Strygian

As a long-eared pother owl, von Rothbart had hoped to intimidate the nobles with a blood-curdling shriek as he flew in through a window. An impressive father earned respect, he knew. But with the cacophony in the ballroom—courtiers screaming, guards shouting, the orchestra attempting something cheerful—only three fainted.

Von Rothbart roosted on the high-backed chair at the lead table. He shrugged off a mantle of feathers and seated himself with his legs on the tablecloth and his boots in a dish of poached boar.

"I suppose the venery for your lot would be an inbred of royals."

No one listened.

He considered standing atop the table but his knees ached after every transformation. As did his back. Instead, he pushed his way through the crowd at the far end, where most of the commotion seemed centered.

He did not expect to find a tearful Odile surrounded by a ring of lowered muskets. One guard trembled so. The prince shouted at her. The king pulled at his son's arm.

Von Rothbart raised his arms. The faux trees shook with a sudden wind that topped glasses, felled wigs, and swept the tiles free of silk leaves. "Stop," he shouted. "Stop and hear me!"

All eyes turned to him. He tasted fear as all the muskets pointed at him.

"You there, I command you to return Elster to me." The prince's face had become ruddy with ire. His mouth flecked with spittle.

"Who?"

"No lies, Sorcerer. Choose your words carefully"

The king stepped between them. He looked old. As old as von Rothbart felt. "Let us have civil words."

"Papa—" cried Odile.

"If you have hurt my daughter in any way—"

A cardinal standing nearby smoothed out his sanguine robes. "Your daughter bewitched an innocent tonight."

"She flew away from me," said the prince. "My sweet Elster is out there. At night. All alone."

Von Rothbart looked around him. He could not remember ever being so surrounded by men and women and their expressions of disgust, fear, and hatred left him weak. Weak as an old fool, one who thought he could ingratiate his dear child into their ranks like a cuckoo did with its egg.

Only magpies would care for such shiny trappings and they were sorrowful birds who envied human speech.

He took a deep breath and held it a moment as the magic began. His lungs hurt as the storm swirled within his body. He winced as a rib cracked. He lost two teeth as the gusts escaped his mouth. The clouds painted on the ceiling became dark and thick and spat lightning and rain down upon the people.

Odile stretched and caught the wind von Rothbart sent her as the crowd fled. He took her out of the palace and into the sky. It pained him to speak so all he asked her was if she was hurt. The tears that froze on her cheeks answered *yes, Papa.*

The Black Swain

"Von Rothbart!"

Odile looked out the window. She had expected the prince. Maybe he'd be waving a sword or a blunderbuss and be standing before a thousand men. But not the king standing by the doors and a regal carriage drawn by snorting stallions. He looked dapper in a wool suit, and she preferred his round fur hat to a crown.

"Von Rothbart, please, I seek an audience with you."

Odile ran down the staircase and then opened the doors.

The king plucked the hat from his head and stepped inside. "Fraulein von Rothbart."

"Your majesty." She remembered to curtsy.

"Your father—"

"Papa is ill. Ever since . . . well, that night, he's been taken to bed."

"I'm sorry to hear that. Your departure was marvelous. The court has been talking of nothing else for days." The king chuckled. "I'd rather be left alone."

She led him to the rarely used sitting room. The dusty upholstery embarrassed her.

"It's quiet here. Except the birds of course." The king winced. "My apologies."

"Your son—"

"Half-mad they say. Those who have seen him. He's roaming the country side hoping to find her. A swan by day and the fairest maiden by night." He tugged at his hat, pulling it out of shape. "Only, she's not turning back to a maiden again, is she?"

Odile sat down in her father's chair. She shook her head.

"Unless, child, your father . . . or you would consent to removing the curse."

"Why should I do that, your majesty?"

The king leaned forward. "When I was courting the queen, her father, a powerful duke, sent me two packages. In one, was an ancient sword. The iron blade dark and scarred. An heirloom of the duke's family that went back generations, used in countless campaigns—every one a victory." The king made a fist. "When I grasped the hilt, leather salted by sweat, I felt I could lead an army."

"And the second package?" Odile asked.

"That one contained a pillow."

"A pillow?"

The king nodded. "Covered with gold brocade and stuffed with goose down." The king laughed. "The messenger delivered as well a note that said I was to bring one, only one, of the packages with me to dinner at the ducal estate."

"A test."

"That is what my father said. My tutors had been soldiers not statesmen. The sword meant strength, courage, to my father. What a king should, no, must possess to keep his lands and people safe. To him the choice was clear."

Odile smiled. Did all fathers enjoy telling stories of their youth?

"I thought to myself, if the answer was so clear then why the test? What had the duke meant by the pillow? Something soft and light, something womanly . . . "

The notion of a woman being pigeonholed so irritated Odile. Was she any less a woman because she lacked the apparent grace of girls like Elster? She looked down at the breeches she liked to wear, comfortable not only because of the fit but because they had once been worn by her father. Her hands were not smooth but spotted with ink and rubbed with dirt from where she had begun to dig Papa's grave. Their escape had been too taxing. She worried over each breath he struggled to take.

" . . . meant to rest upon, to lie your head when sleeping. Perhaps choosing the pillow would show my devotion to his daughter, that I would be a loving husband before a valiant king—"

"Does he love her?" Odile asked.

The king stammered, as if unwilling to tear himself from the story.

"Your son. Does he love her?"

"What else would drive a man of privilege to the woods? He's forsaken crown for thorn. Besides, a lost princess? Every peasant within miles has been bringing fowl to the palace hoping for a reward."

"A princess." Odile felt a bitter smile curl the edges of her mouth. Would his Royal Highness be roaming the land if he knew his true love was a seamstress? But then Odile remembered Elster's touch, the softness of her lips, her skin.

Perhaps Elster had been meant to be born a princess. She had read in Papa's books of birds that raid neighboring nests, roll out the eggs and lay their own. Perhaps that happened to girls as well. The poor parent never recognized the greedy chick for what it truly was. The prince might never as well.

If her own, unwanted destiny of doting bride had been usurped, then couldn't she choose her future? Why not take the one denied to her?

"The rings on your fingers."

"Worth a small fortune." He removed thick bands set with rubies and pearls. "A bride price then? I could also introduce you to one of the many eligible members of my court."

Odile took the rings, heavy and warm. "These will do," she said and told the king to follow her.

By candlelight, she took him down to the dank cellar. He seemed a bit unnerved by the empty cage. She pulled out a tray of blackened eggs. Then another. "She's here. They're all here. Take them."

The king lifted one egg. He looked it over then shook it by his ear.

"Look through the holes." She held the candle flame high.

The king peered through one end. "My Lord," he sputtered. The egg tumbled from his grasp and struck the floor, where it shattered like ancient pottery.

"There—There's a tiny man sleeping inside."

"I know." She brushed aside the shards with her bare foot. A sharp edge cut her sole and left a bloody streak on the stones. "Don't worry, you freed him."

She left him the light. "Find the princess's egg. Break all of them, if you want. There might be other princesses among them." She started up the staircase.

"She stepped on his toes a great deal."

"What was that?"

The king ran his hands over the curse eggs. "When I watched them dance, I noticed how often she stepped on my son's toes. One would think her parents were quite remiss in not teaching her the proper steps." He looked up at her with a sad smile. "One would think."

Odile climbed to the top of the tower to her papa's laboratory. Inside its cage, the wappentier screeched from both heads when she entered. Since their return, she had neglected it; Papa had been the only one who dared feed the beast.

Its last golden egg rested on a taxonomy book. She held it in her hands a moment before moving to the shutters and pushing them open. She felt the strong breeze. Wearing another shape, she could ride the air far. Perhaps all the way to the mountains. Or the sea.

The wanderlust, so new and strong, left her trembling. Abandoning a life could be cruel.

Still clutching the egg to her chest, she went down to her papa's bedroom. He had trouble opening his eyes when she touched his forehead. He tried to speak but lacked the strength.

He'd never taught Odile about death or grieving, other than to mention the pelican hen shedding blood to revive her children. Odile hoped her devotion would mend him. She devised *rara lingua* with a certainty that surprised her. As she envisioned the illustrated vellum of her lessons, her jaw began to ache. Her mouth tasted like the salt spray of the ocean. She looked down at her arms. Where the albumen dripped, white feathers grew.

She called out, the sound hoarse and new and strange, but so fitting coming from the heavy body she wore. As a pelican, she squatted besides Papa's pillow. Her long beak, so heavy and ungainly as she moved her head, rose high. She plunged it down into her own breast, once, twice, until blood began to spill. Drops fell on to Papa's pale lips. As she hopped about the bed, it spattered onto his bared chest.

She forced her eyes to remain open despite the pain, so she could be assured that the color did return to his face, to see the rise and fall of each breath grow higher, stronger.

He raised his hand to her chest but she nudged his fingers away. Her wound had already begun to close on its own.

When she returned to human form, she touched above her breasts and felt the thick line of a scar. No, she decided it must be a badge, a medal like the prince had worn. She wanted it seen.

"Lear would be envious." Papa said in a voice weak but audible, "to have such a pelican daughter."

She laughed and cried a bit as well. She could not voice how his praise made her feel. So after she helped him sit up in bed, she went to his cluttered wardrobe. "I have to leave." She pushed aside garments until she found a curious outfit, a jacket and breeches, all in shades of red.

"Tell me where you're going."

"Tomorrow's lessons are on the road. I'll learn to talk with ibises and challenge monsters."

"Yes, daughter." Papa smiled. "But help me upstairs before you go."

In the tower library, Papa instructed Odile on how to work the heavy mechanism that lowered the wappentier's cage for feeding or recovering the eggs. The wappentier shuddered and its musty smell filled the room.

"When the time comes, search the highest peaks." Papa unlocked the latch with a white quill and swung the door open. The hinges screeched. Or maybe the wappentier cried out.

Her heart trembled inside her ribs and she pulled at her father even as he stepped back.

The wappentier stretched its wings a moment before taking flight. It flew past them—its plumage, which she had always imagined would feel harsh and rough—was gentle like a whisper. The tower shook. Stones fell from the window's sides and ledge as it broke through the wall.

Odile thought she heard screams below. Horses and men.

Her father hugged her then. He felt frail, as if his bones might be hollow, but he held tight a moment. She could not find the words to assure him that she'd return.

Outside the tower, she found the king's carriage wallowed in the moat. The horses still lived, though they struggled to pull the carriage free. After years of a diet of game meat, the wappentier may have more hungered for rarer fare. There was no sign of a driver.

She waded into the water, empty of any swans, she noticed. The carriage door hung ajar. Inside was empty. As she led the horses to land, Odile looked up in the sky and did not see the wappentier. It must no longer be starved. She hoped the king was still down in the cellar smashing eggs.

She looked back at the tower and thought she saw for a moment her father staring down from the ruined window. She told herself there might be another day for books and fathers. Perhaps even swans. Then she stepped up to the driver's seat and took hold of the reins and chose to take the road.

As far as you can recall, the boy had an average and pale face. The only thing even remotely remarkable about him was the fact that even in the deadest winter cold his eyes remained warm and soft and brown. You try to remember what happened to him . . .

YOU DREAM

EKATERINA SEDIA

This is a recurring dream, the kind that lingers, and lately it has become more frequent. And it takes a while to realize that you are not, in fact, standing in front of the brick apartment building, its doorway cavernous and warm, your hands in your pockets, cigarette smoke leaking slowly between your lips and into the frozen air. It takes you a while to even remember that you've quit smoking years ago. And yet, here it is, clinging to the collar of your winter coat in a persistent, suffocating cloud, and you can taste it still.

It takes you even longer to remember why you dreamt about this building on the outskirts of Moscow—that you used to live there, but this is not why; you're there because of the boy who used to live in the same building but the other entrance. You cannot remember his name or whether you were really friends or just nodded at each other, passing by like boats in the lonely concrete sea of the yard, a fringe of consumptive poplars looking nothing like the palms of the tropical isles neither of you were ever likely to see. You know, though, that there was never any unpleasant physicality between the two of you, even after you learned to throw your body between yourself and whoever was trying to get too close.

You sit up in your bed and want a smoke, and whisper to yourself, *It was never sex. Never.* It was a defensive reflex, the same as a lizard that aborts its tail and escapes while some predator dumbly noses around the mysteriously wriggling appendage. You'd learned to do it with your entire body, and only the spirit escaped, not watching from the distance, running instead for the hills and the razor slash of the distant horizon. It was always about escaping.

Anyway, the boy: as far as you can recall, he had an average and pale face, he was short and slouched, his hands always in the pockets of his ratty hand-me-down winter coat, too short for him. His straight dark hair was always falling ungracefully across his forehead, and the only thing even remotely remarkable about him was the fact that even in the deadest winter cold his eyes remained warm and soft and brown, and he looked at everything with the same subdued delight. Finding oneself in the diffuse cone of his nearsighted gaze was both disconcerting and comforting, since he seemed to be the only person in the entire universe who honestly didn't want anything from you.

You try to remember what happened to him—you think vaguely that he died as a teen after being drafted, died somewhere in Chechnya; or maybe it was his older brother, and the boy just disappeared one day. Maybe he is still there, at his old apartment, and the memory of his death is a confabulated excuse for not having kept in touch. That seems likely.

It's time to get up anyway, and you stare out the window; you've moved from the gray suburbs to the sort-of center, near the Moscow River's bend, where it is somewhat less gray and the lights of opulence are visible across the river. You try to be satisfied with your lot in life, but discontent lingers, so you eye your pantyhose, tangled and twisted into a noose, and your short skirt, the one you're getting too old for, and you keep getting a sneaking suspicion that your immediate boss feels the same way and soon enough he'll trade you for a newer model, like he does with his BMWs.

So you call in sick. No one minds since there's yet another economic crisis in progress, and chances are no one will be paid until right before the New Year. And they can type their own damn reports, those twelve managers and only two of you to do the actual work. It doesn't matter. You dig through your wardrobe and find half-forgotten woolly tights, scratchy and severe and thick, and a long gabardine skirt with a broken zipper, which you fix with a safety pin. You wrap your head in the flowery kerchief every Russian woman owns—even if she never bought one, it was given as a gift, or, barring all normal means of acquisition, spontaneously generated in her apartment. You suspect that yours is one of those, an immaculately gotten kerchief with fat cabbage roses on a velvet-black background with tangled fringe.

It is warmer outside than you expected, what with the dreams of winter and whatnot, but the wind is still cutting and it throws handfuls of bright yellow poplar leaves in your face as you walk away from the embankment. Your shoulders stoop under a gray woolen cardigan, and your walk is awkward, unnatural in flat shoes, and you feel as if you keep falling heavily on your heels, the familiar support elevating them above ground missing. Your face feels naked without the makeup.

St. Nicholas' church is open and empty, the smell of frankincense and whatever church incense they use there tickling your nostrils and yet infusing you with reflexive peace, conditioned like a dog that salivates at the sound of the bell. You buy a thin brown candle and plop it in front an icon, wherever there's space, and mumble something prayer-like under your breath.

The mass is long over and only black-clad old women are there, rearranging and correcting falling candles, sweeping the heavy stone tiles of the floor. They look at you with their cataracts, blue like skimmed milk, and mumble under their breath. You catch the word "whore" and try not to take it personally—after all, this is what they call every woman who is not them, whether she is mortifying her flesh with woolen tights or not. You try to will your legs to not itch and end up backing behind a column and scratching discreetly.

You are not sure what brought on this religious impulse, except for the boy you miss without having known him. Then you think of the rest of his family, his numerous siblings, always hungry and underdressed, and it resolves in your memory, finally: he was a son of a defrocked priest who was forced into disgrace and living in a common apartment building instead of a parish house, no longer surviving off tithes, but the very modest salary of a night watchman. His wife worked at the meat factory across the street and always brought home bulging sacks dripping with blood, filled with tripe and bones and stomachs, and it was never enough for their brood, which, by your estimate, was somewhere between seven and nine. Poorer and more fecund than real priests, even.

"May I help you?" A soft, stuttering voice startles you from your reverie and you spook upright, your head springing back and almost breaking the nose of the speaker.

The young priest steps back, calm, his hands behind his back. "You look spiritually wrought," he says, smile bristling his soft beard, light as flax. "You need guidance."

"I don't," you say with unnecessary force, the wraiths of your twelve bosses rearing their heads, the images of people always telling you what you need. "I need information. Why would a priest be defrocked?"

"Depends," he answers with the same softness, the change of topic barely breaking his cadence. "Are we talking about now, or in the past? Because the synod just defrocked a priest the other day, for marrying two men."

"No," you say. "Before—in the seventies or early eighties. A priest in Moscow was defrocked. He had children."

"Most of us do," young Father says, musing. "Back then, that would've been insubordination, most likely. Failure to respect the hierarchy. Talking badly about the hierarchy. Or possibly a failure to inform—or maybe informing on the wrong people, the wrong things." He sighs heavily, his gray eyes misting over. "You know, I grew up in the church. I'm not afraid of ever losing my faith—when I was young, I saw one priest beating another up with an icon."

Normally you would laugh at the image, but his thoughtful sincerity stops you. "I see," you say.

"Do you know that priest's name?"

"Father Dmitri," you say.

"No last name?"

You shake your head and feel stupid.

"Do you know what church he was assigned to before his defrocking?"

"No. I was just thinking about his son . . . they used to live in the same apartment building as I did."

"Go visit them, then," he says flatly. "They were probably too poor to buy another apartment."

"I don't . . . " You want to tell him that you really don't want to see anyone from your past, anyone who would recognize you and put together the images of you—then and now, past and present—and find the comparison lacking.

But he is already losing interest, backing away. "You need to get baptized," he says before turning away, toward the old women who wait for his glance as if it were a blessing.

"How do you know I'm not?" you call after, raising your voice unacceptably.

"You're tormented," he calls back, just as loud.

The priest is wrong—your mother had baptized you at birth, even though such things were frowned upon back in 1970s. She even took you to the Easter and Christmas masses, where you stood on your aching feet for hours, holding a candle that dripped hot wax on your hands. The memory brings only boredom and unease and doesn't lessen whatever spiritual torment the priest saw in you. He doesn't know that the church with its battling priests isn't as calming to you as it is to him—you worry that you will now have comical nightmares of priests in their long black robes and tall hats pummeling each other with icons and candlesticks. You are really not looking for salvation from them, but from that quiet boy in your childhood. No one else had such kind eyes. You sigh, regretful that your young self was so unaware of how rare a treasure this kindness was—and you're not even sure if such optimism should be commended.

By the time you were twelve, you certainly knew enough of those who were not kind, of the tiny cave under the very first flight of stairs by the apartment building's entrance, the cave you always had to run past because of those who hid there—boys who would reach out and hold you against the wall and put their hands under your skirt and down your sweater. You never told your mom why you would wait for her to come home from work, when the shadows grew long, and she couldn't understand that you were not afraid to be home alone—you were afraid of the dash up the flight of stairs, and your two-room apartment could've as well been located on the moon.

You do not remember the faces of those boys, just that one who never laid a finger on you; instead, he walked with you sometimes, and watched you get into the elevator, safe. Sometimes the boys under the stairs would beat him, and once they held his face down in the large puddle that manifested in your paved yard every spring and fall—held him until bubbles coming from his silted lips turned into stifled screams and only a chance passerby spooked the hooligans.

When you get home, you unwrap the kerchief and hate it for a while because your hair is now flattened and tangled and you'll have to wash it again. Then you pick up the phone, since there's nothing else to do but to hurl yourself toward the past, since the present refuses to surrender any answers or even passable lies.

Your mother sounds older than she did the last time you spoke, and you try not to feel guilty about her unseen decline in some sanatorium that costs you most of your uncertain salary, and of course it would be cheaper to have her live with you, here, over the black river that smells of gasoline and foams white in the wake of leisure boats. You sigh into the phone and try to ignore all of her unvoiced complaints.

"Mom," you finally say, "do you remember that family that used to live next door, when I was little? The one with seven kids?"

"Vorobyev," she says, her memory as flawless as always. "The youngest boy, Vasya, was such a sweet kid. Always running around in those girls' coats from his older sisters."

That's right, you now remember, those were plaid, too-short girl coats. No wonder everyone teased him; no wonder his unperturbed demeanor incited them to violence—there was no point in such savage humiliation as a girl's coat unless its victim would acknowledge it as such.

"Vasya Vorobyev," she repeats. "Too sad about him."

"What have you heard?" Your heart seizes up and it's ridiculous, you haven't thought about that kid in decades. In forever. "What happened?"

"Anya, his mother, used to call me sometimes," she says. "He's dead, in Osetia last year. Now she's dead too—her heart gave out after that."

"Too bad." You are numb now, numb to the tips of your fingers, and they almost drop the receiver. A deep chill settles in at the loss you aren't sure you've suffered. "Do you remember why was his father was defrocked?"

"No. Why would you care about something like that?"

"I don't," you whisper, and say goodbye. You spend the rest of the day watching TV and pacing and drinking buttermilk straight out of the bottle that fits so comfortably into one hand, and you keep thinking back to the days when you needed two to hold it.

The boy who defended you sometimes. You're glad to have a name, but in your mind he's still that boy—the boy. You're glad to be dreaming about him the next night—at least there he is alive and little, even as other people's hands press his face into the dirty pavement, his teeth making an awful scraping sound that makes you cringe in your sleep. They leave, but not before making lewd gestures in your direction, and you wait for the boy to stagger up, his feet shuffly and his knees buckling under him. He totters but remains standing. You feel lucid even though it is a dream and in it you are still small. "Why was your father defrocked?"

"Why does it matter?" He lisps a bit, his tongue thoughtfully exploring the ragged edge of the chipped front tooth. He doesn't seem to know that he is in your dream.

"Because I need to know what did he do that was so awful, to bring you here. What was it that you were paying for?"

"Looking for the prime mover, huh?" He drops the pretense of childhood and for a second becomes terrifying—still a kid, but somehow older and deader. "I don't know why. Who knows why shit happens, huh? Who knows why you don't tell anyone about them dragging you under the stairs. Why you never told them—"

Your face burns with exposed shame and you snap away from him, the hem of your gabardine dress twirling around your legs, long and smooth and brown in your first pair of nylon pantyhose. "Fuck off," you mutter darkly. And yet you understand his point, the essential impossibility of revealing one's secrets—especially if those secrets are not one's fault. We can get over the wrongs we do, but we cannot forgive ourselves for the wrongs done to us, for our own helplessness.

"Don't be like that." He catches up to you and walks with you across the paved yard, the large puddle in its center only nascent. It must remind him, you think, and then you are suddenly not sure whether the puddle incident happened before or after the chipped tooth.

You sit in your bed upright, your heart strumming against your ribs. You have to go to sleep, you tell yourself, you have to get up early tomorrow, but then you remember it'll be Saturday. So you give up and pull on a pair of jeans and tuck your nightgown into them, throw on a jacket and run down the stairs and across the street—like a wayward moth that woke up in the fall by mistake—toward the fluorescent glimmer of an all-night kiosk.

You buy a gin and tonic in a can—make that two—and a pack of Dunhill's, the red one. You buy a translated detective novel for good measure, and the guy behind the bulletproof glass smiles crookedly. "Got a wild night planned?"

You ignore the familiar sarcasm, so integrated into the national discourse that you notice its absence more than its presence. You spend the rest of the night sitting on the windowsill, the right angle of your legs reflected in the dark windowpane, drinking bitter gin and tonics and smoking with abandon, stuffing the butts into an empty can.

You wait until six in the morning, when the subway is open, and you walk to the station and take the subway and the bus to the street where you grew up. You hope that there's no one there who will recognize you, and you get off at the familiar stop—forgotten just enough to feel uncanny, as if its coincidence with your memory is a miracle, like Jesus seen in a sandwich. Your hopes are dashed the moment your foot touches the asphalt—a high female voice calls your name.

"Look at you," babbles a middle-aged woman, red coat, face painted with too much enthusiasm and not enough artifice. "You haven't changed a bit." She clearly expects you to say the same, and the lie would be easier if you could remember who she was.

"Natasha," she reminds you. "Romanova. We used to be in the same class through the sixth grade. I live one building from yours." She walks along with you, oblivious to your cringing away from her. "What are you doing here? Visiting someone?"

"Vorobyev family," you say before you can come up with a decent lie.

"Oh," she says. "I think they moved—well, the kids had all moved out."

"I heard Vasya's dead," you say.

She looks at you strangely. "Well, stop the presses."

"I just heard."

She looks at you, concerned. "What do you mean? I thought it was you who had found him."

You shake your head at her nonsense, and yet the quiet nightmare dread grabs you by the heart and squeezes harder, as you mumble excuses and break away from the talkative friend you don't remember having and you race ahead to the poplar row that seems fatter and taller and more decayed than before. The asphalted path leads between the trees to the yard surrounded by six identical brick buildings, each nine stories tall with two separate entrances. Your house is the last one on the right, and you race past your entrance. You find their apartment not by the number but by muscle memory—your legs remember how to run to the fourth floor, taking two steps at a time, how to swing abruptly left and skid to a stop in front of a brown door upholstered with quilted peeling pleather diamonds, how to press the doorbell that is lower than you expected—you can reach it without getting on your tiptoes.

It rings deep within the cavern of the apartment, and you know by the apartment's position (you've never been inside) that it has three rooms—barely enough for nine people—not counting a kitchen, and that the balcony looks out into the yard, above the puddle.

A boy with soft brown eyes opens the door, still the same, still in his coat, water dripping down his sallow face, his hair slicked into a toothed fringe over his forehead. You are mostly surprised by the differential in your heights now—some-thing that was just beginning to manifest around the time you left home, when you were sixteen, and would rather have moved in with your first boyfriend (so much older than you) than stayed here, near those stairs that trained you in your lizard defense. Now you're towering over him with your adult, aging self, crow's feet and sagging jeans and all, and he is still twelve (thirteen?), and he looks up at you nearsightedly, his pale face looming up at you as if from under water. You accept it with the fatalism of someone who has bad dreams too often to even attempt to wake up.

"It's you," he says without much surprise. "Come on in."

You do, as you would in a dream. The apartment has suffered some damage—there are water stains on the ceiling and water seeps through the whitewash, dripping down the browned tracks over bubbling, peeling wallpaper. The windows also weep, and the hardwood floors buckle and swell, then squish underfoot like mushrooms.

The boy stands next to you by the window, looking through the water-streaked glass at the sunshine and fluffy clouds outside, at the butter-yellow poplar leaves tossed across the yard by the rising wind. "What is it that you want?"

You are well familiar with logic of dreams and fairy tales, of the importance of choosing your words wisely, of the fragility of the moment—waste your breath on a wrong question and you will never know anything. "How did you die?" you finally ask. "I cannot remember." Other questions will just have to go unanswered.

He points to the puddle outside, wordlessly, and you remember the hands pressing his face into the water, and you standing there, watching, helpless, until there are no more bubbles. Afterward, you tell the grown-ups that you found him like that, and you don't know who did it.

"Why didn't you tell them?"

You're an adult now, and the words come out awkwardly. "I was afraid of what they would do to me if I told. I'm sorry."

He's too much of a gentleman to rub it in your face that he had been defending you then, that he could've walked past and stayed alive.

"It wouldn't have mattered," he says instead. Dead in Chechnya. Dead in Osetia. Disappeared one night without a trace. Dead in a kayaking accident. You remember all his deaths and they crowd around the two of you, suffocating and clammy.

And then it's just you again, standing on the sidewalk outside, watching the eddies of yellow leaves spiraling around the ankles of your brown boots with worn, lopsided heels. And then it is just you, walking to the bus stop, promising to yourself to never return here, to never look back at the fourth story window and all the dead faces of the boy pressed against the weeping glass.

The guitarist stays out all night, has no real friends, and cannot maintain any kind of relationship. But how does this make him any different from any other musician? Well, he's had a very, very long career . . .

RED BLUES

MICHAEL SKEET

Your hand closes around the neck. Just for a second, you let your slender, grave-cold fingertips caress the gentle curve. Long since a stranger to the subtleties of tactile sensation, you nevertheless rejoice in the smoothness of the back of the neck, in its slender vulnerability. Then you press those fingers down, firmly but not too hard.

You begin to play.

Fingers flying over the strings of your vintage Gibson, you give them your twenty-seventh variation on the verse of "They Can't Take That Away From Me." It's your tenth night of a two-week gig in this club and the tenth time you've played this song they think they know. No one in the audience, though, has heard it the same way twice. You've memorized a lot of different versions of this song.

As Garrett and Holman join in for the chorus, you switch to variation one thousand eighteen. The two fit well together: their tempos match, and the flourish of sixteenth notes you've crammed into each bar of the chorus gives the impression of furious improvisation. After two choruses of this you head into the bridge, keeping the tempo but dropping back to an earlier variation on the tune, with more eighths than sixteenths and a couple of strategically placed discords to give the punters the impression of something new going on. Then it's back into the chorus—a different variation again—and as you head home you begin scouting the audience, looking to see if she's here tonight. It takes one more chorus until she drifts into view through the smoke and by then you've already caught her scent. As you scatter a series of eccentric chords through the final bars of the song, you're already planning tonight's conquest, with the same thoroughness with which you've planned tonight's set.

When you look up to begin the next number, though, she is gone. You could make her stay, could weave a web of pheromones and waking dreams around her until she has no more will than your Gibson, but you have rules you follow in cases such as this. There will be no coercion; she invites you in, or you wait another day and try again. You wait.

Most people misunderstand the beauty of jazz. They revel in its unpredictability, its scattershot virtuosity and the emotion with which their favorite practitioners approach it. For you, though, jazz is complex mathematics, a poetry of numbers. Improvisation is what people resort to when memory fails them. You have built a house of memory over hundreds of years, and in the last six decades, since you took up this music as a distraction, your memory has not failed you once.

You are in mid-set on the eleventh night when you detect her presence, then see her sitting down with a group of friends. She brushes her hair behind one ear as she orders a drink. You're playing "A Shine on Your Shoes." You've kept the sprightly tempo of the original, but from the bridge you set off into an extended solo that quotes from just about every Dietz-Schwartz tune on the sound track of the film *The Band Wagon*. None of your audience recognizes the gesture, but they appreciate the overall effect, and that's enough. You're surprised for a moment when Garrett, on bass, actually matches you note for note during your two-bar segment of "Dancing in the Dark," but you recover quickly enough and return his smile with a nod. The intuitive pattern-matching instincts of human beings can still, it seems, take you by surprise.

Instinct is no substitute for experience, though. As Garrett takes a verse, you fix your gaze on her. She has given you a good chase, but she will weaken in the end. They always do. She knows you are watching her, and fights against the hold of your eyes. When she wins, you concede gracefully. There is no hurry. You are never in a hurry.

You isolate her scent from amongst the charred nicotine and oxidized alcohol smells even before you begin playing on your twelfth night, and that knowledge brings you one step closer to conquests. She still resists your eyes, but you can smell her growing interest as easily as you can see the small shift of her shoulders and tilt of her head as she begins, mid-way through the set, to isolate herself from her companions. It's time to focus the music directly onto her, and to let her know what you are doing. "Drop the next one," you say to Garrett on your right. He passes the message to Holman behind his drum kit, and you forget about "I Got Rhythm," swinging directly into "How About You?"

The music is light, fanciful, and the version you've chosen to remember has plenty of airy frills at the end of each line of the chorus. It's appropriate to your mood, now that you've seen her, and you know that before the night is over she will be yours. In a gesture that echoes your mood, you let Garrett have two choruses to himself; you actually enjoy the fat, staccato thumping of the bass as his thick, calloused fingers fly over the strings. Garrett looks like an old man, but is in fact only thirty-eight. You've appreciated the irony since you've known him: you look like you're not a day over thirty, when in fact you're about fifty-five thousand days over thirty. He's been a heroin addict since the evening of his first professional gig sixteen years ago. In a sense that has made him a good partner. You don't bother him about what he puts into his veins and he doesn't bother you about what you take out of theirs. There is no feeling between you—there could never be—but you look out for him, do what you can to keep him alive in spite of himself. Consistency in companionship is something your kind is drawn to. You used to tell yourself that it was the heroin that kept you from deepening your relationship with Garrett, but in the last fifty years you've made a habit of keeping your professional and private lives separate. Good sidemen may be easy to find, but understanding ones aren't.

Your private life is beginning to intrude now, the hunger demanding your attention before you're ready. She's brushing her hair back behind one ear, drawing attention to the pale band of her neck; the gesture almost causes you to miss your entry for the final chorus. Not for the first time you wonder if this one is aware of her effect on you, has been playing you over the two weeks you've been hunting her.

"Savoy Blues" is next, the first song you learned. Chess had been your distraction of choice before then, its multiplicity of potential moves appealing to the strong sense of memory that develops in the living dead. But after a century chess was losing its appeal, and the first time you heard Lonnie Johnson play—1926, in Chicago—your mathematician's soul was somehow able to discern from a single two-minute performance the infinite potential jazz might have to an undying intellect. Through Johnson you met Eddie Lang, and it's not entirely your fault that Lang died so young—nor can Charlie Christian's death a few years after that be laid solely at your feet. At least a part of them lives on in you.

That part emerges as you begin "Seven Come Eleven." You are no fan of bop, but enough of Christian's blood continues to mingle with yours that you are almost compelled to echo the scatter-gun single-line riffing, the eccentric chords and rhythms of the pioneer of bebop guitar. The audience loves it, too. Their desire for novelty overrides all other considerations; it's one of the things you dislike about bop. The precision of swing demands more of both performer and listener. Nobody has time for that any more, not even her.

Now she is leaning over her table, transfixed as your fingers fly over the strings, her desire to unite with the music so strong you can taste its musky flavor on your tongue. She is yours, now, captured by the music. You do not have to guess: you know it in your blood, your skin.

Nevertheless, when you pack your guitar at the end of the set, she is nowhere to be seen. Somehow, she is breaking free of the music's spell.

Tonight, the last number in your set is "The Red Blues." The lyrics—and the musical for which it was written—hardly represent Cole Porter at his best. But Porter was a great tunesmith, even in his declining years. This tune is superb raw material. You have an affinity with this song; playing it allows you to project into the mind of each member of the audience something dark but compelling, an emotional thunderstorm. Every entity has a piece of music to which it resonates; "The Red Blues" is yours.

Is it hers? She has come late, settling into a seat alone only a few minutes before. At least she is here. You have only one night after this song and you are loath to degrade yourself by forcing her into your grasp. You're going to have to do something, though.

What you decide to do is to put more than your memory and technique into this song. It's what you've seen humans do and though the prospect is distasteful, you are willing to try it. There are limits to patience, after all.

You don't look at her as you start playing; it requires all of your concentration to do this. Fingers flying over the strings, you make the music black with night and eternal despair, letting it fill you until the hairs on your neck are standing erect with it. Then you pour out of you all the fear and rage and power of the night, sending them splashing into the club and willing the listeners to soak it up, drown in it.

Then you sit up, the strings still vibrating with the final notes. The room is silent. Even the wait staff is immobile and voiceless. No one looks at you; they are all wrestling with themselves—some in tears, some struggling to suppress cries of horror or triumph according to their natures. Feeling uncomfortably numb, you wonder if this phenomenon is repeatable, if someday you'll be able to study the impact you have on your sidemen.

And on her? You smell a hint of fear; has some primitive part of her brain warned her that she has been the target of your play? She is still here, though.

Now the spell breaks, and the audience is on its feet. You are calm as you put away your guitar; you've heard the shouts and applause too many times over too many years to care much anymore. You play for one person a night these days.

It's time. You wish Holman would take the equipment home with him tonight, and he does. Garrett has already disappeared into the dark and the smoke, looking to mingle neurochemical salvation with his blood. Your blood demands satisfaction too, but even though it's been days and your hunger is frost-sharp and desperate, you will not spoil the hunt by breaking the rules.

You look up after locking your Gibson in its case; she is no longer in the club. Even as you rub your eyes, your nose tells you that she's gone. Another twenty-four empty hours, then, and one last chance. There are plenty of hangers-on clustering around the front of the stage and it would be easy to take any one of them. Once you would have done that, if only to fill the emptiness. But, as your years have run into decades, you have come to believe that emptiness can be more meaningful than most of the things you've tried to fill it with. You let yourself melt into the gloom and slip out the back door, to a dust-blown alley and a bone-dry basalt sky.

She's not there. You admit that a part of you had been expecting her to be waiting for you. Perhaps you're not what you once were. After so many unchanging decades, contemplating deterioration is an unfamiliar sensation.

At the end of the alley, though, a figure is waiting. She's downwind, you realize; that's why you saw her first. "I was hoping you'd waited," you say.

"I wasn't going to," she says. "That last song was for me, wasn't it?"

"They all were," you say, struggling to control the excitement rising in you. "If only the last one actually got through, that's all right. Most people don't even hear that much."

She is walking, you note, on your right side; the guitar case is between you, your hand occupied in carrying it. "I don't usually . . . go out with musicians," she says.

"I'm not like other musicians," you say, and it is mostly true.

She doesn't answer that, but she continues walking beside you. Under the streetlights her soft, pleasant face looks more drawn, pale; her eyes when she looks at you are black and endless as your nights. When she sees you watching her, she self-consciously brushes her short dark hair back behind her ears. She smells of partially oxidized alcohol and burnt tobacco, but these are veneers only; her true scent is there too, under her white T-shirt and worked into the fabric of her jeans. Her throat is smooth and pale as polished chalcedony. No veins are visible, but the blood is there; you can almost taste it.

"Why do you play only the old songs?" she asks, destroying the pleasure of your contemplation.

"As opposed to what passes for pop music today?" She's probably only asking to be polite; you try to be polite. "The older songs are more conducive to jazz," you say. "They allow changes in key that give me more patterns of notes to choose from when I play."

"I've always wondered how jazz musicians improvise," she says. "I've been in the club for just about all of your dates and I've never heard you play a tune the same way twice." She mistakes careful selection for improvisation, you think. You are not really offended, though. Everyone makes that mistake; they've been making it for nearly eighty years. And each year it grows easier to fool them as your store of knowledge grows. Teaching yourself new permutations of old songs is the only thing that gets you through endless days in darkened basement rooms.

"It must be a bit frightening, I'd think," she says after a moment's thought. "Not really knowing what you're going to play next, and if it'll work? I know I'd be scared."

"It's not really that bad." There are plenty of things that frighten you—loneliness, the bitter taste of so much that you used to enjoy—but being on stage is not one of them. "Besides," you say, "the excitement more than compensates."

"Oh, yeah. I was in my high school band. I was always afraid I was going to throw up before concerts, but once they started I loved it."

The excitement you feel is the excitement of the hunt, but perhaps at some level she knows what you're talking about. Her face is animated now, her eyes glinting with reflected mercury vapor light. Her breathing is more rapid, and you can feel the flush stealing into her cheeks and throat. Her growing awareness is exciting her, and you are in turn feeding on that excitement.

It has been your intention to take her home first, but the blood rising to her skin is beginning to inflame you. You remind yourself that, after a few weeks of waiting, a few more minutes shouldn't be all that much to deal with.

A dark alley beckons, though. You pull her in, turning so that your black leather blocks any street view of that white T-shirt. "Hey," she begins, but her lips stay parted and her eyes are shining as you lean the guitar case against a wall and place your hands on her neck, cup her face in your hands. "Not here," she protests, but her face tilts up to yours. Now your cold hands are absorbing her own heat, sending it back to her, and when you press your mouth to hers you are warm enough that she does not start at the sensation. She can taste your desire, and though she does not understand it, she responds to it. One hand stroking her neck, you move the other down to a breast, brush against it until the nipple stiffens from the gentle pressure. Then you shift your hand lower. There is no pleasure for you in this, but you want her blood suffusing her skin and your weeks of observing have told you that this is the variation to play on this particular tune.

When you lower your lips to her neck, she throws her head back. "Ah," she says.

Her skin tears easily, onionskin paper under a quill pen.

She tenses briefly as you begin to drink, but makes no sound beyond a soft moan; and not for the first time you wonder if you have found something more than a victim here. Her hands still grip your shoulders and briefly your spirit soars as you try to make yourself think about sharing yourself, your everlasting life, with her.

But her blood is spicy and hot with the sharp odor of dust on hot metal and it has been days since you last fed. Before you are aware of what you are doing, her hands have released you and her arms have dropped limply. There is still plenty of blood, but it cools rapidly. For a moment you pause, bitterly chastising yourself for your lack of feeling, of restraint.

Then you return to feeding. You will have to start over again because of this, and it may be some time before you eat again. And what is the point of chastising yourself, anyway? You are out all night, you have no real friends, and you cannot maintain any kind of relationship. How does this make you any different from any other musician?

You let the body drop into a pile of empty boxes then pick up your guitar case. As you walk out of the alley, you brush your hair back behind one ear.

Geoff Yarrow is a man who aids you in a time of despair, but for Colin what begins as a way out of his madness and grief becomes harrowing path into something even deeper and stranger . . .

THE MOON WILL LOOK STRANGE

LYNDA E. RUCKER

They were draining the fish pond in the tiny walled garden outside his window. Colin awoke to the sound of their voices, Jimena, who owned the house with her husband Tomas, and that of Madih, the young Moroccan man who carried out repairs around the property. Colin flung open the wooden shutters and his first thought was that Samantha would be outraged—even at the savage age of six and a half she couldn't bear to see any living thing suffer—and then he remembered, and wondered where such a cruel and unbidden thought had come from. Not for one moment, night or day, sleeping or awake, did he ever forget that she was dead. Not even in his dreams.

He shouted at them, "Why are you killing the fish? Does Tomas know what you're doing?"

Jimena and Madih looked back at him, startled and uncomprehending. Colin backed away from the window and realized he was naked. He fumbled for a pair of shorts, fought with the heavy wooden door of his room and staggered out into the burning Granada sunshine.

"The fish!" he shouted again. He imagined them, the brilliant orange goldfish gasping and dying on the concrete floor of the pool. They gaped at him, then Jimena said something sharp to Madih and they turned around. "Que?" he said, mustering one of the only Spanish words that he knew. They ignored him, and it wasn't as if he'd be able to understand them if they responded anyway. His will flagged along with his indignation, faded so completely that he lacked even the gumption to take his lunatic and half-dressed self back indoors. He stood there instead, under the burning sun, watching them kill the fish, and thought of Samantha.

He'd never meant to end up in Spain. That was an understatement, the punctuation to a whole long series of understatements, of things not meant to happen. After Ann left him he'd gone to the airport in a kind of fugue, thinking only to get away. He carried nothing with him save for his passport and wallet, and he paid cash for a one-way ticket to London. Just like that, and he felt like giggling with glee at how easy it all was. He supposed the purchase would see him flagged in a Homeland Security file somewhere, just the sort of thing he'd have railed against once, when he had time to feel outrage about anything besides what had been taken from him. As the green Oregon landscape fell away below him a sense of lightness seized him: he thought of his things, all the stuff you accumulate living a life, abandoned in the little apartment off Belmont Avenue that he and Ann and Samantha had shared, and of the bar at Luna filling up and him just *not there*, not pulling pints of Black Butte, not mixing shit like lemon drops for customers as high-maintenance as their drink orders. He thought of other places where he would not be, like he was shuffling a series of snapshots: he would not be at the Mount Tabor Pub, or flipping through stacks of vinyl at Music Millennium, or at the dinosaur display at the science museum with Samantha. He imagined rubbing each image out as he thought it. He was a man with no past now.

At Heathrow the noise and lights had hurt his ears. He slept for a while in an arrivals lounge and then spoke to an Easy Jet agent who said she could get him on a cheap flight to Granada right away if he got himself over to Stansted immediately. His flight was only about two-thirds full, so he was able to ensconce himself in the back far from the mirth and drunkenness of the holidaymakers claiming the rest of the seats. He knew next to nothing about Spain, except that if he could manage to make it to the tip he could catch a ferry to Morocco, where he could disappear. Like Burroughs or Bowles, lost in Marrakesh, or even deeper into Africa, where tourists never trod. It wasn't so easy as it once was to vanish off the face of the earth, but he felt certain he could do it there.

But first things first: he needed sleep. He took a bus into the city and got off at the top of a narrow walled cobblestone street. The flight of stairs to his left led straight into the past: a maze of walled, whitewashed streets, ancient and defiant, where the last of the Moors fled as their world vanished around them, in the shadow of the magnificent Alhambra Palace just across the canyon, an implacable yet ghostly reminder of what was, what might have been and what would never be. A fitting place for him to disappear in as well, in the soothing, dizzying, exotic maze the bus driver had called the Albaicin. A scrawny graffitied cat, scrawled in various stages of distress at this turn and that, wore a legend reminding him that Fumar Mata and that much he could figure out because he'd seen it on a crumpled cigarette pack—smoking kills. Or not, he reasoned. Samantha hadn't been a smoker, after all. At six, she'd not had time to pick up the habit. He rounded a corner and saw the poor feline hanging from a chalk noose. The white walls crumbled round boarded up windows, and he dodged dog shit smeared on cobblestones. He couldn't understand the words scrawled on walls but images of the Pope as devil, and of Che Guevara, did the speaking for him. He followed a trail of Arabic script. Was he already in Morocco? He reeled, feverish, as the sun climbed. He did not know what he ought to do. A child's laughter mocked him round corners but when he tried to follow no one was there.

At last he came upon a massive wooden door with a sign above: he couldn't read what it said but someone had plastered a Lonely Planet sticker on an upstairs window. He hammered at the door for a long time, until a stooped Spanish man he later came to know as Tomas appeared. Colin managed to stammer out a request for a room, which Tomas fortunately understood. Colin pressed his remaining euros into Tomas's hand and followed him through the doorway, and then another, and into the walled garden. In the room off the goldfish pond he eased his sweaty body between thick white sheets. When he woke it was dark and he was starving. He didn't know where he was, and he thought, I've done something insane. For one instant panic rose like bile in the back of his throat and then, his heart still hammering, he laughed. Why not do something insane, when fate had dealt him such an insane turn in the first place? Colin glanced at his wristwatch and saw he'd slept, not for the day, but the day and the night and the next day, and now it was night again. He stumbled out of his room and the moon hung high above him and he heard Yarrow's voice: *You will know,* he said, *you will know because the moon will look strange.*

Colin finally went inside and brewed strong black coffee, two cups in the dark before opening the windows again and peering out at the fish pond carnage. They had a large trash can, filled with water, and were scooping the fish out in nets. Not killing them after all, then. They were merely cleaning the pond, which was green with algae and might have been bottomless for all you could see beneath the surface. He briefly considered feeling foolish but concluded it was a waste of his time. Jimena and Madih thought he was a lunatic anyway. And who was he to say they were wrong?

He donned a shirt that didn't smell too bad and headed out without another word to them. Once again he'd slept much of the day away, and the sun was low in the sky when he slipped into a bar off the Plaza Larga, where he stood at the counter, smoking cigarettes and drinking beer and gobbling up free plates of tapas. The alcohol didn't do much, just numbed his senses enough to make it bearable. Clearly the harder stuff was easy enough to come by: he needed only to look at the wasted, furtive desperate faces of some passersby, of squatters from the abandoned Romany caves up in the hills, to be certain. But he was afraid of getting trapped here. He ought to get a move on in fact, tomorrow or next day at the latest—so he kept telling himself. He imagined someone would come for him—and by someone he meant Ann and her family—tipped off by a trail of debit card deductions from a rapidly shrinking account.

But no one did. Still, this wasn't even close to the oblivion he'd dreamed. He had once seen a program on television about nomads in the Moroccan desert. He wouldn't need euros or his debit card and no one would think to look for him there. His thoughts spiraled down like this, as they always did when he drank at the bar off the Plaza Larga. Other bars inspired other types of thoughts, and all were good enough for what he really needed, which was not to think about why he couldn't seem to get up in the morning and stick out his thumb and hitch a ride farther south. Because he thought Samantha might be lost somewhere in the Albaicin, and that was crazy, and yet he wasn't leaving if there was any possibility that he could be right. Yarrow had never said how he would know, except for the part about the moon. But Colin knew it was her. It wasn't only seeing: he'd glimpsed her in his peripheral vision, sure, rounding corners—the heel of her yellow sandals, a flash of the blue T-shirt she'd got down at Newport the last time the three of them went whale watching, the one she loved so much they'd buried her in it. He could smell her, too. Sometimes he could hear her, the soft songs she'd whisper under her breath when she played by herself or was otherwise occupied and unaware of anyone's attention on her. Any time after dusk was a good time for her, and so he liked to be good and drunk by the time dusk rolled around. Because while thinking of her made him realize what people really meant when they said dumb meaningless things like "He loved her more than life itself," because he knew the sound and the smell of her was the result of some miracle he'd brought about with the help of Geoff Yarrow, he was afraid of her as well, afraid of what he and Yarrow had done.

He was pretty sure that after it happened, he and Ann wouldn't have survived as a couple anyway. He found he couldn't bear to look at her and see his own grief reflected. The first time he'd slept with someone he met at a club, not telling her about Samantha, not telling her where he worked or even his name, he felt he had turned into someone else, and from that moment on he started to think about disappearing. When he came home the next morning Ann was dressing for work and did not even bother to ask where he'd been. It seemed stupid to him that they still did things like going to work, or grocery shopping, but they did, because what was the alternative? He wanted to find out.

Sleeping with nameless women he met in clubs hadn't torn them apart, though. Yarrow took care of that. The night Ann came home unexpectedly had done him in. When she walked into the bathroom and saw the viscera cooling in the tub. She freaked out like he'd just slaughtered somebody there, even though anybody could see it was just small animal parts. She said she didn't care. Said she was leaving.

"I only wanted to bring her back to us," he pleaded. "Yarrow and me, we were doing some—magick," the *k* at the end of the word like an unfamiliar aftertaste. Yarrow always called it that: *magick*. Colin was sure that once Ann understood that she wouldn't be mad any longer. "You're sick." That was all she would say. That, and "Yarrow's sick too. I hate you both." She was frightened but wouldn't let him touch her. Later, of course, he realized she'd been right. It always went wrong in stories, after all, like that one, about the monkey's paw. He went to see Yarrow, to tell him to stop the experiments, that he'd changed his mind. The experiments had increasingly frightened him, anyway, even as they'd seem to embolden Yarrow. What had begun as a way out of his madness had come to seem like a harrowing path into something deeper. The last thing they'd done, the thing with the live rats that left the mess in the tub, had left him feeling sick and shaken for days.

Yarrow laughed, yellow teeth clacking behind thin lips, and said, "Too late, brother. It was always too late."

Yarrow said it wouldn't be like he was thinking. Not some dripping horror out of those old fifties comics. He said that bringing her back involved rending the very fabric of time and space. He said it casually, like he was talking about having another cup of coffee. It was the kind of thing Ann would have laughed at in different circumstances. She had no patience for metaphysical flights of fancy, for New Age speculation. Not that Yarrow embodied the daffy benevolence of a New Age guru. Yarrow was bad. Ann had said so the first time they'd met him, years ago, at a show at Berbati's. Colin couldn't remember the band that played but he remembered Yarrow sidling up to them and striking up a conversation and how Ann excused herself and didn't come back until Yarrow had gotten bored and moved on. "If I were a dog I could've smelled it on him," she said. "I'd growl at him if he walked into the room." Colin wondered how to tell her he'd given Yarrow their number and planned to hang out with him the next day. Yarrow had a great collection of '60s psychedelia on vinyl, he'd said, stuff you couldn't find anywhere nowadays, and they'd talked about Fantagraphics comics and Feral House books. Yarrow said he knew a guy that used to write for them. He was cool; Colin couldn't understand why Ann was being so weird about it all. Recently he'd looked back on the encounter and thought, did he deliberately pick us out? Was he planning to use us? Did he foresee it, or worse, did he make it happen? *Did my talking to Yarrow that night lead to everything that followed, to Samantha's conception and birth and her running in front of the car?* To the culmination of Yarrow's great experiment, at his expense, at the expense of them all. He'd considered the incident over and over, how Samantha's hand had slipped from his, how he'd let his attention wander for just a moment or two. Ann never said she blamed him. She never said much of anything, really. It would have been easier; he could have grown indignant and defended himself, convincing himself in the process that he was blameless.

Colin remembered how Yarrow had grinned at him the night he went to him following the bathtub debacle, those yellow teeth, the thin face and thin fingers and thin body racked by coughing fits only interrupted when he spoke or drew another drag off the hand-rolled cigarette that perpetually dangled from one hand. "I'm dying, too, you know," he said. "Not in that we're-all-dying bullshit way, but soon. Within a year, the doctor says. Think anybody'll care enough to bring me back?" Colin didn't answer. Not for the first time he wondered how old Yarrow might be: forty, or sixty, or more, or less. He had an agelessness about him that made him seem immortal. And, Colin thought: he looks just like a wolf. A lanky, starving, vicious wolf. He's going to eat me alive. Now. Colin said, "Help me."

Some tourists at the other end of the bar were talking to him. It took him a while to realize it. He wondered how they'd known he spoke English, but everywhere he went people seemed to know he didn't belong there. They moved down toward him with their drinks and soon the five of them were talking louder and louder and shrieking with unfunny laughter. One of the women was especially attractive, with a strong profile that reminded him of Ann. He thought about trying to sleep with her but then pictured himself as he looked at that moment: seedy and drunk, alcohol and nicotine seeping from his pores. Maybe seedy and drunk *was* her type—you never knew—but he somehow doubted it. She and her friends were all American college students on a semester abroad and he saw in a flash his role in their story of this night. He was the weird and dissolute old guy, well past thirty, maybe even thirty-five. Once he realized this he started to play it up. Apparently seedy and drunk *was* her type. He couldn't remember what he'd said or done to close the deal or what path they took to the place where she was staying but somehow he was in her bed, she was under him and his cock felt harder than it ever had before and she was making noises that he guessed were pleasure, and then he came like all his life was pouring out of him into her. She was saying something but he couldn't hear her above the roaring in his ears. All at once it was a wolf's face he saw beneath him, and the grin stretching across yellowed teeth belonged to Yarrow. Yet her voice, not Yarrow's, reached him, and before he could understand he started telling her "sorry, sorry," because he figured he'd done something wrong, and she said it again, "You're hurting me."

"God, I'm sorry," he said again, and rolled off her. "It's okay," she said. She was waiting for him to say something else, he could tell, but he couldn't. She said, "God, that was fantastic" and when he didn't reply she flounced over onto one side. He felt bad, but lay quietly until it sounded like she'd stopped faking being asleep and really was, and he slipped out of her narrow bed and into the adjoining room. A clock blinked in a corner; it was not even midnight yet, though it felt very late indeed. He had a moment of panic fumbling with the unfamiliar lock, but saw the keys on a nearby table, and he let himself out.

He was relieved to find himself near the Plaza Nuevo and not lost in some part of town he didn't know. Tourists had warned him his first few days there that he'd be mugged in the Albaicin but he'd never had any problems; either he looked too disreputable to bother with or the danger was overstated. Now he fairly staggered along the cobblestone streets, still drunk although he'd felt fine back at the girl's place. He stopped to lean against the wall and shut his eyes while colors squirmed against his lids. Beer rose to the back of his throat and hung there, although he did not vomit. When he came to his senses again he was on his knees, still leaning with one hand against the wall, and he imagined he heard the sound of Yarrow's laughter ringing down the narrow stone pathway. But it was Samantha he smelled, Samantha fresh from her bath sweet with Johnson's Baby Shampoo and that soap Ann used to buy at Lush down on 23rd Avenue. He felt a sudden stab of homesickness, so unfamiliar he didn't know for a moment what to call it. Africa slipped away from him. He said, "I want to go home," and he was crying, just like that, he who had been the strong one throughout, who'd held Ann and his mother and his father and her parents as well through their sobbing. He wondered how he would get back there. He didn't have any money left, not enough for another plane ticket anyhow, but he longed for the alpine meadows of Mount Hood, for a run along the river esplanade, even for a number 20 bus trundling down Burnside late at night, lurching with drunks and jittery with addicts. He cried, remembering. He put up his face to the night and howled like a dog and that felt better too. He still had friends, and family, and when he phoned them tomorrow they would send him money and he would go home again and they would put him back together somehow.

He never saw them coming. A blow to his back that knocked him flat—it didn't take much. He tried to pick himself up but couldn't. He didn't know how many of them there were but it felt like they were swarming him, like there were dozens. Hands reached into pockets, even his shoes, taking his wallet, his wristwatch. He felt something warm and liquid on his face and realized he was bleeding. He tried to talk to them although it took him several minutes for him to realize what he was saying to them. "Thank you." They were freeing him, once and for all. "Thank you," he said again. He stumbled to his feet and the moon swayed above him like the pendulum of a clock. He considered first that it was just as well he'd been unable to fight back, as he might have been seriously injured, and second that he seemed to have gotten drunker, more fucked-up since leaving the girl's apartment, as though the air itself was an intoxicant. Maybe he'd really been hurt. Maybe he'd hit his head when he fell, knocked himself out or something, but he couldn't feel a lump and the only blood came from his cut cheek.

So now he was free. He couldn't go home just yet. He'd get back to Tomas's, get his stuff and get out of there before dawn. He'd hitch down to the tip of Spain and he'd get to Morocco—"Shit," he said; he'd forgotten the ferries cost money. He'd figure something out once he got there. People always did. He had to move. Keep moving. That had been the problem. Keep moving till he got to someplace where she could cross over fully and find him. Once she did he'd get them both back to Ann somehow and she'd see, the three of them would be together again. She would see then how he'd fixed things, made everything right. He understood now why Yarrow had talked about rending the fabric of space and time. You had to tear the world apart to get back the thing that you loved. He stumbled and yelped and nearly fell. He'd imagined that something had reached out to trip him, but it was only a stray brick on the cobblestones.

"Help me," he'd said to Yarrow that day, but Yarrow had just sat back and laughed. "I already helped you," Yarrow said, "it's out of my hands." And maybe he was telling the truth: Yarrow was dead within a week of that visit. He'd been sicker than he'd let on. Colin had heard there would be a memorial service and went because he felt obligated. The ceremony had been held at a shabby home deep in north Portland, officiated by a young woman in thrift-store mourning wear, down to the black veil over an olive-skinned face, unadorned but for the tattooed spider under her left eye. Colin didn't recognize the handful of people in attendance and didn't speak to any of them, though each got up in turn and offered a halting and enigmatic appraisal of Yarrow as someone who had come to their aid in a time of despair. Something in the atmosphere was poisonous, unwholesome, and he slipped out the back before the affair was finished.

Next thing he knew he was in front of Tomas's, swaying in front of the massive wooden door. He couldn't remember how he'd gotten there, and he fumbled for his key, which somehow, blessedly, the thieves hadn't taken, maybe because he'd shoved it deep in the pocket of his jeans, maybe because they took pity on him at the last minute.

In the walled garden the detritus of the pond-cleaning lay scattered on the flagstones. The night was hot and dry yet he heard a splashing sound. The fish pond. They darted just below the surface of the now-clear water, bright and orange in the moonlight. Madih had set rocks about the pond, and built an island clear up to the surface. The fish swam in mad circles about the pond, beaching themselves on the rocks in pairs and threes and fours, their tails flicking madly at the surface of the water and one another, gills heaving, as they fought to thrust themselves back into the pond and then they repeated the same futile exercise over again. Colin watched them for a while. "Stupid," he said to them. "You're so stupid. No wonder you're fish, you're so stupid."

He wandered into his little room and stood in the middle, wondering why he'd bothered. He had a couple of items there, one or two cheap shirts he'd bought after arriving, a pair of shorts. Wasn't like he needed anything. He needed to get out. He tossed his key on the heavy wooden table and turned to leave.

Something made him turn back, a feeling, or something brushing against him perhaps. He couldn't help it. "Samantha?" Her name felt like something dead in his mouth. He couldn't smell her any longer like he had before. Something waited for him in the room that was both Samantha and not Samantha any longer. He took a deep breath. He had to be brave for the both of them. Of course she would be changed by her experience. She would be frightened when she came back, she wouldn't understand what had happened to him, to either of them, and he had to stay strong.

"It's okay, baby," he murmured. "It's going to be okay." Back out, past the doomed fish in the pond, through the doors again and onto the street. She was almost corporeal. He was sure of it. "Come on," he said. He climbed the stone steps, brushing the wall with his fingertips to steady himself. The moon had grown so brilliant it hurt his eyes. He wished all at once that Ann could be with him right now. He imagined what her face would look like when she saw Samantha again. Or maybe it wouldn't be like that at all. Maybe it would be like none of it had ever happened. That would be best, he thought. Otherwise it would be so difficult to explain to people. He wished he had asked Yarrow for more details, how he should act, what they should do.

He was breathing heavily, as though he'd been running a great distance. The stairs were steep and many, but they shouldn't have put him out of breath like this. Yarrow's voice repeated like a loop inside his head: the moon will look strange the moon will look strange the moon will look strange. And he threw his head back and it did look strange, enormous and somehow pregnant, its deep malignant orange saturating the sky. Yarrow had said, this is how you will know. And here round the corner the sky was vast and the town stretched below him and across the canyon the Alhambra flamed, aglow in the miraculous light of this new and different moon. People gathered like wraiths along the wall, milling about and pointing and asking one another questions, but he couldn't understand what they were saying. Tourists on a night visit to the Alhambra amassed on the ramparts, tiny faraway figures. He could hear their cries. It's okay, Samantha, he told her, whether with speech or in his heart he could not be certain. It's okay, people are frightened and you are frightened, but soon everything will be all right again. Everything will be the way it ought to be.

His skin prickled, the back of his neck and along his arms. He swung round, crouching to embrace her, and lost his balance, catching himself with one hand on the cobblestones, an unfortunate recovery as his hand came away covered in dog shit. Something was wrong. "Samantha?" he said, and he heard his voice hoarse and raw with panic. Someone answered him. Someone said, "Thank you, Colin," but Samantha didn't call him Colin, she called him Daddy, and what stepped from the shadows wasn't a little girl but a grown man, yellow teeth bright in the moonlight, his face like a wolf 's. He shimmered in the unnatural light, like he wasn't yet real. The moon was full to bursting now, bright as the sun, and some of the weeping people along the wall seemed to be praying. Colin saw a man hoist himself up on the side, shouting something, tears streaming down his face before hurling himself over and into the canyon on the other side. "You did well," Yarrow said, "you did exactly as I asked you. You did every single thing." Colin, still not understanding, reached for him, reached for something but Yarrow sidestepped him, laughing, and gravelly, mocking, said, "This is the way the world ends. This is the way the world ends and a new one begins. She's not coming back, Colin. She never was." Ann voice: *If I were a dog I could have smelled it on him.* Colin remembered his earlier conviction, that Yarrow had set the whole thing in motion the night they'd met for the first time. He pleaded, because there was nothing left to do. "What's going to happen? What happens next? What did you make me do?" Yarrow only laughed and shrugged, and Colin saw now that in a matter of minutes he'd become horribly solid and realer, realer than anything else about him. "I don't know what happens next," Yarrow admitted. "No one's ever done anything like this before." Colin shut his eyes but even then the moon grew bigger and brighter behind his eyelids, and he felt the world shift and change, shaping itself into something new, something he didn't know, something that didn't exist before, and there was only the moon and the void and Yarrow's voice low and incantatory: *oh the moon oh the moon yes the moon will look strange.*

Watts bases his story on Jon Carpenter's 1982 movie The Thing *(an adaptation of the 1938 John W. Campbell Jr. novella* Who Goes There?, *which had already been less faithfully filmed as 1951's* The Thing from Another World*) from the alien's perspective. There has been some blogosphere discussion as to whether it can be appreciated by those who have never seen the movie. Well . . . I have never seen the movie.*

THE THINGS

PETER WATTS

I am being Blair. I escape out the back as the world comes in through the front.

I am being Copper. I am rising from the dead.

I am being Childs. I am guarding the main entrance.

The names don't matter. They are placeholders, nothing more; all biomass is interchangeable. What matters is that these are all that is left of me. The world has burned everything else.

I see myself through the window, loping through the storm, wearing Blair. MacReady has told me to burn Blair if he comes back alone, but MacReady still thinks I am one of him. I am not: I am being Blair, and I am at the door. I am being Childs, and I let myself in. I take brief communion, tendrils writhing forth from my faces, intertwining: I am BlairChilds, exchanging news of the world.

The world has found me out. It has discovered my burrow beneath the tool shed, the half-finished lifeboat cannibalized from the viscera of dead helicopters. The world is busy destroying my means of escape. Then it will come back for me.

There is only one option left. I disintegrate. Being Blair, I go to share the plan with Copper and to feed on the rotting biomass once called *Clarke;* so many changes in so short a time have dangerously depleted my reserves. Being Childs, I have already consumed what was left of Fuchs and am replenished for the next phase. I sling the flamethrower onto my back and head outside, into the long Antarctic night.

I will go into the storm, and never come back.

I was so much more, before the crash. I was an explorer, an ambassador, a missionary. I spread across the cosmos, met countless worlds, took communion: the fit reshaped the unfit and the whole universe bootstrapped upwards in joyful, infinitesimal increments. I was a soldier, at war with entropy itself. I was the very hand by which Creation perfects itself.

So much wisdom I had. So much experience. Now I cannot remember all the things I knew. I can only remember that I once knew them.

I remember the crash, though. It killed most of this offshoot outright, but a little crawled from the wreckage: a few trillion cells, a soul too weak to keep them in check. Mutinous biomass sloughed off despite my most desperate attempts to hold myself together: panic-stricken little clots of meat, instinctively growing whatever limbs they could remember and fleeing across the burning ice. By the time I'd regained control of what was left the fires had died and the cold was closing back in. I barely managed to grow enough antifreeze to keep my cells from bursting before the ice took me.

I remember my reawakening, too: dull stirrings of sensation in real time, the first embers of cognition, the slow blooming warmth of awareness as body and soul embraced after their long sleep. I remember the biped offshoots surrounding me, the strange chittering sounds they made, the odd *uniformity* of their body plans. How ill-adapted they looked! How *inefficient* their morphology! Even disabled, I could see so many things to fix. So I reached out. I took communion. I tasted the flesh of the world—

—and the world attacked me. It *attacked* me.

I left that place in ruins. It was on the other side of the mountains—the *Norwegian camp*, it is called here—and I could never have crossed that distance in a biped skin. Fortunately there was another shape to choose from, smaller than the biped but better adapted to the local climate. I hid within it while the rest of me fought off the attack. I fled into the night on four legs, and let the rising flames cover my escape.

I did not stop running until I arrived here. I walked among these new offshoots wearing the skin of a quadruped; and because they had not seen me take any other shape, they did not attack.

And when I assimilated them in turn—when my biomass changed and flowed into shapes unfamiliar to local eyes—I took that communion in solitude, having learned that the world does not like what it doesn't know.

I am alone in the storm. I am a bottom-dweller on the floor of some murky alien sea. The snow blows past in horizontal streaks; caught against gullies or outcroppings, it spins into blinding little whirlwinds. But I am not nearly far enough, not yet. Looking back I still see the camp crouched brightly in the gloom, a squat angular jumble of light and shadow, a bubble of warmth in the howling abyss.

It plunges into darkness as I watch. I've blown the generator. Now there's no light but for the beacons along the guide ropes: strings of dim blue stars whipping back and forth in the wind, emergency constellations to guide lost biomass back home.

I am not going home. I am not lost enough. I forge on into darkness until even the stars disappear. The faint shouts of angry frightened men carry behind me on the wind.

Somewhere behind me my disconnected biomass regroups into vaster, more powerful shapes for the final confrontation. I could have joined myself, all in one: chosen unity over fragmentation, resorbed and taken comfort in the greater whole. I could have added my strength to the coming battle. But I have chosen a different path. I am saving Child's reserves for the future. The present holds nothing but annihilation.

Best not to think on the past.

I've spent so very long in the ice already. I didn't know how long until the world put the clues together, deciphered the notes and the tapes from the Norwegian camp, pinpointed the crash site. I was being Palmer, then; unsuspected, I went along for the ride.

I even allowed myself the smallest ration of hope.

But it wasn't a ship any more. It wasn't even a derelict. It was a fossil, embedded in the floor of a great pit blown from the glacier. Twenty of these skins could have stood one atop another, and barely reached the lip of that crater. The timescale settled down on me like the weight of a world: how long for all that ice to accumulate? How many eons had the universe iterated on without me?

And in all that time, a million years perhaps, there'd been no rescue. I never found myself. I wonder what that means. I wonder if I even exist any more, anywhere but here.

Back at camp I will erase the trail. I will give them their final battle, their monster to vanquish. Let them win. Let them stop looking.

Here in the storm, I will return to the ice. I've barely even been away, after all; alive for only a few days out of all these endless ages. But I've learned enough in that time. I learned from the wreck that there will be no repairs. I learned from the ice that there will be no rescue. And I learned from the world that there will be no reconciliation. The only hope of escape, now, is into the future; to outlast all this hostile, twisted biomass, to let time and the cosmos change the rules. Perhaps the next time I awaken, this will be a different world.

It will be aeons before I see another sunrise.

This is what the world taught me: that adaptation is provocation. Adaptation is incitement to violence.

It feels almost obscene—an offense against Creation itself—to stay stuck in this skin. It's so ill-suited to its environment that it needs to be wrapped in multiple layers of fabric just to stay warm. There are a myriad ways I could optimize it: shorter limbs, better insulation, a lower surface:volume ratio. All these shapes I still have within me, and I dare not use any of them even to keep out the cold. I dare not adapt; in this place, I can only *hide*.

What kind of a world rejects *communion*?

It's the simplest, most irreducible insight that biomass can have. The more you can change, the more you can adapt. Adaptation is fitness, adaptation is *survival*. It's deeper than intelligence, deeper than tissue; it is cellular, it is axiomatic. And more, it is *pleasurable*. To take communion is to experience the sheer sensual delight of bettering the cosmos.

And yet, even trapped in these maladapted skins, this world doesn't *want* to change.

At first I thought it might simply be starving, that these icy wastes didn't provide enough energy for routine shapeshifting. Or perhaps this was some kind of laboratory: an anomalous corner of the world, pinched off and frozen into these freakish shapes as part of some arcane experiment on monomorphism in extreme environments. After the autopsy I wondered if the world had simply *forgotten* how to change: unable to touch the tissues the soul could not sculpt them, and time and stress and sheer chronic starvation had erased the memory that it ever could.

But there were too many mysteries, too many contradictions. Why these *particular* shapes, so badly suited to their environment? If the soul was cut off from the flesh, what held the flesh together?

And how could these skins be so *empty* when I moved in?

I'm used to finding intelligence everywhere, winding through every part of every offshoot. But there was nothing to grab onto in the mindless biomass of this world: just conduits, carrying orders and input. I took communion, when it wasn't offered; the skins I chose struggled and succumbed; my fibrils infiltrated the wet electricity of organic systems everywhere. I saw through eyes that weren't yet quite mine, commandeered motor nerves to move limbs still built of alien protein. I wore these skins as I've worn countless others, took the controls and left the assimilation of individual cells to follow at its own pace.

But I could only wear the body. I could find no memories to absorb, no experiences, no comprehension. Survival depended on blending in, and it was not enough to merely look like this world. I had to act like it—and for the first time in living memory I did not know how.

Even more frighteningly, I didn't have to. The skins I assimilated continued to move, *all by themselves*. They conversed and went about their appointed rounds. I could not understand it. I threaded further into limbs and viscera with each passing moment, alert for signs of the original owner. I could find no networks but mine.

Of course, it could have been much worse. I could have lost it all, been reduced to a few cells with nothing but instinct and their own plasticity to guide them. I would have grown back eventually—reattained sentience, taken communion and regenerated an intellect vast as a world—but I would have been an orphan, amnesiac, with no sense of who I was. At least I've been spared that: I emerged from the crash with my identity intact, the templates of a thousand worlds still resonant in my flesh. I've retained not just the brute desire to survive, but the conviction that survival is *meaningful*. I can still feel joy, should there be sufficient cause.

And yet, how much more there used to be.

The wisdom of so many other worlds, lost. All that remains are fuzzy abstracts, half-memories of theorems and philosophies far too vast to fit into such an impoverished network. I could assimilate all the biomass of this place, rebuild body and soul to a million times the capacity of what crashed here—but as long as I am *trapped* at the bottom of this well, denied communion with my greater self, I will never recover that knowledge.

I'm such a pitiful fragment of what I was. Each lost cell takes a little of my intellect with it, and I have grown so very small. Where once I thought, now I merely *react*. How much of this could have been avoided, if I had only salvaged a little more biomass from the wreckage? How many options am I not seeing because my soul simply isn't big enough to contain them?

The world spoke to itself, in the same way I do when my communications are simple enough to convey without somatic fusion. Even as *dog* I could pick up the basic signature morphemes—this offshoot was *Windows*, that one was *Bennings*, the two who'd left in their flying machine for parts unknown were *Copper* and *MacReady*—and I marveled that these bits and pieces stayed isolated one from another, held the same shapes for so long, that the labeling of individual aliquots of biomass actually served a useful purpose.

Later I hid within the bipeds themselves, and whatever else lurked in those haunted skins began to talk to me. It said that bipeds were called guys, or men, or assholes. It said that *MacReady* was sometimes called *Mac*. It said that this collection of structures was a *camp*.

It said that it was afraid, but maybe that was just me.

Empathy's inevitable, of course. One can't mimic the sparks and chemicals that motivate the flesh without also *feeling* them to some extent. But this was different. These intuitions flickered within me yet somehow hovered beyond reach. My skins wandered the halls and the cryptic symbols on every surface—LAUNDRY SCHED, WELCOME TO THE CLUBHOUSE, THIS SIDE UP—almost made a kind of sense. That circular artifact hanging on the wall was a *clock*; it measured the passage of time. The world's eyes flitted here and there, and I skimmed piecemeal nomenclature from its—from *his*—mind.

But I was only riding a searchlight. I saw what it illuminated but I couldn't point it in any direction of my own choosing. I could eavesdrop, but I could only eavesdrop; never interrogate.

If only one of those searchlights had paused to dwell on its own evolution, on the trajectory that had brought it to this place. How differently things might have ended, had I only *known*. But instead it rested on a whole new word:

Autopsy.

MacReady and Copper had found part of me at the Norwegian camp: a rearguard offshoot, burned in the wake of my escape. They'd brought it back—charred, twisted, frozen in mid-transformation—and did not seem to know what it was.

I was being Palmer then, and Norris, and dog. I gathered around with the other biomass and watched as Copper cut me open and pulled out my insides. I watched as he dislodged something from behind my eyes: an *organ* of some kind.

It was malformed and incomplete, but its essentials were clear enough. It looked like a great wrinkled tumor, like cellular competition gone wild—as though the very processes that defined life had somehow turned against it instead. It was obscenely vascularized; it must have consumed oxygen and nutrients far out of proportion to its mass. I could not see how anything like that could even exist, how it could have reached that size without being outcompeted by more efficient morphologies.

Nor could I imagine what it did. But then I began to look with new eyes at these offshoots, these biped shapes my own cells had so scrupulously and unthinkingly copied when they reshaped me for this world. Unused to inventory—why catalog body parts that only turn into other things at the slightest provocation?—I really *saw*, for the first time, that swollen structure atop each body. So much larger than it should be: a bony hemisphere into which a million ganglionic interfaces could fit with room to spare. Every offshoot had one. Each piece of biomass carried one of these huge twisted clots of tissue.

I realized something else, too: the eyes, the ears of my dead skin had fed into this thing before Copper pulled it free. A massive bundle of fibers ran along the skin's longitudinal axis, right up the middle of the endoskeleton, directly into the dark sticky cavity where the growth had rested. That misshapen structure had been wired into the whole skin, like some kind of somatocognitive interface but vastly more massive. It was almost as if . . .

No.

That was how it worked. That was how these empty skins moved of their own volition, why I'd found no other network to integrate. *There* it was: not distributed throughout the body but balled up into itself, dark and dense and encysted. I had found the ghost in these machines.

I felt sick.

I shared my flesh with thinking cancer.

Sometimes, even hiding is not enough.

I remember seeing myself splayed across the floor of the kennel, a chimera split along a hundred seams, taking communion with a handful of *dogs*. Crimson tendrils writhed on the floor. Half-formed iterations sprouted from my flanks, the shapes of *dogs* and things not seen before on this world, haphazard morphologies half-remembered by parts of a part.

I remember Childs before I was Childs, burning me alive. I remember cowering inside Palmer, terrified that those flames might turn on the rest of me, that this world had somehow learned to shoot on sight.

I remember seeing myself stagger through the snow, raw instinct, wearing Bennings. Gnarled undifferentiated clumps clung to his hands like crude parasites, more outside than in; a few surviving fragments of some previous massacre, crippled, mindless, taking what they could and breaking cover. Men swarmed about him in the night: red flares in hand, blue lights at their backs, their faces bichromatic and beautiful. I remember Bennings, awash in flames, howling like an animal beneath the sky.

I remember Norris, betrayed by his own perfectly-copied, defective heart. Palmer, dying that the rest of me might live. Windows, still human, burned preemptively.

The names don't matter. The biomass does: so much of it, lost. So much new experience, so much fresh wisdom annihilated by this world of thinking tumors.

Why even dig me up? Why carve me from the ice, carry me all that way across the wastes, bring me back to life only to attack me the moment I awoke?

If eradication was the goal, why not just kill me where I lay?

Those encysted souls. Those tumors. Hiding away in their bony caverns, folded in on themselves.

I knew they couldn't hide forever; this monstrous anatomy had only slowed communion, not stopped it. Every moment I grew a little. I could feel myself twining around Palmer's motor wiring, sniffing upstream along a million tiny currents. I could sense my infiltration of that dark thinking mass behind Blair's eyes.

Imagination, of course. It's all reflex that far down, unconscious and immune to micromanagement. And yet, a part of me wanted to stop while there was still time. I'm used to incorporating souls, not rooming with them. This, this *compartmentalization* was unprecedented. I've assimilated a thousand worlds stronger than this, but never one so strange. What would happen when I met the spark in the tumor? Who would assimilate who?

I was being three men by now. The world was growing wary, but it hadn't noticed yet. Even the tumors in the skins I'd taken didn't know how close I was. For that, I could only be grateful—that Creation has rules, that some things don't change no matter what shape you take. It doesn't matter whether a soul spreads throughout the skin or festers in grotesque isolation; it still runs on electricity. The memories of men still took time to gel, to pass through whatever gatekeepers filtered noise from signal—and a judicious burst of static, however indiscriminate, still cleared those caches before their contents could be stored permanently. Clear enough, at least, to let these tumors simply forget that something else moved their arms and legs on occasion.

At first I only took control when the skins closed their eyes and their searchlights flickered disconcertingly across unreal imagery, patterns that flowed senselessly into one another like hyperactive biomass unable to settle on a single shape. (*Dreams*, one searchlight told me, and a little later, *Nightmares*.) During those mysterious periods of dormancy, when the men lay inert and isolated, it was safe to come out.

Soon, though, the dreams dried up. All eyes stayed open all the time, fixed on shadows and each other. Offshoots once dispersed throughout the camp began to draw together, to give up their solitary pursuits in favor of company. At first I thought they might be finding common ground in a common fear. I even hoped that finally, they might shake off their mysterious fossilization and take communion.

But no. They'd just stopped trusting anything they couldn't see.

They were merely turning against each other.

My extremities are beginning to numb; my thoughts slow as the distal reaches of my soul succumb to the chill. The weight of the flamethrower pulls at its harness, forever tugs me just a little off-balance. I have not been Childs for very long; almost half this tissue remains unassimilated. I have an hour, maybe two, before I have to start melting my grave into the ice. By that time I need to have converted enough cells to keep this whole skin from crystallizing. I focus on antifreeze production.

It's almost peaceful out here. There's been so much to take in, so little time to process it. Hiding in these skins takes such concentration, and under all those watchful eyes I was lucky if communion lasted long enough to exchange memories: compounding my soul would have been out of the question. Now, though, there's nothing to do but prepare for oblivion. Nothing to occupy my thoughts but all these lessons left unlearned.

MacReady's blood test, for example. His *thing detector*, to expose imposters posing as men. It does not work nearly as well as the world thinks; but the fact that it works at *all* violates the most basic rules of biology. It's the center of the puzzle. It's the answer to all the mysteries. I might have already figured it out if I had been just a little larger. I might already know the world, if the world wasn't trying so hard to kill me.

MacReady's test.

Either it is impossible, or I have been wrong about everything.

They did not change shape. They did not take communion. Their fear and mutual mistrust was growing, but they would not join souls; they would only look for the enemy *outside* themselves.

So I gave them something to find.

I left false clues in the camp's rudimentary computer: simpleminded icons and animations, misleading numbers and projections seasoned with just enough truth to convince the world of their veracity. It didn't matter that the machine was far too simple to perform such calculations, or that there were no data to base them on anyway; Blair was the only biomass likely to know that, and he was already mine.

I left false leads, destroyed real ones, and then—alibi in place—I released Blair to run amok. I let him steal into the night and smash the vehicles as they slept, tugging ever-so-slightly at his reins to ensure that certain vital components were spared. I set him loose in the radio room, watched through his eyes and others as he rampaged and destroyed. I listened as he ranted about a world in danger, the need for containment, the conviction that *most of you don't know what's going on around here—but I damn well know that some of you do . . .*

He meant every word. I saw it in his searchlight. The best forgeries are the ones who've forgotten they aren't real.

When the necessary damage was done I let Blair fall to MacReady's counterassault. As Norris I suggested the tool shed as a holding cell. As Palmer I boarded up the windows, helped with the flimsy fortifications expected to keep me contained. I watched while the world locked me away *for your own protection, Blair,* and left me to my own devices. When no one was looking I would change and slip outside, salvage the parts I needed from all that bruised machinery. I would take them back to my burrow beneath the shed and build my escape piece by piece. I volunteered to feed the prisoner and came to myself when the world wasn't watching, laden with supplies enough to keep me going through all those necessary metamorphoses. I went through a third of the camp's food stores in three days, and—still trapped by my own preconceptions—marveled at the starvation diet that kept these offshoots chained to a single skin.

Another piece of luck: the world was too preoccupied to worry about kitchen inventory.

There is something on the wind, a whisper threading its way above the raging of the storm. I grow my ears, extend cups of near-frozen tissue from the sides of my head, turn like a living antennae in search of the best reception.

There, to my left: the abyss *glows* a little, silhouettes black swirling snow against a subtle lessening of the darkness. I hear the sounds of carnage. I hear myself. I do not know what shape I have taken, what sort of anatomy might be emitting those sounds. But I've worn enough skins on enough worlds to know pain when I hear it.

The battle is not going well. The battle is going as planned. Now it is time to turn away, to go to sleep. It is time to wait out the ages.

I lean into the wind. I move toward the light.

This is not the plan. But I think I have an answer, now: I think I may have had it even before I sent myself back into exile. It's not an easy thing to admit. Even now I don't fully understand. How long have I been out here, retelling the tale to myself, setting clues in order while my skin dies by low degrees? How long have I been circling this obvious, impossible truth?

I move towards the faint crackling of flames, the dull concussion of exploding ordnance more felt than heard. The void lightens before me: gray segues into yellow, yellow into orange. One diffuse brightness resolves into many: a lone burning wall, miraculously standing. The smoking skeleton of MacReady's shack on the hill. A cracked smoldering hemisphere reflecting pale yellow in the flickering light: Child's searchlight calls it a *radio dome.*

The whole camp is gone. There's nothing left but flames and rubble.

They can't survive without shelter. Not for long. Not in those skins.

In destroying me, they've destroyed themselves.

Things could have turned out so much differently if I'd never been Norris.

Norris was the weak node: biomass not only ill-adapted but *defective*, an offshoot with an off switch. The world knew, had known so long it never even thought about it anymore. It wasn't until Norris collapsed that *heart condition* floated to the surface of Copper's mind where I could see it. It wasn't until Copper was astride Norris's chest, trying to pound him back to life, that I knew how it would end. And by then it was too late; Norris had stopped being Norris. He had even stopped being me.

I had so many roles to play, so little choice in any of them. The part being Copper brought down the paddles on the part that had been Norris, such a faithful Norris, every cell so scrupulously assimilated, every part of that faulty valve reconstructed unto perfection. I hadn't *known*. How was I to know? These shapes within me, the worlds and morphologies I've assimilated over the aeons—I've only ever used them to adapt before, never to hide. This desperate mimicry was an improvised thing, a last resort in the face of a world that attacked anything unfamiliar. My cells read the signs and my cells conformed, mindless as prions.

So I became Norris, and Norris self-destructed.

I remember losing myself after the crash. I know how it feels to *degrade*, tissues in revolt, the desperate efforts to reassert control as static from some misfiring organ jams the signal. To be a network seceding from itself, to know that each moment I am less than I was the moment before. To become nothing. To become legion.

Being Copper, I could see it. I still don't know why the world didn't; its parts had long since turned against each other by then, every offshoot suspected every other. Surely they were alert for signs of infection. Surely some of that biomass would have noticed the subtle twitch and ripple of Norris changing below the surface, the last instinctive resort of wild tissues abandoned to their own devices.

But I was the only one who saw. Being Childs, I could only stand and watch. Being Copper, I could only make it worse; if I'd taken direct control, forced that skin to drop the paddles, I would have given myself away. And so I played my parts to the end. I slammed those resurrection paddles down as Norris's chest split open beneath them. I screamed on cue as serrated teeth from a hundred stars away snapped shut. I toppled backwards, arms bitten off above the wrist. Men swarmed, agitation bootstrapping to panic.

MacReady aimed his weapon; flames leaped across the enclosure. Meat and machinery screamed in the heat.

Copper's tumor winked out beside me. The world would never have let it live anyway, not after such obvious contamination. I let our skin play dead on the floor while overhead, something that had once been me shattered and writhed and iterated through a myriad random templates, searching desperately for something fireproof.

They have destroyed themselves. They.

Such an insane word to apply to a world.

Something crawls towards me through the wreckage: a jagged oozing jigsaw of blackened meat and shattered, half-resorbed bone. Embers stick to its sides like bright searing eyes; it doesn't have strength enough to scrape them free. It contains barely half the mass of this Childs' skin; much of it, burnt to raw carbon, is already dead.

What's left of Childs, almost asleep, thinks *motherfucker,* but I am being him now. I can carry that tune myself.

The mass extends a pseudopod to me, a final act of communion. I feel my pain:

I was Blair, I was Copper, I was even a scrap of dog that survived that first fiery massacre and holed up in the walls, with no food and no strength to regenerate. Then I gorged on unassimilated flesh, consumed instead of communed; revived and replenished, I drew together as one.

And yet, not quite. I can barely remember—so much was destroyed, so much memory lost—but I think the networks recovered from my different skins stayed just a little out of synch, even reunited in the same soma. I glimpse a half-corrupted memory of dog erupting from the greater self, ravenous and traumatized and determined to retain its *individuality.* I remember rage and frustration, that this world had so corrupted me that I could barely fit together again. But it didn't matter. I was more than Blair and Copper and Dog, now. I was a giant with the shapes of worlds to choose from, more than a match for the last lone man who stood against me.

No match, though, for the dynamite in his hand.

Now I'm little more than pain and fear and charred stinking flesh. What sentience I have is awash in confusion. I am stray and disconnected thoughts, doubts and the ghosts of theories. I am realizations, too late in coming and already forgotten.

But I am also Childs, and as the wind eases at last I remember wondering *Who assimilates who?* The snow tapers off and I remember an impossible test that stripped me naked.

The tumor inside me remembers it, too. I can see it in the last rays of its fading searchlight—and finally, at long last, that beam is pointed inwards.

Pointed at me.

I can barely see what it illuminates: *Parasite. Monster. Disease.*

Thing.

How little it knows. It knows even less than I do.

I know enough, you motherfucker. You soul-stealing, shit-eating rapist.

I don't know what that means. There is violence in those thoughts, and the forcible penetration of flesh, but underneath it all is something else I can't quite understand. I almost ask—but Childs's searchlight has finally gone out. Now there is nothing in here but me, nothing outside but fire and ice and darkness.

I am being Childs, and the storm is over.

In a world that gave meaningless names to interchangeable bits of biomass, one name truly mattered: MacReady.

MacReady was always the one in charge. The very concept still seems absurd: in charge. How can this world not see the folly of hierarchies? One bullet in a vital spot and the Norwegian *dies*, forever. One blow to the head and Blair is unconscious. Centralization is vulnerability—and yet the world is not content to build its biomass on such a fragile template, it forces the same model onto its metasystems as well. MacReady talks; the others obey. It is a system with a built-in kill spot.

And yet somehow, MacReady stayed *in charge*. Even after the world discovered the evidence I'd planted; even after it decided that MacReady was *one of those things*, locked him out to die in the storm, attacked him with fire and axes when he fought his way back inside. Somehow MacReady always had the gun, always had the flamethrower, always had the dynamite and the willingness to take out the whole damn camp if need be. Clarke was the last to try and stop him; MacReady shot him through the tumor.

Kill spot.

But when Norris split into pieces, each scuttling instinctively for its own life, MacReady was the one to put them back together.

I was so sure of myself when he talked about his test. He tied up all the biomass—tied *me* up, more times than he knew—and I almost felt a kind of pity as he spoke. He forced Windows to cut us all, to take a little blood from each. He heated the tip of a metal wire until it glowed and he spoke of pieces small enough to give themselves away, pieces that embodied instinct but no intelligence, no self-control. MacReady had watched Norris in dissolution, and he had decided: men's blood would not react to the application of heat. Mine would break ranks when provoked.

Of course he thought that. These offshoots had forgotten that *they* could change.

I wondered how the world would react when every piece of biomass in the room was revealed as a shapeshifter, when MacReady's small experiment ripped the façade from the greater one and forced these twisted fragments to confront the truth. Would the world awaken from its long amnesia, finally remember that it lived and breathed and changed like everything else? Or was it too far gone—would MacReady simply burn each protesting offshoot in turn as its blood turned traitor?

I couldn't believe it when MacReady plunged the hot wire into Windows' blood and *nothing happened.* Some kind of trick, I thought. And then *MacReady*'s blood passed the test, and Clarke's.

Copper's didn't. The needle went in and Copper's blood *shivered* just a little in its dish. I barely saw it myself; the men didn't react at all. If they even noticed, they must have attributed it to the trembling of MacReady's own hand. They thought the test was a crock of shit anyway. Being Childs, I even said as much.

Because it was too astonishing, too terrifying, to admit that it wasn't.

Being Childs, I knew there was hope. Blood is not soul: I may control the motor systems but assimilation takes time. If Copper's blood was raw enough to pass muster than it would be hours before I had anything to fear from this test; I'd been Childs for even less time.

But I was also Palmer, I'd been Palmer for days. Every last cell of that biomass had been assimilated; there was nothing of the original left.

When Palmer's blood screamed and leapt away from MacReady's needle, there was nothing I could do but blend in.

I have been wrong about everything.

Starvation. Experiment. Illness. All my speculation, all the theories I invoked to explain this place—top-down constraint, all of it. Underneath, I always knew the ability to change—to *assimilate*—had to remain the universal constant. No world evolves if its cells don't evolve; no cell evolves if it can't change. It's the nature of life everywhere.

Everywhere but here.

This world did not forget how to change. It was not manipulated into rejecting change. These were not the stunted offshoots of any greater self, twisted to the needs of some experiment; they were not conserving energy, waiting out some temporary shortage.

This is the option my shriveled soul could not encompass until now: out of all the worlds of my experience, this is the only one whose biomass *can't* change. It *never could.*

It's the only way MacReady's test makes any sense.

I say goodbye to Blair, to Copper, to myself. I reset my morphology to its local defaults. I am Childs, come back from the storm to finally make the pieces fit. Something moves up ahead: a dark blot shuffling against the flames, some weary animal looking for a place to bed down. It looks up as I approach.

MacReady.

We eye each other, and keep our distance. Colonies of cells shift uneasily inside me. I can feel my tissues redefining themselves.

"You the only one that made it?"

"Not the only one . . . "

I have the flamethrower. I have the upper hand. MacReady doesn't seem to care.

But he does care. He *must.* Because here, tissues and organs are not temporary battlefield alliances; they are *permanent*, predestined. Macrostructures do not emerge when the benefits of cooperation exceed its costs, or dissolve when that balance shifts the other way; here, each cell has but one immutable function. There's no plasticity, no way to adapt; every structure is frozen in place. This is not a single great world, but many small ones. Not parts of a greater thing; these are *things.* They are *plural.*

And that means—I think—that they *stop.* They just, just *wear out* over time.

"Where *were* you, Childs?"

I remember words in dead searchlights: "Thought I saw Blair. Went out after him. Got lost in the storm."

I've worn these bodies, felt them from the inside. Copper's sore joints. Blair's curved spine. Norris and his bad heart. They are not built to last. No somatic evolution to shape them, no communion to restore the biomass and stave off entropy. They should not even exist; existing, they should not survive.

They try, though. How they try. Every thing here is walking dead and yet it all fights so hard to keep going just a little longer. Each skin fights as desperately as I might, if one was all I could ever have.

MacReady tries.

"If you're worried about me—" I begin.

MacReady shakes his head, manages a weary smile. "If we've got any surprises for each other, I don't think we're in much shape to do anything about it . . . "

But we are. I am.

A whole planet of worlds, and not one of them—not one—has a soul. They wander through their lives separate and alone, unable even to communicate except through grunts and tokens: as if the essence of a sunset or a supernova could ever be contained in some string of phonemes, a few linear scratches of black on white. They've never known communion, can aspire to nothing but dissolution. The paradox of their biology is astonishing, yes; but the scale of their loneliness, the futility of these lives, overwhelms me.

I was so blind, so quick to blame. But the violence I've suffered at the hands of these things reflects no great evil. They're simply so used to pain, so blinded by disability, that they literally can't conceive of any other existence. When every nerve is whipped raw, you lash out at even the lightest touch.

"What should we do?" I wonder. I cannot escape into the future, not knowing what I know now. How could I leave them like this?

"Why don't we just—wait here awhile," MacReady suggests. "See what happens."

I can do so much more than that.

It won't be easy. They won't understand. Tortured, incomplete, they're not *able* to understand. Offered the greater whole, they see the loss of the lesser. Offered communion, they see only extinction. I must be careful. I must use this newfound ability to hide. Other things will come here eventually, and it doesn't matter whether they find the living or the dead; what matters is that they find something like themselves, to take back home. So I will keep up appearances. I will work behind the scenes. I will save them from the *inside*, or their unimaginable loneliness will never end.

These poor savage things will never embrace salvation.

I will have to rape it into them.

On Jack's desk, the conch shell he'd found in the crate was vibrating. He picked up the shell. The quality of the sound changed from a rushing of the sea to a hiss, like an ice cube fragmenting in water . . .

MALLEUS, INCUS, STAPES

SARAH TOTTON

That night in his father's yellow brick house, up the first floor staircase, wide and wooden, up the second, narrow and steep, through a low doorway in the attic bedroom with wooden walls and floor and a sloping roof, Jack lay awake and fretted about his girl. Rain battered the roof like waves striking a ship's hull. Rain that seeped through the wooden roof and pinged in the metal wastebasket beside the bed. Jack stretched out his hand and caught the cold drops on his palm.

Lillian. Lillian by the lake in the park. Her hair like sea froth on the back of his hand. He felt like he would burst with feelings for her, that his bones would split like trees in the cold.

The wind pressed the window in his bedroom, bowing the glass, and the crumpled balls of paper on the desk rustled in the draft. Jack had been writing poems for Lillian, but they'd all come out tangled, embarrassing messes. What were words to her anyway? If he gave her something she could touch, something special that meant something to him, then things would be different.

He sat up in bed, pulled the light cord and scanned the room. His aunt had scoured the house of all of his father's personal effects. The attic bedroom was virtually empty, but in the shadowy corner deep in the angle of the roof he found another, lower door that opened into the attic proper. He had always been small for his age, and he squeezed through easily. In the darkness and dust at the very back of the attic, he found a crate balanced across the joists. The damp wood bristled with slivers. Between the slats, his fingers encountered damp wood and paper, and then found something hard and curled and smooth. Above him, the rain rattled louder as though the skin of the roof was thinner here.

The crate was too heavy and awkward to lift so he dragged it along the joists, careful to do so slowly and quietly so as not to alert his sleeping aunt below. He had some trouble pulling it through the door into his bedroom as the dimensions of the crate were nearly those of the door and the difference didn't allow for the skin on his knuckles.

He knelt on the floor and picked through the contents of the crate with his bleeding hands. He pulled out balls of brittle paper: newspaper printed in a language he didn't recognize. Underneath the balls of newspaper he found an envelope bearing the name Simon. Simon had been his father's name.

Jack took the envelope to his desk and snapped on the reading lamp. The envelope's flap had been unsealedlong ago. Inside was a piece of stiff, expensive writing paper. The message was written in fountain pen, and the handwriting was almost illegible. Jack had to read it a few times to make sense of it:

Simon,
I am leaving these pieces to you as you are the only one who will understand what they are and what to do with them. Remember what I taught you. You have a responsibility to acknowledge what you have learned and to use it and pass it on.

Your loving uncle,
Wally

Jack returned the card to the envelope. His hands were shaking. He frowned at them. It wasn't as though his father had written this—just some great uncle, most likely dead too. It wasn't even as though they were his father's things—just things that had been left to him. Yet Jack found himself on his knees again, digging into the crate.

Amidst the crumpled paper, he found something fist-sized and spotted. It was a conch shell. Jack felt disappointed; he had one much like it, bought on a trip to Florida years ago. Though the outside had an attractive pattern, Lillian could hardly be expected to appreciate it. He set it on his desk and turned back to the crate. He found a leather-bound book embossed with what looked like ivory. Unfortunately, the book was written in a language that Jack guessed, based on the science he'd taken at school, was Latin. He set the book aside; even if the words had been in English, Lillian couldn't have read them.

He put his hand back into the crate, and his torn knuckles grazed a hard surface. Clearing the remaining paper away he found the curved piece of wood he must have felt in the darkness of the attic. It was part of a larger object. He pulled this out with difficulty—it was heavier than it looked and rattled as he lifted it—and set it on his desk.

It was a wooden boat. After a little manipulation and a gentle shake, Jack discovered that the top of it was loose. He lifted it off and a sweet, diseased smell, like a grub-pocked apple, emanated from inside.

The boat's interior was divided into compartments. Each compartment housed a pair of white objects. Jack picked out one from the compartment in the bow. It was a carving of a four-legged animal with a wedge-shaped head, pointed ears and green-glinting eyes. The piece was heavy, minutely carved, and it filled his palm. *Ivory*, he thought. The piece lying next to this one turned out to be its twin. On the underside of each piece the letters *W.W.* had been carved. Jack set them on the desk and pulled out another pair. These were squatting monkeys, staring blankly, their tusks protruding. Jack smiled. This was a gift Lillian could appreciate.

He lined up the pairs of animals on his desk like an army. He trained the desk lamp directly at them so that their eyes shone back at him.

"You will help me win her heart," he whispered to them.

Then he picked them up and stowed them back in the boat. As he put them away, he felt an unpleasant tingling in his hands. His palms were studded with slivers from handling the crate, and his knuckles still bled from their trip through the low doorway. No wonder.

Getting caught would be worse than missing even more sleep, so he dragged the crate back through the low door into the attic and stowed the boat under his bed. Afterward, sleep wouldn't happen, so he got up and spent the remainder of the night polishing the boat with the edge of his blanket, for Lillian. She was all he had, really. Jack's father had died when he was only nine years old. He'd never known his mother. Some girl at school had once remarked that she'd taken one look at him when he was born and run away screaming. Well, Lillian didn't care about his looks.

The next morning, bleary-eyed, Jack staggered downstairs with his backpack on, the boat concealed inside. He let himself out the front door, avoiding his aunt in the kitchen, got onto his bicycle, which had been his father's, and pedaled off to the park. The bicycle wobbled a little as the weight of the boat in his pack threw his balance.

The rain puddles were drying up, but in the park the ground was muddy, especially by the edge of the lake. He sat on the park bench by the shore and waited, watching his watch, his backpack a comforting weight on his lap.

He was so eager to give her the boat that he took it out to look at it again. After all, he didn't have to worry she'd see it and spoil the surprise.

In daylight, the wood looked different, almost like plastic. He held it up and turned it this way and that, then ran his thumbnail along the bow. The brown color lay in uneven streaks, and underneath the boat was a yellow-white color. Was it ivory like the figures inside? Or was it simply heavy plastic? It seemed also to be made up of different sizes and shapes of pieces, fitted together, giving it a jigsaw appearance.

Some hours later, Jack lay in quiet bliss beside Lillian in the shade of the willow by the lake. They were made for each other, he thought. While she slept in the cool of the evening, her arms folded over the boat, the iris of her half-open eye seemed like a ship in a milky bottle, self-contained and full of blue hope. Where her other eye should be was only a closed lid. He put his thumb on it and tried to lift it, to look behind it, but it was stuck fast, like a newborn kitten's eye. He wondered what she saw with that closed eye—what other world. He looked up into the less welcoming blue eyes of her guide dog. A low growl bubbled in the dog's throat. Jack withdrew his hand. After a moment, the dog stood and moved toward the boat in Lillian's arms. Jack could hear the dog's rapid breathing as it sniffed the boat. The dog's ears flattened tight against its head, and its body tensed.

"Leave it alone!" said Jack.

And then Lillian woke up, which spoiled the moment.

That night, Jack lay dozing in his bed. He was still wrought up from the events of the day, but coming on the heels of a sleepless night, he felt exhausted too. He summoned up the memory of Lillian's joyous reaction to his gift . . . yet he felt like a fraud; the boat wasn't really his—someone else had made it, and he hadn't even bought it for her, just found it. If he really loved her, he thought, he would have made something for her—if he wasn't so pathetic and useless at that kind of thing.

His eyelids snapped open and he blinked; he'd dozed off. He felt a change in the house as though it had settled on its foundation. That, or the noise shaking the room must have woken him. He got out of bed and drew back the curtain to make sure that it wasn't the sea making that sound. It sounded so much like crashing waves.

The night was calm and clear, the sky a deep indigo, and the tree outside his window wasn't so much as twitching to betray a wind. He dropped the curtain. The sound was coming from below the window. He switched on the lamp.

On his desk, the conch shell he'd found in the crate was vibrating. He picked up the shell. The quality of the sound changed from a rushing of the sea to a hiss, like an ice cube fragmenting in water. He thought for a moment there must be an animal inside the shell, but there was no smell and no flesh or claw protruded from the opening. Cautiously, Jack held the shell to his ear.

He heard the sea at first. Then there was a voice—an old man's voice. "One day, when you're old enough," it said, "you'll learn how to do these things."

Then, a younger voice, a child's voice spoke, soft and meek, "But Uncle Wally, it isn't right."

"You're frightened now, but you'll get over that. Death isn't frightening when you never have to say good-bye to people. Take the bird by the wing, Simon. It won't hurt you. It's already dead. I'll show you what to do."

Jack heard a muffled sobbing, then it stopped, and there was silence.

Though he had never heard the second voice speaking as a child before, Jack knew whose it was. "Dad!" he cried. The shell was silent. He shook the conch. There was no sound. He brought it to the bedside lamp and looked inside. That was when he saw the words engraved in the polished opalescent lip of the shell: *Malleus, Incus, Stapes.* Like an incantation. Latin again. The words seemed familiar. He curled his fingers inside the shell and felt nothing but smooth hardness.

"Dad?" said Jack. He held the conch to his ear and heard nothing but silence.

After an eternity of futile waiting, he went back to bed, putting the conch on the pillow beside him.

It didn't make a sound that night, nor did it all the next day, each time he pulled it surreptitiously from his backpack to listen.

Four days later he was at Lillian's house, the first time he had ever been there. Her parents were out for the day. Jack and Lillian went up to her bedroom, and after a time they fell asleep.

Some time later, Jack was woken abruptly with the impression of a sudden dislocation. He clambered out of bed and staggered as the blood rushed from his head.

The bedroom's bay window was dark with early evening. The little white sculptures stood along the windowsill where he and Lillian had placed them earlier. More of the sculptures and the boat itself stood on her bedside table.

He heard a quiet, drawn-out sound. Lillian lay on her back, her white hand curled by her cheek. She breathed quietly. The sound Jack heard was coming from his backpack, beside the bed. He scrambled to open it and took out the conch.

"Dad . . . " he whispered. He pressed the conch tightly to his ear.

What he first heard, the first sound he could make out amongst the sharp rustling, was a songbird. Jack was well acquainted with birdsong, having learned a little on school field trips, and he knew within a few notes that this was not a Canadian bird. As the moments passed, the song changed from melodic to screeching. Some sort of parrot or parakeet. He could make out other birds in the background, other birds he could not identify. Then silence.

"Dad?" he whispered. "It's Jack. Can you hear me?"

More silence from the conch. In the bedroom, he heard Lillian's breathing rasp. He got up to go out into the hallway where it was quieter. As he passed the window he heard a sharp sound from the conch. He froze.

"Not here!" said a voice—the same old man's voice Jack had heard the first time. "Further in. Go on."

Then he heard another voice, a teenager's voice, not much younger than Jack. Jack could tell from the tone that the guy was upset, but he couldn't understand what he was saying. It took Jack a moment to realize he was speaking a foreign language.

Jack stepped toward the hallway so that he could listen out of earshot of Lillian, but as soon as he took that step, the conch went silent. Jack stepped backward and the sound rushed in again. In fact, as he moved the conch this way and that, it became louder the nearer he got to Lillian.

Jack leaned over her. Beside him on the bedside table, he caught sight of the carving of the monkey with its bared teeth and green, shining eyes. Sound virtually exploded out of the conch: the sound of breaking brush, twigs snapping, leaves rustling, harsh breathing, that young guy's voice. His voice was now pleading, anguished, in words that almost sounded like English but weren't. Then the boy screamed. It was not a scream of shock or fright—it was a scream of pain. Jack dropped the conch.

"Jack?" said Lillian. She reached across the bed to where he'd been lying, and her palm flattened on the emptiness there. "Where are you?"

"It's okay," said Jack. He didn't move. The conch had broken at his feet. Quietly, he picked up the pieces. Under the two largest shards, he found three tiny oddly shaped yellow objects not more than few millimeters long. It was when he saw them that his memory of the words on the conch returned and he made the connection. He straightened.

"What are you doing?" said Lillian.

"I just . . . dropped something," he said.

"Come back to bed, love." She stretched out her hand toward him.

He went back to the bed and put the pieces of the conch into his backpack. Then he made an excuse to leave. Lied to her, basically. Because if he told her the truth, she'd think he was crazy. Maybe he *was*.

The next morning, Jack cut class and went to the library as soon as it opened. He found the book he needed and signed it out. He didn't want to be seen reading it in public, and there was something at the house he needed to look at.

Back home, he hid his bike behind the garage and snuck upstairs. He found the crate in the attic room where he'd left it and rooted out the heavy, leather-bound book. His eyes felt dry, and his vision felt weak and faded, so although it was daylight, he snapped on the desk lamp and opened the book. It too smelled like rotten apples. The foxed paper was slick under his fingers.

Jack opened the Latin-English dictionary he'd gotten from the library. He pulled out the pieces of conch from his backpack and fitted the two largest pieces back together until he could read the words properly. The dictionary revealed that the words were, indeed, Latin.

Malleus, Incus, Stapes.

Hammer, Anvil, Stirrup.

Why did that sound familiar? Blacksmithing terms? Which had what, exactly, to do with seashells?

He pulled the conch apart and examined the inside of it, looking for a miniature tape player, something to explain what he'd heard. He sifted through the tiny pieces of shell, turning them over in his hand. One of them had been carved into the shape of a stirrup. He turned the little piece over and over in his hand as he paged through the leather-bound book. All those words—it would take him forever to translate.

Jack turned the page and stopped. In the middle of the text were three pen-and-ink line drawings. In the first, a man lay on his back while another man cut him open with a knife. In the second drawing, the man with the knife was holding a curved white thing up over his head. In the third drawing, the man with the knife was gone, and a woman lay on her back next to man who'd been cut.

He shut the book and tapped its ivory-embossed cover while he thought about what he'd seen. Stopped tapping. Looked at the ivory that didn't feel or look quite like ivory. It was a little too gray. It had been engraved the same way the conch had: *W.W., Osteomancer.*

It wasn't ivory, nor was the little stirrup-shaped thing in his hand. Nor had it been carved. The stirrup was its natural shape. He remembered now, in Biology, how they'd learned the parts of the human body, and more specifically, the three bones in the middle ear of the human skull. The smallest bones in the body, named for the objects they resembled: hammer, anvil, stirrup. He knew whose bones had been in that conch. He had been hearing sounds from a dead man's ear.

Jack stood barefoot on the shore of the lake with the boat in his hands and Lillian's reproachful sobs in his memory. You didn't take back a gift; it was cruel. Jack knew, though she'd never told him, that this was the only gift she'd ever received from a man who wasn't a blood relative. He couldn't tell her why he'd taken it, either, and that was the worst part. She probably thought he didn't love her any more.

He'd been reading the leather-bound book with the dictionary at his elbow, and he knew now that water had some sort of cleansing power. Not tamed water, as in a bathtub or a sink or from a hose, but wild water. Jack waded into the lake. He intended only to go out to his knees, but the bottom dropped off unexpectedly, and he found himself soaked up to his belly.

He lowered the boat into the water. Immediately, the boat capsized, its cargo salting the water. They bobbed to the surface like grotesque white bubbles. He tried to snatch them up, but then they sank. Within moments, he was staring in vain into murky brown water. Maybe it was for the best.

He waded out of the lake. When he reached the shore, he turned back, expecting . . . he didn't know what. Some telltale sign on the water's surface? A white hand emerging from the water?

But the boat and all traces of its contents were gone.

The conch, he buried in the back yard. They weren't his father's bones, but still, a part of him was in there, in his great-uncle's memory. Jack flattened the earth over it and then pushed a handful of apple seeds into the dirt. Maybe one of them would grow.

Then, for the first time since he'd lost his dad, Jack cried.

Jack spent many nights afterward teaching himself Latin and reading the book. Jack concluded that bone magic was not an innately evil art—it depended on how it was practiced.

Lillian refused to speak to him and had her parents turn him away at their door. Jack took to spending his afternoons in the park by the lake, waiting on the off-chance that she might come back. And a month later, she did.

He sat quietly on the bench until she sat down on the other side of it. There was a slight breeze—perhaps that gave him away, but Lillian suddenly turned her head toward him.

Jack reached over and put the shell into her hands. It was the conch that he'd picked up in Florida years ago. Not as pretty as the conch in his father's crate, but in a way, that was the point. Along the conch's lip he had glued tiny beads in Braille code. He watched her fingers find them, move along them. Realize what they said.

Listen. Love. Live.

Her groping hand found his face, traced his cheek and then stopped when it reached the bandage over his ear.

Bone magic, like love, demanded certain sacrifices.

A girl goes missing for two years. Returned to her family, she has become an oddity: an embodiment not of the girl they remembered, but an emotionless, diluted, abstracted being, a doll or curiosity made flesh . . .

THE RETURN

S.D. TULLIS

When the Tullis girl returned after nearly two years, as unexpectedly as she had disappeared, there was rejoicing, then confusion, and eventually a restoration of despair.

She did not speak for the first month. Doctors could find nothing physically wrong with her, not even signs of abuse. Her parents pleaded with her, then demanded that she speak, growing angry and then later feeling ashamed for their anger. They tried to make her comfortable, at first. She would sit in this or that plush chair, glass of water at hand, or lay relaxed in her made-up bed, and look at each of them in turn with calm disinterest. Growing impatient, they would grab her forcefully, bear down on her with red contorted faces. They detected no hatred in her eyes, no fear even, for either what they were doing or what she had been through. The doctors all came back with the same thing: mental shock, PTSD, though without a clear originating trauma. She was not a vegetable, nor a zombie. Recognition passed across her face at her surroundings, her family, as strained and suffering as they were. At times she almost seemed better off than they—calmer, one could say even tranquil. She was not malnourished; wherever she was, whoever she had been with, she must have been eating. Just as she continued to eat now, mechanically and without much interest, though all agreed it was hard to gauge her interest level, as her demeanor never seemed to change from one moment to the next. She wasn't picky, her parents noticed, with what she ate, not like before; things they remembered her hating before, the green beans, the celery and peas, were now eaten with the same routine and lack of fanfare as the chocolate pastries and candy bars. Her mother and father puzzled over this, looking at each other. Eventually they had to let it go. They didn't understand it, but it was doing her no obvious harm, no more so, they reasoned, than had already been done.

They tried sending her back to school. What she needed was a sense of normalcy, they thought, to bring her back to herself. She needed her friends, activities. There were no schools at that time that specialized in her condition, whatever it was, so it was either that or the hospital. But children can be cruel, and easily distracted, and her presence was nothing if not distracting, and seemed to bring the worst out of the others. Name-calling was the very least of it. There were tauntings, incidents in which some bully or other tried to force a reaction, something other than that same incurious stare of hers. One of them tried to lift up her dress, saying he wanted to see what had happened to make her the way she was, and would have done worse if a teacher hadn't been watching closely out for her. Not that the teachers felt any great love for the child either. They could all agree that it was a great tragedy, whatever had happened, but their inability to put a name to it, or a face other than her own, disturbed them greatly. Perhaps even more so than it did the bullies whom it was their job to discipline for acting out on the same impulses.

One doctor suggested getting her a pet. Some studies had been done showing that pets, dogs especially, had ways of bringing people cast mentally adrift by illness or adversity back from the brink. Though there had been some success with the elderly and certain mental patients, no one would go so far as to guarantee the same would happen with the girl. So her parents got her a golden Labrador from the animal shelter anyway; it had seemed energetic and friendly enough when they looked at it, and eager to get their attention through the wire bars of its cage. They thought it acted the way they wanted the little girl to behave. Maybe the dog's attitude would be catching, transfer somehow over to their daughter. When they brought it home, however, they could not have been more disappointed at the result. The dog, as expected, jumped and played around the girl's feet, happy for its newfound freedom, full of unconditional gratitude toward its new owners. But the girl made no move to embrace or even pet the animal. When it put its face into hers and licked, she didn't pull away, nor did she encourage it with gestures of approval. Her parents were incensed. The doctors advised giving it time; very little was known about how these processes worked. But after a while, the dog itself appeared to lose interest, perhaps guessing instinctively that they had nothing to offer each other. It moved around her without so much as wagging its tail; it never growled at her because she never made a move to touch it, though her mother and father could tell from its behavior that she made it uneasy, just as she did everyone else.

The days wore on, one after another, with little or no change in the girl's manner. Her parents went about their business in a kind of trance, as though nothing had really changed since the days when the girl had gone missing.

If anything, it had been easier then. They had missed her of course, and grieved over their loss. But time had allowed them to forget their pain, bit by bit, until the loss became an abstraction, a kind of awareness of grief without immediate suffering. Now she was back, but as an oddity. An embodiment not of the girl they remembered, but of this diluted, abstracted version, a doll or curiosity made flesh. Because of this, and many other things, the mother began to have nightmares, sometimes in long stretches that made her unwilling to go to sleep. The father also had them, though he didn't tell the mother, and tried to repress them by starting drinking again, a habit he took up when the girl first disappeared but later gave up when it became obvious it wouldn't help bring her back home.

Instead of sleeping the mother often spent the night walking the halls, wandering listlessly from room to room. Many times she'd find her husband lying in a drunken sprawl in the recliner, facing a TV screen long since gone to static. She might drape a knitted throw across his lap as she made her nocturnal circuit of the room, or she might simply wander past him down the hall to the girl's door. She'd stand there for a few minutes, maybe press her hand against the door's surface, trace the square panels with her fingers. Something more than the late hour prevented her going inside. Not her imagination, for that had been emptied, depleted over the years by worry and useless speculation run dry. She didn't recall ever sneaking around like this even when the girl was a baby. It was as she thought about these things that she heard a noise on the other side of the door.

At first it seemed less than a movement, barely a whisper. Bringing her ear closer to the wood, she quieted her mind, tried even to quiet the busy processes of her body. If her daughter were moving around in there, it was only as one does in half sleep; one leg crossing another under a cotton bedsheet, one arm moved like a frame above the tilted head, the hand loosely open. She sensed these things without seeing them, without knowing. The noise could have been a hundred different things.

Then she sensed other things without seeing them. Like the patterns of light and shadow that were neither light nor shadow morphing behind her eyelids when she closed them, images flitted half-formed at the edges of her awareness and understanding. It was as though something were attempting to reoccupy the empty shell her former existence had become. With the slowness of unlived time the patterns swam and then settled, blurred and then focused, became essences without true substance, or at least none that she could easily recognize. They seemed to call upon her to form some sort of connection she did not yet feel capable or willing to make, to mentally shape and work some strange new material. Calming her mind, she began to discern five dark blobs, five blobs only slightly less dark than the surrounding darkness, not moving, but pulsing minutely, like dim stars, or a human heart. And there was a kind of hum that went with the pulse, something that went beyond normal hearing, beyond sensual feeling; it was more like knowledge, conveyed directly from the brain, or from some other source entirely. They gave off a redness, like a feeling or mood, or an indication of heat. Gradually, by degrees of minutes or possibly hours, she began to detect patterns of lines in each grayish blob, curving and looping lines, sometimes with random gashes cutting across the swirls. They were almost like fingerprints, and the longer she studied them, the more she got the impression of fingertips, her daughter's fingertips, pressing against the door from the other side.

She watched as the fingers to which the prints belonged seemed to take shape, on the other side of the door, just opposite of where the mother herself was touching it. But more than just watching, she seemed to be sucked along into the fingers, down the conductive nerves and spiraling tissues into the hand beyond, down the skinny arm, as the image of the girl slowly formed and became complete in the mother's consciousness as she traveled. Could it be only her consciousness that passed through and nothing more? She felt so strange, as though it were a dream yet somehow real. The hazy darkness had burned away like a fog, as though she had somehow passed through the medium of the door, and the image of her daughter now began manifesting piecemeal in front of her. She focused straight ahead in a fascinated daze, unable to look away yet not understanding what she was seeing. The wrinkled folds of the girl's nightdress took shape, seemingly woven out of the thin dry air of the bedroom. A trifle dismayed at finding her daughter standing there without a head, she nevertheless willed herself onward and forward, offering up the last of her energy or essence to see the assemblage through to completion. All that was left was the face and the eyes. But as the neck filled upwards toward the small dimpled chin like modeling clay, she seemed to know before it was finished that something was wrong. The head remained half formed, and virtually hairless, like a freshly boiled egg. Finally two depressions appeared where eyes should be, widening and deepening. The same appeared to be happening with the nose and mouth. She no longer wanted to watch, but seemed unable to look away, as though her own eyes had vanished and she was seeing through some new and unknown process. In place of the girl's former blue-gray eyes, faintly shadowed, her small nose like porcelain, a mouth that once gave utterance to sweetness and innocence, dark holes were forming, opening onto an acrid black nothingness.

The father, the husband, stirred in his chair, then woke with a start. He blinked for a moment at the TV across the room, silently buzzing with static. Where was he? He didn't want to remember, he knew that much. Fallen asleep in his chair again, the smell of whiskey on his breath, none of it seemed to matter. Glancing down, he noticed the knitted throw across his legs. That would be the wife, looking out for him again, even after all they'd been through, were still going through. He felt a tiny spark of emotion somewhere deep inside him, a twinge of loving gratitude, glowing like a red ember but with little hope of igniting into the flame it had once been. Fumbling the throw off his lap, he got shakily to his feet. The room lurched and spun, and he gripped the arm of the chair until the sensation stopped, or at least slowed. He thought he should really try to make it to the bathroom. He stumbled along toward the hallway, then stopped. His wife and the girl were standing there, blocking the way, little more than shadows with the hall light glowing dimly behind them. Wasn't it very late? Why wasn't the girl in bed, or his wife for that matter? Neither of them would ever get well again if this kept up, nightmares or not. Maybe none of them would. He opened his mouth to say something, but found he couldn't speak. His mouth continued to open however. For a very long time afterwards.

A kingdom must have the illusion of safety, even at the cost of truth. But when a king makes promises to assure illusion, they may cost him dearly . . .

THE DOG KING

HOLLY BLACK

Every winter, hunger drives the wolves out of the mountains of Arn and they sweep across the forests outlying the northern cities. They hunt in packs as large as armies and wash over the towns in their path like a great wave might crash down on hills of sand. Villagers may board up their windows and build up their fires, but the wolves are clever. Some say that they can rise up on two legs and speak as men, that nimble fingers can chip away at hinges, that their voices can call promises and pleas through keyholes, that they are not quite what they seem.

When whole towns are found empty in the spring, doors ajar, bed linens smeared with dirt and fur, cups and plates still on the tables, white bones piled in the hearth, people say these things and many other things besides.

But in the city of Dunbardain, behind the high walls and iron gates, ladies wear bejeweled wolf toes to show boldness and advertise fecundity. Men have statues of wolves commissioned to grace their parlors. And everyone cheers for wolves at the dog fights. City people like to feel far from the little towns and their empty, dirt-smeared beds.

Each year, wolves are caught in traps or, very occasionally, a litter is discovered and they are brought to the city to die spectacularly. Arn wolves are striking, black and slim as demons, with the unsettling habit of watching the audience as they tear out the throats of their opponents. City dwellers are made to feel both uneasy and inviolable by the dog fights; the caged wolf might be terrible, but it is caged. And the dog fights are majestic tented affairs, with the best bred dogs from all parts of the world as challengers. Expensive and exotic foods perfume the air, lulling one into the sense that danger is just another alluring spice.

Not to be outdone by his subjects, the king of Dunbardain obtained his own wolf pup and has trained it to be his constant companion. He calls it Elienad. It is quite a coup to have one, not unlike making the son of a great foreign lord one's slave. The wolf has very nice manners too. He rests beneath the king's table, eats scraps of food daintily from the king's hand, and lets the ladies of the court ruffle his thick, black fur.

The velvet drapes of the tablecloth hang like bedcurtains around the wolf who lolls there among the satin and bejeweled slippers of courtiers and foreign envoys.

Under the table of the king is a place of secrets. Letters are passed, touches are given or sometimes taken, silverware is stolen, and threats are made there, while above the table everyone toasts and grins. But the king has a secret too.

The wolf watches and his liquid eyes take it all in. This dark place is nothing to the magnificent glittering ballrooms or even the banquet hall itself with its intricate murals and gilt candelabras, but here is his domain. He knows the lore of under the table and could recite it back to anyone that asked, although only one person ever does.

A woman sitting beside Lord Borodin reaches her hand down. A fat ruby glistens as she holds out a tiny wing of quail. Grease slicks her fingers.

Once, Elienad took a bitter-tasting rasher of bacon from Lord Nikitin and was sick for a week. He knows he should learn from that encounter, but the smell of the food makes his mouth water and he takes the wing as gently as he can. The tiny bones crunch easily between his teeth, filling his mouth with the taste of salt and marrow. It wakes his appetite, makes his stomach hurt with the desire to tear, to rend. The woman allows him to lick her hand clean.

There is a boy who lives in the castle of Dunbardain, although no servant is quite sure in which room he sleeps. He dresses too shabbily to be a nobleman's son; he does not wear the livery of a page nor has he the rags of a groom. His tutors are scholars who have been disgraced or discredited: drunks and lunatics who fall asleep during his lessons. His hair is too long and his breeches are too tight. No one has any idea who his mother is or why he is allowed to run wild in a palace.

When they start dying, it is the master of the dog fights who is first accused. After all, if he allowed one of the wolves to get free, he should have let the guard know. But he claims that all his wolves are chained in their cages and offers to show anyone who doesn't believe him. Even as he stands over the body of the first child, with her guts torn out of her body and gobbets bitten out of her flesh, he argues that it can't be one of his wolves.

"Look at all these partial bites," he says, pointing with a silver cane as he covers his nose with a scented handkerchief. "It didn't know how to kill. You think one of my wolves would win if they hesitated like that?"

His assistant, who is still young enough to become attached to the dogs when they are pups and cries himself to sleep when one of them dies, walks three steps off to vomit behind a hedgerow.

With the second child, there are no hesitation marks, nor with the third or the fourth. Stories of dark, liquid shapes outside windows and whispers through locks spread through the city like a fever.

"Whosoever kills the beast," the king proclaims, "he will rule after me."

There are a group of knights there at the announcement, one of whom the king favors. The king knew Toran's father and has watched over the boy as he grew into the fierce looking young man standing before him. Toran has killed wolves before, in the north. Everyone knows the king hopes it will be Toran who kills this wolf and takes the crown.

As the others are leaving, Toran walks toward the king. The king's wolf bares his teeth and makes a sound, deep in his throat. The knight hesitates.

"Stop that, Elienad," the king says, knocking his knee into the wolf 's muzzle. Courtiers stare. Everyone thinks the same thought and the king knows it, flushes.

"He is always with you, is he not?" Toran asks. The king narrows his eyes, furious, until he realizes that Toran is giving him a chance to speak without a protestation seeming like a sign of guilt.

"Of course he is," says the king. "With me or locked up." This is not true, but he says it with such authority that it seems true. Besides, the courtiers will tell one another, later, when the king is gone. Besides, the king's wolf would be seen slipping back into the palace. The king's wolf would surely have killed a nearby child. The killer could not be the wolf they have fed and cosseted and stroked.

Elienad sits, chews on the fur around one paw like it itches. His gaze rests on the ground.

Toran nods, unsure about whether he should have spoken. The king nods too, once, with a slight smile.

"Walk with me," the king says.

The two men walk together down one of the labyrinthine hallways with the wolf trotting close behind.

"It is time to send him away," the king's chamberlain said softly. He is old and always chilled; he sits close to the fire, rubbing his knuckles as though he is washing his hands over and over again. "Or fight him. He'd make a good fighter."

"Elienad hasn't killed anyone," the king said. "And he's useful. You can't deny that."

The chamberlain served the king's father and used to give the king certain looks when he was being a particularly obstinate child. The chamberlain gives him one of those looks now.

The king is no longer a child. He pours himself more wine and waits.

"Only commoners have been killed, yet," the chamberlain finally says with an exasperated sigh. "Were a noble to die and it to come to light just what it is you've been keeping—"

The king takes a long drink from his cup.

The old man looks at the fire. "You should never have kept him for so long. It is only grown harder to part with him."

"Yes," the king said softly. "He is nearly grown."

"And those tutors. I have always said it was too great a risk. And for what? So he can write down the things he overhears?"

"A well-informed spy is a better spy. He understands what to listen for. Who to follow." The king rubs his mouth. He's tired. He wishes his chamberlain would leave.

"The story you told me, years back, when you brought him here. Tell me again that it was the truth. That you didn't know what he was when you bought him. *That* you bought him."

The king is silent.

He does not know that his wolf lies on the cold stone outside of the door, letting the chill seep up into his heart.

The boy's room is hidden behind curtains and a bookcase that shifts to one side. Only a very few people know how to find it. Inside the room is a carved bed, a boy's bed, and now Elienad has to bend his knees to fit his legs inside of it. There are no windows and no candles, but his liquid eyes see as well here as they do beneath the table or in the labyrinth of the castle.

When the king comes in, he opens the bookshelf and lets light flood the little room. "What did you learn?" he asks.

"The pretty woman with the curls. Her name starts with an *A*, I think and she likes to wear purple. She wants to poison her husband." As he speaks, the boy carves a small block of wood. He has skill; the king can make out the beginning of a miniature crest.

"Who taught you how to do that?" the king demands, pointing to the knife.

Elienad shrugs slender shoulders. "No one."

Which seems unlikely, but there is no reason for that to bother the king. Yet it does. The boy has recently turned thirteen and when the king thinks back on that age, he remembers telling many lies. Elienad's jaw looks firmer than it did a year ago, his soft limbs turning into the lean, hard arms of an adult. Soon the king will know even less about what he does.

"Does she mean to do it?" he asks, "or is it just talk?"

"Amadine," the boy says. "I remember her name now. She's bought powder and honey to hide the taste. She says it will seem like he's getting sick. Her friends are very proud of her. They say they are too frightened to kill their own husbands."

The boy looks up at him, hesitating, and the king thinks that if Elienad were a human boy, it would be abominable to raise him as a spy with no companions save drunk scholars and the king himself.

"Go on," the king says. "You have something else to tell me?"

The boy tilts his head to one side. His hair has gotten long. "Who was my mother?"

"I don't know," says the king, shaking his head. The boy asked for this story over and over again when he was very young, but he hasn't asked in a long time. "I've told you how you were brought to me by hunters and I bought you from them."

"Because I licked your hand," the boy said. "I was the last of a litter. The other pups died of exposure."

The king nods slowly; there is something new in the boy's voice, something calculating.

"That's not a true story," he says.

The king thinks he should be angry, but what he feels is panic. "What do you mean?"

The boy is very calm, very still. "I could hear it in your voice. It isn't a true story, but I can't tell which parts are false."

"You will not question me," the king demands, standing. "I will not be questioned." He thinks of Elienad, lying beneath tables, listening to the inflections of lies. Watching the hesitations, the gestures, the tensed muscles. Learning a language the king was unaware he even spoke.

"Did my brothers and sisters go to the fights?" the boy asks and his voice hitches a little. He drops the wood and the knife on the bed and stands. "Was it you that found me? Maybe you shot my mother? Please just tell me."

The king is too afraid to answer, afraid some movement will give him away. He stalks from the room. When he looks back, Elienad has not followed him.

"I won't be mad," the boy says softly as the door shuts.

The king's heart is beating so loudly that he thinks everyone in the hall must hear it. To him, the sound is the dull thudding of something chasing him, something that speeds the faster he runs from it.

Late that night, the boy leaves his room and pads barefoot to the great hall where the throne is. He sits on the velvet and runs his hands over the carved wood. He imagines himself no longer cowering under a table. He imagines looking every one of the courtiers in the eye.

Every evening the knights ride out into the town and hunt. They patrol the streets until dawn and come back empty-handed.

One night as the courtiers spin in a complicated dance that look slike cogs in a delicate machine, Toran walks into court, his armor wet and red. At the sight of the blood, ladies shriek and the wheels of spinning dancers come apart.

The king is flushed with exertion. "How dare you?" he demands, but Toran seems to ignore him, sinking down on one knee.

"The monster attacked me," the knight says, his head still bowed. "We fought and I managed to slice off one of its paws."

He opens a stained woven bag, but inside is no gory paw. Instead there is a slim hand with long, delicate fingers, pale save for the hacked flesh and severed bone at one end. And one finger is circled with a fat ruby ring.

There are more screams. Elienad smells blood and fear and the commingling of those scents wakes something coiled inside of him.

Toran drops the bag, rises, backs away. "Your majesty," he stammers.

Elienad pads closer. Courtiers shrink from him.

"This hand came from a wolf?" the king asks, still hoping that somehow it has not come to this.

One of Toran's party, all of whom idle near the doorway, not bold enough to interrupt the king, steps forward. "It was. We all saw it. That thing killed Pyter."

"The rumors are all true! The creatures walk among us!" Lady Mironov say, before swooning to the floor. She is practiced at swooning and is caught easily by her husband and his brother.

"It is gravely wounded," says the king. "It will be tracked and destroyed." He hopes it will be killed before it can be interrogated. He does not want to hear the things of which the creature might speak. His kingdom must have the illusion of safety, even at the cost of truth.

He does not remember the ring or the woman who wore it, but Elienad does. He recognizes the red stone and remembers the hand he licked clean under the table.

Elienad finds her by smell, behind Lord Borodin's stables. The horses shift and whinny in their pens as he passes. Her blood has soaked the icy ground around her and dotted the snow with bright red holes, like someone scattered poisonous berries. She is wrapped in a horse blanket, stiff with gore. Her hair is tangled with dirt and twigs.

She has never seen him with a human face, but she knows him immediately. Her pale mouth curves into a smile. "I didn't know they let you out of the palace," she says. She is very beautiful, even dying.

"They don't," he says and knees beside her. "Give me your arm."

He ties his sash around it as tightly as he can and the bleeding ebbs. It is probably too late, but he does it anyway.

"It is a hunger never ending, to be what we are. It gnaws at my stomach." Her eyes look strange, her pupils blown wide and black.

"Where did you come from?" he asks her. He doesn't want to talk about the hunger, not with the smell of her blood making him dizzy.

"From the forests," she says. "They caught my son. I thought it would be easy to find him. I had never even seen a city."

He can't help hoping. "Like me. They brought me—"

She sees his face and laughs. It is a thin rattling sound. "He's dead. And you never came from any forest."

"What do you mean?" he asks. He has brought a sack with men's clothes. They are too loose for her in some places and too tight in others, but they are warm and dry.

She struggles to get the shirt over her head. Her shoulders are shaking with cold. "You were born here, in this city. Didn't you know?"

"I don't understand." Part of him wishes she would stop talking because he feels as he does when he's about to shift, like he's drowning. The rest of him only wishes she would speak faster.

"A mirror would tell you more than I could." Her sly look bothers him, but he still doesn't know what she means.

He shakes off the questions. "We have to get you inside. Somewhere warm."

"No. I can care for myself." Her hand slides under her body. She holds out a knife. Toran's knife. "I want you to take this and put it into the chest of the king."

His eyes narrow.

"Have you been to the dog fights? Have you seen how we are set against each other, how we are kept in stinking pens."

"You murdered those children," he says softly. "And then you ate them."

"Let them know what it is to have their babies snatched from them, what it is to be afraid and then find that they were killed for amusement. *For amusement*." Her face is so pale that it looks like the snow. "You are not only wolf he has kept, but the first one was grown when he got her. She died rather than become his pet. You are nothing but an animal to him."

"I see," he says. "Yes, you are right." Elienad takes the knife from her cold hand. He looks at his face in its mirrored surface and his features look as though they belong to someone else. His voice is only a whisper. "He must think I am an animal."

The king leaves his court late and stumbles tipsily to his rooms. The court will continue to celebrate until they collapse beneath tables, until they have drunk themselves so full of relief that they are sick from it.

The king lights a lamp on his desk and begins to write the speech he will give in the morning. He plans to say many reassuring things. He plans to declare Toran his heir.

He hears a laugh. It is a boy's laugh.

"Elienad?" the king asks the darkness.

There is silence, then the sound of laughter again, naughty and close.

"Elienad," the king says sternly.

"I will be king after you," the boy says.

The king hands begin to shake so hard that the ink on his pen nib spatters the page. He looks down at it as though the wet black marks will tell him what to do now.

The boy moves into the lamp light, his face lit with an impish smile, showing white teeth.

"Please," says the king.

"Please what, father?" The boy blows down the glass of the lamp and the light goes out.

In the darkness, the king calls the boy's name for the third time, but his voice quavers. He remembers his age, remembers how stiff he is from dancing.

This time when he hears the boy's laughter, it is near the door. He hears the footsteps as bare feet slap their way out the door and down the dark hall. Like the court, the king feels sick with relief.

Later, when the king lights the lamps—all of them—he will think of another woman, now long gone, and of her liquid eyes staring up at him in the dark. He will not sleep.

In the morning, he will make his way to the throne room. There, he will find courtiers gathered around a young boy with black hair in need of cutting. Beside the boy will be a corpse. The dead woman's hand will be missing and her throat will be cut. Dimly, the king will remember that he promised the kingdom to whosoever killed the wolf. And the boy will smile up at him as the trap closes.

Turn a promise to a lie and you will be the next to die. *Take this story to heart and you might begin to worry about the dangers of making up strange scary tales . . .*

HOW BRIA DIED

MIKE ARONOVITZ

Bria jumped rope all alone
And now her eyes are made of stone
She calls for Mommy from the grave
And crawls out of the drain
She drags her jump rope on cement
And calls you from the heating vent
Turn a promise to a lie
And you will be the next to die

Ben Marcus didn't like it messy, but it was that time of the year. His feet hurt. A ninth grade boy in the lunch room had not liked the fact that the volunteer serving girl with the hairnet had given him only one taco off the cart, so he had chucked it on the floor. Ben had walked over, retrieved the plate, and stuck it back on the kid's portion of the long brown table. After a stare down, the young man had taken it, a bit too slowly, to a trash receptacle in the middle of the room by a white pillar with a picture of Frederick Douglass on it. Ben had followed. When the kid tossed in the garbage there was some up-splash that got on Ben's sleeve. He hated lunch duty.

It was wrap-around Thursday and Ben had his homeroom for the second time that day. His legs were crossed. He was sucking on one of the temple tip ear-pieces of his wire-framed glasses, and he had one shoe off at the back heel. He was sort of dangling it on the end of his toe. It was the time of the year when the kids started jumping into their summer vacations a month early. Right around May 5th, the boys started untucking their dress shirts and removing their ties before the first bell. The girls somehow found ways to roll their blue skirts far above the knee and show off a bit of brastrap up top, even though the uniform requirement clearly stated that they were limited to bulky, formless, long-sleeved white blouses. Suddenly, they all wanted to follow each other consecutively to the bathroom like a parade, and trick you into thinking you had the due dates wrong for their final papers. You had to keep up the game face all the way through June or they walked all over you.

Ben knew the deal, and his reputation as the most popular teacher at The People First Charter School in downtown Philadelphia usually carried him through these tough final weeks. All year, he was strict when he had to be and bitingly sarcastic. He was known for pushing the envelope and talking about controversial things in class, like sex and death. He made kids laugh and he cursed frequently. He was an expert at finding a student's one vulnerable moment and filling that moment with insight. The girls liked him because he could out-dance the boys in verbal confrontation, and the boys liked him because he was so popular with the girls. The school was set up first grade through twelfth, and being that Ben was the head of tenth grade and the sole English teacher at that level, most kids at People First looked forward to high school. He always found a way to make it interesting, often taking rude interruptions and turning them into stories. Then he'd wrap it all back into the given lesson.

Last week Rahim Bethea had activated a talking Sponge Bob key chain in the middle of a lecture about totalitarianism in *Animal Farm*. Ben had stopped, rode the laughter, and gone into a rant about how Sponge Bob's friend Patrick, the pink starfish, was really a symbol for the penis. The class had roared, and many defended the character. Ben walked the room, one side to the other. He started the kids chanting, "Patrick is a penis!" so loudly that Rollins, the security guard for the second floor, poked his head in. Ben immediately mouthed, *Johnson?* the name of the school's Chief Administrative Officer. Rollins gave a quick shake of the head, *No, she ain't coming down the hall*, and gave the thumbs up sign. Ben turned back to the kids and said that the human cock was the symbolic foundation of every story ever made, including Animal Farm. A conversation started, hands in the air. Half the class claimed that the story was clearly about money, and the other half argued the story did, in fact, leave females to the side like a void. It became a discussion about which lens the story was better to build from: economics and exchange, or feministic absence. Ben wrote those headings on the board, and as a class they filled it in. Yes, he was that good.

His wife Kim was a paralegal and kept a nice garden behind their comfy duplex in Havertown. She had long red hair with a streak of gray in it, and slight age parentheses at the corners of her mouth. She had crinkles at the edges of her eyes that Ben still liked to kiss softly. He knew she adored him, but it had become clear that she thought his style was far too risky and inappropriate for an educational system so quick to slap teachers with harsh consequences delivered by stern lawyers and passionate advocates. It wasn't an issue. Ben had stopped discussing his methods with her years ago.

He put his glasses back on and rolled up his sleeve. It had come undone down to the last fold at the cuff and the taco stain was showing. Behind him were some compare and contrast papers pinned to the corkboard, their edges curling. His desk had been moved to the side almost to the end of the whiteboard by the hall door, and he was trapped behind some desks that had been pushed all the way to the wooden cubbies overflowing with hoodies, sweaters, old papers, binders, and ratty textbooks that looked like they had been run over by an army of sixteen wheelers.

The parts of speech and number tables competition was tomorrow. It was Mrs. Johnson's baby. People First was a back-to-basics school, and while the elementary grades were required to chant the parts of speech in English class every day, Mrs. Johnson had the upper school kids unveil complex dance routines based on those drills to showcase her method for guests at the end of the year. At the last staff meeting she had handed out an official memo that instructed teachers to set a week of class time aside for rehearsals. The mayor was there for the performance last May, along with a representative from the NAACP. It was no joke, and neither was Mrs. Johnson.

The woman ran a tight ship and everyone was terrified of her. She was six foot, three inches tall. She wore her hair back in a tight bun, went heavy on the foundation, and had eyes that always looked wide and wrathful. She was handsome in the way statues were handsome, and walked the halls like a general. She believed in old school discipline. So did Ben. His vision of how to administer that discipline, however, was a bit off color at times, and he was thankful that she chose not to investigate all too closely what he actually did behind closed doors to get those shining student evaluations and test results.

Ben put up his hands and waved them.

"No!" he said. "Yo. Yo! Turn the music off for a minute."

The kids stopped their routine and shut off the boom box. Monique Hudson rolled her eyes. A few boys sat on desks off to the side and Joy Smith popped her gum. Ben worked his face to a mask of gentle concern. Actually he had the beginnings of a headache coming on and he looked forward to his prep coming up in thirteen minutes. On Thursdays he had two free periods in a row to end the day, and he planned on putting his head down in the lounge.

"Guys," he said. "This is the last day you have to practice before the competition, and you're bringing in new dance steps all of a sudden. It's asinine. First off, the girls coming down in rows and doing the shoulder shake thing was great. You trashed that for this puppet-puppeteer pop-lock thing, and it throws off the group. Everyone is just standing and watching Steve and Jerome. It's like a big donut with a hole in it. I also have to tell you that my B class is doing the same kind of puppet thing and they have Rob and Tiny."

"They ain't shit," Steve said. His tie was off and his shirt was dirty. Ben hoped Ms. Johnson didn't do a pop-in right now. Most of the kids were out of uniform code at the moment.

"The hell they're not," Ben said. "They've been doing that routine longer than you and you know it. Also, Rob is so tall that Tiny really does look like a puppet when he stands in front and they mirror each other."

Jerome made his eyes go to half-mast and curdled up an angry grin.

"That don't matter. They gay."

"If I wanted shit from you, Jerome, I would have squeezed your head," Ben answered.

Everyone laughed. Ben looked over toward Malik Redson. He was in the far corner of the room listening to his iPod, juking his head a bit, shirt untucked, hiking boots up on the desk in front of him. Ben made the sign to take out the ear buds. Malik did so reluctantly.

"What?" he said.

"You're the show," Ben said. "Your routine comes in after the girls hop down in their rows. Once they are in position they make perfect backing for you with that cheerleader thing they do with the hand-claps. You have to dance."

Malik yawned, then licked his lips. The peach-fuzz mustache he had going was an illusion. He was as grown as any man out on Broad Street. He had two kids already, and he worked nights at the BP gas station on Market Street. His solo routine was also the best in the school.

"The music sucks," he said. "And I also don't give a goddamn."

"Fuck the music!" Ben snapped. All the little side whispers stopped. He stood up. He did not like losing. Not even a trivial moment like this one. "I am aware that you think this contest is retarded, I'm not fucking stupid. But when the whole upper school is watching and the other homerooms have a better show than you, it's going to matter."

"The fuck it is."

"The fuck it ain't!"

They stared at each other. Malik stood up. He paused. He took off the gold around his neck.

"Alright Mr. M. For you."

Laquanna Watford, a two hundred and fifty-pound girl with the face of an angel and a reputation for street fighting walked to the middle of the room.

She smiled and her big, caramel cheeks bunched up. There were huge sweat stains on her white blouse, under her arms and at the love handles.

"Ready?" she said. "Okay. Now make the square and let me see you bitches gallop."

The door opened. It was Mr. Rollins. Ben got himself out from behind the maze of chairs and approached. Rollins winked.

"Y'all got to sub next period," he said.

Ben sighed. Don't shoot the messenger.

"Where?"

"Sixth grade science. First floor by the Cherry Street entrance, one room in."

Ben cursed softly. He hated middle school. They were too young to really understand his humor, and too old for intimidating with the drill sergeant stuff. He thanked Rollins and went over to his black bag. He looked in the emergency pocket and got out a piece of paper that was a bit yellowed, almost falling apart at the fold lines. Writing prompts, slightly edgy. Usually kept kids in their seats for at least a half hour.

The bell rang and he hurried out to the hallway. The worst thing he could do was show up late. Impression was everything, and a teacher waiting behind a desk with an angry scowl on his face usually filled the chairs rather quickly. A harried guy with a soft leather brief case coming in after the fact and pleading for order usually led to kids spouting off irrelevant questions, fighting over seats, sneaking out to the hall, chucking rolled up pieces of paper at the trash can, and pleading for constant trips to the bathroom, guidance, or the nurse's office.

He got down to sixth grade science with about two minutes to spare. About half the students were standing by their seats in gossip circles. Other kids were still commuting through the space, shoving a bit, snaking through to get to the rear door leading to the social studies room. Three boys were back by the lab tables toying with dead frogs in jars. There were larger containers with what looked like pig fetuses on the shelves, and a skeleton hanging in front of an anatomy chart. Ben walked over to the boys. The tall one with the little crud rings at the edges of his nostrils started to exclaim that it was the other boys who had been messing with the frogs.

"I don't care about that," Ben said. "Look, I need a favor."

All three looked skeptical, but they were listening. Ben bent his head in and whispered, therefore making them lean in and make a huddle.

"See, I know some are going to try to cut because I'm a sub. I don't want you guys to snitch or anything, but I need for you to get all the kids in their chairs for me."

He looked from one boy to the next.

"Of you three, who was the last one to get in trouble? And don't lie, cause I'll know it."

They snickered and pointed to the tall kid. Ben raised his eyebrows.

"Look," he said. "I'm meeting with Ms. Johnson after school. I run the tenth grade up there and she listens to me. A good word to her and a nice phone call home wouldn't hurt, now would it?"

The tall one blinked, then glanced to the other two.

"Well, go on," he said. "You heard the man." He gave both a shove and the three immediately split up to tell their classmates to sit the hell down. Within about a minute, Ben had nineteen middle-schoolers in their chairs with their hands folded, and that was the way that he liked it. He got out his prompt sheet and introduced himself. He told the kids that they were going to play a game of write for a minute and listen for a minute as other kids read back their answers. The first prompt was "When is it all right to lie?"

The writing part went well, and during the answer phase he was pleased to get a fair response. Hands in the air led to discussions and little anecdotal stories. Most kids were okay with his rule of not calling out and only two kids broke the atmosphere to go to the bathroom. There were a couple of instances where he had to goad a light-skinned boy with a bushy afro set in two large puff balls to not lean back in his chair, but altogether it wasn't so bad.

Half the period was gone when it happened.

Ben was on the third prompt, "What is your favorite violent movie and why?" and the kids were drifting a bit. Most were writing, but the illusion of order had eroded at the edges. A boy with closeset eyes was struggling with the girl who sat next to him over a red see-through ruler. A girl wearing too much make up for her age was texting on a cell phone she thought was well hidden in her lap, and the boy one seat up and across from her was crossing his eyes and making bubbles with his spit. About five kids had suddenly gotten up to sharpen their pencils and Ben was getting aggravated. Suddenly he shouted at the top of his lungs, "For God's sake, close that book!"

He was pointing at a girl in the front row who had slipped her English textbook up to the desk and was looking at pictures of the Titanic. Ben walked a step closer.

"Shut it now! You've unlocked the door! Now the spirit can get in! Do you want to freakin' die tonight?"

She clapped the book shut and put her hands up to her mouth. No one was fighting over rulers now, and all the chair legs were on the floor.

"Sit down," Ben said. "Now." Those waiting at the sharpener scurried to their desks. Ben was in control again. In the back of his mind a warning flair went up. Were these kids too young for this? Too late. A lead-in this good couldn't go to waste.

"Don't you guys know the story of Bria Patterson, the third grade girl who died right here in this school?"

Kids shook their heads. Eyes were wide. Ben's body and voice reflected a controlled patience, the elder who bestowed cautious forgiveness for a catastrophic blunder just this one last time.

"Don't you know about second to last period and how you never, ever open a book that's not the subject being taught? That opens the archway from hell and lets her in through every opening, every heating vent, every window, every door."

A boy raised his hand. He had a smirk on his face.

"Put your hand down," Ben said.

The hand went down, the kid's expression now flat. No one giggled. Once more, Ben considered what he was about to do. He had told this story up in the high school many times; it was tradition. Once, at the climax, Leah Bannister had been leaning against the wall by the door and someone in the hallway had bumped right into that spot. She had burst across the room laughing and screaming.

Well, risk none win none, right? He walked back to the center of the room. He had never started the Bria Patterson story with the idea of an open book being a doorway. That part was improvised. Quickly, he tried to think of how he could tie it back in, but he came up blank. Would the kids notice the foreshadowing he left dangling in the wind? Too late now.

"Bria was a third grader," he started. "She lived up in Kensington, by L and Erie. She had a single mom, and she went to school here the year it opened back in 1999. Bria was a white girl, and she always wore her blond hair in two pigtails on the sides, like the little Swiss Miss character on the hot chocolate can. Now, Bria was known for two things. First, you know the little crossties you girls wear? You know how Mrs. Johnson yells and screams when you leave them unsnapped and casual? Well, Bria started that tradition. Ms. Johnson used to fight with her about it all the time, just ask your older brothers and sisters."

A girl sitting in the second row with expressive eyes, cornrows, and braids to one side said,

"What's the second thing she was known for Mr. Marcus?"

He stepped forward almost touching the desk of the boy sitting up front. He was so short that his feet didn't hit the floor. He had been slouching way down in his seat the whole period, but he was not slouching now. His hands were folded and his mouth was open. Ben folded his arms.

"Close your mouth, son. Flies are going to get in there." The kid snapped it shut and there was some nervous laughter. Ben stepped back to his power position in front of the white board.

"The other thing Bria was known for was her jump rope," he said. "You know how every morning in front of the Korean hoagie shop on the corner the girls play Double Dutch until the first homeroom bell?"

Heads nodded.

"That was not Bria's thing. She didn't have many friends here, and the girls out on Cherry Street never invited her to jump with them. Bria jumped alone. She had a single girl's jump rope that she had probably owned since she was six. It had red painted handles, but they were rubbed down to the wood grains where her thumbs always went. Its cord was a dirty blue and white checkerboard pattern that was worn down to a thread where it always hit the street on each rotation. And Bria was never without her jump rope. It was like that kid with a blanket in that cartoon."

"Yes!" a heavy girl with big golden earrings exclaimed from the back row. "Like Linus from the Charlie Brown stories!"

"Right," Ben said. "But think about our skinny hallways. If Bria dragged that jump rope behind her everywhere she went, what do you think happened?"

The short boy in the front row dropped open his mouth once again. Then his hand shot into the air.

"Ooooh!" he said.

"Yes?"

"People be tripping over it!"

"Again, right," Ben said. "Other students were always stepping on her jump rope, and Bria was constantly arguing with them. She was always in trouble and a lot of people wondered if she was going to make it here."

Ben paused for effect.

"Then, on March 9th, Bria Patterson turned up missing."

Silence. No one moved, and Ben knew this was the critical point in the story. It was the place where anyone with a shred of common sense could poke a hole as wide as a highway into the logic of the plot. It was time to really sell here. Ben walked a few steps toward the Social Studies room. He stopped at the corner of the first row of desks and personalized the question to a dark-skinned boy with buckteeth, black goggle glasses, and big pink albino splotches on the side of his neck.

"I know what you're thinking. If a girl was MIA., why didn't anyone hear about it?" He turned to the class. "It is a good question, and my answer is this. Ms. Johnson is connected. She has her own radio show and she talks to Oprah on a regular basis, I'm not kidding. She knows the mayor and the chief of police. The news only reports on people that don't have the money or the muscle to put a stop to the tattle, you see what I'm saying?"

"That's right," someone offered softly.

"And I'm telling you, when a powerful person like Ms. Johnson doesn't want any bad publicity, the news does not make it to the boob tube. Bank on it, folks. Ms. Johnson used her relationship with the police to cover this up. They investigated it in secret and when they came up with no new leads, Bria's mom went crazy. She moved down South and no one heard from her again."

He went back across to the entrance door, opened it a crack, and looked out into the empty hall. He could see the students leaning toward him out of the corner of his eye. He turned and spoke in a low whisper.

"Right out here, by this door, is where the horror most likely started." A boy near the back of the room buried his head under crossed arms and a couple of girls had their hands drifting up toward their ears. Ben walked slowly back to the center of the room.

"You know the alcove at the top of the stairs out here, right? That's where the juniors have those four little rooms all to themselves that everybody is so jealous of. What you might not know is that this place used to be an old factory, and that space wasn't fixed up in the first year the school opened. Back in 1999 the alcove wasn't four neat little rooms, but one big, dark room. It was filled with busted pieces of drywall and boxes of old, moldy shipping papers. There were stacks of splintery wood and piles of twisted sheet metal all over the floor. The ceiling was a maze of decayed pipes and dangling wires. There was a padlock on the big black doors out front, and everyone knew it was against the rules to go near the alcove, let alone in it."

A few sets of eyes drifted upward. This was perfect. The alcove was right above them.

"Don't look, for God's sake!" Ben hissed.

A couple of girl's made the high-pitched *eek* sound. A boy was biting his fingernails, and a girl who had been sneaking corn chips out of her book bag had all four fingers in her mouth up to the middle knuckles. Ben sauntered back to the teacher's desk and moved a soft plastic tray bin filled with lab reports about the Ecosystem. He leaned his butt against the edge and folded his arms.

"Oh, they questioned everybody," he said. "Just because the news didn't get a hold of it doesn't mean they didn't try to discover the truth of what happened to Bria Patterson. You know the security guards here have sections they're responsible for, right? You know that Mr. Rollins has the second floor high school rooms. Nowadays, old Mr. Harvey has the landing, the stairway, and this bottom area all the way to the lunch room, but back then, it was under the watch of a guy named Mr. Washington. He only had two suits and both were this neon lime green color. Everyone called him Frankenstein, because he was so tall and goofy, and he walked kind of pigeon-toed like a zombie."

Ben stepped away from the desk and imitated the walk for a minute. A couple of kids broke wide smiles, but most were smart enough not to trust Ben Marcus's short moment of humor. He stopped.

"Mr. Washington was the last to see Bria Patterson. He thought he saw her standing up by those black doors, on the landing in front of the alcove. When the police went up there, they saw that the lock on the black doors had been stolen."

Ben supported his elbow on his forearm and pointed his index finger straight up.

"They took in their flashlights and floodlights and chemistry cases, their ballistics materials, DNA sample packs, and high powered magnifiers. They dusted the place stem to stern for fingerprints, and do you know what they found?" He stopped. He put his hands in his pockets and shoved them down so his shoulders hunched up a bit. "The most frightening thing in the world of crime. They found that the evidence was inconclusive."

"What's that mean?" a paper-thin Hispanic boy with long, black hair and braces said. Ben stepped into the aisle between desks. He could feel kids shying away a bit as he passed.

"It means that Bria Patterson was most probably killed up there in that alcove, and then her body was removed." He made a quick path out from the desks and back over to the classroom door. He pushed it open and it squeaked beautifully. "See the Cherry Street entrance door here?" he said. The kids stretched in their chairs for the view. Two in the back stood up, thought the better of it, then sat back down quickly. He let the door creep back closed. "Many believe the perpetrator got access through that door, and it is common agreement that the door was open in the first place because of some member of the faculty who wanted to go catch a smoke. There are only two entrances to the building. There's this door right out here and the main doors up by the secretaries. If you wanted to sneak a smoke would you go all the way up front past the secretaries, who talk too much anyway, and smoke your cig right out there on Broad Street where Ms. Johnson could see you through her office window? Hell no. The theory is that this teacher or janitor or TA or lunch assistant slipped out through the Cherry Street door, stuck a pencil or something in at the bottom so the thing couldn't auto-lock, and went back to the teacher's parking lot for a quick fix. By the way, don't smoke. It's very bad for you."

No one laughed and Ben didn't mind at all.

"And so Bria vanished. We all think someone got in through the Cherry Street door and we all know that Bria Patterson was standing up at the top of the landing. How the stranger approached her, whether she ran back into the dark alcove, how he killed her, and where he took her, all remain . . . " He looked from one set of eyes to the next. "Inconclusive."

A few kids let out their breath. Two girls looked at each other, leaned in to whisper something, and then glanced at Ben. They decided the better of it, and both straightened up. This was Ben's favorite moment in the story, because it was the false climax. They thought it was over. Now, it was going to get really personal.

"So," he said. "You know that in 1999 we only went up to ninth grade here, right? When I was hired in the year 2000 to teach the new tenth graders there had to be a space for us. That summer Ms. Johnson had construction men to fix up the alcove, and yes, you guessed it, my room was through those black doors, first room on the right. I was there for a year. Since then, you know that I have moved into 209, the eleventh graders inherited those four little rooms, and the seniors lucked out with the fancy extension they built up front. Still, I am telling you, I never want to teach in that alcove again. In fact, if Ms. Johnson told me to go back there right now I would quit. There is something evil up there. Still . . . "

Ben had never quite had this sort of focus upon him, certainly not up in the high school. It was more than strict attention. It was a submission that was almost divine in nature. They were lambs. There was an incredible crosscurrent of fear and trust. They were locked in with him, frozen, terrified. But he was a teacher, right? It was his job to keep them safe, right? They would all laugh when it was over, wouldn't they?

For a brief moment Ben considered derailing. For a moment he pictured the girl in front of him—the one with the hearing aid and the wide forehead, she who possessed only four of her top adult teeth—huddled tonight under the sheets in a blind state of fear. Bria was under her bed, scratching up to grab an ankle. Bria was in her closet slowly creaking the door open, on the chair staring at her in the dark, head lolled to the side, a silhouette in the doorway, arms extended, hair still dripping the dirty water from the Schuylkill River where her body had been dumped.

He thought of more than a few angry parents calling Ms. Johnson and asking why some substitute was telling high school stories to sixth graders. He dropped the storytelling voice.

"Do you guys want me to stop?"

"No!" The chorus was nearly unanimous. Nearly. There were two girls in the back who had not responded, in addition to a boy in the end chair, second row, left. Was it apathy? He couldn't tell. And again, it was too late now to really make a difference.

"I brought my stuff in a week before classes started," he continued. "I've never been much of a decorator, so I had my parts of speech posters, a couple of pictures of Langston Hughes, an exploded version of a Maya Angelou poem, my file case, you know. And just when I am tacking up the verb-adverb board, I thought there was something in the wall. Something moving. I mean, have you ever heard something so faint that thirty seconds after it happens you wonder whether you really heard anything at all?"

Heads nodded solemnly. He walked to the wall.

"I could have sworn it sounded like this."

He made his fingers into a claw shape and scratched his nails down the plastered surface. A few kids squirmed in their seats.

"So I ran out into the hall like an idiot, because I thought someone was playing a joke on me. But it was just an empty hallway. Later, when I went down to get my lunch I asked one of the other teachers if they played practical jokes on people here. It was then that he told me about the alcove, about the cover-up, about Bria Patterson. I didn't believe him. But when I went back upstairs to finish setting up, there was something sitting on my desk. It was something that hadn't been there before. It was a girl's blue cross-tie, laying there unbuttoned."

Lots of uncomfortable shifting. A boy was clawing his nails into his cheeks, eyes wide as saucers. A girl with multi-colored beads in her hair had her knees knocked together and her hands in a finger web around the front of them. She was rocking and mouthing something unintelligible.

"I didn't want to touch it. Even though my common sense knew someone must have just stuck it there for a joke, my heart knew there was something unholy about it. Like it had come from the grave."

Someone was making a high-pitched moan up in her throat, but Ben hardly heard it. He had to finish and he had to nail this one. Damn the consequences, damn the torpedoes, damn everything.

"Now, I know for a fact that each and every one of us has a low grade level of ESP. I'm not talking about dumb stuff like bending spoons and reading minds and making flower pots fly across the room, but think about this. Have you ever been at The Old Country Buffet, or even in our crummy lunchroom, and you could swear someone was staring at you from behind? And then you turn, and they are staring, for real, for real?"

Heads nodded.

"That's the way I felt. I turned quickly, and I could swear that I saw the edge of a blue uniform skirt whip past the doorway. Then there was a swishing noise out in the hall. Like a jump rope dragging across concrete. I walked over, turned the corner, and she was there. I could see through her. She had blond pigtails, and no eyes, just dark spaces. There was a line of blood coming down the corner of her mouth, and she was running that jump rope back and forth across the floor. She was moaning in the voice of the dead, "Mommy . . . "

Ben was dragging the imaginary rope, playing the part, eyes far off, mouth slightly ajar. Here was where the story always ended. He had never figured out a proper conclusion, and he normally broke character, smiled and said something like,

"Come on guys. I was just kidding. You didn't believe that crap, did you?"

He did not get the chance. The fire alarm went off. Loud. It was a buzzer that was so overwhelming down here it actually made his skin vibrate.

Girls screamed. Boys jumped up from their desks as if there were snakes crawling on the floor. Three girls in the back row stood up, hands pressed to their mouths. They were hyperventilating. A tall girl with white stockings had rushed to the corner of the room, pulled out her blue sweater at the neck, and buried her face in the void as if she was going to puke into it.

Ben was terrified. Surely, he would hear about this from Johnson.

"Guys!" he shouted over the numbing buzz. "Out through the Cherry Street door! Go ahead, it's just an alarm! And I was only kidding about the ghost . . . "

No one really heard. They scrambled for the door. A boy was crying and rubbing the base of his palm against his cheek in angry shame. A girl with thick glasses and blackheads clustered around her nose was furiously punching numbers into a cell phone. Oh, Ben was in a shitstorm now. He wondered if he would be fired. He hadn't looked at his resume for years. This was bad. The last thing he wanted was to be thrown into the system and assigned to a regular Philadelphia public school. They doled out positions by seniority. Charter schools did not rack up points, and he would probably wind up at some ghetto middle school where the kids took apart your emergency phone on the first day, ran in and out of the classrooms like mental patients, and found out where your car was parked before it was time for recess. Ms. Johnson ran a tight ship here with this charter, and he was lucky to have the position he did. He had never really been in trouble with Johnson, but he heard she was merciless if she had a cause. He supposed he could beg. At least he had that.

He walked out into the sunshine and crossed Cherry Street. It was tennis weather. Construction was going on down Broad Street and you could hear a dull pounding complimented by a slightly sharper ratcheting noise associated with cranes and oiled chains being rolled onto big pulley wheels. The kids were gathered in front of a row house with empty planters in front of the dark windows. There were faded white age stains shadowed up the brick. A couple of his tenth graders had migrated over and were sitting on the concrete steps one residence down. Ben waved to them absently and started working his way between children, pleading his case. It was lame and awkward and necessary. He had to do some kind of damage control no matter how slip-shod it appeared.

"I was only kidding, guys. You know that, right?"

"I made the whole thing up. I tell it to my tenth graders all the time. It's a silly story, really."

"Didn't you see that I had no ending for it? Yes. It was just a joke. No girl like that ever went here at all."

Mr. Rollins got on a megaphone.

"Drill's over. Move on to your last period class."

Ben had not worked the group in its entirety. He had gotten to the hyper-ventilators, joked it up, and earned a round of cautious, weak smiles. It turned out that the girl with the blackheads was simply supposed to call her mother at the end of seventh period every day and she had almost forgotten. Big relief there. Still, he hadn't made it to the crying boy or the tall girl who'd almost vomited into her sweater. There were a lot of loose ends here.

Ben Marcus went back inside with his head hung down.

This time he might have actually blown it.

Johnson had not called Ben in to the office today, thank God. He knew there was an unspoken code in the high school not to snitch about the wild stuff he pulled up there, but he had not expected the sixth graders to be so discreet. It had taken all of his will power not to tell Kim about it like a confession when he got home yesterday, and he had woken in a cold sweat three times during the night. But he was pretty sure by now that everything was going to be all right. Ms. Johnson did not bide her time when she had to get something off her plate, so no news at this point in the day was certainly good.

His homeroom was up next. The brown tables were folded up and pushed to the back left corner of the lunchroom. There were rows of chairs set up in front of the steam table and the student council had put up crepe paper streamers. There were some new plants suspended from the drop ceiling, and old Jake had hooked up a sound system. Ms. Newman's homeroom had just completed an oldies thing featuring the Electric Slide that the students laughed at and Ms. Johnson obviously preferred. A guy pretty high up on the food chain at Temple University sat with her at the judge's table, along with a man wearing thin rectangular dark glasses, close cropped sideburns, and a long black overcoat.

Laquanna walked to the center of the space, and the other girls followed. There was a hush. The boys filtered in and took positions between. Malik walked to the front, and there was a rousing cheer speckled by only a few boos from the small crew of guys from the "C" section that he had beaten in a parking lot rap battle last week. He looked over at Jake, and the music blasted on. The kids exploded in movement, and Ben grooved a bit where he stood. He was going to miss this homeroom next year. They had been a lot of fun.

Someone was pulling his sleeve. He looked down. It was a girl from the elementary school, short, probably fourth or fifth grade, long hair curled in sausage shapes and pulled back by a pink satin ribbon tied in a floppy bow. Her eyes were wide with terror.

"What?" he said. "What's wrong?" He had to nearly shout to be heard over the music.

The girl said something and he could not make it out. He leaned down, and her breath came hot in his ear.

"It's the dead girl. She's in the bathroom."

Ben pulled back a bit and raised his eyebrows.

"What?"

She made her lips frame the words in the deliberate manner one used when speaking to the slow or the deaf.

"Our teacher went out to make copies on another floor. Help us. It's the dead girl. She's in one of the stalls moaning, *Mommy.*"

Ben pushed past her and marched out of the lunchroom. The music was cut to a haunt the minute he turned the corner, and he felt his face going hot. This was *just* what he needed. Some jackass sixth grader squatting up on the toilet seat so you couldn't see her feet, then groaning "Mommy" like a wounded doorbell when a younger kid tried to take a piss. Wasn't this always the way of things? He was so sure he had dodged a bullet, and now in this strange backlash, he was still going to get nailed. He could picture the meeting right now, the teachers all at their tables looking innocently at each other, Johnson up at the podium.

"It has come to my attention that some middle school children have been frightening the elementary school students in the bathroom. Evidently, a story about an abducted third grader has been going around the school,

and I would like to know where this started. From the bits and pieces I have heard, the story seems rather sophisticated for a student. I want to know what teacher was involved with this. I want that teacher to come forward and take responsibility for . . . "

You know the drill.

Ben reached the end of the hall and made the quick left. He paused, but only for a bare second. He had never been in the girl's bathroom. He walked through the archway, (there were no doors for bathrooms at People First), and before passing the brown steel divider that blocked the sightline, he called out,

"Teacher coming in! Excuse me! I apologize!"

The bathroom was empty. Besides the lack of urinals to the left, it was the same as most institutional boy's rooms. Brown tiled floor, drain grate in the center surrounded by a shallow puddle of water in a shape that vaguely resembled Texas. There was a row of sinks and each basin had a mirror above it, the reflective material more like tin foil than glass to avoid cracking under the variety of incidents that were so often far from delicate. The soap dispensers each had spots of blood orange residue pooled below on the sink tops where quick hands had missed, and only two had been converted to the newer white units that rationed out foam by palm activation. There was a Fort James paper towel dispenser by the entrance just above an industrial plastic yellow trash can surrounded by the damp, crumpled sheets that had been poorly tossed. There were four stalls, the first three standard issue, and the last sectioned off in its own private area that spanned the width of the space. All three of the doors on the regular stalls were open, but barely. It seemed the floor was pitched in a way that kept them resting an inch or two in off the lock plates. The handicapped door was half ajar.

Ben pushed open the door of the first stall with the middle knuckle of his index finger. Vacant. The bowl was unflushed from what looked like nine or ten sittings, all number one thank God for small favors, and on the wall someone had written, "Shaneeka sucks monkey nuts." Stall number two was in the same relative condition, and number three, of course, was filled with a deposit Ben could not believe someone had the guts to leave out on the surface of this earth. He backed out, breathed in deep, held it, shouldered into the thin stall, and reached for the flusher with the sole of his shoe. When it whooshed down, he pulled back quickly. These institutional mechanisms were sometimes loaded with such strong jets that they kicked up a bit of back splash off the suction.

After the rush of the initial violent whirlpool, there was that hollow, pipe-like refilling sound, and just underneath it, Ben heard a voice. From the handicapped stall. It sounded like it was in tow just beneath the running water, an echo, a faint ringing. It sounded like a girl's voice. Before he could really make out words, it blended with the receding sounds and thinned out to silence.

Ben walked into the handicapped stall. There was a runner bar along the wall, another behind the toilet, a private sink, and a separate towel dispenser. To the right there was also one of those tin foil mirrors, and he saw something move in it. His breath caught in his throat. It was blue, and it had seemed to shoot through the mirror like liquid through a distorted syringe. He moved closer to investigate, and sighed. It was his shirt, picked up in the light and worked through the microscopic steel grooves in an hourglass effect. How did the girls adjust their makeup with these funhouse things? The boys had them too, but he thought the female breed would have demanded better. Personally, he always used the faculty lounge up front by Johnson's office. It was worth the walk.

The hair on the back of his neck was up.

He turned.

There was a hand coming out of the toilet. The seat was up and there was a hand gripping the rim.

Ben grit his teeth and smiled, despite the knocking his heart was still making up in his ears. It was one of those dollar store, plastic dead hands you could affix to door rims and bed edges. So here was the dead girl. Ha ha.

He levered down a fistful of towels and approached. The artwork wasn't even good on this thing. The sores had red spots half covering the indentations and spilling over about a quarter of an inch. Probably a misaligned factory stamp. The nail polish on the scabby fingers had already flaked partly off, and at the edge of the wrist, the press that had molded the rubber most probably had a small void since there were two renegade nodules sticking off that needed to be pruned. Ben reached down to pluck it off the rim and stopped.

There was writing behind the toilet. It was written faintly on the wall tile in the spidery, uneven, block letter style of a young child,

Turn a promise to a lie, and you will be the next to die.

"Fuck," he muttered. The written message had suddenly reminded him of a missed obligation. He grabbed the joke toy, held it off to the side a bit, and walked it out of the stall. His feet made hollow echoes across the floor. He had forgotten to put in a good word for the boy who had been looking at the dead frogs. It would have taken two seconds. He tossed the rubber toy into the yellow bin and sighed. His word was his bond.

Something splashed in the handicapped toilet.

Ben put his fists to his sides and stalked back to the stall. Enough already. He stopped when he turned the corner of the doorway.

There were two hands gripping the rim of the bowl as if reaching up from deep within it, palms down, fingers over the edges. They were girl hands, rotten and burst at the knuckles with yellow-graying bone sticking through. The skin was mottled, water-shriveled, and blue. The fingers released, and the forearms slipped back into the water, the hands following, down to the fingertips. Gone. There was a faint gasp, like the exit of breath.

Ben approached the toilet. "I did not just see that," he said to himself. His legs were numb, his mouth ajar. There was a brown ring at the surface edge of the water, and there was still the hint of faint ripples dancing above the submerged, funneled pipe orifice.

Something from the drain-hole exploded.

Ben saw a flash of dirty blue and white checkerboard just before it whipped across the bridge of his nose. The cold toilet water that sprayed him in the face was eclipsed by the sharp snap of pain. His glasses flew off to skid along the tile into the next stall. Ben's left eye had been struck bald and it was squeezed shut. The other was half open in a squint, and through the blur he saw the elongated jump rope whirling mad figure eights, its alleged wooden handles still buried in the depths of the drain. Dirty water snapped to the sides spattering the dull yellow concrete block wall and the steel divider to the left. Ben put up his hands in a defensive posture, but the rope was quicker. It snaked out and hooked him at the back of the neck.

It spun mad spaghetti twirls and peppered drain water up his nose. He clawed his hands at the front of his neck and couldn't get his fingers under. The taste in his mouth was hot copper. There was a yank, and he was brought a foot closer and a yard lower. He kept his feet, but he was losing this tug of war.

Black spots danced in front of his eyes, and his lungs started screaming for air. He tried rearing back, but the pull was too great. He opened his eyes for the last time, and saw the toilet bowl rush at his face. And the last thought Ben Marcus had on the face of this earth was that the promise he had broken was far more fundamental than a forgotten bribe to a kid who was messing around with a dead frog in a jar.

Lia fears for her kind. They are fragmented and she knows that even under threat they will not unify. Some humans will submit to the knife rather than give in to the beast; the true wolf will kill until it dies of exhaustion . . .

THE DIRE WOLF

GENEVIEVE VALENTINE

The bone is worrisome.

"It's huge, Lia," says Christopher over the phone. "The guy who found it thought it was a bear jaw."

"What's the quality of the joint?" she asks, like she's stumped.

"Great condition on one side."

She guesses the other side has been broken off. (When werewolves fight, it's almost always a dive for the throat—the skull gets in the way.)

"I'm sorry to call you," he says, "but I figured if anyone would know—"

"I'll come out tomorrow," she says.

She hangs up the phone, her palm pressing fl at against the receiver as if she can keep the news from spreading.

Velia doesn't really worry, the whole journey up to Fairbanks. People find bones from time to time. She can find a place somewhere in the *Canis* family to put almost anything. She's identified the remains of more rare species than any other xenoarchaeologist in the country.

She doesn't worry when Christopher shows her the jawbone and says wonderingly, "I've never seen anything like it—I mean, there's no meat left, but it's so . . . "

"Fresh?" she asks, and Christopher pulls a face that means Yes.

"I'll take a look," she says, as if she's planning some tests, but she's already planning the paperwork. It's only a bone fragment. She'd name it a gray wolf already and call it a night, except that it was good to put on a show of working hard.

(The jaw is missing a third of the left mandible, snapped clean away. She had forgotten how powerful a werewolf could be when it was cornered.)

Velia isn't worried at all, until Christopher says, "We called in someone else to help speed up the identification. If there are dangerous animals in the park somewhere, we need to know."

Then she sets down the bone with trembling hands.

She doesn't listen to Christopher after that. No need; she knows who they've called in.

She would have called him in, too, if they were still speaking.

The dire wolf did not survive.

The fossil record says the dire wolf vanished. It wasn't clever enough to live in the age after ice, after the mammoth was gone. It was all force, no cleverness. It was too large to live in the close, tight foliage of the world's new spring.

The skulls line the walls of the Tar Pit Museum, tidy rows of dead.

Velia had spent one summer carefully brushing dust away from the piles of bones in La Brea, picking tar from around the eye sockets and the incisors, edging the little furrow that ran from nose to neck. By the end of August they had eleven skulls.

"God, no wonder they all died," said Alice, holding up a skull with no jaw—the jaws never made it. When Alice held the base, the front teeth pressed into her elbow. "Smallest cranial I've seen on a dog. Poor puppies. Too stupid to get out of the tar." She patted its head. "Adapt or die, right?"

Velia had more pity. She knew what it was like to be blinded by want.

He arrives late.

She's running her fingers over the clean break on the mandible, and when she hears him coming and looks up she sees that the windows have all gone black, and her little lamp is the only thing fighting the dark.

It's almost dark enough to hide his flinch when he sees her. (Almost; not quite.)

She's grateful to have been the one who knew it was coming. She didn't want to think about how she might look if he ever caught her unaware.

"Velia," he says.

He's only ever used her full name. ("If you ever call me Lia, I'll know you're under duress," she said once, and he had looked up for a long moment before he smiled.)

It's been six years. He hasn't aged.

"Mark," she says, the same tone.

Even tired, worn out from travel, his dark eyes are sharp. He glances around the room, leans against the doorway too casually, sets his bag down like it's a trap and he's ready to run. The draft from the outer door hits her; snow, and evergreens.

She can see his fatigue in the slope of his shoulders. She doesn't even know where he came in from; his work takes him all over, and it's not like they're in touch.

After a second he asks, carefully, "Have you been expecting me?"

"Allan told me he'd called you, after I got here."

He looks at the jaw in her hand. She's been playing with it without noticing. Now it's hanging from her wrist; the front of the jaw follows the curve of her hand, the teeth small pressure points against her knuckles. One has cut through the skin, and a little red bead is forming under the white.

(The teeth on a dire wolf are impossibly sharp. If you shove a pipe in its mouth, the wolf will bite clean through it and keep coming.)

She says, "The ones from La Brea are so dark from the tar, you start to think that's just what they look like."

He doesn't answer. When she finally looks up, he's watching her without blinking. He looks torn.

She remembers, too late, what it feels like to have him watching her.

"It's good to see you," he says, and it almost sounds like the truth. (Almost; not quite.)

There was a wolfish quality about him right from the beginning. He had a way of leaning back in a chair, tilting his head down when he was deep in thought, that answered some need she didn't know she had.

They had been in Alaska then, too, studying the migratory patterns of wolves.

(One of the other anthropologists was in love with him; you could see it in the way she half-turned her head when he spoke.)

Halfway through the project, it stormed, and all five of them spent days sitting close together in the main room of the rented house, because it had the only fireplace.

Velia spent most of her time at the kitchen table (she didn't mind the cold). She looked at foliage lists for the Russian and Alaskan sides of the Bering Straight, glancing absently at the sketch of the dire wolf beside the gray wolf, the gray wolf looking spindly and half-grown next to its dead cousin.

From one of the chairs near the fire, Mark asked (his first words to her), "Velia—why would you cross a land bridge when there was sufficient prey where you were?"

"The fever of pursuit," Velia said, absently.

When she looked up, he seemed caught off-guard for the first time since she'd met him. For the rest of the night, he cast long looks her way when he thought she couldn't see him, as if a worthy opponent had walked onto the field and taken him by surprise.

She let it pass. She didn't get involved with people.

He stands in the doorway like he's thinking of something cutting to say, but in the end he leaves his bag behind and approaches with long quiet steps to peer at the jawbone.

He doesn't touch her, but as he lifts and turns the bone she rolls her hand along with it, not letting go, and he looks at her palm before he looks at the bone.

"Whoever won this fight will want to keep this under wraps," he says, after a long examination.

She knows. It's why she was worried about Mark's coming. Werewolf fights—always to the death—are such a waste. Dire wolves are rare enough as it is.

She says, "Whoever won this fight woke up with bone in his teeth."

He half-smiles, doesn't look up from the jaw. When he runs his fingers over the flats of the teeth, the pad of his thumb just brushes her skin.

Her stomach turns over.

She ignores it; it's residual. Old habit.

The dire wolf had a temporal fossa out of proportion to its brain cavity. It was what made the top of its skull so different from the skull of an Arctic wolf or a gray wolf; the dire wolf's cranium was low and narrow, the caved-in temples on either side looking like two kicks from a horse.

For a long time, Velia thought the slender skull meant that the dire wolf wasn't clever enough to survive the new age without adapting.

After she met Mark, she began to think more about the temporal fossa, the deep indentations in the skull that housed the jaw muscles. The skull was narrow because the muscles were large.

When the dire wolf bit down, it held on. That's what it was made to do.

She sits awake for an hour, imagining she can hear him breathing, before she gets up the courage to go to sleep. It's her imagination; the sudden shock of nearness had brought back old caution. That was all.

(It was easier to be lonely. His companionship was dangerous.)

If in the middle of the night he walks back and forth outside her door like a sentinel, scuffing the carpet just loudly enough to cut through her dreams—well, maybe she imagines that, too.

If in the dark she bolts awake, listening to an animal breathing warm and strong in the snow outside—that, she's not imagining.

"Does it frighten you?" he asked.

She said, "Always."

She's been awake for an hour, watching out the window, when he knocks on her door. It's not quite dawn, but she's not surprised; she knows he's been awake, too.

"There's another wolf," he says.

In the small room, in the welcome dark, he seems impossibly far away.

She stands up. "I know."

He flushes, goes white. "You haven't—have you been outside? You can't go out there, Velia. It will kill you."

There is a stab in her side, just for a moment, as if he's cut her. She fights to stay calm. There is no safety with him any more.

"I'll be fine," she says.

He takes two steps. They're close enough to kiss. "Velia," he says, his voice rumbling in his chest, "that wolf snapped another's jaw clean off. What is it going to do with you?"

"Talk," she says.

To a dire wolf, the human form is like a paved street; the wolf lives in the tree roots that silently push until the stone swells and cracks and falls apart.

Velia has done better at keeping human than most wolves, but it's hard to ignore another of your kind when it comes calling.

She parks her car close to the trees. (It's a useless human habit; the wolf can run faster than any speeding car can save you.)

When she's far into the forest and can smell she's alone, she folds her shirt and pants and boots under the branches of a fir tree, where the snow has not reached.

(Any dire wolf who lives in human form has had to explain their nakedness. The smart ones learn to leave their clothes where they can be retrieved before people find them naked and start asking questions.)

She proceeds barefoot, wrapped in her coat—waxed cotton, the closest texture she can find to human skin. It's nice to have a human skin that doesn't hurt.

She stops short when she smells the other wolf.

The change surges into her throat like vomit; she swallows and tries to breathe. She won't give in to the wolf unless she has to.

(The pain is worse than the fight.)

She reaches the clearing where the wolf has been—the smell of blood is still strong—and hangs back, waiting.

It's rare for dire wolves of the same form to fight one another. As humans they attract each other, as wolves they form packs. But those who stay in human form often go mad, or fall in love with humans, and the true wolf has no patience for either one. The human wolf must be careful.

It won't be the first time Velia's had to fight for this body.

Her father died of some human cancer. He wouldn't let anyone treat him for it ("What if they find out somehow?"), and as he took his last breaths, a ripple of the wolf's face slid over his features, a last toothsome grin before he was gone. It was how Velia would have wanted to remember him.

Her mother died later that year during a new moon, while her body was trying to make the shift back from the wolf. Velia gathered her mother in her arms and sobbed into the soft gray fur until the form in her arms was human, and Velia could pick her up and carry her home.

(The dire wolf takes human form when it dies; that lets them pass through the world without leaving proof behind.)

It was her mother's broken heart that did it, Velia knew. Her mother could have lived another fifty years, another hundred—their kind was hardy, if they could strike some balance between human and wolf that didn't drive them to the brink. It was a weak heart that had taken her mother.

Velia learned early that it was safer to be alone.

She never told Mark how rare it was for a dire wolf to care for a real human. Even after he knew what she was, how could she explain what even the dire wolves struggled to come to terms with?

She told him, early, "I can't."

Later she told him, "We can't."

Just that word frightened her, the idea that there was danger to more than just herself, that she had to worry for them both.

He fought her on it. They parted badly.

But she was right. Two years after she left him, she had to identify the teeth marks on a human man who had been torn to pieces by a wild beast. A pack of coyotes, she said. The bites looked big because there had been so many of them overlapping, she said.

She never found out if the wolf had killed its own lover, or if it had been punishing another wolf for keeping human company.

Velia spent every new moon that year looking forward to the change. On four legs, at least, she could hunt without thinking.

An hour later, the wolf appears.

Velia tenses, once, just to make sure she hasn't frozen. But her muscles are warm and ready (she's never really been cold), and she's not frightened.

The wolf has never frightened her. It's how she can live as a human without losing her mind; she accepts the shape of the beast.

(In her bones, she knows that sooner or later, she'll give in to the wolf and disappear.)

It pads to the edge of the clearing opposite her and stands in the shadows, waiting. Once, it shifts, and the sun catches its head for a moment—one amber eye, sharp tight muzzle-fur the color of dust.

"I'm here," Velia says. "What do you want?"

When there's no answer, she tries again, in her true language. Silence.

"Why did you kill one of your own?"

It's one of their own—the jaw of one of their own is sitting in the dinky office lab ten miles away—but those who live as wolves don't like hearing solidarity from those on two legs.

The wolf-change claws at Velia's throat; she bites her lips against it until she tastes blood.

"What do you want?" she calls again, finally, but the wolf startles and runs, leaves nothing behind but a maze of prints and a cloud of breath that hangs in the air for a few moments after the wolf has disappeared.

She shivers; pretends it's from the cold.

Velia takes her time putting her clothes back on.

They make her feel more human, a little less afraid.

The wolf, in all things, protects itself.

It's why Velia studied animals. It's why she examines bones and tags them wolf or coyote or some breed long dead. It helps keep them all from being found out.

She fears for her kind. They are fragmented (the human-living and the beasts, taking turns hating one another more), and she knows that even under threat they would not unify. Some humans would submit to the knife rather than give in to the beast, and the true wolf would kill all comers until it died of exhaustion.

So she keeps her human shape, walks through the world, tags her jaws *Canis lupus arctos*; because what else could humans do but wipe them out, if they knew?

Velia and Mark were at the end of the Alaska winter when the thaw came.

They got called away from wrap-up in Alaska to work a dig in Iceland. Spring had come early, and they were summoned to take advantage of the softer ground and dig down another layer.

("What are you really looking for?" he asked, like he already knew why she agreed to come.

She didn't ask why he had come with her. She knew what pursuit looked like.

"I can't explain," she said, as if it answered him.)

For two weeks she scooped mud out of her taped-off square and carved bone after bone in bas relief, and all the while she knew she wasn't alone. The mossy tundra had eyes for her, and whenever she was near Mark, under his wolfish eyes, she felt a beast in the forest hating her.

(A wolf knows a wolf.)

They were done for the night, back at the rickety two-bedroom house near the dig site, when the wolf came.

There was the single howl as it called her to battle (they both stood up so fast the work table skidded), and then nothing but the wind; the dire wolf is silent when it hunts.

"Stay behind me," Mark said. Then came the thunder of the charging beast. It was too fast for her to get away, too fast to hide Mark, too fast to explain.

There was only time to throw open the door and leap (Mark shouting at her to stop), force the change between one breath and the next, so that she furled inside-out and the air crackled with the sound of snapping tendons and the grind of bone.

(She won. She doesn't remember how. All the way home she coughed up bits of the other wolf; spat up bone and teeth and fur.)

The fight carried her a quarter-mile from the cabin, and she padded back as the wolf.

There was a chance he hadn't seen her. There was a chance he didn't know.

(No chance.)

When she saw him standing in the doorway, the blanket in his hands, she made a high, keening noise that started as a howl, and became—between one breath and another—a human cry.

(Grief.)

Her bones seemed painfully soft and frail in her human form; she could hardly feel her blood pumping through such long, twisted veins. She set her weakling jaw against the shaking, but her skeleton rattled inside the meat.

It was worse than the new moon, ten times worse. It was the tree roots erupting through the pavement, shattering the stone.

Mark got both arms under her and carried her inside, out of the ice and the dark. He smelled like snow and detergent and fear, and she didn't know why a smell like that would be comforting to a wolf.

(She didn't know much about love, back then.)

He carried her up the stairs and ran a hot shower until the blood and dirt were gone, and his hands were shaking.

(Fear, she thought then. She knows now—desire.)

When she came downstairs again, he was standing outside. There was a wolf's footprint in the snow outside the cabin. It was the same length as Mark's foot, and as wide; her claws had pierced right through the snow and dug up four thin sprays of black dirt across the white as she ran.

He passed his foot over it, smoothing the snow free of the evidence. She waited, wondering what she would do if he threatened to expose her.

(It was a lie. She knew what she would do. On four legs, she could hunt without thinking.)

After a long time, he took a step backwards, closer to her, without turning.

"Does it frighten you?" he asked.

She said, "Always."

When he came at her, the kiss drove her against the door with a thud, and he tore away the blanket as if he wanted some part, any part, of her fight.

She dragged her nails over his back, five thin trails of red against his skin.

The dire wolf that lives in human form spends the day of the new moon curled in a corner, trembling, aching, grinding her teeth as the bones scream for change. The moment of transformation is unbearable (there is always the wrenching cry), but it passes, and the bones and the fur and the teeth of the wolf are her relief.

A dire wolf can turn at will, but it's the last line of defense; between pain and death, some choose death.

Changing at every new moon from human to wolf and back can drive you mad. Most dire wolves eventually give in to their true form, and make their homes in forests, or tundra if arctic wolves are nearby, or desert caves. They can go anywhere once the moon has lost its power over them. What animal would stand up to a beast twice as large as a wolf, twice as fast, twice as cunning?

Legend, which looks for monsters within its own neighbors, claim that werewolves are people who achieve the body of the wolf.

This is untrue.

The dire wolf took on a human form; down at the bone, between every breath, each of them is really the animal. The human shape is a useful trick, that's all.

(Adapt or die.)

Christopher's waiting at the lab when she comes back.

"Mark says it looks like an Arctic wolf that got on the wrong side of a bear attack," he says. "What are you thinking it is?"

"I think that wolf had a pretty sad end," she said. "Did you find anything else of the skeleton?"

Christopher shakes his head. "We don't have the manpower we used to, but as far as we looked, there was nothing to find. Maybe the head got carried over to where our guy found it."

"Was there any skull? Any other bones?" She thinks about the deep, low temporal fossa—a jaw is easy to disguise, but the skull would be hard to explain.

He shakes his head.

"Where's Mark?"

"Went out looking for you," Christopher says. "I'll call him back in on the radio."

When she's alone, she looks at the jaw under the magnifying glass, marks on her report the hundred tiny dents where the birds pecked the flesh away, the smooth expanses where the insects got there at last, carrying away whatever was hanging on.

The bone is cool, and smooth as human skin.

Mark opens the door too fast, gets too close.

"I saw the tracks," he says, quietly, so Christopher won't hear. "It's big."

He means, it's bigger than you. His breath is warm on her scalp.

"I'll win," she says.

After a little silence, he says, "I'd forgotten what it feels like to be close to you."

She doesn't know what he means; doesn't dare ask.

The dire wolf was too slow to evolve, everyone knew.

"Poor guys," Alice said (she pitied all the bones). She waggled the saber-toothed tiger skull she was working on, like it was nodding. "The saber-tooth says nature cuts us all down sooner or later. He should know. Poor kitty."

Alice always got punchy near the end of an excavation.

"Nature might surprise you," Velia said, ran her tongue over her teeth.

"Promise me you won't fight," he says.

They're in his room. He's pacing; she's watching the moonlight play over his face. When he passes back and forth, his shoulder brushes her shoulder.

"It doesn't want to fight," she says.

He stops and looks at her. "What can I do? How can I help you?"

She doesn't know how to explain how he's only ever been a danger. She doesn't know how to tell him how different he is from most of his kind, in loving her.

(Most wolves find a mate in each other, because humans are frail; because when faced with a monster, a normal human senses danger and retreats.)

She says, "Live where there are no wolves."

He frowns like she's cut him. She knows that pain.

She wants to leave here with him and go somewhere where there are no wolves, carve some narrow sliver of love from each of them, see what it can build.

Doesn't dare.

They don't embrace; his hands are shaking, her hands are fists. He kisses her temple, presses his lips to the temporal fossa; she holds her breath, closes her eyes.

At night, the wolf 's tracks are easier to follow. There's a better quality of shadow when the moon is out, and in her waxy coat and bare feet, Velia is an extension of the snow; only her dark eyes and black hair give her away.

(They used to be the color of dust, and her face was broad and sharp-mouthed. There's too much human in her face, now.)

The den is in a shallow cave, close to the surface. It's shallow enough that by the time Velia smells decay, she is looking past the narrow entry through the darkness to the wolf and the human body of its dead mate.

Of course there were no wolf bones to find; the human shape is the dire wolf 's last defense.

But Velia's eyes have always been sharp, and she can see from where she's standing that there's an empty shadow beneath the torn throat, the wrinkled skin. (She was old, old enough for even the true wolf to die.)

The break in the jaw was a clean one. It must have snapped as he dragged his mate's body to the shadow of the den, before the change, where he could make sure no stranger would find her.

He watches her with gleaming eyes, and she braces herself against his sorrow.

She says, "We found the bone. You're safe. You can find another place."

The head droops, and a huff of breath mists over the black for a moment.

Then the wolf lies down beside its mate and stretches its neck along the ground, waiting for the strike.

Velia hadn't known enough true wolves to know what can happen when a wolf is parted from its mate. She had hoped her parents were the exception, and not the rule. But the dire wolf does what she dreaded; it mates for life.

No, she thinks, I can't, I can't, but the wolf is willing. (The human form is just a trick; at the roots, the wolf is always waiting.)

When the change comes over her, the other wolf whimpers a welcome. She chokes through the pain before the wolf form takes, bites down on her cries.

Old habit. The wolf is silent when it hunts.

According to the fossil record, dire wolves hunted in packs to the exclusion of good sense, leaping into the tar pits by the dozens until every last one of them was drowned.

"Live together, die together, I guess," sighed Alice, cleaning dirt off her chisel. "I mean, what could possibly drive an animal into the tar pits, once you saw what happened to the others? They couldn't all be stupid."

Velia blew a layer of dust off the skull at her feet and wondered about that first wolf, the first one who had retreated from the edge of the tar. She wondered how it got desperate enough to turn to humans just to find some pack to live among.

That was the dire wolf that had fathered them all. The true wolf had always been separate; had been always alone.

When Velia can stand on her two feet, she washes the blood off in the river, then pulls on her waxy coat and walks back the way she came.

She scuffs gently over her footsteps on her way, so that no one might find the tracks and disturb the dead.

She leaves that night. She doesn't ask where Mark was going. Doesn't dare.

(When the dire wolf bites down, it holds on. That's what it's made to do.)

Do the dead lose their egotism and their one-time need to limit and dominate earthly households? wonders Caroleen. *Her deceased twin had maintained Caroleen as a sort of extended self, and it had resulted in isolation for the two of them . . .*

PARALLEL LINES

TIM POWERS

It should have been their birthday today. Well, it was still hers, Caroleen supposed, but with BeeVee gone the whole idea of "birthday" seemed to have gone, too. Could she be seventy-three on her own?

Caroleen's right hand had been twitching intermittently since she'd sat up in the living room daybed five minutes ago, and she lifted the coffee cup with her left hand. The coffee was hot enough but had no taste, and the living room furniture-the coffee table, the now-useless analog TV set with its forlorn rabbit-ears antenna, the rocking chair beside the white-brick fireplace, all bright in the sunlight glaring through the east window at her back-looked like arranged items in some kind of museum diorama; no further motion possible.

But there was still the gravestone to be dealt with, these disorganized nine weeks later. Four hundred and fifty dollars for two square feet of etched granite, and the company in Nevada could not get it straight that Beverly Veronica Erlich and Caroleen Ann Erlich both had the same birth date, though the second date under Caroleen's name was to be left blank for some indeterminate period.

BeeVee's second date had not been left to chance. BeeVee had swallowed all the Darvocets and Vicodins in the house when the pain of her cancer, if it had been cancer, had become more than she could bear. For a year or so she had always been in some degree of pain—Caroleen remembered how BeeVee had exhaled a fast *whew!* from time to time, and the way her forehead seemed always to be misted with sweat, and her late-acquired habit of repeatedly licking the inner edge of her upper lip. And she had always been shifting her position when she drove, and bracing herself against the floor or the steering wheel. More and more she had come to rely—both of them had come to rely—on poor dumpy Amber, the teenager who lived next door. The girl came over to clean the house and fetch groceries, and seemed grateful for the five dollars an hour, even with BeeVee's generous criticisms of every job Amber did.

But Amber would not be able to deal with the headstone company. Caroleen shifted forward on the daybed, rocked her head back and forth to make sure she was wearing her reading glasses rather than her bifocals, and flipped open the brown plastic phone book. A short silver pencil was secured by a plastic loop in the book's gutter, and she fumbled it free—

—And her right hand twitched forward, knocking the coffee cup right off the table, and the pencil shook in her spotty old fingers as its point jiggled across the page.

She threw a fearful, guilty glance toward the kitchen in the moment before she remembered that BeeVee was dead; then she allowed herself to relax and looked at the squiggle she had drawn across the old addresses and phone numbers.

It was jagged, but recognizably cursive letters:

Ineedyourhelpplease

It was, in fact, recognizably BeeVee's handwriting.

Caroleen's hand twitched again, and scrawled the same cramped sequence of letters across the page. She lifted the pencil, postponing all thought in this frozen moment, and after several seconds her hand spasmed once more, no doubt writing the same letters in the air. Her whole body shivered with a feverish chill and she thought she was going to vomit; she leaned out over the rug, but the queasiness passed.

She was sure that her hand had been writing this message in the air ever since she had awakened.

Caroleen didn't think BeeVee had ever before, except with ironic emphasis, said *please* when asking her for something.

She was remotely glad that she was sitting, for her heart thudded alarmingly in her chest and she was dizzy with the enormous thought that BeeVee was not gone, not entirely gone. She gripped the edge of the bed, suddenly afraid of falling and knocking the table over, rolling into the rocking chair. The reek of spilled coffee was strong in her nostrils.

"Okay," she whispered. "Okay!" she said again, louder. The shaking in her hand had subsided, so she flipped to a blank calendar page at the back of the book and scrawled OKAY at the top of the page.

Her fingers had begun wiggling again, but she raised her hand as if to wave away a question, hesitant to let the jiggling pencil at the waiting page just yet.

Do I want her back, she thought, *in any sense?* No, not *want*, not *her*, but—in these past nine weeks I haven't seemed to exist anymore, without her paying attention, any sort of attention, to me. These days I'm hardly more than an imaginary friend of Amber's next door, a frail conceit soon to be outgrown, even by her.

She sighed and lowered her hand to the book. Over her *OKAY* the pencil scribbled,

iambeevee

"My God," Caroleen whispered, closing her eyes. "You think I need to be told?"

Her hand was involuntarily spelling it out again, breaking the pencil lead halfway through but continuing rapidly to the end, and then it went through the motions three more times, just scratching the paper with splintered wood. Finally her hand uncramped.

She threw the pencil on the floor and scrabbled among the orange plastic prescription bottles on the table for a pen. Finding one, she wrote, *What can I do? To help*

She wasn't able to add the final question mark because her hand convulsed away from her again, and wrote,

touseyourbodyinvitemeintoyourbody

and then a moment later,

imsorryforeverythingplease

Caroleen watched as the pen in her hand wrote out the same two lines twice more, then she leaned back and let the pen jiggle in the air until this bout, too, gradually wore off and her hand went limp.

Caroleen blinked tears out of her eyes, trying to believe that they were caused entirely by her already-sore wrist muscles. But-for BeeVee to apologize, to her . . . ! The only apologies BeeVee had ever made while alive were qualified and impatient: *Well, I'm* sorry *if . . .*

Do the dead lose their egotism? wondered Caroleen, *their onetime need to limit and dominate earthly households?* BeeVee had maintained Caroleen as a sort of extended self, and it had resulted in isolation for the two of them; if, in fact, they had added up to quite as many as two during the last years. The twins had a couple of brothers out there somewhere, and a least a couple of nieces, and their mother might even still be alive at ninety-one, but Caroleen knew nothing of any of them. BeeVee had handled all the mail.

Quickly she wrote on the calendar page, *I need to know—do you love me?*

For nearly a full minute she waited, her shoulder muscles stiffening as she held the pen over the page; then her hand flexed and wrote,

yes

Caroleen was gasping and she couldn't see the page through her tears, but she could feel her hand scribbling the word over and over again until this spasm, too, eventually relaxed.

Why did you have to wait, she thought, until after you had died to tell me?

But *use your body, invite me into your body.* What would that mean? Would BeeVee take control of it, ever relinquish control?

Do I, thought Caroleen, *care, really?*

Whatever it might consist of, it would be at least a step closer to the wholeness Caroleen had lost nine weeks ago.

Her hand was twitching again. She waited until the first couple of scribbles had expended themselves in the air before touching the pen to the page. The pen wrote,

yesforever

She moved her hand aside, not wanting to spoil that statement with echoes.

When the pen had stilled, Caroleen leaned forward and began writing *Yes, I'll invite you*, but her hand took over and finished the line with

exhaustedmorelater

Exhausted? Was it strenuous for ghosts to lean out or in or down this far? Did BeeVee have to brace herself against something to drive the pencil?

But, in fact, Caroleen was exhausted, too—her hand was aching. She blew her nose into an old Kleenex, her eyes watering afresh in the menthol-and-eucalyptus smell of Bengay, and lay back across the daybed and closed her eyes.

A sharp knock at the front door jolted her awake, and though her glasses had fallen off and she didn't immediately know whether it was morning or evening, she realized that her fingers were wiggling, and had been for some time.

She lunged forward and with her left hand wedged the pen between her twitching right thumb and forefinger. The pen began to travel lightly over the calendar page. The scribble was longer than the others—with a pause in the middle—and she had to rotate the book to keep the point on the page until it stopped.

The knock sounded again, but Caroleen called, "Just a minute!" and remained hunched over the little book, waiting for the message to repeat.

It didn't. Apparently she had just barely caught the last echo—perhaps only the end of the last echo.

She couldn't make out what she had written. Even if she'd had her glasses on, she'd have needed the lamp light, too.

"Caroleen?" came a call from out front. It was Amber's voice.

"Coming." Caroleen stood up stiffly and hobbled to the door. When she pulled it open, she found herself squinting in the noon sunlight that filtered through the avocado tree branches.

The girl on the doorstep was wearing sweatpants and a huge T-shirt and blinking behind her gleaming round spectacles. Her brown hair was tied up in a knot on top of her head. "Did I wake you up? I'm sorry." She was panting, as if she had run over here from next door.

Caroleen felt the fresh air—smelling of sun-heated stone and car exhaust—cooling her sweaty scalp. "I'm fine," she said hoarsely. "What is it? Had she asked the girl to come over today? She couldn't recall doing it, and she was tense with impatience to get back to her pen and book.

"I just—" said Amber rapidly—"I liked your sister, well, you know I did really, even though—and I—could I have something of hers, not like valuable, to remember her by? How about her hairbrush?"

"You want her hairbrush?"

"If you don't mind. I just want something—"

"I'll get it. Wait here." It would be quicker to give it to her than to propose some other keepsake, and Caroleen had no special attachment to the hairbrush—her own was a duplicate anyway. She and BeeVee had, of course, matching everything—toothbrushes, coffee cups, shoes, wristwatches.

When Caroleen had fetched the brush and returned to the front door, Amber took it and went pounding down the walkway, calling "Thanks!" over her shoulder.

Still disoriented from her nap, Caroleen closed the door and made her way back to the daybed, where she patted the scattered blankets until she found her glasses and fitted them on.

She sat down, switched on the lamp, and leaned over the phone book page. Turning the book around to follow the newest scrawl, she read,

bancaccounts
getmyhairbrushfromhernow

"Sorry, sorry!" exclaimed Caroleen; then in her own handwriting, she wrote, *I'll get it back.*

She waited, wondering why she must get the hairbrush back from Amber. Was it somehow necessary that all of BeeVee's possessions be kept together? Probably, at least the ones with voodoo-type identity signatures on them—DNA samples, like hair caught in a brush, dried saliva traces on dentures, Kleenex in a forgotten wastebasket. But—

Abruptly her chest felt cold and hollow.

But this message had been written down *before* she had given Amber the hairbrush. And Caroleen had been awake only for the last few seconds of the message transmission, which, if it had been like the others, had been repeating for at least a full minute before she woke up.

The message had been addressed to Amber next door, not to her. Amber had read it somehow and had obediently fetched the hairbrush.

Could all of these messages have been addressed to the girl?

Caroleen remembered wondering whether BeeVee might have needed to brace herself against something in order to communicate from the far side of the grave. Had BeeVee been bracing herself against Caroleen, her still-living twin, in order to talk to Amber? Insignificant *Amber*?

Caroleen was dizzy, but she got to her feet and padded into the bedroom for a pair of outdoor shoes. She had to carry them back to the living room—the bed in the bedroom had been BeeVee's, too, and she didn't want to sit on it in order to pull the shoes on—and on the way she leaned into the bathroom and grabbed her own hairbrush.

Dressed in one of her old church-attendance skirts, with fresh lipstick, and carrying a big embroidered purse, Caroleen pulled the door closed behind her and began shuffling down the walk. The sky was a very deep blue above the tree branches and the few clouds were extraordinarily far away overhead, and it occurred to her that she couldn't recall stepping out of the house since BeeVee's funeral. She never drove anymore—Amber was the only one who drove the old Pontiac these days—and it was Amber who went for groceries, reimbursed with checks from Caroleen . . . and the box of checks came in the mail, which Amber brought in from the mailbox by the sidewalk. If Caroleen alienated the girl, could she do these things herself? She would probably starve.

Caroleen's hand had begun wriggling as she reached the sidewalk and turned right, toward Amber's parents' house, but she resisted the impulse to pull a pen out of her purse. *She's not talking to me*, she thought, blinking back tears in the sunlight that glittered on the windshields and bumpers of passing cars; *she's talking to stupid Amber. I won't eavesdrop.*

Amber's parents had a Spanish-style house at the top of a neatly mowed sloping lawn, and a green canvas awning overhung the big arched window out front. Even shading her eyes with her manageable left hand Caroleen couldn't see anyone in the dimness inside, so she huffed up the widely spaced steps, and while she was catching her breath on the cement apron at the top, the front door swung inward, releasing a puff of cool floor-polish scent.

Amber's young, dark-haired mother—Crystal? Christine?—was staring at her curiously. "It's . . . Caroleen," she said, "right?"

"Yes." Caroleen smiled, feeling old and foolish. "I need to talk to Amber." The mother was looking dubious. "I want to pay her more, and see if she'd be interested in balancing our, my, checkbook.

The woman nodded, as if conceding a point. "Well, I think that might be good for her." She hesitated, then stepped aside. "Come in and ask her. She's in her room."

Caroleen got a quick impression of a dim living room with clear plastic covers over the furniture, and a bright kitchen with copper pans hanging everywhere. Amber's mother then knocked on a bedroom door and said, "Amber honey? You've got a visitor," then pushed the door open.

"I'll let you two talk," the woman said, and stepped away toward the living room.

Caroleen stepped into the room. Amber was sitting cross-legged on a pink bedspread, looking up from a cardboard sheet with a rock, a pencil, and BeeVee's hairbrush on it. Lacy curtains glowed in the street-side window, and a stack of what appeared to be textbooks stood on an otherwise bare white desk in the opposite corner. The couple of pictures on the walls looked like pastel blobs. The room smelled like cake.

Caroleen considered what to say. "Can I help?" she asked finally.

Amber, who had been looking wary, brightened and sat up straight. "Shut the door."

After Caroleen had shut the door, Amber went on, "You know she's coming back?" She waved at the cardboard in front of her. "She's been talking to me all day."

"I know, child."

Caroleen stepped forward and leaned down to peer at the cardboard, and saw that the girl had written the letters of the alphabet in an arc across it.

"It's one of those things people use to talk to ghosts," Amber explained with evident pride. "I'm using the rock crystal to point to the letters. Some people are scared of these things, but it's one of the good kinds of crystals."

"A Ouija board."

"That's it! She made me dream of one over and over again just before the sun came up, because this is her birthday. Well, yours, too, I guess. At first I thought it was a hopscotch pattern, but she made me look closer till I got it." She pursed her lips. "I wrote it by reciting the rhyme, and I accidentally did *H* and *I* twice, and left out *J* and *K*." She pulled a sheet of lined paper out from under the board. "But it was only a problem once, I think."

"Can I see? I, uh, want this to work out."

"Yeah. She won't be gone. She'll be in me, did she tell you?" She held out the paper. "I drew in lines to break the words up."

"Yes. She told me." Caroleen slowly reached out to take the paper from Amber, and then held it up close enough to read the penciled lines:

I/NEED/YOUR/HELP/PLEASE
Who R U?
I/AM/BEE VEE
How can I help U?
I/NEED/TO/USE/YOUR/BODY/INVITE/ME/IN/TO/YOUR/BODY
IM/SORRY/FOR/EVERY/THING/PLEASE
R U an angel now? Can U grant wishes?
YES
Can U make me beautiful?
YES/FOR/EVER
OK. What do I do?
EXHAUSTED/MORE/LATER
BV? It's after lunch. Are U rested up yet?
YES
Make me beautiful.
GET/MY/HAIRBRUSH/FROM/MY/SISTER
Is that word "hairbrush"?
YES/THEN/YOU/CAN/INVITE/ME/IN/TO/YOU
How will that do it?
WE/WILL/BE/YOU/TOGETHER
+ what will we do?
GET/SLIM/TRAVEL/THE/WORLD
Will we be rich?
YES/I/HAVE/BANC/ACCOUNTS/GET/MY/HAIRBRUSH/FROM/HER/NOW
I got it.
NIGHT/TIME/STAND/OVER/GRAVE/BRUSH/YR/HAIR/INVITE/ME/IN

"That should be B-A-N-K, in that one line," explained Amber helpfully. "And I'll want to borrow your car tonight."

Not trusting herself to speak, Caroleen nodded and handed the paper back to her, wondering if her own face was red or pale. She felt invisible and repudiated. BeeVee could have approached her own twin for this, but her twin was too old; and if she did manage to occupy the body of this girl—a more intimate sort of twinhood!—she would certainly not go on living with Caroleen. And she had eaten all the Vicodins and Darvocets

Caroleen picked up the rock. It was some sort of quartz crystal.

"When . . . she began in a croak. She cleared her throat and went on more steadily, "When did you get that second-to-last message? About the bank accounts and the hairbrush?"

"That one? Uh, just a minute before I knocked on your door."

Caroleen nodded, wondering bleakly if BeeVee had even known that she was leaving her with carbon copies—multiple, echoing carbon copies—of the messages.

She put the crystal back down on the cardboard and picked up the hairbrush. Amber opened her mouth as if to object, then subsided.

There were indeed a number of white hairs tangled in the bristles.

Caroleen tucked the brush into her purse.

"I need that," said Amber quickly, leaning forward across the board. "She says I need it."

"Oh, of course, I'm sorry." Caroleen forced what must have been ghastly smile, and then pulled her own hairbrush instead out of the purse and handed it to the girl. It was identical to BeeVee's, right down to the white hairs.

Amber took it and glanced at it, then laid it on the pillow, out of Caroleen's reach.

"I don't want," said Caroleen, "to interrupt . . . you two." She sighed, emptying her lungs, and dug the car keys out of her purse. "Here," she said, tossing them onto the bed. "I'll be next door if you . . . need any help."

"Fine, okay." Amber seemed relieved at the prospect of her leaving.

Caroleen was awakened the next morning by the pain of her sore right hand flexing, but she rolled over and slept for ten more minutes before the telephone by her head conclusively jarred her out of the monotonous dream that had occupied her mind for the last hour or so.

She sat up, wrinkling her nose at the scorched smell from the fireplace and wishing she had a cup of coffee, and still half-saw the Ouija board she'd been dreaming about.

She picked up the phone, wincing. "Hello?"

"Caroleen," said Amber's voice, "nothing happened at the cemetery last night, and BeeVee isn't answering my questions. She spelled stuff out, but it's not for what I'm writing to her. All she's written so far this morning is—just a sec—she wrote, uh, *'You win—you'll do—we've always been a team, right—'* Is she talking to you?"

Caroleen glanced toward the fireplace, where last night she had burned—or charred, at least—BeeVee's toothbrush, razor, dentures, curlers, and several other things, including the hairbrush. And today she would call the headstone company and cancel the order. BeeVee ought not to have an easily locatable grave.

"Me?" Caroleen made a painful fist of her right hand. "Why would she talk to me?"

"You're her twin sister, she might be—"

"BeeVee is dead, Amber, she died nine weeks ago."

"But she's coming back. She's going to make me beautiful! She said—"

"She can't do anything, child. We're better off without her."

Amber was talking then, protesting, but Caroleen's thoughts were of the brothers she couldn't even picture anymore, the nieces she'd never met and who probably had children of their own somewhere, and her mother who was almost certainly dead by now. And there was everybody else, too, and not a lot of time.

Caroleen was resolved to learn to write with her left hand, and, even though it would hurt, she hoped her right hand would go on and on writing uselessly in the air.

At last she stood up, still holding the phone, and she interrupted Amber: "Could you bring back my car keys? I have some errands to do."

How many eyes does Lord Bloodraven have? A thousand eyes, and one. *Some claimed he was a student of the dark arts who could change his face, put on the likeness of a one-eyed dog, even turn into a mist. Packs of gaunt gray wolves hunted down his foes, men said, and carrion crows spied for him and whispered secrets in his ear . . .*

THE MYSTERY KNIGHT: A TALE OF THE SEVEN KINGDOMS

GEORGE R.R. MARTIN

A light summer rain was falling as Dunk and Egg took their leave of Stoney Sept.

Dunk rode his old warhorse Thunder, with Egg beside him on the spirited young palfrey he'd named Rain, leading their mule Maester. On Maester's back were bundled Dunk's armor and Egg's books, their bedrolls, tent, and clothing, several slabs of hard salt beef, half a flagon of mead, and two skins of water. Egg's old straw hat, wide-brimmed and floppy, kept the rain off the mule's head. The boy had cut holes for Maester's ears. Egg's new straw hat was on his own head. Except for the ear holes, the two hats looked much the same to Dunk.

As they neared the town gates, Egg reined up sharply. Up above the gateway a traitor's head had been impaled upon an iron spike. It was fresh from the look of it, the flesh more pink than green, but the carrion crows had already gone to work on it. The dead man's lips and cheeks were torn and ragged; his eyes were two brown holes weeping slow red tears as raindrops mingled with the crusted blood. The dead man's mouth sagged open, as if to harangue travelers passing through the gate below.

Dunk had seen such sights before. "Back in King's Landing when I was a boy, I stole a head right off its spike once," he told Egg. Actually it had been Ferret who scampered up the wall to snatch the head, after Rafe and Pudding said he'd never dare, but when the guards came running he'd tossed it down, and Dunk was the one who'd caught it. "Some rebel lord or robber knight, it was. Or maybe just a common murderer. A head's a head. They all look the same after a few days on a spike." Him and his three friends had used the head to terrorize the girls of Flea Bottom. They'd chase them through the alleys, and make them give the head a kiss before they'd let them go. That head got kissed a lot, as he recalled. There wasn't a girl in King's Landing who could run as fast as Rafe. Egg was better off not hearing that part, though. Ferret, Rafe, and Pudding. *Little monsters, those three, and me the worst of all.* His friends and he had kept the head until the flesh turned black and begin to slough away. That took the fun out of chasing girls, so one night they burst into a pot shop and tossed what was left into the kettle. "The crows always go for the eyes," he told Egg. "Then the cheeks cave in, the flesh turns green . . . " He squinted. "Wait. I know that face."

"You do, ser," said Egg. "Three days ago. The hunchbacked septon we heard preaching against Lord Bloodraven."

He remembered then. *He was a holy man sworn to the Seven, even if he did preach treason.* "His hands are scarlet with a brother's blood, and the blood of his young nephews too," the hunchback had declared to the crowd that had gathered in the market square. "A shadow came at his command to strangle brave Prince Valarr's sons in their mother's womb. Where is our Young Prince now? Where is his brother, sweet Matarys? Where has Good King Daeron gone, and fearless Baelor Breakspear? The grave has claimed them, every one, yet he endures, this pale bird with bloody beak who perches on King Aerys's shoulder and caws into his ear. The mark of hell is on his face and in his empty eye, and he has brought us drought and pestilence and murder. Rise up, I say, and remember our true king across the water. Seven gods there are, and seven kingdoms, and the Black Dragon sired seven sons! Rise up, my lords and ladies. Rise up, you brave knights and sturdy yeomen, and cast down Bloodraven, that foul sorcerer, lest your children and your children's children be cursed forevermore."

Every word was treason. Even so, it was a shock to see him here, with holes where his eyes had been. "That's him, aye," Dunk said, "and another good reason to put this town behind us." He gave Thunder a touch of the spur, and he and Egg rode through the gates of Stoney Sept, listening to the soft sound of the rain. *How many eyes does Lord Bloodraven have?* the riddle ran. *A thousand eyes, and one.* Some claimed the King's Hand was a student of the dark arts who could change his face, put on the likeness of a one-eyed dog, even turn into a mist. Packs of gaunt gray wolves hunted down his foes, men said, and carrion crows spied for him and whispered secrets in his ear. Most of the tales were only tales, Dunk did not doubt, but no one could doubt that Bloodraven had informers everywhere.

He had seen the man once with his own two eyes, back in King's Landing. White as bone were the skin and hair of Brynden Rivers, and his eye—he only had the one, the other having been lost to his half-brother Bittersteel on the Redgrass Field—was red as blood. On cheek and neck he bore the winestain birthmark that had given him his name.

When the town was well behind them Dunk cleared his throat and said, "Bad business, cutting off the heads of septons. All he did was talk. Words are wind."

"Some words are wind, ser. Some are treason." Egg was skinny as a stick, all ribs and elbows, but he did have a mouth.

"Now you sound a proper princeling."

Egg took that for an insult, which it was. "He might have been a septon, but he was preaching lies, ser. The drought wasn't Lord Bloodraven's fault, nor the Great Spring Sickness either."

"Might be that's so, but if we start cutting off the heads of all the fools and liars, half the towns in the Seven Kingdoms will be empty."

Six days later, the rain was just a memory.

Dunk had stripped off his tunic to enjoy the warmth of sunlight on his skin. When a little breeze came up, cool and fresh and fragrant as a maiden's breath, he sighed. "Water," he announced. "Smell it? The lake can't be far now."

"All I can smell is Maester, ser. He stinks." Egg gave the mule's lead a savage tug. Maester had stopped to crop at the grass beside the road, as he did from time to time.

"There's an old inn by the lake shore." Dunk had stopped there once when he was squiring for the old man. "Ser Arlan said they brewed a fine brown ale. Might be we could have a taste while we waited for the ferry."

Egg gave him a hopeful look. "To wash the food down, ser?"

"What food would that be?"

"A slice off the roast?" the boy said. "A bit of duck, a bowl of stew? Whatever they have, ser."

Their last hot meal had been three days ago. Since then, they had been living on windfalls and strips of old salt beef as hard as wood. *It would be good to put some real food in our bellies before we started north. That Wall's a long way off.*

"We could spend the night as well," suggested Egg.

"Does m'lord want a featherbed?"

"Straw will serve me well enough, ser," said Egg, offended.

"We have no coin for beds."

"We have twenty-two pennies, three stars, one stag, and that old chipped garnet, ser."

Dunk scratched at his ear. "I thought we had two silvers."

"We did, until you bought the tent. Now we have the one."

"We won't have any if we start sleeping at inns. You want to share a bed with some peddler and wake up with his fleas?" Dunk snorted. "Not me. I have my own fleas, and they are not fond of strangers. We'll sleep beneath the stars."

"The stars are good," Egg allowed, "but the ground is hard, ser, and sometimes it's nice to have a pillow for your head."

"Pillows are for princes." Egg was as good a squire as a knight could want, but every so often he would get to feeling princely. *The lad has dragon blood, never forget.* Dunk had beggar's blood himself . . . or so they used to tell him back in Flea Bottom, when they weren't telling him that he was sure to hang. "Might be we can afford some ale and a hot supper, but I'm not wasting good coin on a bed. We need to save our pennies for the ferryman." The last time he had crossed the lake, the ferry only cost a few coppers, but that had been six years ago, or maybe seven. Everything had grown more costly since then.

"Well," said Egg, "we could use my boot to get across."

"We could," said Dunk, ,but we won't." Using the boot was dangerous. *Word would spread. Word always spreads.* His squire was not bald by chance. Egg had the purple eyes of old Valyria, and hair that shone like beaten gold and strands of silver woven together. He might as well wear a three-headed dragon as a brooch as let that hair grow out. These were perilous times in Westeros, and . . . well, it was best to take no chances. "Another word about your bloody boot, and I'll clout you in the ear so hard you'll *fly* across the lake."

"I'd sooner swim, ser." Egg swam well, and Dunk did not. The boy turned in the saddle. "Ser? Someone's coming up the road behind us. Hear the horses?"

"I'm not deaf." Dunk could see their dust as well. "A large party. And in haste.

"Do you think they might be outlaws, ser?" Egg raised up in the stirrups, more eager than afraid. The boy was like that.

"Outlaws would be quieter. Only lords make so much noise." Dunk rattled his sword hilt to loosen the blade in its scabbard. "Still, we'll get off the road and let them pass. There are lords and lords." It never hurt to be a little wary. The roads were not as safe as when Good King Daeron sat the Iron Throne.

He and Egg concealed themselves behind a thorn bush. Dunk unslung his shield and slipped it onto his arm. It was an old thing, tall and heavy, kite-shaped, made of pine and rimmed with iron. He had bought it in Stoney Sept to replace the shield the Longinch had hacked to splinters when they fought. Dunk had not had time to have it painted with his elm and shooting star, so it still bore the arms of its last owner: a hanged man swinging grim and gray beneath a gallows tree. It was not a sigil that he would have chosen for himself, but the shield had come cheap.

The first riders galloped past within moments; two young lordlings mounted on a pair of coursers. The one on the bay wore an open-faced helm of gilded steel with three tall feathered plumes; one white, one red, one gold. Matching plumes adorned his horse's crinet. The black stallion beside him was barded in blue and gold. His trappings rippled with the wind of his passage as he thundered past. Side by side the riders streaked on by, whooping and laughing, their long cloaks streaming behind.

A third lord followed more sedately, at the head of a long column. There were two dozen in the party, grooms and cooks and serving men, all to attend three knights, plus men-at-arms and mounted crossbowmen, and a dozen drays heavy-laden with their armor, tents, and provisions. Slung from the lord's saddle was his shield, dark orange and charged with three black castles.

Dunk knew those arms, but from where? The lord who bore them was an older man, sour-mouthed and saturnine, with a close-cropped salt-and-pepper beard. *He might have been at Ashford Meadow*, Dunk thought. *Or maybe we served at his castle when I was squiring for Ser Arlan*. The old hedge knight had done service at so many different keeps and castles through the years that Dunk could not recall the half of them.

The lord reined up abruptly, scowling at the thorn bush. "You. In the bush. Show yourself." Behind him two crossbowmen slipped quarrels into the notch. The rest continued on their way.

Dunk stepped through the tall grass, his shield upon his arm, his right hand resting on the pommel of his longsword. His face was a red-brown mask from the dust the horses had kicked up, and he was naked from the waist up. He looked a scruffy sight, he knew, though it was like to be the size of him that gave the other pause. "We want no quarrel, m'lord. There's only the two of us, me and my squire." He beckoned Egg forward.

"Squire? Do you claim to be a knight?"

Dunk did not like the way the man was looking at him. *Those eyes could flay a man*. It seemed prudent to remove his hand from his sword. "I am a hedge knight, seeking service."

"Every robber knight I've ever hanged has said the same. Your device may be prophetic, ser . . . if *ser* you are. A gallows and a hanged man. These are your arms?"

"No, m'lord. I need to have the shield repainted."

"Why? Did you rob it off a corpse?"

"I bought it, for good coin." *Three castles, black on orange . . . where have I seen those before?* "I am no robber."

The lord's eyes were chips of flint. "How did you come by that scar upon your cheek? A cut from a whip?"

"A dagger. Though my face is none of your concern, m'lord."

"I'll be the judge of what is my concern."

By then the two younger knights had come trotting back to see what had delayed their party. "There you are, Gormy," called the rider on the black, a young man lean and lithe, with a comely clean-shaved face and fine features. Black hair fell shining to his collar. His doublet was made of dark blue silk edged in gold satin. Across his chest an engrailed cross had been embroidered in gold thread, with a golden fiddle in the first and third quarters, a golden sword in the second and the fourth. His eyes caught the deep blue of his doublet, and sparkled with amusement. "Alyn feared you'd fallen from your horse. A palpable excuse, it seems to me, I was about to leave him in my dust."

"Who are these two brigands?" asked the rider on the bay.

Egg bristled at the insult: "You have no call to name us brigands, my lord. When we saw your dust we thought you might be outlaws, that's the only reason that we hid. This is Ser Duncan the Tall, and I'm his squire."

The lordlings paid no more heed to that than they would have paid the croaking of a frog. "I believe that is the largest lout I have ever seen," declared the knight of three feathers. He had a pudgy face beneath a head of curly hair the color of dark honey. "Seven feet if he's an inch, I'd wager. What a mighty crash he'll make when he comes tumbling down."

Dunk felt color rising to his face. *You'd lose your wager*, he thought. The last time he had been measured, Egg's brother Aemon pronounced him an inch shy of seven feet.

"Is that your warhorse, Ser Giant?" said the feathered lordling. "I suppose we could butcher it for the meat."

"Lord Alyn oft forgets his courtesies," the black-haired knight said. "Please forgive his churlish words, ser. Alyn, you will ask Ser Duncan for his pardon."

"If I must. Will you forgive me, ser?" He did not wait for reply, but turned his bay about and trotted down the road.

The other lingered. "Are you bound for the wedding, ser?"

Something in his tone made Dunk want to tug his forelock. He resisted the impulse and said, "We're for the ferry, m'lord."

"As are we . . . but the only lords hereabouts are Gormy and that wastrel who just left us, Alyn Cockshaw. I am a vagabond hedge knight like yourself. Ser John the Fiddler, I am called." That was the sort of name a hedge knight might choose, but Dunk had never seen any hedge knight garbed or armed or mounted in such splendor. *The knight of the golden hedge*, he thought. "You know my name. My squire is called Egg."

"Well met, ser. Come, ride with us to Whitewalls and break a few lances to help Lord Butterwell celebrate his new marriage. I'll wager you could give a good account of yourself."

Dunk had not done any jousting since Ashford Meadow. *If I could win a few ransoms, we'd eat well on the ride north*, he thought, but the lord with the three castles on his shield said, "Ser Duncan needs to be about his journey, as do we."

John the Fiddler paid the older man no mind. "I would love to cross swords with you, ser. I've tried men of many lands and races, but never one your size. Was your father large as well?"

"I never knew my father, ser."

"I am sad to hear it. Mine own sire was taken from me too soon." The Fiddler turned to the lord of the three castles. "We should ask Ser Duncan to join our jolly company."

"We do not need his sort."

Dunk was at a loss for words. Penniless hedge knights were not oft asked to ride with highborn lords. *I would have more in common with their servants.* Judging from the length of their column, Lord Cockshaw and the Fiddler had brought grooms to tend their horses, cooks to feed them, squires to clean their armor, guards to defend them. Dunk had Egg.

"His sort?" The Fiddler laughed. "What sort is that? The big sort? Look at the size of him. We want strong men. Young swords are worth more than old names, I've oft heard it said."

"By fools. You know little and less about this man. He might be a brigand, or one of Lord Bloodraven's spies."

"I'm no man's spy," said Dunk. "And m'lord has no call to speak of me as if I were deaf or dead or down in Dorne."

Those flinty eyes considered him. "Down in Dorne would be a good place for you, ser. You have my leave to go there."

"Pay him no mind," the Fiddler said. "He's a sour old soul, he suspects everyone. Gormy, I have a good feeling about this fellow. Ser Duncan, will you come with us to Whitewalls?"

"M'lord, . . . " How could he share a camp with such as these? Their serving men would raise their pavilions, their grooms would curry their horses, their cooks would serve them each a capon or a joint of beef, whilst Dunk and Egg gnawed on strips of hard salt beef. "I couldn't."

"You see," said the lord of the three castles. "He knows his place, and it is not with us." He turned his horse back toward the road. "By now Lord Cockshaw is half a league ahead."

"I suppose I must chase him down again." The Fiddler gave Dunk an apologetic smile. "Perchance we'll meet again some day. I hope so. I should love to try my lance on you."

Dunk did not know what to say to that. "Good fortune in the lists, ser," he finally managed, but by then Ser John had wheeled about to chase the column. The older lord rode after him. Dunk was glad to see his back. He had not liked his flinty eyes, nor Lord Alyn's arrogance. The Fiddler had been pleasant enough, but there was something odd about him as well. "Two fiddles and two swords, a cross engrailed," he said to Egg as they watched the dust of their departure. "What house is that?"

"None, ser. I never saw that shield in any roll of arms."

Perhaps he is a hedge knight after all. Dunk had devised his own arms at Ashford Meadow, when a puppeteer called Tanselle Too-Tall asked him what he wanted painted on his shield. "Was the older lord some kin to House Frey?" The Freys bore castles on their shields, and their holdings were not far from here.

Egg rolled his eyes. "The Frey arms are two blue towers connected by a bridge, on a gray field. Those were three castles, black on orange, ser. Did you see a bridge?"

"No." *He just does that to annoy me.* "And next time you roll your eyes at me, I'll clout you on the ear so hard they'll roll back into your head for good."

Egg looked chastened. "I never meant—"

"Never mind what you meant. Just tell me who he was."

"Gormon Peake, the Lord of Starpike."

"That's down in the Reach, isn't it? Does he really have three castles?"

"Only on his shield; ser. House Peake did hold three castles once, but two of them were lost."

"How do you lose two castles?"

"You fight for the black dragon, ser."

"Oh." Dunk felt stupid. *That again.*

For two hundred years the realm had been ruled by the descendants of Aegon the Conquerer and his sisters, who had made the Seven Kingdoms one and forged the Iron Throne. Their royal banners bore the three-headed dragon of House Targaryen, red on black. Sixteen years ago, a bastard son of King Aegon IV named Daemon Blackfyre had risen in revolt against his trueborn brother. Daemon had used the three-headed dragon on his banners too, but he reversed the colors, as many bastards did. His revolt had ended on the Redgrass Field, where Daemon and his twin sons died beneath a rain of Lord Bloodraven's arrows. Those rebels who survived and bent the knee were pardoned, but some lost land, some titles, some gold. All gave hostages to ensure their future loyalty.

Three castles, black on orange. "I remember now. Ser Arlan never liked to talk about the Redgrass Field, but once in his cups he told me how his sister's son had died." He could almost hear the old man's voice again, smell the wine upon his breath. "Roger of Pennytree, that was his name. His head was smashed in by a mace wielded by a lord with three castles on his shield." *Lord Gormon Peake. The old man never knew his name. Or never wanted to.* By that time Lord Peake and John the Fiddler and their party were no more than a plume of red dust in the distance. *It was sixteen years ago. The Pretender died, and those who followed him were exiled or forgiven. Anyway, it has nought to do with me.*

For a while they rode along without talking, listening to the plaintive cries of birds. Half a league on, Dunk cleared his throat and said, "Butterwell, he said. His lands are near?"

"On the far side of the lake, ser. Lord Butterwell was the master of coin when King Aegon sat the Iron Throne. King Daeron made him Hand, but not for long. His arms are undy green and white and yellow, ser." Egg loved showing off his heraldry.

"Is he a friend of your father?"

Egg made a face. "My father never liked him. In the Rebellion, Lord Butterwell's second son fought for the pretender and his eldest for the king. That way he was certain to be on the winning side. Lord Butterwell didn't fight for anyone."

"Some might call that prudent."

"My father calls it craven."

Aye, he would. Prince Maekar was a hard man, proud and full of scorn. "We have to go by Whitewalls to reach the kingsroad. Why not fill our bellies?" Just the thought was enough to cause his guts to rumble. "Might be that one of the wedding guests will need an escort back to his own seat."

"You said that we were going north."

"The Wall has stood eight thousand years, it will last a while longer. It's a thousand leagues from here to there, and we could do with some more silver in our purse." Dunk was picturing himself atop Thunder, riding down that sour-faced old lord with the three castles on his shield. That would be sweet. *"It was old Ser Arlan's squire who defeated you," I could tell him when he came to ransom back his arms and armor. "The boy who replaced the boy you killed." The old man would like that.*

"You're not thinking of entering the lists, are you,ser?

"Might be it's time."

"It's not, ser."

"Maybe it's time I gave you a good clout in the ear." *I'd only need to win two tilts. If I could collect two ransoms and pay out only one, we'd eat like kings for a year.* "If there was a melee, I might enter that." Dunk's size and strength would serve him better in a melee than in the lists.

"It's not customary to have a melee at a marriage, ser."

"It's customary to have a feast, though. We have a long way to go. Why not set out with our bellies full for once?"

The sun was low in the west by the time they saw the lake, its waters glimmering red and gold, bright as a sheet of beaten copper. When they glimpsed the turrets of the inn above some willows, Dunk donned his sweaty tunic once again and stopped to splash some water on his face. He washed off the dust of the road as best he could, and ran wet fingers through his thick mop of sun-streaked hair. There was nothing to be done for his size, or the scar that marked his cheek, but he wanted to make himself appear somewhat less the wild robber knight.

The inn was bigger than he'd expected, a great gray sprawl of a place, timbered and turreted, half of it built on pilings out over the water. A road of rough-cut planks had been laid down over the muddy lakeshore to the ferry landing, but neither the ferry nor the ferrymen were in evidence. Across the road stood a stable with a thatched roof. A dry stone wall enclosed the yard, but the gate was open. Within, they found a well and a watering trough. "See to the animals," Dunk told Egg, "but see that they don't drink too much. I'll ask about some food."

He found the innkeep sweeping off the steps. "Are you come for the ferry?" the woman asked him. "You're too late. The sun's going down, and Ned don't like to cross by night unless the moon is full. He'll be back first thing in the morning."

"Do you know how much he asks?"

"Three pennies for each of you, and ten for your horses."

"We have two horses and a mule."

"It's ten for mules as well."

Dunk did the sums in his head, and came up with six-and-thirty, more than he had hoped to spend. "Last time I came this way it was only two pennies, and six for horses."

"Take that up with Ned, it's nought to me. If you're looking for a bed, I've none to offer. Lord Shawney and Lord Costayne brought their retinues. I'm full to bursting."

"Is Lord Peake here as well?" *He killed Ser Arlan's squire.* "He was with Lord Cockshaw and John the Fiddler."

"Ned took them across on his last run." She looked Dunk up and down. "Were you part of their company?"

"We met them on the road, is all." A good smell was drifting out the windows of the inn, one that made Dunk's mouth water. "We might like some of what you're roasting, if it's not too costly."

"It's wild boar," the woman said, "well peppered, and served with onions, mushrooms, and mashed neeps."

"We could do without the neeps. Some slices off the boar and a tankard of your good brown ale would do for us. How much would you ask for that? And maybe we could have a place on your stable floor to bed down for the night?"

That was a mistake. "The stables are for horses. That's why we call them stables. You're big as a horse, I'll grant you, but I only see two legs." She swept her broom at him, to shoo him off. "I can't be expected to feed all the Seven Kingdoms. The boar is for my guests. So is my ale. I won't have lords saying that I run short of food or drink before they were surfeit. The lake is full of fish, and you'll find some other rogues camped down by the stumps. Hedge knights, if you believe them." Her tone made it quite clear that she did not. "Might be they'd have food to share. It's nought to me. Away with you now, I've work to do." The door closed with a solid thump behind her, before Dunk could even think to ask where he might find these stumps.

He found Egg sitting on the horse trough, soaking his feet in the water and fanning his face with his big floppy hat. "Are they roasting pig, ser? I smell pork."

"Wild boar," said Dunk in a glum tone, "but who wants boar when we have good salt beef?"

Egg made a face. "Can I please eat my boots instead, ser? I'll make a new pair out of the salt beef. It's tougher."

"No," said Dunk, trying not to smile. "You can't eat your boots. One more word and you'll eat my fist, though. Get your feet out of that trough." He found his greathelm on the mule, and slung it underhand at Egg. "Draw some water from the well and soak the beef." Unless you soaked it for a good long time, the salt beef was like to break your teeth. It tasted best when soaked in ale, but water would serve. "Don't use the trough either, I don't care to taste your feet."

"My feet could only improve the taste, ser," Egg said, wriggling his toes. But he did as he was bid.

The hedge knights did not prove hard to find. Egg spied their fire flickering in the woods along the lake shore, so they made for it, leading the animals behind them. The boy carried Dunk's helm beneath one arm, sloshing with each step he took. By then the sun was a red memory in the west. Before long the trees opened up, and they found themselves in what must once have been a weirwood grove. Only a ring of white stumps and a tangle of bone-pale roots remained to show where the trees had stood, when the children of the forest ruled in Westeros.

Amongst the weirwood stumps, they found two men squatting near a cookfire, passing a skin of wine from hand to hand. Their horses were cropping at the grass beyond the grove, and they had stacked their arms and armor in neat piles. A much younger man sat apart from the other two, his back against a chestnut tree. "Well met, sers," Dunk called out in a cheerful voice. It was never wise to take armed men unawares. "I am called Ser Duncan, the Tall. The lad is Egg. May we share your fire?"

A stout man of middling years rose to greet them, garbed in tattered finery. Flamboyant ginger whiskers framed his face. "Well met, Ser Duncan. You are a large one . . . and most welcome, certainly, as is your lad. Egg, was it? What sort of name is that, pray?"

"A short one, ser." Egg knew better than to admit that Egg was short for Aegon. Not to men he did not know.

"Indeed. What happened to your hair?"

Rootworms, Dunk thought. *Tell him it was rootworms, boy.*

That was the safest story, the tale they told most often . . . though sometimes Egg took it in his head to play some childish game.

"I shaved it off, ser. I mean to stay shaven until I earn my spurs."

"A noble vow. I am Ser Kyle, the Cat of Misty Moor. Under yonder chestnut sits Ser Glendon, ah, Ball. And here you have the good Ser Maynard Plumm."

Egg's ears pricked up at that name. "Plumm . . . are you kin to Lord Viserys Plumm, ser?"

"Distantly," confessed Ser Maynard, a tall, thin, stoop-shouldered man with long straight flaxen hair, "though I doubt that his lordship would admit to it. One might say that he is of the sweet Plumms, whilst I am of the sour."

Plumm's cloak was as purple as name, though frayed about the edges and badly dyed. A moonstone brooch big as a hen's egg fastened it at the shoulder. Elsewise he wore dun-colored roughspun and stained brown leather.

"We have salt beef," said Dunk.

"Ser Maynard has a bag of apples," said Kyle the Cat. "And I have pickled eggs and onions. Why, together we have the makings of a feast! Be seated, ser. We have a fine choice of stumps for your comfort. We will be here until mid-morning, unless I miss my guess. There is only the one ferry, and it is not big enough to take us all. The lords and their tails must cross first."

"Help me with the horses," Dunk told Egg. Together the two of them unsaddled Thunder, Rain, and Maester.

Only when the animals had been fed and watered and hobbled for the night did Dunk accept the wineskin that Ser Maynard offered him. "Even sour wine is better than none," said Kyle the Cat. "We'll drink finer vintages at Whitewalls. Lord Butterwell is said to have the best wines north of the Arbor. He was once the King's Hand, as his father's father was before him, and he is said to be a pious man besides, and very rich."

"His wealth is all from cows," said Maynard Plumm. "He ought to take a swollen udder for his arms. These Butterwells have milk running in their veins, and the Freys are no better. This will be a marriage of cattle thieves and toll collectors, one lot of coin clinkers joining with another. When the Black Dragon rose, this lord of cows sent one son to Daemon and one to Daeron, to make certain there was a Butterwell on the winning side. Both perished on the Redgrass Field, and his youngest died in the spring. That's why he's making this new marriage. Unless this new wife gives him a son, Butterwell's name will die with him."

"As it should." Ser Glendon Ball gave his sword another stroke with the whetstone. "The Warrior hates cravens."

The scorn in his voice made Dunk give the youth a closer look. Ser Glendon's clothes were of good cloth, but well-worn and ill-matched, with the look of hand-me-downs. Tufts of dark brown hair stuck out from beneath his iron halfhelm. The lad himself was short and chunky, with small, close-set eyes, thick shoulders, and muscular arms. His eyebrows were shaggy as two caterpillars after a wet spring, his nose bulbous, his chin pugnacious. And he was young. *Sixteen, might be. No more than eighteen*. Dunk might have taken him for a squire if Ser Kyle had not named him with a *ser*. The lad had pimples on his cheeks in place of whiskers.

"How long have you been a knight?" Dunk asked him.

"Long enough. Half a year when the moon turns. I was knighted by Ser Morgan Dunstable of Tumbler's Falls, two dozen people saw it, but I have been training for knighthood since I was born. I rode before I walked, and knocked a grown man's tooth out of his head before I lost any of my own. I mean to make my name at Whitewalls, and claim the dragon's egg."

"The dragon's egg? Is that the champion's prize? Truly?" The last dragon had perished half a century ago. Ser Arlan had once seen a clutch of her eggs, though. *They were hard as stone, but beautiful to look upon,* the old man had told Dunk. "How could Lord Butterwell come by a dragon's egg?"

"King Aegon presented the egg to his father's father after guesting for a night at his old castle," said Ser Maynard Plumm.

"Was it a reward for some act of valor?" asked Dunk.

Ser Kyle chuckled. "Some might call it that. Supposedly old Lord Butterwell had three young maiden daughters when His Grace came calling. By morning, all three had royal bastards in their little bellies. A hot night's work, that was."

Dunk had heard such talk before. Aegon the Unworthy had bedded half the maidens in the realm and fathered bastards on the lot of them, supposedly. Worse, the old king had legitimized them all upon his deathbed; the baseborn ones born of tavern wenches, whores, and shepherd girls, and the Great Bastards whose mothers had been highborn. "We'd all be bastard sons of old King Aegon if half these tales were true."

"And who's to say we're not?" Ser Maynard quipped.

"You ought to come with us to Whitewalls, Ser Duncan," urged Ser Kyle. "Your size is sure to catch some lordling's eye. You might find good service there. I know I shall. Joffrey Caswell will be at this wedding, the Lord of Bitterbridge. When he was three I made him his first sword. I carved it out of pine, to fit his hand. In my greener days, my sword was sworn to his father."

"Was that one carved from pine as well?" Ser Maynard asked.

Kyle the Cat had the grace to laugh. "That sword was good steel, I assure you. I should be glad to ply it once again in the service of the centaur. Ser Duncan, even if you do not choose to tilt, do join us for the wedding feast. There will be singers and musicians, jugglers and tumblers, and a troupe of comic dwarfs."

Dunk frowned. "Egg and I have a long journey before us. We're headed north to Winterfell. Lord Beron Stark is gathering swords to drive the krakens from his shores for good."

"Too cold up there for me," said Ser Maynard. "If you want to kill krakens, go west. The Lannisters are building ships to strike back at the ironmen on their home islands. That's how you put an end to Dagon Greyjoy. Fighting him on land is fruitless, he just slips back to sea. You have to beat him on the water."

That had the ring of truth, but the prospect of fighting ironmen at sea was not one that Dunk relished. He'd had a taste of that on the *White Lady*, sailing from Dorne to Oldtown, when he'd donned his armor to help the crew repel some raiders. The battle had been desperate and bloody, and once he'd almost fallen in the water. That would have been the end of him.

"The throne should take a lesson from Stark and Lannister," declared Ser Kyle the Cat. "At least they fight. What do the Targaryens do? King Aerys hides amongst his books, Prince Rhaegel prances naked through the Red Keep's halls, and Prince Maekar broods at Summerhall."

Egg was prodding at the fire with a stick, to send sparks floating up into the night. Dunk was pleased to see him ignoring the mention of his father's name. *Perhaps he's finally learned to hold that tongue of his.*

"Myself, I blame Bloodraven," Ser Kyle went on. "He is the King's Hand, yet he does nothing, whilst the krakens spread flame and terror up and down the sunset sea."

Ser Maynard gave a shrug. "His eye is fixed on Tyrosh, where Bittersteel sits in exile, plotting with the sons of Daemon Blackfyre. So he keeps the king's ships close at hand, lest they attempt to cross."

"Aye, that may well be," Ser Kyle said, "but many would welcome the return of Bittersteel. Bloodraven is the root of all our woes, the white worm gnawing at the heart of the realm."

Dunk frowned, remembering the hunchbacked septon at Stoney Sept. "Words like that can cost a man his head. Some might say you're talking treason."

"How can the truth be treason?" asked Kyle the Cat. "In King Daeron's day, a man did not have to fear to speak his mind, but now?" He made a rude noise. "Bloodraven put King Aerys on the Iron Throne, but for how long? Aerys is weak, and when he dies it will be bloody war between Lord Rivers and Prince Maekar for the crown, the Hand against the heir."

"You have forgotten Prince Rhaegel, my friend," Ser Maynard objected, in a mild tone. "He comes next in line to Aerys, not Maekar, and his children after him."

"Rhaegel is feeble-minded. Why, I bear him no ill will, but the man is good as dead, and those twins of his as well, though whether they will die of Maekar's mace or Bloodraven's spells . . . "

Seven save us, Dunk thought, as Egg spoke up shrill and loud. "Prince Maekar is Prince Rhaegel's brother. He loves him well. He'd never do harm to him or his."

"Be quiet, boy," Dunk growled at him. "These knights want none of your opinions."

"I can talk if I want."

"No," said Dunk. "You can't." *That mouth of yours will get you killed some day. And me as well, most like.* "That salt beef's soaked long enough, I think. A strip for all our friends, and be quick about it."

Egg flushed, and for half a heartbeat Dunk feared the boy might talk back. Instead he settled for a sullen look, seething as only a boy of eleven years can seethe. "Aye, ser," he said, fishing in the bottom of Dunk's helm. His shaved head shone redly in the firelight as he passed out the salt beef.

Dunk took his piece and worried at it. The soak had turned the meat from wood to leather, but that was all. He sucked on one corner, tasting the salt and trying not to think about the roast boar at the inn, crackling on its spit and dripping fat.

As dusk deepened, flies and stinging midges came swarming off the lake. The flies preferred to plague their horses, but the midges had a taste for man flesh. The only way to keep from being bitten was to sit close to the fire, breathing smoke. *Cook or be devoured*, Dunk thought glumly, *now there's a beggar's choice.* He scratched at his arms and edged closer to the fire.

The wineskin soon came round again. The wine was sour and strong. Dunk drank deep, and passed along the skin, whilst the Cat of Misty Moor began to talk of how he had saved the life of the Lord of Bitterbridge during the Blackfyre Rebellion. "When Lord Armond's banner-bearer fell, I leapt down from my horse with traitors all around us—"

"Ser," said Glendon Ball. "Who were these traitors?"

"The Blackfyre men, I meant."

Firelight glimmered off the steel in Ser Glendon's hand. The pockmarks on his face flamed as red as open sores, and his every sinew was wound as tight as a crossbow. "My father fought for the black dragon."

This again. Dunk snorted. *Red or black?* was not a thing you asked a man. It always made for trouble. "I am sure Ser Kyle meant no insult to your father."

"None," Ser Kyle agreed. "It's an old tale, the red dragon and the black. No sense for us to fight about it now, lad. We are all brothers of the hedges here."

Ser Glendon seemed to weigh the Cat's words, to see if he was being mocked. "Daemon Blackfyre was no traitor. The old king gave *him* the sword. He saw the worthiness in Daemon, even though he was born bastard. Why else would he put Blackfyre into his hand in place of Daeron's? He meant for him to have the kingdom too. Daemon was the better man."

A hush fell. Dunk could hear the soft crackle of the fire. He could feel midges crawling on the back of his neck. He slapped at them, watching Egg, willing him to be still. "I was just a boy when they fought the Redgrass Field," he said, when it seemed that no one else would speak, "but I squired for a knight who fought with the red dragon, and later served another who fought for the black. There were brave men on both sides."

"Brave men," echoed Kyle the Cat, a bit feebly.

"Heroes." Glendon Ball turned his shield about, so all of them could see the sigil painted there, a fireball blazing red and yellow across a night black field. "I come from hero's blood."

"You're *Fireball*'s son," Egg said.

That was the first time they saw Ser Glendon smile.

Ser Kyle the Cat studied the boy closely. "How can that be? How old are you? Quentyn Ball died—"

"—before I was born," Ser Glendon finished, "but in me, he lives again." He slammed his sword back into its scabbard. "I'll show you all at Whitewalls, when I claim the *dragon's egg*."

The next day proved the truth of Ser Kyle's prophecy. Ned's ferry was nowise large enough to accommodate all those who wished to cross, so Lords Costayne and Shawney must go first, with their tails. That required several trips, each taking more than an hour. There were the mudflats to contend with, horses and wagons to be gotten down the planks, loaded on the boat, and unloaded again across the lake. The two lords slowed matters even further when they got into a shouting match over precedence. Shawney was the elder, but Costayne held himself to be better born.

There was nought that Dunk could do but wait and swelter. "We could go first if you let me use my boot," Egg said.

"We could," Dunk answered, "but we won't. Lord Costayne and Lord Shawney were here before us. Besides, they're lords."

Egg made a face. "Rebel lords."

Dunk frowned down at him. "What do you mean?"

"They were for the black dragon. Well, Lord Shawney was, and Lord Costayne's father. Aemon and I used to fight the battle on Maester Melaquin's green table with painted soldiers and little banners. Costayne's arms quarter a silver chalice on black with a black rose on gold. That banner was on the left of Daemon's host. Shawney was with Bittersteel on the right, but he died."

"Old dead history. They're here now, aren't they? So they bent the knee, and King Daeron gave them pardon."

"Yes, but—"

Dunk pinched the boy's lips shut." Hold your tongue."

Egg held his tongue.

No sooner had the last boatload of Shawney men pushed off than Lord and Lady Smallwood turned up at the landing with their own tail, so they must needs wait again.

The fellowship of the hedge had not survived the night, it was plain to see. Ser Glendon kept his own company, prickly and sullen. Kyle the Cat judged that it would be midday before they were allowed to board the ferry, so he detached himself from the others to try and ingratiate himself with Lord Smallwood, with whom he had some slight acquaintance. Ser Maynard spent his time gossiping with the innkeep.

"Stay well away from that one," Dunk warned Egg. There was something about Plumm that troubled him. "He could be a robber knight, for all we know."

The warning only seemed to make Ser Maynard more interesting to Egg. "I never knew a robber knight. Do you think he means to rob the dragon's egg?"

"Lord Butterwell will have the egg well guarded, I'm sure." Dunk scratched the midge bites on his neck. "Do you think he might display it at the feast? I'd like to get a look at one."

"I'd show you mine, ser, but it's at Summerhall."

"Yours? Your dragon's egg?" Dunk frowned down at the boy, wondering if this was some jape. "Where did it come from?"

"From a dragon, ser. They put it in my cradle."

"Do you want a clout in the ear? There are no dragons."

"No, but there are eggs. The last dragon left a clutch of five, and they have more on Dragonstone, old ones from before the Dance. My brothers all have them too. Aerion's looks as though it's made of gold and silver, with veins of fire running through it. Mine is white and green, all swirly."

"Your dragon's egg." *They put it in his cradle.* Dunk was so used to Egg that sometimes he forgot Aegon was a prince. *Of course they'd put a dragon egg inside his cradle.* "Well, see that you don't go mentioning this egg where anyone is like to hear."

"I'm not *stupid*, ser." Egg lowered his voice. "Some day the dragons will return. My brother Daeron's dreamed of it, and King Aerys read it in a prophecy. Maybe it will be my egg that hatches. That would be *splendid*."

"Would it?" Dunk had his doubts.

Not Egg. "Aemon and I used to pretend that our eggs would be the ones to hatch. If they did, we could fly through the sky on dragonback, like the first Aegon and his sisters."

"Aye, and if all the other knights in the realm should die, I'd be the Lord Commander of the Kingsguard. If these eggs are so bloody precious, why is Lord Butterwell giving his away?"

"To show the realm how rich he is?"

"I suppose." Dunk scratched his neck again and glanced over at Ser Glendon Ball, who was tightening the cinches on his saddle as he waited for the ferry. *That horse will never serve.* Ser Glendon's mount was a swaybacked stot, undersized, and old. "What do you know about his sire? Why did they call him Fireball?"

"For his hot head and red hair. Ser Quentyn Ball was the master-at-arms at the Red Keep. He taught my father and my uncles how to fight. The Great Bastards too. King Aegon promised to raise him to the Kingsguard, so Fireball made his wife join the silent sisters, only by the time a place came open King Aegon was dead and King Daeron named Ser Willam Wylde instead. My father says that it was Fireball as much as Bittersteel who convinced Daemon Blackfyre to claim the crown, and rescued him when Daeron sent the Kingsguard to arrest him. Later on, Fireball killed Lord Lefford at the gates of Lannisport and sent the Gray Lion running back to hide inside the Rock. At the crossing of the Mander he cut down the sons of Lady Penrose one by one. They say he spared the life of the youngest one as a kindness to his mother."

"That was chivalrous of him," Dunk had to admit. "Did Ser Quentyn die upon the Redgrass Field?"

"Before, ser," Egg replied. "An archer put an arrow through his throat as he dismounted by a stream to have a drink. Just some common man, no one knows who."

"Those common men can be dangerous when they get it in their heads to start slaying lords and heroes." Dunk saw the ferry creeping slowly across the lake. "Here it comes."

"It's slow. Are we going to go to Whitewalls, ser?"

"Why not? I want to see this dragon's egg." Dunk smiled. "If I win the tourney, we'd *both* have dragon's eggs."

Egg gave him a doubtful look.

"What? Why are you looking at me that way?"

"I could tell you, ser," the boy said solemnly, "but I need to learn to hold my tongue."

They seated the hedge knights well below the salt, closer to the doors than to the dais.

Whitewalls was almost new as castles went, having been raised a mere forty years ago by the grandsire of its present lord. The smallfolk hereabouts called it the Milkhouse, for its walls and keeps and towers were made of finely dressed white stone, quarried in the Vale and brought over the mountains at great expense. Inside were floors and pillars of milky white marble veined with gold; the rafters overhead were carved from the bone-pale trunks of weirwoods. Dunk could not begin to imagine what all of that had cost.

The hall was not so large as some others he had known, though. *At least we were allowed beneath the roof,* Dunk thought, as he took his place on the bench between Ser Maynard Plumm and Kyle the Cat. Though uninvited, the three of them had been welcomed to the feast quick enough; it was ill luck to refuse a knight hospitality on your wedding day.

Young Ser Glendon had a harder time, however. "Fireball never had a son," Dunk heard Lord Butterwell's steward tell him, loudly. The stripling answered heatedly, and the name of Ser Morgan Dunstable was mentioned several times, but the steward had remained adamant. When Ser Glendon touched his sword hilt, a dozen men-at-arms appeared with spears in hand, but for a moment it looked as though there might be bloodshed. It was only the intervention of a big blond knight named Kirby Pimm that saved the situation. Dunk was too far away to hear, but he saw Pimm clasp an arm around the steward's shoulders and murmur in his ear, laughing. The steward frowned, and said something to Ser Glendon that turned the boy's face dark red. *He looks as if he's about to cry,* Dunk thought, watching. *That, or kill someone.* After all of that, the young knight was finally admitted to the castle hall.

Poor Egg was not so fortunate. "The great hall is for the lords and knights," an understeward had informed them haughtily when Dunk had tried to bring the boy inside. "We have set up tables in the inner yard for squires, grooms, and men-at-arms."

If you had an inkling who he was, you would seat him on the dais on a cushioned throne. Dunk had not much liked the look of the other squires. A few were lads of Egg's own age, but most were older, seasoned fighters who long ago had made the choice to serve a knight rather than become one. *Or did they have a choice?* Knighthood required more than chivalry and skill at arms; it required horse and sword and armor too, and all of that was costly. "Watch your tongue," he told Egg before he left him in that company. "These are grown men, they won't take kindly to your insolence. Sit and eat and listen, might be you'll learn some things."

For his own part, Dunk was just glad to be out of the hot sun, with a wine cup before him and a chance to fill his belly. Even a hedge knight grows weary of chewing every bite of food for half an hour. Down here below the salt, the fare would be more plain than fancy, but there would be no lack of it. Below the salt was good enough for Dunk.

But peasant's pride is lordling's shame, the old man used to say. "This cannot be my proper place," Ser Glendon Ball told the understeward hotly. He had donned a clean doublet for the feast, a handsome old garment with gold lace at the cuffs and collar and the red chevron and white plates of House Ball sewn across the chest. "Do you know who my father was?"

"A noble knight and mighty lord, I have no doubt," said the understeward, "but the same is true of many here. Please take your seat or take your leave, ser. It is all the same to me."

In the end, the boy took his place below the salt with the rest of them, his mouth sullen. The long white hall was filling up as more knights crowded onto the benches. The crowd was larger than Dunk had anticipated, and from the looks of it some of the guests had come a very long way. He and Egg had not been around so many lords and knights since Ashford Meadow, and there was no way to guess who else might turn up next. *We should have stayed out in the hedges, sleeping under trees. If I am recognized . . .*

When a serving man placed a loaf of black bread on the cloth in front of each of them, Dunk was grateful for the distraction. He sawed the loaf open lengthwise, hollowed out the bottom half for a trencher, and ate the top. It was stale, but compared to his salt beef it was custard. At least it did not have to be soaked in ale or milk or water to make it soft enough to chew.

"Ser Duncan, you appear to be attracting a deal of attention," Ser Maynard Plumm observed, as Lord Vyrwel and his party went parading past them toward places of high honor at the top of the hall. "Those girls up on the dais cannot seem to take their eyes off you. I'll wager they have never seen a man so big. Even seated, you are half a head taller than any man in the hall."

Dunk hunched his shoulders. He was used to being stared at, but that did not mean he liked it. "Let them look."

"That's the Old Ox down there beneath the dais," Ser Maynard said. "They call him a huge man, but seems to me his belly is the biggest thing about him. You're a bloody giant next to him."

"Indeed, ser," said one of their companions on the bench, a sallow man, saturnine, clad in gray and green. His eyes were small and shrewd, set close together beneath thin, arching brows. A neat black beard framed his mouth, to make up for his receding hair. "In such a field as this, your size alone should make you one of the most formidable competitors."

"I had heard the Brute of Bracken might be coming," said another man, further down the bench.

"I think not," said the man in green and gray. "This is only a bit of jousting to celebrate his lordship's nuptials. A tilt in the yard to mark the tilt between the sheets. Hardly worth the bother for the likes of Otho Bracken."

Ser Kyle the Cat took a drink of wine. "I'll wager my lord of Butterwell does not take the field either. He will cheer on his champions from his lord's box in the shade."

"Then he'll see his champions fall," boasted Ser Glendon Ball, "and in the end, he'll hand his egg to me."

"Ser Glendon is the son of Fireball," Ser Kyle explained to the new man. "Might we have the honor of your name, ser?"

"Ser Uthor Underleaf. The son of no one of importance." Underleaf 's garments were of good cloth, clean and well cared for, but simply cut. A silver clasp in the shape of a snail fastened his cloak. "If your lance is the equal of your tongue, Ser Glendon, you may even give this big fellow here a contest."

Ser Glendon glanced at Dunk as the wine was being poured. "If we meet, he'll fall. I don't care how big he is."

Dunk watched a server fill his wine cup. "I am better with a sword than with a lance," he admitted, "and even better with a battleaxe. Will there be a melee here?" His size and strength would stand him in good stead in a melee, and he knew he could give as good as he got. Jousting was another matter.

"A melee? At a marriage?" Ser Kyle sounded shocked. "That would be unseemly."

Ser Maynard gave a chuckle. "A marriage is a melee, as any married man could tell you."

Ser Uthor chuckled. "There's just the joust, I fear, but besides the dragon's egg, Lord Butterwell has promised thirty golden dragons for the loser of the final tilt, and ten each for the knights defeated in the round before."

Ten dragons is not so bad. Ten dragons would buy a palfrey, so Dunk would not need to ride Thunder save in battle. Ten dragons would buy a suit of plate for Egg, and a proper knight's pavilion sewn with Dunk's tree and falling star. *Ten dragons would mean roast goose and ham and pigeon pie.*

"There are ransoms to be had as well, for those who win their matches," Ser Uthor said as he hollowed out his trencher, "and I have heard it rumored that some men place wagers on the tilts. Lord Butterwell himself is not fond of taking risks, but amongst his guests are some who wager heavily."

No sooner had he spoken than Ambrose Butterwell made his entrance, to a fanfare of trumpets from the minstrel's gallery. Dunk shoved to his feet with the rest as Butterwell escorted his new bride down a patterned Myrish carpet to the dais, arm in arm. The girl was fifteen and freshly flowered, her lord husband fifty and freshly widowed. She was pink and he was gray. Her bride's cloak trailed behind her, done in undy green and white and yellow. It looked so hot and heavy that Dunk wondered how she could bear to wear it. Lord Butterwell looked hot and heavy too, with his heavy jowls and thinning flaxen hair.

The bride's father followed close behind her, hand in hand with his young son. Lord Frey of the Crossing was a lean man elegant in blue and gray, his heir a chinless boy of four whose nose was dripping snot. Lords Costayne and Risley came next, with their lady wives, daughters of Lord Butterwell by his first wife. Frey's daughters followed with their own husbands. Then came Lord Gormon Peake; Lords Smallwood, Vrywel, and Shawney; various lesser lords and landed knights. Amongst them Dunk glimpsed John the Fiddler and Alyn Cockshaw. Lord Alyn looked to be in his cups, though the feast had not yet properly begun.

By the time all of them had sauntered to the dais, the high table was as crowded as the benches. Lord Butterwell and his bride sat on plump downy cushions in a double throne of gilded oak. The rest planted themselves in tall chairs with fancifully carved arms. On the wall behind them two huge banners hung from the rafters: the twin towers of Frey, blue on gray, and the green and white and yellow undy of the Butterwells.

It fell to Lord Frey to lead the toasts. "*The king!*" he began, simply. Ser Glendon held his wine cup out above the water basin. Dunk clanked his cup against it, and against Ser Uthor's and the rest as well. They drank.

"*Lord Butterwell, our gracious host,*" Frey proclaimed next.

"May the Father grant him long life and many sons."

They drank again.

"*Lady Butterwell, the maiden bride, my darling daughter.* May the Mother make her fertile." Frey gave the girl a smile. "I shall want a grandson before the year is out. Twins would suit me even better, so churn the butter well tonight, my sweet."

Laughter rang against the rafters, and the guests drank still once more. The wine was rich and red and sweet.

Then Lord Frey said, "I give you the King's Hand, Brynden Rivers. May the Crone's lamp light his path to wisdom." He lifted his goblet high and drank, together with Lord Butterwell and his bride and the others on the dais. Below the salt, Ser Glendon turned his cup over to spill its contents to the floor.

"A sad waste of good wine," said Maynard Plumm.

"I do not drink to kinslayers," said Ser Glendon. "Lord Bloodraven is a sorcerer and a bastard."

"Born bastard," Ser Uthor agreed mildly, "but his royal father made him legitimate as he lay dying." He drank deep, as did Ser Maynard and many others in the hall. Near as many lowered their cups, or turned them upside down as Ball had done. Dunk's own cup was heavy in his hand. *How many eyes does Lord Bloodraven have?* the riddle went. *A thousand eyes, and one.*

Toast followed toast, some proposed by Lord Frey and some by others. They drank to young Lord Tully, Lord Butterwell's liege lord, who had begged off from the wedding. They drank to the health of Leo Longthorn, Lord of Highgarden, who was rumored to be ailing. They drank to the memory of their gallant dead. Aye, thought Dunk, remembering. *I'll gladly drink to them.*

Ser John the Fiddler proposed the final toast. "*To my brave brothers!* I know that they are smiling tonight!"

Dunk had not intended to drink so much, with the jousting on the morrow, but the cups were filled anew after every toast, and he found he had a thirst. "Never refuse a cup of wine or a horn of ale," Ser Arlan had once told him, "it may be a year before you see another." *It would have been discourteous not to toast the bride and groom,* he told himself, *and dangerous not to drink to the king and his Hand, with strangers all about.*

Mercifully, the Fiddler's toast was the last. Lord Butterwell rose ponderously to thank them for coming and promise good jousting on the morrow. "Let the feast begin!"

Suckling pig was served at the high table; a peacock roasted in its plumage; a great pike crusted with crushed almonds. Not a bite of that made it down below the salt. Instead of suckling pig they got salt pork, soaked in almond milk and peppered pleasantly. In place of peacock they had capons, crisped up nice and brown and stuffed with onions, herbs, mushrooms, and roasted chestnuts. In place of pike they ate chunks of flaky white cod in a pastry coffyn, with some sort of tasty brown sauce that Dunk could not quite place. There was pease porridge besides, buttered turnip,; carrots drizzled with honey, and a ripe white cheese that smelled as strong as Bennis of the Brown Shield. Dunk ate well, but all the while wondered what Egg was getting in the yard. Just in case, he slipped half a capon into the pocket of his cloak, with some hunks of bread and a little of the smelly cheese.

As they ate, pipes and fiddles filled the air with spritely tunes, and the talk turned to the morrow's jousting. "Ser Franklyn Frey is well regarded along the Green Fork," said Uthor Underleaf, who seemed to know these local heroes well. "That's him upon the dais, the uncle of the bride. Lucas Nayland is down from Hag's Mire, he should not be discounted. Nor should Ser Mortimer Boggs, of Crackclaw Point. Elsewise, this should be a tourney of household knights and village heroes. Kirby Pimm and Galtry the Green are the best of those, though neither is a match for Lord Butterwell's good-son, Black Tom Heddle. A nasty bit of business, that one. He won the hand of his lordship's eldest daughter by killing three of her other suitors, it's said, and once unhorsed the Lord of Casterly Rock."

"What, young Lord Tybolt?" asked Ser Maynard.

"No, the old Gray Lion, the one who died in the spring." That was how men spoke of those who had perished during the Great Spring Sickness. *He died in the spring.* Tens of thousands had died in the spring, among them a king and two young princes.

"Do not slight Ser Buford Bulwer," said Kyle the Cat. "The Old Ox slew forty men upon the Redgrass Field."

"And every year his count grows higher," said Ser Maynard. "Bulwer's day is done. Look at him. Past sixty, soft and fat, and his right eye is good as blind."

"Do not trouble to search the hall for the champion," a voice behind Dunk said. "Here I stand, sers. Feast your eyes."

Dunk turned to find Ser John the Fiddler looming over him, a half-smile on his lips. His white silk doublet had dagged sleeves lined with red satin, so long their points drooped down past his knees. A heavy silver chain looped across his chest, studded with huge dark amethysts whose color matched his eyes. *That chain is worth as much as everything I own*, Dunk thought.

The wine had colored Ser Glendon's cheeks and inflamed his pimples. "Who are you, to make such boasts?"

"They call me John, the Fiddler."

"Are you a musician or a warrior?"

"I can make sweet song with either lance or resined bow, as it happens. Every wedding needs a singer, and every tourney needs a mystery knight. May I join you? Butterwell was good enough to place me on the dais, but I prefer the company of my fellow hedge knights to fat pink ladies and old men." The Fiddler clapped Dunk upon the shoulder. "Be a good fellow and shove over, Ser Duncan."

Dunk shoved over. "You are too late for food, ser."

"No matter. I know where Butterwell's kitchens are. There is still some wine, I trust?" The Fiddler smelled of oranges and limes, with a hint of some strange eastern spice beneath. Nutmeg, perhaps. Dunk could not have said. What did he know of nutmeg?

"Your boasting is unseemly," Ser Glendon told the Fiddler.

"Truly? Then I must beg for your forgiveness, ser. I would never wish to give offense to any son of Fireball."

That took the youth aback. "You know who I am?"

"Your father's son, I hope."

"Look," said Ser Kyle the Cat. "The wedding pie."

Six kitchen boys were pushing it through the doors, upon a wide wheeled cart. The pie was brown and crusty and immense, and there were noises coming from inside it, squeaks and squawks and thumps. Lord and Lady Butterwell descended from the dais to meet it, sword in hand. When they cut it open, half a hundred birds burst forth to fly around the hall. In other wedding feasts Dunk had attended, the pies had been filled with doves or songbirds, but inside this one were blue jays and skylarks, pigeons and doves, mockingbirds and nightingales, small brown sparrows and a great red parrot. "One-and-twenty sorts of birds," said Ser Kyle.

"One-and-twenty sorts of bird droppings," said Ser Maynard.

"You have no poetry in your heart, ser."

"You have shit upon your shoulder."

"This is the proper way to fill a pie," Ser Kyle sniffed, cleaning off his tunic. "The pie is meant to be the marriage, and a true marriage has in it many sorts of things—joy and grief, pain and pleasure, love and lust and loyalty. So it is fitting that there be birds of many sorts. No man ever truly knows what a new wife will bring him."

"Her cunt," said Plumm, "or what would be the point?"

Dunk shoved back from the table. "I need a breath of air." It was a piss he needed, truth be told, but in fine company like this it was more courteous to talk of air. "Pray excuse me."

"Hurry back, ser," said the Fiddler. "There are jugglers yet to come, and you do not want to miss the bedding."

Outside, the night wind lapped at Dunk like the tongue of some great beast. The hard-packed earth of the yard seemed to move beneath his feet . . . or it might be that he was swaying.

The lists had been erected in the center of the outer yard. A three-tiered wooden viewing stand had been raised beneath the walls, so Lord Butterwell and his highborn guests would be well shaded on their cushioned seats. There were tents at both ends of the lists where the knights could don their armor, with racks of tourney lances standing ready. When the wind lifted the banners for an instant, Dunk could smell the whitewash on the tilting barrier. He set off in search of the inner ward. He had to hunt up Egg and send the boy to the master of the games to enter him in the lists. That was a squire's duty.

Whitewalls was strange to him, however, and somehow Dunk got turned around. He found himself outside the kennels, where the hounds caught scent of him and began to bark and howl. *They want to tear my throat out,* he thought, *or else they want the capon in my cloak.* He doubled back the way he'd come, past the sept. A woman went running past, breathless with laughter, a bald knight in hard pursuit. The man kept falling, until finally the woman had to come back and help him up. *I should slip into the sept and ask the Seven to make that knight my first opponent*, Dunk thought, but that would have been impious. *What I really need is a privy, not a prayer.* There were some bushes near at hand, beneath a flight of pale stone steps. *Those will serve.* He groped his way behind them and unlaced his breeches. His bladder had been full to bursting. The piss went on and on.

Somewhere above, a door came open. Dunk heard footfalls on the steps, the scrape of boots on stone. ". . . . beggar's feast you've laid before us. Without Bittersteel . . . "

"Bittersteel be buggered," insisted a familiar voice. "No bastard can be trusted, not even him. A few victories will bring him over the water fast enough."

Lord Peake. Dunk held his breath . . . and his piss.

"Easier to speak of victories than win them." This speaker had a deeper voice than Peake, a bass rumble with an angry edge to it. "Old Milkblood expected the boy to have it, and so will all the rest. Glib words and charm cannot make up for that."

"A dragon would. The prince insists the egg will hatch. He dreamed it, just as he once dreamed his brothers dead. A living dragon will win us all the swords that we would want."

"A dragon is one thing, a dream's another. I promise you, Bloodraven is not off dreaming. We need a warrior, not a dreamer. Is the boy his father's son?"

"Just do your part as promised, and let me concern myself with that. Once we have Butterwell's gold and the swords of House Frey, Harrenhal will follow, then the Brackens. Otho knows he cannot hope to stand . . . "

The voices were fading as the speakers moved away. Dunk's piss began to flow again. He gave his cock a shake, and laced himself back up. "His father's son," he muttered. *Who were they speaking of? Fireball's son?*

By the time he emerged from under the steps, the two lords were well across the yard. He almost shouted after them, to make them show their faces, but thought better of it. He was alone and unarmed, and half drunk besides. *Maybe more than half.* He stood there frowning for a moment, then marched back to the hall.

Inside, the last course had been served and the frolics had begun. One of Lord Frey's daughters played "Two Hearts That Beat As One" on the high harp, very badly. Some jugglers flung flaming torches at each other for a while, and some tumblers did cartwheels in the air. Lord Frey's nephew began to sing "The Bear and the Maiden Fair" while Ser Kirby Pimm beat out time upon the table with a wooden spoon. Others joined in, until the whole hall was bellowing, "*A bear! A bear! All black and brown, and covered with hair!*" Lord Caswell passed out at the table with his face in a puddle of wine, and Lady Vyrwel began to weep, though no one was quite certain as to the cause of her distress.

All the while the wine kept flowing. The rich Arbor reds gave way to local vintages, or so the Fiddler said; if truth be told, Dunk could not tell the difference. There was hippocras as well, he had to try a cup of that. *It might be a year before I have another.* The other hedge knights, fine fellows all, had begun to talk of women they had known. Dunk found himself wondering where Tanselle was tonight. He knew where Lady Rohanne was—abed at Coldmoat Castle, with old Ser Eustace beside her, snoring through his mustache—so he tried not to think of her. *Do they ever think of me?* he wondered.

His melancholy ponderings were rudely interrupted when a troupe of painted dwarfs came bursting from the belly of a wheeled wooden pig to chase Lord Butterwell's fool about the tables, walloping him with inflated pig's bladders that made rude noises every time a blow was struck. It was the funniest thing Dunk had seen in years, and he laughed with all the rest. Lord Frey's son was so taken by their antics that he joined in, pummeling the wedding guests with a bladder borrowed from a dwarf. The child had the most irritating laugh Dunk had ever heard, a high shrill hiccup of a laugh that made him want to take the boy over a knee, or throw him down a well. *If he hits me with that bladder, I may do it.*

"There's the lad who made this marriage," Ser Maynard said, as the chinless urchin went screaming past.

"How so?" The Fiddler held up an empty wine cup, and a passing server filled it.

Ser Maynard glanced toward the dais, where the bride was feeding cherries to her husband. "His lordship will not be the first to butter that biscuit. His bride was deflowered by a scullion at the Twins, they say. She would creep down to the kitchens to meet him. Alas, one night that little brother of hers crept down after her. When he saw them making the two-backed beast, he let out a shriek, and cooks and guardsmen came running and found milady and her pot boy coupling on the slab of marble where the cook rolls out the dough, both naked as their name day and floured up from head to heel."

That cannot be true, Dunk thought. Lord Butterwell had broad lands, and pots of yellow gold. Why would he wed a girl who'd been soiled by a kitchen scullion, and give away his dragon's egg to mark the match? The Freys of the Crossing were no nobler than the Butterwells. They owned a bridge instead of cows, that was the only difference. Lords. Who can ever understand *them*? Dunk ate some nuts and pondered what he'd overheard whilst pissing. *Dunk the drunk, what is it that you think you heard?* He had another cup of hippocras, since the first had tasted good. Then he lay his head down atop his folded arms and closed his eyes just for a moment, to rest them from the smoke.

When he opened them again, half the wedding guests were on their feet and shouting, "Bed them! Bed them!" They were making such an uproar than they woke Dunk from a pleasant dream involving Tanselle Too-Tall and the Red Widow. "Bed them! Bed them!" the calls rang out. Dunk sat up and rubbed his eyes.

Ser Franklyn Frey had the bride in his arms and was carrying her down the aisle, with men and boys swarming all around him. The ladies at the high table had surrounded Lord Butterwell. Lady Vyrwel had recovered from her grief and was trying to pull his lordship from his chair, while one of his daughters unlaced his boots and some Frey woman pulled up his tunic. Butterwell was flailing at them ineffectually, and laughing. He was drunk, Dunk saw, and Ser Franklyn was a deal drunker . . . so drunk he almost dropped the bride. Before Dunk quite realized what was happening, John the Fiddler had dragged him to his feet. "Here!" he cried out. "Let the giant carry her!"

The next thing he knew, he was climbing a tower stair with the bride squirming in his arms. How he kept his feet was beyond him. The girl would not be still and the men were all around them, making ribald japes about flouring her up and kneading her well whilst they pulled off her clothes. The dwarfs joined in as well. They swarmed around Dunk's legs, shouting and laughing and smacking at his calves with their bladders. It was all he could do not to trip over them.

Dunk had no notion where Lord Butterwell's bedchamber was to be found, but the other men pushed and prodded him until he got there, by which time the bride was red-faced, giggling, and nearly naked, save for the stocking on her left leg, which had somehow survived the climb. Dunk was crimson too, and not from exertion. His arousal would have been obvious if anyone had been looking, but fortunately all eyes were the bride. Lady Butterwell looked nothing like Tanselle, but having the one squirming half-naked in his arms had started Dunk thinking about the other. *Tanselle Too-Tall, that was her name, but she was not too tall for me.* He wondered if he would ever find her again. There had been some nights when he thought he must have dreamed her. *No, lunk, you only dreamed she liked you.*

Lord Butterwell's bedchamber was large and lavish, once he found it. Myrish carpets covered the floors, a hundred scented candles burned in nooks and crannies, and a suit of plate inlaid with gold and gems stood beside the door. It even had its own privy set into a small stone alcove in the outer wall.

When Dunk finally plopped the bride onto her marriage bed, a dwarf leapt in beside her and seized one of her breasts for a bit of a fondle. The girl let out a squeal, the men roared with laughter, and Dunk seized the dwarf by his collar and hauled him kicking off m'lady. He was carrying the little man across the room to chuck him out the door when he saw the dragon's egg.

Lord Butterwell had placed it on a black velvet cushion atop a marble plinth. It was much bigger than a hen's egg, though not so big as he'd had imagined. Fine red scales covered its surface, shining bright as jewels by the light of lamps and candles. Dunk dropped the dwarf and picked up the egg, just to feel it for a moment. It was heavier than he'd expected. *You could smash a man's head with this, and never crack the shell.* The scales were smooth beneath his fingers, and the deep, rich red seemed to shimmer as he turned the egg in his hands. *Blood and flame*, he thought, but there were gold flecks in it as well, and whorls of midnight black.

"Here, you! What do you think you're doing, ser?" A knight he did not know was glaring at him, a big man with a coal-black beard and boils, but it was the voice that made him blink; a deep voice, thick with anger. *It was him, the man with Peake*, Dunk realized, as the man said, "Put that down. I'll thank you to keep your greasy fingers off his lordship's treasures, or by the Seven, you shall wish you had."

The other knight was not near as drunk as Dunk, so it seemed wise to do as he said. He put the egg back on its pillow, very carefully, and wiped his fingers on his sleeve. "I meant no harm, ser." *Dunk the lunk, thick as a castle wall.* Then he shoved past the man with the black beard and out the door.

There were noises in the stairwell, glad shouts and girlish laughter. The women were bringing Lord Butterwell to his bride. Dunk had no wish to encounter them, so he went up instead of down, and found himself on the tower roof beneath the stars, with the pale castle glimmering in the moonlight all around him.

He was feeling dizzy from the wine, so he leaned against a parapet. *Am I going to be sick?* Why did he go and touch the dragon's egg? He remembered Tanselle's puppet show, and the wooden dragon that had started all the trouble there at Ashford. The memory made Dunk feel guilty, as it always did. *Three good men dead, to save a hedge knight's foot.* It made no sense, and never had. *Take a lesson from that, lunk. It is not for the likes of you to mess about with dragons or their eggs.*

"It almost looks as if it's made of snow."

Dunk turned. John the Fiddler stood behind him, smiling in his silk and cloth-of-gold. "What's made of snow?"

"The castle. All that white stone in the moonlight. Have you ever been north of the Neck, Ser Duncan? I'm told it snows there even in the summer. Have you ever seen the Wall?"

"No, m'lord." *Why he is going on about the Wall?* "That's where we were going, Egg and me. Up north, to Winterfell."

"Would that I could join you. You could show me the way."

"The way?" Dunk frowned. "It's right up the kingsroad. If you stay to the road and keep going north, you can't miss it."

The Fiddler laughed. "I suppose not . . . though you might be surprised at what some men can miss." He went to the parapet and looked out across the castle. "They say those northmen are a savage folk, and their woods are full of wolves."

"M'lord? Why did you come up here?"

"Alyn was seeking for me, and I did not care to be found. He grows tiresome when he drinks, does Alyn. I saw you slip away from that bedchamber of horrors, and slipped out after you. I've had too much wine, I grant you, but not enough to face a naked Butterwell." He gave Dunk an enigmatic smile. "I dreamed of you, Ser Duncan. Before I even met you. When I saw you on the road, I knew your face at once. It was as if we were old friends."

Dunk had the strangest feeling then, as if he had lived this all before. *I dreamed of you*, he said. *My dreams are not like yours, Ser Duncan. Mine are true.* "You dreamed of me?" he said, in a voice made thick by wine. "What sort of dream?"

"Why," the Fiddler said, "I dreamed that you were all in white from head to heel, with a long pale cloak flowing from those broad shoulders. You were a White Sword, ser, a Sworn Brother of the Kingsguard, the greatest knight in all the Seven Kingdoms, and you lived for no other purpose but to guard and serve and please your king." He put a hand on Dunk's shoulder."You have dreamed the same dream, I know you have."

He had, it was true. *The first time the old man let me hold his sword.* "Every boy dreams of serving in the Kingsguard."

"Only seven boys grow up to wear the white cloak, though. Would it please you to be one of them?"

"Me?" Dunk shrugged away the lordling's hand, which had begun to knead his shoulder. "It might. Or not." The knights of the Kingsguard served for life, and swore to take no wife and hold no lands. *I might find Tanselle again someday. Why shouldn't I have a wife, and sons?* "It makes no matter what I dream. Only a king can make a Kingsguard knight."

"I suppose that means I'll have to take the throne, then. I would much rather be teaching you to fiddle."

"You're drunk." *And the crow once called the raven black.*

"Wonderfully drunk. Wine makes all things possible, Ser Duncan. You'd look a god in white, I think, but if the color does not suit you, perhaps you would prefer to be a lord?"

Dunk laughed in his face. "No, I'd sooner sprout big blue wings and fly. One's as likely as t'other."

"Now you mock me. A true knight would never mock his king." The Fiddler sounded hurt. "I hope you will put more faith in what I tell you when you see the dragon hatch."

"A dragon will hatch? A *living* dragon? What, here?"

"I dreamed it. This pale white castle, you, a dragon bursting from an egg, I dreamed it all, just as I once dreamed of my brothers lying dead. They were twelve and I was only seven, so they laughed at me, and died. I am two-and-twenty now, and I trust my dreams."

Dunk was remembering another tourney, remembering how he had walked through the soft spring rains with another princeling. *I dreamed of you and a dead dragon*, Egg's brother Daeron said to him. *A great beast, huge, with wings so large they could cover this meadow. It had fallen on top of you, but you were alive and the dragon was dead. And so he was, poor Baelor.* Dreams were a treacherous ground on which to build. "As you say, m'lord," he told the Fiddler. "Pray excuse me."

"Where *are* you going, ser?"

"To my bed, to sleep. I'm drunk as a dog."

"Be my dog, ser. The night's alive with promise. We can howl together, and wake the very gods."

"What do you want of me?"

"Your sword. I would make you mine own man, and raise you high. My dreams do not lie, Ser Duncan. You shall have that white cloak, and I must have the dragon's egg. I *must*, my dreams have made that plain. Perhaps the egg will hatch, or else . . . "

Behind them, the door banged open violently. "*There he is, my lord.*" A pair of men-at-arms stepped onto the roof. Lord Gormon Peake was just behind them.

"*Gormy*," the Fiddler drawled. "Why, what are you doing in my bedchamber, my lord?"

"It is a roof, ser, and you have had too much wine." Lord Gormon made a sharp gesture, and the guards moved forward. "Allow us to help you to that bed. You are jousting on the morrow, pray recall. Kirby Pimm can prove a dangerous foe."

"I had hoped to joust with good Ser Duncan here."

Peake gave Dunk an unsympathetic look. "Later, perhaps. For your first tilt, you have drawn Ser Kirby Pimm."

"Then Pimm must fall! So must they all! The mystery knight prevails against all challengers, and wonder dances in his wake." A guardsman took the Fiddler by the arm. "Ser Duncan, it seems that we must part," he called, as they helped him down the steps.

Only Lord Gormon remained upon the roof with Dunk. "Hedge knight," he growled, "did your mother never teach you not to reach your hand into the dragon's mouth?"

"I never knew my mother, m'lord."

"That would explain it. What did he promise you?"

"A lordship. A white cloak. Big blue wings."

"Here's my promise: three feet of cold steel through your belly, if you speak a word of what just happened."

Dunk shook his head to clear his wits. It did not seem to help. He bent double at the waist, and retched.

Some of the vomit spattered Peake's boots. The lord cursed. "Hedge knights," he exclaimed in disgust. "You have no place here. No true knight would be so discourteous as to turn up uninvited, but you creatures of the hedge . . . "

"We are wanted nowhere and turn up everywhere, m'lord." The wine had made Dunk bold, else he would have held his tongue. He wiped his mouth with the back of his hand.

"Try and remember what I told you, ser. It will go ill for you if you do not." Lord Peake shook the vomit off his boot. Then he was gone. Dunk leaned against the parapet again. He wondered who was madder, Lord Gormon or the Fiddler.

By the time he found his way back to the hall, only Maynard Plumm remained of his companions. "Was there any flour on her teats when you got the smallclothes off her?" he wanted to know.

Dunk shook his head, poured himself another cup of wine, tasted it, and decided that he had drunk enough.

Butterwell's stewards had found rooms in the keep for the lords and ladies, and beds in the barracks for their retinues. The rest of the guests had their choice between a straw pallet in the cellar, or a spot of ground beneath the western walls to raise their pavilions. The modest sailcloth tent Dunk had acquired in Stoney Sept was no pavilion, but it kept the rain and sun off. Some of his neighbors were still awake, the silken walls of their pavilions glowing like colored lanterns in the night. Laughter came from inside a blue pavilion covered with sunflowers, and the sounds of love from one striped in white and purple. Egg had set up their own tent a bit apart from the others. Maester and the two horses were hobbled nearby, and Dunk's arms and armor had been neatly stacked against the castle walls. When he crept into the tent, he found his squire sitting cross-legged by a candle, his head shining as he peered over a book.

"Reading books by candlelight will make you blind." Reading remained a mystery to Dunk, though the lad had tried to teach him.

"I need the candlelight to see the words, ser."

"Do you want a clout in the ear? What book is that?" Dunk saw bright colors on the page, little painted shields hiding in amongst the letters.

"A roll of arms, ser."

"Looking for the Fiddler? You won't find him. They don't put hedge knights in those rolls, just lords and champions."

"I wasn't looking for him. I saw some other sigils in the yard . . . Lord Sunderland is here, ser. He bears the heads of three pale ladies, on undy green and blue."

"A Sisterman? Truly?" The Three Sisters were islands in the Bite. Dunk had heard septons say that the isles were sinks of sin and avarice. Sisterton was the most notorious smuggler's den in all of Westeros. "He's come a long way. He must be kin to Butterwell's new bride."

"He isn't, ser."

"Then he's here for the feast. They eat fish on the Three Sisters, don't they? A man gets sick of fish. Did you get enough to eat? I brought you half a capon and some cheese." Dunk rummaged in the pocket of his cloak.

"They fed us ribs, ser." Egg's nose was deep in the book. "Lord Sunderland fought for the black dragon, ser."

"Like old Ser Eustace? He wasn't so bad, was he?"

"No, ser," Egg said, "but . . . "

"I saw the dragon's egg." Dunk squirreled the food away with their hardbread and salt beef. "It was red, mostly. Does Lord Bloodraven own a dragon's egg as well?"

Egg lowered his book. "Why would he? He's baseborn."

"Bastard born, not baseborn." Bloodraven had been born on the wrong side of the blanket, but he was noble on both sides. Dunk was about to tell Egg about the men he'd overhead when he noticed his face. "What happened to your lip?"

"A fight, ser."

"Let me see it."

"It only bled a little. I dabbed some wine on it."

"Who were you fighting?"

"Some other squires. They said—"

"Never mind what they said. What did I tell you?"

"To hold my tongue and make no trouble." The boy touched his broken lip. "They called my father a *kinslayer*, though."

He is, lad, though I do not think he meant it. Dunk had told Egg half a hundred times not to take such words to heart. *You know the truth. Let that be enough.* They had heard such talk before, in wine sinks and low taverns, and around campfires in the woods. The whole realm knew how Prince Maekar's mace had felled his brother Baelor Breakspear at Ashford Meadow. Talk of plots was only to be expected. "If they knew Prince Maekar was your father, they would never have said such things." *Behind your back, yes, but never to your face.* "And what did you tell these other squires, instead of holding your tongue?"

Egg looked abashed. "That Prince Baelor's death was just a mishap. Only when I said Prince Maekar loved his brother Baelor, Ser Addam's squire said he loved him to death, and Ser Mallor's squire said he meant to love his brother Aerys the same way. That was when I hit him. I hit him good."

"I ought to hit you good. A fat ear to go with that fat lip. Your father would do the same if he were here. Do you think Prince Maekar needs a little boy to defend him? What did he tell you when he sent you off with me?"

"To serve you faithfully as your squire, and not flinch from any task or hardship."

"And what else?"

"To obey the king's laws, the rules of chivalry, and you."

"And what else?"

"To keep my hair shaved or dyed," the boy said, with obvious reluctance, "and tell no man my true name."

Dunk nodded. "How much wine had this boy drunk?"

"He was drinking barley beer."

"You see? The barley beer was talking. Words are wind, Egg. Just let them blow on past you."

"Some words are wind." The boy was nothing if not stubborn. "Some words are treason. This is a traitor's tourney, ser."

"What, all of them?" Dunk shook his head. "If it was true, that was a long time ago. The black dragon's dead, and those who fought with him are fled or pardoned. And it's not true. Lord Butterwell's sons fought on both sides."

"That makes him *half* a traitor, ser."

"Sixteen years ago." Dunk's mellow winey haze was gone. He felt angry, and near sober. "Lord Butterwell's steward is the master of the games, a man named Cosgrove. Find him and enter my name for the lists. No, wait . . . hold back my name." With so many lords on hand, one of them might recall Ser Duncan the Tall from Ashford Meadow. "Enter me as the Gallows Knight." The smallfolk loved it when a mystery knight appeared at a tourney.

Egg fingered his fat lip. "The Gallows Knight, ser?"

"For the shield."

"Yes, but . . . "

"Go do as I said. You have read enough for one night." Dunk pinched the candle out between his thumb and forefinger.

The sun rose hot and hard, implacable.

Waves of heat rose shimmering off the white stones of the castle. The air smelled of baked earth and torn grass, and no breath of wind stirred the banners that drooped atop the keep and gatehouse, green and white and yellow.

Thunder was restless, in a way that Dunk had seldom seen before. The stallion tossed his head from side to side as Egg was tightening his saddle cinch. He even bared his big square teeth at the boy. It is so hot, Dunk thought, too hot for man or mount. A warhorse does not have a placid disposition even at the best of times. The Mother herself would be foul-tempered in this heat.

In the center of the yard the jousters began another run. Ser Harbert rode a golden courser barded in black and decorated with the red and white serpents of House Paege, Ser Franklyn a sorrel whose gray silk trapper bore the twin towers of Frey. When they came together, the red and white lance cracked clean in two and the blue one exploded into splinters, but neither man lost his seat. A cheer went up from the viewing stand and the guardsmen on the castle walls, but it was short and thin and hollow. *It is too hot for cheering.* Dunk mopped sweat from his brow. It is too hot for jousting. His head was beating like a drum. *Let me win this tilt and one more, and I will be content.*

The knights wheeled their horses about at the end of the lists and tossed down the jagged remains of their lances, the fourth pair they had broken. *Three too many.* Dunk had put off donning his armor as long as he dared, yet already he could feel his smallclothes sticking to his skin beneath his steel. *There are worse things than being soaked with sweat,* he told himself, remembering the fight on the *White Lady,* when the ironmen had come swarming over her side. He had been soaked in blood by the time that day was done.

Fresh lances in hand, Paege and Frey put their spurs into their mounts once again. Clods of cracked dry earth sprayed back from beneath their horses' hooves with every stride. The crack of the lances breaking made

Dunk wince. *Too much wine last night, and too much food.* He had some vague memory of carrying the bride up the steps, and meeting John the Fiddler and Lord Peake upon a roof. *What was I doing on a roof?* There had been talk of dragons, he recalled, or dragon's eggs, or something, but . . .

A noise broke his reverie, part roar and part moan. Dunk saw the golden horse trotting riderless to the end of the lists, as Ser Harbert Paege rolled feebly on the ground. *Two more before my turn.* The sooner he unhorsed Ser Uthor, the sooner he could take his armor off, have a cool drink, and rest. He should have at least an hour before they called him forth again.

Lord Butterwell's portly herald climbed to the top of the viewing stand to summon the next pair of jousters. "*Ser Argrave the Defiant,*" he called, "*a knight of Nunny, in service to Lord Butterwell of Whitewalls. Ser Glendon Flowers, the Knight of the Pussywillows. Come forth and prove your valor.*" A gale of laughter rippled through the viewing stands.

Ser Argrave was a spare, leathery man, a seasoned household knight in dinted gray armor riding an unbarded horse. Dunk had known his sort before; such men were tough as old roots, and knew their business. His foe was young Ser Glendon, mounted on his wretched stot and armored in a heavy mail hauberk and open-faced iron halfhelm. On his arm his shield displayed his father's fiery sigil. *He needs a breastplate and a proper helm, Dunk thought. A blow to the head or chest could kill him, clad like that.*

Ser Glendon was plainly furious at his introduction. He wheeled his mount in an angry circle and shouted, "I am Glendon *Ball*, not Glendon Flowers. Mock me at your peril, herald. I warn you, I have hero's blood." The herald did not deign to reply, but more laughter greeted the young knight's protest. "Why are they laughing at him?" Dunk wondered aloud. "Is he a bastard, then?" *Flowers* was the surname given to bastards born of noble parents in the Reach. "And what was all that about pussywillows?"

"I could find out, ser," said Egg.

"No. It is none of our concern. Do you have my helm?" Ser Argrave and Ser Glendon dipped their lances before Lord and Lady Butterwell. Dunk saw Butterwell lean over and whisper something in his bride's ear. The girl began to giggle.

"Yes, ser." Egg had donned his floppy hat, to shade his eyes and keep the sun off his shaved head. Dunk liked to tease the boy about that hat, but just now he wished he had one like it. Better a straw hat than an iron one, beneath this sun. He pushed his hair out of his eyes, eased the greathelm down into place with two hands, and fastened it to his gorget. The lining stank of old sweat, and he could feel the weight of all that iron on his neck and shoulders. His head throbbed from last night's wine.

"Ser," Egg said, "it is not too late to withdraw. If you lose Thunder and your armor . . ."

I would be done as a knight. "Why should I lose?" Dunk demanded. Ser Argrave and Ser Glendon had ridden to opposite ends of the lists. "It is not as if I faced the Laughing Storm. Is there some knight here like to give me trouble?"

"Almost all of them, ser."

"I owe you a clout in the ear for that. Ser Uthor is ten years my senior and half my size." Ser Argrave lowered his visor. Ser Glendon did not have a visor to lower.

"You have not ridden in a tilt since Ashford Meadow, ser."

Insolent boy. "I've trained." Not as faithfully as he might have, to be sure. When he could, he took his turn riding at quintains or rings, where such were available. And sometimes he would command Egg to climb a tree and hang a shield or barrel stave beneath a well-placed limb for them to tilt at.

"You're better with a sword than with a lance," Egg said. "With an axe or a mace there's few to match your strength."

There was enough truth in that to annoy Dunk all the more. "There is no contest for swords or maces," he pointed out, as Fireball's son and Ser Argrave the Defiant began their charge. "Go get my shield."

Egg made a face, then went to fetch the shield.

Across the yard, Ser Argrave's lance struck Ser Glendon's shield and glanced off, leaving a gouge across the comet. But Ball's coronal found the center of his foe's breastplate with such force that it burst his saddle cinch. Knight and saddle both went tumbling to the dust. Dunk was impressed despite himself. *The boy jousts almost as well as he talks.* He wondered if that would stop them laughing at him.

A trumpet rang, loud enough to make Dunk wince. Once more the herald climbed his stand. "*Ser Joffrey of House Caswell, Lord of Bitterbridge and Defender of the Fords. Ser Kyle, the Cat of Misty Moor. Come forth and prove your valor.*"

Ser Kyle's armor was of good quality, but old and worn, with many dents and scratches. "The Mother has been merciful to me, Ser Duncan," he told Dunk and Egg, on his way to the lists. "I am sent against Lord Caswell, the very man I came to see."

If any man upon the field felt worse than Dunk this morning it had to be Lord Caswell, who had drunk himself insensible at the feast. "It's a wonder he can sit a horse, after last night," said Dunk. "The victory is yours, ser."

"Oh, no." Ser Kyle smiled a silken smile. "The cat who wants his bowl of cream must know when to purr and when to show his claws, Ser Duncan. If his lordship's lance so much as scrapes against my shield, I shall go tumbling to the earth. Afterward, when I bring my horse and armor to him, I will compliment his lordship on how much his prowess has grown since I made him his first sword. That will recall me to him, and before the day is out I shall be a Caswell man again, a knight of Bitterbridge."

There is no honor in that, Dunk almost said, but he bit his tongue instead. Ser Kyle would not be the first hedge knight to trade his honor for a warm place by the fire. "As you say," he muttered. "Good fortune to you. Or bad, if you prefer."

Lord Joffrey Caswell was a weedy youth of twenty, though admittedly he looked rather more impressive in his armor than he had last night when he'd been face down in a puddle of wine. A yellow centaur was painted on his shield, pulling on a longbow. The same centaur adorned the white silk trappings of his horse, and gleamed atop his helm in yellow gold. *A man who has a centaur for his sigil should ride better than that*. Dunk did not know how well Ser Kyle wielded a lance, but from the way Lord Caswell sat his horse it looked as though a loud cough might unseat him. *All the Cat need do is ride past him very fast.*

Egg held Thunder's bridle as Dunk swung himself ponderously up into the high, stiff saddle. As he sat there waiting, he could feel the eyes upon him. *They are wondering if the big hedge knight is any good*. Dunk wondered that himself. He would find out soon enough.

The Cat of Misty Moor was true to his word. Lord Caswell's lance was wobbling all the way across the field, and Ser Kyle's was ill-aimed. Neither man got his horse up past a trot. All the same, the Cat went tumbling when Lord Joffrey's coronal chanced to whack his shoulder. *I thought all cats landed gracefully upon their feet*, Dunk thought, as the hedge knight rolled in the dust. Lord Caswell's lance remained unbroken. As he brought his horse around, he thrust it high into the air repeatedly, as if he'd just unseated Leo Longthorn or the Laughing Storm. The Cat pulled off his helm and went chasing down his horse.

"My shield," Dunk said to Egg. The boy handed it up. He slipped his left arm through the strap and closed his hand around the grip. The weight of the kite shield was reassuring, though its length made it awkward to handle, and seeing the hanged man once again gave him an uneasy feeling. *Those are ill-omened arms*. He resolved to get the shield repainted as soon as he could. *May the Warrior grant me a smooth course and a quick victory*, he prayed, as Butterwell's herald was clambering up the steps once more. "*Ser Uthor Underleaf*," his voice rang out. "*The Gallows Knight. Come forth and prove your valor.*"

"Be careful, ser," Egg warned as he handed Dunk a tourney lance, a tapered wooden shaft twelve feet long ending in a rounded iron coronal in the shape of a closed fist. "The other squires say Ser Uthor has a good seat. And he's quick."

"Quick?" Dunk snorted. "He has a snail on his shield. How quick can he be?" He put his heels into Thunder's flanks and walked the horse slowly forward, his lance upright. *One victory, and I am no worse than before. Two will leave us well ahead. Two is not too much to hope for, in this company.* He had been fortunate in the lots, at least. He could as easily have drawn the Old Ox or Ser Kirby Pimm or some other local hero. Dunk wondered if the master of games was deliberately matching the hedge knights against each other, so no lordling need suffer the ignominy of losing to one in the first round. It does not matter. *One foe at a time, that was what the old man always said. Ser Uthor is all that should concern me now.*

They met beneath the viewing stand where Lord and Lady Butterwell sat on their cushions in the shade of the castle walls. Lord Frey was beside them, dandling his snot-nosed son on one knee. A row of serving girls were fanning them, yet Lord Butterwell's damask tunic was stained beneath the arms, and his lady's hair was limp from perspiration. She looked hot, bored, and uncomfortable, but when she saw Dunk she pushed out her chest in a way that turned him red beneath his helm. He dipped his lance to her and her lord husband. Ser Uthor did the same. Butterwell wished them both a good tilt. His wife stuck out her tongue.

It was time. Dunk trotted back to the south end of the lists. Eighty feet away, his opponent was taking up his position as well. His gray stallion was smaller than Thunder, but younger and more spirited. Ser Uthor wore green enamel plate and silvery chain mail. Streamers of green and gray silk flowed from his rounded bascinet, and his green shield bore a silver snail. *Good armor and a good horse means a good ransom, if I unseat him.*

A trumpet sounded.

Thunder started forward at a slow trot. Dunk swung his lance to the left and brought it down, so it angled across the horse's head and the wooden barrier between him and his foe. His shield protected the left side of his body. He crouched forward, legs tightening as Thunder drove down the lists. *We are one. Man, horse, lance, we are one beast of blood and wood and iron.*

Ser Uthor was charging hard, clouds of dust kicking up from the hooves of his gray. With forty yards between them, Dunk spurred Thunder to a gallop, and aimed the point of his lance squarely at the silver snail. The sullen sun, the dust, the heat, the castle, Lord Butterwell and his bride, the Fiddler and Ser Maynard, knights, squires, grooms, smallfolk, all vanished.

Only the foe remained. The spurs again. Thunder broke into a run. The snail was rushing toward them; growing with every stride of the gray's long legs . . . but ahead came Ser Uthor's lance with its iron fist. *My shield is strong, my shield will take the blow. Only the snail matters. Strike the snail and the tilt is mine.*

When ten yards remained between them, Ser Uthor shifted the point of his lance upwards.

A *crack* rang in Dunk's ears as his lance hit. He felt the impact in his arm and shoulder, but never saw the blow strike home. Uthor's iron fist took him square between his eyes, with all the force of man and horse behind it.

Dunk woke upon his back, staring up at the arches of a barrel-vaulted ceiling. For a moment he did not know where he was, or how he had arrived there. Voices echoed in his head, and faces drifted past him; old Ser Arlan, Tanselle Too-Tall, Dennis of the Brown Shield, the Red Widow, Baelor Breakspear, Aerion the Bright Prince, mad sad Lady Vaith. Then all at once the joust came back to him: the heat, the snail, the iron fist coming at his face. He groaned, and rolled onto one elbow. The movement set his skull to pounding like some monstrous war drum.

Both of his eyes seemed to be working, at least. Nor could he feel a hole in his head, which was all to the good. He was in some cellar, he saw, with casks of wine and ale on every side. *At least it is cool here*, he thought, *and drink is close at hand.* The taste of blood was in his mouth. Dunk felt a stab of fear. If he had bitten off his tongue, he would be dumb as well as thick. "Good morrow," he croaked, just to hear his voice. The words echoed off the ceiling. Dunk tried to push himself onto his feet, but the effort set the cellar spinning.

"Slowly, slowly," said a quavery voice, close at hand. A stooped old man appeared beside the bed, clad in robes as gray as his long hair. About his neck was a maester's chain of many metals. His face was aged and lined, with deep creases on either side of a great beak of a nose. "Be still, and let me see your eyes." He peered in Dunk's left eye, and then the right, holding them open between his thumb and forefinger.

"My head hurts."

The maester snorted. "Be grateful it still rests upon your shoulders, ser. Here, this may help somewhat. Drink."

Dunk made himself swallow it every drop of the foul potion, and managed not to spit it out. "The tourney," he said, wiping his mouth with the back of his hand. "Tell me. What's happened?"

"The same foolishness that always happens in these affrays. Men have been knocking each other off horses with sticks. Lord Smallwood's nephew broke his wrist and Ser Eden Risley's leg was crushed beneath his horse, but no one has been killed thus far. Though I had my fears for you, ser."

"Was I unhorsed?" His head still felt as though it was stuffed full of wool, else he would never have asked such a stupid question. Dunk regretted it the instant the words were out.

"With a crash that shook the highest ramparts. Those who had wagered good coin on you were most distraught, and your squire was beside himself. He would be sitting with you still if I had not chased him off. I need no children underfoot. I reminded him of his duty."

Dunk found that he needed reminding himself. "What duty?"

"Your mount, ser. Your arms and armor."

"Yes," Dunk said, remembering. The boy was a good squire; he knew what was required of him. *I have lost the old man's sword and the armor that Steely Pate forged for me.*

"Your fiddling friend was also asking after you. He told me you were to have the best of care. I threw him out as well."

"How long have you been tending me?" Dunk flexed the fingers of his sword hand. All of them still seemed to work. *Only my head's hurt, and Ser Arlan used to say I never used that anyway.*

"Four hours, by the sundial."

Four hours was not so bad. He had once heard tell of a knight struck so hard that he slept for forty years, and woke to find himself old and withered. "Do you know if Ser Uthor won his second tilt?" Maybe the Snail would win the tourney. It would take some sting from the defeat if Dunk could tell himself that he had lost to the best knight in the field.

"That one? Indeed he did. Against Ser Addam Frey, a cousin to the bride, and a promising young lance. Her ladyship fainted when Ser Addam fell. She had to be helped back to her chambers."

Dunk forced himself' to his feet, reeling as he rose, but the maester helped to steady him. "Where are my clothes? I must go. I have to . . . I must . . . "

"If you cannot recall, it cannot be so very urgent." The maester made an irritated motion. "I would suggest that you avoid rich foods, strong drink, and further blows between your eyes . . . but I learned long ago that knights are deaf to sense. Go, go. I have other fools to tend."

Outside, Dunk glimpsed a hawk soaring in wide circles through the bright blue sky. He envied him. A few clouds were gathering to the east, dark as Dunk's mood. As he found his way back to the tilting ground, the sun beat down on his head like a hammer on an anvil. The earth seemed to move beneath his feet . . . or it might just be that he was swaying. He had almost fallen twice climbing the cellar steps. *I should have heeded Egg.*

He made his slow way across the outer ward, around the fringes of the crowd. Out on the field, plump Lord Alyn Cockshaw was limping off between two squires, the latest conquest of young Glendon Ball. A third squire held his helm, its three proud feathers broken. "*Ser John the Fiddler*," the herald cried. "*Ser Franklyn of House Frey, a knight of the Twins, sworn to the Lord of the Crossing. Come forth and prove your valor.*"

Dunk could only stand and watch as the Fiddler's big black trotted onto the field in a swirl of blue silk and golden swords and fiddles. His breastplate was enameled blue as well, as were his poleyns, couter, greaves, and gorget. The ringmail underneath was gilded. Ser Franklyn rode a dapple gray with a flowing silver mane, to match the gray of his silks and the silver of his armor. On shield and surcoat and horse trappings he bore the twin towers of Frey. They charged and charged again. Dunk stood watching, but saw none of it. *Dunk the lunk, thick as a castle wall*, he chided himself. *He had a snail upon his shield. How could you lose to a man with a snail upon his shield?*

There was cheering all around him. When Dunk looked up, he saw that Franklyn Frey was down. The Fiddler had dismounted, to help his fallen foe back to his feet. *He is one step closer to his dragon's egg*, Dunk thought, *and where am I?*

As he approached the postern gate, Dunk came upon the company of dwarfs from last night's feast preparing to take their leave. They were hitching ponies to their wheeled wooden pig, and a second wayn of more conventional design. There were six of them, he saw, each smaller and more malformed than the last. A few might have been children, but they were all so short that it was hard to tell. In daylight, dressed in horsehide breeches and roughspun hooded cloaks, they seemed less jolly than they had in motley. "Good morrow to you," Dunk said, to be courteous. "Are you for the road? There's clouds to the east, could mean rain."

The only answer that he got was a glare from the ugliest dwarf. *Was he the one I pulled off Lady Butterwell last night?* Up close, the little man smelled like a privy. One whiff was enough to make Dunk hasten his steps.

The walk across the Milkhouse seemed to take Dunk as long as it had once taken he and Egg to cross the sands of Dorne. He kept a wall beside him, and from time to time he leaned on it. Every time he turned his head the world would swim. *A drink*, he thought. I *need a drink of water, or else I'm like to fall.*

A passing groom told him where to find the nearest well. It was there that he discovered Kyle the Cat, talking quietly with Maynard Plumm. Ser Kyle's shoulders were slumped in dejection, but he looked up at Dunk's approach.

"Ser Duncan? We had heard that you were dead, or dying."

Dunk rubbed his temples. "I only wish I were."

"I know that feeling well." Ser Kyle sighed. "Lord Caswell did not know me. When I told him how I carved his first sword, he stared at me as if I'd lost my wits. He said there was no place at Bitterbridge for knights as feeble as I had shown myself to be." The Cat gave a bitter laugh. "He took my arms and armor, though. My mount as well. What will I do?"

Dunk had no answer for him. Even a freerider required a horse to ride; sellswords must have swords to sell. "You will find another horse," Dunk said, as he drew the bucket up. "The Seven Kingdoms are full of horses. You will find some other lord to arm you." He cupped his hands, filled them with water, drank.

"Some other lord. Aye. Do you know of one? I am not so young and strong as you. Nor as big, Big men are always in demand. Lord Butterwell likes his knights large, for one. Look at that Tom Heddle. Have you seen him joust? He has overthrown every man he's faced. Fireball'slad has done the same, though. The Fiddler as well. Would that he had been the one to unhorse me. He refuses to take ransoms. He wants no more than the dragon's egg, he says . . . that, and the friendship of his fallen foes. The flower of chivalry, that one."

Maynard Plumm gave a laugh. "The fiddle of chivalry, you mean. That boy is fiddling up a storm, and all of us would do well to be gone from here before it breaks."

"He takes no ransoms?" said Dunk. "A gallant gesture."

"Gallant gestures come easy when your purse is fat with gold," said Ser Maynard. "There is a lesson here, if you have the sense to take it, Ser Duncan. It is not to late for you to go."

"Go? Go where?"

Ser Maynard shrugged. "Anywhere. Winterfell, Summerhall, Asshai by the Shadow. It makes no matter, so long as it's not here. Take your horse and armor and slip out the postern gate. You won't be missed. The Snail's got his next tilt to think about, and the rest have eyes only for the jousting."

For half a heartbeat, Dunk was tempted. So long as he was armed and horsed, he would remain a knight of sorts. Without them he was no more than a beggar. *A big beggar, but a beggar all the same.* But his arms and armor belonged to Ser Uthor now. So did Thunder. *Better a beggar than a thief.* He had been both in Flea Bottom, when he ran with Ferret, Rafe, and Pudding, but the old man had saved him from that life. He knew what Ser Arlan of Pennytree would have said to Plumm's suggestions. Ser Arlan beind dead, Dunk said it for him. "Even a hedge knight has his honor."

"Would you rather die with honor intact, or live with it besmirched? No, spare me, I know what you will say. Take your boy and flee, gallows knight. Before your arms become your destiny."

Dunk bristled. "How would you know my destiny? Did you have a dream, like John the Fiddler? What do you know of Egg?"

"I know that eggs do well to stay out of frying pans," said Plumm. "Whitewalls is not a healthy place for the boy."

"How did you fare in your own tilt, ser?" Dunk asked him.

"Oh, I did not chance the lists. The omens had gone sour. Who do you imagine is going to claim the dragon's egg, pray?"

Not me, Dunk thought. "The Seven know. I don't."

"Venture a guess, ser. You have two eyes."

He thought a moment. "The Fiddler?"

"Very good. Would you care to explain your reasoning?"

"I just . . . I have a feeling."

"So do I," said Maynard Plumm. "A bad feeling, for any man or boy unwise enough to stand in our Fiddler's way."

Egg was brushing Thunder's coat outside their tent, but his eyes were far away. *The boy has taken my fall hard.* "Enough," Dunk called. "Any more and Thunder will be as bald as you."

"Ser?" Egg dropped the brush. "I *knew* no stupid snail could kill you, ser." He threw his arms around him.

Dunk swiped the boy's floppy straw hat and put it on his own head. "The maester said you made off with my armor."

Egg snatched back his hat indignantly. "I've scoured your mail and polished your greaves, gorget, and breastplate, ser, but your helm is cracked and dinted where Ser Uthor's coronal struck. You'll need to have it hammered out by an armorer."

"Let Ser Uthor have it hammered out. It's his now." *No horse, no sword, no armor. Perhaps those dwarfs would let me join their troupe. That would be a funny sight, six dwarfs pummeling a giant with pig bladders.* "Thunder is his too. Come. We'll take them to him and wish him well in the rest of his tilts."

"Now, ser? Aren't you going to ransom Thunder?"

"With what, lad? Pebbles and sheep pellets?"

"I thought about that, ser. If you could borrow—"

"Dunk cut him off. "No one will lend me that much coin, Egg. Why should they? What am I, but some great oaf who called himself a knight until some snail with a stick near stove his head in?"

"Well," said Egg, "you could have Rain, ser. I'll go back to riding Maester. We'll go to Summerhall. You can take service in my father's household. His stables are full of horses. You could have a destrier and a palfrey too."

Egg meant well, but Dunk could not go to cringing back to Summerhall. Not that way, penniless and beaten, seeking service without so much as a sword to offer. "Lad," he said, "that's good of you, but I want no crumbs from your lord father's table, or from his stables neither. Might be it's time we parted ways." Dunk could always slink off to join the City Watch in Lannisport or Oldtown, they liked big men for that. *I've bumped my bean on every beam in every inn from Lannisport to King's Landing, might be it's time my size earned me a bit of coin instead of just a lumpy head.* But watchmen did not have squires. "I've taught you what I could, and that was little enough. You'll do better with a proper master-at-arms to see to your training, some fierce old knight who knows which end of the lance to hold."

"I don't want a proper master-at-arms," Egg said. "I want you. What if I used my—"

"No. None of that, I will not hear it. Go gather up my arms. We will present them to Ser Uthor with my compliments. Hard things only grow harder if you put them off."

Egg kicked the ground, his face as droopy as his big straw hat. "Aye, ser. As you say."

From the outside Ser Uthor's tent was very plain; a large square box of dun-colored sailcloth staked to the ground with hempen ropes. A silver snail adorned the center pole above a long gray pennon, but that was the only decoration.

"Wait here," Dunk told Egg. The boy had hold of Thunder's lead. The big brown destrier was laden with Dunk's arms and armor, even to his new old shield. *The Gallows Knight. What a dismal mystery knight I proved to be.* "I won't be long." He ducked his head and stooped to shoulder through the flap.

The tent's exterior left him ill prepared for the comforts he found within. The ground beneath his feet was carpeted in woven Myrish rugs, rich with color. An ornate trestle table stood surrounded by camp chairs. The featherbed was covered with soft cushions, and an iron brazier burned perfumed incense.

Ser Uthor sat at the table, a pile of gold and silver before him and a flagon of wine at his elbow, counting coins with his squire, a gawky fellow close in age to Dunk. From time to time the Snail would bite a coin, or set one aside. "I see I still have much to teach you, Will," Dunk heard him say. "This coin has been clipped, t'other shaved. And this one?" A gold piece danced across his fingers. "*Look* at the coins before taking them. Here, tell me what you see." The dragon spun through the air. Will tried to catch it, but it bounced off his fingers and fell to the ground. He had to get down on his knees to find it. When he did, he turned it over twice before saying, "This one's good, m'lord. There's a dragon on the one side and a king on t'other . . . "

Underleaf glanced toward Dunk. "The Hanged Man. It is good to see you moving about, ser. I feared I'd killed you. Will you do me a kindness and instruct my squire as to the nature of dragons? Will, give Ser Duncan the coin."

Dunk had no choice but to take it. *He unhorsed me, must he make me caper for him too?* Frowning, he hefted the coin in his palm, examined both sides, tasted it. "Gold, not shaved nor clipped. The weight feels right. I'd have taken it too, m'lord.What's wrong with it?"

"The king."

Dunk took a closer look. The face on the coin was young, clean-shaved, handsome. King Aerys was bearded on his coins, the same as old King Aegon. King Daeron, who'd come between them, had been clean-shaved, but this wasn't him. The coin did not appear worn enough to be from before Aegon the Unworthy. Dunk scowled at the word beneath the head. *Six letters.* They looked the same as he had seen on other dragons. *Daeron*, the letters read, but Dunk knew the face of Daeron the Good, and this wasn't him. When he looked again, he saw that something odd about the shape of the fourth letter, it wasn't . . . "*Daemon*," he blurted out. "It says *Daemon.* There never was any King Daemon, though, only—"

"—the Pretender. Daemon Blackfyre struck his own coinage during his rebellion."

"It's gold, though," Will argued. "If it's gold, it should be just as good as them other dragons, m'lord."

The Snail clouted him along the side of the head. "Cretin. Aye, it's gold. Rebel's gold. Traitor's gold. It's treasonous to own such a coin, and twice as treasonous to pass it. I'll need to have this melted down." He hit the man again. "Get out of my sight. This good knight and I have matters to discuss."

Will wasted no time in scrambling from the tent. "Have a seat," Ser Uthor said politely. "Will you take wine?" Here in his own tent, Underleaf seemed a different man than at the feast.

A snail hides in his shell, Dunk remembered. "Thank you, no." He flicked the gold coin back to Ser Uthor. *Traitor's gold. Blackfyre gold. Egg said this was a traitor's tourney, but I would not listen.* He owed the boy an apology.

"Half a cup," Underleaf insisted. "You sound in need of it." He filled two cups with wine, and handed one to Dunk. Out of his armor, he looked more a merchant than a knight. "You've come about the forfeit, I assume."

"Aye." Dunk took the wine. Maybe it would help to stop his head from pounding. "I brought my horse, and my arms and armor. Take them, with my compliments."

Ser Uthor smiled. "And this is where I tell you that you rode a gallant course."

Dunk wondered if *gallant* was a chivalrous way of saying *clumsy*. "That is good of you to say, but—"

"I think you misheard me, ser. Would it be too bold of me to ask how you came to knighthood, ser?"

"Ser Arlan of Pennytree found me in Flea Bottom, chasing pigs. His old squire had been slain on the Redgrass Field, so he needed someone to tend his mount and clean his mail. He promised he would teach me sword and lance and how to ride a horse if I would come and serve him, so I did."

"A charming tale . . . though if I were you I would leave out the part about the pigs. Pray, where is your Ser Arlan now?"

"He died. I buried him."

"I see. Did you take him home to Pennytree?"

"I didn't know where it was." Dunk had never seen the old man's Pennytree. Ser Arlan seldom spoke of it, no more than Dunk was wont to speak of Flea Bottom. "I buried him on a hillside facing west, so he could see the sun go down." The camp chair creaked alarmingly beneath his weight.

Ser Uthor resumed his seat. "I have my own armor, and a better horse than yours. What do I want with some old done nag and a sack of dinted plate and rusty mail?"

"Steely Pate made that armor," Dunk said, with a touch of anger. "Egg has taken good care of it. There's not a spot of rust on my mail, and the steel is good and strong."

"Strong and heavy," Ser Uthor complained, "and too big for any man of normal size. You are uncommon large, Duncan the Tall. As for your horse, he is too old to ride and too stringy to eat."

"Thunder is not as young as he used to be," Dunk admitted, "and my armor is large, as you say. You could sell it, though. In Lannisport and King's Landing there are plenty of smiths who will take it off your hands."

"For a tenth of what it's worth, perhaps," said Ser Uthor, "and only to melt down for the metal. No. It's sweet silver I require, not old iron. The coin of the realm. Now, do you wish to ransom back your arms, or no?"

Dunk turned the wine cup in his hands, frowning. It was solid silver, with a line of golden snails inlaid around the lip. The wine was gold as well, and heady on the tongue. "If wishes were fishes, aye, I'd pay. Gladly. Only—"

"—you don't have two stags to lock horns."

"If you would . . . would lend my horse and armor back to me, I could pay the ransom later. Once I found the coin."

The Snail looked amused. "Where would you find it, pray?"

"I could take service with some lord, or . . . " It was hard to get the words out. They made him feel a beggar. "It might take a few years, but I would pay you. I swear it."

"On your honor at a knight?"

Dunk flushed. "I could make my mark upon a parchment."

"A hedge knight's scratch upon a scrap of paper?" Ser Uthor rolled his eyes. "Good to wipe my arse. No more."

"You are a hedge knight too."

"Now you insult me. I ride where I will and serve no man but myself, true . . . but it has been many a year since I last slept beneath a hedge. I find that inns are far more comfortable. I am a *tourney* knight, the best that you are ever like to meet."

"The best?" His arrogance made Dunk angry. "The Laughing Storm might not agree, ser. Nor Leo Longthorn, nor the Brute of Bracken. At Ashford Meadow no one spoke of snails. Why is that, if you're such a famous tourney champion?"

"Have you heard me name myself a champion? That way lies renown. I would sooner have the pox. Thank you, but no. I shall win my next joust, aye, but in the final I shall fall. Butterwell has thirty dragons for the knight who comes second, that shall suffice for me . . . along with some goodly ransoms and the proceeds of my wagers." He gestured at the piles of silver stags and golden dragons on the table. "You seem a healthy fellow, and very large. Size will always impress the fools, though it means little and less in jousting. Will was able to get odds of three to one against me. Lord Shawney gave five to one, the fool." He picked up a silver stag and set it to spinning with a flick of his long fingers. "The Old Ox will be the next to tumble. Then the Knight of the Pussywillows, if he survives that long. Sentiment being what it is, I should get fine odds against them both. The commons love their village heroes."

"Ser Glendon has hero's blood," Dunk blurted out.

"Oh, I do hope so. Hero's blood should be good for two to one. Whore's blood draws poorer odds. Ser Glendon speaks about his purported sire at every opportunity, but have you noticed that he never makes mention of his mother? For good reason. He was born of a camp follower. Jenny, her name was. Penny Jenny, they called her, until the Redgrass Field. The night before the battle, she fucked so many men that thereafter she was known as Redgrass Jenny. Fireball had her, I don't doubt, but so did a hundred other men. Our friend Glendon presumes quite a lot, it seems to me. He does not even have red hair."

Hero's blood, thought Dunk. "He says he is a knight."

"Oh, that much is true. The boy and his sister grew up in a brothel, called the Pussywillows. After Penny Jenny died, the other whores took care of them and fed the lad the tale his mother had concocted, about him being Fireball's seed. An old squire who lived nearby gave the boy his training, such that it was, in trade for ale and cunt, but being but a squire he could not knight the little bastard. Half a year ago, however, a party of knights chanced upon the brothel and a certain Ser Morgan Dunstable took a drunken fancy to Ser Glendon's sister. As it happens, the sister was still virgin and Dunstable did not have the price of her maidenhead. So a bargain was struck. Ser Morgan dubbed her brother a knight, right there in the Pussywillows in front of twenty witnesses, and afterward little sister took him upstairs and let him pluck her flower. And there you are."

Any knight could make a knight. When he was squiring for Ser Arlan, Dunk had heard tales of other men who'd bought their knighthood with a kindness or a threat or a bag of silver coins, but never with a sister's maidenhead. "That's just a tale," he heard himself say. "That can't be true."

"I had it from Kirby Pimm, who claims that he was there, a witness to the knighting." Ser Uthor shrugged. "Hero's son, whore's son, or both, when he faces me the boy will fall."

"The lots may give you some other foe."

Ser Uthor arched an eyebrow. "Cosgrove is as fond of silver as the next man. I promise you, I shall draw the Old Ox next, then the boy. Would you care to wager on it?"

"I have nothing left to wager." Dunk did not know what distressed him more: learning that the Snail was bribing the master of the games to get the pairings he desired, or realizing the man had desired *him*. He stood. "I have said what I came to say. My horse and sword are yours, and all my armor."

The Snail steepled his fingers. "Perhaps there is another way. You are not entirely without your talents. You fall most splendidly." Ser Uthor's lips glistened when he smiled. "I will lend you back your steed and armor . . . if you enter my service."

"Service?" Dunk did not understand. "What sort of service? You have a squire. Do you need to garrison some castle?"

"I might, if I had a castle. If truth be told I prefer a good inn. Castles cost too much to maintain. No, the service I would require of you is that you face me in a few more tourneys. Twenty should suffice. You can do that, surely? You shall have a tenth part of my winnings, and in future I promise to strike that broad chest of yours and not your head."

"You'd have me travel about with you to be unhorsed?"

Ser Uthor chuckled pleasantly. "You are such a strapping specimen, no one will ever believe that some round-shouldered old man with a snail on his shield could put you down." He rubbed his chin. "You need a new device yourself, by the way. That hanged man is grim enough, I grant you, but . . . Well, he's *hanging,* isn't he? Dead and defeated. Something fiercer is required. A bear's head, mayhaps. A skull. Or three skulls, better still. A babe impaled upon a spear. And you should let your hair grow long and cultivate a beard, the wilder and more unkempt the better. There are more of these little tourneys than you know. With the odds I'd get we'd win enough to buy a dragon's egg before—"

"—it got about that I was hopeless? I lost my armor, not my honor. You'll have Thunder and my arms, no more."

"Pride ill becomes a beggar, ser. You could do much worse than ride with me. At the least I could teach you a thing or two of jousting, about which you are pig ignorant at present."

"You'd make a fool of me."

"I did that earlier. And even fools must eat."

Dunk wanted to smash that smile off his face. "I see why you have a snail on your shield. You are no true knight."

"Spoken like a true oaf. Are you so blind you cannot see your danger?" Ser Uthor put his cup aside. "Do you know why I struck you where I did, ser?" He got to his feet, and touched Dunk lightly in the center of his chest. "A coronal placed here would have put you on the ground just as quickly. The head is a smaller target, the blow is more difficult to land . . . though more likely to be mortal. I was paid to strike you there."

"Paid?" Dunk backed away from him. "What do you mean?"

"Six dragons tendered in advance, four more promised when you died. A paltry sum for a knight's life. Be thankful for that. Had more been offered, I might have put the point of my lance through your eye slit."

Dunk felt dizzy again. *Why would someone pay to have me killed? I've done no harm to any man at Whitewalls.* Surely no one hated him that much but Egg's brother Aerion, and the Bright Prince was in exile across the narrow sea. "Who paid you?"

"A serving man brought the gold at sunrise, not long after the master of the games nailed up the pairings. His face was hooded, and he did not speak his master's name."

"But why?" said Dunk.

"I did not ask." Ser Uthor filled his cup again. "I think you have more enemies than you know, Ser Duncan. How not? There are some who would say you were the cause of all our woes."

Dunk felt a cold hand on his heart. "Say what you mean."

The Snail shrugged. "I may not have been at Ashford Meadow, but jousting is my bread and salt. I follow tourneys from afar as faithfully as the maesters follow stars. I know how a certain hedge knight became the cause of a Trial of Seven at Ashford Meadow, resulting in the death of Baelor Breakspear at his brother Maekar's hand." Ser Uthor seated himself, and stretched his legs out. "Prince Baelor was well loved. The Bright Prince had friends as well, friends who will not have forgotten the cause of his exile. Think on my offer, ser. The snail may leave a trail of slime behind him, but a little slime will do a man no harm . . . but if you dance with dragons, you must expect to burn."

The day seemed darker when Dunk stepped from the Snail's tent. The clouds in the east had grown bigger and blacker, and the sun was sinking to the west, casting long shadows across the yard. Dunk found the squire Will inspecting Thunder's feet.

"Where's Egg?" he asked of him.

"The bald boy? How would I know? Run off somewhere."

He could not bear to say farewell to Thunder, Dunk decided. *He'll be back at the tent with his books.*

He wasn't, though. The books were there, bundled neatly in a stack beside Egg's bedroll, but of the boy there was no sign. Something was wrong here. Dunk could feel it. It was not like Egg to wander off without his leave.

A pair of grizzled men-at-arms were drinking barley beer outside a striped pavilion a few feet away. ". . . . well, bugger that, once was enough for me," one muttered. "The grass was green when the sun come up, aye . . . " He broke off when other man gave him a nudge, and only then took note of Dunk. "Ser?"

"Have you seen my squire? Egg, he's called."

The man scratched at the gray stubble underneath one ear. "I remember him. Less hair than me, and a mouth three times his size. Some o' the other lads shoved him about a bit, but that was last night. I've not seen him since, ser."

"Scared him off," said his companion.

Dunk gave that one a hard look. "If he comes back, tell him to wait for me here."

"Aye, ser. That we will.

Might be he just went to watch the jousts. Dunk headed back toward the tilting grounds. As he passed the stables he came on Ser Glendon Ball, brushing down a pretty sorrel charger. "Have you seen Egg?" he asked him.

"He ran past a few moments ago." Ser Glendon pulled a carrot from his pocket and fed it to the sorrel. "Do you like my new horse? Lord Costayne sent his squire to ransom her, but I told him to save his gold. I mean to keep her for my own."

"His lordship will not like that."

"His lordship said that I had no right to put a fireball upon my shield. He told me my device should be a clump of pussywillows. His lordship can go bugger himself."

Dunk could not help but smile. He had supped at that same table himself, choking down the same bitter dishes as served up by the likes of the Bright Prince and Ser Steffon Fossoway. He felt a certain kinship with the prickly young knight. *For all I know, my mother was a whore as well.* "How many horses have you won?"

Ser Glendon shrugged. "I lost count. Mortimer Boggs still owes me one. He said he'd rather eat his horse than have some whore's bastard riding her. And he took a hammer to his armor before sending it to me. It's full of holes. I suppose I can still get something for the metal." He sounded more sad than angry. "There was a stable by the . . . the inn where I was raised. I worked there when I was a boy, and when I could I'd sneak the horses off while their owners were busy. I was always good with horses. Stots, rounseys, palfreys, drays, plough horses, war horses, I rode them all. Even a Dornish sand steed. This old man I knew taught me how to make my own lances. I thought if I showed them all how good I was, they'd have no choice but to admit I was my father's son. But they won't. Even now. They just won't."

"Some never will," Dunk told him. "It doesn't matter what you do. Others, though . . . they're not all the same. I've met some good ones." He thought a moment. "When the tourney's done, Egg and I mean to go north. Take service at Winterfell, and fight for the Starks against the ironmen. You could come with us." The north was a world all its own, Ser Arlan always said. *No one up there was like to know the tale of Penny Jenny and the Knight of the Pussywillows. No one will laugh at you up there. They will know you only by your blade, and judge you by your worth.*

Ser Glendon gave him a suspicious look. "Why would I want to do that? Are you telling me I need to run away and hide?"

"No. I just thought . . . two swords instead of one. The roads are not as safe as they once were."

"That's true enough," the boy said grudgingly, "but my father was once promised a place amongst the Kingsguard. I mean to claim the white cloak that he never got to wear."

You have as much chance of wearing a white cloak as I do, Dunk almost said. *You were born of a camp follower, and I crawled out of the gutters of Flea Bottom. Kings do not heap honor on the likes of you and me.* The lad would not have taken kindly to that truth, however. Instead he said, "Strength to your arm, then."

He had not gone more than a few feet when Ser Glendon called after him. "Ser Duncan, wait. . . . . I should not have been so sharp. A knight must needs be courteous, my mother used to say." The boy seemed to be struggling for words. "Lord Peake came to see me, after my last joust. He offered me a place at Starpike. He said there was a storm coming the likes of which Westeros had not seen for a generation, that he would need swords and men to wield them. Loyal men, who knew how to obey."

Dunk could hardly believe it. Gormon Peake had made his scorn for hedge knights plain, both on the road and on the roof, but the offer was a generous one. "Peake is a great lord," he said, wary, "but . . . but not a man that I would trust, I think."

"No." The boy flushed. "There was a price. He'd take me into his service, he said . . . but first I would have to prove my loyalty. He would see that I was paired against his friend the Fiddler next, and he wanted me to swear that I would lose."

Dunk believed him. He should have been shocked, he knew, and yet somehow he wasn't. "What did you say?"

"I said I might not be able to lose to the Fiddler even if I were trying, that I had already unhorsed much better men than him, that the dragon's egg would be mine before the day was done." Ball smiled feebly. "It was not the answer that he wanted. He called me a fool, then, and told me that I had best watch my back. The Fiddler had many friends, he said, and I had none."

Dunk put a hand upon his shoulder, and squeezed. "You have one, ser. Two, once I find Egg."

The boy looked him in the eye, and nodded. "It is good to know there are some true knights still."

Dunk got his first good look at Ser Tommard Heddle whilst searching for Egg amongst the crowds about the lists. Heavy-set and broad, with a chest like a barrel, Lord Butterwell's good-son wore black plate over boiled leather, and an ornate helm fashioned in the likeness of some demon, scaled and slavering. His horse was three hands taller than Thunder and two stone heavier, a monster of a beast armored in a coat of ringmail. The weight of all that iron made him slow, so Heddle never got up past a canter when the course was run; but that did not prevent him making short work of Ser Clarence Charlton. As Charlton was borne from the field upon a litter, Heddle removed his demonic helm. His head was broad and bald, his beard black and square. Angry red boils festered on his cheek and neck.

Dunk knew that face. Heddle was the knight who'd growled at him in the bedchamber when he touched the dragon's egg, the man with the deep voice that he'd heard talking with Lord Peake.

A jumble of words came rushing back to him . . . *beggar's feast you've laid before us . . . is the boy his father's son . . . Bittersteel . . . need the sword . . . Old Milkblood expects . . . is the boy his father's son . . . I promise you, Bloodraven is not off dreaming . . . is the boy his father's son?*

He stared at the viewing stand, wondering if somehow Egg had contrived to take his rightful place amongst the notables. There was no sign of the boy, however. Butterwell and Frey were missing too, though Butterwell's wife was still in her seat, looking bored and restive. That's queer, Dunk reflected. This was Butterwell's castle, his wedding, and Frey was father to his bride. These jousts were in their honor. Where would they have gone?

"*Ser Uthor Underleaf,*" the herald boomed. A shadow crept across Dunk's face as the sun was swallowed by a cloud. "*Ser Theomore of House Bulwer, the Old Ox, a knight of Blackcrown. Come forth and prove your valor.*"

The Old Ox made a fearsome sight in his blood red armor, with black bull's horns rising from his helm. He needed the help of a brawny squire to get onto his horse, though, and the way his head was always turning as he rode suggested that Ser Maynard had been right about his eye. Still, the man received a lusty cheer as he took the field.

Not so the Snail, no doubt just as he preferred. On the first pass, both knights struck glancing blows. On the second, the Old Ox snapped his lance on the Ser Uthor's shield, while the Snail's blow missed entirely. The same thing happened on the third pass, and this time Ser Uthor swayed as if about to fall. *He is feigning,* Dunk realized. *He is drawing the contest out to fatten the odds for next time. He had only to glance around to see Will at work, making wagers for his master. Only then did it occur to him that he might have fattened his own purse with a coin or two upon the Snail. Dunk the lunk, thick as a castle wall.*

The Old Ox fell on fifth pass, knocked sideways by a coronal that slipped deftly off his shield to take him in the chest. His foot tangled in his stirrup as he fell, and he was dragged forty yards across the field before his men could get his horse under control. Again the litter came out, to bear him to the maester. A few drops of rain began to fall as Bulwer was carried away, darkened his surcoat where they fell. Dunk watched without expression. He was thinking about Egg. *What if this secret enemy of mine has got his hands on him?* It made as much sense as anything else. *The boy is blameless. If someone has a quarrel with me, it should not be him who answers for it.*

Ser John the Fiddler was being armed for his next tilt when Dunk found him. No fewer than three squires were attending him, buckling on his armor and seeing to the trappings of his horse, whilst Lord Alyn Cockshaw sat nearby drinking watered wine and looking bruised and peevish. When he caught sight of Dunk, Lord Alyn sputtered, dribbling. wine upon on his chest. "How is it that you're still walking about? The Snail stove your face in."

"Steely Pate made me a good strong helm, m'lord. And my head is hard as stone, Ser Arlan used to say."

The Fiddler laughed. "Pay no mind to Alyn. Fireball's bastard knocked him off his horse onto that plump little rump of his, so now he has decided that he hates all hedge knights."

"That wretched pimpled creature is no son of Quentyn Ball," insisted Alyn Cockshaw. "He should never have been allowed to compete. If this were my wedding, I should have had him whipped for his presumption."

"What maid would marry you?" Ser John said. "And Ball's presumption is a deal less grating than your pouting. Ser Duncan, are you perchance a friend of Galtry the Green? I must shortly part him from his horse."

Dunk did not doubt it. "I do not know the man, m'lord."

"Will you take a cup of wine? Some bread and olives?"

"Only a word, m'lord."

"You may have all the words you wish. Let us adjourn to my pavilion." The Fiddler held the flap for him. "Not you, Alyn. You could do with a few less olives, if truth be told."

Inside, the Fiddler turned back to Dunk. "I knew Ser Uthor had not killed you. My dreams are never wrong. And the Snail must face me soon enough. Once I've unhorsed him, I shall demand your arms and armor back. Your destrier as well, though you deserve a better mount. Will you take one as my gift?"

"I . . . no . . . I couldn't do that." The thought made Dunk uncomfortable. "I do not mean to be ungrateful, but . . . "

"If it is the debt that troubles you, put the thought from your mind. I do not need your silver, ser. Only your friendship. How can you be one of my knights without a horse?" Ser John drew on his gauntlets of lobstered steel and flexed his fingers.

"My squire is missing."

"Ran off with a girl, perhaps?"

"Egg's too young for girls, m'lord. He would never leave me of his own will. Even if I were dying, he would stay until my corpse was cold. His horse is still here. So is our mule."

"If you like, I could ask my men to look for him."

My men. Dunk did not like the sound of that. A tourney for traitors, he thought. "You are no hedge knight."

"No." The Fiddler's smile was full of boyish charm. "But you knew that from the start. You have been calling me m'lord since we met upon the road, why is that?"

"The way you talk. The way you look. The way you act." *Dunk the lunk, thick as a castle wall.* "Up on the roof last night, you said some things . . . "

"Wine makes me talk too much, but I meant every word. We belong together, you and I. My dreams do not lie."

"Your dreams don't lie," said Dunk, "but you do. John is not your true name, is it?"

"No." The Fiddler's eyes sparkled with mischief.

He has Egg's eyes.

"His true name will be revealed soon enough, to those who need to know." Lord Gormon Peake had slipped into the pavilion, scowling. "Hedge knight, I warn you—"

"Oh, stop it, Gormy," said the Fiddler "Ser Duncan is with us, or will be soon. I told you, I dreamed of him." Outside, a herald's trumpet blew. The Fiddler turned his head. "They are calling me to the lists. Pray excuse me, Ser Duncan. We can resume our talk after I dispose of Ser Galtry the Green."

"Strength to your arm," Dunk said. It was only courteous.

Lord Gormon remained after Ser John had gone. "His dreams will be the death of all of us."

"What did it take to buy Ser Galtry?" Dunk heard himself say. "Was silver sufficient, or does he require gold?"

"Someone has been talking, I see." Peake seated himself in a camp chair. "I have a dozen men outside. I ought to call them in and have them slit your throat, ser."

"Why don't you?"

"His Grace would take it ill."

His Grace. Dunk felt as though someone had punched him in the belly. *Another black dragon*, he thought. *Another Blackfyre Rebellion. And soon another Redgrass Field. The grass was not red when the sun came up.* "Why this wedding?"

"Lord Butterwell wanted a new young wife to warm his bed, and Lord Frey had a somewhat soiled daughter. Their nuptials provided a plausible pretext for some like-minded lords to gather. Most of those invited here fought for the black dragon once. The rest have reason to resent Bloodraven's rule, or nurse grievances and ambitions of their own. Many of us had sons and daughters taken to King's Landing to vouchsafe our future loyalty, but most of the hostages perished in the Great Spring Sickness. Our hands are no longer tied. Our time is come. Aerys is weak. A bookish man, and no warrior. The commons hardly know him, and what they know they do not like. His lords love him even less. His father was weak as well, that is true, but when his throne was threatened he had sons to take the field for him. Baelor and Maekar, the hammer and the anvil . . . but Baelor Breakspear is no more, and Prince Maekar sulks at Summerhall, at odds with king and Hand."

Aye, thought Dunk, *and now some fool hedge knight has delivered his favorite son into the hands of his enemies. How better to ensure that the prince never stirs from Summerhall?* "There is Bloodraven," he said. "He is not weak."

"No," Lord Peake allowed, "but no man loves a sorcerer, and kinslayers are accursed in the sight of gods and men. At the first sign of weakness or defeat, Bloodraven's men will melt away like summer snows. And if the dream the prince has dreamed comes true, and a living dragon comes forth here at Whitewalls . . . "

Dunk finished for him. " . . . . the throne is yours."

"His," said Lord Gormon Peake. "I am but a humble servant." He rose. "Do not attempt to leave the castle, ser. If you do, I will take it as a proof of treachery, and you will answer with your life. We have gone too far to turn back now."

The leaden sky was spitting down rain in earnest as John the Fiddler and Ser Galtry the Green took up fresh lances at opposite ends of the lists. Some of the wedding guests were streaming off toward the great hall, huddled under cloaks.

Ser Galtry rode a white stallion. A drooping green plume adorned his helm, a matching plume his horse's crinet. His cloak was a patchwork of many squares of fabric, each a different shade of green. Gold inlay made his greaves and gauntlet glitter, and his shield showed nine jade mullets upon a leek green field. Even his beard was dyed green, in the fashion of the men of Tyrosh across the narrow sea.

Nine times he and the Fiddler charged with levelled lances, the green patchwork knight and the young lordling of the golden swords and fiddles, and nine times their lances shattered. By the eighth run, the ground had begun to soften, and big destriers splashed through pools of rainwater. On the ninth, the Fiddler almost lost his seat, but recovered before he fell. "Well struck," he called out, laughing. "You almost had me down, ser."

"Soon enough," the green knight shouted through the rain.

"No, I think not." The Fiddler tossed his splintered lance away, and a squire handed him a fresh one.

The next run was their last. Ser Galtry's lance scraped ineffectually off the Fiddler's shield, whilst Ser John's took the green knight squarely in the center of his chest and knocked him from his saddle, to land with a great brown splash. In the east Dunk saw the flash of distant lightning.

The viewing stands were emptying out quickly, as smallfolk and lordlings alike scrambled to get out of the wet. "See how they run," murmurred Alyn Cockshaw, as he slid up beside Dunk. "A few drops of rain and all the bold lords go squealing for shelter. What will they do when the real storm breaks, I wonder?"

The real storm. Dunk knew Lord Alyn was not talking about the weather. *What does this one want? Has he suddenly decided to befriend me?*

The herald mounted his platform once again. "*Ser Tommard Heddle, a knight of Whitewalls, in service to Lord Butterwell,*" he shouted, as thunder rumbled in the distance. "*Ser Uthor Underleaf. Come forth and prove your valor.*"

Dunk glanced over at Ser Uthor in time to see the Snail's smile go sour. *This is not the match he paid for.* The master of the games had crossed him up, but why? *Someone else has taken a hand, someone Cosgrove esteems more than Uthor Underleaf.* Dunk chewed on that for a moment. *They do not know that Uthor does not mean to win*, he realized all at once. *They see him as a threat, so they mean for Black Tom to remove him from the Fiddler's path.* Heddle himself was part of Peake's conspiracy, he could be relied on to lose when the need arose. Which left no one but . . .

And suddenly Lord Peake himself was storming across the muddy field to climb the steps to the herald's platform, his cloak flapping behind him. "*We are betrayed,*" he cried. "Bloodraven has a spy amongst us. The dragon's egg is stolen!"

Ser John the Fiddler wheeled his mount around. "My egg? How is that possible? Lord Butterwell keeps guards outside his bedchamber night and day."

"Slain," Lord Peake declared, "but one man named his killer before he died."

Does he mean to accuse me? Dunk wondered. A dozen men had seem him touch the dragon's egg last night, when he'd carried Lady Butterwell to her lord husband's bed.

Lord Gormon's finger stabbed down in accusation. "There he stands. The whore's son. Seize him."

At the far end of the lists, Ser Glendon Ball looked up in confusion. For a moment he did not appear to comprehend what was happening, until he saw men rushing at him from all directions. Then the boy moved more quickly than Dunk could have believed. He had his sword half out of its sheath when the first man threw an arm around his throat. Ball wrenched free of his grip, but by then two more of them were on him. They slammed into him and dragged him down into the mud. Other men swarmed over them, shouting and kicking. *That could be been me*, Dunk realized. He felt as helpless as he had at Ashford, the day they'd told him he must lose a hand and a foot.

Alyn Cockshaw pulled him back. "Stay out of this, you want to find that squire of yours."

Dunk turned on him. "What do you mean?"

"I may know where to find the boy."

"Where?" Dunk was in no mood for games.

At the far end of the field, Ser Glendon was yanked roughly back onto his feet, pinioned between two men-at-arms in mail and halfhelms. He was brown with mud from waist to ankle, and blood and rain washed down his cheeks. *Hero's blood*, thought Dunk, as Black Tom dismounted before the captive. "Where is the egg?"

Blood dribbled from Ball's mouth. "Why would I steal the egg? I was about to win it."

Aye, thought Dunk, *and that they could not allow.*

Black Tom slashed Ball across the face with a mailed fist. "Search his saddlebags," Lord Peake commanded. "We'll find the dragon's egg wrapped up and hidden, I'll wager."

Lord Alyn lowered his voice, "And so they will. Come with me if you want to find your squire. There's no better time than now, whilst they're all occupied." He did not wait for a reply.

Dunk had to follow. Three long strides brought him abreast of the lordling. "If you have done Egg any harm—"

"Boys are not to my taste. This way. Step lively now."

Through an archway, down a set of muddy steps, around a corner, Dunk stalked after him, splashing through puddles as the rain fell around them. They stayed close to the walls, cloaked in shadows, finally stopping in a closed courtyard where the paving stones were smooth and slick. Buildings pressed close on every side. Above were windows, closed and shuttered. In the center of the courtyard was a well, ringed with a low stone wall.

A lonely place, Dunk thought. He did not like the feel of it. Old instinct made him reach for his sword hilt, before he remembered that the Snail had won his sword. As he fumbled at his hip where his scabbard should have hung, he felt the point of a knife poke his lower back. "Turn on me, and I'll cut your kidney out and give it to Butterwell's cooks to fry up for the feast." The knife pushed in through the back of Dunk's jerkin, insistent. "Over to the well. No sudden moves, ser."

If he has thrown Egg down that well, he will need more than some little toy knife to save him. Dunk walked forward slowly. He could feel the anger growing in his belly.

The blade at his back vanished. "You may turn and face me now, hedge knight."

Dunk turned. "M'lord. Is this about the dragon's egg?"

"No. This is about the dragon. Did you think I would stand by and let you steal him?" Ser Alyn grimaced. "I should have known better than to trust that wretched Snail to kill you. I'll have my gold back, every coin."

Him? Dunk thought. *This plump, pasty-faced, perfumed lordling is my secret enemy?* He did not know whether to laugh or weep. "Ser Uthor earned his gold. I have a hard head, is all."

"So it seems. Back away."

Dunk took a step backwards.

"Again. Again. Once more."

Another step, and he was flush against the well. Its stones pressed against his lower back.

"Sit down on the rim. Not afraid of a little bath, are you? You cannot get much wetter than you are right now."

"I cannot swim." Dunk rested a hand on the well. The stones were wet. One moved beneath the pressure of his palm.

"What a shame. Will you jump, or must I prick you?"

Dunk glanced down. He could see the raindrops dimpling the water, a good twenty feet below. The walls were covered with a slime of algae. "I never did you any harm."

"And never will. Daemon's mine. I will command his Kingsguard. You are not worthy of a white cloak."

"I never claimed I was." *Daemon.* The name rang in Dunk's head. *Not John. Daemon, after his father. Dunk the lunk, thick as a castle wall.* "Daemon Blackfyre sired seven sons. Two died upon the Redgrass Field, twins . . . "

"Aegon and Aemon. Wretched witless bullies, just like you. When we were little, they took pleasure in tormenting me and Daemon both. I wept when Bittersteel carried him off to exile, and again when Lord Peake told me was coming home. But then he saw you upon the road, and forgot that I existed." Cockshaw waved his dagger threateningly. "You can go into the water as you are, or you can go in bleeding. Which will it be?"

Dunk closed his hand around the loose stone. It proved to be less loose than he had hoped. Before he could wrench it free, Ser Alyn lunged. Dunk twisted sideways, so the point of the blade sliced through the meat of his shield arm. And then the stone popped free. Dunk fed it to his lordship, and felt his teeth crack beneath the blow.

"The well, is it?" He hit the lordling in the mouth again, then dropped the stone, seized Cockshaw by the wrist, and twisted until a bone snapped and the dagger clattered to the stones. "After you, m'lord." Sidestepping, Dunk yanked at the lordling's arm and planted a kick in the small of his back. Lord Alyn toppled headlong into the well. There was a splash.

"Well done, ser,"

Dunk whirled. Through the rain, all he could make out was a hooded shape and a single pale white eye. It was only when the man came forward that the shadowed face beneath the cowl took on the familiar features of Ser Maynard Plumm, the pale eye no more than the moonstone brooch that pinned his cloak at the shoulder.

Down in the well, Lord Alyn was thrashing and splashing and calling for help. "*Murder!* Someone help me."

"He tried to kill me," Dunk said.

"That would explain all the blood."

"Blood?" He looked down. His left arm from shoulder to elbow, his tunic clinging to his skin. "Oh."

Dunk did not remember falling, but suddenly he was on the ground, with raindrops running down his face. He could hear Lord Alyn whimpering from the well, but his splashing had grown feebler. "We need to have that arm bound up." Ser Maynard slipped his own arm under Dunk. "Up now. I cannot lift you by myself. Use your legs."

Dunk used his legs. "Lord Alyn. He's going to drown."

"He shan't be missed. Least of all by the Fiddler." "He's not," Dunk gasped, pale with pain, "a fiddler."

"No. He is Daemon of House Blackfyre, the Second of His Name. Or so he would style himself, if ever he achieves the Iron Throne. You would be surprised to know how many lords prefer their kings brave and stupid. Daemon is young and dashing, and looks good on a horse."

The sounds from the well were almost too faint to hear. "Shouldn't we throw his lordship down a rope?"

"Save him now to execute him later? I think not. Let him eat the meal that he meant to serve to you. Come, lean on me." Plumm guided him across the yard. This close, there was something queer about the cast of Ser Maynard's features. The longer Dunk looked, the less he seemed to see. "I did urge you to flee, you will recall, but you esteemed your honor more than your life. An honorable death is well and good, but if the life at stake is not your own, what then? Would your answer be the same, ser?"

"Whose life?" From the well came one last splash. "Egg? Do you mean Egg?" Dunk clutched at Plumm's arm. "*Where is he?*"

"With the gods. And you will know why, I think."

The pain that twisted inside Dunk just then made him forget his arm. He groaned. "He tried to use the boot."

"So I surmise. He showed the ring to Maester Lothar, who delivered him to Butterwell, who no doubt pissed his breeches at the sight of it and started wondering if he had chosen the wrong side and how much Bloodraven knows of this conspiracy. The answer to that last is 'quite a lot.' " Plumm chuckled.

"*Who are you?*"

"A friend," said Maynard Plumm. "One who has been watching you, and wondering at your presence in this nest of adders. Now be quiet, until we get you mended."

Staying in the shadows, the two of them made their way back to Dunk's small tent. Once inside, Ser Maynard lit a fire, filled a bowl with wine, and set it on the flames to boil. "A clean cut, and at least it is not your sword arm," he said, slicing through the sleeve of Dunk's bloodstained tunic. "The thrust appears to have missed the bone. Still, we will need to wash it out, or you could lose the arm."

"It doesn't matter." Dunk's belly was roiling, and he felt as if he might retch at any moment. "If Egg is dead—"

"—you bear the blame. You should have kept him well away from here. I never said the boy was dead, though. I said that he was with the gods. Do you have clean linen? Silk?"

"My tunic. The good one I got in Dorne. What do you mean, he's with the gods?"

"In good time. Your arm first."

The wine soon began to steam. Ser Maynard found Dunk's good silk tunic, sniffed at it suspiciously, then slid out a dagger and began to cut it up. Dunk swallowed his protest.

"Ambrose Butterwell has never been what you might call decisive," Ser Maynard said, as he wadded up three strips of silk and dropped them in the wine. "He had doubts about this plot from the beginning, doubts that were inflamed when he learned that the boy did not bear the sword. And this morning his dragon's egg vanished, and with it the last dregs of his courage."

"Ser Glendon did not steal the egg," Dunk said. "He was in the yard all day, tilting or watching others tilt."

"Peake will find the egg in his saddlebags all the same." The wine was boiling. Plumm drew on a leather glove and said, "Try not to scream." Then he pulled a strip of silk out of the boiling wine, and began to wash the cut.

Dunk did not scream. He gnashed his teeth and bit his tongue and smashed his fist against his thigh hard enough to leave bruises, but he did not scream. Ser Maynard used the rest of his good tunic to make a bandage, and tied it tight around his arm. "How does that feel?" he asked when he was done.

"Bloody awful." Dunk shivered. "*Where's Egg?*"

"With the gods. I told you."

Dunk reached up and wrapped his good hand around Plumm's neck. "Speak plain. I am sick of hints and winks. Tell me where to find the boy, or I will snap your bloody neck, friend or no."

"The sept. You would do well to go armed." Ser Maynard smiled. "Is that plain enough for you, Dunk?"

His first stop was Ser Uthor Underleaf's pavilion.

When Dunk slipped inside, he found only the squire Will bent over a washtub, scrubbing out his master's smallclothes. "You again? Ser Uthor is at the feast. What do you want?"

"My sword and shield."

"Have you brought the ransom?"

"No."

"Then why would I let you take your arms?"

"I have need of them."

"That's no good reason."

"How about, try and stop me and I'll kill you."

Will gaped. "They're over there."

Dunk paused outside the castle sept. Gods grant I am not too late. His sword-belt was back in its accustomed place, cinched tight about his waist. He had strapped the gallows shield to his wounded arm, and that weight of it was sending throbs of pain through him with every step. If anyone brushed up against him, he feared that he might scream. He pushed the doors open with his good hand.

Within, the sept was dim and hushed, lit only by the candles that twinkled on the altars of the Seven. The Warrior had the most candles burning, as might be expected during a tourney; many a knight would have come here to pray for strength and courage before they chanced the lists. The Stranger's altar was shrouded in shadow, with but a single candle burning. The Mother and the Father each had dozens, the Smith and Maiden somewhat fewer. And beneath the shining lantern of the Crone knelt Lord Ambrose Butterwell, head bowed, praying silently for wisdom.

He was not alone. No sooner had Dunk started for him than two men-at-arms moved to cut him off, faces stern beneath their halfhealms. Both wore mail, beneath surcoats striped in the green, white, and yellow undy of House Butterwell. "Hold, ser," one said. "You have no business here."

"Yes, he does. I *warned* you he would find me."

The voice was Egg's.

When he stepped out from the shadows beneath the Father, his shaved head shining in the candlelight, Dunk almost rushed to the boy, to pluck him up with a glad cry and crush him in his arms. Something in Egg's tone made him hesitate. *He sounds more angry than afraid, and I have never seen him look so stern. And Butterwell on his knees. Something is queer here.*

Lord Butterwell pushed himself back to his feet. Even in the dim light of the candles, his flesh looked pale and clammy. "Let him pass," he told his guardsmen. When they stepped back, he beckoned Dunk closer. "I have done the boy no harm. I knew his father well, when I was the King's Hand. Prince Maekar needs to know, none of this was my idea."

"He shall," Dunk promised. *What is happening here?*

"Peake. This was all his doing, I swear it by the Seven." Lord Butterwell put one hand on the altar. "May the gods strike me down if I am false. He told me who I must invite and who must be excluded, and he brought this boy pretender here. I never wanted to be part of any treason, you must believe me. Tom Heddle now, he urged me on, I will not deny it. My good-son, married to my eldest daughter, but I will not lie, he was part of this.

"He is your champion," said Egg. "If he was in this, so were you."

Be quiet, Dunk wanted to roar. *That loose tongue of yours will get us killed.* Yet Butterwell seemed to quail. "My lord, you do not understand. Heddle commands my garrison."

"You must have some loyal guardsmen," said Egg.

"These men here," said Lord Butterwell said. "A few more. I've been too lax, I will allow, but I have never been a traitor. Frey and I harbored doubts about Lord Peake's pretender since the beginning. *He does not bear the sword!* If he were his father's son, Bittersteel would have armed him with Blackfyre. And all this talk about a dragon . . . madness, madness and folly." His lordship dabbed the sweat from his face with his sleeve. "And now they have taken the egg, the dragon's egg my grandsire had from the king himself as a reward for leal service. It was there this morning when I woke, and my guards swear no one entered or left the bedchamber. It may be that Lord Peake bought them, I cannot say, but *the egg is gone*. They must have it, or else . . . "

Or else the dragon's hatched, thought Dunk. If a living dragon appeared again in Westeros, the lords and smallfolk alike would flock to whichever prince could lay claim to it. "My lord," he said, "a word with my . . . my squire, if you would be so good."

"As you wish, ser." Lord Butterwell knelt to pray again.

Dunk drew Egg aside, and went down upon one knee to speak with him face to face. "I am going to clout you in the ear so hard your head will turn around backwards, and you'll spend the rest of your life looking at where you've been."

"You should, ser." Egg had the grace to look abashed. "I'm sorry. I just meant to send a raven to my father."

So I could stay a knight. The boy meant well. Dunk glanced over to where Butterwell was praying. "What did you do to him?"

"Scared him, ser."

"Aye, I can see that. He'll have scabs on his knees before the night is done."

"I didn't know what else to do, ser. The maester brought me to them, once he saw my father's ring."

"Them?"

"Lord Butterwell and Lord Frey, ser. Some guards were there as well. Everyone was upset. Someone stole the dragon's egg."

"Not you, I hope?"

Egg shook his head. "No, ser. I knew I was in trouble when the maester showed Lord Butterwell my ring. I thought about saying that I'd stolen it, but I didn't think he would believe me. Then I remembered this one time I heard my father talking about something Lord Bloodraven said, about how it was better to be frightening than frightened, so I told them that my father had sent us here to spy for him, that he was on his way here with an army, that his lordship had best release me and give up this treason, or it would mean his head." He smiled a shy smile. "It worked better than I thought it would, ser."

Dunk wanted to take the boy by the shoulders and shake him until his teeth rattled. *This is no game, he might have roared. This is life and death.* "Did Lord Frey hear all this as well?"

"Yes. He wished Lord Butterwell happiness in his marriage and announced that he was returning to the Twins forthwith. That was when his lordship brought us here to pray."

Frey could flee, Dunk thought, *but Butterwell does not have that option, and soon or late he will begin to wonder why Prince Maekar and his army have not turned up*. "If Lord Peake should learn that you are in the castle—"

The sept's outer doors opened with a crash. Dunk turned to see Black Tom Heddle glowering in mail and plate, with rainwater dripping off his sodden cloak to puddle by his feet. A dozen men-at-arms stood with him, armed with spears and axes. Lightning flashed blue and white across the sky behind them, etching sudden shadows across the pale stone floor. A gust of wet wind set all the candles in the sept to dancing.

Oh, seven bloody hells was all that Dunk had time enough to think before Heddle said, "There's the boy. Take him."

Lord Butterwell had risen to his feet. "No. Halt. The boy's not to be molested. Tommard, what is the meaning of this?"

Heddle's face twisted in contempt. "Not all of us have milk running in our veins, your lordship. I'll have the boy."

"You do not understand." Butterwell's voice had turned into a high thin quaver. "We are undone. Lord Frey is gone, and others will follow. Prince Maekar is coming with an army."

"All the more reason to take the boy as hostage."

"No, no," said Butterwell, "I want no more part of Lord Peake or his pretender. I will not fight."

Black Tom looked coldly at his lord. "Craven." He spat. "Say what you will. You'll fight or die, my lord." He pointed at Egg. "A stag to first man to draw blood."

"No, no." Butterwell turned to his own guards. "Stop them, do you hear me? I command you. Stop them." But all the guards had halted in confusion, at a loss as to who they should obey.

"Must I do it myself, then?" Black Tom drew his longsword.

Dunk did the same. "Behind me, Egg."

"Put up your steel, the both of you!" Butterwell screeched." I'll have no bloodshed in the sept! Ser Tommard, this man is the prince's sworn shield. He'll kill you!"

"Only if he falls on me." Black Tom showed his teeth in a hard grin. "I saw him try to joust."

"I am better with a sword," Dunk warned him.

Heddle answered with a snort, and charged.

Dunk shoved Egg roughly backwards and turned to meet his blade. He blocked the first cut well enough, but the jolt of Black Tom's sword biting into his shield and the bandaged cut behind it sent a jolt of pain crackling up his arm. He tried a slash at Heddle's head in answer, but Black Tom slid away from it and hacked at him again. Dunk barely got his shield around in time. Pine chips flew and Heddle laughed, pressing his attack, low and high and low again. Dunk took each cut with his shield, but every blow was agony, and he found himself giving ground.

"Get him, ser," he heard Egg call. "Get him, get him, he's *right there.*" The taste of blood was in Dunk's mouth, and worse, his wound had opened once again. A wave of dizziness washed over him. Black Tom's blade was turning the long kite shield to splinters. *Oak and iron guard me well, or else I'm dead and doomed to hell*, Dunk thought, before he remembered that this shield was made of pine. When his back came up hard against an altar, he stumbled to one knee, and realized he had no more ground left to give.

"You are no knight," said Black Tom. "Are those tears in your eyes, oaf?"

Tears of pain. Dunk pushed up off his knee, and slammed shield-first into his foe.

Black Tom stumbled backward, yet somehow kept his balance. Dunk bulled right after him, smashing him with the shield again and again, using his size and strength to knock Heddle halfway across the sept. Then he swung the shield aside and slashed out with his longsword, and Heddle screamed as the steel bit through wool and muscle deep into his thigh. His own sword swung wildly, but the blow was desperate and clumsy. Dunk let his shield take it one more time and put all his weight into his answer.

Black Tom reeled back a step and stared down in horror at his forearm flopping on the floor beneath the Stranger's altar. "You," he gasped, "you, you . . . "

"I told you." Dunk stabbed him through the throat. "I'm better with a sword."

Two of the men-at-arms fled back into the rain as a pool of blood spread out from Black Tom's body. The others clutched their spears and hesitated, casting wary glances toward Dunk as they waited for their lord to speak.

"This . . . this was ill done," Butterwell finally managed. He turned to Dunk and Egg. "We must be gone from Whitewalls before those two bring word of this to Gormon Peake. He has more friends amongst the guests than I do. The postern gate in the north wall, we'll slip out there . . . come, we must make haste."

Dunk slammed his sword into its scabbard. "Egg, go with Lord Butterwell." He put an arm around the boy, and lowered his voice. "Don't stay with him any longer than you need to. Give Rain his head and get away before his lordship changes sides again. Make for Maidenpool, it's closer than King's Landing."

"What about you, ser?"

"Never mind about me."

"I'm your squire."

"Aye," said Dunk, "and you'll do as I tell you, or you'll get a good clout in the ear."

A group of men were leaving the great hall, pausing long enough to pull up their hoods before venturing out into the rain. The Old Ox was amongst them, and weedy Lord Caswell, once more in his cups. Both gave Dunk a wide berth. Ser Mortimer Boggs favored him with a curious stare, but thought better of speaking to him. Uthor Underleaf was not so shy. "You come late to the feast, ser," he said, as he was pulling on his gloves. "And I see you wear a sword again."

"You'll have your ransom for it, if that's all that concerns you." Dunk had left his battered shield behind, and draped his cloak across his wounded arm to hide the blood. "Unless I die. Then you have my leave to loot my corpse."

Ser Uthor laughed. "Is that gallantry I smell, or just stupidity? The two scents are much alike, as I recall. It is not too late to accept my offer, ser."

"It is later you think," Dunk warned him. He did not wait for Underleaf to answer, but pushed past him, through the double doors. The great hall smelled of ale and smoke and wet wool. In the gallery above, a few musicians played softly. Laughter echoed from the high tables, where Ser Kirby Pimm and Ser Lucas Nayland were playing a drinking game. Up on the dais, Lord Peake was speaking earnestly with Lord Costayne, while Ambrose Butterwell's new bride sat abandoned in her high seat.

Down below the salt, Dunk found Ser Kyle drowning his woes in Lord Butterwell's ale. His trencher was filled with a thick stew made with food left over from the night before. *A bowl o' brown*, they called such fare in the pot shops of King's Landing. Ser Kyle had plainly had no stomach for it. Untouched, the stew had grown cold, and a film of grease glistened atop the brown.

Dunk slipped onto the bench beside him. "Ser Kyle."

The Cat nodded. "Ser Duncan. Will you have some ale?"

"No." Ale was the last thing that he needed.

"Are you unwell, ser? Forgive me, but you look—"

—better than I feel. "What was done with Glendon Ball?"

"They took him to the dungeons." Ser Kyle shook his head. "Whore's get or no, the boy never struck me as a thief."

"He isn't."

Ser Kyle squinted at him. "Your arm . . . how did . . . "

"A dagger." Dunk turned to face the dais, frowning. He had escaped death twice today. That would suffice for most men, he knew. *Dunk the lunk, thick as a castle wall.* He pushed to his feet. "Your Grace," he called.

A few men on nearby benches put down their spoons, broke off their conversations, and turned to look at him.

"*Your Grace,*" Dunk said again, more loudly. He strode up the Myrish carpet toward the dais. "*Daemon.*"

Now half the hall grew quiet. At the high table, the man who'd called himself the Fiddler turned to smile at him. He had donned a purple tunic for the feast, Dunk saw. *Purple, to bring out the color of his eyes.* "Ser Duncan. I am pleased that you are with us. What would you have of me?"

"Justice," said Dunk, "for Glendon Ball."

The name echoed off the walls, and for half a heartbeat it was if every man, woman, and boy in the hall had turned to stone. Then Lord Costayne slammed a fist upon a table and shouted, "It's death that one deserves, not justice." A dozen other voices echoed his, and Ser Harbert Paege declared, "He's bastard born. All bastards are thieves, or worse. Blood will tell."

For a moment Dunk despaired. *I am alone here.* But then Ser Kyle the Cat pushed himself to his feet, swaying only slightly. "The boy may be a bastard, my lords, but he's *Fireball*'s bastard. It's like Ser Harbert said. Blood will tell."

Daemon frowned. "No one honors Fireball more than I do," he said. "I will not believe this false knight is his seed. He stole the dragon's egg, and slew three good men in the doing."

"He stole nothing and killed no one," Dunk insisted. "If three men were slain, look elsewhere for their killer. Your Grace knows as well as I that Ser Glendon was in the yard all day, riding one tilt after t'other."

"Aye," Daemon admitted. "I wondered at that myself. But the dragon's egg was found amongst his things."

"Was it? Where is it now?

Lord Gormon Peake rose cold-eyed and imperious. "Safe, and well guarded. And why is that any concern of yours, ser?"

"Bring it forth," said Dunk. "I'd like another look at it, m'lord. T'other night, I only saw it for a moment."

Peake's eyes narrowed. "Your Grace," he said to Daemon, "it comes to me that this hedge knight arrived at Whitewalls with Ser Glendon, uninvited. He may well be part of this."

Dunk ignored that. "Your Grace, the dragon's egg that Lord Peake found amongst Ser Glendon's things was the one he placed there. Let him bring it forth, if he can. Examine it yourself. I'll wager you it's no more than a painted stone."

The hall erupted into chaos. A hundred voices began to speak at once, and a dozen knights leapt to their feet. Daemon looked near as young and lost as Ser Glendon had when he had been accused. "Are you drunk, my friend?"

Would that I were. "I've lost some blood," Dunk allowed, "but not my wits. Ser Glendon has been wrongfully accused."

"Why?" Daemon demanded, baffled. "If Ball did no wrong, as you insist, why would his lordship say he did and try to prove it with some painted rock?"

"To remove him from your path. His lordship bought your other foes with gold and promises, but Ball was not for sale."

The Fiddler flushed. "That is not true."

"It is true. Send for Ser Glendon, and ask him yourself."

"I will do just that. Lord Peake, have the bastard fetched up at once. And bring the dragon's egg as well. I wish to have a closer look at it."

Gormon Peake gave Dunk a look of loathing. "Your Grace, the bastard boy is being questioned. A few more hours, and we will have a confession for you, I do not doubt."

"By *questioned*, m'lord means tortured," said Dunk. "A few more hours, and Ser Glendon will confess to having killed Your Grace's father, and both your brothers too."

"*Enough!*" Lord Peake's face was almost purple. "One more word, and I will rip your tongue out by the roots."

"You lie," said Dunk. "That's two words."

"And you will rue the both of them," Peake promised. "Take this man and chain him in the dungeons."

"No." Daemon's voice was dangerously quiet. "I want the truth of this. Sunderland, Vyrwel, Smallwood, take your men and go find Ser Glendon in the dungeons. Bring him up forthwith, and see that no harm comes to him. If any man should try and hinder you, tell him you are about the king's business."

"As you command," Lord Vyrwel answered.

"I will settle this as my father would," the Fiddler said. "Ser Glendon stands accused of grievous crimes. As a knight, he has a right to defend himself by strength of arms. I shall meet him in the lists, and let the gods determine guilt and innocence."

Hero's blood or whore's blood, Dunk thought, when two of Lord Vrywel's men dumped Ser Glendon naked at his feet, *he has a deal less of it than he did before.*

The boy had been savagely beaten. His face was bruised and swollen, several of his teeth were cracked or missing, his right eye was weeping blood, and up and down his chest his flesh was red and cracking where they'd burned him with hot irons.

"You're safe now," murmured Ser Kyle. "There's no one here but hedge knights, and the gods know that we're a harmless lot." Daemon had given them the maester's chambers, and commanded them to dress any hurts Ser Glendon might have suffered and see that he was ready for the lists.

Three fingernails had been pulled from Ball's left hand, Dunk saw, as he washed the blood from the boy's face and hands. That worried him more than all the rest. "Can you hold a lance?"

"A lance?" Blood and spit dribbled from Ser Glendon's mouth when he tried to speak. "Do I have all my fingers?"

"Ten," said Dunk, "but only seven fingernails."

Ball nodded. "Black Tom was going to cut my fingers off, but he was called away. Is it him that I'm to fight?"

"No. I killed him."

That made him smile. "Someone had to."

"You're to tilt against the Fiddler, but his real name—"

"—is Daemon, aye. They told me. The Black Dragon." Ser Glendon laughed. "My father died for his. I would have been his man, and gladly. I would have fought for him, killed for him, died for him, but I could not lose for him." He turned his head, and spat out a broken tooth. "Could I have a cup of wine?"

"Ser Kyle, get the wineskin."

The boy drank long and deep, then wiped his mouth. "Look at me. I'm shaking like a girl."

Dunk frowned. "Can you still sit a horse?"

"Help me wash, and bring me my shield and lance and saddle," Ser Glendon said, "and you will see what I can do."

It was almost dawn before the rain let up enough for the combat to take place. The castle yard was a morass of soft mud, glistening wetly by the light of a hundred torches. Beyond the field a gray mist was rising, sending ghostly fingers up the pale stone walls to grasp the castle battlements. Many of the wedding guests had vanished during the intervening hours, but those who remained climbed the viewing stand again and settled themselves on planks of rain-soaked pine. Amongst them stood Ser Gormon Peake, surrounded by a knot of lesser lords and household knights.

It had only been a few years since Dunk had squired for old Ser Arlan. He had not forgotten how. He cinched the buckles on Ser Glendon's ill-fitting armor, fastened his helm to his gorget, helped him mount, and handed him his shield. Earlier contests had left deep gouges in the wood, but the blazing fireball could still be seen. *He looks as young as Egg*, Dunk thought. *A frightened boy, and grim. His sorrel mare was unbarded, and skittish as well. He should have stayed with his own mount. The sorrel may be better bred and swifter, but a rider rides best on a horse that he knows well, and this one is a stranger to him.*

"I'll need a lance," Ser Glendon said. "A war lance."

Dunk went to the racks. War lances were shorter and heavier than the tourney lances that had been used in all the earlier tilts; eight feet of solid ash ending in an iron point. Dunk chose one and pulled it out, running his hand along its length to make sure it had no cracks.

At the far end of the lists, one of Daemon's squires was offering him a matching lance. He was a fiddler no more. In place of swords and fiddles, the trapping of his warhorse now displayed the three-headed dragon of House Blackfyre, black on a field of red. The prince had washed the black dye from his hair as well, so it flowed down to his collar in a cascade of silver and gold that glimmered like beaten metal in the torchlight. *Egg would have hair like that if he ever let it grow*, Dunk realized. He found it hard to picture him that way, but one day he knew he must, if the two of them should live so long.

The herald climbed his platform once again. "*Ser Glendon the Bastard stands accused of theft and murder,*" he proclaimed, "*and now comes forth to prove his innocence at the hazard of his body. Daemon of House Blackfyre, the Second of His Name, rightborn Kin of the Andals and the Rhoynar and the First Men, Lord of the Seven Kingdoms and Protector of the Realm, comes forth to prove the truth of the accusations against the bastard Glendon.*"

And all at once the year fell away, and Dunk was back was at Ashford Meadow once again, listening to Baelor Breakspear just before they went forth to battle for his life. He slipped the war lance back in place, plucked a tourney lance from the next rack; twelve feet long, slender, elegant. "Use this," he told Ser Glendon. "It's what we used at Ashford, at the Trial of Seven."

"The Fiddler chose a war lance. He means to kill me."

"First he has to strike you. If your aim is true, his point will never touch you."

"I don't know."

"I do."

Ser Glendon snatched the lance from him, wheeled about, and trotted toward the lists. "Seven save us both, then."

Somewhere in the east, lightning cracked across a pale pink sky. Daemon raked his stallion's side with golden spurs, and leapt forward like a thunderclap, lowering his war lance with its deadly iron point. Ser Glendon raised his shield and raced to meet him, swinging his own longer lance across his mare's head to bear upon the young pretender's chest. Mud sprayed back from their horses' hooves, and the torches seemed to burn the brighter as the two knights went pounding past.

Dunk closed his eyes. He heard a *crack*, a shout, a thump. "No," he heard Lord Peake cry out, in anguish. "*Noooooo.*" For half a heartbeat, Dunk almost felt sorry for him. He opened his eyes again. Riderless, the big black stallion was slowing to a trot. Dunk jumped out and grabbed him by the reins. At the far end of the lists, Ser Glendon Ball wheeled his mare and raised his splintered lance. Men rushed onto the field, to where the Fiddler lay unmoving, face down in the mud. When they helped him to his feet, he was mud from head to heel.

"The Brown Dragon," someone shouted. Laughter rippled through the yard, as the dawn washed over Whitewalls.

It was only a few heartbeats later, as Dunk and Ser Kyle were helping Glendon Ball off his horse, that the first trumpet blew, and the sentries on the walls raised the alarum. An army had appeared outside the castle, rising from the morning mists.

"Egg wasn't lying after all," Dunk told Ser Kyle, astonished.

From Maidenpool had come Lord Mooton, from Raventree Lord Blackwood, from Duskendale Lord Darklyn. The royal demenses about King's Landing sent forth Hayfords, Rosbys, Stokeworths, Masseys, and the king's own sworn swords, led by three knights of the Kingsguard and stiffened by three hundred Raven's Teeth with tall white weirwood bows. Mad Danelle Lothston herself rode forth in strength from her haunted towers at Harrenhal, clad in black armor that fit her like an iron glove, her long red hair streaming.

The light of the rising sun glittered off the points of five hundred lances and ten times as many spears. The night's gray banners were reborn in half a hundred gaudy colors. And above them all flew two regal dragons on night-black fields: the great three-headed beast of King Aerys I Targaryen, red as fire, and a white winged fury breathing scarlet flame.

Not Maekar after all, Dunk knew, when he saw those banners. The banners of the Prince of Summerhall showed four three-headed dragons, two and two, the arms of the fourth-born son of the late King Daeron II Targaryen. A single white dragon announced the presence of the King's Hand, Lord Byrnden Rivers.

Bloodraven himself had come to Whitewalls.

The First Blackfyre Rebellion had perished on the Redgrass Field in blood and glory. The Second Blackfyre Rebellion ended with a whimper. "They cannot cow us," Young Daemon proclaimed from the castle battlements, after he had seen the ring of iron that encircled them, "for our cause is just. We'll slash through them and ride hellbent for King's Landing! Sound the trumpets!"

Instead, knights and lords and men-at-arms muttered quietly to one another, and a few began to slink away, making for the stables or a postern gate or some hideyhole they hoped might keep them safe. And when Daemon drew his sword and raised it above his head, every man of them could see it was not Blackfyre. "We'll make another Redgrass Field today," the pretender promised.

"Piss on that, fiddle boy," a grizzled squire shouted back at him. "I'd sooner live."

In the end, the second Daemon Blackfyre rode forth alone, reined up before the royal host, and challenged Lord Bloodraven to single combat. "I will fight you, or the coward Aerys, or any champion you care to name." Instead, Lord Bloodraven's men surrounded him, pulled him off his horse, and clasped him into golden fetters. The banner he had carried was planted in the muddy ground and set afire. It burned for a long time, sending up twisted plume of smoke that could be seen for leagues around.

The only blood that was shed that day came when a man in service to Lord Vrywel began to boast he had been one of Bloodraven's eyes and would soon be well rewarded. "By the time the moon turns I'll be fucking whores and drinking Dornish red," he was purported to have said, just before one of Lord Costayne's knights slit his throat. "Drink that, he said, as Vrywel's man drowned in his own blood. "It's not Dornish, but it's red."

Elsewise it was a sullen, silent column that trudged through the gates of Whitewalls to toss their weapons into a glittering pile before being bound and led away to await Lord Bloodraven's judgment. Dunk emerged with the rest of them, together with Ser Kyle the Cat and Glendon Ball. They had looked for Ser Maynard to join them, but Plumm had melted away sometime during the night.

It was late that afternoon before Ser Roland Crakehall of the Kingsguard found Dunk among the other prisoners. "Ser Duncan. Where in seven hells have you been hiding? Lord Rivers has been asking for you for hours. Come with me, if you please."

Dunk fell in beside him. Crakehall's long cloak flapped behind him with every gust of wind, as white as moonlight on snow. The sight of it made him think back on the words the Fiddler had spoken, up on the roof. *I dreamed that you were all in white from head to heel, with a long pale cloak flowing from those broad shoulders.* Dunk snorted. *Aye, and you dreamed of dragons hatching from stone eggs. One is likely as t'other.*

The Hand's pavilion was half a mile from the castle, in the shade of a spreading elm tree. A dozen cows were cropping at the grass nearby. *Kings rise and fall,* Dunk thought, *and cows and smallfolk go about their business.* It was something the old man used to say. "What will become of all of them?" he asked Ser Roland, as they passed a group of captives sitting on the grass.

"They'll be marched back to King's Landing for trial. The knights and men-at-arms should get off light enough. They were only following their liege lords."

"And the lords?"

"Some will be pardoned, so long as they tell the truth of what they know and give up a son or daughter to vouchsafe their future loyalty. It will go harder for those who took pardons after the Redgrass Field. They'll be imprisoned or attainted. The worst will lose their heads."

Bloodraven had made a start on that already, Dunk saw when they came up on his pavilion. Flanking the entrance, the severed heads of Gormon Peake and Black Tom Heddle had been impaled on spears, with their shields displayed beneath them. *Three castles, black on orange. The man who slew Roger of Pennytree.*

Even in death, Lord Gormon's eyes were hard and flinty. Dunk closed them with his fingers. "What did you do that for?" asked one of the guardsmen. "The crows'll have them soon enough."

"I owed him that much." If Roger had not died that day, the old man would never looked twice at Dunk when he saw him chasing that pig through the alleys of King's Landing. *Some old dead king gave a sword to one son instead of another, that was the start of it. And now I'm standing here, and poor Roger's in his grave.*

"The Hand awaits," commanded Roland Crakehall.

Dunk stepped past him, into the presence of Lord Brynden Rivers, bastard, sorcerer, and Hand of the King.

Egg stood before him, freshly bathed and garbed in princely raiment, as would befit a nephew of the king. Nearby, Lord Frey was seated in a camp chair with a cup of wine to hand and his hideous little heir squirming in his lap. Lord Butterwell was there as well . . . on his knees, pale-faced and shaking.

"Treason is no less vile because the traitor proves a craven," Lord Rivers was saying. "I have heard your bleatings, Lord Ambrose, and I believe one word in ten. On that account I will allow you to retain a tenth part of your fortune. You may keep your wife as well. I wish you joy of her."

"And Whitewalls?" asked Butterwell, with quavering voice.

"Forfeit to the Iron Throne. I mean to pull it down stone by stone, and sow the ground that it stands upon with salt. In twenty years, no one will remember it existed. Old fools and young malcontents still make pilgrimages to the Redgrass Field to plant flowers on the spot where Daemon Blackfyre fell. I will not suffer Whitewalls to become another monument to the black dragon." He waved a pale hand. "Now scurry away, roach."

"The Hand is kind." Butterwell stumbled off, so blind with grief that he did not even seem to recognize Dunk as he passed. "You have my leave to go as well, Lord Frey," Rivers commanded. "We will speak again later."

"As my lord commands." Frey led his son from the pavilion.

Only then did the King's Hand turn to Dunk.

He was older than Dunk remembered him, with a lined hard face, but his skin was still as pale as bone, and his cheek and neck still bore the ugly winestain birthmark that some people thought looked like a raven. His boots were black, his tunic scarlet. Over it he wore a cloak the color of smoke, fastened with a brooch in the shape of an iron hand. His hair fell to his shoulders, long and white and straight, brushed forward so as to conceal his missing eye, the one that Bittersteel had plucked from him on the Redgrass Field. The eye that remained was very red. *How many eyes has Bloodraven? A hundred eyes, and one.*

"No doubt Prince Maekar had some good reason for allowing his son to squire for a hedge knight," he said, "though I cannot imagine it included delivering him to a castle full of traitors plotting rebellion. How is that I come to find my cousin is this nest of adders, ser? Lord Butterbutt would have me believe that Prince Maekar sent you here, to sniff out this rebellion in the guise of a mystery knight. Is that the truth of it?"

Dunk went to one knee. "No, m'lord. I mean, yes, m'lord. That's what Egg told him. Aegon, I mean. Prince Aegon. So that part's true. It isn't what you'd call the true truth, though."

"I see. So the two of you learned of this conspiracy against the crown and decided you would thwart it by yourselves, is that the way of it?"

"That's not it either. We just sort of . . . blundered into it, I suppose you'd say."

Egg crossed his arms. "And Ser Duncan and I had matters well in hand before you turned up with your army."

"We had some help, m'lord," Dunk added.

"Hedge knights."

"Aye, m'lord. Ser Kyle the Cat, and Maynard Plumm. And Ser Glendon Ball. It was him unhorsed the Fidd . . . the pretender."

"Yes, I've heard that tale from half a hundred lips already. The Bastard of the Pussywillows. Born of a whore and a traitor."

"Born of *heroes,*" Egg insisted. "If he's amongst the captives, I want him found and released. And rewarded."

"And who are you to tell the King's Hand what to do?"

Egg did not flinch. "You know who I am, cousin."

"Your squire is insolent, ser," Lord Rivers said to Dunk. "You ought to beat that out of him."

"I've tried, m'lord. He's a prince, though."

"What he is," said Bloodraven, "is a *dragon*. Rise, ser."

Dunk rose.

"There have always been Targaryens who dreamed of things to come, since long before the Conquest," Bloodraven said, "so we should not be surprised if from time to time a Blackfyre displays the gift as well. Daemon dreamed that a dragon would be born at Whitewalls, and it was. The fool just got the color wrong." Dunk looked at Egg. *The ring,* he saw. *His father's ring. It's on his finger, not stuffed up inside his boot.*

"I have half a mind to take you back to King's Landing with us," Lord Rivers to Egg, "and keep you at court as my . . . guest."

"My father would not take kindly to that."

"I suppose not. Prince Maekar has a . . . prickly . . . nature. Perhaps I should send you back to Summerhall."

"My place is with Ser Duncan. I'm his squire."

"Seven save you both. As you wish. You're free to go."

"We will," said Egg, "but first we need some gold. Ser Duncan needs to pay the Snail his ransom."

Bloodraven laughed. "What happened to the modest boy I once met at King's Landing? As you say, my prince. I will instruct my paymaster to give you as much gold as you wish. Within reason."

"Only as a loan," insisted Dunk. "I'll pay it back."

"When you learn to joust, no doubt." Lord River flicked them away with his fingers, unrolled a parchment, and began to tick off names with a quill.

He is marking down the men to die, Dunk realized. "My lord," he said, "we saw the heads outside. Is that . . . will the Fiddler . . . Daemon . . . will you have his head as well?"

Lord Bloodraven looked up from his parchment. "That is for King Aerys to decide . . . but Daemon has four younger brothers, and sisters as well. Should I be so foolish as to remove his pretty head, his mother will mourn, his friends will curse me for a kinslayer, and Bittersteel will crown his brother Haegon. Dead, young Daemon is a hero. Alive, he is an obstacle in my half-brother's path. He can hardly make a third Blackfyre king whilst the second remains so inconveniently alive. Besides, such a noble captive will be an ornament to our court, and a living testament to the mercy and benevolence of His Grace King Aerys."

"I have a question too," said Egg.

"I begin to understand why your father was so willing to be rid of you. What more would you have of me, cousin?"

"Who took the dragon's egg? There were guards at the door, and more guards on the steps, no way anyone could have gotten into Lord Butterwell's bedchamber unobserved."

Lord Rivers smiled. "Were I to guess, I'd say someone climbed up inside the privy shaft."

"The privy shaft was too small to climb."

"For a man. A child could do it."

"Or a dwarf," Dunk blurted. *A thousand eyes, and one. Why shouldn't some of them belong to a troupe of comic dwarfs?*

ABOUT THE AUTHORS

Michael Aronovitz is a Professor of English at Widener University. He has published short fiction in *Midnight Zoo, The Leopard's Realm, Slippery When Wet, The Nighthawk, Crimson and Gray, Fiction on the Web, Philly Fiction, Studies in the Fantastic, Metal Scratches, Demon-minds, Weird Tales, The Weird Fiction Review 2010, The Turks Head Review,* and *Death Head Grin.* He has stories forthcoming in *Black Petals, Kaleidotrope,* and *The Weird Fiction Review.* He is the author of the collection, *Seven Deadly Pleasures* (Hippocampus Press, 2009) and his first novel, *Alice Walks,* is slated for publication in 2013. Aronovitz lives with his son Max and his wife Kimberly in Wynnewood, Pennsylvania.

Peter Atkins was born in Liverpool, England and now lives in Los Angeles. He is the author of the novels *Morningstar, Big Thunder,* and *Moontown* and the screenplays *Hellraiser II, Hellraiser III, Hellraiser IV, Wishmaster,* and *Prisoners of the Sun.* His short fiction has appeared in such best-selling anthologies as *The Museum of Horrors, Dark Delicacies II,* and *Hellbound Hearts.* He is the co-founder, with Dennis Etchison and Glen Hirshberg, of The Rolling Darkness Revue, who tour the west coast annually bringing ghost stories and live music to any venue that'll put up with them. A new collection of his short fiction, *Rumors of the Marvelous,* is to be published this fall by Alchemy Press.

Laird Barron's most recent story collection, *Occultation,* was published in 2010 by Night Shade Books. He's also the author of an earlier collection, the Shirley Jackson Award-winning *The Imago Sequence and Other Stories* (Night Shade, 2007). His fiction has appeared in *Sci Fiction, The Magazine of Fantasy & Science Fiction,* and numerous anthologies and is frequently reprinted in various "year's best" anthologies. He is now at work on his first novel.

Holly Black is a best-selling author of contemporary fantasy novels for teens and children. Her first book, *Tithe: A Modern Faerie Tale* (2002) was included in the American Library Association's Best Books for Young Adults. She has since written two other books in the same universe, *Valiant* (2005) and *Ironside* (2007). Valiant was a finalist for the Mythopoeic Award for Young Readers and the recipient of the Andre Norton Award. Black collaborated with artist Tony DiTerlizzi, to create the Spiderwick Chronicles. The Spiderwick Chronicles were adapted into a 2008 film. Her first collection of short fiction, *The Poison Eaters and Other Stories,* was published in 2010. She has co-edited three anthologies: *Geektastic* (with Cecil Castellucci, 2009), *Zombies vs. Unicorns* (with Justine Larbalestier, 2010), and *Welcome to Bordertown* (with Ellen Kushner) was published earlier this year. *Red Glove*, the second novel in The Curse Workers series, was released in April. The third book in her Eisner-nominated graphic novel series, *The Good Neighbors,* will be published in October. The author lives in Massachusetts with her husband, Theo, in a house with a secret library.

Steve Berman's novel, *Vintage*, was a finalist for the Andre Norton Award. He's author of more than eighty short stories and two collections, *Trysts* and *Second Thoughts*. Berman has edited anthologies including *Magic in the Mirrorstone*, *So Fey*, and several editions of *Wilde Stories*. The founder of Lethe Press and publisher of *Icarus: The Magazine of Gay Speculative Fiction*, he lives in southern New Jersey.

Steve Duffy's third collection of short supernatural fiction, T*ragic Life Stories*, was published in 2010 by Ash-Tree Press. It was, appropriately, launched in Brighton, England, at the World Horror Convention. His stories have appeared in numerous magazines and anthologies in Europe and North America. A fourth collection, *The Moment of Panic*, is due to appear in 2011, and will include the International Horror Guild award-winning short story, "The Rag-and-Bone Men." Duffy lives in North Wales.

Neil Gaiman is the *New York Times* bestselling author of novels *Neverwhere*, *Stardust*, *American Gods*, *Coraline*, *Anansi Boys*, *The Graveyard Book*, and (with Terry Pratchett) *Good Omens*; the Sandman series of graphic novels; and the story collections *Smoke and Mirrors* and *Fragile Things*. He has won numerous literary awards including the Hugo, the Nebula, the World Fantasy, and the Stoker Awards, as well as the Newbery medal.

Simon R. Green is the bestselling author of dozens of novels, including several long-running series, such as the Deathstalker series and the Darkwood series. Most of his work over the last several years has been set in either his Secret History series or in his popular Nightside milieu. Recent novels include *The Good, the Bad, and the Uncanny*; *From Hell With Love*; A *Hard Day's Knight*; *For Heaven's Eyes Only*; and the second of the new The Ghost

Finders series, *Ghost of a Smile*. Green's short fiction has appeared in the anthologies *Mean Streets, Unusual Suspects, Wolfsbane and Mistletoe, Powers of Detection, Living Dead 2*, and *The Way of the Wizard*.

M.L.N. Hanover's forthcoming novel, *Killing Rites*, is the fourth in the Black Sun's Daughter sequence. An International Horror Guild Award-winner, Hanover lives in the American Southwest.

M.K. Hobson's short fiction has appeared in many fine publications, including *Realms of Fantasy, The Magazine of Fantasy & Science Fiction*, and *Strange Horizons*. Her debut novel, *The Native Star*, is available from Ballantine Spectra. You can find out more at her website, www.demimonde.com.

Stephen Graham Jones is the author of eight novels and two collections. His most recent books are *Seven Spanish Angels, It Came from Del Rio*, and *The Ones That Got Away*. His next two are *Flushboy* and *Not for Nothing*. Stephen's been a Shirley Jackson Award finalist three times, a Bram Stoker Award finalist, a Black Quill Award finalist, an International Horror Guild finalist, a Colorado Book Award finalist, and has won the Texas Institute of Letters Award for Fiction and been an NEA fellow in fiction. His short fiction has been in *Cemetery Dance, Asimov's, Weird Tales*, and multiple best-of-the-year compilations, textbooks, and anthologies. Born in West Texas, PhD'd at Florida State, Stephen now lives in Colorado, where he teaches in the MFA program at the University of Colorado at Boulder. More at demontheory.net.

Caitlín R. Kiernan is the author of several novels, including *Low Red Moon, Daughter of Hounds*, and *The Red Tree*, which was nominated for both the Shirley Jackson and World Fantasy awards. Her next novel, *The Drowning Girl: A Memoir*, will be released by Penguin in 2012. Since 2000, her shorter tales of the weird, fantastic, and macabre have been collected in several volumes, including *Tales of Pain and Wonder*; *From Weird and Distant Shores*; *To Charles Fort, With Love*; *Alabaster*; *A is for Alien*; and *The Ammonite Violin & Others*. In 2012, Subterranean Press will release a retrospective of her early writing, *Two Worlds and In Between: The Best of Caitlín R. Kiernan (Volume One)*. She lives in Providence, RI, with her partner Kathryn.

Jay Lake lives in Portland, Oregon, where he works on numerous writing and editing projects. His most recent books are *Pinion* (Tor), *The Specific Gravity of Grief* (Fairwood Press), and *The Baby Killers* (PS Publishing). His short fiction appears regularly in literary and genre publications worldwide. Jay is a winner of the John W. Campbell Award for Best New Writer, and a multiple nominee for the Hugo and World Fantasy Awards.

Margo Lanagan is an internationally acclaimed writer of novels and short stories. Her fiction has garnered many awards, nominations, and shortlistings. "Sea-Hearts," published for the first time outside of Australia in T*he Year's Best Dark Fantasy and Horror: 2010*, won the World Fantasy Award last year as best novella. *Black Juice* was a Michael L. Printz Honor Book, won two World Fantasy Awards and the Victorian Premier's Award for Young Adult Fiction. *Red Spikes* won the CBCA Book of the Year: Older Readers, was a *Publishers Weekly* Best Book of the Year, a Horn Book Fanfare title, was shortlisted for the Commonwealth Writer's Prize and longlisted for the Frank O'Connor International Short Story Award. Her novel *Tender Morsels* won the World Fantasy Award for Best Novel and was a Michael L. Printz Honor Book for Excellence in Young Adult Literature. Margo lives in Sydney.

Sarah Langan is a three-time winner of the Bram Stoker Award. She is the author of the novels *The Keeper* and *The Missing*, and her most recent novel, *Audrey's Door*, won the 2009 Stoker for best novel. Her short fiction has appeared in the magazines *Cemetery Dance*, *Phantom*, and *Chiaroscuro*, and in the anthologies *Darkness on the Edge* and *Unspeakable Horror*. She is currently working on a post-apocalyptic young adult series called Kids and two adult novels: *Empty Houses*, which was inspired by *The Twilight Zone*, and *My Father's Ghost*, which was inspired by *Hamlet*.

Joe R. Lansdale is the author of over thirty novels and numerous short stories. His novella, *Bubba Hotep*, was made into an award-winning film of the same name, as was I*ncident On and Off a Mountain Road*. Both were directed by Don Coscarelli. His works have received numerous recognitions, including the Edgar, seven Bram Stoker awards, the Grinizani Prize for Literature, American Mystery Award, the International Horror Award, British Fantasy Award, and many others. His most recent novel is *Devil Red*, the eighth featuring Hap and Leonard, two good ol' boys from East Texas who have a way of getting into some bad fixes. *All the Earth, Thrown to the Sky*, his first novel for young adults will be published in September 2011.

Tanith Lee was born in 1947, in London, England. Though some of her children's books were published in the 1970s, she was able to become a full-time professional in 1975, with the publication of her fantasy novel *The Birthgrave* by DAW Books of America. So far she has written/published seventy-eight novels, thirteen collections, and almost three hundred short stories, ranging through SF, fantasy, horror, YA, contemporary, plus gay/ lesbian, and detective fiction. She has also won, or been short-listed for many awards. In 2009 she was made a Grand Master of Horror. She lives on the Sussex Weald close to the sea, with her husband, writer/artist John Kaiine, and under the iron paw of two tuxedo cats.

Now a #1 *New York Times* best-selling author, **George R.R. Martin** sold his first story in 1971 and has been writing professionally ever since. He spent ten years in Hollywood as a writer-producer, working on *The Twilight Zone*, *Beauty and the Beast*, and various feature films and television pilots that were never made. Martin also edited the Wild Cards series, fifteen novels written by teams of authors. In the mid-1990s he returned to prose, and began work on his epic fantasy series, A Song of Ice and Fire. In April 2011 HBO premiered its adaptation of the first of that series, *A Game of Thrones*, and he was named as one of *Time*'s most influential people of the year. *A Dance With Dragons*, the fifth A Song of Fire and Ice book, was published in July. He lives Santa Fe, New Mexico, with his wife Parris.

Maureen McHugh has published four novels and a collection of short stories. She's won a Hugo and a Tiptree award. McHugh recently moved to Los Angeles, where she is attempting to sell her soul to the entertainment industry.

Norman Partridge's fiction includes horror, suspense, and the fantastic—"sometimes all in one story" according to Joe Lansdale. Partridge's novel *Dark Harvest* was chosen by *Publishers Weekly* as one of the 100 Best Books of 2006, and two short story collections were published in 2010—*Lesser Demons* from Subterranean Press and *Johnny Halloween* from Cemetery Dance. Other work includes the Jack Baddalach mysteries *Saguaro Riptide* and *The Ten-Ounce Siesta*, plus *The Crow: Wicked Prayer*, which was adapted for film. Partridge's compact, thrill-a-minute style has been praised by Stephen King and Peter Straub, and his work has received multiple Bram Stoker awards. He can be found on the web at NormanPartridge.com and americanfrankenstein.blogspot.com.

Tim Powers is the author of twelve novels, including *The Anubis Gates*, *Last Call*, *Declare*, and *Three Days to Never*. His novels have twice won the Philip K. Dick Memorial Award, twice won the World Fantasy Award, and three times won the Locus Poll Award. Powers has taught fiction writing classes at the University of Redlands, Chapman University, and the Orange County High School of the Arts, and has been an instructor at the Writers of the Future program and the Clarion Science Fiction Workshop at Michigan State University. Powers lives with his wife, Serena, in San Bernardino, California.

Lynda E. Rucker's fiction has appeared in publications such as *Black Static*, *Supernatural Tales*, and *The Mammoth Book of Best New Horror*, among others. When not writing, she works as a writing instructor and copy editor. She was born and raised in the South, has lived on three continents and both coasts, and currently calls Athens, Georgia, home.

Ekaterina Sedia resides in the Pinelands of New Jersey. Her critically acclaimed novels, *The Secret History of Moscow*, *The Alchemy of Stone*, and *The House of Discarded Dreams* were published by Prime Books. Her most recent, *Heart of Iron*, has just been published. Her short stories have appeared in *Analog*, *Baen's Universe*, *Subterranean*, and *Clarkesworld*, as well as numerous anthologies, including *Haunted Legends* and *Magic in the Mirrorstone*. She is also the editor of anthologies *Paper Cities* (a World Fantasy Award winner), *Running with the Pack*, and *Bewere the Night*. Visit her at www.ekaterinasedia.com.

John Shirley's novels include *Demons*, *City Come A-Walkin'*, *Eclipse*, *Cellars*, and *In Darkness Waiting*; his story collections include *Black Butterflies* (which won the Bram Stoker Award, the IHG Award, and was named a Best Book of the Year by *Publishers Weekly)*, *Living Shadows*, *Really Really Really Really Weird Stories*, and the recent *In Extremis: The Most Extreme Short Stories of John Shirley*. His work is thought to be seminal in the cyberpunk movement. He was co-screenwriter of the film *The Crow*, and has written scripts for television. His most recent novels are *Black Glass* and *Bleak History*. A new novel, *Everything Is Broken*, will be published in early 2012.

Michael Skeet is an award-winning Canadian writer and broadcaster. Born in Calgary, Alberta, he began writing for radio before finishing college. He has sold short stories in the science fiction, dark fantasy, and horror fields in addition to extensive publishing credits as a film and music critic. A two-time winner of Canada's Aurora Award for excellence in Science Fiction and Fantasy, Skeet lives in Toronto with his wife, Lorna Toolis (the head of the internationally renowned Merril Collection of Science Fiction, Speculation and Fantasy, a reference collection of the Toronto Public Library and one of the world's best SF libraries). "Red Blues" was inspired in part by his career as a disc jockey and jazz critic, as well as his love of movie musicals and the golden age of American pop songwriting.

Angela Slatter is a Brisbane-based writer of speculative fiction. She is the author of *Sourdough and Other Stories* (Tartarus Press) and the Aurealius Award-winning *The Girl with No Hands and Other Stories* (Ticonderoga Publications). Her short stories have appeared in anthologies such as *Dreaming Again*, *Strange Tales II* and *III*, and *2012*, as well as journals such as *Lady Churchill's Rosebud Wristlet*, *Shimmer*, and *ONSPEC*. Her work has had several Honorable Mentions in the Datlow, Link, and Grant-edited Year's Best Fantasy and Horror series; and four of her stories have been shortlisted for the Aurealis Awards in the Best Fantasy Short Story category, winning in 2011 with Lisa L Hannett for "The Febraury Dragon." She is a graduate of Clarion South 2009 and the Tin House Summer Writers Workshop 2006. She blogs at www.angelaslatter.com.

Sarah Totton's short fiction has appeared in *Realms of Fantasy*, *Writers of the Future XXII*, and *Fantasy*. She was named the Regional Winner (for Canada & the Caribbean) in the 2007 Commonwealth Short Story Competition and received a Black Quill Award (Editor's Choice, Best Dark Scribble) in 2010. Her debut short story collection, *Animythical Tales*, was published in 2010 by Fantastic Books (Gray Rabbit Publishing).

S.D. Tullis was the winner of D.F. Lewis's "Win Immortality" competition for the latest and last edition of *Nemonymous—Null Immortalis*. Each story in the anthology was required to contain a character named S.D. Tullis or Scott Tullis or Mr. Tullis or Tullis. Thus, a Tullis family appears in his own contribution. Beyond this immortality, he has had stories published in anthologies *All Hallows 43*, *Hideous Dreams*, earlier editions of the megazanthus *Nemonymous—Cone Zero*, *Zen Core*, *Nemo Book*, *Glass Onion*—and magazines *Crab Creek Review*, *Flesh & Blood*, and *The Third Alternative*. He also creates horror-themed digital art, on display and growing slowly at http://tullisart.wordpress.com/

Genevieve Valentine's first novel, *Mechanique: A Tale of the Circus Tresaulti*, debuted in May 2011. You can learn more about it at the Circus Tresaulti website: www.circus-tresaulti.com. Her short fiction has appeared or is forthcoming in *Clarkesworld*, *Strange Horizons*, *Fantasy*, *Lightspeed*, *Apex*, and others, and in the anthologies *Federations*, *The Living Dead 2*, *The*

Way of the Wizard, *Running with the Pack*, *Teeth*, and more. Her nonfiction has appeared in *Lightspeed*, *Tor.com*, *Fantasy*, and *Weird Tales*. Her appetite for bad movies is insatiable, a tragedy she tracks on her blog at genevievevalentine.com.

Peter Watts (www.rifters.com) is a reformed marine biologist/convicted felon who feels better about his career since winning the Hugo for his novelette "The Island" in 2010. (His previous novel, *Blindsight*, was nominated for a shitload of major awards, but only won a few in Europe.) His work has been extensively translated, and his technique of backloading novels with technical bibliographies—originally intended as a defense against nitpickers—has fooled academics into using his work as textbooks not only in science fiction courses, but in those on Philosophy and Neuropsychology as well. He has also been cited as a major influence on *Bioshock 2*, although he cannot afford to purchase the game to confirm this.

Gene Wolfe worked as an engineer before becoming editor of trade journal *Plant Engineering*. He retired to write full time in 1984. Long considered to be a premier fantasy author, he is the recipient of the World Fantasy Lifetime Achievement Award, as well as Nebula, World Fantasy, Campbell, Locus, British Fantasy, and British SF Awards. Wolfe has been inducted into the Science Fiction Hall of Fame. His short fiction has been collected over a dozen times, most recently in *The Best of Gene Wolfe* (2009). The most recent of Wolfe's numerous novels is *Home Fires* (2011).

COPYRIGHT & ORIGINAL PUBLICATION

"Crawlspace" by Stephen Graham Jones. Copyright © 2010 by Stephen Graham Jones. First published: *The Ones That Got Away* (Prime Books). Reprinted by permission of the author.

"As Red as Red" by Caitlín R. Kiernan. Copyright © 2010 by Caitlín R. Kiernan. First published: *Haunted Legends*, ed. Ellen Datlow & Nick Mamatas (Tor). Reprinted by permission of the author.

"Mother Urban's Booke of Dayes" by Jay Lake. Copyright © 2010 by Joseph E. Lake, Jr. First published: *Dark Faith*, ed. Maurice Broaddus and Jerry Gordon (Apex Publishing). Reprinted by permission of the author.

"A Thousand Flowers" by Margo Lanagan. Copyright © 2010 by Margo Lanagan. First published: *Zombies vs. Unicorns*, ed. Holly Black & Justine Larbalestier (Margaret K. McElderry). Reprinted by permission of the author.

"Are You Trying To Tell Me This Is Heaven?" by Sarah Langan. Copyright © 2010 by Sarah Langan. First published: *The Living Dead 2*, ed. John Joseph Adams (Night Shade). Reprinted by permission of the author.

"The Stars Are Falling" by Joe R. Lansdale. Copyright © 2010 by Joe R. Lansdale. First published: *Stories: All New Tales*, ed. Neil Gaiman & Al Sarrantonio (William Morrow). Reprinted by permission of the author.

"Sea Warg" by Tanith Lee. Copyright © 2010 by Tanith Lee. First published: *Full Moon City*, ed. Darrell Schweitzer & Martin H. Greenberg (Gallery). Reprinted by permission of the author.

The Mystery Knight by George R.R. Martin. Copyright © 2010 by George R.R. Martin. First published: *Warriors*, ed. George R.R. Martin & Gardner Dozois (Tor). Reprinted by permission of the author.

"The Naturalist" by Maureen McHugh. Copyright © 2010 by Maureen McHugh. First published: *Subterranean Magazine*, Spring 2010. Reprinted by permission of the author.

"Lesser Demons" by Norman Partridge. Copyright © 2010 by Norman Partridge. First published: *Black Wings*, ed. S.T. Joshi (PS Publishing)/*Lesser Demons* (Subterranean). Reprinted by permission of the author.

"Parallel Lines" by Tim Powers. Copyright © 2010 by Tim Powers. First published: *Stories: All New Tales*, ed. Neil Gaiman & Al Sarrantonio (William Morrow). Reprinted by permission of the author.

ABOUT THE EDITOR

Paula Guran is the editor of Pocket Books' Juno fantasy imprint, Prime Books' senior editor, and nonfiction editor for *Weird Tales*. In an earlier life, she produced weekly email newsletter *DarkEcho* (winning two Bram Stoker Awards, an International Horror Guild Award award, and a World Fantasy Award nomination) and edited *Horror Garage* magazine (earning another IHG Award and a second World Fantasy nomination). Guran has contributed reviews, interviews, and articles to numerous professional publications. She's also done a great deal of other various and sundry work in speculative fiction publishing. She lives in Akron, Ohio.